THE MARY HOUSE

The Mary House

A novel
by

J D BALLAM

Adelaide Books
New York/Lisbon
2019

THE MARY HOUSE
A novel
By J D Ballam

Published by Adelaide Books, New York / Lisbon
adelaidebooks.org

Editor-in-Chief
Stevan V. Nikolic

For any information, please address Adelaide Books
at info@adelaidebooks.org

or write to:

Adelaide Books
244 Fifth Ave. Suite D27
New York, NY, 10001

ISBN-10: 1-951214-44-7

ISBN-13: 978-1-951214-44-9

Printed in the United States of America

Contents

Preface to this Book

To generations of her admirers, the discovery and publication of Mary White's literary journals will feel like the arrival of a packet of long-delayed love letters. For not only do the journals include drafts of so many previously unpublished stories, they also allow us to see something of the woman herself, something never before revealed about her journey from grief and loneliness towards the happiness that so distinguished the later years of her life. Here, for the first time, is a precious insight into the workings of the author's mind and imagination in that period of her life when, after so much success, she fell silent, dealing with the private pain she concealed behind the masks of her characters.

So much of Mary's story is well-known: her early successes, critical acclaim for novels like *Living it Down*, prizes for collections of stories like *Backwater*, all kept her at or near the front row of writers known first to other writers, and only then to a wider public. Comparisons were never far away: Dorothy Parker, Katherine Anne Porter, or that sisterhood of Southern women unfolding their arms to join hands with the world around them. All of this had, of course, come as a surprise to Mary, who had never sought anything for her stories except to represent accurately the uncertainty and isolation of people somehow destined to stand alone on the banks of the mainstream. Loneliness, as is well-known, was always her theme.

Perhaps, that is why the sudden loss of her husband (he took his own life) followed almost at once by the disappearance of her only child in the early days of the Vietnam War, threatened to end even Mary's relationship with herself and her art. For several years, she published nothing new. But the writing was still very much alive. Looking back now, it is possible to see how this writer, who had said so much so feelingly about being a woman, was also passionately concerned with what it means to be a man. We can see in these pages her struggle to untangle the influences she perceives as shaping men's lives, from boyhood to manhood, as well as the blame she affords herself for not having attempted to chronicle these things with such insight previously. In the opening pages of her journal, even before she gets going on her own story, she notes a small scene she witnessed on her doorstep: a group of boys bullying and tempting one another. It is clear that what interests her is the unspoken code that exists among them and what reinforces that terrible code. In light of the twin losses of her husband and son, her anger and perplexity are understandable. As she says, the imaginative mind sees the end before it sees the beginning.

I can recall from her letters the decision to move herself, alone, from the beautiful home near the Chesapeake Bay – a place which had seen the triumph of her work and the tragedy of her family – to live in, of all places, a tiny dwelling (a former slave house) in the foothills of the Blue Ridge Mountains, where she would watch a small band of men restore another old, empty house. Anyone could see that she hoped to leave some things behind. What was harder to see was that, for Mary, this was a plunging in. The front porch of the old Mary House in Harmony, Maryland was her lookout on to a world of men and women still connected to centuries of American life. She wrote to me of the characters she met in the dusty roads around her – people driven by habits, bigotries and a deep greatness of soul that she felt had been so far unexpressed. She liked to say that her tiny house echoed with the voices of the women who had lived there before her – those who had never known any other world, those who were imprisoned by the one they found themselves in. She claimed these voices were as real to her as those of the women she met, and reading her stories, I am reluctant to contradict her.

These are the voices you will find here, the voices that tell these stories. She lets them speak for themselves, and in doing so they speak for her (maybe for all of us). There is the voice of the mute Catoctin woman, known as Red Mary, whose real name (Little Wound) no one else ever really knows. There is the voice of Black Mary, the slave whose patience and wisdom give her endurance. And there is a version of Mary's own voice, less beaming, more searching than that of the Mary I knew; a voice that yearns for itself in the lives of others.

But most importantly, there is the "real" Mary, the Mary of the journal itself, laughing and crying in her new environment. It is the voice of a very capable woman trying to make sense of her experiences: lives of men growing, living, dead and far away; of women who for two centuries have found ways not merely of coping with their worlds, but to sustain hope within them. Because that is Mary's own journey. The journal chronicles not just Mary's rebuilding of a ramshackle house, but her rebuilding of a ramshackle life, tearing out the forlorn attachments to old suffering, and as time passes, letting more and more sunlight and music in. Together these form the pathway from the experience of separation and longing to that of joy and community.

AGW, June 21, 1981

PART I:

Red County

A Country Mile

August 29, 1963

3pm. The end. It always comes first. First, in the imagination.

*This morning I was standing on the high porch (the name they give the balcony here) at The Corner, looking straight down the Harmony Road. There is an old house down the road on the left, & a little further on, one on the right. Between them, on the right, the ground rises very steeply & is covered with honeysuckle, briars, and small trees. There were some boys gathered here, clowning around in the road & in the bushes. Six boys, the oldest about 15. He had very white hair, & a thin animal look on his face, the grin-like look that comes before a bite. Two of the other boys were obviously his brothers, each about two years younger than the next, all with the same white hair & manic look. Not feral exactly, but more like they had recently escaped from confinement, & were now seeking adventure, with pain if necessary. The other boys hovered round these three. The shortest was a skinny frog-face kid, whose eyes constantly darted back & forth between the white-haired ones, checking, it seemed, to make sure they weren't about to turn on him. There was another very tall, very thin boy, short straight hair sticking up, who looked to be watching for the right thing to say or do, something that wouldn't risk too much. Then there was the one at the center. Obviously the poorest one of them all, his hair huge, his body like a stunted man's, heavy for his age, his movements slow and ponderous. He listened to everything they all said, & never spoke. In a minute, it was clear what they were doing. Taking turns, the white-haired ones climbed into the bushes & emerged on the top of the embankment. Then recklessly, each would jump off & like a trapeze artist, at the very last second, grab on to a branch, swing out over the road, & letting out a squeal, fall to their feet in the gravel below, where they would squat like monkeys. They were trying to talk the sluggish boy into copying them. Finally, when he disappeared into the bushes, I felt myself holding my breath. I saw him stand on the edge of the embankment & look. He was so much larger and more burdened with his body than the others, that I was afraid for him. Then he spat on his hands (I've never seen anyone really do this, & I suspect he had no idea why he did it himself) & he leaped out. He sailed downwards like the others had & caught the branch just as they had. But being so heavy, his body swung on with the momentum, leaving him absolutely flat, parallel to the ground below. His fingers slipped loose, probably with the suddenness, & down he fell. He landed on the gravel road perfectly horizontal, all parts of him arriving at the ground at precisely the same moment. The others circled round him, & I wanted to scream at them, at everyone, though there was no one else to hear. Just then, they all started whooping & shouting & laughing. Just then, a filthy pick-up truck drew up towards them from the opposite direction. There were two people inside. A man hopped out & without hurrying walked over to the boys & stood among them. They didn't say much or anything, & then another boy, tall, thin and wearing heavy glasses, got out of the truck and joined the others. The heavy boy in the road got up smiling faintly & all the original gang climbed into the back of the truck. The man stood closer to the boy in glasses, probably his son, & pointed to the heavy one. —See that? he said. —Now that's a real boy. Then he got into the truck. The son, evidently used to this ritual of humiliation, followed, getting into the cab beside his father. Then they drove off. Such is the world of boys and men.

*Today I took possession of my new home. It is called The Corner, & Mr Hartsock, the architect overseeing (I am tempted to say overlooking) the project tells me it was built as a mill in the 1760s & is older than everything else in the area. I don't know whether to be proud or ashamed of this. It is a very big building, with stone & brick walls 4 foot thick on three sides, & it has lots of rooms & windows. It is in a poor state of repair, having only been a house since the 1890s, & while the work is being done on it, I will be living across the road in a brick-covered log cabin called The Mary House. This is mine also. Hartsock tells me it is as old as The Corner, wasn't always bricked, & used to be the slave quarters for the mill. It was inhabited until the 1930s or so, & the interior reflects this. Around the back & sides of The Corner there are somewhat steep lawns, walnut trees, ornamentals, and a lot of abandoned dreams, I'd say. The Harmony Road runs past the eastern side & over an iron bridge in front. It is intersected to the left by the Hollow Road, also over an iron bridge. The Mary House (surrounded by an enormous vegetable patch) sits in this intersection, surrounded on the two other sides by two different streams that come together just beyond the vegetable garden. I also now own a piece of land across the small stream, & another across the Harmony Road (this big one is called The Patch). In front of

The Corner, the Brethren Church Road meets the Harmony Road. I've got a little land the other side of this one too. All & all, the original builders of this place could not have sited it better, or built it any stronger. Hartsock agrees.

*I have sold up and come here for Alex's sake. I think it is best that when this business in Vietnam is over & he finally comes home, that it will do him good to be far away from all those things that drove him away in the first place. It will be a new start for both of us. I cannot wait to get started.

10pm. Foggy & drizzly this morning & rainy this afternoon. Quite warm for the time of year.

*Extraordinary sights on the evening news. Rev King led a march in DC they are saying had ¼ million people in it. Not violent. Thank God. Have been watching & reading the news more than ever lately, since last week's crackdown in South V. Perhaps, martial law will bring some news of Alex. It is very hard.

Way down in the Blue Ridge Mountains

The men in Virgil Summers's family had been fortunate in the timing of their births. One by one, for generations they came into the world at a time that left them to reach maturity too soon or too late to become soldiers in the country's latest war. His great-grandfather had watched Maryland vote overwhelmingly for John C. Breckenridge for president. He himself had voted for John Bell. But the war came anyway, and he had married late, and become a father late, and he was too old to enlist, and then too old to be drafted. His sons were too young. One of them, Virgil's grandfather, was too old to fight the Spanish. His son, too young to fight the Germans. And then Virgil would be too old to fight the Japanese. Throughout it all the wars kept coming, and the farmers and merchants and tradesmen kept going for soldiers, many of them not returning. Those that returned were never the men they were when they left. Some were broken, others made into something either silent or talkative. But esteemed, always esteemed.

Instead, Virgil's great-grandfather had made money. When Mr Lincoln's war started, and everyone else with something to lose took it out of the banks and buried it in crocks under oak trees, he began to buy land. It was cheap at first - $5.34 an acre. But then, just as he predicted, the war ended and the price of land, newly-free land, rose to $28.07 an acre. He grew rich. By the time Virgil entered manhood, he became the third generation of his family to go to Baltimore and to study at Johns Hopkins. He was the first to become a doctor. He returned to Middletown, the place nearest to his family's original farm, and set up his practice there, accepting the gifts in lieu of payment from the patients made too poor by the Depression to pay in any other way. He was given so many eggs he had to give them away to his neighbours.

But Virgil was lonely. He had always been lonely. In his memory, he had not been a boy like other boys, and was now not a man like other men. He recalled vividly how, as a child, he had been sucker-punched by a boy half his size. Much later, as a teenager, he had been playing football with his classmates and his speed enabled him to tackle the opposing quarterback again and again until in frustration the quarterback punched Virgil hard, directly in the nose, so that blood covered his whole face. But because Virgil neither fought back nor even winced, the other boy followed him for half an hour, desperately apologizing. He remembered a boy named Alan who caught and killed rabbits for the sole purpose of dismembering them and playing tricks with their limbs. He knew a boy named Jeff who rode his horse wildly up and down the main street whooping and carousing, shouting out nonsense and laughing so that everyone who saw him laughed too. There had been a case of some boys riding their bicycles all over an old man's potato patch, incensing him, so that he drew out a shotgun and tried to kill them all. But Virgil knew he could never have been one of those boys, and he knew he would never become one of those men.

He wanted to be loved. Physically loved. Everything he did he did so that he would be loved. Yet everywhere he saw it, love confused him. At first, there were the terrible stories. Stephen, who claimed his little sister would dance naked for a quarter. Vincent, who claimed he saw Kimberly sleeping naked. The gentle kindly old Mr Ford whose bitter wife was rumoured to have married him only after he raped her in a cornfield. In college he knew boys with successions of girlfriends. The ginger-haired athlete who boasted of three girls, the swimmer who boasted of three as well. With his own eyes, he had seen Jeanine, the beautiful Irish girl, walk off into the woods with the blonde-haired Irish boy. And it was all the boys talked of, laughing, in circles, like tall-tales. Frieda with her legs wrapped around Scotty.

Where he loved he loved in vain, invisible, untouched. As a man, his medical practice kept him busy, decently fed and with one suit to wear and two in his closet. He stitched wounds, set broken bones, prescribed drugs, delivered babies and administered advice. His family, married brothers and sisters, described him as slower than molasses in January and not worth a hill of blue beans.

But Virgil, lonely and ashamed of loving, nevertheless, was not ready for his story to end. Every day, for his lunch, he walked up Main Street to the diner. Within two months, he had tasted everything on the menu. But it was not food that kept him returning. There was a waitress there named Grace Bidle.

Grace was Virgil's age, more or less. She was short, very thin and small featured, with long dull hair, but dark russet eyes. Eyes that laughed with joy at absolutely everyone she met. Virgil liked to see this, even though there was nothing special in the way she looked at or spoke to him. He appreciated her joyfulness. They chatted sometimes, laughed sometimes. He always kept a place in his memory for the jokes that came his way so that he could repeat them to Grace the next time he saw her. It surprised him just how often people joked with him, since they only came to him when there was something wrong, some pain that needed ending.

But Grace never came to him in a professional context. Perhaps, that was what he was waiting for. She was never ill, never injured, never got a rash, never had an unexplained ailment which required his treatment. She was as well as she was joyful. A few times, in the evenings, he tried cancelling his office hours, so that he could be walking home past the diner at about the time he judged her shift to be finished, and a few times they met this way. Sometimes she seemed pleased. Sometimes she was in a hurry or in a mood he couldn't quite understand. These moods troubled him when he went back to his own house and cooked his small supper, listening to the baseball game on the radio.

The truth was, as Virgil himself knew, that there was no crisis between them. No look of anger or desire, or that shock of transparency that comes to people when they realize they have been understood when they least expected to be. Virgil had grown so used to crises, other people's crises, that he had lost the vital connection between crisis and passion. Passions have names, but crises are all the same, and he feared to light the powder when he could not see the keg.

It happened in May. The red-bud trees glistened in the sun, the days lengthening tenderly into evening. Virgil entered the dim waiting room from the back as he always did, having left the front door of his office open for thirty minutes prior to his scheduled opening time so that his patients might enter and seat themselves at their own pace. He knew that country people are shy and afraid of offending, and so they always arrived early for any appointment. To his astonishment there were only three people in the room: a mother with her bespectacled daughter and, sitting across the room, Grace, looking very shaken and pale. He took the mother and daughter into his examination room, looked down the daughter's throat at the pus-white sores, and gave the mother a small bottle of medicine for the daughter to take thrice daily.

When he followed them back into the waiting room, Grace had already risen and looked as though she had lost her nerve and was preparing to leave. His return had startled her somewhat and left her indecisive.

She came in and sat down, laying her small handbag on the stainless steel table near his medicine cabinet. He thought about sharing the newest joke he had learned, but then changed his mind. Instead, he praised the weather.

What can we do for you today? he asked.

She hesitated for a moment and he found himself unable to discover her eyes' focus as she looked around the room. Finally, she replied, Female troubles.

He nodded and made a non-committal gesture with his hands, as if to say this was nothing uncommon in his line of work. This seemed to relax her enough so that she began to recite the tale of her symptoms. He tried his hardest to be as professional as he knew how, to look as business-like and as old-hand-at-this-sort-of-thing as he could, but a cold numbness crept over him, fingering through his ribs and locking its clutch on to his throat. What she described were undoubtedly the symptoms of syphilis.

That evening Virgil sat alone at his kitchen table. He did not switch the radio on, and the house – kitchen, living room, study, bathroom, three bedrooms – echoed with silence. He stared into his favourite white bowl, filled neatly with Campbell's soup. Beyond it, on the table, lay a rolled copy of the *Valley Register*, listing, as it always did, the names and beloved memory of people who had died in the past week – many of them, people he had known. He sat dry-eyed, too familiar with sadness to feel that anything in particular had been emptied or drained or in some way taken away from him. Whatever he might have hoped, or imagined he had hoped, he was far from wanting anything that he could understand or name. He sat with his fingertips together until the night fell outside his windows. Then he went to bed, wondering whether he would dream.

August 30, 1963

2pm. At lunchtime Hartsock sent the crew of workmen 'round to meet me. He warned me not to be disappointed by their appearance. It's good he did this, as it would be easy to be disappointed by their appearance. There are four of them in the crew. The youngest one, about 30, is named Davy. Everything about him is oval, his face, his torso, each half of each leg. He is very smooth and egg-like. The next oldest is called Dicky Bird. His face always looks as though he has just stopped laughing at something you didn't quite catch, all lines & small eyes. He wears his trousers low, which makes his back & chest seem elongated. The next one, who may be a brother to Dicky Bird, is known as Rip. His face is more serious, more intelligent, more genuinely humble. But then there was the boss of the crew. I'm not quite sure of his name. From what Hartsock said, I thought it was Maurice, but it may be Morris or Morse. They called him something sounding like Marce. I hope it isn't Mars. Anyway, he is quite something. Tall, well-built, good-looking in a way that a man might be after he has beaten up all the other men you know. He clearly rules the others with more nuances of intimidation than I could ever understand. Looking at him, I thought I recognized him somewhat, though I couldn't imagine how. Just then we were joined by the glasses-wearing boy I had seen yesterday in the truck. It was clear then, that Marce was the man I'd seen with the truck. The boy's name was John John. When they drove away (I hadn't recognized the truck, as they'd parked it in a triangle called The Common, near the Hollow Road) Marce drove with Rip and Dicky Bird beside him. Davy and John John rode in the truck bed, holding on to the edges.

10.30pm. Foggy again this morning. Warmer even than yesterday.

Cumberland Gap

I, LittleWound, tell this story.

It was in the time before the Washechu came. There was a hunter named CloudMan. As a boy he brought his mother gifts of groundhog, squirrel, turkey and deer. His father was proud of him. He was also a warrior. Though the Catoctin did not like war, CloudMan wore two feathers of the eagle as symbols of the two men he had killed.

CloudMan watched his brothers choose wives and marry, making lodges of their own. He was proud of them and he was not jealous. He wished to know what they knew.

There came a day when CloudMan's mother gripped her stomach and died, and after that, CloudMan's father took less care on the hunt. It was as if his wisdom had deserted him. One day, ahead of his brothers, he rushed upon a wounded bear with his hatchet, and the bear killed him. CloudMan buried his father with honour and mourned him as a son should mourn. From this, CloudMan also learned lessons in love.

There was a girl named FourSkies whose father had seen the bear kill CloudMan's father. He had also seen his daughter look at CloudMan and this upset him. He was afraid that the madness that had led to the warrior's death might be a madness that his son shared. For this reason, he quickly gave his daughter in marriage to another man.

FourSkies had been a daughter of honour and she became a wife of honour. She did not wear feathers, except at those times when the Manitoes are honoured. She did not sit with her ankles crossed. She knew how to make sugar from birch, from boxelder and from maple. As a girl, she loved to be among the other girls and throw the wand. But as a wife she behaved in a way befitting a wife. Her one extravagance was that she loved to swim. When the locusts sang and the only thing in the sky was the sun and the circling buzzards, she would leave her work and go for a swim. The place she favoured was among the sycamores in the valley below the lodges. Here the shade fell and the water lay unmoving, slowed by the rocks.

It happened that one day in summer CloudMan's brothers were talking. FourSkies had had no children and for this they blamed her husband. They had once heard a rumour that before her marriage, FourSkies had looked at CloudMan. They began by asking him whether he had heard this himself. He had not. They began to tease him, saying that he could become the man she needed. They said their own wives had cooked his meals and mended his clothes for too long. They also said he had lived too long in his parents' lodge, and it was time he made it his own by bringing his own wife to it. CloudMan said nothing, but he now had thoughts he had not had before.

CloudMan began to take notice of FourSkies. He watched her tasks throughout the year. When the frosts came, he saw her work alongside the other wives when the people moved from their homes from the mountaintop to the valley in time for the migration of the deer. He watched her hair and her hands. He saw her shoulder-blades move beneath her clothes. He saw her eyes close when the wind blew. He saw the muscles in her legs tense and flex and his heart ached with longing.

But she was another warrior's wife.

The frost began to come to CloudMan's hair. It also came to FourSkies'. Their days continued to pass in honour and the dignity of their lives remained. CloudMan did not become like his father, though he did gain two more eagle feathers. In the time he loved FourSkies he saw his brothers' children learn to hold the bow and kill the ak uk o jesh. There were times when his loneliness overwhelmed him and he lost the light of his spirit. He would wait for the hearth to cool and plunging his hands among the coals he would blacken his face and go to the cave above the stream and fast, waiting for the truth to appear. His reputation for wisdom grew.

The time of blossoms came again. The warriors put on their robes and played the flute, dancing. The chaperones followed the couples wanting to be married. The love-calls of the men sweetened the air. The mothers with babies sat by the doors of their lodges and CloudMan saw nothing but the returning of his pain.

The afternoon heated until there was nothing but silence and lethargy. The mountain itself and everything that lived on it drowsed and the sun refused to cool or set.

Looking out from her lodge, FourSkies saw that everyone was taken up by exhaustion. They had eaten, drunk, caroused and now they slept in groups, chatted, drew in the dirt with sticks, spun tops and enjoyed the peace of satiety and repletion. She turned her eyes away and walked towards the valley where the sycamores surrounded the pool in the stream.

When she reached the rocks above the water FourSkies looked around. There was no one following her. Alone in the quiet, she undressed and lay down softly in the water. She shivered and watched her skin harden in the coolness. She lay looking over her body, watching the grasshoppers leap over the grass on the bluff where the sun still burned furiously. She wanted to sleep, and although the gravel pillowed her back and hips, her head rested on the stones. She tried closing her eyes.

When she opened them, she saw sitting on the limb of the sycamore nearest the sun, the shape of a man. He did not move.

She squinted. It was CloudMan. Had she slept? Did he follow her while she was sleeping and now sat down, knowing her shame? Had he been there all along? Why didn't he move?

She knew why he hadn't spoken. It was the same reason he had never spoken to her. All the frustration, the heartache, the loneliness, pain, loss and desperation she had felt because of him for so long mounted up inside her as anger, and she screamed. Her voice lifted itself as a wail of anguish and desire of a kind none of the people had ever heard spoken before. They roused themselves at once and ran towards the sound of her screams.

When they arrived, FourSkies had dressed again. Her hair soaked her shoulders and breasts and she quivered in fear and rage. When they asked her what had happened – had she been bitten by a snake? – she could not answer. She only pointed to the sycamore trees and said she had seen something. Perhaps, it had been a paukauk, an evil spirit that frightened her. Her husband took her back inside his lodge and she stayed indoors for several days.

In his despair, CloudMan had looked down at FourSkies in the water below. His spirit beat within him and his pride echoed in his ears. He thought himself bewitched as the love he felt translated into a torment that should have been lust. When she screamed he knew he had been freed. As the people drew around FourSkies leading her away he stayed hidden in the laurels on the ridge. When they were gone, he returned to the water and plunged his hands amid the lichens and moulds, darkening them. Once again, he blackened his face for what would become another fasting meditation. He turned from the stream and walked towards the mountain he could see in the distance. In his shame, he ate no more and never saw any of his people again. Not until he found the SpiritRoad.

August 31, 1963

10am. I have finished unpacking the necessaries in the Mary House. A good thing I brought a cupboard, as there is only one downstairs, & none upstairs, although there are hooks everywhere there is room for them. I feel a little (more?) like a nun.

*The Mary House is about 25' x 20', with one room downstairs and one upstairs. There are no windows on the south side, one to the north, two to the east, and four to the west (one downstairs). The door is on the west side, towards the intersection of the roads & The Corner. The downstairs has a linoleum floor, a 1-piece enamel sink, an electric stove & a fireplace. I have added a chair, a lamp, a bookshelf with books, rug, & a dinette for one. The stairs go up opposite the door & along the east wall. Upstairs has a very old bed, evidently built right into the walls & nailed to the floor. It has pegs in the frame for the ropes that once held the mattress. It looks as though there was a second one built into the opposite wall. Beside the stairs is a curtained corner with a commode. There is no bathtub or shower, so I'll have to get used to washing like Granny did. Outside there is a lean-to on the south wall piled up with very dry firewood. I must ask whether this will be enough for the winter. The walls seem very solid. Must also ask about the nearest A & P.

2.45pm. Having walked all around The Corner inside & out I started to feel as though I were being watched, though I could see no one. Once more on the high porch, I saw a woman from the house to my right (there are four in sight in that direction, & 1 church, all at least 100 years old) come outside and throw something into the bushes at the end of her yard. She scolded someone, presumably a child, telling him not to go near whatever she had thrown out. She then looked my way and stared at me very hard. I waved and smiled, but she shut her door & disappeared. I wonder whether she'd scold me if I went near those bushes?

5.30pm. About 30 minutes ago I saw an old woman wobbling down the Harmony Road from the houses behind The Corner, so I made an excuse to myself (and I hope to her) to be on the Mary House porch when she passed. She was, I thought, shaped like an upturned bucket, & was dressed in a brown calico dress to suit. I introduced myself, telling her my name. She smiled, in embarrassment, I thought. I had to ask her name directly. Pointless, as her voice was so garbled, I'm not sure what she said. I think it might have been Agatha, though it sounded more like Agassy. I asked her where the nearest A & P store is, and she looked worried, possibly afraid. Frederick, she finally said, & left it there. 12 miles or so, I think. Agassy then smiled, more relieved, and headed up the Brethren Church Road. I fiddled around on the porch, waiting to see where she'd go. She knocked on the door at the house where the staring scolding bush-contaminating woman lived. Agassy opened the door & vanished, & a moment later I heard the other woman's voice call out -Come in!

8.30pm. Interesting evening. About 6.30 I found myself outside defacing my own bushes with dishwater & peelings, when I heard music coming from somewhere. It turns out there is a younger couple (late 30s?) who live in the house just across the little stream to the right of The Corner. They were out on their long porch, sitting in wooden chairs & playing instruments. The man had a fiddle and the woman a dulcimer. There was no singing, but the music had an odd Irish gait to it. I learned that their names are Joanie & Paul, they have no children, he's a groundskeeper, she's a florist, he is a Korean War vet, she did a year of college, the nearest A & P is in Frederick & there is an Acme store in Middletown (6 miles). They are both very nice. I like his curly hair, & I like her hand-clapping laugh.

9.45pm. Have made so many lists I have run out of paper. Added -more paper- to shopping list, and pencil point broke.

10.45pm. Not sleepy. Nice warm dry day.

Throw 'way your pen, John, John

There really wasn't anything else she could do. She had done all a woman could. All a woman like her could do. She was sure of that. Mae Burkhardt had given birth four times, three of them alone, on the floor in her own parlour. The one time she had help was the third one, her only daughter, whose birthing was so bad Hiram had got a neighbour to come and see what could be done. The child lived for two days. After the funeral Hiram tried to comfort her by telling her not to worry – one day, she'd forget the whole thing. Perhaps, he did.

Her home life was stark but not impossible. She and Hiram had a bed, and each of the boys had one of his own. In the winter there would be ice on the floors downstairs, until Hiram got the fires re-started, but there was always food enough. Hiram was a good shot, and they were lucky with their chickens, which he killed one by one as they needed them. She sometimes watched him strike them with a stick of wood before cutting their heads off with the hatchet, leaving their bodies flailing and coursing blood round the block near the woodpile. She sometimes remembered those moments whenever she heard about a neighbour's suicide. Bill Williams jumping down his silo. Ross Weddle shooting himself with a pistol.

The boys had been bad, but not that bad. They learned to drink in the beer joints that would sell a bottle to anyone who could see above the counter. They stole firewood, traps, sometimes even barbed wire, or anything else they could find in the woods. They overturned outhouses, bought cars they couldn't keep running, tried to impress any girl they could find. She had watched Hiram training them in the manhood he understood. He taught them how to throw punches and how to dodge them. He taught them how to throw and hit a baseball. He taught them about lust and goaded them about sex. When his own mother died, he even showed them that he could cry. He never said sorry.

Mostly Hiram worked until he was exhausted and drank whiskey in a manner so careful that no one, not even Mae, ever saw him drink it, though the whole family knew where it was kept, knew it disappeared regularly, and saw him buy more. When he was in the mood, he washed himself thoroughly, doused himself with Old Spice and set to a regular pattern of groping Mae. Sex was something that belonged to him, beginning, middle and end.

In the autumn after her youngest son joined the others who had already left home – one to the army, one to the foundry, and the last one as a labourer at the brickworks – Hiram realized there was no one left to help him outdoors. He was forty-four years old, had lived on the same road all his life, and he had no friends to speak of. He took to spending more time indoors, reading the newspaper, listening to the radio. When he went outside to farm what was left of his little farm, everything he did had a worn-out, busted feel to it. He sold all the cows except the best eight, all the hogs except the best four. Even the chickens were living more than one generation.

Around Thanksgiving he decided he would have a butchering again as he had every year when the boys still lived with them. This time though, instead of four hogs, he would only kill one. Partly he knew that he and Mae weren't likely to eat more than that in one winter, but also because he didn't think he could handle killing more than that by himself, as it all had to be finished in one day, to make sure nothing spoilt. He told Mae she'd have to help him herself, even though she had helped him with the butchering every year since they were married.

He started even before the late sun rose above the mountaintop. By nine o'clock he had the carcass shot, stuck, scalded, scraped, on the poles, head off and gutted. Mae had the one-piece poplar butchering table scrubbed and Hiram was cutting up the first side while she was crouching over a trio of washtubs. One of them held the hog's head which she had shaven with a straight razor and trimmed of its ears and eyes, ready for Hiram to collect and cut up. Another tub held all the useful organs to be made into pudding – liver, kidneys, and two or three things she knew by sight but not by name. In the third tub, the one she was bent over, coiled the intestines. She had a smooth washed board in front of her, against which she delicately stretched the small intestine, slowly rubbing it inside out so that the contents of the hog's last few meals spilled over the side. When she was done, she would wash the whole rope of empty intestines in warm water, ready to turn them into the casings for the sausages she would make with the trimmings from the table.

It was then that Hiram called out to her with some instruction. But because she was concentrating, he was a little too far away, she had her back to him and he had a chaw of tobacco in his jaw, she couldn't hear what he said. She looked up and called back to him. In spite of the cold (there was three inches of snow on everything), he was hot and already getting tired. He laid down the long knife he was using and walked towards her, more or less blocking the sunshine behind him. She looked down again at her work.

Hiram was about ten feet away when he stopped and put his greasy bloody hands on his hips. Mae braced herself for a complaint.

Hell, woman, ain't y'all done that yet? he said.

Mae wiped the loose hair from her face with the back of her wrist and looked up. She stood at the same moment, straightening her stiff back, and then she saw it. Galloping clumsily towards Hiram, attracted by the smell of the offal, the blood, or the fresh faeces, was a bear. Hiram neither heard it nor saw it.

Mae looked down for a weapon. She had been sitting on the chopping block, and in the chips near her feet lay Hiram's hatchet.

With nothing in her mind at all, she grabbed the hatchet at the moment the bear lifted himself on to his haunches. All of the animal's attention was on Hiram, and he didn't see Mae coming at all. Just as his front legs opened outwards for his first swipe she plunged straight into the bear's chest, her momentum causing the blade of the hatchet to completely disappear in the animal's trunk. She had cut through several of its ribs and nearly cut its heart in two. There was a moment when she felt the bear's breath exhaling on her head and neck even as it perceived its own death. At last, it wobbled, and fell to her right, its massive foreleg striking her shoulder with the weight of two men, knocking her to the ground alongside it.

Hiram looked down and saw her lying on the ground with a circle of blood the size of a pie dish on her chest. The bear was motionless and he couldn't tell whether it was injured or dead. He thought Mae was dead. When she finally moved, he stumbled and fell towards her. They sat perfectly still until the snow began to melt under them, soaking their clothes.

By sunset, the butchering was complete – cooked, crocked, salted, and smoking. The bear's corpse lay exactly where it had fallen. Later, within a week, Hiram had sold the bearskin to a neighbour for dressing, and he cut up the bear's corpse with his axe and dragged the debris to the edge of the woods to rot away or be eaten by the carrion birds and animals. He found the hatchet, saved it and hung it over his workbench in the barn.

By Christmas, Hiram had stopped drinking altogether and gave what was left of his whiskey to a neighbour. Though Mae never said a word about the incident to anyone, Hiram told everybody he met. Not everything he thought about Mae had changed, but enough had. Mae saw it and accepted it, though she never asked him for an explanation, and luckily, she thought, he never asked her for one. But sometimes, at night, when they were both lying in bed awake, one or the other of them crept a hand over looking for the other's hand. And then they slept.

September 1, 1963

12.30pm. What a special morning it has been. It seems as though the whole of Harmony went to church on foot today. Little groups of families, couples & old people in their finest paraded round the bend at The Corner, heading for one of the two churches on the Brethren Church Road. (It seems the Almighty has a sense of economy, as he had His Lutherans build their temple about 250 yards from His Brethrens.) Anyway, they all looked very spiffy, the men in clean pants and shirts; the older men with ties and jackets, the boys with their shirt tails in. The girls looked like small women, and the women looked like large cakes, all hairspray, beads, gloves and hats (the Brethren women with a kind of net veil). I swept the Mary House porch for about 30 minutes just to get a look at them all. Quite a few said –How do? as they passed. Some were chatty & said –Ain't y'all coming? and –It ain't fancy. You look fine. Just fine. Others, I'm quite sure, smelt slightly of brimstone. No doubt having seen me sweeping on a Sunday they will have prayed for my salvation, the quality of my fried chicken, & the morals of any man likely to come within 6 feet of me, as nobody trusts a widow. About 11 o'clock, the parade reversed direction & they all came back. By now the children were climbing, throwing, hitting, shouting and generally creating reasons for doubting the effectiveness of contemporary Sunday School teaching. The women, mostly, went off in little groups, sometimes pointing at women in other little groups, shaking their heads, giggling, & finding two hours on a pew tightens the girdle unacceptably. The men, somehow, seemed to walk with wider steps then they set off with, laughed more, & found the time right to swear when required.

*The last ones to go by were Agassy & two other women who appearance-wise had everything in common with her.

The tallest, & I think the oldest (70s?) introduced them all as —Mrs Zittle, Mrs Fisher and Mrs Ford. Unfortunately, it all happened so unexpectedly, I'm not sure which one is Zittle & which one Fisher, though I'm clear that Mrs Ford was the shortest. Fisher and Zittle waved goodbye, one heading left up the Harmony Road, one down the Hollow Road. Mrs Ford watched them go and then looked at me. I looked at her, expecting her to say something. She just smiled. —I like your necklace, Mrs Ford, I said. Her hand went to her throat and she twisted them. —Ain't they purdy? she said. Then she leaned over towards me and rolled some really unusual green eyes at me. —Miss Mary, she said. You better just call me Cinch. I won't know who you're a-talkin to if you call me anythin' else. Then she smiled and shrugged her shoulders like a little girl. She turned and walked away, saying quietly —See ya tamarr.

7.30pm. Have been thinking of Cinch Ford. I know I am going to like her.

9.30pm. Another nice day — warm & bright. At 10, hoping to watch "The DuPont Show of the Week".

September 2, 1963

9am. Monday. Today is Labor Day, so naturally the men aren't working. That sounds like a joke, though it doesn't feel like one.

11.30am. After breakfasting on bread without butter & tea without milk, I decided to take a walk. I turned right from the Mary House door, & walked up the Harmony Road, counting houses until I came to the Coxey Brown Road. There are 6 on the left & 6 on the right, all but 2 at least a century old. I glimpsed 1 man, 1 woman & heard 2 children shouting. 2 cars drove past, both slowing down to look at me, their drivers (1 man and 1 woman) simply raising a finger from the steering wheel by way of greeting.

5.00pm. What an afternoon! I have discovered that, being in the center of things, The Corner is a place magnetized by habits. Over about 3 hours, at least 25 people variously came & went in small groups. The men & boys paid their respects (that is, nodded awkwardly) at the women, before all going to a piece of land that lay between mine and the embankment where the boys were jumping the other day, & "pitched horseshoes" into sandy pits where they'd already driven metal stakes. They shouted, whooped, laughed, swore & joked, coming & going, for about 2 hours or more. Meanwhile, the women all stood or sat like damp hens around a pair of benches (that is, an old church pew & a bridge plank on tree stumps) under the walnut trees beside the bridge directly in front of the Mary House & The Corner. The girls who joined them busied themselves by risking their lives walking along the outer tension railings on the iron bridge.

*I thought it would be prudent to join the women, as it is better to gossip from within than from without. Here are some of the conversations:

*–Sure nice to meet ya, Miss White. – Oh, please call me Mary. –Well.

*–How long ya been widowed? –Three years. –Uh huh. It sure is hard.

*–What did your husband do 'fore he died? –He was a doctor. –Uh huh. –A psychiatrist. –Uh huh. I heard you was from Sykesville. –Yes. –He work in … that place? –Yes. Springfield Hospital. Since we were married. –Uh huh. How long you married? –Twenty-three years. –Uh huh. Don't know how he could stand it, working in that place. –It takes a toll. –Uh huh.

*–My sister-in-law Irene says you're some kinda writer. That right? –Yes. Stories. Mainly. –Uh huh. Huh! Ain't that something? A real live writer. Huh!

*Then Cinch Ford, who had been listening to all this, spoke up. —Miss Mary, you got children?

*There is something timeless or infinitely old in her face and in her look, & her hopeful earnest glance reached very far into me, & unexpectedly, I felt my eyes tear up. —Yes. One, I said. —Uh huh. —He's a soldier. Now. —Uh huh.

*I looked at her face, lined in every direction like a scratched mirror. She was reading everything inside me. Finally, her high cheekbones raised and those mysterious eyes of hers twinkled. —Now won't it just be something when he comes here and sees all this? You'll both be so proud. —Yes, I said. Yes.

*I made myself listen to the women, & watch the men for another 15 minutes before I came inside & cried till I shook.

11.15pm. For some reason, the TV news tonight announced that it would now go from 15 to 30 minutes. Perhaps, we now have twice as much going on as we used to. Perhaps, they will tell us twice as much about what is going on. Perhaps, they will spend the last 15 minutes apologizing for the first 15. What strange times. More trouble in Ala. Gov Wallace now made the police surround schools to keep the black children out. What terror those children must all feel.

*Foggy again this morning, though it got very warm this afternoon.

Ida Red

I, LittleWound, tell this story.

It was in the time after my capture by the Washechu but before the menses began. I no longer wore doeskin and dyed the toes of my boots with pokeberries. I could not plait my hair because of the mourning. It was in the time after the Catoctin warriors went to the mountain beyond the valley to look for deer, because of the winter's violence and deer on this mountain had grown scarce. The story came to us that the Catoctin warriors had met with others and they were all killed in a battle. None came home and the winter worsened. The HomeWind blew in the morning and at night. Before long the old began to die. The women and fathers collected wood for the fires and we were not cold. We trapped what we could and ate all the fruits and nuts we had saved. But it was not enough. The women and fathers began to die. They died lying down at night and they died in silence sitting by the fires. Our mothers too began to die, have given everything they had to eat to us. Before long we grew afraid and began to walk down the hillsides following the small streams to where the Washechu lived. I was found by two men, a father and son, and they brought me to a village beside the stream. There was a building there built of logs, one they used to store the goods they needed for their large building, the one where the Washechu stream passed through. The wife of the man gave me food and clothes and blankets, and they put me upstairs in the small building. They decided to name me Mary.

I worked every day for the family who fed me and whose fire kept me warm. Though I never dishonoured myself with tears, I thought often of my mother who died lying in the snow and my father who had died on the mountain across the valley. The Washechu worked very hard, the men and the women, and they wished me to look like them. They gave me dresses. When my boots wore out they sought to give me boots like their own, and this is where my story begins.

In the stream behind the building where I live there were once trout. If you shot an arrow twice in the direction of the water's flow, you would come to a pool that the Catoctin made to catch trout. The water was dammed with earth and stones and the Catoctin women would catch the fish in baskets. Here another man from the Washechu village had made buildings of his own. In one of these he lived, in one he dressed hides, and in another he used tools to make things from the leather. I was taken here to be given boots.

The workroom was full and had windows in the walls. There were shelves that looked like bunks in which hides of all kinds were stacked. There was a table with tools and tools and strips of leather hung from the ceiling and the room smelt of oak and fruit. The shoemaker sat on a bench in the centre of the room. He measured my foot with a ruler and nodded. This was how I learned to know his face. He smiled and spoke to me, touching my shoulder.

She can't talk, the Master said.

Can't talk or won't talk? the shoemaker asked.

Can't talk, he said.

On the day when the food is given, the shoemaker came to the building where I lived and gave me the boots. Say, he said, Can you hear me? I nodded. You see that house over there? he said. He pointed to another house across the road from us. Do you know who lives there? he said. Miss Mamie. Do you know her? I shook my head. She's a widow. Her husband died. You ever see anybody else go around there, any gentlemen? I shook my head. You're a good girl, he said. Now I want you to do something for me. You keep watching that house and if you see anybody go in there, you come and get me, you hear? All right, then, he said, and left the boots.

Day after day I watched the house where the widow Miss Mamie lived. I saw her do her chores, empty her buckets, and sometimes talk to people who passed by. No one went to her house. Sometimes in the evening she walked through the water of the stream where it lay over the road and walked towards the meadow, stopping before she got to the hillside. Here there was a stable and blacksmith. She seldom spoke to the blacksmith, though she did sometimes chat with his wife. Mostly she liked to look at the horses that were kept in the stables. It seemed to be a task of hers to walk each one down to the stream to drink and then walk them back again. Her favourite horse was the stallion that belonged to the smith and his wife.

It happened that the smith burnt his arm and had to stay indoors, where his wife tended him. At this time, no more horses came, and the widow used to come more often to visit the stallion, walking him down to the stream. Sometimes she would let him come on to her side of the water, where she would tether him with a rope while he grazed on the grass between her house and the road. It was on one of these days that I remembered my promise to the shoemaker.

Is it man or a woman? he said. I shook my head.

He came with me at once, and I stood in the road, pointing towards the house where Miss Mamie lived. The horse was no longer on the tether but I could not see his hindquarters through the stable-door. I took the shoemaker by the hand and led him towards the house. He made as if to go to the door, but I pulled him towards the back, by the stream.

Where you taking me, girl? he said.

I pointed and he looked into the shade between the house and the stream, where the chestnuts and walnuts overhung the grass. Here was the horse. The shoemaker looked at me, ready to laugh, but I pointed. Through the horse's legs I could see the widow's skirts. She was standing behind the horse. He saw them too. He shook his head and started to walk towards her. Miss Mamie heard the steps and looked up. Her face stiffened and she stepped back. Her ears stood back in pain and her colour grew like the sunset. The stallion stamped and Miss Mamie hid her hands in the folds of her dress. The shoemaker opened his mouth to speak, but his jaw froze.

Evening, ma'am, he said. Blacksmith 'round? I ... I come to get some hasps. Rivets. Hardware.

No sir, she said. They went to Fredericktowne early this morning.

Sorry to trouble you, ma'am.

He touched his fingers to his hat and coughed. Then he walked back down the road without looking at me.

Get on out of here, girl, she said. You get back where you belong, she said, wiping the grease from her hands on to a rag as the stallion pulled against his halter.

September 3, 1963

10am. Tuesday. The first day of work on The Corner. Hooray! All four of the men showed up by 8 o'clock. I'm pretty sure that Marce was there from 7.45. Just after 8 I walked over to see what they were going to do. I was met with a chorus of 3 –Morn, Ma'am-s & 1 –Hey! from Marce. I brought them a pot of coffee and 4 cups. Marce said he prefers tea.

*They are starting work on the ground outside & around the building. Pruning, clearing away & making room to get a truck close to the old wash house to haul away junk & debris. They are going to rip out the old oil tank, dig a hole for the septic system, & a trench for pipes to connect to a new well.

4.30pm. The men have cleared off. They certainly do work hard, I must say. Davy is in charge of sweating, & never seems to slacken. Dicky Bird sings throughout everything. Rip concentrates & for light relief, smiles sometimes. Marce exhibits mastery through swagger & cajoling, though he works almost non-stop. Crouched on their haunches, they seemed to eat spam or ham sandwiches, cheese and fruit for lunch. I brought them more coffee (& tea!) when I heard the hammering & whacking stop at about 12. At 4 John John showed up looking skinny & fed up & was greeted by his father with –Where in the hell have you been? John John then spent 30 minutes piling up branches, cut bushes, briars, honeysuckle & rusty metal beside the wash house. Then they drove off, & his first day in 6th grade was over. I hope.

7.30pm. Joanie and Paul just finished an hour of music. Paul played the mandolin & Joanie played the autoharp.

9.30pm. Sleepy this evening. Beautiful full moon after a stunning dry warm day.

September 4, 1963

1pm. Shortly after 8 a large rusty flat-bed truck pulled into the cleared space near the wash house. It has been loaded, driven off & back, reloaded etc at least 4 times. In between, the men have been digging holes and trenches. Same coffee & tea routine.

*I spent some time inside The Corner this morning, arranging things in my mind. Outside, the men had their usual WFMD on the radio, & Dicky Bird started to sing along with a Sam Cooke tune. All at once Marce shouted out –Shut up the G[]d d[]mn n[]gg[]r music!

5.30pm. John John came as before after school. Dicky Bird asked him whether there are any pretty girls in his class. He blushed and looked away. His dad grunted –Sh[]t!

10pm. Very even sort of day, breezy dry and warm.

Kitty alone at night.

Now I don't know nothing. But I tell you what I know. I know that knowing nothing is 'bout the best you can know. That's for sure and all. People say, How you know what you can't never see? I say I can imagine, can't I? I seen it all. Yes sir, I seen it all.

I tell you what, when I was brung here, me being just a girl and all, they put me in the building 'cross the road from The

Corner. They was a woman already live there, and they called her Mary, and they took to calling me Little Mary, but that didn't last too long. The other Mary was a Injun so soon they took to calling her Red Mary and me Black Mary, and that's just the way it took on.

Anyways, when I come it was in the springtime, 'fore it got too hot and all, and the folks 'round here was a talking about the summer coming, and whether it was gonna be like the last one. Pray Lord, they said, it ain't gonna be like the last one when Miss Odessa died. That's all they wanted and that's all they talked about.

Now Miss Odessa was Mister Paul's daughter. Mister Paul, he owned The Corner, and the house, and one that after I come folks took to calling the Mary House, the one where I lived with ole Red Mary. The Corner was the biggest mill 'round here and Mister Paul owned it from his daddy. A side of the Mary House was a creek no bigger than you could've stepped over, I 'spect, but it was into that creek that the water from the mill run. It was just a little bitty thing till the mill-water run in. Anyhow, that water run down the big ole ditch and then into the big creek behind the Mary House – the one where the mill water come from to start with, if you was to walk all the way up to Fisher's Hollow.

Like I said, the mill was a big one, bigger than all them others, and it had a big ole wheel right in the middle, not on the side like them others does, and then they was mill on both sides. The waggons full of wheat and oats and barley and I don't know what all, come down the hill on the road aside the race, and the fellas took the sacks over the race and to the back porch of the mill, where they went through the door and up the big steps to the top. Then when the flour done ground, they collected it from the porch 'round the front, by the pond and where them roads meet in front of our porch. Cross the creek is where Mister Paul kept his stables, but that don't concern me none.

Well, like I say, it was coming on for summer again, and all folks wanted to say was 'bout Miss Odessa. She was a real pretty young thing, and I 'spect she was all right, but from what I hear, she didn't have sense enough to pour sand down a rat hole, leastwise where men was concerned. Maybe nobody showed her nothing, and maybe nobody told her neither. Anyway, whatever talk she did hear she believed, and white folks, being what they is, was always full of talk 'bout the negro men, and how dangerous they was for white women. Mm, mm. If they was to be believed, all a black man had to do was see a white gal and he like a bull in high rye. So whatever Miss Odessa didn't know 'bout men general, she sure knew that much for certain.

Well, 'cause the summer was hot by then, Mister Paul was a handling the grain just about as fast as the farmers could get it dry enough to work. So he thought he'd hire hisself some extra help. Now Mister Paul didn't keep no men negroes of his own, so he'd hire some when he wanted them. 'Course, by now everybody was as busy as he was, so he had to go looking for somebody to hire him a fella for the summer. So he come home with a big young fella they called Rook, who used to work a-lifting timber where they was building the railroads, picking up ties and poles for the telegraph. Something had fallen on his foot and left it twisted in towards the other one, so he kind of went up and down when he walked. But he still could lift, and Mister Paul set him to work a carrying sacks off the waggons and up the steps to the top floor.

Well, like I say, it was hot as the devil's breath that summer, and anybody that could took to finding a place that was cool. Ole Red Mary had come back with her pans full of blackberries, stinking of tar to keep the chiggers off, and went to get herself a nap before Mister Paul's wife, start thinking about her supper. But just the same, the waggons was sitting up the Harmony Road, waiting to be unloaded, and the men had took the horses down to the shade by the creek.

Now it seems like everybody else, Miss Odessa didn't have nothing on her mind but getting cool in the shade somewhere. She went into The Corner, on the same floor where the big stairs get started, and all the big stones sit a-grinding all day. This is the place where some of the fellas does the work a watching the stones a-grinding, but mostly they is upstairs, pouring in the grain, or downstairs a catching up the flour. So they weren't nobody round to see her. So on the side of floor where the big wheel turns was the only wall without no windows, 'cause that's the bit where the machinery is, and where the water runs. They ain't no windows but for one, and it ain't a real window, though it's a hole like one. 'Stead of glass and all, it's got big shutters, and if you open 'em up, you could look out at the wheel and the water from the underneath. Well, what Miss Odessa found out was that if you was to open them windows good and wide, the air from underneath that wheel was all wet and cold like the springhouse, and a body could set there and it was like the breeze after a thunderstorm. So she'd go there when there wasn't nobody to tell her not to.

So the thing is, she was a sitting there when ole Rook was still working, carrying all them sacks out of the waggons, over the bridge and up the steps to the top floor. I 'spect she didn't see him none and he didn't see her none. But the trouble was, 'cause it was so hot, ole Rook didn't have nothing on cept his britches, and they was so full of holes, cause he weren't nothing but a hired-out negro, that he might has well have left them off too. Anyway, what with all the white folks cooling theyselves someplace, they wasn't no one to notice him neither.

So what happened is he was taking one of them full sacks up the steps, when he slipped, maybe on his own sweat, maybe on his crooked foot, I don't know, and busted one of them sacks so the grain run on the steps. Now he didn't know what to 'spect from Mister Paul, or the man that owned that sackful, so he thought he'd better get that grain gone, and in a hurry. So he put the thing down and went to looking around the machinery to find hisself a brush or a broom. Now when he come into the floor where Miss Odessa was, she was a-sitting on that windowsill with the cool and the water all running behind her, and she had her eyes shut, I guess, and I 'spect the machinery made that fuzz fuzz noise it makes, so she didn't see him or hear him. He was a-looking around for that broom, when he comes up to her, and they both jumps, 'cause he didn't 'spect to see her neither. That have all still been all right, I 'magine, 'cept she must have looked down and through all the cracks and the holes and tears in his pants, she seen his little man, just as plain as could be. Now knowing what she been told, she jumped right back like she been bit on by a dog, and the next thing ole Rook knew she went right out the window.

Folks round here says that when they found her stuck down there where the pond goes over the gate into the creek, she was all soft like a doll and the colour of a bruise all over. Mister Paul like went crazy all to hisself too, and he shut The Corner till the fall come and the apples dropping, never mind the waggons that still wanted him seeing to them. They buried her down Middletown with they people. They put ole Rook in the jail for a while, and I 'spect they whip him, but his master say they couldn't prove nothing, and Mister Paul had to pay that master $20 for the rest of what he owed on Rook's hire, and the damages from the whipping.

September 5, 1963

8am. Foggy again this morning and cooler. Hope it improves. Men just arriving. Dicky Bird has a cough.

1.30pm. Trenches all finished now, & the men working on the big hole for the septic system, taking turns to dig and wheelbarrow. For some reason, Marce is fussing about ladders (?).

10.30pm. Very mild all day, then drizzle turned to rain.

September 6, 1963

9.30am. After the usual start, Marce had the men unloading ladders from his truck, together with buckets & tools. I asked & was told this is for the roof. About 8.30 an old man driving a truck showed up to deliver a very long wooden ladder.

2.30pm. Some of the men have been on the roof all morning, ropes tied around their waists, ladders running down the roof on both sides to give them footing. They must be 40' off the ground at times. Davy holds the ladders to the ground, ropes up & back & goes up and down the ladders with things; Dicky Bird and Rip are pounding away at the tin roof with huge hammers, taking nails from their mouths & Marce is everywhere on the ground giving directions. For some reason he keeps sticking a knife or file into the mortar between the bricks & stones, evidently checking for something.

6.30pm. John John arrived after school today to be greeted with –Get the Hell out of the way!

*Before leaving, Marce saw me pulling up weeds from what will one day be a vegetable garden again. He shouted out that the well driller will be coming on Monday, early. I thanked him for the news, all the while wondering where I might best put a hen house.

10pm. Nice autumnal day today. Dry & bright. Leaves will change quickly if this keeps up.

Mississippi Sawyer

I, LittleWound, tell this story.

It was in the time after the Washechu's war of many winters – the one where the Ford men came home missing fingers and toes – but before the Washechu war when refugees came to

45

the valley. The village grew to be called Harmony and more men and women came to live there, speaking languages not like one another. In the hollow where the stream begins, beyond the site where once the Catoctin deer-lodges stood, trees were being cut. Day after day the trees were cut and made into shapes to be used in the villagers' work. They used cedar to store their clothes and sourwood to make their canes. They used maple and cherry and walnut for their furniture, and they made instruments from birch. They cleaned their teeth with blackgum and cooked with poplar and ash. They built their lodges with chestnut when they could, and pine when they could not. But of all the trees on the Catoctins' Mountain it was oak they loved. They used it for baskets and barrels, for their roofs and their floors and their spinning wheels, and they saved the bark to tan their hides.

The need for so much wood brought men to the village. Sawyers set up their frames or their pits in the hollow, and the shriek of blades could be heard in the morning and afternoon. Two of these sawyers came to see my master when he needed timber to replace those parts of the mill which its turning wheels wore away. These men lived only among men in the forest near their saw-pits and they looked about them at the village's women whenever they came into the valley. Sometimes they made bargains with Master Routzahn at the mill, trading their timber for the use of his horses, his waggon or the labourers he sometimes hired to dig and repair the millrace.

It was on a day when the walnuts were dropping their leaves in the wind and the nuts had begun to drop around the mill, the Master's house and my own quarters, that the two sawyers came to the mill to find Master Routzahn. They found him in his house on the hill above the millrace and he took them into the dooryard. At the same time, his wife watched from the window. The two sawyers stared at Mrs Routzahn in the window and their mouths dampened and they rubbed their chins. As they were talking, I came outdoors on to the porch to sit down again and knock hulls from the walnuts in my pail. After talking, the three men shook hands and the sawyers turned to leave. Then they stopped and looked downhill towards me.

Would you look at that, one of them said.

She's a injun, ain't she? said the other.

She yours? the first one said.

She's a servant we keep, Master Routzahn said. Her name is Mary. She helps my wife, sweeps the mill, does chores.

How much you want for her? the first one asked.

She's not for sale, Master Routzahn said.

No, sir, we don't want to buy her, the first sawyer said. He looked at his companion. We just want to rent her for a little.

The window where Mrs Routzahn stood crashed down and Master turned to look. He turned back and said something else to the sawyers. They shook their heads and walked back up the road towards the hollow. That afternoon Master Routzahn saddled his horse and rode off towards the hollow. He came back before nightfall.

The two sawyers did not come back, and after that day Master Routzahn made deals with other sawyers. Sometimes the deal would be that he would send his waggon up to the hollow, where they would load it with timber, then bring it back to mill to load with flour and other stores for a trip to one of the villages further up the valley to where the farmers were beginning to live. Mrs Routzahn would sometimes go along with her son on these trips and come back with supplies like wool for spinning, sassafras for tea or shellbarks for cake.

It happened in the time when the wheat was ripe that Master Routzahn and his son had to go to Fredericktowne to make a bargain over land for brick-burning, and Mrs Routzahn was left to manage the mill by herself. At this time her husband had forgotten that he had made a deal with some sawyers to deliver their goods along with his own in the valley towards Mount Pleasant. The men were busy keeping the mill working, and there was no one to ride on this journey with her but me. I hid my face in my apron and refused to go, knowing that if I went I would die. Mrs Routzahn pleaded with me, promised me pies and shook her fist at me. I ran out of my quarters before she could catch me and took the road towards Hawbottom as fast as I could. As there was no one else to take, and she was afraid of losing the Master's deal, Mrs Routzahn decided to make the journey alone just as she had made it many times before with her son.

It happened that the two sawyers who had once tried to buy me had not forgotten what had cost them their deal with the Master. On the morning that Mrs Routzahn set off with the waggon full of supplies they were splitting shingles on the rise before the Delauter homestead. They recognized the waggon making its way up the road and then saw that it was a woman on her own driving the horses. They stopped working and consulted. In the silence, Mrs Routzahn took the horses into the shade at the top of the hill to rest them. It was then that the men came out towards her.

Well, I'll be damn, the first one said. What's your hurry, missus?

You keep back now, you hear?

Whoa, there. Ain't nobody done nothing now, have they?

Mrs Routzahn sat back down on the waggon-seat and the second man came closer.

What you got in there, then, huh?

She looked over her shoulder at the waggon.

Not in there. In there. He put his hands on her breasts. She writhed and fell off the seat and on to the ground. She stood up as the men laughed.

You ain't so high and mighty now.

Mrs Routzahn stood with her back to the waggon. Beside her hand lay the reins and the whip in its sheath. Behind her back, on the edge behind the waggon's side, was a bucket of pitch that she had agreed to sell for her husband's partners. She threw her hands back on both sides as if to steady herself against the waggon. She made a decision and said something to the sawyer with the teeth like a fox.

Shit, Karl, you hear that?

Hell, I did!

They both raised their chins and looked at her. Karl ran his hands over his shirt where the sweat marked it in rings like the heart of a tree. They were thinking.

Mrs Routzahn lowered her hands and started to gather up her skirts. She said something else and looked at the man she thought believed himself to be most like a rabbit, least like a bull.

It's him, she said, her skirts now showing the place where her knees became her thighs. I'll bet he's the biggest.

Like Hell he is, the other sawyer said. Both men began to fumble with their belts and their buttons.

Just then Mrs Routzahn dropped her skirts, taking hold of the whip with one hand and plunging the other into the bucket of pitch. Like a horse kicking she brought the whip down in a stroke on to first man's crotch. Something fell into the leaves and he made a sound like a dying possum as his shirttails flowered in blood.

The other sawyer lunged towards her but stumbled over the trousers at his feet. Mrs Routzahn's hand full of pitch came straight into his eyes. She pulled her hand away as if he were on fire and the man fell to the ground clutching his face as it disappeared in blood. He groaned and tried to touch his face but couldn't. She had torn away his eyelids, and the skin from his nose and cheeks.

With her one good hand, she took the reins and got on to the waggon's seat. She swung the reins above the horses' backs and turned the waggon in the road, driving away from the place where the two sawyers rolled, stumbling into the ruts as hard as troughs dried in the sun.

Later that night I used the Master's razor to shave Mrs Routzahn's hand. I washed it in my own basin with lye-soap that I had made. She did not sleep much and until the day of her death spoke only with the voice of a foal.

September 7, 1963

7.30am. Woke up suddenly, afraid of my own dreams. Alex running through the woods and someone shouting. I listened to the shouting for a moment before I realized it was my own voice. And that I was already awake.

1pm. Drove to Frederick today, eventually finding the A & P. Spent nearly $23, but then I needed everything. Also visited the C Burr Artz (Arts?) library, joined, & got a 2 vol history of western Maryland. Discovered there is a bookshop on North Market Street & something more like a news & magazine shop on Patrick Street.

4pm. Sat down for a cup of tea & realized what day it is. It is my (our?) wedding anniversary. 26 years. Tried to think of Tom but couldn't. Not as a boyfriend, or a fiancé or a young husband or even a middle-aged one. Couldn't keep a single image or memory in mind for very long. It all slips away. I look around me & it seems that everything in my life has grown smooth & sleek & undulating & I cannot catch hold, get a good grip on anything. All I could picture was the Tom I never met, the boy he was in the stories he told me about himself, the old man he never lived to become. I forgive everything else about him for the sake of those two people, the ones I imagine. Happy anniversary, Tom.

10.30pm. I've been thinking about the moment that will come when I have to unpack Alex's clothes & hang them in what will become his new room. How will I feel? Will he still want them? Will they still fit? Perhaps, he will return before The Corner is ready. Don't run, Alex, in case you fall. Remember?

*Very still and quiet today, with fog this morning. Temperature like yesterday.

September 8, 1963

9am. I woke up early this morning, washed dressed & walked over to The Corner. I don't even know why. I was surprised to see four squirrels with the speed of piece-rate workers making off with walnuts. They made no sound other than the scratching & hopping & clicking knock as they scampered about. I crept back down to the bottom floor and went in the front door. This will be our kitchen & dining room. Now it is so dirty & piled with decades of abandonment. I know where I will put a table & which chair Alex will want to sit in when he reads the papers. I wonder if his hair is still the color of Tom's?

*I was upstairs when the people going to the churches passed by. One boy was told off for whistling. Another for walking with his hands in his pockets. I envied both mothers.

10.45pm. Foggy again this morning. It makes the hills look magical, especially as these cold mornings and downright warm (over 80) afternoons are making the leaves yellow, orange and red.

Sowing on the mountain,

Rex was from Philadelphia, Amos from a backwater near York. They met one summer on a dirt road near Lancaster when they were both looking for a cheap place to spend the night. Rex was on the road with a suitcase full of samples from the brush company he worked for, and Amos had been on his own since he ran off from the metal shop where he'd been training to work in tin, copper and brass. They fell to talking about the world and their lives when the night grew thick and they were both too worn out to sleep. Rex had some money saved up and was pretty sure he was about to be fired because his boss suspected him of cheating on his receipts – an accusation that he had to admit was partly true. Amos had a little as well, and he had also made an important discovery: with the Depression now old enough to have grown familiar, housewives and farmers were both very ready to have their broken things mended rather than pay to replace them. The two of them decided to pool their talents and resources and become itinerant sellers and menders.

They had strayed south into Maryland chasing what was left of the sunshine as the days were getting shorter. They worked their way down the county from Emmitsburg and Thurmont, learning that the same things were true in Maryland as in Pennsylvania. If they timed their arrival right, they could always get the lady of the house to admit to having something that didn't work as well as it ought – a splayed broom, a dented ladle, a fork without a tine. By the time the wage-earning husband appeared, tired and sceptical even as he stood in his own doorway, the job would already be started, and there was nothing for him to do but accept the situation as he found it.

But what Rex and Amos found hardest was the fact that there were few diners, restaurants, boarding houses or anything useful to a traveller in the towns they visited. They sometimes bought food from women on their porch steps; but they had soon grown tired of whatever they were offered. Half of what they bought or were given was pickled or smoked. And sleeping was no easier. There were churches everywhere – most places had two or three – yet the spirit of Christian giving never extended to letting a pair of wayfaring tinkers sleep indoors. Not once.

Usually, they found themselves provided for in barns, sheds and small stables at the far end of town lots.

That was the situation when they strode into Myersville. On the north end of town they sold a mop and two toothbrushes, and Amos had fixed the tang on a bucket. Their last job was for him to braze a cracked Dutch oven at a fairly large farm just on the edge of town after the crossroads towards Harmony. Hats in hand, they asked whether there might be any space for them to sleep for the night, and the farmer and his wife – Baptists whose children had moved out ten years previously – huddled for a few minutes with the kitchen door closed, before saying they could have the old tack-room side of the waggon shed.

They followed the farmer as he walked them towards the building, probably 150 yards from the house. This waggon shed, like all the others they'd seen in Maryland, looked like a covered bridge with no stream under it. It was rectangular, open and without doors at the narrow ends, but with what looked like very thick walls on both of the long sides. One of these sides was a corn crib, the other had been used to hang up the harness, tools and other necessaries in the days when the farm used horses. Now there was a tractor parked in the space where the waggons had once been.

The farmer opened the door and turned up his lantern to show them the space. He said he'd fetch them some straw for the floor, and they could help themselves to the pump down nearer the house, beside where the old well was. Amos and Rex hung up their straps on the hooks and set down their cases by moonlight, and the farmer came back carrying two bales of musty hay by the twines, one in each hand. He set both bales on the floor and cut the strings, scattering the hay around with his boots. He left them the lantern and told them they weren't to smoke except outside. When he was gone, Amos and Rex began their bedtime routines.

As they were getting settled, Amos drew his tin cup out of his pack and said he'd go and find that pump the farmer had told them about. He left the lantern with Rex, thinking there'd be enough moonlight to show him the way, but when he got outside again, the moon had shrunken behind the clouds and he couldn't get his bearings. He remembered the farmer had said the pump was near the house, and he saw lights on at a window, so he headed that way. After a few minutes of looking, he still couldn't find the pump, so he decided to go over towards the house and stand with his back near the wall to let his eyes settle a little and to get the light from the window to shine in his favour towards the garden and barnyard. It wasn't a cold night, and the farmhouse still had its windows open with the screens in, and Amos listened to the farmer and his wife talking.

God-damn rats, the farmer said.

You ain't seen none in a coon's age, his wife said.

Hell, I ain't, he answered.

Well, in the corn crib maybe.

You think they'll stay in that corn crib when they smell them fellers in that tool shed? Hell, they'll have company tonight.

Maybe the lantern'll scare 'em off.

Smoke 'em out, more like.

What if they burn it down?

Then the preacher won't have nothing much to bury.

Though the night was as dark and still as a mine shaft, Amos couldn't hear everything the pair said, and he found these mountaineers hard to understand in daylight when they were standing right in front of him. What he heard clearly was God-damn rats, fellers in that tool shed, smoke em out, burn it down, nothing much to bury. He forgot about his thirst and soft-footed it back to where Rex lay dozing in the frowzy hay.

We got to get outta here, Amos said.

What in the Hell you talking about? Rex opened his eyes.

Their fixing to burn us up.

Who is?

That God-damn farmer.

What the Hell for? We ain't done nothing to him. He say that to you?

No. But I heard 'em talking.

Why they wanna do that?

Not much to bury, he said.

Maybe they think we got some money. But why don't they just knock us on the head or something?

You hear that? Amos said.

There was a rustling nearby, sounding like it was underfoot. Or maybe overhead. Rex scrambled to his feet, and they both ran outside. They couldn't see anyone.

Look here, Amos said, I ain't staying here and waiting for no hick farmer to cook me up. I'm getting the Hell outta here.

Where you think you're gonna go? Hell, it's black as shit out here, and the town's shut up till morning.

We got a lantern.

You wanna know what I think? Rex said. I think they're hiding something.

What they got worth hiding?

Hell, boy, all these tight-arse farmers got money stuck in the cracks everywhere.

Rex looked around. Where you think they hid it? Must be close.

Why would they bed us down if they hid their God-damn money close?

'Cause they ain't got nowhere else to put us, and they're too Christian to turn out a couple of bums on the night, that's why.

How do you know it ain't in the house?

You ain't never had no money, have you? Nobody in the country hides money in the house. Some reason they don't trust it. No sir, they'll hide it outside.

What you wanna do, dig up all the fields we can find?

No, it'll be easier than that. Let's look around.

How come you're putting the lantern back?

'Cause even a hillbilly knows enough to look out the window, and if they see that light moving around, we'll be up shit creek.

Amos did his best to follow Rex's example and started to look around at everything he could see in the dark, even though he had no idea what he should be looking for. All at once, Rex made a loud quiet noise.

Hsst! he said.

He had gone down the slope towards the house, and even though Amos could barely see him, he had the feeling that Rex was calling him over, so he walked carefully towards the direction of the noise.

There, Rex said.

There what?

Rex was standing beside the pump and pointing at a low round wall to the side. It'll be down there, he said.

Amos looked. Ain't that the old well? he said.

Yes, sir, it is.

Ain't nobody dumb enough to hide money in no well.

Shit, Rex said. Ain't you ever seen a wishing well? Money don't rust. And who do you know ever kept a old well when they got themselves a new one right beside it? And look here, he said, leaning over the edge. Amos looked. They done built a cage over it and put a lock on it. These ain't the sort of people to spend money on a lock if they ain't got nothing worth locking up. Now listen here, he said. You get your kit and grab a piece of rope off one of them hooks and get on back down here.

Amos came back with his tools and a coil of rope over his shoulder. He laid the rope down and took out a piece of canvas from the rucksack. Rolled up inside the roll of canvas was a set of tools like a dentist's. He took a long, hooked probe, found the lock's keyhole and started gingerly twisting and feeling inside it.

In about two minutes there was a quiet chink and the mechanism opened softly in his hand. He slipped the lock out of the hasp and dropped it in the grass. He then lifted off the iron cage and looked in the hole. Pure blackness.

While he was doing this, Rex had tied one end of the rope around his waist and spooled out the length of what was left – about fifteen feet, he supposed. Here, he said to Amos. Tie this around your waist.

What in the Hell for?

'Cause you're gonna stay here and help pull me up in a minute.

Amos looked at Rex. Although Rex was slightly taller than him, Amos was slightly broader. They must be evenly matched, he thought.

Rex climbed up on the edge of the low wall. Now listen here, he said. I'll walk up and down them walls easy as anything. We used to do it between buildings when I was a kid.

He gestured with his hands and feet to show Amos what he meant.

When I get to the bottom, Rex said, I'll have a good feel around, fill my pockets and give you a tug so you know to hold the rope snug when I'm climbing back up. You got that?

Amos nodded.

Like taking candy from a baby, Rex said.

Amos watched as Rex lowered himself into the hole. Just as he said, his arms and legs stretched out and he seemed to be crab-walking right down the inside of the well. Amos braced himself by sitting on the ground with his back to the low wall. He heard a tiny splash, and a faint noise that sounding like someone saying, Shit! He leaned over the side and called as quietly as he could, All right?

Rex spoke in what sounded like a normal volume. There's water down there, he said.

How much? Amos asked.

How in the Hell do I know? Rex answered. But it's wet and a bit slippery.

There was a pause.

I'm coming out, Rex said.

Amos sat down again and braced himself. He remembered then to draw the slack rope up towards himself. But what he couldn't see is that this had drawn a loop around Rex's forearm.

All at once there was a scraping noise. Then more scraping. Rex was half-sliding, half-flailing, but definitely sinking. The rope was tumbling away faster than Amos could get a grip, until finally it pulled against his waist, threatening to lift him off the ground.

Holy shit! Amos said.

Get me the Hell out of here, Rex shouted.

Shut up now, Amos said, or we'll have 'em all out here, law included.

Then pull, God damn it, Rex hissed.

Amos tried pulling with his hands but couldn't gain any purchase on the rope. He spun around and tried lifting upwards by straightening his legs against the wall of the well. But all that did was to raise Rex by about two feet. When Amos stood up, he nearly went head first into the well himself. He tried leaning away from the well and walking like a plough horse, thinking he'd use the whole length of the rope to raise Rex to the surface, or at least to where the well was dry enough to get some grip. But the rope was too low on Amos's body and there was no slack.

They were stuck.

They were still stuck when the cows started crying out in the morning to be milked. The farmer saw Amos sitting by the wellside and thought Amos was dead. Or dead drunk. He walked over to them and looked down the well.

Good God Almighty, he said.

He ran down towards the waggon shed and started up his Farmall tractor. Minutes later he was idling it beside Amos and taking a log chain from where it was wrapped around the tractor's steel seat. He leaned over Amos's exhausted terrified body and sunk the log chain's hook into the loop of rope around Amos's torso, then he climbed back on the tractor's seat, and inched it forward. Amos stumbled to his feet, and slowly walked forward as the farmer lifted Rex out of the well at the end of the long rope. Rex looked nearly dead, and both men could barely stand to touch their abdomens. The farmer took out his knife and cut the rope off both of them.

I ain't never seen nothing like this, he said. His wife had not yet looked out the door, and he didn't call her.

The farmer chewed his lips and pondered. As they were both weak, he could kick the shit out of them. He could even shoot them. He could probably tie them up long enough to get the sheriff's department out. But what good would any of it do? Instead, he grabbed hold of Rex's shirt and dragged him close to Amos.

Y'all listen to me, he said. You get down there and get your shit and get yourselves off my land or I'll see you both hung. Go on now.

He gave them both a push and headed towards his barn where the cows were getting impatient.

Clutching their bruised waists, Amos and Rex got back to the waggon shed. The door was open and the lantern still burned. Most of their things were just where they left them. But sometime in the night, the rats had chewed into their rucksacks and eaten about three days' worth of their food. When Amos and Rex left the farm they headed back north. To Pennsylvania. To winter.

September 9, 1963

10am. I think Marce must have arrived (alone?) by about 7.30 as he was certainly there at 7.45 when the well-drilling rig arrived. It has parked & unfolded itself like a yellow praying mantis just beyond the old wash house. By 9.00 there started the most awful low thumping, then a steady dull roar. How long will this last?

*About an hour ago I looked out the window & saw Dicky Bird climbing up the stone retaining wall near the small stream. I couldn't imagine what he could be after, until about a half hour later I saw Davy headed the same way. He hopped down the wall & walked along until he disappeared under the bridge. I opened the door and walked out into the road. As I got near the bridge I listened for a moment until I heard the sounds of what could have been an animal being strangled, & then I realized what was happening. I have promised myself never to go under that bridge or to allow anything I love to do so.

5pm. The well-driller fell silent at 4. I walked over to ask how long it was likely to go on & Marce replied —How deep would you like your hole, ma'am? I assumed the most naïve expression I am capable of & said I understood. He then said it could take up to a week to hit a good stream. The other men carried on working as if nothing had been said. Marce looked at them all with the faintest of smirks, & I thought how he might graffiti their very backs if he chose & they would say nothing.

*Dicky Bird and Rip spent the whole day on & off the roof today, painting the whole thing with a thick silver paint. Davy and Marce at the bottom as usual, though Marce's truck left & came back once, unloading something, I think.

7.30pm. Paul and Joanie just finished playing. Guitar & dulcimer this time.

10.30pm. On the news this evening that the government is taking away Wallace's power to use the police to surround schools. Let's hope the locals don't turn into vigilantes.

*Weather a complete copy of yesterday, only a shade warmer.

September 10, 1963

10am. Well-driller like an organ grinder for the past two hours. I find myself singing songs in my head to its rhythm.

5pm. Saw the men off today & tried to account for what they've been doing. They finished silvering the roof today, & now the whole thing shines like a pair of baking trays. Marce unloaded some mason's tools, a large tub, a funny hoe etc, as well as bags of cement & piles of sand. He evidently mixed some of this up, and together they made a concrete floor at the bottom of the big hole for the septic system.

*When he arrived at 4, John John was given a brush & a bucket of water & made to clean all the tools, including the tub and hoe.

11pm. In the paper this morning that there was a terrible landslide in Italy. Thousands feared dead. So many families, such loss. Evening news showed black children entering schools in Ala. I can't imagine how frightened their mothers must be. Children on the threshold of a new era. Children so exposed. I can't stop thinking about them.

*Dry, sunny and warm all day. Spent some time reading the history of Maryland books.

September 11, 1963

9.30pm. Sleepy today. Such a fine day though, really. Mild, sunny, dry.

*Well-driller snoring violently since 8.

3pm. Heard shouts & laughter so walked over the road to check. Well-driller silent as a slain dragon. The men standing about & Marce looking triumphant. Well is now producing 30 gallons a minute, he says. Good news.

5pm. Well-drilling rig folded up like a dead wasp & now gone. Men left on time. I walked around to have a look at their progress. There are now block walls for my septic tank, long black pipes in absurdly deep trenches & anonymous machinery, tools & supplies under tarpaulins everywhere. The grass is beaten flat, grey dust covers everything, there is mud that has come somehow without rain spattered on the fences, & the look as though Vikings or pirates have raided the village.

Don't you feel like shouting sometime?

Home. Home, she thought. What an impractical idea.

Emma Wachter looked across her wide kitchen. At the big table sat her three sons. The eldest, Denny, was five. She let them get started on the fried chicken, the mashed potatoes, the sweet-corn and carrots while her husband, Clyde, was still at the sink, washing off the last spots of manure from his upper arms. She liked the glimpse of his arms as he flexed and unflexed them, turning them around to check whether they were clean.

She loved everything about his body – the one he used to make her a gift of her own. She remembered the first time his tongue had touched hers. She remembered sitting in his lap, his hands tracing the curves of her leg, feeling that her own mouth was small, his breath warm and sweet. She remembered his lifting her shirt, lowering her clothes, breathing in her scent. She liked it when they made love, or rather, as she liked to think of it, when he made love to her. She liked to put her hands in his hair, on his neck, his shoulders, his back, and her favourite, his waist as it rocked back and forth and back again. She liked to raise her legs in the air, and she liked to stroke his calves with her feet. She told him they were soulmates, and that she would never say no.

He was a good husband and a good father. He liked to make her laugh. He told everyone they knew what a fine woman she was. He was good with money and was glad she was too. He loved making gifts to the children. He told them how handsome and strong they were. He never frightened them, and he told them that they would grow up to be taller, stronger and cleverer them him, and that he was just as proud of them as he could be.

He had moved to the area in 1931 from Virginia, and bought the little farm on Wistman Lane, a mile from Harmony, with money that he'd brought with him. It had come from the sale of his mother's house, he'd said. He'd come north looking for work, drifting from Baltimore to Frederick, Middletown to Myersville. When he'd found out he had enough money to buy a place to live on, he decided he liked the looks of Catoctin Mountain enough to settle there, even if earning a living made him scratch where it didn't itch. He met Emma the same summer at the Fire Department carnival, and they were married before Thanksgiving. Denny was born on Labor Day.

Clyde was ten years older than Emma. She liked that too. She liked the sound of his voice, his soft drawl, when he knoatched the boys. Emma had been raised in a family where her father, for better or for worse, was never seen to hug, whip, kiss, smack, or otherwise touch anybody. Her mother had been the same. She and her sisters grew up starved of touching, and they all three were married by the time they were nineteen.

Emma watched Clyde sit down, his shirt open half way down his chest, his sleeves still rolled up. He teased Denny, pretending to steal a chicken leg from his plate. He smiled at Wayne, the middle one, and he made exaggerated chewing faces at little Jeff. Emma reached for his plate to fill it up for him, and he passed it to her, smiling. She was pouring the gravy when there was a knock at the door.

No one in their experience had ever been known to knock on a door up Wistman Lane. Neighbours simply called out and walked in. Strangers stood silently outside, until someone in the family noticed. A knock on the door spelt out something foreign. An emergency.

Just a minute, Emma said, passing Clyde his full plate. She stood up, wiped her hands on her apron, and made a perfunctory swipe at her hair, as if touching it suddenly would conceal or correct anything out of place. She walked, almost ran, to the door and looked through the screen where a man's outline was visible. He was from the County Sheriff's department. Emma pushed open the door very very slowly.

How do, ma'am, he said. My name's Tucker, and I'm from the sheriff's office. How y'all doing?

He tried on a very tight smile, and Emma just squinted at him. Over his shoulder, parked in the dried puddles of the gravel near their barn, was a car, a Ford. Beside it, stretching and loosening the clothes that stuck to them hotly, were a man in a suit, aged about forty and balding, and three children – two girls and a boy, eleven, nine, and maybe seven. The sheriff's man took off his hat.

Ma'am, he said, I believe your name's Wachter. Is that right?

Emma nodded.

Is your husband Clyde Wachter?

Emma turned instinctively and looked back into the kitchen where her husband sat, eating with one hand, and distracting their boys with the other.

Clyde, she called. Clyde. Feller wants to see you.

She let the screen door bang shut, and the sheriff stepped back, putting his hat on again. He glanced towards the people beside the car.

Emma went back to her dinner table. Her eyes looked at Clyde, all over, as if at once. Her heart was beating like water in a storm. Clyde's jaw had gone rigid and as he walked towards the door his hands clenched and unclenched, as if he were shaking things from his grasp.

Clyde pushed the screen door open with a crack and stepped on to the porch. Hey, he said very quietly. The sheriff stepped towards him, then stepped back again.

Mr Wachter? he said.

Clyde was silent. He nodded.

Clyde Wachter?

Uh huh.

Sir, he said, I've brought some people here to see you.

Emma sat at the table trembling, willing herself to be motionless for the boys' sake.

Who's that? Denny said.

Eat your corn, Emma replied.

The sheriff turned to the people at the car and motioned with his hand for them to come nearer. The man in the suit took a couple of steps, and then remembered the children. He looked at them and gestured for them to stay put.

Mr Wachter, the sheriff said, this here is Mr Conroy. He's a lawyer from Loudon County, Virginia. He has some business with you.

The sheriff stood back another step, letting his hands find rest on his belt, where his pistol sat in its holster, and sundry other little pouches lay discreetly.

Mr Conroy came on to the porch holding a piece of paper in front of him.

Mr Wachter, he said, I've come as a representative of the family of the late Mrs Josephine Wachter. That is, sir, your own late wife. I'm sorry to tell you, well, first off, that she's dead. She died peaceful. Anyhow, sir, the thing is, my office has done some tracing and some rooting around and looks now like we've found you out.

He handed the paper to Clyde.

Mr Wachter, Mr Conroy said, whatever I might say about you leaving your wife like that, and with three kids to keep, I ain't saying nothing, 'cause it ain't none of my business any more. But in the eyes of the law, your coming up here and marrying another woman is plain double-dealing bigamy, and you ought to be made to pay for it. But the truth is, that ain't what's gonna happen now. Them kidses' grandmother is too old to give 'em what they need, and she don't want to press any charges against ya, and now that her daughter's dead, it don't seem to serve any purpose anyhow. But the fact is, them kids is your responsibility now. They always was and now it's your job to see to it you do the right thing.

Conroy stepped back and watched Clyde looking at the paper. Clyde was still silent, so Conroy spoke up.

I've brought Mr Tucker here along as a witness that this is how things've got to be.

Tucker touched his hat and rolled his eyes towards Clyde. I don't expect we'll have no trouble now, will we, Mr Wachter? he said.

Conroy turned towards the car and waved his arm. Children, he said, come on up here now.

The children walked over the blue gravel and on to the edge of the porch slowly, eyes too open, mouths too closed.

Y'all gonna be just fine now, Conroy said to the children. Just fine.

Just fine, Tucker said.

Both Tucker and Conroy stepped back. We'll leave y'all in peace now, Tucker said.

Hang on a minute, Conroy said. He turned and jogged to the car, opened the trunk and took out a leather suitcase tied with baler twine. He trotted back to the porch and placed it beside the girl.

There ya are, Mary Beth, he said. All you need.

Tucker and Conroy walked back to the car not talking. They got inside and the engine started. Take care now, y'all Conroy's voice called. Tucker waved a listless farewell.

Clyde was still holding the paper. The three children who had just arrived, looked at him. Y'all best come inside now, ya hear? he said.

He held open the screen door and one by one the children filed inside, looking around them, as if they had stumbled into a museum.

Clyde looked into the kitchen. His three youngest sons were still in their places, their plates as clean as could be. All three stared at him. All six children stared at him.

He thought Emma must be just around the corner in the kitchen, washing some plate or something, or maybe looking for a spoon for the strawberries.

Emma, honey, he called out. But there was no answer.

September 12, 1963

9.30am. Loud music plays behind The Corner & when the announcer (Happy Johnny?!) talks between songs, Dicky Bird reprises whatever number has just finished. When I brought the tea & coffee they had covered the septic "tank" (HOW I learn the lingo!) with a mesh of steel rods on a wooden bed, and were mixing concrete. Rip hoes it, Dicky Bird measures it (apparently with shovelfuls) & Davy is busy burying the pipes. Marce not in evidence. Gone to Middletown, they said.

2.30pm. Marce evidently brought back more masonry supplies, bags, bricks & some orange square clay pipes.

10.30pm. Much warmer today. Possibly near 90 this afternoon. Felt bad for the men, especially Davy, as he looked near to drowning with sweat. All of them are chestnut coloured from the sun. A light breeze blew though.

*Joanie & Paul played until 7; fiddle and dulcimer.

September 13, 1963

1pm. Septic tank is now fully installed & covered. I hope for the sake of the flora & fauna under the bridge that a working commode is soon attached.

*The ladders are raised against the walls and Rip and Dicky Bird are on them scraping away at the bricks and mortar. Why? Davy is everywhere, but Marce only shows occasionally. I think he is inside.

10.45pm. So much cooler today, though still dry and sunny.

September 14, 1963

1pm. Went to Middletown this morning & bought some groceries at the Acme store. Walked around quite a bit. Most of the town is 100+ years old, the smaller older houses grouped at one end, the huge Gay 90s ones at the other. Some of these are beautiful. Remembered to buy birthday card for Sis.

6pm. Spent the afternoon blistering those places on my hands not already scratched by briars. Cleaning up the vegetable garden. Found a small pile of rusted ends of garden tools (I think). One leaf rake with dental abnormalities, unfit to use. On the bank leading down to the smaller stream I noticed little piles of black droppings. As tomorrow is Sunday, I will remember to pray these belong to a quadruped.

10.30pm. Getting cooler now, not even 70 today. Nice & sunny again. Tired and sleepy this evening. Tried reading Western Maryland book but kept nodding off.

September 15, 1963

10.30am. Overslept and was woken by church bells this morning (Lutheran, as the Brethren consider them sinful.

Honoring both, I only listened with one ear.) Back slightly sore from so much crouching yesterday.

10pm. Even cooler today, drizzle this morning, then rain. Wet now, I think. Just finished watching "Bonanza", though picture a little fuzzy.

September 16, 1963

9am. Rip and Dicky Bird back up the ladders. Marce on the high porch, all working on bricks and stones. Davy piling and mixing cement?

5pm. This afternoon Rip and Dicky Bird on adjacent ladders on the east side of The Corner, carefully putting cement into the places they have spent a day & ½ chipping at. This goes slowly. Marce on the high porch. All of them shout out orders to Davy (–More mud!) who lumbers along obligingly. At 4 John John given the job of washing the tools again. How much he must look forward to coming home after school…

11.15pm. In the paper this morning that those KKK clowns have killed people in a church in Ala. Others shot on their bicycles. I want to say to the victims' families I feel as helpless as they are.
*Cool 50s-60s all day. Mostly rainy this evening.

Billy in the Lowground

Little Sonny Gilbert went missing. No one knew where he had gone, and no one really knew how. But everyone knew why.

Sonny had grown up in Harmony. He was born with two older sisters in the little house across the creek and just beyond the orchard below the Mary House. His father was a man who had no temper about him at all, and who was most often away from home, working with the charcoal burners up towards Catoctin Furnace. His mother was a shrunken whiney sort of woman who kept one eye on all her neighbours in case there was a way she could claim a little money from them – damage done to something that belonged to her or hers, credit from someone for some kind of unsought-for work she'd done, that sort of thing. Sonny's two sisters both left home early, married to the first men who showed any interest in them at all.

Sonny grew up without much respect from the local boys. One winter, he tried to keep up with their bravado, and had attempted to sled down the steep hill on the other side of the Harmony Road, opposite his house. Like the others, he started at the top of the hill and by half way was already travelling at the speed of a galloping horse. The others knew that the secret to it was to roll off about three quarters of the way down the hill, pitching and turning into the soft snow that drifted there. But when Sonny tried it, he lost his nerve about the rolling off, instead shooting down the hill to where the multiflora bushes piled as high as a stables and as dense as coils of wire. He hit the barbed entanglement at full speed, his clothes being nearly torn off, and his face saved by the sheer luck of the sled's rising up in front of him. He stood up, unable to see because his face was lost in blood from the cuts across his forehead. The scars lasted him well into manhood.

He made two other attempts to convince the boys in Harmony that he had some respectable violence inside him. He joined them on the frozen creeks when they all went sliding. But he fell and broke his left arm above the wrist. Though none of the boys were witnesses to the doctor setting it, some claimed they could hear the screaming, even though their windows had been shut. Sonny's other outburst came when one of the stringy German farm labourers whose family had just moved nearby took to calling Sonny Steer Ham (for no reason anyone else understood).

Sonny startled everybody when he tripped the German boy and pushed him over. But to no one's surprise, the German leapt to his feet and punched Sonny in the nose, once again blanketing his face in blood. The fight in him seemed to end there.

After that, about the time that puberty started, Sonny gave up on boys altogether and thought he'd try his luck with girls. He made a valentine and sent it to the undertaker's daughter. But he didn't put his name inside it. He wrote a ballad for the horse-breaker's daughter, but nothing whatsoever came of it. She seemed not to understand at all that this was in any way significant and remained completely unchanged towards him. At seventeen he wrote more poems, mostly to the fiancée of the local carpenter, a girl for whom he was sure he would be a better match. Unlike his earlier muse, she seemed to understand just what the gesture meant, although she seemed very unsure about what emotion she ought to prefer in response. She tried anger, then embarrassment, and then explored gossip about the experience as a way of humiliating him. That, she decided, worked best after all. The carpenter seemed to agree, and he never mentioned it to anyone without also laughing.

That was how things stood until Sonny turned eighteen. It was then that his neat handwriting and his proximity to The Corner – his family's house was only about 100 yards away – enabled him to gain some employment there as an amanuensis, writing letters, copying documents, keeping simple accounts. Within two years, he was given the desk inside the door where the principal buying and selling was done. It was then that the long-dormant sense of his own wrongs began to find some life again.

Every working day, throughout the entire year, they came: farmers, men who once had been boys he knew, or their wives, girls he had known, even yearned for. They came bearing the marks of advance, prosperity, expansion, growth, success. He looked at their clothes, their horses, their servants. He thought about the places where they lived, their furnishings, their children. He even envied their petty strife, the bickering, the teasing, the cajoling, the unspoken communications between them. He envied all the things which, to him, signalled intimacy; something which existed for each one of them, all of them, but for which he had been deemed unsuitable, and from which he now felt excluded.

And so his plan was a simple one. It started at no particular time, and with no particular impetus or goal. As each load of grain arrived, he accompanied the millman upstairs where the sacks were weighed, and he recorded the figure in his ledger. None of these people could read more than their own names, and sometimes not even that, and all he had to do was to subtract a plausible amount from each load he accepted for milling. When it was weighed out as flour on the shop floor behind his desk, he added a small amount to the total in his ledger for each sack full of flour. In this way, he cheated each customer twice: each got less credit than he deserved for what he brought in and was charged more than was due for what he took away. No one, least of all the family of millowners up in the big house, were any the wiser.

This amused Sonny for most of a year. But as satisfying as it was to see so many people who didn't love him exploited in this manner, he still felt there was something missing. When he sat down to his supper at night – potatoes, greens, roots, cornbread and molasses – his senses were assaulted by the void. Every day the tastes were the same; the sounds of the room, the road, the village – the same; the sights, the smells, unchanging; and every day, he touched nothing, no one, and nothing and no one touched him. His only real companion was the boy inside him, the boy whose thin arms waved inside his own, whose legs walked inside his steps, and whose heart throbbed with an empty pain until his eyes filled and his teeth set so hard that he often woke in the morning with aching jaws. No, Sonny thought, if he were to feel better, he must give them pain like his own.

In the early summer of his fourth year as clerk at The Corner, Sonny stopped making fraudulent entries in the ledger, and began to swap one farmer's goods for another, so that soon, he could have guaranteed that almost no one went home with flour from his own grain.

It was such a small thing, it was ridiculous. And yet, it gave Sonny a kind of pride to think he was making fools of so many people. He looked at everyone now with a private contempt, as if he knew at least something about each one that that person didn't even know himself. Sonny thought of himself as having stolen just a little bit of their pride from every mouthful they swallowed.

He thought of other stratagems too. He thought of pouring rust in the meal sacks, grasshoppers in the grain. He thought of pissing on the sieves. His disdain for these people who smiled patronizingly at him grew softly and delicately into something like hatred, something like despising. By autumn, he began to think of ways that poisons might be strewn in the different sackfulls as they left The Corner.

But he did nothing else, nothing new, nothing brave and nothing craven. He lost interest in his experiments with vice and by Thanksgiving, everyone who came to The Corner got true measure for their goods and left with their own produce. Until one morning, Sonny just didn't show up to take his place at the desk. Mid-morning, the owners sent a millman down to Sonny's house to find out whether he was ill. His mother said she thought he had gone out early, as he wasn't in the house. None of his things were missing, nothing was out of place, but Sonny was gone.

There were rumours for months, suicide being the favourite. Nobody thought he went west or had gone for a soldier. Sonny? Never. Maybe he had gone to Baltimore. Or Philadelphia. They pitied his mother. They even thought they pitied Sonny. He had always been strange, they said. Always.

September 17, 1963

5pm. Rip & Dicky Bird on ladders all day, Marce on the lower porch, same as yesterday. Evidently, this is called "pointing". It looks tedious. Davy hoeing and carrying cement all day.

10.45pm. Very dark tonight. No moon. A good autumn day again, cool then warm. Leaves going golden and falling a bit. Walnut trees stripping themselves shamelessly.

September 18, 1963

5pm. Men worked like yesterday, but now on the west side. Marce beside them, but at ground level.

10.30pm. Odd day today. Warm but foggy. Like living in a lighthouse. The tree trunks on the mountainside like black waves. Joanie & Paul sat outside, playing a little half-heartedly, I felt. Guitar & autoharp.

September 19, 1963

5pm. Men spent most of the day pointing the west side, Marce 'round the back (north side), ground level. The others joined him about 2. John John came at 4 & tried skulking, throwing fallen walnuts at those still on the trees. Tried talking to Davy. Marce put a trowel in his hand & told him to scrape up all the gobs of cement that had fallen near the walls, put them in a bucket, & then spread them out on the ground near where the new oil tank is going.

10.30pm. The leaves growing richer now. Warm this morning, very warm (mid 80s) this afternoon, and sunny sunny sunny. Paul & Joanie on fire tonight, with mandolin & dulcimer.

September 20, 1963

5pm. Pointing all finished this afternoon. After that, with a lot of shouting and insulting, Marce had the ladders raised to the roof again, & Rip went up alone, near the chimney on the east side. He chipped & hacked, dismantling some bruised-looking bricks, tossing them on to the ground below, 1 by 1. About ½ the protruding chimney was removed. They then moved the ladders to the west chimney, repeating this all, taking about 1/3 of it off. When he came down to go home Rip's hands were the colour of bricks & soot, his face like raw beef (from the heat). They left the ladders and ropes in place.

10.45pm. Weather like yesterday, only hotter this afternoon, near 90. Lucky the men were working mostly on the north side today.

Go down, Old Hannah –

I, LittleWound, tell this story.

It was around the time that the Lutherans built their church, tobacco was expensive and the Washechu liked to speak of the Old Line. Most of the Washechu men without families, and some with families, had gone to be soldiers and the village felt as though it were made up of women and boys.

The Harmony Road, which runs in front of my porch was a route for waggons full of flour to be taken to Ellerton, Wolfsville, and to the farms beyond. Some went to Fredericktowne to be taken to the soldiers. The road runs just outside my door. On the side near where I grow vegetables the Hawbottom Road runs over the stream and up the hill. In front of my door the road to the Brethren meeting house comes together with the Harmony Road. It lay over a bridge because the water from the mill crosses the road here and runs to the stream and then this stream joins the one behind my quarters. The mill is only footsteps away, over the road from my quarters. The wheels that power the machines in the mill are on the other side, spilling their water into the pool near the road. In this pool the water rests for a while in the shade of the walnut trees. Here there are many crayfish and worms sleep under the stones.

Beside the mill there is another place for vegetables and then a house. On the bend in the road there is a barn and farmhouse and beyond them lay the Washechu dead beside the Brethren meeting house. Across the road from the barn the Lutherans built their church. Beside the barn the villagers built a school. Almost every day, unless they worked with their fathers, the boys from the village went here. The Mosers, Grossnickels, Blicken-staffs, Bakers, Delauters, Hubbles, Haineses and others walked up the road, throwing walnuts into the stream, shouting, hitting, laughing, chasing. But when the chestnut-flowers grew and the maple-wings spun to the ground they stopped below the mill's wheels and looked into the water to see the crayfish. The took the worms from under the stones and hooked the crayfish out, pinching their backs until they died. Every day, they hid the cray-fish they killed in the hollow of a tree and as the evening came, collected them again on their way home, because everyone loves to eat crayfish.

The mistress of the school was Mrs Warrenfeltz. Her hair was the colour of quartz and her voice like the call of a hawk. The boys' laughter brought the anger to her hands and to her eyes and to see them catch the crayfish caused her to resent them and their joy. It is also true that like everyone else, Mrs Warrrenfeltz liked to eat crayfish, but she was afraid that her dignity would suffer if anyone saw her try to catch them in the pool. I saw with my eyes and heard with my ears the anguish she brought to these boys because of their love for fishing, and the wet they trailed to her classroom from their boots and their breeches. Sometimes she hit their legs with the birch, and sometimes spoke to them until she ruined their manhood with tears. I watched them all from the bench by my quarters and my heart became like a stone in my hand.

It was after the day when she made the Runkles boy throw his dead crayfish into the pool, the crayfish that glistened like magnolias in the sun, that I knew revenge would find her. I watched as the boys stopped their fishing, stopped their antics. Now, every day, instead of walking on the road, the boys walked over the paddock, a patch of land beside the stream, on the other side away from the pool, where the Master had his chickens and horses, and I knew that they were planning their surprise. They walked where the horses grazed and then up to the road, wading to their ankles in the stream. Mrs Warrenfeltz watched them from under the schoolhouse bell to see whether any of them stopped to catch crayfish, but none did. Finally, an afternoon came when, instead of walking home on the road, as she did every day, she crossed over the water as the boys did, tracing their steps towards the stable, and looking inside, she saw the door to the feed-bins open. She looked inside, and there, wrapped in a gunny sack, was a mess of crayfish. The light of the sun on the stream still shone on their backs. She looked around and saw no one, so she took the sack home, cooking the crayfish for her dinner. That night, she brought the sack back, and replaced it in the bin where she found it.

In the afternoon of the following day, though she saw no one fishing, the sack was filled again. So once more she took the sack home, cooked the crayfish, and brought the sack back to its place of hiding.

It happened then that a night came when I could not sleep. The owl called and I went outside to smoke redwillow and look for the Spirit Road. I saw by the stable a boy walking with a sack. He went inside, and then left with nothing in his hands. I waited until he had gone and then I crossed to the paddock and went to the feedbin. I picked up the sack and looked inside. There were crayfish the size of oakleaves, such as would fill the hand and make one praise the waters of the stream. But these crayfish, I knew, had not been caught in this pool, and had not been caught on this day. I went to bed, smiling because of the boys' patience and expectation of joy.

The afternoon followed as the others had before it. Mrs Warrenfeltz took the sack home, her lips springing up and down as she walked, anticipating the savour of the crayfish. Though I watched from the porch, I saw no boys anywhere – none to see whether she had taken the bait. But I had an idea.

The morning came and I rose before the sun came over the hill towards Hawbottom. As I expected, there were already boys creeping and running down the roads towards the stables. They went inside, and I listened, but I could hear nothing. Just to be sure, I went to the stables myself and made as though I was feeding the Master's horses. I could feel them in the loft above, but they made no sounds that a Washechu would hear. I went outside and hid myself behind the chicken-coop.

When the hour for school came, as was her habit, Mrs Warrenfeltz came into the paddock, crossing as if to go towards the school. Her cheeks were without colour, her lips were like the stones in the wall, her hands shook and she bent like a willow in the wind. She carried the sack as far from her as she could. She went into the stables to put it in the bin as she always did, but something about its smell affected her. As I looked upward I saw the boys faces appear at the opening of the hay-hole above the stable-yard. Mrs Warrenfeltz came out holding her body. Her mouth was open and she stepped about, as if her legs were going without her. She swayed back and forth, clicking her head like a whip, pushing her middle, holding her mouth, twisting her waist. She looked first towards the road to the Lutheran church, and then towards the Harmony road. She saw no one and so she stumbled to the corner of the fence near to where I was hiding. She pulled up her dress to her waist and squatted. Saying uh uh uh, a stream flew beneath her, splashing on to the stones and earth. She grunted and held her eyes tight as the flood pulsed on to the ground.

EEEEEEEEEeeeeeeeee! Yip! Yip! Yip! the boys howled in the air above us.

Mrs Warrenfeltz looked at the stables, but there was nothing to be seen. She wiped her mouth with her hand, padded her thighs with her petticoats and ran across the paddock back the way she had come. I went back to my quarters and boiled a she-hocah and its eggs for my breakfast.

September 21, 1963

10am. Got a letter from Ags today, expressing continued sympathy about Alex & asking whether there is any news. I want to write back & say yes, the news is my heart is frozen, the gray in my hair looks like it means to stay, & Webster's has asked my permission to use my name as a definition for exhausted. She has asked how the writing is going, & I'll have to think of an answer.

7pm. Realized I forgot to mail Sis's card. As penance I wrote her a good long letter. That'll teach me.

10.30pm. Autumn is back. Cool this morning, warm this afternoon, & rain off & on all day. Nice on the tin roof.

September 22, 1963

3pm. Slept a bit later again. Went outside & watched as the leaves spun down. I was sitting on the bench when the church-goers began their walk home. Tom would have said I had subconsciously timed my arrival to be there when they neared, as if daring myself or them to include me. I don't think I did this, but as a wife I don't like to contradict my husband, even when he's dead. As they all arrived, the families who were still walking together (many had already split up into single-sex groups) divided, with the men standing near the culvert where the little stream crosses the road, and the women sitting on the benches. Every one of them, to my surprise, asked me how things were. They told me I should come and see them (though none told me where she lived), & all promised to visit me. 2 or 3 worried I might be cold in the winter & promised me their spare quilts. Cinch Ford patted me on the knee and asked me whether I liked apple butter. I thought this seemed enigmatic but couldn't see the risk in saying yes.

5.30pm. I haven't seen a car or heard a human voice for what may be hours. It is hard to be strong when the quiet is so overcoming.

11pm. Much cooler today, though sunny. Some windiness this morning. Realized when I sat down at 10 to watch "Gun-smoke" that it was on last night.

Johnson Boys

They is some things I seen with my own eyes, but I don't hardly believe 'em. Umnh Umnh. No sir. Ya just gotta get on, that's all. That's all they is.

I was just a young woman at the time. Ole Red Mary, she took good care of me. 'Deed she did. I cough the once, she be down there picking the horehound and I don't know what all. The only reason I is this big is cause when I was growing she used to give me half what she should've been eating her own self. That's what she was like. Some folks is like that, and some ain't, I guess. You lucky if you get one.

I knowed a fella, his name was Columbus. He worked down the road there, down towards Middletown, for a woman they call

Miss Opal. He come up from a place down 'round New Market, where he used to belong to Miss Opal's sister. When she died, he got sent up here, 'long with her other belongings. They was another servant too, and she was called Guiney. They weren't married or nothing, and nobody think they should've been. But they get along all right. Anyhow, they come up here and they live with Miss Opal. And she didn't know nothing 'bout no servants, 'cause she didn't have none herself. She was an ole maid, and she come into the house when her pappy died, and I 'spect he left her some money or something, 'cause she didn't do no work that I can ever recall. Anyhow, ole Columbus and Guiney come along, and I don't know if she was pleased or put out, 'cause she was so awful contrary that ain't nobody knew whether she was glad to be living or not.

Well, she come up to Harmony sometimes in her buggy, buying flour, going to the blacksmith for the horse and all that, visiting folks, ya know. Anyhow, what I seen of her weren't that pretty. No, sir. Ole Columbus, he druve the buggy, and he loaded up anything she buy, and mostly he sit 'round here, spitting in the dust and shaking his head and waiting for another chewing out.

Columbus, she say, Lord a mercy, you is slow as molasses in January.

She tell everybody how hoodly he was, losing this and wasting that. Long-fingered too. Like most folks, she had a barrel where she kept the cider for to making vinegar. Well, she say, 'bout half the cider end up gone down his ole gizzard, for it turn. Umnh umnh. I saw him my own self put the box of butter she bought from that Leatherman girl in the buggy, and Miss Opal, she don't like the sound it make when it hit the floor, and she lit out. Y'all trying to make my new butter all kerflooey? she say. She half laid a egg right there front of The Corner.

Anyhow, all us servants hear all this, and we talks when we can, and they ain't nothing we can do, though we want to. It ain't so bad as some folks has it, but nobody thought it right or fitting the way she shame that fella every chance she get. Men ain't much to look at, but they got they pride too. Ole Guiney was probably the same, but I don't know, 'cause I never seen her so much. Anyhow, we was all studying how we might get something going for him, when the Lord Hisself come in with one.

Now it started on a Sunday. Ole Miss Opal was a Lutheran, and she used to come up to go to the church in Harmony two three times a month. 'Specially if they was a holiday or something, the way folks did. Well, the womenfolk on they way out used to stand 'round under the walnut trees if the weather was good and waste they time while the men chewed the fat over on the bench 'side the mill pond. Well, one Sunday Miss Opal starts up a-talking 'bout her dreams, the way some folks'll always do. She talks about 'em till the white ladies start to look a little green 'round the gills. Anyhow, she kept on saying it so finally one of them white women says maybe she bewitched or something. Maybe somebody done put the hex on her. Set the hants a-running.

Well, that set Miss Opal all to thinking. The next Sunday come, and she can't stop herself talking 'bout all the things gone funny for her since last Sunday. You hexed, for sure, they say. Lord a-mercy, yes, they say. I surely glad I ain't you. She feel so put out, she get in the buggy and give ole Columbus a awful look, half kill him with spite, even 'fore he get home.

Well, what happened then, was the next Sunday come and she druve herself to church, and she brought Guiney 'long to keep her company. She tell folks ole Columbus done gone down with some kind of fever in the liver or something, and anyway, he lazy as the devil hisself. So then she tell everybody 'bout this dream of hers. In this dream, she say, she think she seen the witch his own self. Seen him for sure. She say, in that dream, this witching fella, he climb up and sit right on her chest so she can't half breathe or nothing. But she say she run him off cause she retch up and scratch some big scratches down his face with her nails.

Well, Guiney and me is standing on the porch of the Mary House when she say that, and all at once Guiney look at me and I look at her and we both get to smiling.

The next Sunday come, and just like we thought, Columbus druve Miss Opal like always, and he take hisself a nap under the trees till the church is over, and all the white folks come walking down the road to have they get together. So just as they get to talking, and all the women is there in one big hive, I up and says good and loud, Columbus, I declare, what's the matter with that face of yours? You done look like a turkey buzzard come down and put the talons on you cheeks and chin. Now Columbus, he jump like the flea done bit him, and he swing round to see how Miss Opal taking the sound of that. Sure enough, all them women is a-looking to if what I says is true, and they see them scratches. And I knows, and he knows and Guiney knows just who put them there, but Miss Opal, she don't know nothing 'bout it, and she ain't got no ideas connecting them things. But them women all starts to look at each other real funny, and faster than you say jack rabbit, they all a-turning and a-grinning and hiding they faces in they gloves and fans.

I don't know whether Miss Opal ever did think what it was they found so funny. But I know this much: she might have brung Columbus with her just like she used to, but nobody paid her no mind no more whenever she start in on his this and that. Lord a-mercy, I think. Ole Guiney and Columbus they sure fix that. Yes, sir.

September 23, 1963

8.30am. After delivering tea and coffee to the men, I mailed card to Sis. So proud of myself, I may even do so again next year. When I came back with the tray I noticed on the plant stand that someone had left me 2 pints of apple butter. I was so touched by this I gasped & felt on the edge of tears.

5pm. Quite theatrical out there today. Rip back up the ladder, Marce at the bottom, Dicky Bird on the ropes, Davy at the cement trough. Piece by piece the clay boxes (chimney flues!) were hoisted to the top, cemented on the edges, and then lowered down the chimney by rope. After a while Rip looked exhausted and he swapped places with Dicky Bird. They then rebuilt the chimney top. By lunchtime, they started the east chimney, and it was done by 4. The whole crew of them looked broken. No sign of John John.

10.30pm. Real chill in the air now, and not that warm this afternoon. Sunny though.

September 24, 1963

11am. Men working as usual from 8, but strangely quiet, apart from Dicky Bird's customary singing. (Treated today to "Moon River", which in his accent sounds more like Moan Raver.) Marce busy sawing and nailing something large. Dicky Bird & Rip back & forth unloading bricks from the truck, some of them yellow. Davy hoeing his concrete again. They stayed so quiet that at 10 I walked over to investigate. The timbers went into molding a frame into which they had poured a load of concrete, near the place where John John had been directed to dump his scrapings the other day. Presumably this will hold the oil tank. The back door was propped open and they were all busy, one way & another, building fireplaces. Marce was on the bottom floor building the big fancy colonial one in the kitchen & dining room; Rip was on the middle floor building the smaller one for the living room; and Dicky Bird was upstairs putting in the small one at the end of the big hall. Davy, who really should have wheels, was carrying supplies to all three.

6pm. I was outside when John John arrived at 4, so I spoke to him alone for the first time. He was looking at the big concrete base for the oil tank, & I thought barely resisting the urge to step in it. In the corner, I noticed Marce had scratched "1963". I asked him how school was, & then immediately thought how stupid that sounded. —S'allright, he said. He was still looking at the concrete. —Why don't you write your initials in it? I said. He didn't look at me. —He'd skin me alive, if I did that. —Tell you what, I said. Just press your hand right there above the date. He looked at me a moment to be sure I wasn't teasing him. Then he knelt down and pressed his palm and fingers gently into the wet cement. He nearly wiped his hand on his pants, but then thought better of it & rinsed it in a bucket, shaking it dry. He smiled at me, then went inside. A minute later I heard Marce call him. —Get a bucket & start picking up them broken pieces of brick 'fore Davy Crockett trips & falls & breaks his ass.

10.30pm. Weather like yesterday, though not much breeze today. Getting cold at night now.

September 25, 1963

5pm. Men worked today much the same as yesterday.

10.30pm. Cold again tonight (and this morning). Dry and sunny, but not quite 70 today. No music from J & P for a while. Too cold, I guess. Watched "The Beverly Hillbillies" & "The Dick Van Dyke Show".

September 26, 1963

5pm. Still working on the fireplaces. Meticulous work. I am always impressed by the way they clean up their tools & work spaces by the end of the day. I'd tell them so, if I thought they'd like it. Or not like it too much, as I am a little afraid of them. I was relieved to see Hartsock's drawings of each fireplace stuck with nails to 2x4s beside where each man is working. Both the smaller ones look finished to me.

10.45pm. A little warmer today. Foggy nearly all day. Soupy, the locals call it. Spent some time with MD history book again.

September 27, 1963

2.30pm. Truck just delivered big silver oil tank, a furnace and a lot of small parts, most of which the men have taken inside. I think they have finished all the fireplaces now.

5pm. They spent the afternoon wrestling the oil tank into place & with a lot of swearing, not all of it funny, they levelled it up before leaving.

10.30pm. Very pretty sunshine today, and now warmer again. Leaves in colored bands now, red, orange, yellow in stripes, presumably as the wind blows the cold over them. Must get a rake.

*Paul & Joanie played for an hour; dulcimer and fiddle.

Jerusalem's Ridge

I, LittleWound, tell this story.

It was in the time before the Washechu came to the mountain and to the valley. The Catoctin nation walked with the pride of the StoneGods in their veins and the breath of the Thunderbird in their lungs.

There lived among the people a warrior named FearlessBear and his fame spread like the mists over the hills. His eyes were above the eyes of other warriors and his bow was strung with his sisters' hair. He was the one to seek danger in combat and the one to seek glory in the hunt. His threefletched arrows never missed their mark and his twofletched arrows outsped even the wind. But FearlessBear had no wife and this grieved his family and his elders. He did not make himself a suitor to any and he left no gifts of game on the maidens' doorsteps. But there was a maiden who loved him above all others and her name was WhiteFootprint. Because her love was seen by all, the elders persuaded FearlessBear to take her to his lodge as a wife.

Still, the days passed and though WhiteFootprint lived with him every day, she could never persuade FearlessBear to accept her love. The reason for this was not that he found no joy in her; she was all that eye or ear or hand might desire. Instead, inside his heart he doubted that she could love him as a man, knowing him as others did as the bearer of reputation, a warrior, a hunter and a prince.

Unable to bear it any longer, WhiteFootprint took his hand into her own and spoke to him. Husband, how can I convince you that my love for you is without end?

FearlessBear looked into his wife's eyes and spoke. I will believe that you love me, he said, when throughout those nights when the hearthfire keeps the cold from our door, and the ice clouds the air, you can change the nature of my dreams from winter to summer.

He looked away and left her to her own imaginings.

All that summer, when she was not helping among the women and toiling in honour among her friends and family, she spent her hours in the meadows, along the streams and on the rocks. She gathered the honeysuckle, the multiflora, the bay, the rose, the bluebell and the clover and she dried them in the sunshine. In secret, she sewed them all into a bag and hid the bag inside the doeskins piled by her bed. Then, when the winter came, she waited for FearlessBear to sleep, and night after night, she slipped the bag of herbs and flowers beneath his head and filled his dreams with the imagining of summer.

Husband, she said. I have kept my vow and filled your dreams with summer. Do you believe that I love you?

I will believe you love me, he said, when you capture the sunshine on the water and place it in the palm of my hand.

The days passed once again and the leaves returned to the trees. Finally, WhiteFootprint remembered a tale she had heard as a girl. On the far side of the Catoctin's mountain there ran a stream and it was to this stream that she determined to go. She set out on the journey alone, not wanting to wait for anyone's advice about the perils she would face as a woman travelling without husband or friends.

After days of walking she found the stream she sought. There, at the base of the mountain, where the stream slowed, it twisted to the side. In the past, the waters here had run in torrents, and on the side of the stream away from her a bank of sand and gravel had accumulated. The water ran over this shoal like fingers in the hair, and in WhiteFootprints' eyes the sunshine sparkled here as it did nowhere else she had ever seen. She waded into the water and came to the shoal, where she lowered her hand, scooping up the stones. Among them were grains the size of acorn shells, each made of gold, the colour of the sun. She filled the pouch she brought and walked again to the summit of the mountain.

On the day she arrived, she took FearlessBear's hand into her own, and poured out the pouch of gold into his palm.

Husband, she said. Once again, I have been true to my vow and brought you the light of the sunshine upon the water. Do you believe that I love you?

FearlessBear closed his hand and thought. He shut his eyes. Wife, he said, I will believe you love me when you bring the sound of the birds' singing into the closeness of our lodge.

WhiteFootprint was silent throughout the season when the fruits are gathered. During the time of the snows and the frosts and the braying of the coyotes she often kept away from the other wives. No one spoke of her grief until one day the other wives saw her take up the empty antler of a deer and examine it. She took the knife from her belt, she gathered together a parcel of meat and nuts and with these she walked off into the woods, towards the height where the stream leaps above the stones.

It was an evening when WhiteFootprint returned to her lodge. In the darkness, she could see FearlessBear beside the fire, staring into the flames, buffing an arrowpoint with hide.

Husband, she said, you must close your eyes and listen to the noise I bring you. When his eyes were shut, she drew forth from her pouch the antler. She had cut and shaped it, bored holes in its sheath, and smoothed an end to fit her lips. She closed her own eyes and blew her breath into the pipe the way she had practised. In FearlessBear's mind he heard the song of the robin and the blackbird, the call of the owl and the coo of the dove. He listened, and there came to him the music of all the birds he had ever known. Finally, WhiteFootprint opened her eyes and spoke. Husband, she said, I have kept my vow, and brought the voices of the birds to our lodge. Do you believe that I love you?

FearlessBear's spirit was moved as it was only moved when the battleblood pounded in his ears. Wife, he said, I will only believe you love me when I see you against the sky, soaring like an eagle.

That night WhiteFootprint did not sleep. But in the morning she spoke to her husband. Come with me, she said, and I will show you and all the Catoctin how much a woman may love.

WhiteFootprint led the way outdoors, beyond the village and into the forest. She walked with FearlessBear behind her until the sun was at the crescent of the sky. She told FearlessBear to stand, leaning against a poplar until he should look up and see her in the sky above him. FearlessBear stood as he was told and waited. At the same time, WhiteFootprint walked up the side of the ridge where the trees cannot grow, to the rocks the colour of water and at last to the rock that stands alone, jutting upwards, the shape of a wolf's head. As FearlessBear looked up, he saw her there, her outline a shadow against a sky the colour of a jay's wing. From the height where she stood, WhiteFootprint looked down and saw her husband in the valley below. To her he was the size of swallow's egg.

FearlessBear looked up and squinted in the brightness. He saw her lift her arms outward, away from her chest. He saw the step she took and the snap of her clothes as the wind caught them, pushing them away from her body. It seemed for a moment that she hung in the air and that the forest itself made no sound. At this moment, he knew that her love for him was like the fire of the stars and his yearning for her would never end. But then within himself he felt the scream rise into his own ears as downward she soared, her body tearing into pieces on the pillars of stone beneath her.

She had kept her vow. And so, FearlessBear too, would keep his own. For the rest of the days he walked as a Catoctin, he could never again dream of summer, see the sunshine on the water, hear the birds singing in the forest, or even look at the sky over his head without feeling the truth and longing of the woman who had loved him, and proved her love with miracles.

September 28, 1963

9am. Plans to clean the house today & to wash clothes.

5.30pm. Clothes took so long to do by hand the house is still messy. Now too dark to dust. (Hooray! Shh!)

10.45pm. Weather a little better than yesterday even, in the 80s this afternoon. Tried using a garden rake for the leaves, but it is too heavy. No witnesses.

September 29, 1963

10am. Ran out especially this morning to try & catch Cinch Ford on her way to church. Finally saw her coming up the road from about 100 yards away. At 50 she spotted me, started smiling, & didn't stop until she came over the bridge. I ran up & hugged her, & I can't remember when anything has felt so good. She crumpled up like a toddler, giggled & hardly hugged me back, but she plainly loved it. —Thank you so much for that surprise! —Ya said ya liked it. —And you remembered. —I got plenty more.

*She was wearing a mint green dress, cream sweater, shoes, hat & gloves, and a green necklace.

11am. Telephoned Sis to wish her happy birthday. She liked being called & enjoyed telling me her plans, Roy's plans, the girls' plans & about her Angel Food cake surprise (square not round – only imagine!) When I said I had to go, as I was phoning long distance and on a party line, she remembered to ask how I am. She reminded me that she thinks this whole enterprise is crazy, & then evidently thinking it prudent not to use the word "crazy" too freely with me, wished me all the luck in the world. Resolution about my sending next year's birthday card now thrown into serious doubt.

12.30pm. Chatted with the church women again just now. Today's topics were aches & pains, women's & men's troubles, children's teeth, what kind of winter we're likely to have, the president, & the young woman who sang on Lawrence Welk a week ago whose name no one could recall. Cinch didn't talk long as she said she had to cook dinner for her daughter's family today. Something to ask her about.

11pm. Such a strange day. Mild this morning and foggy again, then humid and outright sticky this afternoon, in the 80s. How close are we to Fla?

September 30, 1963

1pm. Eerily quiet over the road today, nobody really visible except Davy back & forth as always, fetching things like pipes & small tanks of gas & heavy things in pasteboard boxes. Tea & coffee still disappearing from trays though.

5.30pm. Have just come back from The Corner. At 4pm there was a small knock on the Mary House door, & I was surprised to see John John. Marce sent him over to tell me that the furnace & oil tank were all set up. They had also checked the draw on the fireplaces and said all three were "just fine". Just then Marce blew the horn on his truck & John John ran off, barely making it on to the tailgate before Marce spun away in the gravel.

10.30pm. So much nicer today. Cool this morning, and dry and sunny. It is the end of my first full month in the Mary House. Things I have learned:
+It is possible to be impressed by people you don't really like.
+It is possible to like people you cannot understand.

+It is not possible to be so busy that you stop feeling lonely because of it.

+A diarist is a pilgrim who does not yet know what is possible and what is not possible.

Adam's Ale

October 1, 1963

9am. Glimpsed out the window this morning that Marce seems to have arrived a little earlier than usual. He spent some time unloading his truck, which was parked in front of the lower porch. He had tarpaulins, buckets of tools & tubs of something, & he was fussing about ladders again. At 8 I took their tray over & asked Rip what they were going to do next. He looked embarrassed to be spoken to, garbled something low in his throat, & nodded emphatically towards Marce. Marce spoke without stopping work (he & Dicky Bird were setting up the long ladder). —Windas, he said. —Fix them windas. They're in a helluva shape. And the doors. They ain't much better.

1pm. Dicky Bird & Rip have spent all morning up ladders scrapping & digging at the windows. Marce has spent the whole time on the back door. Davy holds ladders, fetches & is generally abused for being lazy. Dicky Bird sings of how he will "Act Naturally" & that "Love's Gonna Live Here Again".

5pm. Same as the morning. When John John arrived, he was given the job of sweeping up the tarpaulins, covered in paint chips & splinters & crumbs of "putty". The result of the day's work is that a wall full of windows now looks like they have been chewed. When the men left, I counted the windows. There are 23.

7pm. Remembered to add John Updike to shopping list. Wonder whether he would be pleased? Must look for something else by Mary McCarthy before I am tempted to reread The Group.

10.30pm. Cool this morning and warmer by afternoon. Very dry & sunny. Leaves browning.

October 2, 1963

9.30am. Men still working on the windows. East side finished, now they have joined Marce on the north side. He is working on a window as well.

5pm. Radio on all afternoon while they worked. Baseball. Two sides of the house now have scraped windows, & one of the three doors is finished.

10.45pm. Weather today much like yesterday. A little warmer this afternoon.

October 3, 1963

11am. Sleepy this morning after a restless night, I rushed to get the coffee & tea across the road by 8. I was upstairs making the bed, which I'd left, as I wanted to change the sheets, & as it is fine this morning, I opened the windows to get some fresh air in. On the east side, where the vegetable garden is narrowest, near the wide creek, I could hear some women talking at my neighbors' in the white house. I couldn't see them for the trees & I didn't recognize the voices. I caught the sounds of –Never seen nobody visiting.

You? —No, siree, not a soul. —Always over there a-eyeing up them men, I betcha. —They better watch out then.

*I can't be sure they were talking about me, but am I wrong to wonder? If they mean me, surely this is pure malignancy. Who would say I (me!) have ever 'eyed up' any men, let alone this bunch? Why would they say that? As for anyone to visit, who do they think would come? Sis hasn't been to Maryland since Tom's funeral & Tom's family think everything below Philadelphia should have been let go in 1861 to die in boondocks full of hillbillies & rivers full of cottonmouths. Where would I put them anyway?

1pm. Should I be more visible? Go to church? Quilting bees, hoedowns, hootenannies, barn-raisings? But seriously, church? Public auctions?

2.30pm. I can't invite Sis. Not here. Not yet.

3.30pm. I have thinking about Alex. I started crying & then got very angry. First with Tom, then with him. Then I grew afraid of being angry with him in case it brought more bad luck. I miss him so badly it hurts.

5.30pm. Men spent the whole day scraping at the windows on the south side, using the lower porch and high porch for footing. More work for Davy, as he has to walk all the way around the house (or through it) to get to them. Mostly he has been out of sight, and hammering at something, I think. Radio on all afternoon again. World Series.

11pm. Very dark tonight. No moon. Another dry sunny day. Can't sleep.

*Thinking about Tom, & decided pity feels better than anything else. Tom was his own victim.

*I loved loving him, for a while because of this. Then love becomes a habit.

*It's never been a habit to love Alex. I don't think so.

*I wish I knew how to be angry with him without being afraid. I don't know if I ever will.

*Come home, Alex. Be alive & come home.

*Or just be alive.

Earl's Breakdown

Monday July 4, 1927 was dry and overcast, cooler than the day before. Newt Harne had spent the day baling hay with the help of four of his six sons. The other two were too young to help, so they stayed near the house, helping their mother and sister shell what was left of the peas, and then pick and snap three bushels of green beans. It had been a good day. The baler only jammed twice on wet grass where the field dipped on the corner, and by early evening, they had baled, transported, unloaded and stacked nearly 200 bales. The whole family was exhausted, but as the evening was coming on, getting cooler and with no smell of a storm on the air, they were all looking forward to their night out at the Fire Department carnival, and the fireworks afterwards. They would all go, the boys and girls meeting up with friends they hadn't seen in weeks, drinking Coca Colas, eating ham sandwiches, riding the Ferris Wheel. The grown-ups would play Bingo at the long trestle tables, listen to the music from the band on the hay waggon, throw darts or nickels, discuss the weather, eat standing up.

The ritual had started right away, as soon as they headed in from the barn. It was the same whenever they made plans to go anywhere as a family. They were lucky. Their house, their whole farm, was quite a new one compared to their neighbours. It was built for them in 1911, the land coming from a piece cut away from Elsie's family farm, one they'd owned since the area was first settled in the 1700s. All of the old-timers in her family were buried in the little triangle plot on the side of Catoctin Mountain, facing Frederick, all of them with their names and dates and poetry carved in German on skinny slabs of slate under the pine trees. Elsie was her parents' only daughter, and they made her the present when she got married, keeping the home farm for her younger brother. The house, barn and outbuildings had been built especially for them. Newt's family had put up the money. There were good relations all around.

The ritual was like this. Elsie washed the younger children, saw them dressed and then ordered them to stay on the long porch till it was time to go. She and the girls washed and fixed their hair but didn't put on their going-out clothes until the last minute, as there always seemed to be something else for them to do in the meantime. Really, something for Elsie to do, as the girls tended to sit on the porch and wait, gossiping, scolding their siblings, discussing who they'd see at the carnival. The boys would barrel upstairs and wash, shave if necessary, and dress until they too congregated on the porch. By the time Newt got himself to the bathroom, there was such a smell of wet on the air, scent and soap everywhere, that he felt clean just to walk in his own upstairs hallway.

He liked the bathroom. It was one of the features of the house he liked best of all. He liked to peel off his sweaty clothes and sink into the water of the bath, even though he never drew it deeper than his own navel as he lay flat in the tub. He was shaven, but his hair was unbrushed, and hung loosely over his forehead and ears. He was relaxed in the way he had longed for all day – it was all meeting his expectations. Through the screened windows he could hear them below, outside. The thin chains on the porch swing gently creaking, the porch glider ticking and tocking while someone eased it back and forth. One of the children, probably one of the boys, had put the Victrola on, and the music hissed brightly, lazily.

Newt would have fallen asleep except for one idea he had. On these occasions, before they went out, Elsie liked to hang the dress she planned to wear on the back of the bathroom door. She had the idea that the steam from the room would soften it, keep it fresh looking. And now Newt was looking at the dress, how it hung, how its colours looked, how it waited for someone to become themselves inside it.

It was not one he recognized. Had he ever seen Elsie inside it? He tried to picture her in the dress. Her hands below the cuffs, the hemline as it shone around her legs. He pictured the press of her thighs in the upper reaches, below the belt, the shape of her backside as the material clung to her form when she walked, or just shifted her weight. He looked at the neckline and saw where the skin of her chest would be revealed, where the weight of her breasts would give definition to the dress's contours.

But something was wrong.

It was not Elsie he saw in the dress. It was their neighbour Maud Stine.

Was it her dress? Had Elsie borrowed it for the occasion? He tried to remember whether he had ever seen Maud in the dress, but he couldn't think of a single time. Not one. He thought of how and when he had seen Maud in the past, how she looked, and what she wore. Why did he see her as the woman belonging in this dress?

He sat up and the cooling water ran through the hair on his chest, down the tired muscles of his arms. He looked at the dress, willing himself to see Elsie inside it. But it was no good. The ghostly woman wearing it in his mind leaned towards him, the vee of the collar opening. The glimpsed flesh was not Elsie's.

Newt stood up and the bath water sunk downward to his shins. In his mind he could hear Maud's voice, chatting, laughing, and he shivered. He stepped out of the bath on to the rug he had placed beside it. He took up his towel from the chair where it lay heaped and began to dry himself: hair, face, chest, arms. He looked at the dress and wanted powerfully to touch it, to put his hands on its flattened hips, his face on its flattened chest. He felt with surprise how solid, how real, how present his own body was, and he turned his back to the door, wrapping the towel around his waist.

There was a slight sudden knock, and the bathroom door opened quickly, as Elsie's hand fired in, reaching for the dress.

Sorry, honey, she said. Just gonna get dressed now. Y'all bout done in here?

The door shut before Newt could answer. Still holding the towel with one hand, he accidentally looked in the mirror, catching the surprise in his own eyes. He heard the music and the voices outside and he recognized them. Then he recognized himself. Then he recognized everything. Almost everything.

October 4, 1963

9am. Rip up the ladder on the west side, Davy at the bottom. Dicky Bird and Marce both at work on doors, one above, one below. Dicky Bird crooning "Only Make Believe". Have to give him credit for trying, I suppose.

5pm. I waited on the Mary House porch, & as I expected, John John was sent to give me an update before they left for the day. All the windows & doors are now ready for priming and painting, & all the glass is "re-bedded" (I think he said.)

*I asked John John what he was going to do tomorrow. He said they had fences to fix, wood to stack & "brush to burn". I asked if he had seen any of the World Series. He hadn't. Would he watch any? —I might could, he said. —Do you like baseball? I asked. —Yes, ma'am, he said. He smiled. At last he looked like a boy who just might be able to be happy. Just then Marce blew the horn on his truck, and John John ran off, leaping into the back with Davy.

11pm. Not quite as cold today or as warm. Nice breeze, dry, sunny. On the news that there is a huge hurricane south of Florida. Just watched "The Alfred Hitchcock Hour".

October 5, 1963

8.30am. Made too much coffee this morning (habit) so had a second cup & now feel sick. Funny dreams last night. Dreamed Mother telling me things I couldn't hear, but I was certain she was wrong anyway.

12.45pm. Saw Joanie outside raking leaves so I walked over & asked her directly whether I might come 'round in a week or so (I thought they'd like to think this over) & ask them about their music. She blushed & asked whether they were too loud. I said I just wanted to understand it, and she nodded. She'll speak to Paul but thinks it will be just fine.

2pm. Having a cup of tea after lunch. A bit fatigued & slight headache. Went shopping in Frederick this morning: A & P ($16). Also bought Rabbit Run (finally). Nothing by MM. Found a store with some pretty things in this new "Orlon". Walked around Sears. Nothing really for The Corner, I think.

4pm. Joanie saw me outside & came over to The Corner porch to tell me Paul said it was fine to come 'round whenever it suited me. She looked very pleased. That makes me happy.

11pm. Very cold last night. Near freezing. Quite warm, sunny & dry today. Hurricane still menacing Cuba & its neighbors.

October 6, 1963

8.45am. Chilly this morning. Some sun. Had tea instead of coffee.

12pm. Made a mental list of things I never told Tom & now wish I had. Decided to tell Alex 4 of them. But which 1 first?

7pm. For John John's sake (and maybe for Alex's?) I watched the World Series. All over now, in four games. 2-1 Dodgers, & Dodgers took the Series. At home. I hope John John saw it.

9.30pm. These early nights are very dull. Cold out there. Odd, as it was over 80 this afternoon & sunny.

October 7, 1963

9am. Marce and the others here by 8, all unloading paint and brushes.

2pm. All morning they have been painting grey primer on the east-side windows. Very careful & slow. Davy inside & hammering, I think. Marce at work on the back door.

5.30pm. Afternoon passed much like the morning; priming windows, door and frames.

*I waited at the window until I saw John John walking down the Harmony Road, & then I rushed out & met him by the picket fence near the old Band Hall. –Hi there, John John. Did you see the game yesterday? –Yes, ma'am, he said, smiling. –What did you like best? Mantle's homer? –No, ma'am, he said. I just like to watch Sandy Koufax pitchin'. He's somethin'. –Would you like to be a pitcher? I said. He looked suddenly at the ground, his smile ended, & he shook his head. –No, ma'am, he said. He hesitated, then spoke right out. –Daddy says eyes like mine ain't worth nuthin'. He started to move forward again, humiliated to echo words he'd probably heard many times. Or maybe even only once. –I think you can see a long way, John John, I called after him. He kept going & I suddenly felt very foolish.

10pm. Not so cold this morning, but even warmer this afternoon. Leaves still clinging on a little. Pictures on the news of hurricane in Haiti.

Beware you young and tender ladies

In the first year of the war, they was Yankees 'most everywhere 'round here. We heard they was there in they thousands and thousands over at Frederick. We see 'em coming up and down the road, and sometimes they stop at the mill and load up they waggons with the flour and the cornmeal. They always paid for what they took, but that don't mean that folk liked it too much. They go to the farmers with the cows, specially the farmers with servants, and they make 'em sell 'em them cows, and we see 'em a-herding 'em up and down the road on they way to Frederick. They march 'long flinging they knapsacks on to the cows' backs so the soldiers didn't have to carry them or nothing. Mostly, they sing a song they called Gay and Happy. Once the war get to going little more, they don't sing that no more.

Anyway, down the Middletown road, after she turn down the hill to where the valley done flatten, and to where the road towards Hawbottom comes in, they was a little farm stuck in between the big ones. The fella what lived there farmed it mostly hisself, but his wife, whose name was Ursa, had a woman she kept with her to do the house chores, and she was married to one of the servants on the Remsburg place down the road. Now that woman had a boy of her own that lived with her, cause they both belonged to Miss Ursa. That boy was named Josephus, and he was 'bout twelve thirteen year old when the war started.

Now Ursa husband – I don't know his first name, but his pap was one of them Warrenfeltzes from towards Shookstown – 'course, he weren't no Yankee, and when the war gets going, he rode off with the others down to Virginia to join up with the

Sesesh. His neighbours on the big places 'greed they'd send they servants over to farm his land till the war over.

Lordy, it must've been hard for them wives of them fellas that went south, cause once the Yankees all come, they couldn't come home no more for no visits or nothing, and they wives couldn't send 'em nothing 'cause they was on the wrong side of the river. Anyhow, when the spring come, Miss Ursa she got a letter from somebody that her man got hisself shot a little, but that he was recovering and would be all right soon. Well, she was fit to be tied, she was so worried. How she took on. She was a nice little thing, never doing no harm and not wishing none neither. But she sure love her husband, she truly did.

Well now, Josephus saw all that was happening and he started to get a little inclined to her more than he should've. He weren't outright fool enough to say or do nothing, least his mammy would've seen it and skinned him alive. But it was true that he began to thinking about Miss Ursa more than was good for him or any boy besides.

He's already working like a man, and that means he was out in the fields and 'round the house and in the barn and I don't know what all from the rooster crowing to the milking, so he plenty of time on his own to think for hisself. Seemed that what he was thinking was how he could make Miss Ursa pay him some mind and get just a little sweet on him like she was sweet on her husband. I don't think he wanted too much, and he weren't no dirty dog or nothing. But I just think he wanted her to look at him sometimes and make him feel like her nice was for him too.

So he got to thinking 'bout how she went all funny when she got the news bout her man getting hisself a little shot, even though he was all right in his own self, and he thought maybe that's what he ought to do too. But no matter how hard that boy tried, he couldn't think of no way to get his self a little shot without maybe getting hisself shot a whole lot, so he gave up. He thought he could steal a gun and maybe shoot hisself a little, but if the padarolles had have found out he got a gun, they'd a skun him for sure, no difference who owned him or nothing.

He got the idea then that maybe he could get hisself a good bruising or maybe a broken arm or leg or something like that. So next thing he was up there in the hay mow walking on the beams, but ever time he looked down, he got so whoozy he just couldn't jump. He tried falling in to the hay, but whenever he did that the way his belly felt like it swung up into his neck made him feel so sick, he didn't think he do it no more. He tried jumping off the pigpen roof twice. The first time he didn't hurt hisself at all. But the second time, he landed funny, and twisted his foot a little. He tried limping for a week, but Miss Ursa didn't take no notice.

The whole summer he tried everything he could think of to hurt hisself. He tried hittin' his head against the house wall, 'cause it was made of bricks. He started off kind of gradual, but soon as his scalp started to push down on his ears, he gave up. He tried to put his fingers in the clothes boiling, but the fire was so hot he couldn't get close enough to reach without his shirt tails threatening to set on fire. He tried sticking his hand in the fire, and got the hair on his knuckles singed, but he couldn't hold on to the heat long enough to do no damage. He tried sticking his head under the water down Middle Creek way, but when he got a taste of the sand and the weeds he gagged so bad he couldn't hold out. He tried hitting his own fingers with a hammer, or swinging the sledge on to his foot, but while he was getting the steam up for the big one by smacking at spiders and crickets and katydids, the sight of they yellow guts made him feel so bad he had to quit that too. He took one of the boss's files, one with the handle fall off and the point end sticking out sharp, and he looked over hisself to see just where he might stab it. He didn't want to hit no organs, and his hands and feet and arms and legs looked so full of bones and veins and leaders and stuff that he didn't think there was nothing he could poke no hole in without doing hisself some kind of permanent damage.

Then he got to thinking how lucky them white men was, getting shot when they couldn't see it coming. So he started to thinking maybe that was the trouble. Everything he did he could see coming. He needed to give hisself a surprise. The same way you surprised a rabbit to catch it. 'Cept there wasn't no use in getting his foot caught in no ole snare. It have to be like a mousetrap, giving hisself a big ole whack with something when he couldn't see it coming.

So what he did was to go up the path between the piece of ground where the grape arbour and the smokehouse was, towards the place at the top where the ground flatten and where the ice house was to get dug. They was a little hickory tree growing on the side, and Josephus took his hatchet and cut off all the branches right down to the trunk, which was 'bout the size of ya arm. He twisted that down on to the ground and tied a piece of plough line to it in a kind of bow, with the long piece running across the path. The idea was that one day when he was carrying a bucket or something to slop the hogs, he forget about it, and pull that cord with his foot and that hickory tree hit good and hard fore he could see it coming. He took a bean pole and lay on the ground and touched it off once and it come 'round in the air half like a club and half like lightning.

Well, the Fall come and he never did forget about that plough line, and he never did hit hisself with it, 'cause he didn't want to do it on purpose. Meantime, Miss Ursa get word from somebody she know in the army that her husband got hisself shot again, this time more serious, and that he was captured by the Yankees and being kept in a prison somewhere down below Baltimore or something. Well, she was half-crazy, running this way and that, fixing herself and everything else up on the place, 'cause she was going off to see if she could fetch him home. Ole Josephus knowed that soon as she was to get him back she wouldn't pay her servants no more mind than nothing, so he best get a move on if he was to get some attention of his own, so he followed her round the place like a peepy to a cluck.

Well, just about the time she was fixing to go, she decided to walk 'round over the whole place to make sure everything looked like it ought, fore she went and left it to her servants and her neighbours' people. Up that hill she went, past the smokehouse to get a good look at them hogs. She was out in front, and Josephus saw her going and remembered that big mousetrap he built for hisself. Faster than he could say nothing, she went up the hill just fine, 'cause she must've missed the cord. So he high-tailed it after her, and just as she was coming back down he got to the place and she hollered at him so that he jumped fit to beat the band. His foot caught the rope and out come that hickory tree like a bucking horse and caught him up side the open mouth. Two of his teeth shot loose from one side of his face to the other, and the little end of that tree went straight through, shooting them like bullets into the field.

I don't think Miss Ursa ever did figure out how that hickory trap got there, or just how it sprung on ole Josephus like that. While she was gone to Baltimore, it healed up though. She come back with her husband like she said she would, 'cause they Yankees exchanged him or something. His left arm didn't work too good no more and they say he had burns like birthmarks all over it. He was glad to see everybody, and when he made Josephus smile at him, he said from now on, he was going to call him Whistle. He surely did. And I don't think they never was no more trouble 'bout Miss Ursa.

October 8, 1963

9.45am. Men all here by 8, but weather not fit to work outside. They are indoors on the very top floor, where there are no stairs. They have all joined Davy pulling down lathing from under the rafters. A terrible mess as far as I can see through the trap-door hole in the ceiling. Davy relegated to removing the debris & piling it into Marce's truck.

6pm. Much of the men's work out of sight today. Lots of hammering & shrill pulling of nails. Truck loaded, driven off & driven back empty several times. No sign of John John today.

10pm. Pretty warm all day, though drizzly when I woke up and rain by afternoon. Can't hear any rain now. On the news tonight that Hurricane Flora may have killed as many as 6000 people. No person, no family, no town & no country that suffers this much can be our enemy.

October 9, 1963

9.30am. Everyone now shifted to the south side of the house, priming windows and doors. Davy not here as he has taken Marce's truck to fetch supplies of some kind.

2pm. Priming operation looks set to continue. Davy returned mid-morning with long boards & spouting pieces. He has unloaded the boards & is painting them with primer.

5.45pm. The men finished the day with everything unloaded & carefully stacked. No sign of John John.

10.15pm. Quite cool this morning, & never got much over 60. No rain, & sun by lunchtime.

October 10, 1963

2pm. Last of the priming finished this morning, the men have put up the ladders again as always and have torn off old boards near the roof.

4.45pm. Odd business this afternoon as the men used Davy's primed boards to replace the ones they tore down this morning. A lot of cutting, fitting, lifting & swearing involved. Dicky Bird booming out "He'll Have To Go" at least 30 times. I kept expecting his neck to swell like a tree frog's.

10.45pm. Very cold again this morning, and then nice by afternoon. No wind to speak of and lovely sun. The mountains are now looking gray with orange and brown flecks.

October 11, 1963

5pm. Men worked much like yesterday, replacing boards near roof with new ones. This afternoon they tore out the ceiling of the high porch & dismantled everything about it they didn't like the looks of. Now entire house looks like it lost fight with a bigger house.

*At 4, Marce approached the Mary House porch & I met him outside. He said they'd be painting the windows & doors, "soffits" (sockets?) next week & putting up the spouting. Then they'd work on the high porch. —Now don't you go up there, ya hear? he told me.

*I asked Marce about John John, why I hadn't seen him. He looked incredulous at the boy's stupidity. —He done fell at school & cut the hell out of his head. He showed me, pointing above his left eye. —Broke his glasses all to hell. That's what did it, he said. I asked if he had had stiches. —Hell no, he said. God-damn doctors. Then he smirked. —Just as pretty as he ever was, I 'spect. He turned & walked back to his truck. Poor poor John John. I'd like to meet his mother.

11.30pm. Warmer this morning & dry & bright all day.

*Can't relax. On the news pictures of a dam break in Italy. Maybe 2000 killed this time. God have mercy on so much suffering.

Well, I was young and in my prime

Beulah Pearl was seventeen years old when she married Emory. He had come from Ohio and he was twenty-five years older than her, though he too had never been married. He had been in the army, and he was known to be a man with a temper. He never struck Beulah Pearl, though he often pushed, slapped, whipped or threw the children about. He had learned to box in the army – real boxing – footwork and everything, and most of the local men were afraid of him, though he was quite a small man. He was also known to be a rare shot with a rifle. He had been a marksman in the army, and during the war he had killed more men than he could remember. He spoke without feeling of shooting them in the head or the chest, always to kill, never to wound. He left the army after the war and bumped around Ohio looking for work in factories until the Crash came in '29, and he slowly came eastward into the mountains, eventually finding a job with Beulah Pearl's daddy, who was a moonshiner. Emory's sole chore was to make it known to everyone that if they came too near the operation, he would shoot them. He never had to kill a civilian, though he beat-up a few and intimidated plenty of others. He was jealous of his teenage wife, and she knew better than to give him any cause to become angry with her. She seldom went into town, seldom dressed up or saw her friends. Sadly, for Beulah Pearl, the sheer scale of Emory's jealousy gave their neighbours cause to suspect he had reasons to be jealous of her. No one had any genuine stories to tell, but there was talk that Beulah Pearl sometimes had visits from men when Emory was out of the house. Or maybe that she sometimes visited men herself.

Beulah Pearl had five children living – three boys and two girls. She had given birth to at least two others, and possibly one more that she knew of, though she wasn't completely certain about one of them. That is, one had been stillborn, one had made a few desperate gasps before dying, and the third time, Beulah Pearl had been so sick and weak and giddy, that they took away whatever she'd given birth to, and didn't allow her even to see it. Because they were poor – their house had one room upstairs and one down – they couldn't afford funerals for babies who had never even had names. Most of their neighbours would have agreed that the expense would have been a waste of the little money that Beulah Pearl and Emory had. Instead, they did what a lot of people did, and quietly saw to it that the child's remains found their way to the gravedigger who, with no authority but his own, secreted the body in a small, out-of-the-way grave in the big cemetery on the edge of town. Beulah Pearl was pretty sure this had happened twice, but the third time, all she could remember were the blood-stained blankets being taken away, and the shocked looks on the women's faces. It was, she felt, the one unanswered question in her life, and the one thing that after years of hardship, she really wanted to know.

Because Beulah Pearl had made up her mind to leave Emory. She was going to do it suddenly, at night, when they were all asleep. She was going to run off and try to catch the trolley on the old line near Middletown, hoping to get away before anyone recognized her (though she'd been seen so seldom, there was really no chance that anyone was likely to recognize her). Her plan, as far as she had a plan, was to get as far as Hagerstown. There she hoped to find a boy she had once known, a carpenter, who, the year before she married Emory, had told her he loved her. She knew he had gone there, and she'd heard some talk that he was earning some money repairing rolling stock for the railroad. It was the only hope she had, and she was so afraid of losing even it, that she would never have told it to anyone, even if there had been anyone she could have told it to.

There was only one thing she still wanted to do before she left. She wanted to speak to the gravedigger, Mart Stull, at the big

Methodist cemetery and ask him if he could remember anything about the graves he had dug for her two (or three) dead children. She wanted to know for certain that they had been treated decently, to know that she no longer had to fear that Emory had simply put them in the ground somewhere nearby, convenient and out of sight. Or worse. She had made up her mind to leave the living ones as they were - bullied, cruel, harassed, set for trouble – because she could see them, had seen them, and what their likely fates were. But she was haunted by fears for the ones she'd never met, the ones whose failure to live rested on her conscience as a pain more intense than anything she felt for the others.

But she had to be careful. Mart had a reputation for drink and for womanizing. On the night Beulah Pearl left, she waited until after midnight, hoping the rumours about him were true. She had heard that after a deep debauch, Mart would wander up to the Methodist church, where he had a key, and sleep it off on one of the pews inside, until he was sober enough to find his way back to the boarding house where he lived, where the landlord wouldn't allow anyone drunk to come inside. If she could find him in the church, a little worse for drink, she'd get him to tell her where the children were buried, if he had, in fact, buried them. She also knew and accepted what his price for this information might be. She had paid higher prices already.

When Beulah Pearl got to the cemetery there was still only starlight and half a moon to see with. She went straight off the main street to the church door, but it was locked. She remembered there was also a small door on the back, facing the long field where the graves were, so she went 'round the building to try it. It was locked as well, but outside it sat a pair of men's boots caked in mud. Leaning against the wall were a pickaxe, a shovel, a digging iron and a carpenter's folding wooden ruler. Mart had obviously been there recently, and maybe was close by still. Beulah Pearl stared out over the tombstones, straining for any signs of movement.

To the right, on the slope facing the school house, she could see a black mound, probably of earth from a grave being dug. Beulah Pearl thought it was just possible that Mart could be there, resting or perhaps drunk. She walked cautiously towards the mound and looked. There was, as she thought, a grave, just dug, smelling smoky and wet, rooty and cool. But there was no sign of Mart. She sat down on the earth, thinking she would wait.

Minutes later Beulah Pearl heard footsteps on the gravel path near the church. She nearly called out, but then it occurred to her that it might not be Mart at all, it might be anyone, anyone at all.

Then she thought it might be Emory. Perhaps, he had followed her. What would he do? And then she thought, even if it were Mart, suppose he wouldn't help? Could, but wouldn't. Suppose he just took what he wanted and laughed at her, or told her what she wanted to hear, even though it was all lies?

Beulah Pearl was lying on her chest, looking over the top of the piled soil, gazing with all her senses into the darkness, trying to see who it was near the church door. She could hear someone, someone she was certain was a man, but she couldn't tell who it was. Listening and looking she felt her footing give way, and with two or three bumps, she slid downwards into the open grave.

Beulah Pearl sat on the floor of the grave gasping. As she slipped, she wanted to call out, but it happened so fast that her mouth filled up with the wet clay, and now she spat out the lumps and rubbed at her face, trying not to cough or gag.

Now she could only listen. Was the man still there? Was he looking for her? She waited, hearing only the sounds of the night, and the pulsing of her blood in her ears. When she was finally too sick with care and too exhausted to fret any longer about the consequences, she tried climbing up the wall of the grave to get out. But it was no good. The soil was such heavy clay, and so slick with dew that she couldn't get a foothold. Feeling the despair pressing upwards from deep inside her body, she screamed, daring anyone to hear her, to reach down for her. But no one did. There was no one nearby.

Dawn came, and Beulah Pearl was surprised when she woke up – surprised that she had been sleeping. She looked around. In the darkness, she hadn't seen the two ropes hanging down in the corners of the grave; ropes that would, eventually, be positioned to lower the coffin. She tried one and found it firm. She used her hands and legs to grapple her way to the surface. It took three attempts to make it all the way on to the level ground.

Beulah Pearl walked home before the sunrise made its way down the slopes of Catoctin Mountain, though it was already lighting the tops of South Mountain to the west. She was filthy, her face reddened with the clay, her clothes black, green and tobacco-coloured with grime. She stripped to her underwear where the creek crosses Monument Road and scrubbed what would be the visible parts of her body and ground her dress together in her fists beneath the surface of the water to loosen the mould. She walked home half-naked and no one saw her. She got to the back-door side of her house without being seen and unpegged one of her own dresses from where it had been hanging on the line overnight, further evidence of her slovenly ways, and pulled it on. When she got inside the house, no one else was there. Evidently, Emory had sent them off to do something early. Or the boys had gone fishing, the girls looking for mushrooms or dandelions. Emory's gun was, as usual, not in its place by the fire. The box of shells was open on the table. He was hunting.

Beulah Pearl sat down between the two beds where her children – the children she had given names – slept; boys in the one bed, girls in the other. For the first time since any of them had been born, she wept, weeping for everyone she'd ever known.

October 12, 1963

8.15. Saturday. Columbus Day. Windy & dry.

9.30am. Found a trio of Indian corn cobs on the Mary House doorstep this morning, the husks pulled back & tied, the kernels an autumn rainbow. This can only have come from one source, so I will keep an eye out for her tomorrow. I tied them to the door with string.

1pm. Back from the A & P ($15). Also found a store & bought Paul a box of Toledo cigars & Joanie a bottle of Yardley.

4pm. Wrote two letters & put them in the box for Monday (Sis & Ags.)

10pm. Cool this morning, & quite a strong breeze today. Still very dry & bright though. About ½ way through Rabbit Run. Beautiful, in a manly way, & yet a horror story in so many others.

October 13, 1963

11am. As expected, I saw Cinch Ford coming home from church. She started grinning as soon as she saw me. When she got close enough I said thank you & kissed her on the cheek. –Your cheek's cold! I said. –Boo! It's cold this morning, she said. –How was the sermon? I asked. She leaned over close & said in a hushed tone –His throat hurt so it weren't too long to the "Amen". She fluttered her eyelids & grinned.

*Must try to get her inside for tea. Bet she likes cake.

10.30pm. Gosh it was cold this morning. Freezing, I think. Mild this afternoon. Still very dry and nicely sunny.

October 14, 1963

5pm. Just saw John John. His face has a brown-blood & bruise jagged line above his left eye, & he's wearing a pair of glasses too small for his face. Obviously, an old pair he's outgrown. He didn't come near the Mary House.

*Ladders up all day, Rip & Dicky Bird painting the windows white. Marce at the back door. This all goes faster, it seems. East wall & door done, & back door finished.

10.30pm. Another pretty day, cool then warm. Sun finishing off the leaves, now mostly brown.

October 15, 1963

2pm. Ladders up & down all over the house today as the windows all being painted.

7pm. Windows all done except on south side. Woodwork everywhere now gleaming. Broken up porches look worse alongside this.

*John John's face healing. His job today to wash the paint brushes in a bucket of gasoline.

10pm. Near freezing again this morning, but very warm even before lunchtime. No wind at all & still sunny.

October 16, 1963

1.30pm. Took lunchtime tea & coffee over to men, working on south side. As I am obviously a man-eating flirt, I decided to throw caution out one of my newly-painted windows & ask Marce why the wall on the west side of The Corner is ½ as thick as the other three walls. He said the building used to be much bigger, extending out beyond where the wash house now stands. The bank falls away here because it was where the mill-wheel was, right in what was the middle of the building. As some stage, it was dismantled and the wash house was probably built with the leftovers. I told him Hartsock said the Mary House hadn't always been bricked & asked whether he thought they might have used the old bricks to cover it. He said he didn't know, but probably. Besides, he said —Hartsock's a crock of sh[]t. I thanked him, using all my womanly wiles to look as unalluring as I could.

3pm. South side wood & windows all done now. Men working on spouting at corner farthest from the road (towards the wash house).

10.45pm. Cold again this morning & very foggy, but over 80 this afternoon.

Pike County Breakdown

Yes sir, whatever folks say after the war — and believe me, they say plenty — afore the war they weren't nobody saying nothing 'bout no abolition and 'mancipation nor no nothing of the kind. Sure enough they was folks what might have believed it, like the Dunkers who didn't have no servants no how and didn't even drink no liquor, and they was some families that had a reputation, like the Wentz's for being friendly with the underground railroad; but they wasn't nobody singing out for no freedom. Most folks just tolerate the things they find, whatever they is.

They was a family up the ole road up the mountain, the one you gets to 'fore the Fisher's Hollow, way up there where the hill flat out on the little shelf for you get to the big one on the topside, that was called Coblentz. His name was Hobart, and hers was Dory. It might have been Eudora or something like that, but everybody just call her Dory. Anyhow, they had two children, a boy and a girl that grow up and get married. The girl, she ended up near Jugtown way, and the boy married hisself a girl from all the way over in Keedysville, 'fore he headed out west to Missouri. I never did know they names, 'cause all that was when I was still little. So the mammy and the daddy, that's Hobart and Dory, was home by theyselves farming that little farm of theirn, when Miss Dory starts to acting like she sick with nobody know what. She took this and that, but nothing was doing no good, and all she want to do was lay 'round on a couch and fan in the summer and crochet in the winter. Now Mr Hobart, he think the world of his missus, and they weren't nothing he wouldn't do for Miss Dory, and he was getting powerful worried about her, 'cause they weren't nothing that made her happy no more. And besides, they was all the woman chores to be doing. So he asked her what he ought to do to fix things, and she said they ought to get them a servant of some kind. So Mr Hobart, he asked around, and 'fore long he come back from Frederick on the spring waggon with a young gal named Tildy.

She was a fine gal, ole Tildy, and she was 'bout my age, I think, when she come to live with them. They put her in the room up side of the porch, and she had a fireplace of her own. Miss Dory took to her like a she cat with kittens. She never had her no servant before, and now she weren't sure what to think of the one she had, and she treat that girl more like a daughter than a servant. She was giving her clothes to wear and asking her what she liked to eat and fussing over her like she was her own natural born child. Mr Hobart just as happy as a pig in clover, cause Miss Dory looking like her old self again, now that she had somebody to do for.

So Mr Hobart, he go back to the outside, and he do the things that the menfolk do on the farm, and he feeling like he brought the harvest home early. But 'fore long, Miss Dory start to say things like, You see the way that girl wash them clothes of mine? She make them cleaner than I ever got 'em in all my born days. You see her ironing? Umnh umnh. Like she born with the flat iron in her hand.

Same thing every day. You see ole Tildy sweep them floors? They bright as ashes in the sunshine. You eat any them fried tomatoes she cook? No sir, I ain't never had 'em so good. Ole Mr Hobart he learn to think they wasn't nothing that Tildy do weren't better than everything Miss Dory ever do in her life. But that didn't make Miss Dory mad or sad or nothing of the kind. No, sir. She seem happier than ever. 'Fore long, she back sitting on her couch and a-singing songs to herself, just like she a child again. She pick up the sewing again, and sure enough, she start to making things for Tildy to wear. Colours she like, patterns that fit her. She even send Mr Hobart down to the store in Ellerton to get her some calico for to make her a dress to wear on Sundays.

Now I ain't saying they was nothing the matter with any of that. No, sir, I ain't. But all I got to say is they all sure is lucky that Tildy was the kind of gal she was. She act like she know just how good she got it all the time. She didn't try to act like no white girl nor nothing. And I think she love Miss Dory like she her own mama. Mr Hobart love her like she his own child, and he just so grateful to God Hisself for sending them somebody that make Miss Dory so happy again.

It looked like everything set to be fine, till one day he come in from stacking the wood for house fires, and he see Tildy come a running towards him on the porch. It nearly broke her heart, but she say that something the matter with Miss Dory, cause she was a-sitting on her couch, and she won't answer no questions. Tildy was sure she was dead, but she was too scared to say nothing. Sure enough, Miss Dory had done died, and they was both, Mr Hobart and Tildy, in a awful fix 'bout what they gonna do.

Ain't nobody could tell 'em neither. They buried poor Miss Dory just like the Christian folks they was, and Mr Hobart, he send letters to his son out west, but he don't hear nothing. His daughter come to the burying, but she got a family of her own, and her husband ain't got nothing to say about what Mr Hobart ought to do. See, everybody 'fraid of what it look like if he was to live in that ole house with just Tildy round there. Maybe he get to interfering with her or something. They all got to talk and use they jaws for something besides eating. Anyhow, Tildy say to me, Lord, Mary, what I supposed to do now then? Mr Hobart gonna sell me, sure as shooting, and I gonna end up somewhere where I don't know nobody. Ain't nobody ever treat me so good. And he don't know nothing 'bout looking after hisself no how. She worry herself half sick.

Well, Mr Hobart, he live with the preacher for while, while he think things over, leaving Tildy in the house by herself. He grieve like a gentleman ought, you ask me. Anyway, when he come out from the preacher's, he head hisself off to Frederick again. He got a idea. He come back with a fella, called Grudge — bout the shyest negro man I ever laid eyes on. He took him back to the house, and he gave him the room side of Tildy's. There, he said, now y'all can live like you sister and brother. Tildy say ole Grudge, who got his name 'cause his last master say he had some kind of grudge against talking, 'bout the nicest quietest fella she ever see and he work long side of Mr Hobart like he his own son. Tildy say she do the cooking and Mr Hobart sometimes even eat his dinner and his supper with them. Lord, lord, lord.

Anyhow, folks stop they threats to chin wagging. Mr Hobart die, he left instructions in his will that Tildy and Grudge get they free papers. They go on living there till Mr Hobart's daughter's husband say they got to move so he can sell the farm. I hear they move to New York or somewhere.

October 17, 1963

5pm. Rest of the spouting went up today. Main part of the building looks so much better. Porches like the slum end of things. They seem to have over-bought spouting, as more remains piled outside.

*While the ladders were up, they attached a new TV aerial to the eastern chimney. Rip was at the top of the ladder, serenaded by Dicky Bird's rendition of "16 Tons".

10.45pm. Dark & starless tonight. No moon. Slightly warmer this morning & reliably foggy. Over 80 again this afternoon.

October 18, 1963

8.45am. Men just a little later this morning, as they came with some lumber and some different tools.

12.30pm. Men having their lunch. This morning, after they unloaded their own truck another big one came and delivered piles of lumber. They have stacked all this under the over-hanging porch on the wash house.

3.45pm. Men just finishing up cleaning up the mess they made after pulling out everything they didn't like on the porches. Truck piled high. Not sure where Davy & John John will sit.

5pm. John John came to my door and knocked just after 4. His face looks much better, but he'll definitely have a scar. I'm no expert, but I'd guess he should have had about 6 stitches. Anyway, he said the windows & doors are all done now & so is the spouting. Next week starts work on the porches.

*As John John headed back to the truck for his ride, Marce had obviously got Davy & the others to tease him that I had become his girlfriend. John John looked so angry & so ashamed & so so used to it. He joined Davy, sitting dangerously high on the pile of rubbish filling the back of Marce's truck.

9pm. Just back from visiting Joanie & Paul & being serenaded on all their instruments. Wonderful to hear them talk about their music. I gave them the presents I bought & think I may have overwhelmed them. They were very grateful, but I think just a little uncomfortable too? Their house is just as I expected, a good mix of old & fairly new. I liked watching them together, intimacy in silent forms between them.

10pm. Much warmer this morning, over 80 this afternoon. No rain still & things looking parched. Cornfields dead & yellow until plowed brown.

October 19, 1963

8.00am. Very quiet morning. Shopping later.

11.30am. Didn't go to Frederick but went to Acme in Middletown instead. $11 but selection not as good.

12.15pm. Just listened to the siren blowing in Myersville (3 miles). It is so quiet. They blow this, Cinch told me, at 12 so that the farmers know what time it is. I bit my tongue holding back the tidal wave of possible replies. I've decided after all that there is something quaint about it. That's a better viewpoint, I think.

10pm. Cool but not cold this morning. Yet again over 80 this afternoon. Indian summer? No wind at all.

October 20, 1963

11.45am. Usual crowd of churchgoers, there & back. I went out to join in & the women all chirpy as robins. I watched for tell-tale signs of future betrayal or present hypocrisy but saw nothing definite. Cinch wearing an orange dress (!) with a white collar. All her clothes look homemade, clean, simple, looked after. She has 1 daughter, a granddaughter and a grandson. I asked her to point out her husband from among the men. She looked like she suddenly tasted lemons & said he was out with his metal detector "huntin' up relics". I think she means Civil War ones.

*Must make a list of locals I want to meet: Marce's wife (John John's mother); Cinch's husband; woman opposite Paul & Joanie (was it her I overheard?) etc.

10.30pm. Probably 40 this morning, & not quite as warm this afternoon. Another day that started foggy. No wind & no rain. Finished RR. Nicely written, but a foreign language to me.

October 21, 1963

2pm. Glorious sawings & hammerings going on as the porches are being rebuilt. Dicky Bird is on a Johnny Cash binge, all prisons, trains etc. Rip busy & serious, Marce doing the finer work, & Davy chiefly responsible for holding, carrying & metaphorically showing his backside for kicking. (I would love to meet his wife too, as I would like to know whether she is a dear soul, or more like Marce.)

5.30pm. Men long gone & lower side of porches looking better. Very solid. (I walked over & had a look, Marce be d[] mned.) Is it possible that the place could smell of aftershave, or is that just sawdust?

10pm. Terrible fog this morning, though not so cold. Over 80 again this afternoon. The men show up in flannel & end up in tee shirts.

*Just watched "Wagon Train".

Black-eyed Susie

Danny, Tim and Cliff were friends. They had grown up within a quarter mile of one another, up the old gravel road between Harmony and Ellerton, about half-way up the mountainside. Danny lived with his grandfather, a groundhog-eating mountaineer who wore the same clothes winter and summer. Tim's father had been a soldier in the last war, but when the war ended and he came home, he didn't stay long, before he left Tim and his mother to look after themselves as best they could. His mother got a job as a waitress at a joint just over the county line, and stayed away from home most nights, sometimes with men, sometimes with women. Cliff was the youngest in his family and he lived with his brother, sister, mother and father, all of whom worked wherever they could, though money was always short.

The boys had all tried drinking and found it pretty unsatisfying. They had all tried smoking, but none of them seemed very interested in it as a habit. What they hadn't tried, and so what they talked about most, was sex. Danny claimed he had seen the older Schumacher girl asleep naked, and he and Cliff had been together when they both saw the Willards' little girl skinny dipping in the creek, though she was only four. Tim claimed he had seen Sue Fink peeing in the woods. These were the only sightings of usually-covered living female flesh anyone of them confidently asserted. Touching was rarer still. Only Danny had an offering, and that was that when Miss Draper washed his hair after the accident at school he had felt her breasts through her dress as she leaned against his shoulder.

They had listened to older boys talking. Three claimed to have done it with Maggie Remsburg. They had overheard Pip Flook talking with his cronies about doing it with Poozer Schildknecht, even though his wife Dottie suspected them. One night after he'd been drinking, Tim's father had confessed to Tim's mother that he nearly did it with a black girl in France. Cliff had watched his father almost drooling with lust once when he saw Cliff's brother Bobby with a girl at the Mount Airy carnival. Cliff said the old man just never got his eyes above the girl's waist. Cliff and Tim had heard the older men teasing Melvin Ricketts about those summer nights when everyone had their windows open and they could all hear the bed springs squeaking in his house. All the older men stood there saying, Squeak! Squeak! Squeak! until Melvin told them to shut the hell up, and they didn't know nothing about it. And, of course, they had seen pictures. Danny's grandfather had a pile of old cards in a tin box, but the women all looked so silly that there was nothing sexy about their dimpled buttocks or tilting breasts.

A rumour finally came to the boys the same summer they all turned sixteen. A little further uphill from where they all lived, between the places where the old Fisher's Lodge Road ended and the Hawbottom Road started, there lived a woman named Irene Zimmer. Folks thought of her as a widow, though no one could recall her husband, and she didn't seem to have any children. Her house was bigger than a shack and had one room on each of two floors – a clapboard cabin, unpainted and patched with tar-paper, and surrounded by trees where chickens pecked and hogs sometimes rooted. The rumour the boys heard was that Irene could be very accommodating to folks who came around and did the sort of chores that she found it hard to do for herself. If she liked the work you'd done, she found a way to reward you.

Cliff was the first of the boys to try and discover whether the rumour was true. This came about through big talk. He boasted how he could think of so many things to do that Irene would just fall on her back without his even having to ask her.

Cliff went up the road towards Irene's house on a day he knew that both Danny and Tim would be up at Thurmont picking peaches at the big orchards there. He didn't want any witnesses, just in case things went wrong. When he got near the wire fence between Irene's yard and her porch he saw her looking down the hill away from him, one hand on her hip and the other holding a hat. When she turned around towards him, Cliff's arms fell to his sides and his throat dried. There were a few wrinkles at the corners of her eyes, and he couldn't have said for sure whether her hair was red, or blonde or grey.

What can I do for ya? she said.

I come to do some work, Cliff said.

Irene looked at him a moment. How old are ya? she said.

Eighteen, he lied.

Uh huh, she said. What's your name?

Cliff told her the truth.

See that pile of wood down there under them trees?

He nodded.

You saw that about this long and split the big pieces and stack it all up under that roof over there. I'll be in the house.

Cliff looked at her and she looked back. Then she walked past him, and the screen door slammed behind her. At least she's smaller than me, Cliff thought.

When the wood was cut and chopped, Cliff went up to the house and tried looking in the door to the inside. He couldn't see her.

Ma'am? Miss Irene. I'm done here now.

I'm upstairs, she said.

That was all she said, so Cliff opened the door and went inside.

The next day he told his story to Danny and Tim. It was a story that Irene certainly would not have recognized. Cliff almost didn't recognize it himself.

Two days later, Tim used some old lumber from a broken-down barn to strengthen the walls around Irene's hog pen. A week later, and Danny had stolen 100 cedar shingles from his grandfather's loafing shed and fixed all the leaks in Irene's roof. Without telling the others, Cliff even went back once and cut down the elm tree that was threatening to fall over Irene's springhouse.

Then came the week of the Walkersville carnival. Danny, Tim and Cliff were washed, wearing shoes that tied, and had their hair parted and shiny. Between them, they had finished a pint of 'shine from a man down from Spruce Run, and now they were taking turns swinging a nine-pound hammer and trying to drive a stubborn weight thirty feet into the air in order to ring a bell that could be heard over the whole carnival ground. All three had taken their three swings, and all three had failed. They were all shaking their heads when Little Mose, a volunteer fireman who smoked cigars, took the hammer from Cliff and with a single swing sent the weight to the top of the mast, clanging the bell solidly. A small cheer went up as people walked by. Little Mose looked at the three boys, each one stubbornly grinning, forlorn and defiant.

Keep tryin', boys. One day you'll get it.

As Little Mose was walking away, Danny said just loud enough to let them all think Little Mose might hear, We're already getting it.

He laughed and hit Cliff on the shoulder. Then the three of them drifted towards the mid-way, to where the rides were, to where the music came from, and to where the hootchy-kootchy would be later.

You ain't, Cliff said.

Huh? Danny said. What y'all talkin' 'bout?

Cliff looked at Tim. We heard you ain't getting any.

What the hell you mean? Danny stopped and looked at them.

The way we heard it, you done what you done on that woman's sheets.

Danny looked first at Cliff and then at Tim, his mouth open, his fists clenching, and tears on the rims of his eyes.

Tell him, Tim, he said. Tell him what we heard.

Cliff looked at Tim, but Danny did the talking.

We heard you couldn't even get it up, he said.

Oh, yeah? Cliff said.

Yeah, Tim said.

Both Danny and Cliff looked at Tim.

Don't you go shootin' off your mouth none, Cliff said.

Yeah, dumb ass, Danny said. We know all 'bout you too.

Tim looked at them both ready to explode.

It's a god damn lie, he said.

Cliff looked at Danny. Didn't she tell us, he said, that that short one got about the littlest wiener she ever saw, and if he did get it in, she sure couldn't tell.

The three of them stood there ready to murder something, ready to let the humiliation that was breaking their ribs tear everything down, burnt, destroyed, wasted.

Tim walked away first, disappearing into the rainbow lights. Cliff went towards the food tents, led on by the greasy smells. Danny felt in his pockets for more nickels, thinking it still might not be too late to win something, some prize to take home and put on the windowsill.

It was the last carnival any of them went to that summer.

October 22, 1963

5.45pm. Men busy on porches all day. Lower one looks nearly done. Ceiling very pretty in tongue & groove.

 *Got a glimpse of John John. He has new glasses. Black frames.

11pm. Windy, dry & sunny again today. On this evening's news that over 200,000 students in Chicago refused to go to school in protest. Every night I am made angry or afraid. It is like falling asleep under water.

 *Today Dicky Bird was singing "The Battle of New Orleans". "They ran through the briars etc". Young men, poor men, frightened men. So many. Who remembers them?

October 23, 1963

9.30am. I was in the vegetable garden piling up dead weeds to burn when I saw a large white cat across the Common at the gray house. I went to where the fence is most collapsed and tried to call it over, holding my hand out. It just looked at me. I went into the road & the cat seemed wary but curious. I crossed the road, hand still out when all at once the back screen door snapped open & the old woman who lives there appeared. The cat ran off as if death loomed. The woman called out – He ain't knoatchy. I said hello. She said –Y'all can have him if ya can catch him. I thanked her & said I'd try another day. She looked at me a minute and then closed her back door. Wonder what she's heard?

5pm. Men all at work on high porch today. Heavy pieces around the edges all done, floor finished & ceiling coming along.

*Dicky Bird tried giving his version of "Walking After Midnight", but the others soon crushed the life out of it.

9.30pm. Not so cold this morning and not so hot this afternoon. Hardly 70. Still no rain.

October 24, 1963

1pm. Just back with tray things. Very hungry myself. Living on poached eggs, it feels.

6pm. High porch ceiling & floor finished now & railing started. This looks like slow work to me.

10pm. Cool this morning & foggy. No breeze. Warm this afternoon.

October 25, 1963

5pm. Not only did they finish fitting that railing today, they have started priming the lower porch. Davy came into his own as a gray paint slinger.

*I brought them ice tea at about 3, as it seems so dull today. I tried talking to Davy. So long as he forgot the others were (literally) over his head he seemed relaxed. His wife is from Germany, he told me. He has a son named Tim. He showed me a picture. If I were just a little older, I'd have kissed him on the cheek. Dear Davy. Does she ask him about his day? Will he say, "They let me prime the wood-work today"? Would she be proud of him? How often is she proud of him? Does she tell him?

*Suddenly had the thought the maybe some of the neighbors are witches & read my mind. If so, scratch that last entry. They already think I live in some kind of a permanent Sadie Hawkins Dance.

11pm. Cool this morning, foggy again. Heavy & oppressive all day. No breeze at all. No rain.

Oh, stingy woman

'Round 'bout the time that ole Red Mary was a getting sick with the swelling in her legs, she used to like if I was to tell her all the stories that I hear from folks a-coming and a-going. Being so much younger than her I got through the chores a whole lot faster, the cooking and the washing and the cleaning and fixing and all the things they want in the big house. So I took up the garden for ourselves and spanded it right round the whole backside of the Mary House, right over to where the creek runs towards the back. I put up a fence of willow I put together to keep the coons and the possums out, and I growed everything I could fit in there, seeings as how I had to tend it in the evenings. I even took a cutting off ole Miss Margaret's pink roses and got us one of our ownself round the window. Anyhow, with what they 'lowed us, we had plenty to eat most times. On Monday, Miss Margaret left me fetch down for us seven pounds of pork – ham and side meat mostly – and two dozen salt herring. We got a gunny sack of cornmeal, and sometimes some flour, and always some molasses till the next Monday. We never got no milk nor coffee, 'cept we buy it our ownselves. I took to selling anything I could, and Miss Margaret, she happy to see us get it, honest, she say. I asked ole man Leatherman, up 'yond the Meeting House, if I could pick up some of the long straw that lay on the ground in his field when the scything was done, and he say, Girl, you get yourself a sack and get out there and take all you want, I don't want it for nothing. So I took it up and taught myself to make hats for folk. I started off with hats for the servants, and I practice till I started making fine ones for the white folks too. I was mighty proud. That's how I hear so many stories 'bout folks.

That all happened cause of the knife I got. Now servants ain't supposed to have theyselves no knives, no sir. No how. When I was a girl child, Red Mary she have to cut up the meat for cooking with a axe from the woodpile. But I got me a knife this away. When I started in to fixing and mending the clothes for Little Bob – he was Miss Margaret's first one – she saw me a-biting the thread, and she say, Lordy, Mary, what y'all doing? I tells her I ain't got no scissors, and she say, Ain't you got no knife or nothing? And I say, No, ma'am, I surely ain't. And she say, Well, next time we gets to Middletown way, we get you a little knife of you own. That's how I met ole Hen Pot.

His real name was Henry, but since I got to know him, everybody just call him Hen Pot. He had been a field servant down there on that big Koogle farm, on the side of Middletown, towards the South Mountain. Ever since he a boy, he busier than a fishworm in a skillet, and he always cheerful – not fool laughing and a-cutting the monkey, but just putting on. Well, he was a good fella, and ole Mr Koogle, he kept him out of the fields and let him get showed how to work in the forge, a-shoeing horses, and working with files and I don't know what all. Well, he so good, pretty soon he fixing everything, 'cluding setting the saws and sharpening the scissors and making knives for the butchering. Mr Koogle think so much of him that when he die, he left Hen Pot his free papers and give him one hundred dollars for hisself. So Hen Pot got hisself a little ole house and stable on the side of town, and set hisself up as a free negro, making knives, and setting saws, and sharpening scissors, and any of the fine iron that the folks wanting. He go out into Middletown, he wore a waistcoat and boots and a straw hat that I made. He looked fine, you ask me.

Thing was, ever since before ole Mr Koogle die, Hen Pot had his eye on a gal servant down the road towards Burkittsville, on a farm belonging to Mr Hahn. He used to have to go over there when Mr Koogle hire him out for the day to work there, and he see her then. Her name was Creola, and she was a sweet young thing, wore her hair pulled back, 'way from her neck. Sometimes I go long with Miss Margaret when she go down to Middletown to get her stuff for dressmaking, and I carry it for her, and sell all the stuff she let me sell. That's when I got my knife, on one of them trips. She say, Now Mary, don't y'all forget to get yourself a little ole knife this time. So I showed her when I got it. Anyhow, most every time I go to Middletown, I see Hen Pot, and I say, How you getting on with Creola? And he shake his head, I don't know Mary, I just don't know. I say, What you mean you don't know? She like ya, don't she? She like me, he say, but she work so good, that Miss Hahn don't want her to get married, lessen' she have a baby or something, and it change her. Why don't you tell her not to work so good? I say. But he just shake his head.

Well, I see Creola when she in Middletown, like me, carrying on all the trading for Miss Hahn, like the servants does. Once, I seen her a-toting all the things down to the waggon for Miss Hahn, and I say to her, Creola, honey, what you gonna do bout Hen Pot? And she say, I can't think 'bout him, 'cause I just cries and cries. I 'bout die for him. Don't do that, I says. Ask Miss Hahn if you could marry him. She want you to be happy, don't she? She mean? No, she ain't mean, she say. But I don't know what she want.

Next thing, she start to cry. I say, Girl, you can't be standing here like this. She say, I know that. But that ain't it, she say. I awful worried. What you worried 'bout, child? I say. It's Mr Hahn, Mr Hahn's boy. He the one called Mahlon. What you worried bout him for? I say. And she just look at me. He been messing with you? I say. No, he ain't, she say. Not yet, anyway. But he just keeps a-trying. He give me stuff all the time. He give me things then say I got to kiss him. But I don't. He chase all the servants? I say. No, just me – I think, she say. You tell Miss Hahn 'bout that?

She give me a look like the cat crawled up her dress. I can't say nothing 'bout that. Mr Hahn whop me sure as shooting. Then you gotta make sure she find out somehow. How I supposed to do that? she say. Well, I don't know, but you just find youself a way. Meantime, we got to get Hen Pot to try and buy you out from ole Mr Hahn. You think Hen Pot got that much money? Maybe not yet, I say, but if they sell you a little at a time, maybe he get that much.

Anyhow, I don't hear nothing for a while. Next thing I hears is from Hen Pot hisself. Miss Margaret was visiting her friend Miss Marker up by the Lutheran Church and I done the trading, so I goes down to the workshop and there is Hen Pot a-smacking away at the big saw-setting bench. How you, Hen Pot? I say. Lord, Mary, I'm so glad to see ya! he say. You right. You as right as right can be.

So he tell me he go along to ole Mr Hahn and he say he want to marry Creola, and how much money would it cost to buy her free papers. Mr Hahn say he can't be selling her nohow, as Miss Hahn don't want her to go, free or not. Well, 'bout a couple of days after that time, Creola was in the washhouse a-battling the sheets, when Mr Mahlon come up behind her, sweet-talking and saying how much he want to come 'round and see Creola when the sun go down. What he don't know is Creola got the windows open 'cause it's hot, and his mammy, Miss Hahn, is trying to get the cat off the washhouse roof and she hear the whole thing. I think it must've got a little worse, but Hen Pot didn't want to say too much 'bout that. Anyway, things then change real fast. 'Fore you know it, Mr Hahn hisself ride down to Hen Pot's and say he take five hundred dollars for Creola, and give Hen Pot five years to pay the whole thing, a hundred or more a year. But 'fore he did, Mr Hahn say, Hen Pot have to 'gree that she be 'lowed to come and live at the forge, so long as she still do the sewing and the fine work for Miss Hahn.

Hen Pot just grin like you ain't never seen a man grin before. He say he give ole Mr Hahn two hundred fifty dollars right away, when the 'countant bring him the papers promising for Creola to be free. I want to ask him what he think change Mr Hahn's mind, but I don't know just how much Creola tell him bout Mahlon, so I don't say nothing.

I say, Where Creola now then?
She gone to buy eggs from the town.
You still 'ford eggs?
Can't 'ford no chickens.
You get that wife a bonnet yet?
I get her one. You help her make it.
She don't need my help, I say.
No, sir, he say. Guess she don't.

October 26, 1963

9.30am. Saw Agassy this morning walking down the road with her husband. They are like chess pieces. Worn little chess pieces. He is like her with shorter hair, green pants, blue shirt, chin that no amount of shaving can bare.

1pm. Still couldn't summon the enthusiasm to got to Frederick, so back to Acme ($18 & guilt over doughnuts & pretzels).

*Saw two of the white-haired boys walk down the Harmony Road with the frog-faced short one.

4.30pm. In a rush of virtue, I took doughnuts up to Paul & Joanie. Wound up trading them for a piece of J's homemade berry pie. She said there is a Halloween party in the Band Hall tonight. Ought I to go?

10.30pm. Back from Band Hall. I was expecting Norman Rockwell, & much of it was. Caught a glimpse of Marce arriving with a short busty woman & John John dressed as a fat (pillow under the shirt) tramp. Her name is Jean & she only spoke to women all evening. I introduced myself & she said a flat "Hi" & hoped I was settling in. I told her her husband was doing good work, & she replied that he "is something". Oh, that he is, I thought.

*John John paraded with the others in his costume but didn't win. I told him he looked good & he seemed pleased, I think. Two of the white-haired boys were there with frogface & the tall kid. No sign of the ponderous one.

*Cinch Ford talked to everyone in the room, poured everyone Dixie cups of cider, & distributed pieces of gingerbread that she'd made herself. 4 big trays of it. I think her husband is a plump balding man. If so, he only spoke to men all evening.

*The moment of truth came when to my (& everyone else's) bafflement, Dicky Bird & Davy showed up … dressed as women! I would never have believed it if I hadn't seen it. Both wore heels (too small), stockings, dresses, necklaces, gloves, hats & fire-engine lipstick. To my incredulous eyes, they did their very best to walk & sway like dames. If they had drink in them, it wasn't obvious. The "crowd" loved them. Anyway, I will have to rethink them both from now on. What can have prompted this? Only The Shadow Knows.

11pm. Weather almost the same as yesterday. Like wearing a wet coat all day. No rain.

*Still picturing Davy's pouty red lips above his Himalayan breasts.

*Was the tall skinny blonde with the little blonde boy his wife?

October 27, 1963

9am. After last night's debauch, I feel depressed to be without a hangover. Did I imagine all that?

1pm. Made soup for lunch. Wish I had more pie.

6.30pm. Acme bread not bad. 10c a loaf. Nice with second round of soup.

10.45pm. Weather much the same. Dreary fog. Slightly warmer.

October 28, 1963

2.30pm. The whole crew have been daintily priming the porch woodwork today & it is finished.

*To my astonishment, they have set up ladders, right into the road, & are working on the porch roof. Hammering. It looks slippery.

5pm. Porch roof evidently sufficiently hammered. Ladders moved away.

*John John given the job of sorting a bucket of mixed nails. He seems to be an intelligent boy & this must be hard for him. His eyes are poor enough that he leans right over the bucket. I want so much to hug him & tell him that it won't always be like this.

10pm. Much warmer this morning. And rain! More drizzle & breezy this afternoon. Never really warmed up.

October 29, 1963

8.30am. Already they have set up the ladders & Rip & Dicky Bird are on the high porch roof painting it with silver paint. Marce is at the very bottom, painting the columns of the lower porch. He is painting the bottom 1/3 green.

1.30pm. Marce has finished his greening of the lower pillars & is painting the upper 2/3 white. Rip & Dicky Bird have joined him & are painting the other woodwork white. They also painted the outer wood white upstairs.

5pm. Once again, John John had to clean all the brushes in a paint can full of gasoline.

10pm. Started nicely today, warmer, but so windy it never really improved. Quite bright. Watched "Petticoat Junction" but found it too realistic, too much like the life I know.

October 30, 1963

1pm. Like a barbershop quartet, all four men are on the high porch painting the woodwork white. The ceiling downstairs, by the way, they painted sky blue.

5.45pm. Yes, the upstairs ceiling of the high porch is blue & all the woodwork, including the railing is now white.

10.30pm. Cool again this morning & windy. Never really warmed up. Lovely sunshine. Leaves virtually all gone now. Nothing but smoke on the air. The mountains like a pile of old gray hats.

October 31, 1963

10am. Ladders in the road again, as the men are putting up the spouting on the porches. (So there is no extra after all.)

2.45pm. Marce has disappeared in his truck. The others are indoors, hammering.

5pm. Marce returned & the men spent some time unloading what look like round paper hay bales for a while. The porches look finished to me. I have to say, the whole outside of The Corner looks wonderful. Hartsock was right, they are good at what they do. I will phone him & say so.

11.45pm. Weather fine all day, cool but not cold. Never warm.

November 1, 1963

9.30am. Took the tray over as usual this morning. Men slightly nervous, when Dicky Bird finally spoke up to tell me to look at my car. Local boys had soaped my windows. I remembered then that last night was Halloween. No children came to the door, maybe because there aren't many of them, they don't do that here, or they've heard "something". I cleaned the windows with hot water & a sponge. In a strangely pathetic way, I feel honoured even to have gained the local boys' disrespect. At least it's notice.

*Men unloaded more round pink bags, which I now know to be insulation. Also a bucket of fittings, lots of copper pipe & other boxed tools.

1pm. Radio playing faintly from The Corner but not much sign of life all morning. Took the lunch coffee/tea over. Rip & Marce busy with putting copper pipes everywhere for the furnace & heating; Dicky Bird & Davy putting insulation on the under-side of the top floor (roof). As always, Davy the one up & down the ladder & stairs. He must eat prodigiously to sustain his weight.

5pm. Day ended quietly. Saw John John, evidently given the job of carrying the insulation wrappers outside & stuffing them into an old oil drum, probably for burning.

10.30pm. Foggy this morning, rain most of the day, drizzling still. 40s-50s all day. Moonlight struggles. Watched "Twilight Zone".

November 2, 1963

11.30am. So damp & wet today I couldn't face going all the way to Frederick, so went to the Acme in Middletown instead ($17).

*Brought in wood & sticks & used newspaper to get fireplace going. So far so good. Smells nice, & not as smoky as I expected.

2pm. Nearly finished Hist of W Md books, so no need to renew any more.

9pm. Fireplace has warmed the house beautifully.

11pm. Weather like yesterday only colder. House still warm though after having fireplace burning all afternoon & evening. Stairs are so open, nothing to obstruct the upward flow of heat (or the downward flow of my body, if I should misstep.)

*Shocking event on news today: President Diem assassinated. Will this end things quickly?

November 3, 1963

7.30am. Have already got the fireplace burning, as it is cold this morning. Raining too.

9.00am. Breakfast feels good when you are in a room warmed only by a fire. Coffee goes right down to the fingertips. Will try drying some clothes on chairs near the fireplace too.

12pm. Watched the churchgoers there & back today, all huddled under umbrellas. More driving there, I think too. Went outside on purpose to say hello to Cinch Ford. She was all bundled up with her head covered. She saw me & spoke first, fingering the red paisley scarf tied under her chin. –Miss Mary, you like my pretty bandanna? –Prettiest thing I've seen today, Cinch. –I seen the smoke a-coming out your chimney. Y'all warm enough in there? –Yes, I said, just like bread in a toaster. –Well, she said. You're gonna need some more wood. –Do you think so? I asked. She didn't say anything, & then I realized she'd already answered that question. Yes, she thinks so. (Why do I, or "people like me" say things like this?) –Ask that Marce. He'll bring ya some. –Is that right? (I did it again!) –Uh huh. –I'll have to ask him. –It'll be good for burning, she said.

3.30pm. Clothes dried nicely, but will they smell of smoke? I may be so used to it now, I can't smell it. Also, I've told myself I could burn the place down if clothes get too close to the fire. I shouldn't think so much.

11pm. Watched "Bonanza". In the 30s & 40s all day, rain & drizzle. I'm finding my day stretched a little because of the need to get the fire going early & not wanting to let it go down too soon. Upstairs stays surprisingly warm.

November 4, 1963

8.30am. Have been up since 6 this morning. VERY cold! Only in the 20s. Fire going by 7.

 *Delivered tray this morning at 8. Men all wrapped in flannel and denim several layers deep. Clutched their mugs with both hands. I spoke to them as a group, trying to see whether I could get Dicky Bird & Rip each to speak. I joked they must be in a hurry to get that furnace working. Dicky Bird added a headshake to his permanent grin. Rip added a grin to his permanent eyes-wide trying-hard face. Davy looked at the others. Marce ignored me.

 *I asked Marce directly whether he knew how to get me any more firewood. Bizarrely, Davy suddenly spoke up with, –Aw, he knows how, all right. Marce ignored him. –How much ya want? he said. –How much will I need? I asked. –Well, he said, How cold are ya? Dicky Bird snorted. Marce tipped out his cup and said, –I'll bring ya a cord this week. I thanked him. –Uh huh, he said.

1.15pm. Lunch tray as usual. Same as yesterday. Insulation now nearly finished.

3.30pm. Noise from across the road increased, with some hammering & the wee hee noise of nail-pulling.

5pm. Men left on time. John John's task today being to straighten all the old nails the others pulled out earlier today. Not sure what they are doing, but they have made the hole into the top floor much larger by removing some floorboards. Cut up bits of copper everywhere. Sharp edges. Pretty stripes of orange in the gloom though.

10pm. Very clear & still all day. Not much above 40 this afternoon.

Jack o' Diamonds was a witness

I, LittleWound, tell this story.

It was in the time after the slaves in Virginia killed their masters, frightening the Washechu.

There were two brothers who lived on a farm near Myersville. To find the place, you must walk from Harmony over the hill towards the mountain where the sun sets. It was here, where the land levels beside a stream with stones like the fists of the Pomola, that their father made their house. Their name was Kopp, and the first to be born was called George, the other, Henry. Their names to one another, as I heard them say, were Georg and Heinrich. Their mother had died of a fever when both were still boys, and their father too followed her as soon as his sons became men.

The brothers ran the farm as they should, but Henry was the one whose work gained the most esteem. They owned one slave, and his name was Moses. He had no wife and he lived in the quarters behind the farmhouse. He too was like Henry, and his work was praised by everyone who saw it. In this way they lived until the hair of all of them began to thin and lose its darkness.

It happened that it was George who did most of the brothers' trading. In Myersville he met a woman whose name was Anna, and she spoke to him in the language of his own Washechu people. They were married and she came to live with the brothers and Moses at the farm. There was no strife between them and their seasons grew like the grasses on the land.

Because Henry was the worker whose decisions pleased all, though not the first born, he had his way in the tasks serving them all. His labour was the labour prized among his neighbours, and it was to him that most honour came. This did not trouble George, and he allowed the benefits to decorate Henry in the eyes of those who knew them both. Even Moses walked with the grace and pride of a man who knows his duties and who uses his hands to profit himself and those who seek honour through him. Indeed, George's pastime when the sun lay upon the sky's cloth was to sleep in the shade, doing no work until the cool of the evening rose again. Henry never spoke to his brother in wrath, and Moses was wise in his station; but both men felt rancour in their hearts.

It was in the springtime when Anna gave birth to a son that she asked her husband for a favour. She asked that along the sinking ground near the kitchen-house, the farm might have a root-cellar and wash-house built. She hoped to lay in more food for the winter, and the earth of the hillside would preserve their produce from the frost and from the heat. Also the laundry of the family was making demands upon her, and with the summer about to flame through the trees, she wished to ease her burden. She made this request in front of both Henry and Moses, thinking it would happen that they would be the ones to make these improvements. To her surprise, George spoke up. His honour, such as it was, had felt the rasp of the men's eyes, and he vowed to undertake the work himself.

Spring lengthened and the tulips fell from the poplar trees. No work on Anna's cellar and wash-house had begun. She asked George whether he would object to Moses digging the foundation into the place where the ground curved against the hillside. He did not, and soon Moses set to work and though the improving days brought the sweat to his face and left him shaking with fatigue, he completed the excavation in the breadth of his pride. Anna gave him a suit of clothes for his trouble, and enough silver to smoke tobacco until the frosts returned.

As the barley, oats and wheat ripened and the cows' udders grew with the meadow's grass, still George took no steps to further the cellar's foundation on which the wash-house walls would rest. She asked George whether he would object to Henry's gathering the stones for the foundation. He did not. So in the evenings, instead of drinking beer and sleeping after the threshing, Henry took a horse and cart and made trips to the stream, transporting the stones up the hill to the place Moses had dug in the spring. Together, Moses and Henry laid the stones into a foundation.

It was then that George began to take notice. He brought out the timbers he and Henry and Moses had cured seasons before and which they had kept above the waggon-shed. These he laid in rows and stacked beside the foundation, in the place where the building would stand. And yet, time passed. When at last the apples began to ripen on the trees and the shelves in the kitchen sagged with the weight of the food that Anna had dried, or canned or salted; when the hogs in the pen slumbered in satiety; and when the cheeses lay on the stairs as there was no other darkness in which to store them, she let her eyes fall from George so that they might never rise again.

Without a word spoken, Henry and Moses built the cellar and above it the wash-house rose. They painted it with lead the colour of blood and its corners with lead the colour of snow. Neither they nor Anna dared show their pride to George. But still, he said nothing, and his habits did not change.

In spite of this, life on the farm was never the same. The respect that had once existed was gone. There was no longer any joy in the richness that the family had made.

When news of the gold that men were finding in the mountains that lay nearest the sun reached the valley of the Catoctins, Henry bought a horse and cart in Middletown. When the last day came, Moses looked on and he touched his hands to Henry's. Henry did not look back at George, though he did glance at Anna as the horse's steps echoed in the lane. He would never come to the valley again.

In the days that followed, Moses remained the man he always was. He ran the farm as though it were his own. At about the time his third son's beard began to show, George died lifting hay in the barn. Besides her sons, Anna had two daughters, both of whom died as girls. She was pregnant when George died, and her last child was stillborn. Anna died of the fever that follows birth. Moses was sold to a widow in Fredericktowne who made his quarters in the smokehouse near the kitchen's cesspit. He died before her and was buried under the pines, near the place where the Methodists built their church.

November 5, 1963

9am. Men arrived before time today. At 8 a flatbed truck came labelled "Ingalls Lumber & Supply" & brought a large pile of thin gray slices of what they called "sheet rock". Plaster, I believe. It is to go at the very top of the house, under the new insulation. They also unloaded some bags & buckets with other related things.

*Marce handled the paperwork-signing with the driver, standing in the road in front of The Corner, where the truck was being unloaded. Dicky Bird, Rip & Davy helped the driver's assistant (a tall muscled young black man, about 30) carry the wobbly sheet rock all the way into the building on the lowest floor. When he had him alone, Marce asked the driver (white & about 45) –Hey, ain't y'all got no more white men down there no more? The driver snorted & shook his head. –Times ain't like they was, he said, a little ambiguously I thought. –Sure ain't, Marce replied. Sh[]t! He spat through his teeth, & together they joined in unloading the truck.

2pm. Outside, I can hear quiet hammering as the top floor windows are open. Lunch tray as usual. Dicky Bird & Davy putting up the sheet rock; Rip & Marce still "running" pipes everywhere.

*Saw Marce boring a hole through a beam using a thing like a steel S with a handle. Curling shavings falling below. He is, no doubt, very strong.

5.30pm. Went over at 4 to check progress. Upper floor now has pipes roughly in place. About 1/3 of top floor ceiling nailed up. Slow work, beams to cut through, sheet rock to raise up on ladders, with one to hold while other one nails. John John sweeping up, separating the copper debris.

10.15pm. A little warmer today, especially this afternoon. Dry & sunny. Not warm enough, it seems, for Joanie & Paul to play (outside).

November 6, 1963

2pm. Trays over first thing & at lunch. All same as yesterday. Pipes now going into lowest floor.

10.30pm. Foggy this morning, but still not as cold. Drizzle then turned to rain. House snug now. Should I not have a fire tomorrow? Woodpile is half depleted. What if Marce doesn't bring any?

November 7, 1963

8.30am. More pipes unloaded this morning. Hammering upstairs already. Radio on. Dicky Bird intoning that he has a hot-rod Ford & a two-dollar bill & knows a spot right over the hill.

5pm. All quiet, as the men have left. Walked upstairs to the top & even went up ladder to look at the uppermost ceiling. All gray now & smooth with white patches (on seams & nails?). Bottom floor pipes look roughly in place too.

10.30pm. Watched "Rawhide". Temperature in the 50s all day. Foggy this morning, then showers then rain. Very windy with the rain lashing against the windows. Had a fire all day & the house so warm I didn't wear a sweater.

November 8, 1963

12.30pm. Just back. Like a party on the top floor, as all four working up there today, Dicky Bird on stilts! They are plastering the whole top floor ceiling & walls.

5.30pm. Plastering jamboree must have broken up at some point, as now new copper pipes protrude from the floor on the top. The huge room is lovely & bright, even without real sun.

*No sign of John John this evening, & no indication of next week's plans.

*I should ask Hartsock to come & inspect things to see if progress is as he expects.

10.30pm. Weather the same as yesterday, but not quite as windy. Woodpile ¾ gone now. If it turns cold, I'm not sure what I'll do.

November 9, 1963

8am. No fire this morning, partly because I'm going out & partly because it feels as though it is going to get warmer (already 52). Sunny too.

2.30pm. At last a moment. Went to Frederick as planned this morning: took back library books (finally); went to bookstore & got two books (JD Salinger & KA Porter); went to Sears & got a leaf rake (desperate!) & a snow shovel (pessimistic?); & A & P ($19 - & remembered coffee). Got home at 1 to find area I had cleared in the vegetable garden covered in pile of firewood & John John (like an ant moving sugar grains) on his own, toting it all the way around the back of the house to pile it in the lean-to. He had evidently been at it a while, as the neatly-stacked wood was already two-foot deep.

*–Where's your father? I said. –Gone home, he replied. –Isn't he going to help you? He just looked at me. –No, ma'am. –When is he coming back for you? -I'll walk home, he said. Then I had a thought. –I've just come back from the grocery store. Would you like some cookies? He didn't answer at once, but walked away a few steps, then turned. –Yes, ma'am, he said. Then he thought. –Can I just get 'em stacked first? If he drives by & sees me at it… He hesitated. –Would he mind if I helped you? I asked. He looked astonished. –No, ma'am. I'll get back sooner. –Would you like that? –I don't mind, he said.

*So I helped him carry the wood all the way around the Mary House, though he did all the stacking himself, very

146

tightly, bark up (I noticed), ends tied together with sideways pieces. He's obviously done this a lot.

*When we were nearly done, I came inside & made two cups of tea & brought them out with some Oreos. He drank the tea hotter than I can even stand it, & either popped Oreos into his mouth whole, or unscrewed them & licked the icing, or bit 'round the middle until it was tiny. All the while his hands were filthy.

*I asked him what his favourite things are. They are baseball, trains, music, the Civil War & drawing. I picked drawing to ask about. —Buildings, he said. (I didn't see that coming.) —Do you want to be an architect? I asked. —You need college for that, he said. I was about to say something foolish, when he spoke up. —I could be a surveyor though. I almost said, "You'll need college for that too". But how could I? This shy boy in his glasses needs something to believe in. —Maybe someday, you'll go to college, I said, in spite of myself. —I gotta get going now, he said.

*I was so pleased that after he'd gone 30 feet up the Harmony Road he turned around & waved goodbye, that I came inside & wrote a letter to Alex, even though I don't know where to send it.

10pm. Stayed sunny & dry all day, but never got more than 60 degrees. Cold wind.

Way over in the new burying ground

Come Christmas time things go bit slow. The Mary House is built out of logs and they caulked real good and they is a fireplace and a chimney on the south side. The ladder to the upstairs is side of the fireplace, way from the door. Ole Mary and me didn't have no beds that you could move 'round. What we had was pallets that stuck to the walls in the corners with one leg out in the room. The mattresses was made of cornshucks and they noisy, but they sleep good. The heat from the fire go up through the boards of the floor and make it nice. We always had firewood and kindling. Some of the bosses don't give us nothing to use for lighting up the place, but sometimes we get the tallow candles, sometimes the grease lamp. Mister Bob gave us all the short candles from the big house, 'cause he say he think we gonna burn ourselves up with them grease lamps. Ole Mary showed me some kind of weed-burning contraption she had in the old days, but it smoke like all get out. After she die, I tried using her bed to keep the apples and the taters in for the winter, but it get too warm at night for that. It weren't till after the war that Mister Crum put the bricks on the house cause Miss Crum told him he had to. Anyway, we get through the winter all right, and the folks give us presents of things like ole quilts and clothes, so we feel good as we could.

We was sure better off than some. Being right side The Corner I hear all the business of the farmers and the traders and the folks a-passing by. Yes, I did. I see the speculators coming for to buy and sell servants, and the padarolles up and down looking for runaways on they way to the line north. Sometimes I heard why they running.

Now I don't know nothing, but I heard they was a woman down Buckeystown way, she name Mae Schroyer, and she was a widow. All her kids out in Ohio or somewheres, and she left on her own with the farm and the servants. She had 'bout five hands outside and a woman and a gal inside. She hire her neighbour overseer to look out for the menfolk and they chores outside, cause she half 'fraid of them anyway. But she say she look out for the woman and the gal, cause she used to them. Well, 'bout the time her husband die, the woman run off and get away, and they never did hear nothing 'bout her no more. So Miss Mae she decide to take it all out on that gal, making her do everything that the woman was supposed to do, even though that gal didn't know how to do none of it. 'Course weren't nothing done the way she like it nohow, so she took to whooping that girl something regular, with whatever she could get in her hand. Then Miss Mae, she start to worry that the menfolk out in they quarters hear the gal a-weeping and a-shouting, so she used to stick the gal mouth full of rags before she whoop her. 'Bout that time then the gal answer back and say Miss Mae a-killing her slow, so Miss Mae think of a new devilment for her. She get herself a stick 'bout the size of you finger and she cut it smooth on the ends with a saw, then use the saw to cut two notches. Then, when the gal round the house and Miss Mae not liking the look of her, she tell the gal to open her mouth, and Miss Mae ram that ole stick in there 'tween her teeth and wedge her mouth open. That how she treat the house gal.

Well, she didn't know nothing 'bout the menfolk, and that's for sure. When the time come for the reaping the overseer tell her that she needs to get some more help in them fields, or the grain gonna go to waste. He say he try to hire her a field hand everywhere, but the weather been so good, all the servants is done hired out. Anyway, he say, you get 'nough help, we might even get in some more hay and fodder fore the frost come. So he say she ought to buy herself another hand.

Now the truth was, his sister husband was a speculator down at the pen in Licksville, and he had a mind to get hisself some of that money in the dealing. Well, like I say, ole Miss Mae don't know nothing, and she a mean ole thing, so she say he was to go and get her somebody, but he weren't to spend more than no thousand dollar. 'Course, everybody know that a field hand cost more than that, specially when the summer was on, and the work high. But that overseer, he go down there and see that other fella and he make a deal. They got a fella in the pen called Manuel, and he was 'bout as shy as the devil his own self, and he done run away more than once, so nobody wanted him for nothing. So the overseer make the deal, and he get the bill writ out for thousand dollar, even though he only pay eight hundred for Manuel. The rest he and the other fella keep.

They come back to the farm, and the overseer he put Manuel in to the quarters with the other menfolk, and they work they way right through the summer and into the Fall. Far as anybody see, ole Manuel change his ways and work like a hand ought to. Only thing funny 'bout him is he keep making pets out of animals. He get hisself a coon that he feed, and a grey fox that come when he whistle.

Come the winter, like everybody else, Miss Mae like to make a show for her neighbours, and make it seem like the servants all wants nothing more than to kiss her foot. So she get some of the farmers and they wives 'round 'bout New Year time, and they in there drinking whiskey and brandy and eating chestnuts and pie, when she say she gonna have all the servants come in to the porch so she give them a present. So all them white folks comes out on to the porch, and the overseer he brung up all the servants and they take they turn a-bowing and a-looking like butter not melt in they mouths. She give all the men a suit of clothes belong her dead husband and the house gal a old dress and some shoes, and they all said thank ya kindly.

Trouble was she forgot all 'bout Manuel, and she didn't have nothing left to give him. Well, she didn't want to be shamed in front of her neighbours, so she say, What you think I ought to give this boy? And they say, maybe give him a fifth of whiskey. But she don't let the hands have no liquor. So while they all a-thinking, Miss Mae, who done had herself some whiskey too, look down the steps at Manuel, and she say, Boy, what for present you think I ought to give ya? You just name it, and I promise right here that you get it. Well sir, quicker than you could say jack robinson, up he rolls them eyes, and he look at her and he smile, and he say,

Why, lord, Miss Mae, y'all been so good to me, all I needs is the chance to kiss you on the cheek.

Well, all them white folk fit to be tied. The women fan theyselves even though it's a cold day. The men just hooted like they out hunting. Go on, Maisie, they say. You done make that boy a promise, and we all heard ya. So sure as your born, Miss Mae lean herself down them steps, and Manuel give her a kiss on the cheek.

Now you knows and I knows that they was no way she was gonna let herself get laughed at for no field hand with no smile on his face. 'Specially in front of all her neighbours and that house gal she done beat like a washboard.

The next day Miss Mae up and sends the house gal for to get the overseer and get him 'round to see to Manuel. They had a big talk 'bout it, and I think Miss Mae want him to whip the hide right off that boy as a zample to all the other hands, and maybe her neighbours too. But the overseer, he say, that won't do no good, 'cause all she do is make him not fit to work, and not fit to sell neither. He tell her that 'bout the only thing she could do is to let him take Manuel somewhere and sell him, someplace where ain't nobody seen him before. She thought maybe she get some ole speculator 'round, but the overseer, he say they knock her right down in the price. 'Stead, he say, he take him up to Hagerstown, cause they got three pens up there, and he see what he could get for him.

'Course, what he done was to get his sister's husband again to ride with him up there, and to do the dealing. They did all the tricks they knew how to, and varnished Manuel right up with grease and told everybody what a portly hand he was, and they got twelve hundred dollar for him. They get the papers made out for a thousand, and each of them keep they share, and give the rest to Miss Mae when they get home. Far as she know, she broke even on Manuel.

November 10, 1963

10am. Looked at the letter to Alex I wrote yesterday. It's so good to tell him that I love him, that I can't bear to say all the other things I need to say to him. I never could bear it & I certainly can't now.

*He blamed himself, I didn't need to blame him, though for a while I know I did. I can admit that now. Tom was stumbling & Alex kept out of his way, letting him fall. Then, when it was desperate, Alex gave him even more to carry, more failures, more silent reproaches, more petty recriminations for things Tom couldn't even remember.

*I was so angry with them both. But then Tom broke down. How could I say I was angry? I pleaded with Alex, & he felt blamed. After it was over, after Tom's funeral, I couldn't make Alex believe I didn't hold him responsible. He had his own grief, his own blame, & his own anger. That's what he took away. That's what took him away.

10pm. Near freezing this morning, but much warmer this afternoon. Foggy all day, and no wind.

*Rotten news this evening from Japan – terrible mining accident with 100s killed & a train crash killing over 150 more people.

November 11, 1963

9.30am. Men working as usual today, so forgot it is Veterans' Day. Tried phoning Hartsock, but naturally, no answer. Probably off today.

*Dicky Bird & Davy on top floor having a private party, sanding the whole thing. They look like red-eyed snowmen.

*Marce & Rip working on pipes on upper middle floor. Blue flames & coils of solder.

5pm. Afternoon the same as the morning. John John obliged to sweep again today; one floor of chips & pipe bits, one of plaster dust. His shoes and pants filthy to the knees when he leapt on to the truck. (Are these his school clothes?)

10.30pm. I ask myself, is Alex a veteran now? When does it start: recruitment, training, posting, fighting? Surviving?

*Please let it start with surviving.

11pm. Not as cold today 40s-60s, but rainy with a cold wind.

November 12, 1963

2.30pm. Quiet over the road all day. Lunchtime tray I had a look, most of the pipes for the heating sticking out of the floors along the walls now on all four floors. Top floor sanding nearly done.

5.15pm. Quiet at The Corner now. From the outside it looks just like a girl waiting for her date to arrive.

9.45pm. Near freezing this morning & only about 50 this afternoon. Very bright & sunny though. May watch "The Fugitive".

November 13, 1963

8.30am. Up early again today, building the fire, as it is so cold outside.

*Davy not in the crew this morning, as he has a cold. Dicky Bird on the top floor just starting to prime plaster. Marce & Rip connecting pipes to furnace. More complicated than it seems.

2pm. By lunchtime things much the same. Pipes & valves & little brass things.

4.30pm. John John alone in the back of the truck as they drove off.

*I left collecting the lunchtime tray until 4 just to have a word with John John. He was idling about for a change, picking up stray things & trying to look busy & where no one could tell him to do anything. I asked him how school was going. He said they are playing football now in gym. –Do you like football? I asked. –I like playing Defence, he said. –Why's that? –'Cause when it's Offence, I don't ever get the ball anyway.

10.45pm. Below freezing this morning, & below 50 all day. Sunny & dry.

November 14, 1963

9am. Davy back at work this morning. They unloaded a big white tank in a box & what I think must be radiators in smaller boxes.

1.30pm. Marce & Rip connecting white tank, which is for hot water. Dicky Bird & Davy priming top floor. Davy still coughing & blowing his nose.

5pm. Top floor priming looks finished. John John washed up the brushes at 4. Hot water tank looks as though it is connected.

10.30pm. Near freezing this morning & cold all day. Sunny.

November 15, 1963

10am. Painting party on the top floor today, with all hands brushing white paint.

4.30pm. John John came & knocked. He looked pleased so I asked him what was new. He told me his grandmother is coming for Thanksgiving. Then he told me that the upstairs was all painted & that next week they'd connect the oil tank, the radiators & the water & try out the heating. I thanked him & he walked off, hands low in his pockets, & not hurrying.

154

10.30pm. Weather same as yesterday.

11pm. Have been thinking about John John & trying to imagine how I would tell him I was angry with him (if I were ever angry with him). I picture his face, I try to imagine my voice, rational, distant, ripe with justice-on-my-side. The truth is I don't know whether I could show my anger to him ever, if I felt it.

*Poor Alex. I have been a bad mother. Afraid of my anger. Frightened to give pain.

Sourwood Mountain

I, LittleWound, tell this story.

It was in the time before the Washechu came, when the whispering of the Manitoes lingered in the breezes of summer.

A boy was born and he was called Chatanna, known as FourthSon. In the tradition of the people, the boys of the village threw the water of the streams upon his brothers, and when the winter came, they rolled them in the snow. FourthSon grew to be a boy of calibre, and he never cried outside his father's lodge, lest the crows carry him away to be eaten by the StoneGods.

At this time too, a girl was born, and she was called Meneyahtah, or BesidetheWater. As a child, she learned to play with the doe-hooves and she knew never to cry at night. As she grew to womanhood her honour increased, and she was praised for the clothing she made for her brothers, her father and her uncles.

Before long, BesidetheWater let her eyes fall on FourthSon and her love for him grew through the seasons. But her yearning was graced with respect, and she knew all the feelings a wife should have for her husband. And yet, she also knew the spirit of pride, a spirit that stood watch over her, never letting her show the love she felt to anyone, least of all to FourthSon.

But FourthSon was not like the other men. He smiled and he knew the joys of living as all men of honour do, yet he did not seek for glory among the warriors or the hunters. Instead, as the beauty of his manhood grew upon him, he began to seek his destiny as a man of wisdom, a healer of wounds, and an interpreter of dreams. Such men are not often found, and his esteem among the Catoctins grew even as BesidetheWater found her love irresistible. More than anything she had ever imagined, she desired that he might love her as she loved him.

But through the days of summer and autumn he never spoke to her with favour, nor groomed his looks to embolden her desire. Instead, he spoke to all the men and women and their children as a priest speaks, full of patience, full of empathy and asking nothing for himself.

Finally, BesidetheWater could wait no longer. She went to him and spoke like the dove, affecting sorrow, as one to whom a dream has come. Her voice shook like the trembling of a spring.

FourthSon, she said, I have dreamt this dream whenever I have shut my eyes. I see a stag that has gone forth from his herd, walking so that his steps linger on the edge of the sunset-rays as they draw back towards the mountain. His feet are always on the rim of this light as it leads him away from his clan. I am afraid for him. I am afraid that he will falter, or that in the darkness that must come he will lose his way back to the clan. For there is one among the clan to whom his being is more than is her own. Tell me, FourthSon, she said, what can this dream mean?

FourthSon's eyes fell from the sky to find their reflection in her own. He stared into the eyes of BesidetheWater and she felt his presence warm the air around them.

She may go, he said, to walk beside this stag, if she can find the courage in her heart to know that the light he seeks will always be before him and never behind. If it is her destiny to walk where none may see her shadow, then she will find peace at his side. If not, then she must seek her road where the clan walks with her, in the cycle of light and darkness that is the lives of the people.

He closed his eyes and raised his chin to the place where the sun lowered itself into the pines. BesidetheWater rose and went her own way to ponder his words.

Though the love she felt never turned to bitterness, it was not long until BesidetheWater began to speak ill of FourthSon. Why, she said to the other women, does he walk where others run? Why does he not join in the festivals? Why does he not claim a wife?

It happened then on a day when the frost hung in cords in the trees that BesidetheWater was walking with the other women, all of them carrying firewood in their arms. As they came into the village they could see men and boys working in the sunshine, sharpening arrows, shaping the wooden talisman, binding the venison returned from the hunt. There, apart from them all stood FourthSon, gazing as still as a rapture into the depths of the flame.

Look at FourthSon! she said. Where is his pride? If the gods favour him in the manner it seems, then let him show us their homes, and let him command even one of them to speak among us.

Everyone looked on at the scene and wondered at the disgrace BesidetheWater had spoken. That night FourthSon disappeared from among the people.

The time of blossoms came again and the bodies of the people expanded with hopefulness and joy in their being. Men sought out women to make their wives, and women grew to resemble the happiness they desired. It was then that BesidetheWater, lost in her tasks, the savour of which had long departed, dreamt in earnest the fable she had once recounted to FourthSon. In the morning, when the sky fanned like a fountain with dawn, the people assembled, for it was the season when the growth of the days is celebrated. BesidetheWater placed herself before all the others and spoke.

I have had a vision, she said. I know the road where FourthSon may be found.

All that day until the sun passed its meridian, she led the people up the side of the mountain to the place where the quartzes lay. There on an outcropping of boulders she rested them and said, Here. He will be found here.

Just then there was a cry. FourthSon's brothers stood before an opening in the stone. There on the ground, but sheltered by the boulders, sat the body of FourthSon. He had shrunken and his skin was like the sand where the sun has dried it. Before him, between his knees, sat something that none of them had ever seen before. He had cut a tree, emptied of its heartwood by time, and across it he had fashioned a hide, tied with leather and decorated around its breadth with foolsgold, bluecopper and jackstones. On the surface of the hide he had made marks with the ink of the pokeweed – lines, circles, and shapes, like the fingerprints of heaven. But as they looked on in wonder the sky above them began to change, and the sun eased its way into the forest on the hillsides beyond them. As they saw it disappear they looked up and recognized the work that FourthSon had created. The surface of the hide was a mandala of the stars above their heads.

As the people returned to the village their arms swung without pride and their eyes lost the lustre of the celebrations they were meant to have. They put the artwork that FourthSon had made in the centre of the village and the sky became like the depths of a cave. Clouds gathered from the west and stood like men in battle. BesidetheWater drew herself up close to the thing that FourthSon had fashioned and looked from it to the worsening sky. Not knowing what she did she began to beat the map of the heavens with her fists and its echoing throat was seconded by a roar from the sky. It was then she and all the people knew that her challenge had been fulfilled. FourthSon had given the Catoctins a glimpse of the homes of the gods, and he had given them a voice of thunder to call them, even as they spoke themselves.

November 16, 1963

10.45pm. Very dark tonight. Warm afternoon, though cold this morning. Nice sunshine. Very disappointed with JDS. Not the man who wrote Catcher in the Rye, surely?

November 17, 1963

12pm. Made an excuse to walk along with Cinch Ford to church this morning. (Said I wanted to look around the graveyard. She pulled a face.) On the way, she asked me about Alex. —Miss Mary, your boy coming home for Thanksgivin'? —No, I'm afraid not. —Aw. Won't them fellers even let a body come & see his mammy? —Well, Cinch, I said, the thing is, … nobody knows where Alex is right now. She looked at me. —I mean, he's in Vietnam, & he's gone missing. He's probably a prisoner. That's what the army thinks. —Uh huh, she said. Well. He'll be back some time then. She touched my arm. —You'll be so happy. We got near the Brethren Meeting House & I stopped near the graves. She leaned in very close. —They'll take care of him. They got to. He'll be back 'fore ya know it. You'll have a high time then. I kissed her on the cheek & she winced in happiness & walked inside. I stood & looked at the graves, & then walked home.

6pm. Joanie & Paul just finished a short session (too dark to see?) She had her dulcimer, he played a fiddle.

11pm. Weather dry & bright all day. Not so cold this morning & over 70 this afternoon.

12am. I am lying in bed. Angry. I don't know who with. I am angry for believing everything I believe. Cinch saw my need to believe & responded with her simple heart. She only spoke what I desperately try to believe.

November 18, 1963

7.30am. Dreamed of Alex as a little boy, playing with tools.

1pm. Sounds of drilling all morning, & Davy in & out burning pasteboard & paper in the oil drum.

5pm. Curious to see what they'd been up to, I went over to The Corner & looked. Radiators now all attached to the floors & walls, but not pipes. Hot water tank looks attached & so does oil tank.

10pm. Not a bad day. Sunny & over 70 by this afternoon.

November 19, 1963

9.15am. Oil tanker has just left, having filled up tank. Not sure who ordered this or what the bill will be. Quiet over there now.

5pm. Quiet still all afternoon. Sometimes saw Rip or Marce outside.

5.45pm. Just back after a look. Radiators now attached to pipes & additional pipes now attached to water tank. Smelt of paint, so I looked & found top floor windows neatly painted white.

10.30pm. Temperature much like yesterday, warmer in the morning, cooler this even as the wind picked up. Drizzle & rain off & on.

November 20, 1963

8.45am. Very cold again this morning & foggy. Fire burning early. Men arrived with some pipe fittings & great coils of grey wire.

9.15am. Just off the phone with Hartsock. He asked for oil delivery (to be paid for by him). He said he will be visiting on Friday, as there is an inspector coming at 10 to look at the heating system.

10.30am. Just back after answering a knock on the door. Rip came to tell me to walk over & see how the heating system is working. I think I saw him smile.

*I followed him over & on the way asked how long he'd been in the construction business. —Since fore I was married, he said. —Does your wife work? I asked. —Yes, ma'am, he said. She works in a school. Cooking dinners, he added. He looked pleased to be asked, & I thought either proud of her, or just happy to be reminded of her.

*I walked around the whole house & it was surprisingly warm, all the radiators on fully. There was a smell of hot grease on the air & something like disinfectant.

*Marce, on his hands & knees with Dicky Bird over some kitchen pipes, didn't look up until he saw me. —Whaddaya think? he said. —Purdy good, huh? —Very good, I said. Thank you. —Uh huh, he said. He looked at Dicky Bird. —We ain't so dumb. They both grinned.

*By the time I got to the Mary House porch I could hear lots of drilling over the road.

2pm. Looked around when collecting lunchtime tray. Pipes for hot & cold water being put in. After washing in a basin for a long time, having 2 ½ baths will be an incredible luxury.

*Dicky Bird singing of his love for a wicked Mexican maiden named Paulina.

4.30pm. John John first on to the truck this evening. I saw him carrying bags of trash.

11pm. Warmed up a little this afternoon. No breeze & fog lasted all day. Have started Ship of Fools.

I wade the water to my knees

Like I say, it was after the war that they brung on the changes at The Corner. They say what with all the steam mills a-being built, nobody want no ole grist mill like thisn no more. So what they done was to tear down all that building there on the other side of the big wheel, so as that wheel out there on the outside now. Then they took out all that machinery for the wheat and the corn and brung in machinery for weaving the wool. They gonna make blankets and I don't know what all. Well, they took off them bricks from the little side and piled 'em up, and the fellas say, What y'all want us to do with them? And Miss Margaret she get in on Mister Robert and she say, ya ought to put them on the Mary House, 'cause I think ole Mary like to freeze in there in the winter. So that's what they did. Only they have to move all the windows and the door too. Mister Robert, he a good ole soul, and he don't seem to mind none.

Well, sir, the fella what did the overseeing of the tearing down was one of them Umphersocks, from up 'round Highland. They poor up there, cause the ground don't grow nothing 'cept rocks and greenbriars mostly. You get there by going up through Ellerton, then past Turkey Hill, then down that ole road back towards Myersville. It still there. Anyhow, he come with a parcel of his boys and they cousins and I don't know who all, and the deal they made was that they could keep all the timber and the flooring for theyselves.

So while they was down at The Corner a-cutting and a-tearing, they leave one of they old fellas, a uncle called Gilbert Umphersock back on the home place to do the unloading of the boards and the beams when the waggons brings 'em up. He was a old bachelor man, live by hisself in the shack they built when they first come to mountain in the old days, while the others mostly live in the houses they built since.

Anyway, he up there by hisself, a-waiting for them waggons to start coming in, when he starts to getting the bellyache. 'Fore long, he got the backdoor trots, and he ain't got nobody to help him none, so he starting to get anxious 'bout them waggons and how he gonna unload 'em with his bellyache, 'cause they ain't gonna send nobody but a boy to drive the waggon, sure as your born. The only fella that lived near that weren't no Umphersock was a negro named Pinkney that up and bought hisself a old shack and a piece of mountain land after the war. Gilbert was on speaking terms with Pinkney, so he go on down there to see if he could talk Pinkney into helping him a little. Time he got there though he see Pinkney standing there by his shed a-looking into the woods and a-cussing.

Hey, Pinkney, he say. Whatinthehell y'all doing out here?

Aw, he say, them hogs is done root they way out there again, and I gots to catch 'em for the get down the road.

Now Gilbert know he ain't gonna get no help from Pinkney today. He think maybe he ought to help him catch them hogs, then maybe he get some ground for asking 'bout helping with the waggons, but his belly feel like it a bag full of cannonballs, so he don't say nothing. Then he gets hisself a idea.

What you want? Pinkney say.

Well, sir, he say. I gotta a weaned calf down there with the runs so bad his ass gone sore. You know how to cure that?

Sure, I do, he say. You help me get them hogs, I give you something for it.

Well, lucky for ole Gilbert, them hogs knows they way in like they knows they way out, so they done in a hurry. They get back to the shack and Pinkney say wait here I get you something. He go out and pull off a whole bunch of leaves from the marshmallow and the agrimony and he give 'em to Gilbert.

Now y'all take these here marshmallow, and you cook 'em and you put the pot liquor in that calf's water and he drink it down. Then you take this here and you cut it up real fine and you mash it with water with a egg beater or something like that, and you put it all over them sores. Ya hear?

So Gilbert got hisself back down to his own shack, and the time he got there the boy come up the road with the first waggon. Ole Gilbert looked mighty green and he have to stop sometimes and head off to the outhouse, but he get that waggonload done and the boy head back for more. Gilbert then get hisself into the house to start making hisself some medicine. Now he don't know nothing bout cooking nothing, and time he get the fire going and the water toted and all that, he have to unload another waggon. They sounding the twelve o'clock whistle by the time he gets to drinking tea and rubbing poultice on his backside. 'Bout the time evening come and all them others get back to they own houses up there, he start to feel pretty good again.

Next morning, when they all gone back to working down at The Corner, and Gilbert he waiting for the first waggon to come up with the wood and the shingles and that, he looked down the road and he see ole Pinkney taking his mule out of the barn.

How do, Pink? he shout.

Pinkney turn 'round and look up the road. Gilbert come a-waving, and Pinkney look him all over.

Morning, sir, he say. How that calf of yourn this morning?

Fine. Fine, he say. Much obliged, thank ya.

Uh huh, Pinkney say. Then he think. There's something I was supposed to tell ya yesterday, but I forgot. That calf a yourn a heifer or a bull?

Gilbert he think for minute then he say, a heifer.

Well, that lucky, say Pinkney. 'Cause that cure only work on a heifer. Y'all give it to a bull calf, his balls fall off in 'bout a week.

Pinkney tell me, 'fore he start a-laughing, he ain't never seen no white man look so scared since the war over.

November 21, 1963

8.30am. Men at work as usual. They seem sluggish, coming to pour coffee as soon as I put the tray down. Still working on pipes, I think. Davy drilling holes.

5pm. Men gone as usual, John John & Davy in the back. Didn't bother to walk over tonight.

10.30pm. Not so cold today. Up to 70 this afternoon. More rain & drizzle. The mountains & fields all now like old photographs in browns & grays, white creases, black streaks.

November 22, 1963

8.30am. Foggy & cold this morning & not much air stirring. I predict it will stay foggy. (How much a local I am becoming!)

11am. Hartsock knocked on my door at 9.40 & wouldn't come in for tea, but said he wanted to look things over with me before the inspector arrived, in case any of us had any questions. He greeted all the men with a handshake, Davy & Dicky Bird looking impressed, Marce barely subduing a sneer. We got as far as the furnace when a voice called from the lower porch behind us. The inspector was 10 minutes early. Hartsock showed him 'round with an attitude ½ way between we've-both-seen-so-many-of-these-it's-simply-too-boring, & that of 2 old lawyers meeting for whiskey in the judge's chambers before arguing different sides of the same case. The men kept working & ignored it all, though I did see Marce shake his head once at something Hartsock said. It was all over by 10.30. Hartsock still refused tea, saying he had another client to visit.

2pm. The president has been shot. I've now put the television on & they have blanked everything else out.

*About 20 minutes ago there was a knock on my door. I opened it to find Rip looking very uneasy. –Ma'am, he said. Uh, we got the radio on. The president's down in Texas & they're sayin' he's been shot. I looked at him for a couple of seconds & said, –Are you sure? –Uh, yes, ma'am. They ain't sayin' how bad or nuthin'. Ya might wanna put your radio on, or something. I thanked him & he smiled very faintly, then walked away. He's a gentle man & I wish I knew what to say to him.

3.15pm. They have announced that the president has died.

4pm. They have already sworn in Johnson.

5pm. I went over to The Corner just after 4 to see what was happening. The men were finishing up the day's work (pipes & holes in the beams & floors) with the radio on. They talked a bit & all seemed uncomfortable. John John had cleaned up everything & was sitting on a coil of wire.

*Marce said the hot & cold were now all "roughed in" & starting Monday they'd "pull cables" (?). I didn't ask. They left & I locked up.

12.30am. Very still tonight. Everything seems forlorn & lonely now.

By the print of the nail in his hand

If her religion had allowed her to do so, Annie Engel would have thought herself unlucky. As it was, she just believed she had a hard row to hoe. Her husband Bill had worked for Union Carbide. It was a good job, and every day he drove his truck the twelve miles to the factory, on the way picking up two friends, Roger and Laffe, who also worked with him. Both Roger and Laffe gave Bill some money to pay for gas and oil, and together they had a pretty good arrangement. Bill was about ten years older than Annie and had spent some time in the navy – just a few months, really. He had had an accident on his first ship, falling down a ladder, and hitting his head all over the steel lining of the ladder well. He had been unconscious for two days, and when he woke up, the doctors thought it best that he end his naval career then. When he came home, he married a woman named Nina, and they had a little boy named Paul. When Paul was three, both he and Nina died of influenza, and Bill lived alone for a few years before he married Annie. Annie had a son they named Roy, after Bill's father. One afternoon, when Roy was four months old, Annie came to pick Roy up after what had been a long nap for him, and she found him dead in his cot. No one, not even the doctor, could determine why. Sometimes, it just happens, he said. But don't worry. You're young. There'll be more to come. But there never were. Something about Roy's death troubled Bill so much he never wanted to touch Annie again. Or maybe he had someone else. Annie couldn't be sure. And then one day, Bill was standing in the line to collect his pay packet and he started to wobble. Laffe was standing behind him, and he said, Hey, son, y'all right? Then, according to Laffe, he thought Bill said no, before he fell down in a heap, gave a big sigh, and died. The doctors said later that it was probably a blood clot in Bill's brain that killed him; something that had been there since his short time in the navy. But because Bill had been in the navy, even for less than a year, Annie got a widow's pension. That's what she lived on.

She kept the house in good order, rented out the field and the woodlot, took in some ironing, made and sold candles and soap, and didn't live too badly. Every Sunday, she walked the mile and a half to the old Church Hill church, where she sang quietly and prayed silently. At thirty-five, childless, thin, a little worn, but shapely, a home-owner and someone about whom no one talked scandal, the local women all thought there was some chance she would get married again. Some chance, they thought.

One Sunday in June when Annie got to church, she found most of the congregation standing around outside shaking their heads. The news was that the preacher, Basil Albright, had died on Saturday night, having taken ill on Friday. He had been a good old fellow, they said. In his seventies. Alan Wolfe, who was the church's deacon, said they might just as well all go home and wait to see what the church would do next. He reckoned the funeral would probably be Wednesday or Thursday.

It was Thursday. And there was a new face at the funeral. The new preacher, Christopher Cline, was there, nodding and shyly being introduced by the preacher who had come up from Middletown to lead the service. He said the church would be back to its regular mission in two weeks, after the new preacher got settled in. He had taken on the little Harne place towards Wolfsville.

Annie went to the new preacher's first service. Everyone went. He was just right somehow. He was gentle, gentler than old Albright used to be. He sang softly, his eyes met the eyes of everyone in the pews, and he seemed able to speak the verses of the readings without even looking at his bible. After the service he stood at the church door and shook hands with everyone, men, women and children. Annie felt that he loved them all.

She was very lonely when she went home that Sunday. Her heart was filled with a formless love, one without design, one which included no one but herself. She sat down after her dinner in the best chair in her tiny parlour and thought she wanted to do something important, to make giving – giving itself – a key. But to what? She had seen the preacher's example, heard his words, almost felt his breath, and she wanted to make herself worthy of feeling as good as she thought she could feel.

She looked at the small crowded room and thought of the small crowded rooms upstairs. Closets and dressers and cedar chests full of clothes and hats and all the things she and Bill had inherited or bought or just somehow accumulated. There were clothes belonging to people long-dead, people she'd never even met, things that mattered to no one where they were.

She went upstairs to the little bedroom, the one that was, for a while where little Paul had lived, and the one where little Roy had died. The room was filled with clutter, piles of good things, dull good things, kept just in case they were needed. She pulled open the old closet door and saw that stacked on the shelves were quilts, folded for so long the creases had grown worn and dusty. Some had been sewn by Annie's mother and grandmother; some, by Nina and the women in her family; some by women Annie would never know. Angry with what felt like the luxuries of the dead, Annie dragged out an armload of these quilts and piled them on the floor. She tipped out an old laundry basket full of fabric that had been bought or saved and never used and piled the quilts inside it. She heaved the whole lot downstairs and on to her porch. She locked the door and headed off towards the old Harne place.

She was sweating when she got there, and she set the basket down on the porch, and rested herself in the shade for a moment. There were no signs of the preacher. After a few minutes she got up and walked to the front door. The inside door was open, with only the screen door shielding the hallway. Anybody home? she called. But there was no answer. She walked around the house's shady side and here she saw him walking towards her.

Howdy, ma'am, he said. My name's Chris Cline. You were in church this morning.

Annie was going to answer when she saw he was carrying two old one-gallon vinegar jugs in his hands. He saw her looking.

Yes, ma'am, I just don't understand it either. Mr Albright had these setting around everywhere on that back porch, every one of 'em full of water. There's water connected to the house, and the old pump is still down there, and I just can't see what he was saving these for.

Annie smiled. He used to keep water in 'em to water his garden, she said. It's better for things when the water is the same temperature as the air.

Is that a fact? the preacher said. Huh. Well, I'll be.

He set the jugs on the porch floor and looked up at her. What can I do for ya?

Annie thought he must be just a few years younger than her.

I brought you some things, she said. I was thinking about your sermon and charity and all. They're here, she said, laying her hand on the old basket, full of quilts. I wasn't using 'em or nothing. There must be folks could though. I thought they'd more likely to take 'em if they was to be give by a preacher. Folks don't like feeling they owe nobody nothing. I got plenty more than this. If you think people'll want 'em.

She was getting nervous now at the sound of her own voice, and she was fidgeting to leave. She knew he could see this, and he looked at the quilts and smiled.

God loveth a cheerful giver, he said.

Annie backed away, smiling as best she could. Well, she said, y'all let me know if you want something else now, ya hear?

She walked away without looking back, and she couldn't be sure whether he was watching her or not.

Annie went to church the following Sunday, and listened to the preacher's sermon, saw the look in his eyes as his words made their way kindly into people's hearts. She shook his hand at the door. There was nothing special about his greeting, no summer lightning that she could feel.

That afternoon she took a stack of old clothes over to the old Harne place. There didn't seem to be anyone at home, so she left them on the porch. He'd know where they came from.

More Sundays passed in just the same way. Annie went along, wearing her hat and her gloves and her necklace, just like all the other women. And then, in the evenings, she went 'round to the preacher's house – it was now being called the New Preacher's Place – and left a pile of things, women's things, domestic, household things that fitted best into women's hands, in a pile on his porch. She never saw him, and he never acknowledged her gifts.

On a Saturday in late August, there was a wedding at the church, the new preacher's first since he came to Church Hill. Annie went along with everyone else. There was a party afterwards down in the old picnic woods near the road, and everyone looked shiny and out-of-place in their good clothes, sitting on the benches under the oak trees, eating chicken and ham and potatoes.

Annie was standing near the pavilion with the old women when the preacher himself arrived. In each hand he was carrying one of the gallon jugs she had seen him with before. But now the jugs were full of something dark. The men walked over to him and took these into their hands.

What y'all got there, Reverend?

Blackberry wine, he said. Made it myself.

By evening, all the men had had a cupful. Annie was the only woman to have a taste, and it was one that no one else saw.

That autumn showed what a good summer it had been. The hay was dry, the corn tall, the wheat ears long. The fruit and vegetable crops were good too. Up the hill from Annie's house, the Getzendammers had seen it coming, and had spent the summer building a new root cellar, or cave as they called it. The old man had supervised his son and son-in-law as they dug a huge hole into the bank behind the garden edge, and then they had brought waggon loads of stones up from the creek and off the old stone ridges to build the walls. They had sneaked down to the roads off the Harmony Road and up the mountain side, where the County had been replacing the old bridges and quietly stole all the worn-out bridge planks to use as roofing for the cave. When it was done, they piled all the earth they'd dug out back on top of the planks, fitted bins inside, and a door outside, and were ready to bring in the harvest.

About a week after Labor Day, Annie heard the shouting and saw the younger kids running down the road. She went outside and heard more shouting up at the Getzendammers, so she walked up the hill to see. By the time she got there, four or five other neighbours were there too. What had happened was when the men were loading up the new bins in the cave full of potatoes, Les, the youngest, hit the wheelbarrow against the wall a little too hard, and the stone wall, which must have been leaning a little inside anyway, fell towards him, and brought the whole roof down on him, trapping him inside. Mrs Getzendammer was screaming the boy's name, his wife had gone yellow with shock, and the grandmother just stood stock still letting tear after tear roll down her face. The men were digging with shovels to try and get enough earth away so they could lift the roof. The door was open a bit, but they couldn't see or hear anything, and they were afraid it might collapse even further.

The children had run to find someone with a telephone so they could get the fire department or the sheriff to come (though nobody knew what good either would do), to find more men with shovels, and to find the preacher for no other reason than because it seemed like he ought to know.

Annie stood near the family women, with the other women neighbours in their aprons or their field bonnets and watched the men trying to do something useful, though none of them had ever seen anything like this. They were digging from the sides, trying to loosen the planks without causing them to fall. All at once Annie saw the preacher himself arrive, not running, not squinting in the sun, not picking up a shovel or pickaxe.

Listen, he said, and raised his hands.

The men stopped momentarily, grudgingly, and even the women hushed.

The preacher got down on his hands and knees near the collapsed doorway and listened. Before anyone could stop him, he was pushing himself into the doorway, feet first.

Christ Almighty, preacher! someone shouted.

What in the hell you think you're doing?

God damn it!

Jesus H Christ, boy!

But by then it was too late. The preacher had slid his way into the doorway and disappeared.

Everything outside fell silent and motionless, like a dream.

Annie heard him first and pointed.

The preacher's arm up to the elbow showed in the doorway. He was clawing at the ground. John Moser ran forward and took the open hand and the preacher's arm went stiff – a signal to pull. John leaned backwards and the preacher's head started to show, then his shoulder. Other men joined John, taking hold of the preacher's clothes and dragging. Then they saw the preacher's other hand clutched under the Getzendammer boy's armpit. Suddenly the men dragged them both into the light. The preacher sat himself up. The boy lay still, his eyes open, visibly breathing. He was alive. The men dropped their shovels and the women screamed. Annie bowed her head.

By January, Annie had the little bedroom nearly emptied, and she was working her way through all the things in every other room, things for which she felt no love and no use. With every Sunday that came and went she felt lighter, freer, more ready for Heaven. When she ran out of the clothes and quilts and tablecloths and aprons and curtains that other women had sewn, she sewed new ones out of all the material that had been saved for so long. Spools of thread, hanks of bias binding, tapes of rickrack, all of it came out of drawers and cupboards and went into her enterprise. By February she had new calluses on her fingers from the pressure of the needle, and a ring shape where she wore her thimble.

That February was cold, colder than usual, and there was ice on everything. The children stayed home from school, sledding on the hills, sliding on the roads. They liked to meet near the farmyard down by the Kuntzler's corner and throw rocks and sticks on to the big pond to see whether they could crack the ice. Annie could see them from the window in the little bedroom and she liked to watch them, listening to the shouts and the promises and the taunts.

She was watching them when little Nevin Brandenburg took his sister's rag doll and threw it as far out on to the ice as he could. Annie heard the girl shout and felt her own throat contract when the girl ran straight on to the ice to fetch the doll. There was no sound, but a shelf of ice leaned down to where the girl stood, and she slipped, falling on to her face, clinging to the doll, and sliding about a foot to where the freezing water began to seep up the ice.

The other children were screaming and flapping their arms when Annie got to the edge of the pond. She took little Nevin by the shoulders and told him to get the preacher. He'd know what to do. Nevin shot off, taking two boys with him.

Annie shut her eyes and prayed. The other children just looked at her. The girl on the ice was too scared to move.

Annie opened her eyes and saw the preacher coming. Nevin wasn't with him. The preacher wasn't coming from the direction of his house. He saw what was happening and took off his coat. Annie opened her mouth to call out to him, but no words came forth. She watched as the preacher stepped on to the ice, the far side of the shelf from where the little girl lay. He walked steadily, as if unafraid, and in a minute he had his hand on her back, lifting her by her coat. He pulled her to his body, turned and walked slowly back to the edge of the water, where he put the girl on her feet. She ran to her friends.

The preacher was buttoning his coat as Annie walked towards him.

I've never been so scared, she said.

There was nothing else to do, he said. Then he smiled at her and walked away.

It was at his Lent service that the preacher announced he would be leaving at Easter. The church had other work for him to do, at a new church being built back where he came from, down on the Eastern Shore.

After that Sunday, Annie stopped coming to church for a while, and she missed the preacher's last few services. Instead, she sat in her favourite chair in her parlour, thinking about her house and the things she had done. The house seemed so much bigger now, so much more light came into the windows, and came further into the rooms. She thought about the things she had given away and wondered whether she felt proud. She didn't know, but she didn't think so. She thought about the preacher. He never thanked her for the things she had given him. Probably, she felt, because he knew she wasn't giving them to him, but to the world that stood on the other side of him. It was a world that couldn't seem to find peace no matter what anyone did. But she had found peace. She had seen it in the things he did, heard it in the things he said. She had remembered to act and forgot to judge. Maybe that's all there was to it. Maybe. She would try again tomorrow. There was nothing else to do.

November 23, 1963

9am. Bad sleep. Warmer this morning, so no fire, thinking I'll go out. I should go shopping & suppose I will. Foggy & some drizzle.

2.30pm. Back from Frederick. Quiet, I felt. Everyone in A & P talking with whomever they met, shaking their heads. Spent $15. Also went to Sears with no real purpose. Looked at Revlon (Xmas for Sis?) & new cookware called Pyrosil. Very pretty.

6.30pm. Johnson has declared Monday a national day of mourning. I should tell the men to take the day off.

7.30pm. Tried phoning Hartsock to get him to tell Marce & the others not to come on Monday. No answer.

9.30pm. Rainy this evening. On the CBS radio news that there's been a terrible fire in an old folks' home in Ohio. As many as 60 dead.

  *Still no answer at Hartsock's, & now probably too late to phone on a Saturday night.

November 24, 1963

8.00am. Cold this morning, so up early building a fire. May work on the vegetable garden (scorning the gossips' scorn) if it stays dry.

12pm. Spoke to the returning church crowd, several ladies, seeing me outside, coming to the old fence to have a word. They still seem shocked by the news. Cinch looked on the edge of tears a few times, doing more listening than the others. When talk turned to the children she turned her head & I thought she said –Them poor little fellers. I gave her a hug, & the other women (Agassy included) looked surprised & somehow grateful.

  *I saw Cinch look at me then & I knew what she was thinking. She feels my pain, my longing, my doubt & my hope & is much too wise ever to say anything.

2pm. Listened to the radio while eating lunch. Evidently Oswald, the assassin, has now been shot dead. Astonishing. How? I put on the television, & there it is again, newsmen talking & explaining. What is happening?

9.15pm. Television news creeping into everything on air. The man who shot Kennedy was filmed being shot himself.

I simply can't believe it. I also can't believe that this is being re-played on television. What if children see this?

10pm. Stayed dry & sunny all day, upper 50s. Whole vegetable patch is clear of weeds now. Not sure whether I should mark out beds, as the ground must surely freeze. Wouldn't hurt to mark them, I think. Maybe should get the men to erect a tool shed? Or lay out pipes for water? But with creeks on two sides, maybe I should just bucket the water up the banks. Or get an Archimedes screw? (Re-reading this, I realize how naïve I am (or am not), as I must never use words like "erect", "lay" or "screw" when Marce is in earshot.)

November 25, 1963

8.45am. Men have showed up for work, & I was a little late bringing their tray. I said that as far as I was concerned, they could all have the day off, & that I'd have said so earlier if I'd known how to reach them. They nodded. I told them I tried phoning Hartsock but couldn't get an answer. Marce spoke up to say that Hartsock had phoned him on Sunday to say they should take the day off, but he (Marce) said there was nothing they could do about it anyway, so they might as well work. I then said to all of them (including John John, who was with them as there is no school today) that they should feel free any time today to come over & watch any of the funeral on television. John John looked hopeful, but Marce looked ready to spit, & snarled —I ain't a-lookin' at that. The others were too intimidated to respond & simply looked away.

2pm. Just brought lunchtime tray back. Men are busy ripping out what passed for the old wiring in The Corner: little white porcelain insulators with round wires & nails. John John's job to pick up whatever the others throw on to the floor. (A rise in status for Davy, it seems.)

4.15pm. The other day when I saw the pictures of Mrs Kennedy, a widow of only a few hours, standing shocked & utterly isolated, still wearing a suit splashed with her husband's blood, I thought my heart was broken. But today, watching that precious innocent little boy join the soldiers to salute his father's coffin, I felt as though I couldn't breathe. How can such things be endured? How long before this terrible cycle ends?

*Men left on time, John John & Davy sitting among the buckets of junk & old wire.

2am. Still awake watching the ghost play of Tom's funeral in my mind. Still seeing Alex's face, & hearing the last words the two of them spoke to one another, before Tom went & kept his hideous promise. Standing there by his grave, the fresh earth discreetly, if incompletely, hidden by a green rug. Seeing Alex's face, his thoughts not yet ready to go from rage to grief. So now this. Must all women be widowed in some way? Must all mothers of sons wait to see their child salute the father they loved or hated or never really knew?

*God, Tom, you deserted us. I loved you but I didn't need you. Alex needed you. You should have seen that. Through it all, you should have seen that. How do men love one another? I've seen how they can hate, I see it every day. Why are you all so lost? Why do we pity you so much? Why are we all doomed to waiting?

It was ole Lost John

Lucy Holter was an only child and her parents loved her dearly. She grew up on a small farm just to the right of where the Harmony Road meets the Middletown Road, right after the humpbacked iron bridge. The farm was pretty and tidy and her parents were happy. Though never well-off, they made sure that things were easy for themselves and their daughter, indoors and out. Lucy herself was a charming girl, nut-brown from being outside, tall, slim, brown-eyed and modest. She liked animals and she liked the feeling of having grown to womanhood with a sense that she held all the accomplishments of her culture in her own two hands. She could cook, sew, handle all the domestic chores with efficiency and sing in the Reformed Church choir on Sundays. Her parents were proud of her and she was proud of herself.

There was only one small shadow that darkened an area of Lucy's life. She was a somewhat superstitious girl who, through the assistance of books and an active imagination, grew into a woman who showed genuine caution, if not outright anxiety, about the powers of the supernatural in her daily life. Unfortunately, for Lucy, her religion gave her little solace in these matters, as Lucy tended to believe that the unseen forces she thought inhabited her environment were not the work of Satan himself, but rather a kind of failed natural religion – an array of accidents of circumstances. These accidents took many forms. Once, when some girls at school had teased Lucy mercilessly for weeks about the curls in her hair, Lucy had had a terrible vision. She was standing by the barn watching her father brushing the burrs from the tail of a calf, and the evening sun was shining low above the hills behind them, the rays focused and precise, making long outlines and crisp-edged shadows. Lucy turned her face slightly, looking at the white barn wall behind her, and as she did so, her breath fell cold inside her. There on the wall, in silhouette, was the gasping face of the girl who tormented her most at school; a cartoon of agony, as the girl seemed to be suffocating and near to death. A rationalist might have argued that it was no more than a trick of sunlight, drawing an exaggerated pattern of the struggling calf, bucking and tossing its head, and leaving a passing sketch on the wall. But the effect on Lucy was profound, she screamed and shook, and had to be taken to her room to lie down. She was even relieved to see the girl in school the next day, and Lucy vowed to pray for her the next Sunday, right after the sermon. And she did.

As Lucy grew older, her wariness of the unseen ripened into a fascination with ghost stories, both worldwide and local. She knew about gothic castles in the Old Country, but she also knew about the ghosts that surrounded her and her neighbours. She knew about the unhappy spirits all over South Mountain, the ghosts of the sixty men whose bodies had been thrown down the well on the Wise Farm, the annihilated Rebel gunners who pushed cars up the hill near Burkittsville. She knew about the practical joking ghost at the South Mountain Inn, and she had heard of all manner of hants and Indian deviltry. This led her, naturally, into tales of witches and cures, and probably would have led her to fortune-telling, if events hadn't overtaken her.

The change in Lucy's life came when Ron Flook fell in love with her. Like Lucy, Ron was an only child. He had been a late-life baby, and he lived with his parents on a fair-sized farm about two miles away, down the Middletown Road, in the valley before the place where the Hawbottom Road joins. Like Lucy, Ron was tall and healthy, with a thick shock of blonde hair, a quiet manner, and a good singing voice. (They met in the choir.) Their love story made pretty much everyone who knew them content. They fell in love at the same time, smiled and laughed a lot, never seemed to quarrel, had a lot in common, and looked pretty together. That things were as they should be, was the general verdict of the church and all the neighbours. When they married, both families attended, and so did most of their neighbours, as well as the whole church congregation. Ron's parents moved to the empty labourer's house about two hundred yards from the farmhouse, so that Ron and Lucy could have the big house in peace and, they thought, in time, and God willing, fill it up with handsome babies, boys and girls.

Lucy was as happy to move in as Ron was to have her under the roof where he'd grown up. Lucy, whose ideas on household style extended only to include the tastes of all the women who surrounded her while she was growing up, fell in easily with the house's décor, but still made just enough changes to stamp her own individuality on to the place. The ideas she'd taken from contemporary magazines were never the radical ones. She replaced the old kitchen table with a new aluminium one, with curved chairs that had modish, red marble-effect plastic seats. But that was about the only risky move she made. Ron's apparent happiness with her decision inspired her to try and think of other little ways to bring more sunshine and innovation into her housekeeping. She sometimes sat in the one of the front parlour's comfortable chairs and, while embroidering pillowcases or crocheting potholders, cast about in her mind for new ideas.

She decided she would give the house a thorough once-over, cleaning and sorting its contents from top to bottom, taking out what they no longer wanted or needed, salvaging and updating what could be revitalized, and ultimately deciding what new things she might bring to their home. She started with the attic.

The doorway into the attic was in the corner bedroom across the hallway from the one where she and Ron slept, a bedroom she hoped one day would belong to the daughter she dreamt of having. The doorway was made of planks and had been covered with the same wallpaper that covered the walls, making the door itself almost invisible, except for the wooden turn-button that kept it closed. In the months she'd been married, Lucy had never ventured into this attic, and she took a little while to prepare herself mentally and physically. She expected dust and clutter and tied her hair up accordingly. She expected neglect and nostalgia, and so braced herself to make some ruthless, if studiously non-judgmental, decisions.

She turned the button and used her fingernails on the door's edge to pull it open. There was a flat landing, and the steps upwards were just out of sight on the right. Lucy looked. The century-old plaster from the walls was visible in thick strips where it had oozed through the lathing and dried. Each step had something piled on both sides of it, leaving a little trail up the centre of the stairway. Light came into the space from the four low windows, two at either end of the house.

Everything looked just as she imagined. There were pasteboard boxes, old shop-tins for King's Syrup, Prince Albert Cigars, Smith Brother's cough lozenges; Mason jars, crocks, racks of clothes, trunks, dried-up leather, dusty books, stacks of magazines and sheet music, balls of string, speckled mirrors, hats in and out of boxes, trays of burnt-out light bulbs, baby clothes, musty blankets, useful pieces of turned wood, brass fireplace tools, tiles that matched the kitchen floor, paint cans, antique milk bottles, a wheel, a squirting oil can, homemade paintings and sketches, warped records, winter coats too good to throw out. There were mousetraps, but no mice, and wasp nests, but no wasps.

After an hour of rummaging, Lucy went back downstairs to cool off, wipe away the dust she now felt covered her, and to sit down again, and think over how she would go about this new plan of hers. At suppertime she told Ron about what she had been up to and he smiled. He was always happy with whatever Lucy did, so long as what she did made her happy.

That night, while Ron was comfortably snoring, Lucy sat up suddenly in bed. She had heard a noise. Or thought she had. It had been a little like footsteps, a little like someone breathing. Ron had worked all day, and she didn't want to wake him, so she lay back down and put her hand on his shoulder. In a while she slept again.

The next morning, after breakfast Lucy went back upstairs into the corner bedroom. The attic door was open, even though she was certain she had shut it. She told herself that she must be mistaken, and of course, it had been her who had left it open. Or the fact that she had turned the button on the door – probably the first time it had been turned in a very long time – had loosened it, so that it fell vertical and the draft pushed the door open. Either way, she decided she would put off working on the attic until the weather was cooler.

The next day was chilly and raining, and just as Lucy hoped, the attic door was firmly shut. She thought though, that before getting started on that, she ought to calm her oddly agitated nerves by doing just a little cross-stitch downstairs. She really couldn't account for why she felt so edgy these days.

Lucy made herself tea and put it on the table beside her chair. She sat down and picked up her stitching. Where were her glasses? Lucy knew she always put her glasses on the end table beside her chair. She was, after all, a creature of habits, and this really was perplexing. She looked in the kitchen, her bedroom, the pantry, the porch, all the other bedrooms, and all over the parlour, but there was no sign of them. She tried looking in the chicken house, the spring house, the smoke house, the wash house, beside the barn, the waggon shed, the loafing shed, and all the places she might even have thought of going the previous day, but her glasses were simply gone. But when she came back inside the house there they were, right in the centre of her new kitchen table.

Now Lucy was sure. As calmly as she could, she went upstairs and took the smaller leather suitcase out from underneath the bed where she and Ron slept. She opened it and packed her favourite dresses, underwear, clothes and sundries, closed the suitcase, and without leaving any note or word for Ron, she left the house through the back door (she never used the front door – no one did), and walked down the road to her parents' house. When she got there, there was no one indoors, so she went inside, unpacked her things in her old room, made herself a cup of tea, and sat in the chair beside the piano.

She was still there when, at dinnertime, Ron came to the house asking whether her parents knew where she'd gone. Ron, still in his overalls, came and stood in front of her. Lucy's parents, not sure whether they should stay and help Ron, or keep out of the couple's way, went back to the kitchen and left the door open.

Lucy explained to Ron just what the matter was, just how things stood. There was a ghost in Ron's house that Lucy had offended and now she couldn't live there. Ron, who loved Lucy just as much, regardless of what she said, asked whether there was anything he could do. Lucy said she loved him and wanted to live with him, but that she needed to know that the ghost was no longer there before she would consent to come back. Ron nodded, and went into the kitchen to talk to Lucy's parents.

There was an old woman they knew of, or rather had heard of, who lived all the way up on the Marker Road, who was known to be someone who still knew how to try for cures. People still rumoured how she had saved the lives of babies the doctors had given up on by circling them with string and hot coals. She would ask a child its name three times and then recite the Lord's Prayer. She would bend a rye straw into a triangle, put it on the sick person's tongue, then blow through it three times. Maybe she could help.

Ron had his dinner with Lucy and her parents, and then he kissed Lucy before he left. He drove in the truck up to the Marker Road and found the old woman's house as best he could. He was back at Lucy's parents' before milking time. He spent a long while in the barn talking to Lucy's father before he hurried home, without seeing Lucy, to do his own milking.

Lucy slept well that night, though she had dreams she couldn't remember in the morning. Back in her parents' house, she suddenly felt oddly superfluous, not a child and not fully an adult either. Because her mother had gone to Myersville for the morning, Lucy thought she would make a peach cobbler. It would be a nice treat for them all at dinner time.

Lucy went to the screen porch to collect the ripest peaches from the baskets there, where all the fruit was waiting to be canned. That was something Lucy didn't feel like starting alone. Anyway, her mother would be back in the afternoon, and they could work on it together. Lucy piled a dozen peaches into her apron and carried them back to the kitchen table for peeling.

Lucy was half-way through peeling the peaches when she discovered what was wrong. She had peeled seven peaches and there were still six remaining on the table. She counted the halves in the bowl. There were fourteen halves. Definitely seven peaches. So why were there still six to peel, when she was sure she had chosen twelve to bring to the kitchen? She shook her head and laughed. An odd thing the mind, she thought.

After dinner was over, and after all the peaches had been canned and the jars sat hotly in the kitchen, their lids clicking and popping as they cooled, Lucy went outside and sat on the porch swing where it was shady and had a breeze. She picked up the book she had brought with her and decided to read a few pages, until she had cooled off completely, and until it was time to help make supper, or to gather in the clothes from the line.

She opened the book to the place she had marked and started to read. But then she stopped. She turned the book over and looked at it. This was not the book she had brought outside, though it was the same colour. It was not the same story. She looked at the bookmark. It was hers all right, the one she had sewn when she was a girl, all white and trimmed with stitching. It was even at the right chapter of the book, and the right page number, as she recalled both. What had happened?

She suddenly wished for Ron.

That night Ron came to supper with Lucy and her parents. He was very apologetic, and so were they. He told her what he had done, how he had seen the old woman up on the Marker Road, and how she had been. She had, he said, lit a broom straw, and while it burnt, told him that the ghost Lucy feared would leave her house. But it was the ghost's destiny to haunt either

Lucy's future or her past. Ron said it would be best if it haunted her past, and so now the ghost had removed itself, following Lucy to the place that was no longer hers. If Lucy left that place, the ghost could no longer follow her. Ron said he was sorry if he had done the wrong thing. Lucy's parents spoke up and said there was only one thing to do, and that was for Lucy to go back to her home with Ron. After supper, Lucy packed her suitcase and Ron drove her back home. She never slept at her parents' house again.

Instead, Lucy and Ron lived like most of their neighbours. The only difference was that Lucy kept almost nothing that was hers from the time before she was married. And she taught herself and her children to look upon their memories as something new every day.

November 26, 1963

7.45am. Exhausted, but up early. Fire going, because it is well below freezing. Coffee brewing, tea steeping. Dry, white & sunny out there. No wind & a thick frost. Come on, Marce, get them here & back on your high wire.

3pm. Fell asleep & was late collecting lunch tray. Still tearing out old wiring & boring holes. Davy given the job of pulling cables through long series of holes.

9pm. Early to bed (fire not yet out). Stayed sunny all day.

November 27, 1963

9am. Whole crew at work drilling holes & hauling thick grey wires through. Looks like very hard work.

4.30pm. Men gone now. Whole day & not much sight of anyone. Wires & holes all day, I think. No signs of John John.

10pm. Breezy fog this morning, but over 60 & bright this afternoon.

November 28, 1963

Thursday. Thanksgiving Day.

9.30am. Got up & made fire early, then back to bed & read for an hour. Below freezing out there. Some fog.

5pm. Roasted a small chicken for lunch today & took much longer than expected. Potatoes fine, but sweet potato dried out a little. Sweetcorn nice. Will pick at leftovers this evening & finish the rest in the next few days.

 *After lunch I let the fire go very low & took a walk, all the way to Fisher's Hollow Road. As I was coming back 8 deer gracefully ran down the long meadow, leapt the fence sideways, ran behind a barn & up the hillside opposite. Beautiful.

November 29, 1963

9am. Wasn't sure the men would work today but risked getting tray ready just in case. Whole crew (with John John) here by 8 as usual. About 40 & foggy this morning.

1.30pm. Still dragging wires through newly-made holes. John John fetches, carries & unspools cable for them.

4.45pm. Everyone gone now, so I looked around. Lower three floors now have large wires running everywhere, I think.

10pm. Temperature got to 60 today & wind blew fog away before midday.

November 30, 1963

8.30am. Very cold this morning & think I may be catching something. No time to make fire, as must go shopping at A & P, I think.

1pm. Got home just in time with groceries ($15) as the drizzle now has some sleet in it.

4pm. Furious snow flurry for 20 minutes petering out now.

10.15pm. Full moon glimpsed a little as clouds part. No snow or sleet, just some showers now. Read some more of Porter novel.

PART II:

White Lightning

Border State

December 1, 1963

8am. Sleepy & heavy-headed this morning. Raspy throat & full sinuses. Already made fire for the day.

12pm. Finished KAP novel this morning, finally. Good, but somewhat uneven, I felt. Am making soup for lunch.

*Churchgoers chatted ("loafed" as they say) around the benches a while this morning. Cinch Ford in a dark brown dress with pink necklace & earrings. She asked again whether I was keeping warm enough in the Mary House. I asked her where she was planning to get her Christmas tree. She laughed. —I'm too old to have a tree, she said. I told her I was going to have one. —You ain't no spring chicken, she said, as if we shared the greatest intimacy over this joke. I have to admit, I laughed with her, as much by surprise as anything. She then asked where I was going to put it. I said I was moving my bed into the garden, so there would be room. She said she hoped it wouldn't snow. What would Sis say if she could hear me now?

3.30pm. Sun so nice, I walked up the Hollow Road to the top & looked back over Harmony. It is just about possible to see Myersville from up there. The fields are in great alternating ribbons of brick dust, cocoa, & lime, the trees beyond all looking as though they have been burnt, except for the patches of pine, like crow feathers in the light.

7pm. I will put the Christmas tree beside my best chair.

10pm. Temperature around about freezing all day, & a little breezy. Lovely sunshine though. Watched some of "Jaimie McPheeters" tonight. Hm. Not as good as the book.

10.45pm. I will put three presents under the tree. I will buy myself exactly what Tom would have bought me, exactly what Alex would buy me, & I will buy a present for Alex, to keep until next Christmas. I have to.

December 2, 1963

8.45am. Really cold this morning. Up early building fire. (Now have lots of ashes for my garden paths!) Thick thick frost. Throat better, but still headachey.

*Men working as expected today, still cutting holes & dragging heavy wires through. I noticed some other coils of wire though in different sizes & colours.

11.45am. Mailed letter to Sis & one to Ags in NYC, both with Christmas cards. Will send Sis's present later.

4.30pm. Saw John John arrive this evening after school, so I walked over to The Corner to see how things were going. By the time I got there, he was sweeping the floor. The others seem to have been measuring out the lighter wires, working on the upper middle floor.

10.30pm. Hardly over freezing all day. Nice sun to melt the frost.

December 3, 1963

9am. Men at work on time today, but also unloaded large boxes full of small boxes (?).

5pm. Just back after walk across the road. They seem to have been adding the small wires to the large ones & cutting grooves in the walls to hide the smaller ones.

*John John tidying up. He was coughing & looked tired. Rip looked at him & said, –Hey, John John. You ain't lookin' so good. Maybe your daddy'll let ya have the day off tomorrow. Marce didn't even look up from the wall he was chiselling at. –Yeah, right, he said.

10.30pm. Freezing all day today. Fog this morning & a snow flurry this afternoon. Throat almost better after lots of tea. Head getting better now.

December 4, 1963

11.45am. Tidied house & washed clothes. Became quite in-volved noticing the scratches, cuts, nicks & marks on the walls & floors & even furniture of this old house. I feel like there is a person unknown to me just on the other side of these marks, another day, another moment, when each of these tiny accidents left its trace for me to find.

2pm. Collected lunchtime tray. Upper floor now has grooves cut into it & wires everywhere for lights & sockets. Davy busy chipping out holes for these.

5pm. Upper floor wires now all seem to be stapled in place with loose fringes at the ends. Davy has cut in most of the holes for the sockets & lights. Dicky Bird, Rip & Marce already started on the middle floor. John John there, I'm sad to say. He coughed once that I heard & rattled for seconds afterwards. I saw Dicky Bird look at the boy, see my notice, & then look away. I asked him whether he had children of his own. He has; two daughters & a son.

7.30pm. It occurred to me I should find out whether Rip has children, find out how old they are (& Dicky Bird's, as

I know about Davy's) & then should give them all some-thing to take to their families for Christmas. What on earth should I give the men? When?

10.30pm. Below freezing this morning, & hardly over 40 all day. Sunshine.

December 5, 1963

7.30am. Late last night there was a kind of dog telegraph up & down through Harmony. First one would bark, & then it passed to another & so on. Gossip? Boasting? Arguing?

5.30pm. Have found out the ages and sexes of all the men's children now & written them down. John John's cough very hoarse this evening.

   *Middle floor now has grooves everywhere for the wires, about ½ stapled in, & Davy cutting holes as before.

10.30pm. Weather just like yesterday. Soil too cold to shovel. Watched "My Three Sons".

I work out on the new road

It wasn't really his fault. No one understood how difficult it was for him. He wished he could make them understand.

Calvin shut the door to the bedroom and looked at the carpeted hallway. It was nearly Christmas and he was heading home from college for the vacation. It was a long way to his parents' house in Hagerstown, so he was spending the night with his Uncle Hubert, known as Judge Horine, in the Judge's house in Braddock Heights. It was a big draughty house built just after the Civil War, and it had a lot of bedrooms and pantries and hall-ways. Too many, Calvin thought, for just the Judge and his wife Bea. They had no children, and their marriage had been a bit of a scandal in the family. The Judge wasn't really Calvin's uncle, after all, he had been married to Calvin's aunt when she died, and then the old man had his second marriage to Bea. Bea was about thirty, Calvin reckoned, and the Judge about sixty. Anyway, they had a lot of space, and their house made a convenient stopping place on the way home. Calvin thought it would be good for him too to keep the old man sweet, as he was, himself, planning to study law just as soon as he got this undergraduate foolishness finished.

Calvin started down the wide mahogany stairs. No, he thought, it had never been easy. His older brother Arnold had got the family farm, and Patrick had taken up their father's business shares in the lumber mills. There was nothing for him to do but to go off and get some sort of pointless qualification that would enable him to transact some boring business until he was so old he stopped caring. The whole thing depressed him. And, of course, there was no chance of him going to a prestigious university. Harvard or Princeton was where he belonged, but instead … well. He didn't want to hear again in his head the same old arguments he had heard there so many times before. He crossed the marble tiles at the bottom of the stairs and went into the curtained parlour looking for company. He hoped his uncle would find him mature enough, enough a man of the world, to offer him a pre-dinner drink.

Bea was sitting in the rose damask chair beside the piano looking at a magazine.

I'm so sorry, she said. Hubert isn't home. He has had to go out again. This happens so often. He won't be long, he promises me.

She laid her magazine on the top of the revolving bookshelf beside her. How is your room? she said.

Calvin replied that he liked it very much.

It will be nice, she said, as soon as the fireplace takes the chill off.

She did not offer him a drink, so Calvin sat down on the leather chesterfield.

We are so flattered, Bea said sweetly, that you asked to come and join us here, rather than staying down the hill.

Bea was referring to Calvin's Aunt Clarice, his father's sister, who lived on the west side of Middletown. She was unmarried and had one of the older, smaller houses on a side street towards the edge of town. Calvin would pass it on his way home tomorrow. He pictured the room that would have been his, with its high iron bed, its rag rug, its quilt, and its wash stand, basin and pitcher. He smiled. If Bea understood, she didn't let on.

There are towels and toiletries in your bathroom, she said. But I expect you'll find them. Will you need extra pillows? she asked.

Before Calvin could reply, Bea rose and walked towards the hallway door. She turned and looked at him. I imagine, she said, you are too polite to ask. I'll show you where they are.

Calvin stood up and followed her. He listened to her heels tishing on the tiled floor, and then he watched her hips swaying up the stairs ahead of him. Calvin thought of the Judge and an angry pain swept down his arms to his fingertips. He followed Bea into the bedroom where his things rested.

Just here, she said, opening a large panelled cherry wardrobe. The scent of meadowsweet crept into the room as she opened the doors. She reached for the pillows on the top shelf but couldn't quite grip them. She turned and drew a small stepping stool out from beneath the high carved bedframe. She placed the stool in front of the wardrobe and tried it with her foot. The legs sank softly into the carpet. Bea raised herself up on the stool to reach the pillows. As she did so she started to wobble. Calvin stepped forward and without any thought in his mind, placed his hands on her waist. Now over-balanced, Bea began to tip sideways, and Calvin's hands rode up her torso and caught a firm hold, his forearms pressing her ribs, his hands cupping her breasts. She started and he released her. She landed on her feet, and he, perhaps melodramatically, fell right down on to one knee.

Bea's mouth was open, and she was hugging a pillow. She looked at Calvin.

I'm so sorry, she said. Are you all right?

Calvin drew himself up to standing, and Bea walked to the window, half-looking at Calvin and half-looking outside.

I can't think what's keeping Hubert, she said.

Two hours later, Calvin was knocking on the door at his Aunt Clarice's. He had had the sudden inspiration, still in the bedroom at his Uncle Hubert's house, to apologize and say that as much as he had hoped to see the Judge while he was passing through, that as the weather was still holding – the radio threatened snow – perhaps it would be best if he were to go and take the opportunity to visit his Aunt Clarice. The poor thing probably had so few visitors, and he was sure she would be pleased to see him. He hoped the Judge wouldn't be too disappointed, and he hoped he hadn't put Bea to too much inconvenience.

His Aunt Clarice answered the knock and gave her nephew an unexpected hug with her bony arms and fingers. Of course, she was so pleased that Calvin had thought to come and see her. And it was so close to Christmas! What a surprise. Did he mind company? she asked. She was, for the week, looking after the son of her neighbours Betty and Pete, who were in Pennsylvania. The boy was eleven, his name was Phil, and he was as bright as button. Just as bright as could be. But a little wilful, she said. He didn't think he ought to help Clarice with any of her chores. Perhaps, Calvin would oblige her and, if the opportunity presented itself, give him a little talking to.

Calvin put down his suitcase in the cold bedroom opposite the room where his aunt slept, and beside the room where Phil had been sleeping. Phil was in his room, Clarice said, in a bit of a sulk because she had asked him to bring in more firewood from the shed at the far end of her yard. Calvin agreed to do what he could.

In the meantime, he sat in Clarice's small parlour, on one of her three chairs, and had tea and sandwiches with her while she told him about Phil's accomplishments. They were ordinary people, she said, her neighbours Betty and Pete. But Phil, well, he was so special. He could already speak very good German and French, which they taught in school. He could play almost any tune on the piano, and some really quite difficult things on the violin. He read books faster than most adults, and she wasn't sure how far he was getting on with it, but he was having special lessons at school with the maths teacher, who said Phil would be doing trigonometry before the year was out. They were all as proud as they could be.

Just then, Phil came into the room. Clarice stood and moved towards him, but he sat down suddenly. Calvin looked at him. He was fine-boned, with dark strokes for eyebrows, a slim build that would give him a good carriage. He probably could run fast, if anyone had bothered to find out. He would be handsome, and popular with the girls one day.

Phil, Clarice said, this is my nephew Calvin. Can you say hello to Calvin?

Phil stood up with a formal, even polished manner, and extended his hand to Calvin.

I'm pleased to make your acquaintance, he said.

Calvin shook his hand politely and looked into the boy's face. There was something patient inside his eyes, something that took him outside this room and probably many other rooms as well.

Phil, Clarice said, if you would help Calvin bring in some more firewood now, I'll make you up some sandwiches and some hot tea. It's going to be cold tonight, and you'll be glad of it.

Clarice looked at Calvin encouragingly.

Calvin stood and gestured to Phil in the direction of the hall doorway. Phil evidently couldn't think of a way to refuse, so he stood up and walked through the doorway into the small hall.

Calvin followed, and they both pulled on their coats in silence and then went through the kitchen and out the back door into the yard.

The darkness was now falling, and the air had turned colder. The wind against their faces dragged like a file. They walked stamping their feet all the way to the shed where the kindling and stove wood was stacked. Calvin watched Phil as he bent and pried loose the slightly frozen pieces of wood, piling them up in the crook of his left arm. Calvin slowly copied him. Phil had no hat on, and Calvin looked at his heavy brown hair. He had no gloves on, and he looked at his small clean fingers. He watched the breath circling his face.

When his arms were full, Phil turned towards the house. He and Calvin hadn't yet spoken a word. Calvin had his left arm piled high, but his right hand swung free. Phil went down the path ahead of him, down the slight slope with its unevenness and its ruts frozen solid. All at once, Phil stumbled and lost his balance, just a little. The armload of wood toppled though, and in trying to keep his hold on it, Phil saw the whole pile scatter on the ground, and he slid a bit sharply down on to his knee. Calvin was right behind him, and he leaned over the boy's shoulder. Once again, Calvin's mind was empty, unoccupied, blank. Before Phil could extend a hand to pick up a piece of the scattered firewood, Calvin reached over the boy's shoulder, his hand going all the way down between Phil's legs. It came up quickly, his hand cupping against Phil's scrotum, first one testicle, then the other. Just as suddenly, Calvin stood up and stepped to the side, and to the front, looking down at Phil. He said something, but Phil didn't hear him. By the time Phil had gathered up the scattered bits of wood, Calvin was standing beside Clarice's back door, opening it to let Phil go inside first.

That night Calvin slept in the small cold bedroom. Before he fell asleep, he tried to remember everything that had happened to him since he began his journey home, everything that he had thought. But he could remember very little. It all seemed so far away from who he really was, or who people thought him to be. It was disappointing. He hoped things would change.

December 6, 1963

9am. Very cold this morning (about 20?) with a frost hanging in the trees & in the windows.

*Much stapling down of wires going on, Dicky Bird in charge; Davy cutting holes; Marce & Rip in the lower floor measuring wires.

2.45pm. Still clearing up the area outside when I saw Agassy coming up the Brethren Church Road with another woman, about my age. Determined to meet them, so walked over the road & stood looking at the smaller creek. As they neared, I turned & Agassy smiled, chuckled & said –How do? I walked straight towards her, said I was much better after my cold, & asked how she was. –Aw, gettin' 'long, she said. I then introduced myself to her comrade, whose smile was so tight she could've bitten the head off a nail with it. The stranger looked wary, smiled as if the feeling were new (it might be?) & said her name was Eileen. I told her I was pleased to meet her & asked where she lived. She pointed to the house opposite Joanie & Paul's. Ah ha! I thought, the scolding bushwhacker. I said how pleased I am that we are neighbours & that come Spring (I actually said that), I'd be making the Patch (the land next to her) something prettier to look at. She drew back & said, –We're all a-lookin' forward to see what y'all doin'. Yes, I thought, I bet y'all are.

5pm. Went over at 4, anticipating John John's arrival. No sign of him. I asked Marce how he was feeling. He said his wife let JJ stay home today.

*The holes are all cut on the middle floor now, wires in & bright fringes sticking out. All four were working on the lowest floor when I arrived. They left without finishing it. Davy swept up. Marce said (ambiguously to me) they'd "get the boxes in" next week.

*They drove off, Davy alone in the back. It must be 32 degrees. Why couldn't one of them keep him company, at least?

10.30pm. Very still today, hardly above freezing. Sun.

December 7, 1963

2.45pm. Back from Frederick. $17 at A & P. Also discovered a gas station called H L Mills, where I can get S & H green stamps. Now all my needs can be met with patience, a small catalogue, & enough spittle to stick down the little wretches. Also went to Sears', Penney's & Wards' fretting over presents for the men's children. Bought Saul Bellow's Henderson the Rain King & Eudora Welty's The Ponder Heart.

7.15pm. With panicked zeal, I've now wrapped all the presents I bought. Worried about what to give John John.

*Perfect pot roast for dinner. Kept wishing Tom & Alex were here to share it. Ridiculous, as I wouldn't be here if they were.

11pm. Weather like yesterday, though a little warmer this afternoon. Frozen spider web on the wash house. Fell asleep watching the 9 o'clock movie.

December 8, 1963

8am. Rainy this morning & cold with fog. Wood at the edge of the pile a little wet, so hissing. I like the fee fee fee noise it makes.

9am. I think there may be a mouse under the roof near where the chimney goes through. Could be a bird. Might be a walnut tree branch.

12.15pm. I wanted to see Cinch & the others today, & knowing the rain would hurry them, I purposefully walked all the way to the new cemetery with my umbrella, so that I could be heading their way when they all came out after church. –My lands, Miss Mary! Cinch said, Where in tarnation you been? I told her I liked walking in the rain, but she looked sceptical, possibly about my sanity. Anyway, walking amongst all those kindly, somewhat dented-by-life people, with the rain washing the smell of mothballs & cedar from their coats, I have learned important information about stores & Christmas tree farms.

*Cinch seemed to be wearing dark green under her coat, & she had a round black hat with a small veil, I think I've seen before.

8.30pm. What would Tom say about my allegiance to Cinch Ford? He never said things like, She's a mother-sister-etc substitute. But he would never think nothing. Anybody else would say I'm studying her, that I'm a student of "character". Not Tom. He always surprised me. He'd say, She's you, somehow. The only character you find truly irresistible. The only one too real to be partial, yet too close for a point-of-view. Like a twin you've only just met.

10.15pm. Watched "Bonanza".

'Tell me, Woman, what's a-troublin' your mind?'

Most the time, I don't have no trouble with the white folks. But I think that got more to do with the respect they got for the family in the big house. Mostly, I stay out of they way, and nobody interfere with me, nor Red Mary neither. Sometimes you hear 'em say something, like they spoiling us with the Mary House and our garden. Once I hear one them ole farmers say something like that, and Mister Bob say, Them two works from sun up to sun down.

I ain't a-complaining. And we did too. All the cooking and the cleaning and the sewing and the washing and the ironing and the gardening for them and us, and the sweeping the mill, and half-tending to the animals and I don't know what all besides. Most nights I sleep like I dead.

They was sure folks had worse than us. Most of the field hands round about didn't have nothing in they quarters 'cept a dirt floor and a bench. Eat 'thout no knives and no forks neither. Down Frederick they work in the tanneries and the brickworks out 'round East Street, and them fellas all look like dogs that somebody mostly cooked. Out on the big farms the servant gals having babies like a cat has kittens, and then they all gets sold for to sending to Georgia, I hear. They say they take 'em to the pens and everybody shaking like they 'bout to die, and a-waiting for to see how they pin the numbers on 'em. If they pin the same number on the woman and the baby, they sells 'em together. But if they get different numbers, they sells 'em separate. That's when the shouting and the crying start. Lord a-mercy.

Some of them farmers like the devil his ownself. They was one up the Harp Hill got a big ole place and 'bout six seven servants out the house and couple more indoors, and I don't know how many he send out to work in Myersville, Middletown, Keedysville, Sharpsburg. All them towns. His name Hiram Bittle, and I don't know what his wife called. But I pity her, sure enough. Everybody know ole Bittle the daddy 'bout half them servants 'round Harp Hill and I don't know how many besides. He come 'round like the stud horse, they say. And he mean as hell too. I don't know nothing, but folks say when he lost some kind of fight over a piece of land with ole Mister Lindbaugh, 'bout a week later all Mister Lindbaugh's sheep like to bleed to death 'cause somebody get in the field and cut they tongues out. They had to butcher them all, 'fore they starved.

Anyway, they was a servant woman come to working up there, 'cause her husband die where she live, and Bittle got hold of her somehow, whether he buyed her or inherited her or traded for her, I don't know. Anyway, her name was Rezin, and she come with a boy of her own, 'bout ten year old. Now ole Rezin worry herself all the time 'bout that boy and how long it gonna be for Mister Bittle sell him or work him in the field. So she say she want to buy him her own self, and she do anything she gotta do to get the money to buy his free papers.

Well, now, Bittle say he a good healthy boy, and he sure gonna cost plenty. But he got an idea. He say that so long as Rezin let him interfere with her as much as he like, and don't make no trouble, she have herself another boy. Then he say 'fore she get 'tached to that one, she let him sell that baby, and that get her the money for buying that first boy. Rezin, 'greed 'cause I 'spect she didn't see no other way to it. And anyhow, Bittle gonna do just as he liked, so she might as well.

Took 'bout a year, but she get 'specting again, and then she have that baby just fine. Thing was, it was a girl baby, and Bittle, he say that ain't the deal he made. So now, Rezin got herself a boy and a girl to worry bout, 'long with everything else.

Now Bittle say, just as evil as Satan, that he make her the same deal, she wanna do it all over gain. What she gonna do?

So it take 'bout another year after the girl baby weaned, and Rezin 'specting again. Just like before, she have it in the woman quarters in the back of the house, and this time it was a boy. Rezin like to die with not knowing how she oughta do, a-handing that baby child over to Mister Bittle. But she done it. Nobody that hear it believe it, but ole Bittle keep his promise and sell the weaned baby and give Rezin the free papers for the first boy.

I don't know what to say bout that. When it's all done, Rezin and her girl still servants, but she got herself a free son. But she and that boy got to live with selling they own flesh and blood to pay for the bill. After the war they all go to live with the grown-up boy, and they all get by, they say. I think 'fore the freedom come Rezin have some more babies. I don't what happened to them though.

December 9, 1963

9.30am. Strange sad story in the paper this morning. Lightning struck the fuel tank on a plane over at Elkton & blew it up. It crashed killing 81 people. How terrified must they have been?

    *Men unloaded bags of what, I think, must be plaster & some additional tools this morning.

    *All four at work on the lowest floor. Dicky Bird crooning "White Christmas".

1.30pm. Downstairs now seems to be wired & stapled. Men now scattered all over the house. Rip in the upper middle, plastering over wires; Dicky Bird & Davy inserting steel boxes into the holes Davy made; Marce threading wires into these & attaching them to light switches & plug sockets.

5.15pm. John John came this evening. Not coughing now, but looks pale, I thought. He swept up the dust & bits of steel boxes & when picking through the bucket of dust & waste, he snagged his finger slightly on the edge of a disk of steel about the size of a quarter. He jumped & put it in his mouth. Marce grinned. –That'll teach ya, dumb[]ss, he said. John John sat beside Davy as they drove off.

10pm. Dark day today. Freezing, but not bitter, fog, then rain then snow then drizzle. Thought I heard the mouse (mice?) at dinnertime.

December 10, 1963

8.45am. Men arrived with more boxes today, some about 2' square.

1.45pm. Men all over the house again, plastering over wires, fitting steel boxes & their contents. Large boxes piled in the lower ground floor. I asked Dicky Bird (between choruses of "I'll be home for Christmas") what was inside them. He said, –Them's your lights. That's your breakers.

4.30pm. John John just driven off on the back with the others. I waved goodbye to him & to Davy. Neither waved back, though I think Davy grinned.

　*I saw John John alone upstairs earlier & asked him what he wanted for Christmas. He wants a new baseball bat, he said. A Louisville Slugger.

10pm. Not much above freezing all day. A little windy this afternoon, but sun still bright. Time for "The Fugitive".

December 11, 1963

7.30am. Mouse has opened a dancing class for all his friends & relations. Rates are obviously reasonable, as classes are well-attended.

2pm. Work at The Corner much as expected. Now Davy doing the wire-into-boxes thing while Rip plasters. Dicky Bird was helping Marce attach the wall sconce lights that Hartsock recommended. I was carrying out the tray & commented idly, that there sure are a lot of them. –Yes, ma'am, Dicky Bird said. –Ain't they ducky looking things? Marce offered. Then he sighed in disappointment, –Umph umph umph.

7.45pm. On a whim, I have made paper decorations out of writing paper, construction paper, paper bags etc. I now have snowflakes, snowmen, Santa Claus, (with sack & one smaller-than-life reindeer) & various jaunty things like presents, stockings & so forth in silhouette. I fully anticipate despairing mockery from my neighbours & Marce & Co.

10pm. Temperature near freezing all day. Snowed "to beat the band" as Cinch might say, but somehow just wouldn't stick. Why? Watched "The Virginian", though picture a little fuzzy.

December 12, 1963

5pm. Work today much as before. I walked over the whole building & it looks as though all the wires are now covered over except some large ones in the kitchen, the bathrooms & the utility room. All the wall lights seem to be in now.

   *If anyone had any thoughts about the decorations in the Mary House windows, they didn't speak them.

10pm. Weather like yesterday, though foggier this morning. Snow less sure of itself, & then turned to rain.

December 13, 1963

5pm. John John knocked at the door as they were preparing to leave. All the lights are attached he said & the sockets connected. He said next week they'll do "the breakers & the appliances" (?). That doesn't sound right to me: refrigerator? Stove?

   *I asked John John whether he liked my decorations. —Yes, ma'am, he said. Who made them? I replied that I did. —Huh, he said. I asked him then whether he was ready for Christmas. —I guess so, he said. I asked whether he likes turkey & stuffing & pumpkin pie, & he smiled. —What you gonna have? he said. I was so surprised by his question, it took me a moment to answer. I teased him & said hot dogs.

He looked at me for a moment, & then shook his head. —See ya tomorrow, he said. Then he went a few steps, turned, & said, —I mean next week.

10.45pm. Below freezing this morning, & not as much as 40 all day, I think. Frost, so long as it stays frozen, makes things smell nice. So peaceful. Sunny.

Oh, bear me away on your snow-white wings

I, LittleWound, tell this story.

It was around the time when the Washechu men from the village went to Fredericktown to vote, before the charcoal-burners moved over the mountaintop and the farmers were forced to hide their horses.

There was a brother and sister by the name of Runkles, he was called Hiram and she was called Judith. Hiram was beginning a beard when Judith was born. Both sister and brother had eyes the colour of limestone, and hair the colour of rust. They lived on a farm beyond the hollow where the water falls into a pool, a farm that they inherited from their parents. They lived here in peace while Hiram grew to his fullness and while Judith grew to womanhood. Though his seasons gave him authority, Hiram did not seek a wife. He worked in his fields and his pastures, and like the other Washechu he let his hogs roam the wildwood, eating the acorns, the chestnuts and the mast. Judith kept the house for both as a wife ought. She filled the shelves of their cellar with jars of pickled cabbage, corn, beets, tomatoes, cucumbers and peppers. She crocked the grapes in molasses. Their lives had bounty and there was no strife between them.

But though she was a woman with few longings, there came inside her body an ache to be loved and to be the giver of joy to another man's eyes. She let herself be open to these urges and, as Providence wills, a man named Kefauver took delight in her.

While there was never any anger between them, Hiram did not esteem Kefauver, because he had no farm and no trade with which to keep a wife. Still, because he knew the passion in his sister's spirit, he gave his blessing to their marriage, so that Kefauver came to live with Hiram and Judith on Hiram's farm.

It was also true that Kefauver did not have the seasons of either Judith or Hiram. A man's breadth of time lay between Hiram and Kefauver, and for a while, this looked as though it would benefit them all. When Hiram's limbs ached with the scything, or his head pulsed with the shelling of the corn, Kefauver could be the one to help accomplish the chores. And so it went through the renewal of the seasons.

As happens with men, there grew an enmity between Hiram and Kefauver. Hiram's lifetime with Judith had been spent seeing her tasks accomplished as pleased him. But now her work took the shape of pleasure in her husband's eyes. When the men worked outdoors there came between them a rivalry over which one might be the labourer of regard. And though Hiram was the one who had seasons of experience in his hands, Kefauver's youth gave him strength, agility and endurance.

When the winter lessened their labour, they still sought ways to provide themselves with challenges. Chopping wood, shovelling the snow, rising before the dawn, repairing their tools into the night. The farm prospered as never before.

But to Judith there came a foreboding. She saw the lines around her brother's face deepen in sorrow and exhaustion. She spoke to him of this in the way that a woman may speak, but his answer acknowledged no truth in her words. The household, he said, had no anger and its fortunes grew.

There came a day about the time when the daffodils begin their journey that Hiram told Judith he would be working alone to fell an elm that had been splintered by the storms. He set out even before the sun had risen, before Kefauver returned from the barns with the milk. The blows of his axe sounded against the hillside and both Judith and Kefauver entered their tasks without reflection.

At about the time when hunger returns to working men, the sound of the axe ceased. Judith thought to herself that soon Hiram would return, but he did not. Because she was baking, she asked Kefauver to walk to the place where the elm was being felled, and seek Hiram, calling him to return for his meal.

Kefauver approached the hillside where the elm still stood. Hiram's axe had done its work in a way that even Kefauver esteemed, and the tree balanced on its threads ready to topple. Why had he not completed his task? Kefauver wondered. He looked and saw Hiram's axe propped against the side of the tree. He walked around but saw no one. He called out but heard no answer. What he did not know was that Hiram had gone to rest in the shade beside the stone-ridge marking the edge of the field and here he had fallen asleep. Now it may have been because he wished not to leave the job undone, or it may have been out of spite, or it may have been as a gift, but regardless, Kefauver picked up Hiram's axe and began to take strokes at the cut in the elm.

Felling trees is the work of men with experience and there is pride in the vision that enables them to see the outcome of their work, to see how the tree will twist, to see how it will jump before falling to its end. Kefauver did not have this experience and he could not see what his actions would lead to. With fewer swings than he thought it would take the cords of the tree began to groan. There came a whistling like that of a woman giving birth, and then the trunk began to twist as the cracking of whips inside it multiplied. Kefauver threw down the axe and leaped to one side as the hurricane of the branches flew downwards and the elm collapsed roaring into the earth. The tree, each limb the size of a man's body, fell down the hillside and on to the stone-ridge where Hiram lay sleeping.

Judith's neighbours came with saws and cut up the elm and the men split the wood and piled it beside the stable where Hiram's horses rested. The men used a gate to carry Hiram's body into the kitchen, where they laid it on the table. Their wives oversaw the cutting off of his clothes, stained with blood, and the washing and dressing of his body. They massaged his cheeks to restore their shape before his face hardened in death.

Kefauver and Judith remained on the farm until the seasons brought them sons and daughters. The hillside where the elm fell became the burial-ground for the family, and when their destiny was upon them, each was buried beside Hiram, below the stone-ridge, facing the south-wind.

December 14, 1963

6am. Oh, my it is bitter this morning! Not sure what to do: must go shopping, so no fire, but almost too cold to move, & looks like snow.

*Mice passing little complaining notes through ceiling, requesting a revised heating schedule etc etc.

12.15pm. Back from Middletown. Found the store & bought the Louisville Slugger. Spent $19 at Acme, but that includes Xmas baking & extras. Fire reluctant now in the cold bricks. Next time Cinch asks me, I may answer differently about the snugness of the Mary House. Bought Max Factor to send to Sis.

*Mailed more cards this morning. I've now had 14 come, 2 I didn't expect, so must now reply in kind. 'Tis the season of hypocrisy.

7.45pm. Enjoying the Bellow book.

9.30pm. Giving up on fire & going for blankets. Not much above freezing all day. Yawn. Movie too dull to watch & I don't think I have the energy to watch "Gunsmoke". Will try to stop picturing Festus or may have nightmares.

*Today reminds me of being a girl again, although I'm not sure why. Smell of the spices? Wanting to get everything right?

December 15, 1963

6.30am. Even colder than yesterday! In the teens. Wind blowing against the window. Fire shooting sparks. Mice so happy they're having a square dance.

9am. Went outside to dump ashes & found a 4' Xmas tree on my porch! Dragged it inside, arranged it in a bucket of water with bricks to hold it. Can't wait to see Cinch, as it must be her doing.

12pm. Cinch & the others commenced the wobble home-wards as expected. I grabbed her by the arm & she shrunk into herself like a toddler. I forced a kiss on to her cheek & thanked her. She said, –I knew ya wanted one, & all the good ones was gettin' gone. I asked how she got it delivered, & to my amazement, she said, –Marce brung it. I had no idea they ever even spoke to one another. I asked her if she wanted to help me to decorate it & eat gingerbread. She said, –You make gingerbread? I said yes, & she replied, –Ain't it cold? I took this to mean she was still feeling too shy to come inside, so I offered to bring her some outside. –You'll spoil my dinner, she said. –You better get in there 'fore ya freeze up & bust, she said. I could see she wanted to go, so I forced another hug on her. The other women were all smiles now & said, –My, my. Bye now!

5pm. Tree is all decorated, just as I had hoped. But every emotion I have ever felt has come back to me while doing it. If only Tom & Alex were here I would throw my arms around them. It is beautiful, strangely beautiful, even without them. Beautiful in its peacefulness, something which their love hardly allowed for.

10pm. Beautiful night. No moon but stars aplenty. A day for the Vikings, sunny & frigid.

*I have just realized I have not bought a present for Cinch.

Why don't you ring, Old Hammer?

Oh, yes sir, I do remember the days when the war was getting started. Umnh umnh. Folks all talked like they wished they could talk faster. Farmers and neighbours all a-watching each other, with the Fed folk a-trying to get the Sesesh folk in trouble with the law, and when they couldn't get that going, they just try to scare 'em. The Seseshes keeping to theyselves, mostly. Some of 'em put up flags of all kinds. Then the others get in there and steal 'em when they could. They was some barn-burnings, and some sheds and some cows and hogs and sheep got killed. They was a time when they try to get you 'rested if you was to whistle Dixie. When all the folks come a-walking out after the church in the mornings, you could hear 'em arguing all the way down to the Mary House. Yes sir, you could. All talking 'bout the 'zaminer and what it was printing. Lord, they didn't need no armies. They was all in a fighting mood.

Well, 'bout that time they was a ole fella down round Sugar Loaf Mountain somewheres, that up and died, and he didn't have but the one servant of his own. He was a ole fella too, called Gideon, and he spent his whole life, I think, with that ole white man and they more like brothers than anything else. Well, when the boss die, he didn't have no child or nothing, so the lawyers, they found that his only kin was a fella live up Highland way, up on the mountain 'hind us, 'bove Harmony. This fella was named

Virgil Ridenour, and he weren't much but a young fella hisself, and he had a wife name Em, and they live on a little place they bought with money she brought to the wedding. Little farm up there in the hills. Anyway, they ain't but the two them on the place, cause they ain't had no children of they own yet, and Lord knows they couldn't 'ford no servants, even if they need one. So next thing they know, up shows this lawyer a toting ole Gideon with him, and he say this here servant is yours, left you by you uncle that died. Well, Mister Virgil, he didn't know just what to do, 'cause he didn't need no old man to help him none, and he thought they ought to sell ole Gideon pretty quick, and see what they get. But Em – lord, lord – she mighty proud to think she had a servant of her own. She think she big now. Ain't neither one of them know what they gonna do with no ole servant, and they spend they time trying to think of things to keep Gideon from sleeping all day. God Hisself know that ole Gideon was a real shite poke, and not worth a hill of blue beans anyhow. So they come up with 'bout a hundred things to keep him busy. He sleep in the bedroom downstairs, right next to the room Miss Em took to calling the parlour. They all a-getting along all right, till the war get going.

'Bout that time, ole Gideon come in from a-shelling the corn down the barn, and he look up by the door, and there on the peg is a hat he never see 'fore. It's a man's hat, and it's got a feather out of a pheasant stuck in the band 'round the head. Now Gideon, he took down that hat he look at it, and sure 'nough, he ain't never seen it afore. So he put it back, and he go on out to the chicken house looking for Miss Em to ask her who they got in the house that he don't know 'bout. He never does find her, so he go back into the kitchen, thinking he gonna get that hat and show it to Mister Virgil and ask him. Thing is, he get to the kitchen and there's Miss Em a-shelling beans and a-washing 'em, and the hat's done gone. Miss Em, he say, y'all see a hat with a big ole feather in it a-hanging here? Miss Em, she give him a look like he crazy, and say, Ain't no hat been up there with no feather. You dreaming, Gideon.

Now Gideon, he get 'spicous. He go on down there to the barn and look for Mister Virgil. He look up in the hay mow, and he can't find him, so he go down to the cellar, and there tied up is Mister Virgil's horse and a big ole mare like he ain't seen before. He look at that horse. Yes sir, he say to hisself, that sure ain't no horse I seen before. He go out in to the barnyard, and he see Mister Virgil coming down the hill following the cows for the milking. Lord, Mister Virgil, he say. Who that horse belong to, sir? I ain't never seen him 'fore. Gideon, he say, I found that horse. Found him? Yes, I did. I was down in the woods looking for flat stones for the wall, when up she come a-nosing round like she lost. I looked everywhere, and I called out loud as I could, and I don't get no answer. So I think she done run off. She have a saddle on? Gideon say. And Mister Virgil he think for a minute. Yes, she did, he say. I took it off and put it in the barn. Rider must've lost her, I reckon. I just hold on to her till he come looking for her. Yes, sir, Gideon say. I see what ya mean. He thinking he ought to say something 'bout the hat he see, but something tell him that he ain't got no hat to show, so he best wait a little and see what happen.

That night, after the supper, Miss Em, she take all the ham and the biscuits and the beans they don't eat and she pile em up on a tin plate and she put em on the top of the range, just like she waiting for someone to come later. What y'all doing that for? Gideon say. Why, she say, sometimes Mister Virgil get powerful hungry 'bout the time he go to bed, and I want him to have something if he want it. Gideon shake his head.

That night Gideon say he sat a-listening to the dark, like he 'specting a ghost or something to come looking for his supper, and sure as you're born, in the morning, that plate all gone, and Gideon didn't hear nothing. No sir, not a thing. Well, that morning was a Saturday, and on Saturday he help carry the washing for Miss Em, and he go round collecting all the sheets and the shirts and I don't know what all. He say when he go up the stairs, Miss Em got the door to the big bedroom in the back shut, and she ain't never got no doors shut, 'cause she say it make the place smell like a church. So Gideon, he think the wind done blow the door shut, but when he try to open it, it stuck and he can't get it open. He go out to the porch where Miss Em's a-washing the clothes and he say the door to the bedroom in the back is stuck and I can't get it open. I know, she say, I shut it. It's gonna be Mister Virgil's birthday soon, and I'm piecing him a quilt in there, and I don't want him to see it no more.

Now ole Gideon, he getting 'spiciouser and 'spiciouser. He decide to set hisself a trap and find out what Miss Em and Mister Virgil up to.

That night, Miss Em fry the ham and cook the beans and make the cornbread and the carrots and just like before, she put a big ole tin plate up on the range, pile high. Gideon, he don't say nothing, but he a-watching and a-waiting for to catch 'em in they game.

Well, it's getting late in the summer and it's getting dark earlier and earlier, and when the folks is gone to bed ole Gideon sat up a-listening. He wait till it all go real quiet, and he start to think he ain't gonna hear nothing, so he have hisself a little nap, he think. He wake up and think he sure 'nough hear something in the back bedroom, and he crep' outa bed in his combinations and head up the steps a-listening and a-looking. He get to the top of the stairs, he see that the door to the bedroom is open and they a splashing a-going on down there. So he get down low and he creep up best he can till he get to the door. He stick his eye up to the crack and he look in. What he see, but Miss Em a-washing her face and hands and not wearing nothing but her shimmy and her skirt? She swing round and she shout, God

Almighty, Gideon, y'all trying to kill me or something. Gideon, jump 'bout a foot, and Mister Virgil he come out and say, What in the Hell, y'all doing out here now? He trying to see me, Miss Em say. And Mister Virgil, he look at Gideon, and he say, That true, you ole fool?

Now Gideon, he don't know what he gon' to do. He say he think they a stranger in there, they think he lost his mind. He say he there a-looking at Miss Em, Mister Virgil like to beat him like a ole rug. So Gideon, he shiver like he cold and he say, I awful sorry, sir. I thought they a ghost up here.

All the rest of that summer and that fall and most of the winter, Gideon keep on a-hearing ghosts in the bedroom in the back of the house. Mister Virgil, he keep on a-finding horses wandering in the woods, and keep 'em in the barn till they owners come and collect 'em. Miss Em, she still a-working on that quilt for the birthday. And sometimes they hats and pipes and boots and cigars in the kitchen that don't belong to Mister Virgil. It ain't till the Sesesh come theyselves with they army till Gideon get the idea that the ghosts he been hearing ain't nothing but fellas trying to get theyselves to Virginia to join in the fighting. He say to Mister Virgil, How come y'all don't want me to know you got them men a-passing through this house? But Mister Virgil, he don't say nothing.

When the war over, Miss Em and Mister Virgil go on a-living in they house just like always and they raise two children of they own. They ain't got no trouble with they neighbours. Gideon try to tell folks 'bout the ghosts, but nobody believe him. He say what he think. 'Fore long, he move to Philadelphia.

December 16, 1963

7am. Another cold start, looks like 17. Windier. Mice pretty quiet this morning. Nothing but the sound of them flicking through travel brochures for Florida.

9.30am. Very tranquil in The Corner today. Rip & Davy attaching larger lights; Marce & Dicky Bird in the lowest floor, but not sure what they are doing & couldn't be bothered with finding out. Could just hear Dicky Bird's "O Holy Night" through the floorboards.

5pm. Men drove off as usual. No sign of John John.

*Went in to have a look at their work. Lights up on three top floors. Fusebox full of black toggles now in the utility room, about ½ the wires in place.

10.30pm. Sunny all day. Never reached freezing. Watched "Wagon Train". Still reading Bellow.

December 17, 1963

7am. Up making the fire. Colder than yesterday. Mice staggering about under the effect of too many brandy toddies.

2pm. Men doing something with wires in the kitchen & bathrooms.

*Last, truly last, Christmas cards sent. Hope they make it. 22 in now.

5pm. Men gone like yesterday. Didn't go to inspect their work. Too cold.

10.45pm. Sunny but below freezing all day. Read more Bellow.

December 18, 1963

3.30pm. Snowing now, but will it last?

4.30pm. John John just knocked at the door. He was sent to tell me (from his father) that the electricity company is coming tomorrow some time to connect (or rather re-connect) The Corner, & could I keep an eye out for them. I said I would.

*I asked JJ how many days of school he has left. He smiled & held up two fingers. I asked him what he was going to do then. —I don't know, he said. —Read books, watch TV, help my dad.

7.30pm. After dinner spent some time recalling Daddy. Clove smell of his pipe. Sweaty ring on his hat in the summer. His wedding ring.

10pm. Weather like yesterday. No real snow. Missed seeing "The Virginian".

December 19, 1963

8.45pm. Cold as can be again today. Wind blowing, so fire flourishes.

10am. Electricity company came as expected. Two men (who might have been Art Carney & Jackie Gleason) hopped out & as I approached, Art touched his hat (Can you believe?) & Jackie asked who was in charge. I answered that I was & he looked at his clipboard. Just then the door on to the high porch opened & Marce called out, —Hey! Art & Jackie turned to face him. Jackie said, —Mornin'. Then he & Art looked at me, smirked in something like politeness & walked away. I went back into the Mary House & boiled the tea kettle. I then (metaphorically, at least), spat into three cups & made them tea with (metaphorical) horse p[]ss.

1pm. Electricity truck left about 20 minutes ago, & I have replaced the tea tray, taking away the old one. There are empty boxes on the floor in the middle room & it sounds like they are all working in the bathrooms. Dicky Bird, perhaps literally, singing in the shower.

4.30pm. Just back from The Corner. The work on the bathrooms & kitchen has to do with fans, the stove & other big electrical things.

*Thinking I was unobserved, I flicked the light switch in what will be my study, just to see what would happen. Nothing happened.

*I tried the same experiment in the big hall with the same result. John John was popping Styrofoam from a box, while the others were flattening the boxes. –It don't work yet, Davy spoke up. –It ain't switched on, Dicky Bird said. –You ain't had your inspection yet, Rip said, adding, –Ma'am.

*Marce came into the room, took the Styrofoam from John John & put it into a box full of the stuff he'd already broken up. –Put that in the can outside, he told him. Then to me, he said, –Inspection's tomorrow morning. Then you can light up your Christmas tree.

10pm. Sunny & dry but not above 20 all day.

December 20, 1963

6.30am. So so cold this morning. 9 degrees (I went out & looked, prying loose frozen wood for later.) Tried to look at roof to see whether mice had established visible architectural features near the chimney. Couldn't see anything as it was still too dark.

8.30am. Just back from Corner. Not sure, but I think Marce looks just a tiny bit nervous. Must be the inspection.

*I made the men some homemade cookies today, partly because I was up early & felt like some, & partly because it was so cold. All of them said, –Thank ya, except Marce. –You make these? he said. I answered yes. –Huh, he said. –Pretty good.

1pm. Inspection over. The Corner passed & the papers should come next week.

*Sawing & hammering going on across the road now. (?)

5pm. John John got a telling off when he arrived. A lot of the Styrofoam he carried outside yesterday had blown around, getting stuck in the bushes & fence & everywhere, as the wind has picked up & he didn't weight it down. He was given a pack of matches & after he had gathered it all up, stood looking like a hobo in a jungle burning (or rather melting) it in the oil drum where they burn trash.

    *I called out to him & said Happy Last Day of School. He turned and smiled at me & waved, his face hot from the fire.

11pm. Wind picked up later today, but still only 20s, sun or no sun. Sleepy & didn't enjoy "Twilight Zone".

    *Realized I forgot to look at what all the sawing & hammering had been about. Toyed with the idea of walking over & turning on all my new lights, but too cold.

December 21, 1963

9.30am. Up early this morning, made fire to the sounds of fox-trot, can-can, & Mexican hat dance between the rafters. Realize (not too late!) I didn't send the little family a Xmas card.

11am. Have baked a very nice ginger cake for Cinch & boxed it prettily. Quite pleased about this.

    *Lost confidence in wrapping, as I thought it looked too much like one of her hats. Replaced bow with a plaid ribbon.

4.30pm. Drinking tea to keep warm. Finished Bellow. Really enjoyed it.

10.30pm. Weather like yesterday. Sky tonight is wonderful.

Randy Lynn Rag

There weren't many ladies who worked at the Valley Merchants' Bank in Middletown. There was old Mrs Chapline with her brushes and mops and vacuum, and there was Berniece, the fat girl who did most of the filing upstairs. The rumour was that she was a little slow, and it gave no man any credit to say he got a smile out of her. So it gave Dennis a little compensatory satisfaction when the new boss, Mr Rhoderick, brought his wife to work with him and installed her as the receptionist in the main lobby. The bank had never had a receptionist, and Mrs Rhoderick, who liked everyone to call her Rose, and who even wore a badge with the words, 'My Name is Rose. How May I Help You?' printed on it, was pretty and sweet-tempered. She was made neither meek nor vain by the fact that her husband was the boss, although there still did seem to be a very slight deference in the bank employees' manner when they spoke to her. Everyone was relaxed, and yet somehow alert, in case they accidentally gave offense.

Dennis was the same. It wasn't that he had singled out Rose for his attention. It was rather that there was no one else on whom he might bestow it. He smiled and said good morning to her when he arrived (she was always at her desk early, before everyone else). Sometimes he even gestured as though he were tipping his hat in quite an old-fashioned way. Sometimes, he made eye-contact with Rose, all the way across the bank's wide lobby, when she was not speaking with customers and he was not handling their requests from behind his counter. Customers liked Rose, liked knowing who she was and why she was there. Dennis felt they liked him too. Or at least, some did. There were those who only trusted the aged tellers, men who had known the secrets of their neighbours' banking for decades. But there were others who gave the young man a chance. Such a nice young man, they said. He knows his stuff, he really does.

Rose treated him with the same kindness she had for all her husband's employees. It was a kindness that was never aloof, at least not on her part. Sometimes, the men around Dennis said, they liked to make it plain that they were only polite to Rose in a most professional fashion, giving her what was due to her as a lady, the boss's wife, a colleague.

But Dennis wasn't sure about Rose. He came from a big family, lots of brothers and sisters, aunts and uncles, and he had had chances to watch how men and women looked at one another. How his mother and step-father looked at one another; how his aunt and uncle seemed to fight constantly, while still producing children. His cousin with two ex-wives; his brother with a succession of girlfriends, all so young. To Dennis, it all tasted like the stale air of the bedroom.

No, there was something about Rose. Definitely. Dennis had seen it in the way she looked at her husband, Mr Rhoderick. He had seen it in the way her eyes lingered over some of the better-looking, better-off male customers. He wanted to call it hunger, but that made Rose seem vulgar and low. Instead, Dennis called it longing. Rose, he felt sure, looked at men with longing. In her eyes was a confession that she wasn't living the life she wanted, wasn't being loved the way she wanted. Dennis understood this and was moved. He, too, felt longing, felt loneliness.

The only time Dennis spoke to Rose was just after 3.00pm on weekdays, when the bank closed. Mr Rhoderick had brought with him a new accounting procedure which meant that each of the tellers had to complete a blue chit confirming the contents of their drawers when they cashed out for the day. The numbered drawers were then taken to the vault, as always, but the blue chits were given to Rose, whose job it was to record them in an accounts book for her husband to review. If he ever truly reviewed them. Some of Dennis's fellow tellers said it was just one of the many tasks old Rhoderick had created to make it seem as though Rose had something to do when there weren't many customers to chat with.

In any case, it was a moment of the day that Dennis looked forward to. He usually timed his arrival at Rose's desk last, so that there would be no one waiting after him, no one to hurry him along. It all started with smiles, mention of the weather, or impending holidays. Before long, Dennis had made subtle enquiries into the lives of Rose and Mr Rhoderick, so that he was able to ask Rose questions about how things were at home. How was Mr Rhoderick's sister faring after her operation? Did those geraniums she bought prosper? Which tea really was better, Lipton or Tetley? Dennis soon was keeping an ear out whenever and wherever he could for new jokes and anecdotes – all chaste, of course – that he could bring to Rose. He liked to make her laugh. He also started smartening up his appearance, new shirts, new ties, new shoes, hoping she might notice and comment.

After a few months, the tellers who worked alongside Dennis began to tease him about his crush on Rose. They couldn't help themselves. He was too old for such puppy love, and there was little else that happened in the bank to make them laugh.

It didn't matter to Dennis. He heard it all, and never responded. It hurt his feelings, naturally, to be mocked and disrespected like this. But what else could he expect from them, from himself? Their teasing was worth the happiness that he felt every day as he walked home at 3.30pm, having chatted with Rose. If she took any notice of what others said about him, or about her, she never let on. That was enough to keep Dennis satisfied. He never felt gloomy. He never felt impatient.

That was why it surprised him so when, on a Friday morning, Mr Rhoderick asked Dennis to stop by his office after he had cashed out for the day. He wanted a word, he said.

Dennis spent all day wondering. Perhaps, he was in line for some sort of promotion. Or a raise. Or, perhaps he was going to be given extra duties, in loans, or mortgages, say.

Dennis knocked at Mr Rhoderick's open door, and Mr Rhoderick looked up. He didn't smile, but with his pen in hand, he gestured for Dennis to sit down on the large leather sofa where the bank's finer clients sometimes sat. Close the door, Mr Rhoderick said.

Rhoderick explained the situation to Dennis very carefully, reluctantly, diffidently, even distractedly, with a slightly routine boredom creeping in. There had been … some discrepancies. It seemed that the amounts on Dennis's blue chits, the sums actually recorded in the drawers, and the those noted on Rose's tally didn't always agree. Where there were differences, those differences implied that there were sums missing. Not large sums, but still, on the whole, all in all, if considered altogether, noticeable. In view of this, Rhoderick said, his eyes on Dennis's new tie, he was letting Dennis go. He would not be taking the matter further, and no one else in the bank would know anything about this. Not unless Dennis himself spoke to anyone about it – something Rhoderick very much hoped Dennis wouldn't do. He also recommended Dennis to find another firm to manage his own private accounts, whatever the nature of those were.

Dennis left the office, carrying his coat and hat. He had no personal items to collect at the counter where he worked, or rather had worked, for the past two years. Tellers were not allowed to keep anything of their own near their stations. He crossed the empty lobby, his own footsteps grown strangely loud in the hollow room. Rose was not at her desk, and he did not say goodbye. He wondered what he might have said if she had been there. He had not protested his innocence to her husband. He was, of course, not guilty of any irregularity – he had committed no fraud, and he knew his accounts were absolutely accurate. He knew what had happened. He knew what he was guilty of. He knew how to feel sorry.

In less than a moment he was outside again, and the automatic door clicked shut behind him.

December 22, 1963

7.30am. Tried to resist giving in to urge to rush down & build fire, but I am too weak. Must be 10 degrees this morning. If this keeps up, may abandon morality & take mice family to bed, just to keep warm. Or worse, take up crochet.

10.30am. Reading the Sunday paper I see today is the last official day of mourning for President Kennedy. When is the last unofficial day?

12pm. Waited for Cinch to pass on her way home from church to give her her cake. –You make this yourself? she asked. I told her I stole it from a windowsill. She looked at it a long time & suddenly said –Well, thank ya. Then she leaned in close to me & almost whispered, –It looks so good! I told her to have a merry Christmas. She said she expected she'd see me 'round sometime.

8pm. I cannot stop brooding on this idea of "mourning". What exactly does this idea even mean? What am I supposed to have been doing for the past month? A bit every day, like exercise? Or am I supposed to be ready, when the mood strikes me, to say, Oh yes, I feel sad now, so this must be a good time to mourn? Or when I'm happy: Ah ah ah, not so fast, remember to mourn. No one who has ever genuinely mourned anything would recognize this.

*I mourned Tom for a part of every minute of every hour for the first month; then every hour of every day; then every day of every week; now, I just don't know. I want an eternity to look at him & to ask him, Why?

*I think, perhaps, what shocked me was not his suicide, or even thinking of him doing it, but the fact that I wasn't completely surprised when they brought me the news. I hated myself for thinking "he is capable of it", & not knowing how to stop it, thinking that not believing it hard enough would be enough to stop it.

*I was so busy mourning myself before he died, that I didn't notice I was mourning him too before he died. He must have seen that. What a terrible burden to be looked upon as someone already gone, whose gifts of joy are returned unopened.

9pm. Now I am so bitterly frightened in case I did the same thing to Alex. I let myself show regret for the happiness he wasn't having. With Tom, with me, with himself. It must have been like saying my Dream Alex has passed away & now only you, his ghost is left to me.

*That's why I can't let go now. I look back & I see myself mourning, grieving even then, so many times, for the happy world we all might have been enjoying, but which, somehow, we all failed to choose. They both resented the fact that no one would open the door for them. But it was already open. I begged them both, but with such hopelessness that it's no wonder they didn't believe me or listen.

*That is what mourning is: not the loss of what has been, or even what hasn't been; but the knowledge, that comes like a sudden choking, that none of it ever will be what it could be & it is always always too late to change it.

*So I am frozen. Afraid to mourn Alex, in case he is alive; afraid to hope in case he is dead. Living in a futile determination to resist despair. Because it is too painful, because it is bad luck, because it is what killed Tom, because it is what drove Alex to leave, & because I may never find my way back.

*So here I am building a real future for imagined time.

10pm. Near freezing only this afternoon. Sun.

December 23, 1963

9am. Foggy this morning & still frost is rock hard.

*Just back from The Corner. All that noise is coming from the top floor. The project seems to be to enlarge the space where the new stairs are to go. Probably the first time there will have ever been stairs up there. Davy & John John mostly watching.

11.15am. About 30 minutes ago another Ingalls truck came full of lumber. (I had no idea they'd be working this close to Christmas.) Davy & John John were the first on the scene, & immediately helped the driver to unload. This time it was the handsome black man on his own. After a while Marce & the others showed up. As soon as he could, Marce set the others to carrying things inside, & called the driver over to sign the paperwork. I came outside & walked over to the porch at The Corner, trying to look as though I were interested in what they were unloading. Marce was speaking to the driver. —Got you working on your own then, huh? —Yes, sir, that's right. —Working ya hard? —No, sir, not too bad. —Uh huh. You like hard work? —Not unless I have to. —Uh huh. Got many more today? —Just two more after this. —You live in Middletown? —Closer to Jefferson. —Go to school in Jefferson, did ya? —Sure did. —Play football? —Not too much. —Uh huh. Ya like it up here? —It's fine. —Not many of your people 'round here. —No, sir. Not too many.

    *I wanted more than anything to read the young man's face when he sat down again behind the wheel, but I couldn't see him clearly. Davy walked out into the road to help him reverse out, & he turned once to face me briefly. He seemed to nod very slowly & then he drove away.

2.30pm. Collected the lunch tray & asked whether they plan to work tomorrow. —It ain't Christmas yet, Marce said.

4.30pm. They men drove away on time, Davy & John John both looking up into the sky as tiny hard snowflakes were falling.

9.30pm. Never made it to freezing again. Some snow this afternoon, very graceful big flakes floating down. No energy for "Wagon Train".

December 24, 1963

8.30am. Slightly warmer this morning. Not sure the men were coming after all, I risked the tray-making. Isolated snowflakes, tiny ones, testing the air, it seems.

1.30pm. Collected the tea tray an hour ago (they always seem to eat early), & not wanting to miss my opportunity, I came back & grabbed up the presents I'd got for the men's children & took them over. All of them stopped work (the hole for the stairs looks very nice now, taking shape neatly). Rip, Davy & Dicky Bird all said —Thank ya, kindly ma'am. That's real nice of ya. Etc. I gave John John his bat & he lit up. He looked almost afraid to touch it. When he did, he took a few practice swings. Marce spoke up, —What do ya say? he asked him. John John looked at me & just a little mechanically, I thought, said thank you. I couldn't quite tell what was the matter, until Rip spoke up. —Chip off the ole block, hey? —He'll be swingin' just like you one day, Marcie, Dicky Bird said. Marce looked disgusted. —I'll say, Davy added in. Then he looked at me, —Ole Marce used to swing one of them good, didn't ya, Marce? Marce looked at him and said half-seriously, —Why don't you get off your []ss and bring up some more of them two by fours? The others looked a little awkward & as Marce passed Rip he muttered, —Gonna take more than bat for him to hit somethin', he said. If John John heard, he showed no signs of it. My thoughts went back to the look on the face of the handsome driver yesterday. The child is father to the man.

3.30pm. John John just knocked on my door. They are finished slightly early today, meaning the place for the stairs is now ready. I told him to enjoy his bat & he said he would. He also said his grandparents ("Nan & Pap") are coming for Christmas dinner. I wanted desperately to give him a hug & would have, but I could feel the men's eyes on him, or feel him feeling they were.

*Did I make a mistake giving him the bat?

*Realize I forgot to ask what day they were returning for work.

8.30pm. I look at the three presents under the tree. Tom would laugh at my choice of perfume for myself. I will open the box tomorrow & imagine his face as it would have been. He liked to give me perfume, he said, because it affected his imagination whenever I was around & whenever I wasn't. The present of slippers, the sort Alex liked to get me, will be useful in this cold winter. He would like that. The little box for him, with its rare baseball cards, Canadian tea & Duke Ellington record, I will keep until we move into The Corner.

*Alex, somewhere, living this moment, without me.

10pm. Not snowing & not not snowing all day. Cold.

Going Across the Sea

I, LittleWound, tell this story.

It was in the era before the Washechu came to the mountain of the Catoctins. It was in the days when Chankpayyuhah, known as CarriestheClub, led the people. His war-bonnet hung to his knees with the feathers of the eagle, and he had touched the bodies of his enemies as often as the raindrops touched the earth.

Esteemed among the Catoctins was the warrior named Red-Hand. He had grown to a stature above the men of his generation, a generation that stood behind that of CarriestheClub. His pride shone in his eyes and his valour was never questioned by any who heard tales of his prowess in the hunt or when the warriors raged. Always the man to count his own worth, RedHand grew impatient with the stars, impatient that so long as CarriestheClub lived, the leadership of the Catoctins could not come into his own hands. He walked with envy and his sleep was disturbed by dreams of violence.

The elders who surrounded CarriestheClub saw what was in RedHand's heart and warned CarriestheClub that he must take care not to shut his eyes while RedHand waked. CarriestheClub had sensed this himself. You must banish him, the elders said, or soon the anger that boils inside him will consume you, and the Catoctins will lose the leader they prize above all others. I will not banish him, said CarriestheClub, for he has the virtues of our people within him. He is the limb that grows from the oak where the sun shines the length of the day. But CarriestheClub was no fool. In his mind he had made a plan that he knew would trap RedHand in the net of his own pride.

At that time of year when the rains are few except when the thunderbird himself commands them, CarriestheClub sent out a message to the villages of the Catoctins on the mountain and in the valley. I proclaim an assembly, he said, where we shall feast and celebrate the achievements of our people. We will meet where the streams cross on the valley-floor, and there for all the days of my hand, we will recount together the pride of our people.

As they were directed, all the Catoctins from the riverside to the highlands came to the place where they might assemble, and a great festival was begun. As the sun rose on the commencement day, CarriestheClub stood before the men and women and spoke these words. Brethren, I have invited you here to help me recognize and exalt the glory of the warrior who stands as the head among you. You see this prince, RedHand, whose strength and courage are known to you. It is to him that this celebration belongs. For those of us here who have never seen him, these days will show why he deserves the honour that surrounds him. Tomorrow will begin the proof of my words. But for today, let us rejoice and consider the debt we owe to those who will stand before us.

All that night the elders of the people wondered. What did CarriestheClub have in mind? In his tent, RedHand could not be sure whether he was about to be made leader of the people, or whether CarriestheClub meant only to woo him to become a supporter of his own for those seasons that remained to him. But in his dreams that night he saw himself like a snake with no legs.

At sunrise the Catoctins crowded together to see what the day would bring. CarriestheClub looked out over the people's faces and he spoke to their understanding. You must know, he said, that RedHand alone is the hero of our nation. Today you will begin to see why he holds this reputation. There is no challenge that he refuses, no task of a living creature in which he does not excel. His stride is like that of the stag and his endurance like that of the wolf. See where he stands before you. I command that as evidence of my words, he will have no difficulty in running from mountaintop to mountaintop, even before the sun sets this evening.

His eyes and the eyes of all the Catoctins fell upon Redhand, and the warrior felt his pride grow within him with the spirit of the wolf and the energy of the stag. At once he set off running towards the top of the mountain nearest to the rising sun. When they could no longer see him from the ground, boys and men climbed trees to watch his progress up the slopes to the mountain's crest like the body of a giant who sleeps. There, as the mid-morning cooking began, he arrived and at once turned himself again to the valley. Down he came, passing beyond the encamped Catoctins, and crossing the hillsides that lay beyond them towards the mountain nearest to the land where the sun sets. Men sought to follow him, but few had the ability to sustain his pace or to dare the distance he had to traverse. By the time the campfires were lit the shouts of the warriors began to echo on the margins of the encampment. As the people drew again to the place where the streams crossed, RedHand once again appeared before them. His legs swung like branches in the wind and his face had lost its colour and his eyes their focus. But, just as CarriestheClub had foretold, Redhand alone could touch the summits of both mountains in the span of a day. The people cheered and shouted and RedHand became to them as one of the Manitoes. But that night, as he lay in his tent, he dreamed that his arms fell away, and in their place, grew fins like those of the trout.

The next morning was like the first. CarriestheClub stood on a tree-stump before the people and beside him stood RedHand, never casting down his eyes. As I have said, spoke CarriestheClub, the earth itself is the servant of RedHand. You may trust your honour to his keeping. But it is not only the earth that obeys him, for the waters too are like a gift to him from the skies. Today, he will demonstrate this mastery when at the place where the valleys cross and the stream swells like a bird full of eggs, he will plunge into the water, fetching forth the beavers' cubs.

The people looked at one another as if they had heard magic and looked at RedHand as though he were a god. They ran before him, each one hoping to get a place in the meadows near the beaver-pool where they could witness the moment when RedHand would prove himself able to withstand the darkness and hold his breath long enough to reach the beavers' deep dens.

At last, RedHand made his way to the edge of the pool. All around him trees lay in mounds, their bark burst by the beavers' teeth. Across the pool, a bowshot away, the men and women watched him as he stripped off his clothes. The water was cool, and even at the length of his body its depths were like the night. To complete this task, he needed to dive into this darkness and swim among the obstructions, feeling with his hands for the places where the animals left openings to enter the nests where they raised their young. He knew too that the beavers would not be sleeping while he was among them, and he knew that he would have to work fast before the air in his lungs left him trapped in the brushwood under the surface of the pool.

Over and over Redhand dove into the pool, each time circling downwards, memorizing the things he felt, working his way closer until each time he had to come back to the surface to breathe. Sometimes, the work was such that he had to haul himself on to the bank and rest, though he looked outwards to no one else, and he never raised his voice to share the anger that filled him. In this way the day passed. Children came back and forth from the encampment, bringing food for those who refused to leave, each one wanting to be there to see if it were true, that RedHand could capture a beaver cub.

They were not disappointed. As the sky grew to the colour of autumn leaves, they saw RedHand climb onto the trunk of a tree on the water's edge, holding something in his hand, his arm pushing outwards from his chest. There, spinning and crying out like a coyote pup was a single beaver cub. The people cheered with the sound of a storm among the hollows, and they rushed to the encampment to tell one another all the things they had witnessed.

CarriestheClub smiled to himself. And that night, with blood on his hands, eyes that swelled and arms that shook, RedHand dreamed of the sky beneath him and the wind in his face.

Even before the dawn showed, the people assembled near the place where the streams cross to see what things CarriestheClub would foretell as further proofs that RedHand was destined to be the one who stood before all the Catoctins.

Family, CarriestheClub spoke, you have seen for yourself that RedHand is the only man who commands the spirits of the earth and of the water. But it is also true that the air is his prisoner.

CarriestheClub pointed behind him to where the ridge of the Catoctins' mountain extended peak after peak, ending in a drop where the springs burst forth from the greenstones. All along this ridge the rocks were home to no trees except the pines. Here, he said, you have seen how even the squirrel flings himself through the treetops, relying on no wings but only upon the strength of his limbs. Even here, with the power befitting a man and a warrior, Redhand will walk from treetop to treetop, from the place where the deer descend, to the place where the mountain ends below us.

A shout of anticipation flew upwards into the sky as the people ran towards the mountain slopes, each one looking for a place where she or he could see the trees above them, and with luck, glimpse RedHand as he walked through the sky.

RedHand himself climbed the mountain without company. When he reached the place where his steps no longer pushed upwards, the place where he could see the valleys that lay on either hand, he climbed easily to the top of pine that stood like a bolt of lightning above the others. Holding his breath within him, he leapt to the tree beside this one, catching himself among the branches that clung to him with their resin.

And so the day passed towards night. From tree to tree, Redhand made his way through the air from the place where the deer descended, to the place where the springs sprouted among the greenstones. Here, at the place where all the valleys joined, Red-Hand looked below him and saw the Catoctins' faces. They stared at him in wonder. There was no man in whom they believed more.

While this was happening, CarriestheClub had remained at the encampment. All through the day he built a pile of brushwood and dry hardwood. By the time he heard the people's cheer the pile had grown to the size of the council-lodge. It was then that he lowered a torch to the tinder and the sky shone with the bonfire.

As the people returned to the encampment, all trailing after RedHand, whose arms, feet, face and body were the colour of soot and who smelt like a winter's night when the pine-knots glow on the hearthstone, they were awed by the fire. CarriestheClub greeted them, outstretching his arms.

Today you have seen wonders, he said. Once again, RedHand has given you a triumph. This man, in whom your trust and loyalty are given, has shown that nothing in the earth, the water or the air quakes him with fear. But tomorrow, you will see that which no man has ever seen before. This fire will burn all night, and tomorrow, RedHand will once more prove his gifts by taking the rest he deserves, sleeping for the whole day in its embers.

The people cheered and stomped until the ground shook and the birds flew away in fear. Everyone felt such excitement that no one wanted to sleep, and all agreed to watch the fire burn throughout the night. All, that is, except RedHand, who crept alone to his tent. That night he dreamt again, and in his dreams, he saw nothing.

As the dawn came the people had formed into a circle around the embers of the bonfire. It glowed like the eye of the sun upon the centre of the nation. Everyone was eager for the vigil to begin. With their hearts beating and their arms waving the people called out for RedHand to appear and prove once more the words that CarriestheClub had spoken. They went to his tent and looked inside. They shook the poles in fear, for no one was there. They ran to tell CarriestheClub, and he brought himself before the assembled Catoctins.

It is plain, he said, that no man with such abilities could live long among mortals. We must all thank the spirits who protect us for the gifts which RedHand bestowed when he was among us. Now that he has gone to live among the Manitoes, let us all remember his name when we fear our courage shrinks within us.

And so it was that CarriestheClub brought honour even to the warrior who had sought his own life.

December 25, 1963

8am. Woke up at the usual time. Tried reading Eudora Welty but couldn't concentrate. Younger mice evidently in Fort Lauderdale, leaving only the old folks behind to lumber about. Got up & made up fire, oddly eager to open presents, the contents of which I know thoroughly. Just eager to begin memories.

11am. Breakfasted on eggs, which feels strange as having chicken for Christmas dinner. Wearing slippers. Thank you, Alex. Merry Christmas to you. We may both thank your father that I smell so good.

2pm. Cannot forgive myself for over-eating, even though I am alone, & even though it was both ridiculous to make so much food, & ridiculous not to eat it. Drank a glass of wine (California) & liked it enough to have another. Quite tipsy now. Hope no one knocks on the door, or I shall truly gain the reputation I fear I may already possess.

5pm. Off the phone with Sis. She liked her present, & sounded slightly surprised, which gives me an added faith in her sincerity. She is fine, apart from her hip, which causes her to think too much of mortality. Mine, not hers, evidently.

8pm. So now, everything is ready for bed, Christmas over & even my teeth & hair brushed. I have respectfully thought of all the people I have ever loved, 1 by 1, & so now feel just a little blessed, in spite of being here alone.

*Forgot to say, I took a walk this afternoon up the Harmony Road, & part way up the Coxey Brown Road, before my breath gave out. Lovely views. Not a soul stirring. A few dogs barked, a cow mooed, and a rooster looked as though he meant business, but I strongly suspect it wasn't me he was thinking of.

10.30pm. Warmer so that even freezing feels better. Windy with sunshine.

December 26, 1963

6.45am. Back to 20 below freezing again. What happens? Fire burning well. Slept better than I ought to have done. Did not dream of anybody I know.

9am. All four men at work today! I was late bringing the tray over. They seem tired, but light-hearted, I think. I asked whether they all enjoyed their dinners. They didn't really answer, but they seemed to like being asked. –Ate too much, Davy said.

*Marce & Dicky Bird working on the new stairs, Davy & Rip, tearing out the ones on the bottom floor, as they say these are rotten.

4.45pm. All quiet now. Had a look. Lots of heavy timber at top for new stairs, bottom ones reduced to rubble of splinters & broken pieces.

10pm. Almost too warm by afternoon, over 50. House is stuffy tonight. Nice sunshine.

December 27, 1963

9.45am. Same sort of work as yesterday, Davy & Rip carrying & wheelbarrowing destroyed old stairs across the road into The Patch.

1pm. Davy & Rip have lit a bonfire in The Patch.

4.30pm. Still a thread of smoke from the bonfire. Everyone gone. Had a look & it seems much of the heavy wood is in place for the top stairs. Also a pile near where the bottom ones will go.

10.30pm. Not nearly so cold today. Sunshine & wet-looking frost this morning.

December 28, 1963

8.45am. Colder again & wind blowing. Looks like snow.

11.30am. Went to Acme in Middletown today ($12). Also drove ½ way to Frederick to find a liquor store, as I had the thought that I really ought to give the men something for themselves. Bought four fifths of whiskey.

2pm. Finished last of chicken for lunch. Endless, some birds. It should say this in the World Book Encyclopaedia, "Chicken: a small feathered bird which expands in volume when cooked."

4.30pm. Watered Xmas tree & tea-ed myself. Pleased with my tidy little home. Would like Alex to see it just as it is, as I think he would smile.

10.45pm. Some light snow, so that everything capped with it, roofs & fences & trees. Reading Welty. So convincing.

December 29, 1963

7am. Very very cold again. Nice early dawn.

10am. Watched them all going to church. Walked over to The Corner & just strolled around the cold rooms, calculating the changes. Hearing my own footsteps. Smelling the food I'll cook, listening to the music I'll play. Dreaming is a great pleasure when it is what you need most.

11.45am. Saw all the folks coming back from church. Realized what a fool I must look as I rush out every Sunday to greet them, as if I am Hester Prynne, unable to join them.

*Cinch, who is shaped like Aunt Jemima, came up to me smiling & said she'd been eating my cake. She says it will be my fault if she gets fat.

*I asked her whether she had a good Christmas. She said she ate too much. She also said she liked listening to her grandson tell her "what a big time he was gonna have with them presents of his'n". The other women all now look on me with the wary affection they'd offer a house-trained tiger.

10pm. Dry & bright today, a little windy. Did I really watch "Lassie", or did I only imagine it?

December 30, 1963

7am. Very cold again. Blue with frost in the early light.

9.45am. Marce & the others (not John John) here at 7.45. At 8, the old man with the flat-bed truck came & all the men spilled out to unload some large machinery. One piece is definitely a saw of some kind, but the others I'm not sure of. They carried all of them around & into the middle floor from the back door.

*Not much noise over there now. Some sawing, I think.

2.15pm. After lunchtime tray, I see that now Dicky Bird & Marce are putting in the heavy timbers on the lowest stairway, effectively starting it all over. Meanwhile, Davy & Rip are taking up pieces of the middle stairway (which I thought was fine).

5pm. Some progress on lowest stairs, middle ones mostly as they were.

*Large machines for working in wood. One is a saw with a round blade, one with a long blade like a rope, a long thin one I don't understand, & a squat one I don't understand. There are also other saws & toolboxes everywhere.

10pm. Glistening full moon tonight. Not above freezing all day, dry as cold dust.

December 31, 1963

6.30am. Coldest morning yet: 0 degrees! Floor & walls are cold. Not much wind, so fire a little reluctant. Afraid I'll choke it with over-eagerness.

9am. Men at work sawing & hammering on stairs. Dicky Bird in fine voice, but on a white theme: one minute about his sport coat & pink carnation, another minute about the brew for which the G Men, T Men & Revenuers too are trying to book his daddy.

*I gave them all their whiskey this morning, not being sure whether they would all leave without a word this evening. Every one of them, Marce included, said –Thank ya! Marce added, –Hot d[]mn!

3.30pm. Rip just knocked on my door to say they were finished early today. Next week, he says they'll get more done on "them steps". I wished him a Happy New Year. –Thank you, ma'am, he said.

9.30pm. Fire still too warm for sleeping, really, but going to trust it is safe. Barely 20 this afternoon, & sky like ice water all day. Can't face "Andy Williams Show".

11pm. Got back out of bed, worried about fire.

*New Year's Eve. Tom is an auld acquaintance more & more forgot. (Sorry, Tom!) But what is Alex? If he were here, right now, tonight, facing me, the fading embers & the paltry dregs of my leftover wine, all I'd have to say to him would sound angry. Mad as Hecuba. Raving for the wrongs he's done me & to the boy I so loved in him.

*I am angry with him for his own faithless, wanton, lusty anger. An anger that couldn't even be true to its real source, but which philandered with every cause it could find. Oh, he spread it about, that boy. So now I want to shout at him & tell him how being a man on those terms is being a child. How loving means throwing everything into the dark stream until you see the island you make rise up before you. Why walking away from tragedy just leaves dirty footprints of pain everywhere you wander. I want to shout at him until he is grown-up enough to hate me properly, to fear his own hatred & not to seek shelter from it. A man should be obliged to cut himself with the edges of everything he breaks. I want to shout out my hatred of him for what he has done, or let be done, to Tom, to me & to himself. I want to hate him just long enough to feel the point of the blade touch my heart before it is pulled away forever. I want to be able to hate him without costing him his life. But I am too afraid.

*Tonight I will sleep in hope that there is no one who can hear my prayers.

January 1, 1964

9am. Hung over with remorse today, not wine. Must try to forgive myself for last night's barbarism. I know it does no real harm, but mothers are always superstitious, at least where their children are concerned.

*Happy New Year, 1964. I wish I knew what my resolutions are.

1.15pm. Had an early lunch and walked up the Brethren Church Road. I tried counting graves in both cemeteries, but both times I doubted myself, recounted, & came up with a different number. Perhaps, there is some metaphor in this that I cannot quite grasp.

2pm. Realized after coming home that I hadn't seen (or heard) Paul & Joanie for a long time, so walked back up to their house & took them a note, wishing them a Happy NY & saying I was looking forward to springtime & more evening music. They weren't home, so I put the note inside their mailbox, then walked ½ way back, realized the mailman might mistakenly take the note, so went back & put it inside their storm door.

4.30pm. Wrote longish letter to Ags, telling her I was keeping busy with project, but promising nothing.

9.45pm. Below 20 this morning & foggy. Hardly got to freezing all day, with rain & snow mixed. Drizzling & windy now. Watched some of "Ben Casey", but gave up.

January 2, 1964,

9am. Men all at work today, showing no ill effects of whiskey consumption. Davy & Dicky Bird gone to the top floor & seem to be prodding at floorboards. Rip & Marce putting in heavy bits of lowest stairway.

11.30am. Ingalls truck came about 10, piled high with lumber & insulation & other things. I walked over to watch what was happening, going around the back, through the hall & on to the high porch. This time there was the original white driver & the black man assisting. All four of the others helped.

*Apart from the insulation, which they unloaded first beside the stairs up to the wash house, they unloaded a very large pile of smoother, prettier wood. It smelled nice even from upstairs. They seemed to be sorting this out, so that some went into the lowest floor, & some they piled on the porch (wider pieces, slightly different color).

    *At one point, Marce said to the white driver, –Hey, your partner here's from Jefferson. Where you from? –H[]ll, he said, I'm from Jefferson too. –Ain't that somethin'? Marce said. Maybe you're related. Dicky Bird made a high-pitched sound, like Eeeeee! The others laughed & I couldn't see anyone's faces.

    *They've only just finished carrying all the wood inside, some of it to middle floor &, I think, the insulation to the upper middle.

5pm. Men gone home now. John John not with them. I had a look inside. Quite a few of the boards on the top floor have been taken up. The lowest stairs seem to be shaping up.

10.30pm. Much warmer today, sunny & dry, in the 40s this afternoon.

January 3, 1964

9.15am. Men all at work today, same arrangement as yesterday.

    *Just had a call from Hartsock. He is coming around this afternoon to have a look.

2.30pm. Saw Hartsock's car on the Common about an hour ago, so walked over to The Corner to collect the lunchtime tea & coffee tray. He had evidently been there a while & was talking to Marce & Rip about the uppermost stairs. If Marce's face were a clock, I could say his mouth had slid to about 4.30 with impatience. Lots of tap tapping on the top floor as Davy straightened old nails. Dicky Bird was sawing replacement floorboards. Hartsock apologized & said he had meant to knock at the Mary House before he left. I walked him to his car (he refused to stay for tea), & he told me things seem to be right on schedule. He asked how I am & I told him I was thinking of emigrating to Monaco (it was the first thing that came into my head). He laughed, finally, & said he thought that was an oil company.

4.45pm. John John just left after coming to update me. (He looks taller?) I said there seems to be a lot going on over there. He said they are going to insulate the top floor, refit the boards, then work their way down the house. All the while they are going to build the new stairways. I asked him how things are back at school. Boring, he said, but he liked doing Music.

10.30pm. Even milder today, from near freezing to mid-50s. Nice sunshine. Just watched "The Farmer's Daughter" for the first time. Another woman shaking up a man & his sons.

Here, Rattler, here!

After all, she was only forty-two. He was only forty-five. It was too soon. Much too soon. What was the problem? What was his problem?

Irene looked at herself in the mirror. She could see nothing the matter. All right, she wasn't the girl she was twenty years ago. But she was in fine shape. Plenty of men thought so, she was sure of it. What was the matter with Harold?

He simply took no notice, that was the problem. He got up so early in the morning, and after he got himself ready to go, and brought her her tea in bed, he ran around the house like a man possessed. He sorted the laundry. He put away the cups and plates and bowls and pans that had dried in the rack overnight. He fed the dog and the cat, laid out the children's clothes for school, tidied up the whole downstairs, organized his papers from his desk and briefcase, scraped the windscreen of the car, and still always managed to be the first one into the school staffroom, the first one into his own classroom every day. It was always the same.

He worked so hard and yet was hopeless when it came to securing anything like a raise, let alone a promotion. Hadn't Irene been the one to persuade him to take on the after-school coaching? Hadn't it been her instigation that led him to coordinate the annual staff barbecue, the Christmas Party, the Easter Egg Hunt, the Thanksgiving Fair? She had steered him into becoming staff representative for the PTA, just so that he would have the support of the parents (he was, of course, so charming when he wanted to be). And now, with the remedial teacher off work for the foreseeable future, she had even had to point out to him how taking on those duties would ingratiate him with the Principal. Honestly, if it weren't for her, he'd be getting nowhere.

He was no better when he came home in the evenings. She had to coax him to help with dinner, and afterwards he acted as though he resented reading bedtime stories to their youngest (who so looked forward to it, because he did the characters' voices so well). Then he spent his time marking papers, and planning lessons. It just never ended with him. Typically, when he finally did crawl into bed, he was asleep as soon as his head found the pillow. He had no time for her at all. None.

She spoke to her girlfriends, of course, and that was some help. They had recommended cocktails, negligees, music. None of it did any good. She didn't dare talk to her mother about the situation (she had always thought Harold a poor excuse for a man anyway). But she did speak to her aunt, whose advice was simple. Biology, she said. Chemistry. You need to take control of his machinery, she said. She had a recipe that was sure to work. It involved making a stew out of ingredients irresistible to the male libido: beef, eggs and red wine. She'd have to fight him off with a club.

Irene waited until Fair Week. Friday would be the day. She had arranged for her mother to take all four of the children to the Fair using their free tickets from school. Harold would come home after his half day, and Irene would be waiting for him. She had prepared everything.

Harold came home at lunchtime, just as she expected, and he was, as he always was these days, ravenous. He sat his briefcase down on the sofa. Something sure smells good, he said. Then he went upstairs to change out of his work clothes and to put on something looser, just the way he liked to every day. (He imagined this afternoon would be a good chance to do that weeding Irene had been reminding him of.)

When he came back downstairs, Irene slid a plateful of her meat and eggs in red-wine gravy on to his placemat at the table. What's all this, he said? Irene sat down opposite him and waited. Her own placemat was empty.

I've had mine, she said. I thought you'd like something special today. After you've been working.

Harold sat down and looked at the plate. He remembered to look up at her then, and he smiled. Golly, he said, if I'd expected this, I wouldn't have …

But he didn't finish his sentence. He didn't like to admit to the doughnuts he'd had from his desk at work.

Tuck in, she said.

Harold picked up his fork and started on a corner of the plate. Irene watched him so closely that there was nothing he could do but finish it all and have a small second helping.

C'mon, she said. I thought you'd like to lie down and rest for a little.

Well, I'm pretty full, Harold said. Anyway, I've got some things to do. He looked around at the house that had somehow grown messy in the few hours he'd been at work.

We'll do it later, Irene said. She took him by the hand and led him upstairs.

Harold hadn't yet put his shoes on (Irene didn't like him to wear them around the house), so it was easy for her to force him to lie down on his side of the bed. He crossed his legs at the ankle and rested his hands on his chest. There was a gurgling just above his belt.

Oh, my, Irene said.

Sorry, he said.

She rested her hand on his thigh and waited. As he stared at the ceiling, she practiced coy looks that she might give him, confident that he couldn't see her face.

Harold rolled over uncomfortably. I'm not so sure this is a good idea, he said.

Mm, she sighed.

Harold belched unexpectedly. I'm so sorry, he said.

He swung his feet to the floor and sat up.

Irene was angry. Are you all right? she said.

Well, he said.

Irene shook her head. He really was hopeless.

Uh, he said, and stood up suddenly, and ran towards the bathroom. In a moment, Irene heard the gasping horrid sounds of vomiting.

Aw, damn, Harold said from the bathroom. There was a shuffling and he came back holding his trousers at arm's length. I got a little on my leg, he said. He dropped them into a heap by the door, then he sat down on the edge of the bed and hooked his socks off with his thumbs. He swung his legs up and lay flat.

Sorry, he said.

Irene just looked at him. She counted. When she reached 98, Harold was asleep.

Irene looked at her husband. Through the gap in his boxer shorts she could see his flaccid genitals. Biting her lip in bitterness, she slipped her hand into the gap and felt around them: hot, a little damp, and altogether inactive. She massaged his scrotum. Harold's face was unchanging. She took his penis, his cock, his dick, his pecker, his manhood into her fingers and rubbed it. Slowly at first, then more quickly. Harold's mouth opened slightly, and he might have been snoring. Irene pulled a little at him, jerked at him, squeezed and shook him. Harold's eyes stayed shut, and Irene took her hand back towards her own body. She went into the bathroom and washed both hands, and then went back downstairs to wait for her mother to return with the children.

The next morning, Harold was awake and dressed by 5.30am. He looked terrible, but he managed to complete all his chores before it was time to leave for work. Before going out the door, he scribbled a note on the envelope from the phone bill. *I'll stop and get more eggs on the way home. I love you. xxx*

January 4, 1964

1.30pm. Back from Frederick: $22 at A & P (bought extra canned goods, dry things & stuff to be eaten cold, as I realized I hadn't put away stores in case the weather really does turn and the power goes off, though it looks now as though it won't).

*Also bought a copy of You Can't Go Home Again as it is the only one I haven't read.

2.30pm. After eating late lunch, I decided to clean the downstairs, starting with the fireplace. I took the ashes out & thought I'd bring some more wood in, when to my complete surprise I see that the lean-to is completely re-filled with wood! They must have brought it this morning, though I hadn't said anything about wanting more. Still, glad they brought it. Must remember to thank them Monday.

8.30pm. In spite of myself, I'm once again feeling randomly angry with Alex. How do I dare?

10.30pm. Weather like yesterday, but a little breezier. Watched some of the 9 o'clock movie, but picture still a little fuzzy.

January 5, 1964

9.45am. Just watched them all going to church. I would like to pray. It seems like such a strange thing. Someone can show you what to do, can do it alongside you, & yet you can never know if you are doing it right. It isn't like a piano lesson, & presumably, there is no rehearsal, as every performance has an Audience.

12pm. Met them all at the benches by The Corner on their way home. Cinch was waving something at me as she approached, & I was flattered that she had evidently expected (hoped?) to see me. —Here, she said, thrusting a very old-fashioned looking little booklet at me. —I brung this'n for ya. I looked and it was an almanac, called "J. Gruber's", & it is for this year. It has all the usual things inside, plus "Household Hints" & "Poultry Notes" & multiplication tables, ads for knives, trusses, cellar doors & everything else I'm every likely to need. —They give 'em out in church, Cinch said.

    *While we were all talking, I noticed the men, none of whom would sit down, all took on a habit of shrugging their shoulders at intervals, as if they felt a sudden draft. It made them look like so many nervous pigeons.

10.45pm. Weather like yesterday, but just a little colder. Below freezing this morning. Watched "Jaimie McPheeters".

January 6, 1964

9.30am. Corner as busy as a hive today, all sawing, insulation-stuffing & hammering.

250

*Marce was sawing when I stopped him to say thanks for bringing me the firewood. He looked at me a moment trying, I felt, to think of what sort of reply he should make. Finally, he just nodded and said, –Uh huh, holding each syllable out to twice its usual length: uuuuuh huuuuuh.

4.30pm. Same end to the working day. John John sweeping (dust everywhere). Most of the floorboards now down upstairs (I climbed the ladder to see!). Can just see outer shape of new stairs coming.

10pm. Much colder today, hardly over freezing. Dark & threatening snow, but just rain all day. Just watched "Wagon Train".

January 7, 1964

8.45am. Foggy this morning & a little above freezing. Men at work as usual.

11am. Can hear all sorts of machinery running over the road.

2pm. Came back with tray. Davy & Dicky Bird now working on the upper middle floor as the top one is finished, I think. Dust everywhere as some of the big machines being used. Smoothing things, it looks like. Dicky Bird giving his all to "Please Release Me".

10.30pm. Mostly rainy all day again, temperature around 40.

January 8, 1964

9.15am. Very cold this morning, below 20. Sunshine though. Men working like yesterday. Upper middle floor is much more complicated & more original floorboards are broken, I notice.

5pm. Men gone. Didn't notice John John until the truck pulled out. Didn't go over to see the afternoon's work.

11pm. Hardly above freezing all day. Nice sunshine & pretty sunset.

January 9, 1964

9.30am. Men all working as yesterday. Can now see how elaborate & complicated these upper stairs are, curving as they do. Rip very skilled, but Marce clearly the boss of this one.

1.30pm. Collected lunch tray. Work as usual going on. Dicky Bird belting out something asking Why, Baby, Why?

3pm. In the paper today that President Johnson, in his state-of-the-union address has declared a "War on Poverty". This comes, I think, after so many many people have had to make peace with it. I suppose it is an initiative of sorts.

5pm. Men gone. I went & had a look before they left. John John cleaning up as usual, lots of long chips, short chips & sawdust. Marce barking at him telling to watch "where'na H[]ll he walks" & not to fall off the beams where the floor should be. Stairs now seem to have sides & places to walk, so when they'd gone I gingerly tried them, holding on to the step in front of me. Upstairs such a beautiful space now. Realized when I came down I may have left footprints on the clean wood.

10.30pm. Temperature around freezing all day. Rainy this morning, then showers, then drizzle. Watched "Rawhide".

Fireball Mail

I, LittleWound, tell this story.

It was in the time after the slave-girl came to live with me, the one they came to call BlackMary. It was around the time that

Master Gledhill cut the holes and put windows into my lodging and removed the last of the mill's stores of sacks and staves. He had the carpenters put in stairs instead of a ladder and build a second pallet, on which BlackMary could sleep. He gave us a table and each of us a chair.

It was at this time up in the hollow that there lived a family named Blickenstaff. They were farmers and labourers and they did their work with respect, though their nest was like that of the wrens. They had a son named Upton who grew to manhood and used to work on the waggons trading barrel-staves, shingles, oak-bark and other wood to Fredericktowne, and so he moved through the valley and into the reaches of the mountain, staying away at nights when the journeys could not be completed in a day.

Once he was travelling to collect a load of planks in the valley that is called the Run, the one where the spruces are thickest. It was here that he met a family named Rinehart – brothers to match all the fingers of a hand, a father and a mother who was dying in her bed. But there was also one daughter and her name was Rachel, and she was the only light in the forest where they lived. Her beauty marked her out beyond all the women Upton saw on his travels, and he desired her for his wife. For this reason, he sought to become friends with her father and brothers.

Upton wooed Rachel as some men woo the women they desire. He never spoke his own praise, he looked at the ground or at the sky whenever she looked at him, and he trembled if ever anything anyone said sounded to him like the voice of a beast. Seeing Upton's joy in Rachel, the men in the family were not filled with pleasure, because they knew that if they lost her they would lose the woman who cooked and cleaned for them, who washed their clothes and who tended them when they were sick. For her part, Rachel liked Upton as he seemed to her and she imagined that becoming the wife of one man would be better than being like the wife of six. She felt she should encourage him.

In front of all the others she praised him and looked upon him with favour. Afraid for what they might be losing, her brothers thought among themselves that they would shame Upton, and so drive him from Rachel's affection. To this end, when the waggon was loaded and darkness began to settle on the Run, they invited him to join them for their dinner.

There is a thing for which the people of the Run are known among the villagers, and this is their ability to drink. It used to be said that the waters of the Run were like the honeysuckle, but in these days, it was as if all the waters had been distilled into whiskey. And like the other folks whose cabins were scattered in this valley, the Rineharts could drink like fish drink. In this way, they hoped to show Rachel that Upton was either a fool or not a man in the way that she knew men could be.

To his credit, Upton was not a fool, and he knew that he did not drink whiskey of any kind, least of all the kind of liquor brewed in the Run. He had grown to manhood drinking spice-wood and birch teas, water and milk. Though he ate the food he was offered, he shunned their drinks, no matter how many times they offered them.

At last, when weariness began to settle over them all and there were no longer any sounds to be heard but the owls, the bobcats and the coyotes, Upton rose from the table and said he would sleep under his waggon, as he always did when travelling. As he stood up to go, Rachel watched him in confusion. She had never seen a man refuse to drink whiskey, a man who stayed sober when those around him didn't, and who was able to refuse their coaxing and even their teasing. Her heart trembled when he turned to look at her before he went out the door. In his face, she read the need for her to make a decision. Her eyes looked then upon her father and brothers and she spoke words that tasted like nettles in her mouth.

I reckon a woman ought to know when a man can hold his drink.

Before the dawn broke through the tent of the trees, Upton had harnessed his horses and led them out of the Run, without seeing anyone in the Rinehart family to say goodbye. As the horses jogged on, and the air heated with the day, he thought over Rachel's words. How should he interpret them? In his mind, he listened to them as if with all the voices he had ever heard. By the time he arrived in Fredericktowne, he had decided what he thought he should do. He would learn to drink as they drank, so that when he returned to them on another day, he would be able to shame them all with his ability to hold his drink in a way that none of them could. And so that night, instead of sleeping under his waggon near the turnpike at Fredericktowne, he went to a tavern and bought a bottle of whiskey to have at once, and another to have on the road back to Harmony.

He found the first bottle easy to drink. People he met, men and women spoke to him, and everyone seemed to be filled with pleasure, and this was a feeling he enjoyed. In the morning, he found that the whiskey even helped the thunder in his head to soothe. But on the road, when there was no one for him to speak to, his thoughts grew to be like the night under the spruces once again, and he could hear Rachel's voice on the wind that scalded his face as he sat in the waggon-seat. The pain from his head moved to his throat and to his limbs, where he longed to put his arms around her and to feel her hair against his neck. The pain entered his chest where he craved to feel her hands holding him, and it slipped down his legs, making him want to lie down. But still, he was determined that he would be the man she would esteem beyond the men her father and brothers were. He opened the bottle he had brought along and drank from this while his horses cooled themselves in the shade by the creek near the cemetery where the Fishers have their farm.

Afraid that he would sleep, he put the bottle into the seat on the waggon and drew the horses back again into their harness. He slipped when he tried to climb into the seat and bruised his face below the eye so that it looked like he had been punched. When, at last, he was in the seat he wetted his mouth with whiskey, and tried to wave his hat at the horses, but his hat had gone, and he had forgotten where. He shouted to the horses and didn't recognize his voice. Still, they moved on and he topped the hill pointing towards the place where the streams cross and the corner mill lay.

As the horses came into the bend, the road lifts its shoulder to the side facing the mountain, and beside it, the land falls away, angling towards the stream. It is here that the driver needs to restrain the animals who want to let their legs stretch and let the slope ease their stride. But Upton was being led now only by the horses. His thirst had grown within him until it scratched at his eyes from the inside. He dropped the reins as he tried to pull the cork from the bottle, and the trace horse, just beneath Upton's feet, felt the pressure loosen, and he let his stride relax. On the inside of the curve his speed outran his partner, and the waggon began to jolt. Upton leant forward to pick up the fallen reins, but as he did so, the waggon tipped towards the stream, and the waggon overturned, throwing him into the ravine below the side of the road. The horses uprighted themselves and dragged what remained of the waggon like a shock of corn until they reached the bottom of the hill, where they stopped and stood, waiting for a command. But Upton had landed with his face in the water, which ran over his shoulders and back until he disappeared. It may have been that he drowned, or it may have been that his bones separated, and he died. It was Mr Fisher who found him. He and his son rode to Upton's family in the hollow, and they agreed to bury him in the cemetery at the top of the hill. They borrowed Mr Fisher's axe to break up the waggon into kindling, though they kept the harness and all the fittings, which they took home in their spring-cart.

January 10, 1964

9.30am. Foggy this morning. Work as usual over the road.

11.15am. Not as loud from machinery this morning.

2pm. Came back with the lunch tray. Marce at work turning spindles for the stairs. Very pretty to watch them made, like a potter's wheel, but sideways. Rip fitting them & measuring pieces.

4.45pm. John John just came to tell me that Davy & Dicky Bird have "got that floor all up now" & will finish it next week. Stairs should be done too. Then next floor, next stairs.

*I asked him whether he had helped stack the firewood & he said he had. I thanked him & he grinned. I asked why they decided to bring it & he told me his father said I needed it, & he didn't want to wait until I got 'round to asking, as he might then be too busy "to do anything about it". Sounds very likely.

*When John John left, I noticed he hopped on to the truck by vaulting over the side. He is taller.

10.30pm. Not as cold today. Freezing this morning, but over 40 this afternoon. Then the wind picked up & it is positively screeching out there now. Watched "The Farmer's Daughter". Glad it is on channel 7, as 4 would be lost completely in this wind.

January 11, 1964

7.30am. Very very cold this morning, well below 20. Dry, it seems.

11.30am. Back from shopping at Acme in Middletown ($11). Bought an "Archie" comic for JJ to say thanks for the firewood.

2pm. Suddenly remembered feeling after a dream I had this morning, though I cannot really recall the dream. Feeling was one of anxious watching, as if something just about to appear over a horizon & the light not good enough to see.

10.30pm. A very pretty day with sunshine, but cold. Hardly above freezing. Movie uninspiring.

January 12, 1964

7.45am. Terrifically cold this morning, 14, I think. Quite foggy. Radio says snow likely tonight.

11.45am. Just got back after walking home with church ladies. They are still trying to talk me into coming to services. Cinch says, —It ain't gonna hurt ya none.

1.30pm. Made soup for lunch thinking, if the electricity goes, I could warm up some tomorrow in a pan on the fireplace (somehow).

11.15pm. Rather gray all day. Just looked outside & there is some snow falling. Watched "Jaimie McPheeters".

January 13, 1964

7am. Even colder this morning than yesterday. Snow about 1" over things & falling lightly. Foggy, too.

9am. Men all here today & talking about snow. Work seems as expected. They arrived with more bags of insulation.

1.45pm. Collected lunch tray. Insulation just about finished on the upper middle floor. Rip sanding the bannister pieces as Marce fits them.

3.15pm. Rip just knocked on my door. He says they're quitting early today before the snow gets bad. —We still gotta get over the mountain, he said.

3.30pm. Snow falling hard now, already 2 more inches. Still very cold, below 20.

11pm. Watched the 9 o'clock movie. Still snowing. Electricity still working (obviously).

January 14, 1964

7am. Even colder this morning! Frosty thermometer looks like 9 degrees. Quiet as can be, & light gone blue with the snow. Looks at least 10" deep.

*Will hold off on coffee & tea until I see them arrive.

8.30am. No sign of the men today, so glad I waited with the tray.

10pm. Never reached 20 degrees today. Snow officially 12" deep. Very dark tonight & no moon.

*Had leftover soup, warmed on the oven. Afterwards, regretted that I didn't experimentally try heating it on the fireplace, just to see.

Cripple Creek

I, LittleWound, tell this story.

It was in the time after the Catoctins no longer made war with the Piscataway, but before the Shawnee came to the mountains toward the setting sun.

It was a custom of the Catoctins that no soul could feel itself to be an orphan. When a man or a woman, a boy or a girl, was left without parents or siblings, aunts, uncles or cousins, the people spoke to one another, and took that person into their lodge so that they might become part of a family once again. It happened that a warrior was killed by the Shawnee and his widow died of the sweating sickness, leaving a daughter named MovingRobe. She was taken as a girl into the lodge of family with one child of their own, a son named RedWing. From that day on, Redwing and MovingRobe were raised as brother and sister.

As they grew to become adults, they spoke together often of how the time would come when each would marry. They spoke of the kind of man that would make a husband of esteem for MovingRobe, and of the kind of woman that would bring honour to RedWing. But all the while, in their hearts they felt a passion for one another. Each felt that the other had no peer among the people. But neither dared to speak or to intimate their feelings, fearing that to do so would bring disgrace to their relationship, to their parents, and to the village altogether. But as time passed, though there was never a cause of shame that arose between them, their relations became much like those of husband and wife. Sometimes, MovingRobe would call out to him, Coo-wah! And indeed, RedWing would come to her, as though it were his wife speaking to him. Sometimes, MovingRobe would speak to him alone, speaking of the things that made her heart sail like the clouds, or fall like the leaves, and he would answer her, To kee, to kee, just as a husband might answer the wife of his spirit.

The rest of the village saw them and wondered, just as people might, what was the relationship between them? No one spoke of dishonour, for no one had seen or heard anything to their shame. But the bond between them was such that RedWing became the suitor of none, and no suitor brought gifts to MovingRobe's door.

The winters grew upon both and the parents who had sheltered and nourished them took their way upon the spirit road. There was no longer anyone in their lodge but themselves, and still the people looked upon them and said, Wakan, wakan – holy, wonderful.

Peace became theirs and remained in their hands and in their acts until such a time as MovingRobe began to pine that neither she nor RedWing had brought children to the people, that they had fostered neither a boy nor a girl to whom they might have given their ways and their happiness. Each of them at night lay in their blankets and raised their eyes to the heavens, asking the gods to remember them if there ever should be a child whose love they might nurture.

But these prayers were not to be fulfilled. It happened that at the time when the dogwoods blossomed the colour of the dawn that RedWing began to feel that the sounds in his head had grown to resemble the hoofbeat of the stags. The roar in his ears tormented him days and nights and the heat in his limbs chilled so that his arm became numb like a branch fallen from a tree. He lay and stared at MovingRobe, and though his mouth opened, no words came to her. He died in silence, holding her hand.

For a time MovingRobe, once again without family, walked like a ghost among the people, her eyes finding joy in no one, her ears closed to the speech that sought to give her comfort. Finally, a day came, when the butterflies fanned the air and the swallows chattered like falling acorns, that she was seen alone, sitting in the hand of an elm, looking towards the sky from where the wind would blow in summer. Her hair swam about her face, and even the children knew she had died. When she was taken down and laid in the place of the spirits the people spoke together of her and her brother Red-Wing, and as one, they chanted, Wakan, wakan. Holy. Wonderful.

January 15, 1964

7.15am. Colder still this morning! Zero!

9.30am. Men on time for work today. I said to Rip that that surprised me. He said they left a ½ hour early because the roads "at Highland" were pretty bad.

*Davy & Dicky Bird inspecting & poking at boards on middle floor. Marce & Rip repairing bits of middle stairs.

2pm. Collected lunch tray. Floorboards up here & there, not as complicated as upstairs. Middle stairway nearly repaired.

*Marce said, —Hey. We're gonna be goin' 'fore too long, 'fore them roads freezes up. I thanked him, though it seems to me they are already frozen.

3.15pm. Men gone for the day.

9.30pm. Pretty day with the snow now very hard to the touch. It goes yellow & orange in places with the sunlight. Below freezing all day. Watched "The Virginian".

January 16, 1964

7am. Only 5 degrees this morning.

8.45am. Men working as usual. I asked Dicky Bird how the roads were this morning. He looked all around the inside of his head for a moment before speaking, & finally said, — Well, pretty good out from under the trees, but the Hollow still ain't fit.

1.30pm. Collected the tray. Insulation looks as though it is all used up. Floorboards going down. Could hear Marce downstairs talking to Rip.

3.15pm. Men left early again today. Not sure why, as it seems so much warmer. Don't think I'll bother going over this evening.

10.15pm. Temperature got to almost 40 this afternoon, & the inevitable run off starting from the snow. The Common has long dirty streaks of water edging down to the bridge on the Hollow Road. Sunny all day. Watched "Perry Mason". I wish everything they say didn't have the tones of cunning, pride or defiance.

January 17, 1964

9am. A bit warmer this morning, but still under 20. Puddles all covered with a silver film of ice, edged with lace flowers.

*Men arrived as usual. All four working on the flooring in the middle floor. I suspect this is to make it easier to use the machines.

2.30pm. Collected lunch tray & noticed that I was right, as the room with the machines (big one near the stairwell) is finished off. Marce & Rip working on the stairs. Davy & Dicky Bird on the flooring.

*Dicky Bird very warmed up, singing about his lover flying too high for his little old sky so now he's moving on.

4.45pm. Saw John John go in earlier, so walked over to save him the trip to the Mary House. When the time came to go, Dicky Bird, Rip & Davy headed for the truck. Marce, obviously waiting to hear John John's report to me, looked at him & said, 'Ain't ya gonna tell her? John John was suddenly so nervous he could hardly speak. He finally got out that they'd finish the floor next week & keep going on the stairs. His father shook his head & walked past the boy & out the door without a word. I told John John to have a good weekend. He said he would. I finally remembered to give him the comic. He lit up when he looked at it, then rolled it & hid it in his shirt before anyone else could see.

10.30pm. Dry all day, a little gray to start, but then sunny after the breeze picked up. Watched "Route 66". Forgot how good this can be.

January 18, 1964

7am. Only 10 degrees again this morning. Don't think I'll go to A & P as the roads might be too frozen.

11am. Made a quick trip to Acme ($11). Fire burning & staying inside now.

10.45pm. Warmed up this afternoon in the sunshine & now water running in the ditches. Some shrinking in the snow & earthy streaks visible in places.

January 19, 1964

8am. Still bitter out there, like yesterday. Now foggy too.

12pm. Met the churchgoers going home today, near to the Mary House. –Where y'all been? they said. They'd been hoping I'd walk them down the road again, I think. After this, I just might.

*Could see the hem of Cinch's dress – dark red. Nice with her coat & gloves.

10.30pm. Stayed foggy all day. Warmed up enough to melt some more. Watched "Jaimie McPheeters" & also "Bonanza". What's going on?

January 20, 1964

9.30am. A little bit warmer this morning, 19, I think. Foggy again.

*Men arrived as usual, more insulation on the truck, unloaded into the lowest floor. Rip & Marce on the stairway, Davy & Dicky Bird on the middle floor.

2pm. Middle floor seems to be all finished now. Stairs ongoing. Davy & Dicky Bird moving things around on the lowest floor. Scattered raindrops.

3pm. Very noisy across the road this afternoon, hammering & sawing.

4.45pm. John John arrived & went in the lower front door. He came back out shortly after, his arms full of splintered up wood. He headed across the bridge with it & dumped it in the Patch where the last bonfire was. I went over to investigate. Apparently lowest floor of all is in worse shape than expected & needs to be replaced. I now have a new stairway starting to rise up from a non-existent floor.

*John John & Davy looked miserable in the back of the truck, rain running on their faces.

10.30pm. Started to rain this afternoon & got warmer. Snow shrinking now.

I think of Handsome Molly

I, LittleWound, tell this story.

It was in the season when the sky was like the centre of a flame. The farmers near the Potomack had sent their slaves and their horses to hide them among their cousins in the valley and on the mountain, to keep them away from the invaders, for the Washechu were again at war. We saw nothing but we were told that the Washechu hatred was such that they left the warriors in sunset coats to rot in the fields where they fell.

It was after this, when the fighting was finished that Sergeant Schroyer came home to his wife and his farm on the hillside below the road to Middletown. The sergeant's wife was named Martha and she was a woman of kindness but not insight, at least none that anyone reckoned. With her children she had grown to the width of a sheaf of wheat. She loved the sergeant like the lark loves the dawn. But there had been something in the fighting that had left him not like the man he had been before. His eyes shone like a man looking for buzzards in the sky, and he turned his head often, like someone who fears the tread of his enemies approaching.

There was a widow who lived in a cabin a half-day's walk from their farm, in the direction of Myersville. She earned her keep in the ways that widows do – sewing, drying herbs, making soaps, spinning cotton. It was to her that the sergeant came looking for a cure for Martha when her headaches kept her in the shade and in the quiet, away from her children and her duties. The widow gave him a paper filled with leaves of feverfew and told him to scatter them on cheese and to give them to Martha with water. When she put the paper full of herbs into his hand her fingers, scented with rose and with the softness of starlight, brushed against his hand. His eyes looked for hers, but he saw only her lashes, and his heart became like water inside him. His breath shivered and he turned away from her, forgetting everything of himself that he had ever known.

The feverfew worked as it should, and Martha's headaches became a memory. But the sergeant became a man without spirit. His tasks sat in his hands like stones and the days shrank his thoughts to shadows. He loved the widow in a mood that was not touched by anger or desire, but with only an echo of his pain and a recollection of the innocence that had been his as a child. He thinned and his presence in his home became no more than a draft in the corners of his family's days and nights.

Ending his sorrow became the only thing that concerned him. And just as a man who has lost his way in the forest will believe that every tree marks the path he seeks, the sergeant began to think that he would be freed if he gave a gift to the widow that somehow held the soul of the love he felt. If he could have given her the blood from his veins he would have done so. Instead, he found the thing that he treasured more than anything else, the thing he held as an emblem of his god as it had stood between him and the deaths he had witnessed, a thing that frightened him with its magic — the sword he had brought back from the war. This sword he took over the mountain to Fredericktowne and sold, trading the money he gained for a ring the colour of the sunlight as it lay upon his children's hair.

The sergeant wrapped the ring, the circle that held all his being, into the same paper the widow had used to hold the feverfew that stopped Martha's pain, and rode towards Myersville to give it to her, not caring whether this would become the day when his life ended.

But the widow was not at home. He waited until the sun melted like wax upon the mountaintop, but she never came into his sight. So he entered her house and lay the paper beneath the pillow where she would rest her head at night, praying to his god that her dreams would direct her steps to his love.

The days silenced and the frosts came again, but the sergeant learned nothing of the widow or her fate. But one day he saw the ring in its place on Martha's hand. She said nothing to explain how it had come to be hers and he never asked. But from that day he looked upon her as someone whose presence he understood as gracing his own. His love for the widow changed then, becoming like the sky forgetting the darkness as it becomes noon. While his love for Martha filled his body so that whenever he saw her, he trembled with joy, and he walked the rest of his days honouring her beyond all women.

January 21, 1964

9.30. At last it is so much warmer. Nearly 40 degrees this morning. Quite windy.

*Davy & Dicky Bird prying & cutting away at the bottom floor. Rip & Marce on the stairs. Bottom of the house smells of new wood & rot.

2.30pm. Collected the lunch tray. They have been trooping broken wood over the bridge all day to the Patch, getting quite a pile of it now.

5pm. Lowest floor now looking as ship-shape as a well-swept 200-year-old dirt floor can look. Davy told me John John was thinking that they'd find some coins under the floorboards & that he'd poked into every corner with a trowel, but "didn't find nothin'".

10.30pm. Got very windy indeed this afternoon, & over 50. No snow left now except the bruise-colored heaps in the corners left by the snow plows & stray bits like gray hairs under trees & bushes. Sunshine felt genuinely warm.

January 22, 1964

9am. Dicky Bird & Davy already burning pile of waste wood in the Patch. Others working on the machines & the stairs, Marce smoothing something, Rip measuring & fitting, with a large pencil over his very large ear.

10.15am. Ingalls truck arrived, piled with lumber. Same two men as last time delivering. Dicky Bird came over the bridge to help unload, leaving Davy to mind the shrinking fire. Nice of him, I thought.

11.30am. They unloaded the wood & sorted it out, piling planks on to the lower porch, & carrying big pieces inside.

*Marce's opening words to the two Ingalls men when they stepped out of the truck was, —Well, if it ain't the Jefferson brothers!

2pm. Large timbers now being cut & fitted for lowest floor. Hot enough working that they had the lower door open. Dicky Bird sweating his way through trying to saw while singing "North to Alaska". Davy looks like he's been dipped in grease.

4.45pm. Men gone now. Had a look around. Utility room floor, (bottom, beside kitchen) looks roughly set up with timbers. Whole kitchen now to do. Stairway now looking graceful. Needs bannister & spindles. Some spindles already in a pile, I see.

10.30pm. Weather much like yesterday, but not nearly so windy. Saw the last 30 minutes of "The Virginian". Easy to imagine the rest.

January 23, 1964

12.45pm. Got lunch tray back early. Floor timbers now filling in. Lots of spindles now. Rip planing pieces of bannister.

4.30pm. Spindles now almost finished, & most of bannister attached. Not much for John John to do. Still treasure-hunting, it looked like.

10.45pm. Just a little colder today. No wind, & beautiful sun. Everything muddy. Watched "Rawhide".

Where the saints abide

Carrie was twenty years old when she died. It was in the springtime, and it was over quickly. Sylvie went to her bedside every day, from her bed at home, to the bed in the hospital, and finally to her bed at home again. She and Carrie had been friends almost their whole lives. Carrie lived on 4th Street, and Sylvie lived on 3rd. Carrie went to the Catholic School, and Sylvie, who went to the local elementary, was fascinated by the little plaid skirt with a giant pin and the snowy white shirt that Carrie had to wear every day. It was what drew them together that very first day in the park. After that they were like sisters. They had no secrets. They grew at the same rate, so they often swapped clothes. They talked about music lessons, menstruation, parents, boys, school cliques, sex, The Future, dying and jobs. Carrie always liked to talk about jobs. At one time or other, she had wanted to be everything, do every job – stewardess, weight lifter, nun. When Carrie left for college, Sylvie started her first job as a secretary in an accountants' office. It was clean and precise, and never left her feeling challenged or even particularly under-valued. She was still working there, on Market Street in the centre of town, when Carrie died.

Almost every day Sylvie had lunch at the Valley Restaurant, a small family-run place down the street a few doors from her office. She liked the crab-and-vegetable soup. She liked the sand-wiches. She liked the way the older women in their tight synthetic uniforms recognized her, smiled, and never asked her questions with answers that were not on the menu.

On the Monday after Carrie's death, Sylvie was surprised, even slightly overwhelmed, by the fact that when she went into the Valley Restaurant, nothing had changed. The counters remained the same; the shelves of crockery, the same; the ashtrays; the scratches on the tables. Even the people who sat at the tables were the same people who were always there, always sitting at the same tables, or in the same booths. There was only one exception. A young man was sitting where Sylvie herself liked to sit – along the wall, at a small table near where the waitresses walked. The young man saw Sylvie looking at him and at his table, and he seemed to guess her thoughts. He stood up gently but quickly.

Please, he said. Have my seat. I was just leaving.

He took up his coffee cup and carried it away with him. Then he turned and looked at Sylvie briefly.

My name is Joe, he said, and smiled. Then he walked away, leaving his cup and saucer on the counter.

Sylvie sat down and thought. Was he just being polite, polite to a stranger? He had not asked her anything. Perhaps, he really was just leaving. Perhaps, he had seen her there before, and noticed that it was where she liked to sit. But then, she had never seen him before, and if he knew she liked to sit there, why did he sit there himself? Unless he wanted to meet her. Or unless he always left just at the moment when Sylvie always arrived, their two lives not touching, just sharing the same point-of-view, one after the other. The waitress came then, and Sylvie ordered the soup.

The next day, Sylvie went back to the Valley Restaurant at the hour of her usual lunch break. Her favourite table was empty. Joe was not there, not in the restaurant at all. She wanted, momentarily, to ask the waitress whether she had seen him today, but she was afraid that might seem strange. She was afraid, in case the waitress knew Joe and told him that a young woman, Sylvie, had asked about him. So when the waitress came, Sylvie only smiled and ordered the club sandwich.

Sylvie went back to the Valley Restaurant every day that week, but she did not see Joe there again. By Friday, she assured herself that the whole thing had been an innocent accident, that nothing had passed between them.

The following Monday was hard for Sylvie. The routine of going to work and then going home to the house where she had lived her entire life began to feel tiresome in a way it had never seemed tiresome before. She thought about Carrie all morning while she was at work, filing, answering calls, booking appointments. She wondered whether being dead was monotonous. What did Carrie have to look forward to now? Sylvie caught herself looking at her own reflection in the window and decided she was like what she saw – transparent, made of light. This shape, she thought, these colours, these are what I am. She felt very guilty having these attributes still being a part of herself when Carrie no longer had them.

By lunchtime Sylvie thought she had a headache. Instead of the Valley Restaurant, she decided she would go somewhere quieter, so she turned in the opposite direction outside the door of her office and went to the Old Town Tavern. In spite of its name, it was a small intimate restaurant with a slightly more upscale menu, and a more genteel clientele. As she went inside, she was pleased that there was no bell on the door. Instead, a nice woman in a print dress smiled at her and gestured Sylvie towards the tiny tables. As she passed by the bar, a dark-haired young man turned towards her. It was Joe.

Hello, he said. It's good to see you again. I have to be going. I work at the furniture store on the corner, and they don't like it if I'm late. Enjoy your lunch.

He smiled and walked away, leaving through the door where Sylvie had just entered. Sylvie sat down and sampled the ice water already on the table waiting for her. Why had he spoken to her in this way? What lay behind his simple words, his candid looks? How would she bear this feeling of her life adding new dimensions when Carrie's was not?

Sylvie did not sleep well that night, and by lunchtime the next day she was completely starving. She needed a lot of food that would be hearty, rough, aggressive, weighty. At lunchtime, she swept down the street and swung through the heavy door of the White Star, home of the best hotdogs anyone had ever seen. She planned to order two of the monsters, with chili and onions. She would drink a Coca Cola from the bottle with a straw, not holding back for the waitress to pour it into one of the little paper cones inside an aluminium goblet. But when she opened the door Sylvie saw how long the line was – men, women, workers of all kinds, were there in front of her, hungry and impatient. Fine, she thought. It would be worth the wait. The hungrier she would get, the more she would enjoy them. Maybe she would order three.

When her turn finally came, and her order was laid on a plate in front of her, Sylvie grabbed up her food and walked to the back of the restaurant to find a table. To her astonishment, all the tables were full, all the chairs taken.

There, someone said.

Sylvie saw a large man seated in the corner, wearing his hat far back so as not to shade his food, pointing to her left. Someone was getting up from the long lunch-counter table that ran along the wall, where people dined sitting on stools.

There, the man said again.

Someone was, indeed, leaving. The figure turned and a young white hand picked up the plate, the Coke bottle, and the soiled paper napkin. Sylvie's eyes travelled up the person's sleeve. It was Joe. Sylvie saw his face in the wall mirror. He saw her eyes find him.

Oh, hello, he said. I didn't know you ever came here.

He smiled and left his things on the waitress's work station, before edging around the crowd still lined up for food. Then he was gone.

Why would he think Sylvie wouldn't come here? Did he think she was a snob? Who did he think he was? Anyway, why shouldn't she go where she liked?

Sylvie chewed through the tough, cooling hotdogs, her temper sitting just beneath her skin. By afternoon, she knew, she would have indigestion.

For the rest of that week, Sylvie brought her own lunch and ate it at her desk. But by the next Monday, a fine warm day, she was eager for a walk outdoors. She made a deal with herself. She would go to the deli up the street on the corner, get something nice, and take it to Court Square to eat beside the fountain. If, just *if,* Joe should come into her view, either at the deli, or the street or the square, she would walk directly up to him and say something. She wasn't sure what she would say, but she was determined to speak up, and she was confident that the words would come if she waited.

Joe was not in the deli, or anywhere on the street, or at the square. Sylvie felt something between relief and disappointment. What had she been hoping to say? As she walked back towards her office, quickly, because it was quite a long walk, she thought she caught a glimpse of someone, a man, in a coat that she thought could be like the one she had seen Joe in. But she couldn't be sure. She wished she could be sure.

The next day it rained, and it rained for the remainder of the week. Sylvie sat at her desk and had sandwiches she made for herself the night before. Tuna, ham, cheese, bologna, BLT. She thought as she took them to pieces, eating them in little morsels. Is this what I have become? Someone who sits thinking gloomy thoughts while eating dull sandwiches? Someone who wonders whether a complete stranger – well, not 'complete', as she knew his name was Joe — is someone she could love, or someone who could love her? What would Carrie say if she knew? Could she ever have said this to Carrie? Would they have laughed over the phone about it, written amusing but kindly-worded letters over it?

Another Monday. The weather had turned warmer still, and Sylvie was feeling bold enough to come to work in her cream dress and sash, her light heels, and carry her white handbag. She had made a decision. At lunchtime, she was going to go to the furniture store on the corner and find Joe, ask him to lunch with her – anywhere! – laugh at his jokes, listen to his stories, touch his arm and be kind. She would be so very very kind. Then she would discover the truth of it all. Afterwards, on her own, she would reflect on the whole thing. She would ask herself questions about it all, asking them in the same way, the same tone, with the same words, that Carrie would have used. Carrie would be so proud of her for being so brave. She would recognize all the motives that Sylvie felt, and maybe she would feel them too. Then Sylvie would know she was doing the right thing. That's how she would know.

When Sylvie entered the department store's wide atrium, she asked the first sales clerk she met where she might find the young man named Joe. The clerk smiled at Sylvie.

He's upstairs, she said. The very top. You can't miss him.

January 24, 1964

9am. Around freezing today & dense fog.
    *Men on time, work as yesterday.

2pm. Last stairway now finished! Very pretty, I think. I said so & they all smiled. Marce said, –Thank ya. But then he also looked at the others like he was a child in possession of a new dirty word.
    *All of them now working on fitting the big floor timbers. It certainly looks strong.

4.45pm. A revelation! John John just gone. He came to give me the Friday update (stairs all done, floor finished next week). But then the bombshell. I asked him whether he had had a chance to try out his new bat. He said no. But then he spontaneously said that "Nan liked it a lot". I said that was nice & then he said (again without coaxing) that she asked him where he got it, "was it Santy Claus?" He said he told her I gave it to him. Then she said I was real nice & made a ginger cake "that was just so good!" He imitated her face & movements, & it was Cinch Ford to a tee! I said, –Is Cinch Ford your grandmother? –Yes, ma'am, he said, looking surprised that I somehow didn't know this. I patted his shoulder & said, –You're a lucky boy. –Yes, ma'am, he said. Then he ran off & vaulted on to truck beside Davy.

*Imagine that. I can't wait to ask Cinch about it all.

*Good heavens. She must be Marce's mother-in-law. (Surely not his mother!)

10.15pm. Just a little colder today, 30s-40s. Fog never let up. Watched "Route 66". Not as good as last week.

January 25, 1964

1pm. Frustrating & ugly drive in Frederick this morning. Wet bag at A & P tore, bouncing apples on the ground. People in a bad mood, I felt. Spent $12.

6pm. Read all afternoon.

11pm. Warmer today from the start. But fog gave way to drizzle, then wind brought rain after I got home.

January 26, 1964

8am. Above freezing this morning, but wind howling through the trees.

12.30pm. Walked home with church ladies. Asked Cinch if she could guess what I'd learned about her, & then told her I had found out John John was her grandson. She smiled fit to burst. —Didn't you know that? she asked. —Don't he just look as purdy as me? she said & laughed outright. I took a risk & said that I was surprised that Marce was her son-in-law, & she didn't come 'round to see his handiwork in The Corner. —Aw, he don't want nobody a-getting' in there, she said. I offered to show her inside, but she said she'd wait until it was all done.

*I had the distinct impression talking about Marce made her uncomfortable, so I let the subject drop.

*Much to think about with those two.

10.30pm. Sunny all day today, upper 40s. But wind never let up. Watched most of the 9 o'clock movie, but as I missed the very beginning, I wasn't completely sure what was happening until it was nearly over.

I've just seen the Rock of Ages —

I, LittleWound, tell this story.

It was in the era when the turnpike was being built across the mountain-passes, and the women pitied the Irishmen and slaves and took them washtubs full of water which they drank with gourds. BigSuper, the Mussers field-hand, delivered corn-meal to them, and he said that at night they lay around their fires cooking the meal-mash in balls, laying them in the ashes.

There came among the Lutherans a preacher and his name was Kline. He stood like a tree without branches, his arms hanging or swinging at his sides. He lived in the cabin next to the church and he had no wife or family with him, and no servants except the Bakers' house-girl and cook whose time he rented by the week. When it rained, he called upon his neighbours, sometimes bringing them gifts and sometimes returning home with gifts of his own. When the sun shone, he could be seen helping those with years upon their backs to attend their gardens, turn down the ears of corn to dry, hang out their clothes, or do their household chores. He was thanked by the whole village, yet his esteem among the men and women was small, as he seemed to have neither the grace of a woman nor the rage of a man. Where, they wondered, was the self-respect of one who sacrificed himself and knew no pride?

In the congregation of his church was a woman of years and stature like his own. She had cousins, aunts and uncles in the hills and valley, but neither father nor mother, as both had died, leaving her their farm and their sheep. This farm she let to her neighbours, though she lived in the farmhouse with no one, accepting as part of her rent for the farm that her chores would be done by her neighbours' servants. She was called MissDraper.

From the time when the geese made arrows in the sky until the time when the sunlight thickened the air before the storms, MissDraper came to church and saw and heard of Kline's deeds among the old and the sick. She saw the elbows and knees of his suit, the bones in his face and wrists and the way he stood near the stove by the pulpit. She saw too the way the farmers, tradesmen and wives looked when they shook his hand leaving the church. Her eyes turned to the ground under the weight of her own plenty, and she longed to bring comfort to this man who comforted others, even when they despised him.

She began to watch the preacher and listen for the stories people told of him. She heard that he had said that what the widow Leatherman needed was firewood and so that Sunday she put a piece of gold in the Lutheran collection-plate, to see what would happen. As she had hoped, before the sun set on the waning moon, the widow's chimney smoked again. She heard that Kline had said that the Lutz's boy needed surgery to remove his arm, and again she put gold into the collection. And so it was done, that a surgeon cut off the boy's arm, saving his life.

The preacher looked with wonder into the faces of his congregation. It seemed that whatever he said needed to be done for the health of the village, whatever he prayed for, came to pass through the charity of the people. But he could never tell through whose hands the bounty of his god was bestowed.

In this way the seasons of the village passed. Kline never turned his face from any task that his people needed, and whenever he spoke his prayers among them, the means to bring them happiness came to him as before.

Neither Kline nor MissDraper ever married. It happened that when the snows began to lighten his hair, he had gone to speak at the funeral of a slave near the Ropp farm, and there, in the rain, he caught a cold, that turned to a fever, that turned to his death. I do not know whether or how MissDraper may have grieved. But she stopped coming to Harmony on Sundays, and when she died, in spite of all her cousins, aunts and uncles, nieces and nephews, she willed that her farm should be sold, and all of the gold be given to the Lutheran Church.

January 27, 1964

8.45am. Just back from taking tray. All hands on the lowest floor, busily inserting some kind of plastic sheeting they've brought.

*Would have liked a chance to speak to Marce about Cinch Ford but thought it best not to talk in front of the others. Also, couldn't think of anything to say about it.

1pm. Back with lunch tray. Dicky Bird & Rip fitting floorboards, Davy carrying & holding, Marce sawing. Insulation visible where they haven't yet nailed down floor.

5pm. Men left now. Utility room all floored.

*Made a special point of buttonholing John John before he got inside today. -Your Grandma tells me, I said, what a good boy you are! He smiled & looked pleased. –Yes, ma'am, he said. –She's very proud of you, I went on. He just looked at me, smiling. –You're very lucky to have her, I said. –Yes, ma'am. –Do you see her much? –Yes, ma'am, he said. Much as I can. –I bet you do, I said. –You keep making her proud, I said. –I'll try, he answered.

10pm. Colder this morning than yesterday, but warmer this afternoon. Some wind, but nice sun. Just watched "Wagon Train".

January 28, 1964

1pm. Men working like yesterday. Sawing, hammering, carrying. Oh, & singing. Dicky Bird renditioning about how things are on Wolverton Mountain.

4.30pm. Men gone as usual. Flooring in kitchen 2/3 done. John John saw me looking around & actually said hi.

10.30pm. Weather the same as yesterday, but not as windy. Fantastic moon tonight, bright as vanilla ice cream.

January 29, 1964

9.30am. Very cold again this morning, below 20.

*Men arrived with a large machine on the truck today & it took two to carry it in the back door.

10.30am. Horrible racket from The Corner. Sounds like a glacier shivering to pieces.

2pm. Back with tray. Terrible noise is upstairs floor being sanded with a huge sander. Dicky Bird at the controls. Others still working on the floor.

4.45pm. Floor looks to be finished. Men gone now. Dicky Bird looking dazzled & red-eyed. John John not with them.

10.45pm. Not much above freezing today, cold breeze but nice sun.

January 30, 1964

9.30am. Davy adding some kind of sealant to top floor. Rip using huge sander on upper middle floor. Marce & Dicky Bird using smaller sanders on stairs.

2pm. Horrible sanding seems to be finished today. Everybody varnishing now.

2.30pm. Sander going again, this time on the middle floor.

5pm. Everyone gone now (no sign of John John again). All of them look exhausted. Can't investigate as the stairs & floors are wet in places.

10.15pm. A little warmer this morning, but not as warm this afternoon. Wind dropped but sun still nice. Watched "Rawhide".

January 31, 1964

9.30am. Only 19 degrees this morning & snowing furiously. Radio says not to expect much.

 *Marce himself sanding middle floor. Others downstairs, clearing away everything, & moving machinery to & fro to be away from sander.

1pm. Davy sanding huge bottom floor. Others varnishing middle floor.

6pm. Men left late this evening, determined to finish sealing lower floor. Didn't finish until 5.15. I waited until I saw lights being turned off & then went over & told them all to

280

have a good weekend. They looked positively worn out. Rip managed to smile, Dicky Bird & Davy both gave a solemn wave. I think Marce muttered, —Yeah, right. No John John again.

10.30pm. No more snow today, but stayed dark all day. Temperature in the 30s. Watched "The Farmer's Daughter".

Shank's Pony

February 1, 1964

8am. Woke up this morning after a good sleep and had such ambitions, & now the weather looks threatening. What to do?

1.30pm. Decided to risk it & went to Frederick. Luckily, weather improved. Went to A & P, which was quiet. I knew it would be better or worse than usual. Spent $20, the penalty of going slowly. They are marketing something they are calling "instant coffee". I can't believe it is any good. Also went to Woolworth's & McCrory's, buying some pots & flower seeds. Not sure about vegetables just yet. Also went to the bookstore & got two books: Big Sur & Reunion. It is hard to imagine JK ever being old or JC ever being young.

6.30pm. Just finished Boston Bean Stew. Very nice. Enough for tomorrow. Made some cornbread muffins that look like little ears of corn, split sideways. Will give some to Cinch tomorrow.

11pm. Foggy this morning & a little snow on the air. This then turned to drizzly rain as it warmed up to the low 40s.

Watched 9 o'clock movie – too sad to be funny too funny to be sad. Picture on channel 4 still fuzzy.

February 2, 1964

8am. Radio reports that bothersome groundhog has seen his shadow, so next six weeks are a write-off. Surely, if groundhogs are at all like humans, there must be groundhogs who disagree?

10am. Bright enough this morning I was tempted outside early, working soil in vegetable garden & generally cleaning up. Yesterday's ambitions still with me.

*Cinch & the ladies saw me outside & waved. –Y'all better get along up here with us now, Cinch called out. She told me once that every shovelful I move on a Sunday I'll have to put back using my nose in The Hereafter. I didn't tell her that after this, I pictured Hell as a flat field full of human moles.

12pm. Made sure my hands were clean & that I had a fresh apron on by the time the ladies were heading home today. I gave Cinch a neat pile of cornbread. –Aw, they look so good, she said. They'll be fine eatin' with molasses.

4pm. Drinking tea I started to think about the men walking home from church behind their women. They walk much slower. Why? Is this because the women are in a hurry to get their Sunday dinners ready? Or do the men think they've worked all week so now they have time to go slow? Time off from being men?

10.45pm. Windy all day & temperature upper 30s-40s. Watched "Jaimie McPheeters". Nearly finished Wolfe novel – which I love.

February 3, 1964

8.45am. Marce & the others arrived before 8 this morning. They started with loading up some of the machines on to his truck, after which he has driven off. Rip has got them cleaning up the upper middle floor (for some reason); all except Davy, who is clearing out the lowest floor, very neatly. Dicky Bird waltzing with his darling to the Tennessee Waltz.

11am. Marce back by 9.30. Around that time Ingalls truck pulled up with very large pile of small thin wood. Usual driver, usual assistant. They all busily carried the wood into the lowest floor. Also more bags of what I think must be plaster and buckets that look heavy, maybe with nails.

*I went over before 9.45 to watch the unloading & to hear if Marce would try provoking the young black man any more. If he said anything too deliberate, I didn't hear it. There might have been some banter about how different people get along with the cold weather, but I'm not certain of this.

*The wood seems to be many small strips, & a lot of thin boards.

2pm. Back with the lunch tray. Rip & Dicky Bird seem to be busy fastening thin strips of wood to the lower half of the walls on the upper middle floor. Marce is cutting up the thin planks (which have shaped edges) & Davy is moving things from the bottom floor upstairs & helping the others.

4.45pm. Men gone now. John John came & spent his time sweeping up as usual. After they all left, I figured out what exactly they are doing. They are putting up wainscoting in all the upstairs rooms. There is a lot here to do, I think.

10.30pm. Only in the 20s this morning, 30s this afternoon. Nice sunshine though. Watched "Wagon Train".

284

February 4, 1964

7am. Very cold this morning, in the teens.

9am. Men at work as usual. Much the same as yesterday, although now Davy given the job of sawing the wainscoting planks to size as the others attach them.

2.30pm. Work as usual across the road. Quite peaceful at the moment. Dicky Bird in full throttle, singing how Mary cried & forgave him, taking him back again. Little falsetto bits even in tune (about which the others don't tease him, surprisingly).

5pm. Men left on time. Saw John John who seemed to be in a bad mood. Bad day at school, I suppose.

8.15pm. Have been thinking about JJ's mood earlier. Ought one to help people to change their bad moods, or are they productive of something? Will JJ's mother even try to help him & ought she?

 *I had no trouble picturing Alex in a bad mood after school. He often was. Tom was the one who would try to deal with it. He would listen, really listen, & try to offer sensible advice (which was not what Alex really needed, I could tell). I thought too that Tom's way of listening had a kind of professional side to it, a kind of couch-side manner that I think Alex grew to find irritating. "How did that make you feel?" I knew how he felt. But I said nothing. Why did I?

10.30pm. Warmed up this afternoon, into the 40s. Sunny all day.

Come to the church in the wildwood

No, sir, I don't know nothing 'bout the war, 'cept what I seen with my own eyes, and what I hear folks a-saying. The soldiers coming and a-going. Yankees mostly. Sometimes the Sesesh. Poorly fellas they was too. They up there in Fisher's Hollow, all 'long the creek. Folks say in the evening they take all they clothes off and put 'em down in the creek with rocks on top so as to drown the lice. I don't know. I sure seen 'em once when they rode up through Harmony – the horses and the cannons. Most all them fellas on the horses didn't have no shoes on they feet at all. 'Bout half the walking ones did. It was in the Fall, but you wouldn't have known it none, it was so hot. They was on they way up to Quebec school-house and they sure meet the Yankees and they horses up there. Umnh umnh. And the red-legged Yankees 'thout horses too. We hear the guns and the cannons. Them Seseshes was polite enough. Speak to the folks in the big house, and we gave 'em some cabbages and some sweet taters and some okra and I don't know what all else. They ask if they was any guns or whiskey, but 'deed I don't know if they got none. I 'member 'cause I was a-cooking at the big house that day. Missy and me was making lemonade and gingerbread, fixing for to get ready for the corn-husking bee. They gave Missy some money for the things they took, but she said it weren't no good anyway. I hear they kill some hogs up on the mountain. That's all they kill for they high-tail it back down and the Yankees come down next day a-following. They didn't ask for nothing 'cept water, and we gave it to 'em by the bucket.

Anyhow, they was times like that they just passed on through, and sometimes they come whole regiments of 'em. I member once they hundreds of 'em slept up there in the field after the patch – not the one top of the hill but the one going down the other side towards Myersville. Well, most folks thinking they best keep away from 'em and all, but they always the ones gets curious, and the ones think they gonna go 'round and sell 'em something. They was even some think a-bringing 'em religion.

Now I don't know, 'cause I wasn't 'lowed no churching. None of the servants 'round here 'lowed in the white folks' churches. 'Cept in the towns where the churches is big and got high porches in the back where the servants could sit theyselves. But I surely did know 'bout ole Dallas Harshman. Yes sir, even I hear that. He the preacher over Myersville for the Methodists and all the folks that goes to his church they say he preach just like the voice of God His own self. Lord, how the people all talk 'bout his preaching. And if you ask me, he just as proud as a baby with a tooth 'bout the way folks is a-talking 'bout him. Anyway, he live over on the Main Street, up near the end towards Church Hill, and he hear that the Yankees in they regiment is done come and camp on the hill 'bout halfway 'tween there and Harmony. Everybody say he oughts to get hisself on out there and read them boys one of his ole sermons and get 'em to thinking 'bout God 'fore they get theyselves killed in the fighting that was surely coming. Now that ole Dallas Harshman, he cluck and he crow and he tell everybody he fixing to do just that. But I knows better. I knows it 'cause his servant Jeremina told me herself. Now she was pretty ole woman that lived with Mister Dallas, and she say she have it good in that house, him being a preacher and all, never lose his temper or nothing. But she say she seen him and the way he acting when all them soldiers starts to marching in the valley and a-sleeping on the hills, and she say, Y'all know what? He just as scared as can be. Scared as can be. I seen her in Myersville myself and she told me, plain as the nose on you face.

Now ole Jeremina, she mostly feel herself too, and she kind of proud the fact that everybody like to talk 'bout Mister Dallas, cause she think it make her look good 'cause she his servant and the one that cook his meals and iron his shirts and do for him. So she say, she just can't believe he ain't already on his way over towards Harmony to see them soldiers and give them the benefit he give to the others. He say he a-fixing too, but he gonna wait to the evening for he start out.

Ole Jeremina, she getting anxious now, 'cause she think he ain't careful, the preacher from them Lutherans down there in Harmony gonna walk up that hill 'hind theyselves and get to them soldiers 'fore Mister Dallas does. So she say she nag and nag him till he fit to be tied and when he can't stand it no more, he get on his hat and take hisself a stick for walking and say that's just where he going. Gonna get over there and give them soldiers the blessed word of God. She just as proud as all get out she hear that.

So he gone for a while, and Jeremina she think she gonna do the evening chores till he get back, 'cause he surely gonna be hungry after the preaching. She say she a-putting things where they goes when she see on his table by the window the book she know he always using when he do his preaching. She think he forget it, and he gonna get a burr under his tail when he find out. So she took up the book and run off towards that hill where the soldiers is all a-sitting 'round they fires and a-cooking and a-laughing and cutting-up. And she say one of them fellas comes a-running towards her a-pointing his gun and shouting for her to stop. What y'all doing here, now? he say. She say she Mister Dallas servant and she come to bring him the book he forget. Who Mister Dallas? he say. She tell him he the preacher. 'Bout then, she say, another one them soldiers come up, and tell the other one to let ole Jeremina in, cause the preacher she looking for down towards the captain's tent. They point where she supposed to go, so she go on down by herself.

When she get to the spot they pointing, she see another white man 'thout no uniform, and he talking with the boss soldiers while the others getting theyselves together in groups like cows and horses. 'Scuse me, mister, she say. I'm looking for Mister Dallas. He come to preach to the soldiers. That white man look at the boss soldiers and he say, Who you say his name is? She say 'gain. And he say, Dallas Harshman? No, we ain't seen him. Then he say, What y'all carrying there? She say it Mister Dallas's book. What book? he say. The book for the preaching. He stuck out his hand. You can show it to me, he say, cause I'm a preacher too.

Now ole Jeremina she say she squint good and hard at that preacher and now she know for certain he must be that ole Harmony Lutheran. She say first thing she wanna do is to put that book where no ole Lutheran get his hands on it. Then she say she think maybe she help Mister Dallas cause she show that preacher that he can have the book, but he ain't never gonna find nothing in it the way Mister Dallas do.

So he took it and give it a look. This ain't no bible, you got here, this is something else, he say. Then she say he look at her like he catched her a-stealing chickens, and he say, And you say he use this here book when he do his preaching?

No, sir, she say. It ain't like that. He set to his table for a while, and he open that book and look at it, and then he writes and writes on the paper, and they is the papers he takes to the church on a Sunday. I ain't never seen him reading no bible. I don't think he needs to.

Y'all know what's in this book? he say. No, sir, I surely don't, Jeremina say. He make to give it back to her. It's a book full of sermons, he say. Costs a lot of money. Y'all take that home and you make sure you put it back where you find it, ya hear? Then he jump and pull his hand back. Wait a minute, he say. He open up the book and there a lady handkerchief inside it. Is this where he stopped reading, he say? 'Deed, I don't know, sir, Jermina say. He always stick that in the book when he done writing, she say.

Then that ole Lutheran turn the page and study it a minute. Uh huh, he say. Just like I thought. He snap the book shut and give it back to her.

That night, Jermina say she didn't hear Mister Dallas come home 'fore dark. But the next day, she think she ask him if he seen the soldiers, and tell him what that ole Lutheran did. But then she think he not gonna like it much if she tell him how she took his own book out to the soldiers her own self, so she didn't tell him nothing.

After that, something funny start to happen to Mister Dallas and his sermons. Folks all gets to talking 'bout the sermons they hearing 'bout over in Harmony, and how the preacher over there seem to be saying the same thing Mister Dallas say, 'cept he saying on the Sunday before Mister Dallas say it. Jeremina say that's how come Mister Dallas have to go all the way to Frederick just to buy hisself a new book for the preaching. She say it a blue one and a little bigger than the ole red one he used to use.

February 5, 1964

9am. Men working as before. Looks like they'll finish the upper middle floor wainscoting today.

2pm. Men working with the windows open in places. Marce now working on fastening strips on to the walls in the lower middle floor, Dicky Bird assisting. He is more quiet when he works alongside Marce, I've noticed. Rip upstairs attaching skirting boards to the fronts of the wainscoting, Davy assisting everywhere at once.

4.45pm. Men gone now, John John sitting in the back with Davy. He looked less bothered this evening, though still not quite his usual self, I think.

*I cannot decide at these times whether it would help him to try & cheer him up a little (maybe get him to thinking about Cinch?) or whether he would feel too inhibited by the others, especially his father? I don't want to make it worse for him.

11pm. Sunny again today & much warmer: nearly 60 this afternoon. Finished Wolfe.

February 6, 1964

9.30am. Men have swapped roles somewhat today. Now Rip & Davy are working on the wainscoting, & Marce & Dicky Bird are doing something to the ceiling on the upper middle floor.

2pm. Upper middle floor seems to be getting a light coat of plastering on its ceiling. Wainscoting as before.

5pm. I'm not sure, but it looks like upper middle floor ceiling is now all coated. Wainscoting below advances.

*John John looking a little better this evening, I asked him how school was going. He said it was okay & that they had hamburgers for lunch.

10.30pm. Foggy this morning, & somewhat wet all day. Over 40 this afternoon. Watched "Rawhide".

February 7, 1964

9am. Men at work as usual, minus Dicky Bird. I asked Rip whether DB was okay, & he said he had toothache. Davy helping Marce upstairs, as Marce is starting to plaster the walls. Rip working alone.

2pm. Quiet over the road. Rip quietly getting on with it. Sound of the radio upstairs. Davy laughing at the announcer's jokes.

5pm. Interesting departure this evening. John John came as always to give me the headlines on work (wainscoting & plastering all next week, probably). I said I thought he must be glad it was the weekend, but he said no, that he had to help his father "plant posts" on Saturday, as it was warm enough. I didn't know what he meant but didn't want to hold him up. I did ask him though whether he'd see his grandmother this weekend. He said they went on Saturday evenings, as she always made them "steamers". (Another thing I didn't understand.)

*When they drove away, I was curious to see how the seating arrangements would change without Dicky Bird in the cab of the truck. As I expected, the three men were inside, John John alone in the back. I waved, but either he didn't see me, or he ignored me.

10.30pm. Temperature around 40 all day, & monotonous rain. Great gusts of wind sometimes though, battering it into the windows. Watched "Route 66" and loved it, which tempted me to watch "Twilight Zone" as it was on right after. Gave up after 10 minutes.

February 8, 1964

11am. Couldn't think of enough reasons to go to Frederick today, so went to Acme in Middletown instead ($12). Might make B Bean S again. Read some of Kerouac when still in bed this morning. A timeless boy. It breaks my heart to have to wonder whether Alex would enjoy reading him. I wish I knew.

2pm. Stew not as good as last time. Went for a walk to try & forget it. Saw a few birds I think must be quail. Drivers of two cars stared at me.

7.15pm. Something about men makes them brood too much on freedom. It's not that women don't want it, probably just as much. But men feel entitled to it. They feel denied it if they haven't got all they want. I marvel at John John's patience & Alex's lack of it.

*Hateful as it sounds, I would like to see JJ lose his temper, if just once. But I suppose if he did Marce would mock him to the point of utter humiliation or simply slap him against the wall for having the impertinence to possess any feelings of his own.

10pm. Thinking about Marce. His power is a kind of predictable anarchy. At guessable times he says or does the unexpected, fulfilling prophecies & yet always with raw force.

*I'll bet as a child he really did steal candy from a baby. Really did put a fly in the ointment. Really did throw sh[]t at the fan. Anarchy started with him or someone just like him.

*Marce's power comes from being the man that all other men are afraid they might become. But do they secretly want to?

10.45pm. Cold again this morning, but over 40 this afternoon. Sunny with a light breeze. Skipped movie and read.

He had great long tushes like a grizzly bear!

It is hard to say how it got started. The Clagetts had all been lawyers for generations, and they were about the only ones any of the ordinary farmers thought of whenever they had a reason to think of a lawyer at all. The most common reason, of course, was a land dispute, and that's where this story began too. In a way.

Earl Runkles's farm lay in the fertile flat lands that ran down the east side of the county, above, through and beyond Walkersville. Earl's family had farmed the same land since the 1830s at least, and Earl knew the shape and the uses of every one of his fields as well as he knew anything else. So when the new folks bought the little place to the east side of him, and started an argument over a triangle of sycamore trees and a half-wet swamp, it didn't matter that Earl knew he was right to say that that small parcel was his, he still had to go down to Walkersville to see Jim Clagett and pay for Jim to prove it.

That would have been fine, if only Earl hadn't taken along his wife Jeanie. Or, maybe, if Jeanie looked a little different than she did. The thing was that the minute Jim Clagett got a look at Jeanie, he made up his mind to add her to the list of women he kept in the back of his mind for thinking of whenever things around the office got slow. Jim had a way with the ladies, and his skill at conquests was frequently abetted through the influence his work could have on their lives. It was amazing what women would do, or what some men might encourage their women to do, for the sake of coming out well where the law was concerned. Jim always found a short road to take him to where he wanted to be.

Like most people who find it easy to get what they want, Jim wasn't one even to try the long road as a first choice either. He wasn't an experimenter, so he usually started out by looking for the very shortest road of all. Knowing the habits and the methods of farmers, Jim found it easy to call in at the Runkles's farm at a time when Earl would be busy somewhere in one of his fields, leaving Jeanie on her own. That was why he first came around to their house only two days after Earl and Jeanie visited him. Of course, Jeanie, being a little afraid of anything to do with the law, was also a little afraid of Jim. She brought him straight into the house, seated him in the parlour and brought him ice tea. She apologized twice that Earl wasn't indoors to answer Jim's questions. Jim said he didn't mind waiting. He liked the company, he said. He liked the way Jeanie kept house. He liked the way she managed to look so fresh and pretty even on an afternoon like this when she couldn't really have been expecting anyone to call. He liked the way she wore her hair. Was it as soft as it looked? It was, he discovered, when he got up and fingered a curl near the back of her neck. It smelled so nice too, he said. But then, he was sure that Jeanie must be used to compliments. All beautiful women were, he said. Jeanie blushed. Why, that Earl is one lucky man. Doesn't know what he's got. If Jeanie were his wife, Jim said, he'd never get any work done. He'd have to spend the whole day indoors. Probably never leave the upstairs. Jim laughed. Jeanie looked strained, and practiced as he was, Jim changed the subject.

After about thirty minutes, Jim left some papers for Earl to read, put his hat on at the door, smiled a long smile at Jeanie, and waved goodbye from the open window of his long ivory Chevrolet.

When Jim got back to his office, he spent an hour finishing up the other work that lay on his desk, and then a further hour leaning back in his chair thinking about Jeanie Runkles. He also thought about Jeanie's brother Roy. Roy had had some trouble of his own a couple of years earlier. Circumstantial evidence, and a slightly im-pure reputation, led some of his co-workers at the livestock auction over in Woodsboro to believe that Roy might have been doctoring some of the animals being taken into the ring to increase their value; hiding blemishes, drugging some to improve their mobility, energy, or mask the pain that might have kept them from fetching top dollar. It was something that farmers selling stock could have paid him a little extra to do. Jim had managed to get Roy's trial suspended on the basis of a lack of firm proof, and he even managed to convince Roy's employer not to fire Roy. This came as a favour to Jim and to Roy's boss (who duly paid for the cover-up), but also as one to Roy, who had never really acknowledged the debt he owed Jim. It was high time, Jim thought, to use this leverage.

That was why Jim went by the livestock auction the very next Tuesday. He found Roy stacking wooden crates full of chickens. Jim wasted no time. He called Roy over and in five minutes told him what he wanted. Roy shook his head mightily and swore that there was nothing he could do. There was no way, even if he wanted to, that he could talk his sister into doing what Jim wanted. Jim only stopped smiling long enough to point out how much damage he could do to Roy (and to his brother-in-law Earl, and even Jeanie), if he were to let some of the information in his files make its way to their enemies' lawyers. Jim explained how trials could be re-opened; he explained how property deeds, especially old ones, could be challenged; how rights of way might be granted right between some people's houses and barns; how some men not only lose their jobs, but go to jail. Roy listened and said he understood. He asked Jim to let him have a little time to work it out. Jim said he shouldn't take too long.

That night Roy went to see his sister Jeanie. He went first to the barn, where he found Earl finishing the milking, and carrying the last two stainless steel buckets to the cooling parlour. Roy did his best to chew the fat with Earl as nonchalantly as he could. He asked Earl whether he had heard anything about the neighbours and the trouble they were all having with thieves. Thieves? Yep. Not the kind that steal from your sheds, or even take your calves, but the kind that come right into your house. Take your radio. Take your silverware. Murder you in your bed. Thieves.

While Earl was washing up the dairy barn floor, Roy went into the house to find Jeanie. She was just starting to put away the ironing she'd finished. She asked him why it took him so long to come up to the house. Didn't he have nothing to say to her? He did, he said. Plenty.

Roy told Jeanie everything that Jim Claggett had said to him, and Jeanie now saw what was happening. She wanted to cry, and she wanted to tell Earl, because so far, she had said nothing about what she hoped hadn't been happening the day Jim Claggett visited her. Roy told her not to. If she did, he said, there wouldn't be anything any of them could do. Roy told her he had a plan, and he told her what it was.

That Friday night at about four thirty, Roy met Jim coming out of his office. He told Jim he had done everything Jim asked him to do, and that Jeanie was willing. He told Jim that he had agreed with Jeanie that he would take Roy out to a bar on Saturday night, and that while they, Roy and Earl, were out, Jeanie would be expecting Jim. But, he said, just so nobody would see

Jim arrive, he'd have to leave his car in the pine trees at the end of the lane, and he'd have to go in to the house through the back-porch door. Jim smiled.

Sunset was at about 8.30 on Saturday night. At 8.45, Jim parked his car in the soft mattress of pine needles near the lane that led to the Runkles's farm. He walked up the road, his grey shoes and his grey suit looking shadowy in the lengthening darkness. When he came into the wide green space separating the barn, the outbuildings and the farmhouse, he looked up. None of Earl's dogs barked at him. Roy must have seen to them somehow. Earl's truck was parked in its usual place, and Jim figured that as it was Roy's invitation, he must have done the driving. There was only one light on in the house, and it was upstairs. That encouraged him.

Jim followed Roy's instructions and went around the back of the house and on to the wide back porch. He walked softly but surely to the back door, turned the knob and pushed. The door was locked. He rattled the lock for a full minute. Jim's shoulders sank and he pursed his lips. If this were some kind of trick, or if something had gone wrong, he'd make sure they would all have Hell to pay.

Jim looked to his left, near where the porch roller and Jeanie's ringer washer stood. The large kitchen window was wide open and the checked curtain was billowing inward on the breeze. So that was it. Jim walked over and looked in. It was dark inside, but he could see the arrangement of the room. He thought it looked as though someone had moved everything away from the window on purpose, maybe to make it easy for him. Or maybe they hadn't. Either way, there was nothing to it – one leg in, duck, and then the other. Not even much of a sound.

Jim walked across the floor, hearing his shoes squeak. He wondered whether he should call out Jeanie's name. Just then he heard a scuttling on the other side of the kitchen door, a door he thought probably went into a hallway or a pantry or a dining room. Dogs, he thought. The dogs have come to have a look. Why didn't they bark? And why were they in the house at all at this hour?

Jim walked over to the doorway where the sound was and gave it a little push. It was latched. He turned the knob and waited. Nothing happened. He slowly opened the door, a little at first, then wide open. He couldn't see anything.

Put your god-damn hands up! a man's voice shouted.

Jim let go the door and turned, looking for the shortest way to the window. But when he did, he heard a shot and then another. The second one spun him around. As he was falling, he saw a glimpse of a man with a shotgun. He saw behind the man a woman standing looking over them both from the stairs. That was the last thing he ever saw.

A month later Earl Runkles was released from custody without charge. A jury of his peers suggested to the judge that Earl was within his rights to do what he did, believing what he believed. The judge ruled in Earl's favour, but also stipulated that he would no longer be permitted to own a shotgun, even for farming purposes. The next summer, Jeanie gave birth to a little girl she named Karen Marie. Roy quit his job at the livestock auction and went to work as a crane operator in Baltimore. Earl settled out of court with his neighbours over the triangle of land, letting them keep it. The neighbours built a spring wall to drain the marshy place and then put up a tree house in the sycamores for their two sons.

February 9, 1964

12.30pm. Walked up to the church today & met the ladies on their way out. They are full of plans. —You like kinklings? Cinch said. I nodded. —Tuesday's doughnut day, she said. If ya ain't too busy ya could get up there to the meeting house & help us to making some for people. What people? I asked. —Aw, just them that knows 'bout it, she said. Folks as put in their orders. It seems that the good Brethren ladies will spend Tuesday in the cellar kitchen of their church (yes, there is a cellar kitchen!) making kinklings for people to collect. I haven't stopped thinking about it since she mentioned it. No one has ever asked me to do anything like this. Never.

4pm. Took ashes outside. Small scattering of gray feathers near the ash pile. Got a bad feeling a fox may have caught a pigeon.

11pm. Not very sleepy tonight. Sunny all day, temperature started below freezing but made it over 40 later. Watched "Jaimie McPheeters", read, watched "Bonanza" then read. Finished Big Sur. Not that big, in my opinion.

February 10, 1964

9.30am. Dicky Bird with the others at work this morning. I tried to see if his jaws showed any bruises but couldn't tell. I asked him how he was & he just grinned & nodded & looked embarrassed. He is working with Rip on the wainscoting while Marce & Davy are plastering upstairs.

3pm. Wainscoting coming along very well, as rooms much simpler on that floor. Didn't venture upstairs.

   *My now-annual February letter from Sis arrived today. Same as last year, generally. Will write & thank her & tell her I'm fine. Really, fine. Really.

5.15pm. Men slightly late leaving, as Marce trying to finish off a room upstairs. I went up after & they all look finished there to me. He seemed in a slightly bad (well, worse than usual) mood to me. I heard him bark at John John to "keep his G[]d[]amn fingers off everything that looked wet."

11pm. Temperature near freezing all day. Wet snow off &
on the whole day. Watched "Wagon Train". Thinking about
tomorrow.

February 11, 1964

6.45am. Up early as I have decided to join Cinch at the
others at the church to make doughnuts. Having no experience, I expect to be laughed at & perhaps prayed for.

8.45am. Left the coffee & tea with the men in serious
discussion on lower middle floor. Marce is of the opinion,
it seems, that some of the ceiling is not as it should be
& wants the others to investigate before he works on it.
He seems angry with them for not having thought of this
without him. I couldn't see them, as I went out the back
door, but he said to one of them, that he wasn't going to
work on the bit near the stairway as it "was G[]d[]mn n[]
gg[]r work" as it was.
   *Just off to the Brethrens now.

1.30pm. Back with the lunchtime tray. Marce downstairs
on lowest floor with Davy, both hacking away at the plaster
on the ceiling, which is coming down in big dirty dusty
chunks. Dicky Bird & Rip on the floor above, looking as
though they are cutting back the ceiling plaster about three
feet from the walls all the way around. This looks like a
compromise of some sort.

3pm. What a wonderful time at the church! Such gossip,
made more fun as it was underneath a church and exclu-
sively about people I know nothing about. The kinklings
(I've brought a bag home) are easily the best doughnuts I've
ever eaten. So many beefy-armed women in little white
bonnets pitching them into huge trays of snowy powdered
sugar. I shall never forget them. Not a single one asked me

whether I believe in God or any of His family. They are a tough, kind, generous bunch. Not easy to love but impossible not to respect.

4.45pm. Davy has spent the past two hours trooping wheelbarrows of plaster debris out of the back door, round the wash house & up on to the back of the truck, where he dumped it. Most of it is gray & earthy looking. From the moment he arrived, John John started following him with bucketsful of smaller bits, evidently swept up when the worst was over. I had a quick look around. The ceiling upstairs is, indeed, chopped back about three feet all the way around. That floor has all been cleaned up. The lowest floor is still piled high with everything that used to be on the ceiling, the clean wood being covered up with canvas. Tomorrow will be a busy day for them.

 *John John & Davy rode away perched on top of the truck bed full of plaster.

10.45pm. Colder today. Snowed seriously a few times, but ground is too wet for it to last. Not above freezing today though. Watched some of "The Fugitive" until I realized I was asleep.

February 12, 1964

7.15am. Bitterly cold this morning; about 9 or 10.

9am. Not sure what happened to the plaster from yesterday, but the truck bed empty this morning. Everyone at work. Marce is plastering the ceiling in the lower middle floor where the wainscoting is done, while Rip & Dicky Bird are back at work on the wainscoting. Davy is the spare hands for everybody, & when they don't need him, he wheelbarrows the remaining plaster junk on to the truck.

1.15pm. Just back with tray. I asked Marce how he got rid of the old plaster so quickly. He said, –There's a ole dump up the Monument Road. Chewing my cheek, I risked asking why he didn't take it to the real dump in Frederick. I thought for a moment that as he looked at me, he was deciding whether to let go of all the laughter he felt inside or knock me into the twilight zone, but all he finally said is, –We ain't got time.

2pm. Davy has driven off in Marce's truck, filled with plaster.
     *Mailed my letter to Sis.

3.15pm. Davy back with the truck & hauling plaster again.

4.30pm. Had some tea & have been reading Cheever. He is so subtle I have to keep checking that I am really holding a book at all or just imagining the words myself.

5pm. Men gone now, all of them having helped load the truck with plaster before going. John John not with them today. Davy, to my horror, rode away sitting on the tailgate of the full truck bed, his hand clutching the chain on one side, his feet a foot above the road.

10.30pm. Sunny all day. Scarcely over freezing.

February 13, 1964

8.45am. Everyone at work as usual. Noticed the truck empty again this morning. Whole house now cleared of debris. Marce readying to plaster upper middle ceiling not yet finished. Dicky Bird & Rip finishing wainscoting. Davy downstairs, moving things about (I think).

1.15pm. Wainscoting all done now. Rip fitting skirting boards with Dicky Bird assisting amid big bolts of song to his special angel (who was sent from Up Above). Davy nailing up little strips downstairs.

5pm. Men gone now. Had a look around. Ceilings on lower middle now done. Walls not started. Skirtings almost done. Kitchen now looks ready for wainscoting.

10.30pm. Weather just like yesterday, but no wind today. Sky filled with stars tonight, but no moon.

12am. Afraid to go to sleep in case I dream.

Just to keep down trouble, don't believe I'll go

Now if you was to go on up there to Wolfsville where the old houses are, the big ole stone ones with the barn, and y'all head to the left towards Myersville, then back in there on the right was a little ole place belong to a fella named Lawson Kepler. He was what some folks call a georgeman, a slave catcher. Most folks calls 'em the soul drivers. Anyhow, he had hisself a farm in there where he keep hisself when he wasn't out a-looking for runaways to catch. Mostly he knowed to look for 'em in the places where they kin was. Servants run away when the beating get too much for em, then they miss they children or they wives and they husbands, and he find out where to look and just go and bring 'em back tied to his horse, sure as shooting. Sometimes he take 'em down to Licksville, sometimes up to Hagerstown. Anyhow, he out a-catching runaways so much he need to get hisself somebody to look after that farm of hisn, so he up and married one of them Flook gals, named Pearl. She 'bout the same age as him but a whole lot prettier. Everybody say so.

Well, the preacher say so too. Ole Mister Emory Doub, down there at the Baptists in Wolfsville, he 'bout twice they own age or more when he married 'em, and he got his eye on her from the day she married. 'Fore long, he coming up there to see her, you know, a-bringing up his bible and a-sitting and a-reading from the word of the Lord. Pretty soon he find out ole Mister Lawson out 'round the county somewhere trying to catch some runaway, he be up there a-praying and a-shaking with Miss Pearl. For long he doing a whole lot more than that. That's what folks say anyhow. Y'all know how they talk. I don't know what to believe. Least I didn't in the beginning.

Well, after the white folks change something 'fore the war start they come a awful lot a runaways a-heading for the line, and Mister Lawson, he busier than the button on the outhouse door running them folks down in the woods and the barns 'fore they could get up to Emmitsburg, 'bout where the line goes. Sometimes he go on up in to Pennsylvania itself 'cause he hear that one of them farmers catch a runaway and want to sell him back south. Anyhow, he start to thinking he gonna need somebody to work that farm of hisn while he off a-chasing, so he get hisself a young fella they calls Yost or something. He a nice looking little white man, not all big like Mister Emory and not half so mean as Mister Lawson, and he 'bout ten years or more younger than Miss Pearl. He live in the attic out there 'bove the washhouse and he work like a good man oughta.

Well, 'deed I don't know if they something in it or not, but 'fore long Mister Emory, he starts to getting jealous of ole Yost, thinking he might be getting after Miss Pearl. He think he something special to Miss Pearl his own self, and he don't seem to mind she Mister Lawson's wife or nothing, so long as she treat him real good. So pretty soon he start to scheming some way to get ole Yost off that farm and 'way from Miss Pearl.

Now ole Mister Emory do like the preachers do, and he 'round all the folks' houses a-bringing them the news, and getting hisself cooked for and I don't know what all. And he listening all the time to what the folks tells him. Well, sure as you born, he up there on the mountain, other side of Wolfsville, where the fields gets short and the rocks gets big, and he talks with a ole farmer who got hisself 'bout six seven servants he hire out to the farmers when the wheat and the hay and the ploughing come on, and he say one of them young boys up and run oft. Now Mister Emory, he say, sure nough, I gonna help y'all out. Y'all got something belong that boy? They go down there to the quarters and they find theyselves a shirt and pants he left in the pallet and a hat they don't think belong to nobody, but they say might have been hisn, 'cept they don't know for sure. Mister Emory say he take all that and give it to Mister Lawson, soon as he see him, and maybe he bring they boy back all right.

Well, sure 'nough, he go on down there to Mister Lawson's, and he get in there with Miss Pearl, and he say she gotta do something for him. He say, they a farmer up the hill towards Five Forks got a ole servant wench that run off and they think she hiding in the woods somewhere down there 'round they farm. He say, he gonna help Mister Lawson catch her, 'cause he got some of that wench's boy's clothes, and they gonna make her think Mister Lawson done took her boy and got him tied up in the barn till she give herself up. Well, Miss Pearl don't know no better, and he say what she gotta do is get that Yost fella to wear them clothes every night just as soon as it get dark, and then they catch the wench when she come in to see her boy.

Miss Pearl, she know what kinda temper Mister Lawson got on him, so she say get ole Yost to do just like Mister Emory say. That's what she do.

Now Mister Emory, he go on up the road towards Hagerstown where they got they the big slave pens, and sure 'nough, he meet Mister Lawson a-coming back home. He get him a-talking, and I 'shamed to say, a-drinking, and he say he see some kinda ole servant boy a-hanging round Mister Lawson back door, and though it shame him as a white man to say it, he got the idea Miss Pearl a-doing something she oughtn't with that boy.

Well, Mister Lawson, he like to die he get so mad, and he ride home just as fast as he can, and he start looking 'round them fields, see if he can see something ain't like it ought to be.

He crept up on the washhouse to see if ole Yost in there, and he not. 'Stead – and Mister Lawson, he don't know this – Yost done gone up to the porch to have his supper like he do. So Mister Lawson, he go 'round the house, and there he see a-sitting on the porch, just as pretty as you please, this here fella look like he a field hand, and it's dark, and Mister Lawson can't see nothing 'bout him, 'cept the way he dressed and that whoever he is, he ain't oughta be there nohow. So 'fore he say anything, he pull out that big ole half-pistol thing he get off of the horse, and he shoot it. Well, ole Yost ain't even got time to jump 'fore he fall over dead.

Miss Pearl she hear the shooting and she run out, and 'bout then Mister Lawson see he done shot hisself a white man. I don't know what Miss Pearl say herself, but Mister Lawson, he get peaceful, and it looks like it's all gonna end right there. Yost didn't have no family or nothing, so Mister Lawson didn't have nobody to worry 'bout complaining.

Least he think he didn't. Ole Mister Emory find out all that's a-going on. And 'deed, I don't know if Miss Pearl told him or how he find out. But 'fore long up comes the sheriff and another fella out of Frederick and they up and 'rest Mister Lawson for shooting ole Yost. They even dug up Yost from down there in the field below the barn and took him 'long with them.

I say to Miss Doris up at the big house, 'cause she like to hear all the speculating that folks do, that I was sure Mister Emory then fixing to marry Miss Pearl, cause she was a widow with the farm, but that ain't what happened. No sir, it ain't. Miss Pearl, with 'bout three men a-chasing her, course soon got the bug up her back, and by the time they hung ole Mister Lawson, that baby starting to show. 'Fore you know it, Miss Pearl up and sell that farm her own self and go off to find her people. I hear she got a brother all the way out in Missouri, but I don't know nothing for sure.

February 14, 1964

9.15am. Everyone at work. Marce plastering lower middle floor walls, Davy assisting. Rip finishing skirtings. Dicky Bird downstairs sawing & crooning that he falls to pieces.

12.45pm. Just back. Skirting done. Marce & Davy plastering, Dicky Bird & Rip wainscoting. They seem to work well together.

5pm. Men gone. John John, I saw, spent most of his time with Dicky Bird & Rip. I could hear Rip chatting with him but couldn't hear what they were saying. I saved JJ the trip over, going over to The Corner myself. Rip, to my mind, looked proudly at John John as he told me they'd finish the upstairs (lower middle) walls next week & see how far they could get on the lowest floor.

7.45pm. Can't put it off any longer. So here I am admitting it to myself. Valentine's Day. The day Tom killed himself. I have done my best all day not to think of it, & so it has been with me like tinnitus, like a shadow, gaslighting my thoughts.

    *Was the timing an accident? The argument he had with Alex was the same one, or one of the same ones. How did it become their last? I spoke up. I was silent. I was unexceptional in every way. I was myself. Only myself. Too much myself.

    *Sis asks how I'm doing. Am I over blaming myself, or blaming Alex? DID I blame anyone, anyone other than Tom?

    *I blame everyone.

    *If there was anything unusual about that day it was the feeling that we all had that time was passing through us somehow, not like the hands on a clock, round & round, but like sand funnelling downwards until there was no sand left. Perhaps, it was just Tom who felt it first.

*As soon as I knew he had done it I tried screaming. But can you believe I stopped because I was embarrassed? Not to think that anyone could hear me. But because I hated the sound of my own voice. Screaming, I sounded like someone unreal, made up.

*I think that is what Alex thought. I think that is why he went away. Not because he thought I was unreal. But because he wanted to know that he wasn't.

*So now, the bitterest of news is that whatever he found out about himself, he has become someone who to me is almost unreal. Alive? Dead? No. Missing. My darling son Alex is missing. Tom's death makes him real. My life, my grief, makes me real. But Alex has disappeared, his fate unknown. All fictions have become true to me now. None has an ending.

11.30pm. Temperature only in the 30s all day. Sunny & dry feeling. Please don't let me dream.

February 15, 1964

8am. Exhausted & sluggish this morning. Dreamed all night but cannot remember anything. Perhaps, that is what Hell is, a dream you experience but cannot recall.

11.15am. Middletown & Acme this morning ($16). Fire feels very nice. Primitive & straightforward.

3.30pm. I want to apologize to Alex & ask him to apologize to me. It was something, I remember now, that he seldom did. (Tom was always apologizing, a man sorry for being alive, in case it interfered with anyone else's plans.) Not Alex. Alex sought to please & was made angry if he thought he hadn't.

*There were the girls. The one whose mother was ill, so he gave her flowers, offending the girl with his attentions.

*The redhead who never said what she meant but kept up a conversation with him entirely in allusions. It wore him out.

*The one that made him roller skate.

*The pretty blonde who dropped him for a married man.

*He loved them all. But in loving them (as I'm sure he did), he gradually made himself more unreal. He was nothing unless he was in love. That must have been what he believed.

*My poor Alex. I was no help to you.

10.15pm. In the teens this morning, over 30 this afternoon. More sunshine. Too tired to read.

February 16, 1964

9.45am. Everyone has just passed by on their way to the churches. The Lutheran bell is ringing. I want to go with them & I am angry with myself for wanting this.

12pm. Just walked back to the Mary House with Cinch & the others. They are much freer now, offering me recipes & quilt patterns. I feel as if I have got 12 new sisters.

*Before the service I stood outside the door listening to their last hymn. I could hear their voices but not their words.

4.30pm. Nice lunch (pork chop) so no cake with my tea. Read some more Cheever.

10pm. Tired this evening. Temperature in the 30s all day. About as windy as I can ever remember. Rain & wet snow this afternoon, fog this morning. Watched "Jaimie McPheeters".

February 17, 1964

9am. All four at work as usual. Marce plastering, Davy helping. Rip & Dicky Bird downstairs on the wainscoting.

2pm. Quiet at The Corner, all working.

5.30pm. Men left as usual tonight. Didn't go over to check progress. Didn't see John John on truck.

    *Feeling a little unsettled this evening. Almost wish there was someone about I could be grouchy at.

    *Or kind to.

10.30pm. Cold but not as cold as yesterday. 20s this morning, 40s this afternoon. Sunshine & not so much wind. Watched "Wagon Train", then fell asleep reading. Again.

I didn't need more power -

At least he wasn't letting himself go, she thought. There was that. It wasn't his fault that his job demanded such a strange combination of clothing. Katy watched Nick pulling on his jacket while trying not to let go of the leather bag in which he carried his papers and his lunch. Nick was a surveyor, and he had to spend half his days in an office, half stomping around muddy or dusty fields, carrying instruments and shouting instructions. He looked like a manager to the waist: jacket, tie, ironed shirt. Below that he wore corduroy trousers or jeans and big firm work boots with long laces. But he had never let himself go. True, when he turned forty she took stock of him, and he was a little rounder than when they'd married. Thirteen years of her cooking, he would have said. His hair was thinner, but always neat, trimmed, scented. He shaved precisely, and his hands, despite his work, were generally soft, and his nails clean. He was a good man, as a man, she thought. Sure, he was a good father (the boys loved him), and a good provider (even her own father thought so); but it was as a man that she was considering him. He kissed her goodbye quickly, told her he loved her, and looked at her just that extra moment, with that extra intensity, that suggested he really did. And then he was gone out the door. Yes, she thought, he still had some gas in the tank, as Ev might have said.

Ev was Katy's next-door neighbour, but one. She came over in the morning for coffee sometimes, or Katy went there. They were the same age, and Katy thought Ev was pretty. Where Katy was very tall and very thin, Ev was shorter, curvier. Katy's hair was mousy and she kept it cut short; Ev's was as black as a winter's night, only lately showing a few clouds of grey, as Ev herself might have said. Ev had two daughters, both in school, both bright, both pretty. Katy's boys knew how to be polite to them, and sometimes, in the summer, they could even be found playing together along the street, or in the backyards. All the houses, though different, were almost the same. They were all built between 1840 and 1900, all white, or burgundy, sometimes pale yellow, pale blue or pale green. All with green shutters. Nick had bought this one to suit Katy when they were first married. He liked old houses. Ev had bought hers with her divorce money about two years later. It was a surprise to all of them when she did. Ev and Nick had gone to high school together over the mountain in Boonsboro. It was Katy and her family who had lived in Middletown. Now here they all were, close and friendly.

Katy liked Ev. She liked the things Ev talked about – not the usual run of child-rearing, aches, men, aging, grandparents, household tips, shopping, soap-opera plots, gossip and fashion. Ev had ideas and she liked talking about them. She was honest, a little quirky, idiosyncratic she might have said. And cheerful. Ev was cheerful. No one could ever be lonely, Katy felt, so long as they stayed as cheerful as Ev.

That was why Katy was surprised the morning she saw Ev standing on her sleeping porch looking out over the backyard, coffee cupped in her hands, her nightdress showing beneath her robe. The children had already gone to school, and Katy had gone outside to peg out her laundry when she looked up and saw Ev standing there, in the dappled sunshine through the birch tree, looking off into space.

Katy waited an hour and then went over to Ev's and knocked on the door. They sat at the kitchen table and drank iced tea, as the day was already warming up. Katy talked brightly at first, trying to raise Ev's mood directly, but it didn't really seem to be working. Finally, Ev sighed, trying to exhale all the things on her mind.

You're lucky, Ev said.

I know, Katy answered. But why?

Best you don't know why, I guess.

Ev looked away out the window, though there was nothing to see there, nothing going on.

A man like Nick, Ev said.

Katy smiled.

You know, Ev said, Did Nick tell you? I had such a crush on him in school. Oh! Terrible. I used to lie in bed at night and imagine him. Him and me. It must have gone on a year. Maybe, two? I don't know. I never told him. Well, not, you know, outright or anything. But he must've known. Everybody knew. But he never let on. Never once. I don't know why. He wasn't going out with anybody else at the time. I guess… I don't know, she said. I just don't know.

Ev looked at Katy, then looked away. Nick ever mention that? she said.

No, he didn't, Katy said. I don't think so.

After that, the talked about the new Phys Ed teacher at the children's school, the one the children called Dud Dudley.

That afternoon, Katy finished her housework early, and sat down on the porch swing to cool off. It was warm for May. Very warm. She thought about Nick, wondering whether, at that moment, he was in the office with a fan on, or outside, squinting down a boundary line in a field somewhere. It was strange, she thought, how things can be real, can be simultaneous, when we can't really be sure of them. Where was Nick *right now*? How did she know if he was even alive? What if, right now, someone was heading into the office to phone her, to tell her something awful had happened, that he had died in some kind of terrible accident, had not had time for last words? How could she have faith that what she wasn't thinking of at that moment was even real?

She tried to think about who Nick was before she met him, who he had been, might have been, must have been. She had seen pictures – Nick in his band uniform, Nick laughing on the beach, Nick with his sister, his friend Paul, all dressed up for the Senior Prom with that girl. What was her name?

Katy thought about Ev, and who she probably was in high school. She thought about her wanting Nick, and Nick not noticing, or not acknowledging what he must have known. Did he know? Had it been in any way as real for him as it was for Ev? If it had been, how might it have been different? Different now?

Katy looked around her, at their house, their street, their town. These things were other people's too, they were their neighbours' neighbours. These things belonged to Ev as well as to them, to Katy and to Nick.

Katy wondered whether Ev thought about Nick now. What could she think? Perhaps, she tried to picture what her life would have been like if Nick had noticed her, had loved and married her. Which of these two houses might they be living in? Perhaps, she imagined their past differently, what could have happened in school before the future, the real future, caught up with them; the future that belonged to Katy, Katy and Nick.

Katy imagined Ev imagining. She saw Ev's mind open before her like one of the comic books Nick had saved from his boyhood. Katy saw Ev picturing herself and Nick like Archie and Veronica, going to a drive-in restaurant and eating plates of hamburgers and French fries and bottles of Pepsi Cola which they took from a tray clipped to the driver's side of the car. She pictured them making out in the back seat of the car, parked down some country lane, Ev with her hands in Nick's hair as he struggled to unhook her brassiere. She pictured Nick shopping at Sears for the Christmas present of perfume that he thought Ev would just love. She imagined Nick bringing Ev home to meet his parents (who looked much younger in the image than they really were, even when Katy met them), beaming at his father, as if to say, She's a pretty one, isn't she, Dad? She pictured Nick ringing his hands after some stupid remark he made to his friends had made its way back to Ev, and Ev, furious with him, was slow to accept his apology until he repeated it in two or three different tones of voice. She saw the laziness that having Ev's undying love brought to Nick, as he grew complacent over their match – her wearing his class ring, him knowing he had been her first 'real' boyfriend. She felt the despair, the emptiness, the hopeless romantic yearning for relief that Ev would have felt when it all came to its end with the summer of graduation.

The phone rang in the hallway, and Katy heard it through the screen door. She got up quickly and ran inside, but she was too late. There was no one there. Strange, she thought. It can only have rung a few times. She pictured someone, a man or a woman, she couldn't tell, at the other end of the phone line, putting down the hand-set.

That night, when Nick came home, when the children were in bed, and when everything except the precious hours of a couple's awakened intimacy is rekindled before exhaustion moves them to sleep, Katy looked at Nick and wondered. She listened when he spoke, and she felt as though she were still listening, even when there was silence between them. Love must always include this wonder, she thought. This faith, this mystery, this wonder.

February 18, 1964

6.45am. Recalled a dream. Tom playing with Alex when A was a little boy; Tom throwing A in the air and catching him; me worrying; Tom saying not to worry, it would make A confident in himself, and in Tom and in the world. What was I afraid of?

9.30am. Slight change of the rota today, as Dicky Bird has gone to join Davy & Marce in the plastering. Rip on the wainscoting.

1.15pm. Rip starting skirting downstairs. Muffled sound of Dicky Bird singing, but I couldn't catch the words.

4.45pm. Men left as usual. Marce looking especially tired. Not sure when John John arrived, but I didn't get to speak to him.

*Interesting spectacle. As they were walking to the truck to leave, Marce held out a bucket of tools for John John to take & sit on the truck bed. John John wasn't looking Marce's way, as he was apparently listening to something Rip & Davy were discussing. All at once, Marce just let go of the bucket & the tools crashed to the ground at John John's feet. JJ jumped, & his father looked disgustedly at him. JJ then picked up all the scattered tools, put them in the bucket, swung the bucket on to the truck, then hopped up himself. His father never looked at him again.

10.15pm. Cold feeling, & not really over freezing all day. Snowed frantically at times, beautifully at others, but took a long time to get settled. Dusting only by nightfall.

February 19, 1964

7.45am. Men due shortly. I hope Spring comes soon. I am growing fed up with starting every day with a fireplace clean-up, a Girl Scout fire-building, and a cold hospital-like wash.

8.45am. Men on time for work. Looks like they'll finish the lower middle floor today.

1pm. Lower middle floor finished. Strange sight to see all four of them working on the lowest floor.

5pm. Kitchen ceiling looks done to me. Men gone, all looking a little tired. No sign of JJ.

10.30pm. Temperature in the 30s all day. Fog this morning gave way to wet snowy drizzle, then just light rain.

February 20, 1964

9am. Just back after delivering tray & watching for a moment or two. Men split up again. Davy & Dicky Bird on upper middle floor sanding plaster (terrible noise!). Rip & Marce working on plastering the walls in the kitchen etc.

2pm. Returned with lunch tray. All as before over the road.

5.15pm. Men gone tonight, John John with them, white to the knees with dust. I suspect upper middle floor now sanded. Looked inside briefly. Lowest floor half done. Deep windows look complicated to me.

10.15pm. More or less freezing all day. Wet like yesterday. Finished Reunion. Wonderful.

February 21, 1964

9.30am. Men working as yesterday. Yes, upper middle floor is now ready. Davy & Dicky Bird working on lower middle floor. They've hung a blanket over the doorway to the stairs, as Marce & Rip are finishing the plaster down there.

5.30pm. Men gone now. Sad moment, as once again, I went over to save John John the trip to the Mary House. The plastering in the lowest floor is now done, & Marce & Rip were helping the others to sand the plaster on the floor above. John John was sweeping a little, but mostly leaning on a broom. I praised their foresight in blocking the doorway, saying the blue-green blanket looked like an Indian one. Marce saw an opening & started gleefully teasing JJ. – It was John John's when he was just a little bitty baby. He used to be so pretty. He sure ain't the pick of the litter now. – Now, Marce, Rip said. He's a fine tall boy, ain't ya, John? Gonna be a big man someday, like your daddy. – He ain't never gonna be big as me, Marce said. Hell, he ain't.

*John John, who never says anything at times like this, went outside the back door. I watched him, idly throwing something (old walnuts?) at the Band Hall wall.

10.45pm. Sunny all day today, no rain at all, but only about freezing all day. Watched "The Farmer's Daughter".

*Troubled all evening by a question: Is being an over-protective mother a species of bullying? Both undermine a child's self-confidence.

Oh, Polly, pretty Polly, would you take me unkind?

That spring when the war get started all the white men talking big. They carry they guns with them everywhere they go, and they hunting up all the ole guns they can lay they hands on, and a-scrubbing the rust off 'em. Down the forge they 'bout as busy making knives 'bout as long as ya elbow to ya hand as they is making horseshoes. The women don't look quite so happy and all they talking 'bout is how the war gonna be over in 'bout a month, or least by summer anyhow.

Well, down the ole Middletown road, they a big farm belong to a man named Ab Gaver, and he got a wife called Martha. They was married when I was a child, and I 'member folks talking 'bout the banding and the celebrating. They 'bout as happy as married folks get most of the time. But time they get a little older and they children growing up, things settle down, like they do. Folks say they ain't nothing wrong 'tween 'em, 'cept ole Mister Ab don't never say nothing nice bout Miss Martha no more, and she spend most her time a-sewing and a-cooking and all that. She ain't got but the one house servant, a ole woman name Goldie, that work for her.

They ain't no story 'tween 'em till that little ole farm next to them gets up and bought by a young fella name Frank Poffenberger. Folk say he spend all the money he got just a-buying that place, and he ain't got nothing left. Not a pot to piss in or a window to throw it out of. Anyhow, 'bout then the war coming on, and all the men's a-talking 'bout who ought to be going soldiering and who ain't. Well, Mr Ab say he got a family and a big place to look after, and it ain't desperate or nothing, so he think he let the young fellas fight this one, till they need him. He say ought to be somebody like Mr Frank doing the fighting. Now Mr Frank, he say if was to go off and join the fighting, his farm up and get ruined for he even half get started on it. They weren't enemies or nothing, but that's how things stood when Mister Frank first meet Miss Martha.

Like I say, Miss Martha probably ten fifteen years older than Mister Frank, but that don't make no difference. Mister Frank, he get to thinking that Miss Martha seem mighty lonely over there in that big house of hern, and he think she a fine woman even though she getting old, and he don't mean no disrespect or nothing, but 'fore he knows it he up and falls in love with her. 'Deed I don't know how it happened, but it did. Anyhow, he hear the talking 'bout how Mister Ab don't pay her no mind, so even though he ain't got nothing his own self, he start finding little ways to bring her things he think she like. He bring cuttings off the roses from the back porch, and he bring up a mess of blackberries he pick, and I don't know what all. Meantime, Mr Ab mostly keep hisself in town, down Middletown, or Myersville, or sometimes all the way down to Frederick to get hisself into meetings and clubs and societies just for talking about the war and what they all fixing to do.

Well, if it ain't plain to Miss Martha what's going on with Mister Frank, and it don't look like it is, it sure 'nough is with ole Goldie. She see Mister Frank a-coming and a-going, asking advice and saying what fine children Miss Martha's children is. Yes sir, Goldie think she know what's coming. But if she right she wrong, 'cause ole Mister Frank he don't seem to say nothing or do nothing to 'courage or 'fend Miss Martha, and things look like they just gonna keep going on same as before.

Well, the war go on for 'bout a year year and a half, and they fight them big battles over South Mountain and Sharpsburg and Keedysville, and the government decide it needs some more Yankees to replace the dead ones, and they start telling the farmers they got to join up now. Well, Mister Ab, he start to worrying 'bout what he gonna do, cause he don't want to be no Yankee, and he done waited too long to be a Sesesh, so he hear that they got a plan that if a fella don't want to go to the war, he could hire hisself another fella to do the fighting for him. So Mister Ab, he go round 'most everybody he know see if can find hisself somebody to go and do his share of the fighting. Well, when he out in town trying to find somebody he don't already know, Mister Frank, he come over to see Miss Martha like he always does, and they get to talking, and she tell him all 'bout what Mister Ab out trying to do. 'Fore long, pretty as you please, Goldie say, Miss Martha say maybe Mister Frank like to hire hisself out as Mister Ab's fighting soldier. Goldie say Mr Frank look like he seen his own ghost, and quick as lightning, he get up and go on home, and stop his visiting, far as she know.

Little while later Mister Ab come home, and he say he been to all the folks he know, and he can't find nobody wants to go to the war 'stead of him, money or no money. So Miss Martha, she say why don't he go over there and see if can talk Mister Frank into doing it for him. Mister Ab say he already thought of that, but Mister Frank done said he can't go to the war nohow. She say he oughta try anyhow, and that's what he do.

Now I don't know nothing but what got said 'tween Mister Ab and Mister Frank, but whatever it was, Mister Ab don't never forget it. He end up going off to the war hisself 'bout Christmas, but he don't do no fighting. He got so sick down 'round Washington that he can't half breathe no more, and he sound like a ole horse if he so much as walk up the porch steps, and the government send him home. I 'spect he blame Mister Frank for everything that happen in the war, and when he get home, and the war get over, he start to looking for ways just to fix Mister Frank for good. He cut down all the trees up on the hill, so the wind blow hard as hell towards the field where Mister Frank try to grow his wheat, and two years together it blow flat. He dig a ditch long the lane and every time it rain it flood down over Mister Frank's hogpen and chicken house. He tell everybody that Mister Frank feeding dead rats to the cows so the milk ain't no good. I don't know why folks believe anything he say, cause they all know he got it in for Mister Frank. Sure 'nough, they did though. 'Bout two years after the war, Mister Frank sell that farm to a fella from down Berlin way. Goldie say she hear Mister Frank say he try his luck someplace else. Maybe Nebraska, she say.

February 22, 1964

7am. Very very cold again. 12, I believe. Going to Frederick today.

3pm. Long day! Just back from Frederick. Decided for a change not to go to bookshop but went to library instead. Found myself absorbed in local history – Indians & Civil War.

Completely forgot to have lunch, so went to A & P hungry, which is always a bad idea (spent $21!). House is utterly freezing, but I've got to eat something. Maybe sandwich with tea?

7.30pm. Late lunch has spoiled my dinner appetite, though I went through the motions & have now got enough corn soup (recipe care of Edna from the church) for at least two days. House warmed up quickly. Expect to sleep well.

10.30pm. Below freezing all day. Sunny & dry. Tired in the shoulders, probably from library table, which was too short. Stomach growling though feels full.

February 23, 1964

6.45am. Near zero this morning! So cold! Have already got the fire burning.

9.45am. Almost no one walking to church this morning. Probably all being driven as it is so cold.

12pm. Luckily, I looked out the window in time to see the handful of people walking home, Edna among them. Told her I had made her corn soup. She looked a little concerned. —Where'd ya get corn this time of year? she said. I told her I imported it from Libby's. She grinned & shook her head. —ou just wait till summer, she said. I'll give ya some of mine.
    *No sign of Cinch today.

10.45pm. Dry & bright today & crept above freezing this afternoon. Watched "Bonanza".

February 24, 1964

9.30am. All four of the men at work today. Davy & Dicky Bird on the lowest floor sanding. Rip & Marce upstairs, very quiet.

2pm. Whole of The Corner seems to smell of Elmer's Glue. Looks the same as this morning.

*Wrote a letter to Sis this morning, warmer than my last one (& sooner). Surprised myself with this. Got it into the mailbox in time.

4.45pm. Men gone now. Had a look inside. Kitchen & utility seem sanded or nearly so now. Glue smell is from upper middle floor. Evidently something on the walls.

10.30pm. Still very cold this morning (below 20) & only in the 30s after lunchtime. Sun & cold wind though. Watched "Wagon Train" while balancing check book.

February 25, 1964

9am. Men at work as before. Downstairs is sanded, as I thought. Dicky Bird & Davy painting glue stuff on, while Marce & Rip doing the same upstairs. Dicky Bird doing his best with bold sweeps of "don't they know it's the end of the whorl hurled" but sounds a little hoarse, probably on the glue fumes.

2pm. Men struggling slightly. They've got the furnace off & the windows open to get rid of the smell, but it is so cold they are finding it hard to keep going.

4pm. Men seem to have gone home early today. Can't blame them. I'm not going in there, as it is still fuming, I suspect.

7.15am. Not much above zero again. Fire sluggish, as quite still (I think.)

10.30pm. Sunny day, but only 30s at best.

But when I die, won't you bury me in the mountains?

I, LittleWound, tell this story.

It was in the time when the Washechu men and their slaves were digging the canal – Irishmen and Germans who fought like wolves, drank like horses and ate like pigs. It was when the leaves hung from the trees like rags and the air was like the breath of a running dog, that they began to die in their footsteps, hiding themselves and vomiting piles of maggots. It was at the time that BlackMary became a modiste to the Master's wife, making all of her clothes, those seen and those not seen.

There was a farmer named Myers, also known as Charles, who lived on the side of Myersville where the HomeWind blows the leaves, even when the grain ripens. His face took its shape from the moon, and his hair, the colour of walnuts, had shrunken to the centre of his head. He wore whiskers to shadow the barrels of his jaws. He had shared his farm with his brother until that brother sold him his portion, and moved to Baltimore, where he loved a woman who was his cousin. But Charles farmed and managed the chores of his household with only the help of two slaves. One was a field-hand whose foot twisted towards his other ankle. It had got broken when another master had beaten him for looking too long with sadness when his woman was sold, and then had left him chained to a log when he tried to run away. The other was a girl he had purchased as a child from a market, who had cost him $1.15 a pound. The neighbours sometimes lent Charles a house-servant to train her in her chores. No one spoke of evil between them, and when she was a woman, Charles gave her to the field-hand as a wife. In respect of her marriage and the kindness she had seen from him, she and the field-hand made him a mattress of rye-straw and a pillow with the down from their ducks.

As these things were happening, Charles felt the fires in his body warm him in the night and melt him in the day. Loneliness lay on his shoulders and sang in his dreams. Letters came from his brother, speaking of his happiness and his children and the laughter of his wife. With his own eyes Charles saw the tenderness and the comradeship between his servants, who soon had a child also.

Charles's neighbour was a farmer named Doub, and he had two daughters, both women. When Doub's sister died, his niece came to live with these daughters and her name was Wolfe, also known as Martha. It was so that Martha was a woman who felt the pressure of her footsteps, who felt the angle of her chin and who felt the turning in the air around her when she moved. Doub's daughters looked on her with esteem, although the farmer himself longed for a day when she would marry. In this way, he came to speak of her to Charles, and brought Charles to his own house on errands so that Charles might see her for himself. This design worked as Doub expected, but only in one respect. Charles felt the heat in his veins spread from his fingertips to his toes whenever Martha was around. But to her, Charles was less than the fruit that grew on the trees, the sound of the birds in the evening, or the scent of the pines as the sun rose.

Season after season, as Doub's daughters married and left home, and his own hair and that of his wife faded like ice, Charles came to their house, bringing in his face all the signs of love and yearning. His slaves had found comfort and solace in one another and their fortunes prospered, so Charles freed both, easing his conscience, and retaining their respect and their labour. Yet though she imposed no tasks upon him, recognized no strengths or promise within him, and offered him no scope to find joy at her hands, so Martha wasted Charles's dreams, and left him to follow her steps.

The news came to Doub then that Charles had found a road for himself and one that would take him from the Catoctin's mountain, to a place where he would become a stranger. His servants had moved themselves, finding work in Harrisburg, and the farm was sold. Charles would seek his path alongside those who followed the setting sun.

The news that Charles would no longer be coming to court her left Martha emptied. She knew now that the music in her was hushed, for there were no other men who came to Doub's threshold seeking her. Pain surrounded her heart and swelled her eyes. When she came to seek him on his farm, a valise in her hand and a bonnet on her head, her mind made up to join him, whether as his wife or anything else, she found he had gone.

And so Martha would outlive Doub by many seasons, but she did not outlive his wife, his daughters or his granddaughters. With them she spent the time when the sunlight lay across their knees, making quilts for them to lay upon their own and their children's beds. They made all the designs they knew. But those which made Martha's fingers tremble with her needle were the four-doves-at-the-well, the lonely-star, the trip-'round the-mountain, and the rocky-road.

February 26, 1964

7am. Below 10 degrees again & foggy.

9.15am. Back from The Corner. Everyone working alone today, sanding the new wainscoting. What a racket! I can't bear it.

12.45pm. Hurried back as the noise of sanding is incessant. Dust everywhere.

5pm. Men gone now. All of them creamy with dust. John John too, on the back of the truck. Rainy as they left, causing streaks to run down their (his & Davy's) faces.

10.15pm. Warmed up a lot today, once rain got going. Mid 40s. Drier this evening.

February 27, 1964

9am. Same as yesterday across the road. Dreadful sanding screech everywhere. Dicky Bird leaving his voice on its roost. Wisely, I think.

5.15pm. Men gone now. Had a look around, & all seems to be quite pleasant & new looking so far. Surprisingly bright. Bucketsful of swept dust still in places.

*Caught a glimpse of the white-haired bully boys going up the Harmony Road earlier. They had the skinny kid, the frog-like one & one I didn't recognize with them. They were solemnly kicking a pair of Coca Cola cans in front of them, all doing their best not to look as cold as they obviously felt.

10.45pm. Sky bright with the moon tonight. Below 20 this morning, but 30s later. Some sun. Watched "Rawhide".

*Have grown angry with myself over thinking about the white-haired boys episode, & that part of me feels completely certain that if Alex were here & a boy with them, he would be completely overawed by them, ridiculed & possibly beaten up. It is a poisonous fantasy of something that has no basis in reality & I am angry for having thought of it.

*No, I am angry with myself for imagining my own son as necessarily the victim of people like that. Is my belief that it would be true the result of my having known Alex as a boy, & therefore "knowing" what he (or I?) could expect? Or did I believe something like this too soon, somehow making my belief true for Alex? Did he become the boy I was afraid he would become because I was so afraid he would become it? Did I teach him to be afraid?

*I am afraid now that he is dead. So now I am making sure he will never know this.

*Unless it is too late. Somehow.

February 28, 1964

7.30am. Cold this morning & have overslept slightly (or feel that I have). Very foggy. Outside and in…

9.30am. Back with tray now. Finishing touches, it looks like to me, as they are obviously restless to get on with something new.

*Marce informed me that they might have to leave early today, as the radio says "it's threatening to make weather".

12pm. Men already gone. Can't imagine they did much this morning except evaluate what they've done & got still to do.

3pm. Couldn't resist a little walk around the empty Corner, watching the snow fall outside through the windows of every room. It is a huge old place. So much space for happiness, for solitude, for expansion of every dream.

*I wish it were all over.

10pm. Snow lasted all day & has piled up a couple of inches out there. Temperature still below freezing. Watched "Route 66".

February 29, 1964

7am. Snowing again this morning, & temperature below freezing. Very pretty. Have made a fire & decided to stay home.

8.30am. Definitely not going to Frederick today, in case it gets colder & the roads freeze.

2.15pm. Quite still for a while & looked settled, so made a quick trip to Middletown Acme for essentials ($8). House a little chilly as I had to let the fire go out before I left.

5pm. Had only a few light snacks this afternoon, so as not to repeat the late-lunch fiasco from a week or so ago. Have started reading The Reivers as just about the only thing on the shelf I haven't read. So far, not that impressed.

10.45pm. Warmed up this afternoon. Snow very pretty for a few hours but sagging a little by dark.

March 1, 1964

7.30am. Woke up early, strangely & lay in bed a bit. Only about 15 degrees out there. In like a very cold lion, it seems.

12pm. As I saw them all walking to church I decided I would trust their instincts & go for a short walk. I went up the Brethren Church Road, crossed US 40 & went as far as Middle Creek, still making it back in time to join the ladies in the walk back from church.

*Some beautiful views on this walk (which I hadn't done before) all along the valley, as if walking in a very wide trough among the mountains. The farmers' fields are like piles of green & brown & gold cushions. The large farms are stripped in fantastic contours like maps.

*Middle Creek made me wish I knew how to fish. Passed farms in red, gray, white & green on the way there.

*Walked back from the church with Agassy & Cinch & the others. I asked them in for a cup of tea, & for the first time the looked very tempted, as they exchanged hopeful glances at one another. Someone needs to make the first move.

*Having fried chicken, potatoes, lima beans & corn for lunch, or dinner, as Cinch calls it. Trying to fit in. What would Sis say?

3.45pm. Have read a lot of Faulkner. Not my favorite of his books, as it feels like the work of one who is aging. An aging giant, anyway. Almost time for more tea.

6.45pm. Wrote letters to Sis & to Ags, so feel entitled to some sort of treat this evening. Too full from lunch to eat dinner, (Cinch's supper!) I'm afraid.

9pm. Stupidly, I've been hungry for an hour now & nibbling on saltines, finished off with graham crackers. Either I won't sleep at all or I will have lurid dreams.

10.30pm. Managed to be quite warm this afternoon, nearly 50. Very sunny all day too. Watched "Bonanza" but felt like I'd seen it all before.

March 2, 1964

9am. Men all at work today. They seem to be scattered all over the house. Marce is on the bottom floor fiddling with the windows. Rip on the next floor up doing the same. Dicky Bird & Davy on the upper middle floor, also tinkering at the windows. What are they up to?

*Remembered to put letters in mailbox.

11.15am. Ingalls truck has just left, having unloaded all sorts of lumber of various sizes, including plywood. As I cannot resist, I went over to watch the unloading. This time, to my surprise (and evidently to Marce's) there were two black men on the Ingalls truck. —Where's the regular fella? Marce asked. —Gone to Baltimore, the new man said. His daughter marrying a fella down there. —Uh huh, Marce said. —Y'all find this place all right? he asked. —Yes sir, the new driver answered. —'Cause I bet y'all ain't from 'round here, Marce said. —No, sir, we ain't, the driver answered. Then pointing to the younger black man I'd seen before, he said, —He's been here though. —Uh huh, Marce answered. All the way from Jefferson. Then they unloaded all the wood into the lower floor.

5pm. All quiet at The Corner. New lumber looks untouched. Windows on three floors seem to have been taken out, with holes left in the frames. Not sure what they've been doing.

10.30pm. Nice day today with plenty of sun. Temperature between freezing & middle 50s. Watched "Wagon Train". Just occurred to me, I didn't dream anything last night.

March 3, 1964

9am. Not so cold this morning, but foggy with a light drizzle. Men at work like yesterday, except that Marce now seems to have turned his attention to the pile of lumber in what will be the kitchen.

1.45pm. Marce busy working on what will be the kitchen cupboards. Meanwhile, Rip & Dicky Bird seem to be dismantling the windows, which seems very worrying. Davy scraping paint on the top floor windows.

3pm. Bored with my own work, I finished The Reivers. The work of a genius gone blind.

5.30pm. Have been inspecting the men's work on the windows. It seems they are re-adjusting the internal mechanisms of the windows, so that all of them slide as they ought to. Poor Davy is busy digging the paint off them. Where does his mind go when he does this? Home? Family? Next Summer? Sex? Marce has made some headway on kitchen, as there now seems to be strips nailed to the wall & plywood cut up.

10.45pm. Damp all day today. Quite a bit of rain at times.

March 4, 1964

9.15am. Marce at work on the kitchen, building the uppermost cupboards. It seems very fussy. Davy scraping windows, with little chips of paint sticking to his sweaty face. The others are carefully removing window bits & scrutinizing them, although I cannot imagine what they are looking for. Dicky Bird, working alone, has found deep resources of song & is piping up fulsomely about his fear that he might cross over love's cheating line. After all, she does belong to another, & can never be his.

2pm. Just the same at The Corner. Evidently Dicky Bird must have set a foot on the wrong side of the cheating line, as he is now crooning that he is sorry, SO sorry, that he was such a fool.

5pm. Men gone now. Marce has, to his credit, executed quite a complicated looking corner cupboard. Davy has stripped bare all of the top floor windows, & the others seem to have done whatever it was to all the other windows, as they now seem to be back where they belong. They look the same to me, but rather like someone has dismantled them, unearthed their secrets, & let them go about their business, like so many foreigners at a border crossing.

*No chance to get a word with John John who looks older almost every time I see him.

10.45pm. Very dull day, 30s & 40s, foggy this morning, rain since lunchtime, then drizzle this evening.

March 5, 1964

9am. Foggy & wet this morning, but in the 40s. Marce in the kitchen (words I bet his wife has never used) & the others busy scraping windows on the middle floors. This warm weather has untightened Dicky Bird, who seems louder & frankly more determined than ever. Today he is pleading for help, as he seems to be fallin'. If no one is willing to shut the door to temptation, he may just walk through. If only she would turn away!

2.30pm. The wind has really picked up, & it is much warmer now. 65 degrees!

*Marce has now completed (I think) a whole wall of the higher cupboards, except for the doors. I watched him for a short while using a kind of saw with a round blade poking through a table. The concentration it requires is inspiring, as it looks dangerous. The interesting thing though is his face after he passes the wood over the saw. He holds the wood up to his face, squints one eye and seems to sight along it as though it were a gun. What is he looking for?

5.30pm. Men left on time as usual. It looks to me as if all the windows above the lowest floor have been stripped to the bare wood. John John was with them today, at the end. He was using a dust pan & brush, & trying to sweep up the paint chips, which seem to be strangely sticky & he was struggling somewhat. His father, unhelpfully, said to him, —For Chr[]st's sake don't get that stuff in your eyes or your mouth. JJ didn't look like he wanted to anyway.

10.30pm. Rain settled down to drizzle this evening, but wind continued. Watched "Rawhide", or think I did, but I kept finding myself thinking of other things.

He picked up a hammer, Lord, Lord.

People say, Don't y'all get lonely down there or nothing? No, sir, I tells 'em, not too much. I see how folks is with each other, what they say, how they treat each other, and I think maybe I'm just fine like I am. Yes, I do. I don't get me no man and no children or nothing, and sometimes I think 'bout that. But what I want an ole man for anyway? His big feet a-trailing in the mud and a-asking me to do for him. No, sir. Me and ole Red Mary 'bout as close as I get to anybody, and then she up and die. That ain't her fault. She make me feel she know when I around and sometimes she do things she know I like. Like putting the jasmine and the basil and the roses down in 'mong my clothes. Or frying up the cucumbers real fast in the grease so they crisp on the outside and still soft in the middle. I cry like a baby when they bury her. Ain't no man never gonna know how to treat me like that. Anyhow, the white folks bust up the negroes so the men don't feel like men 'cept they be acting like they think men supposed to act. And I ain't got time for that. So no, sir, I don't let myself get lonely. Got too much to do being my own self.

I see what it does to folk though. I knowed a gal 'bout my age, name Alvey, live up on the Schildknecht farm, up near Wolfsville. Big ole place, that un. She a house servant and do mostly the cooking and the washing and the cleaning and the chores and the gardening, like me down here at The Corner. 'Cept she got her eye all set a-looking for herself to fall in love. She think everybody oughta be in love just 'bout much as they can. And she always a-looking around, seeing what she can do to get the loving going for everybody.

Well, ole Mister Otha Schildknecht, he got a boy 'bout same age as her, done with school and 'bout the age to be setting hisself up somewhere, and Alvey, she hear him a-having a argument with his daddy 'bout his own loving a girl name Miss Sylvia Ridenour, live up the mountain, half-way into the wildwood. Aw, his daddy say, them ole Ridenours ain't got nothing but a shack up there. What y'all wanna be sniffin' round none of they gals for? She ain't gonna be no good for ya nohow. The boy, whose name was Mister Silas, didn't like the sound of that none. But he knowed better than to say too much, 'cause his daddy not the kind to take no sass from no boy, even if he his daddy's favourite. (He get to be the favourite cause he 'bout the only one left. His mama had herself twins three times a-running, and every time she have a set, one of 'em up and died 'fore they learn to walk. So they weren't but the three children left.)

Anyhow, Alvey get to thinking that she maybe ought to do something for Mister Silas, and Mister Silas, he don't know what to do, 'cept try to keep that Ridenour gal, Miss Sylvia, from falling out of love with him. So he out a-walking 'round and a kickin' the chicken and Alvey say, What y'all gon' do, Mister Silas? And Mister Silas say his daddy done told him he can't go up there to that Ridenour place no more, and his daddy whoop him if he so much as point the horse's nose in that direction.

Now right yare is where Alvey ought to bite down on her tongue so hard she taste the blood. But she don't. 'Stead, Mister Silas, she say, How come y'all don't write Miss Sylvia a letter, tell her what's going on down here. Sure 'nough she wanna know, I 'spect. Now Mister Silas, he just about desperate enough to listen, even to Alvey, and he say, Yes, sir, you sure 'nough right 'bout that. So he up and write her that letter, and he give it to Alvey to take it up there her own self, so ole Mister Otha Schildknecht, don't find out nothing 'bout it.

Now Alvey was mighty lucky, that the Schildknecht place touch the Ridenour road up there 'yond the woods where the apple trees is. 'Cause if she had to be out there on the road, the padarolles get her sure as your born. So what she took to doing, is after dark she say to the missus that she gon' out to watch the guineas and the geese roost theyselves, 'cause she can hear a fox a-barking in the hollow. And the missus, she half-beat with her own working, and not no strong woman nohow, she always mostly sleep anyway by then, so she don't care none. So up the hill ole Alvey high-tail it with Mister Silas's letter. She find Miss Sylvia a-waiting for her down by the end of the road lead up to that loghouse they live in, cause her pap ain't got the sense God give a piss ant, and don't keep no eye on her at all, and her mama know better than to raise Cain round the house with a man that drinks whiskey for his supper. So Alvey give her the letter, and Miss Sylvia always give her something to take back, like some biscuits or a hanky or something, 'cause she don't write too good her own self.

Now if I only knowed what Alvey was up to I'd have told her what she gonna get when them white folks find out what she a-doing. It don't matter that it ain't got nothing to do with her, and she ain't mixed up in it no way her own self. She get her hands on it, and that gonna be 'nough. That's what happen when y'all mix youself up with folkses' dealings in love. I seen it 'nough to be sure that. 'Deed, I do.

That's just what happened too. Just like I said it would. Alvey, she running up the field one night with one of them letters in her hand – not even got the good sense to put it in her apron or nothing – and what she see 'cept ole Mister Otha Schildknecht hisself walking towards her, carrying a groundhog he shot.

Alvey! What in the hell you a-doing out here this time of the evening?

Missus done told me to come and look for you, she say. Say you was out longer than you should be, she say.

Oh, she did, did she? he say. That piece of paper for me?

Alvey know she in trouble now. 'Deed, I don't know, sir, she say. I can't read it or nothing. I just picked it up down by the stone ridge.

Let me see it, he say. They ain't nothing else she can do, so Alvey, she give him the letter Mister Silas wrote. Ole Otha Schildknecht he hold it up to the light and he squint and squint, but he can't see nothing, 'cause it getting dark, and he don't see little stuff too good anyway.

Get on home now, he say. I take care of this my own self.

Alvey don't never find out nothing 'bout what that letter say, and she don't hear no words 'tween Mister Silas and his daddy no more neither. She don't take no more letters though. Mister Silas, he go next day down his uncle way, down Myersville. Alvey, she lucky ole Mister Otha didn't bark the hide clean off her for what she done. Thing was, Mister Otha couldn't find out nohow who responsible. Alvey didn't know nothing and didn't lie no more than most people would have lied. And Mister Silas, he get scared and tell his daddy the whole thing Alvey's idea, and Mister Otha, he say it don't matter whose idea it was nohow, cause I done told you not to be messing with none of them trashy Ridenours.

Anyway, bout a week later, ole Mister Otha, he up and sell Alvey to a speculator. She brung 'bout thousand dollars cause she a good cook and the right age for breeding.

March 6, 1964

7am. Temperature near freezing this morning, & positively the windiest day I've ever seen! Twigs & small branches clattering down from the trees against the roof, here & across the road. March is in like a very large lion.

*Dreamed last night of Alex walking along Middle Creek with a girl whose face I couldn't see. I hope so much that this is prophetic.

9.30am. Men working as usual this morning. Rip downstairs with Davy scraping the big windows in the kitchen. Marce building cupboards. Dicky Bird evidently upstairs, singing away, though I couldn't hear the words this time.

2.30pm. Late to collect the lunch tray today. Marce nearly done the upper cupboards. Davy & Rip nearly done the windows. Made a point of listening at the stairs to hear Dicky Bird's solo, but all I could be sure of was that his pain keeps right on a-hurtin' & the pillow where she laid her head now holds his lonely tears instead. He has a fantastic memory for these song lyrics, & I only wish there was a way for him to find his fortune with this gift. He certainly won't find it for his voice.

4.45pm. John John just left. He says that next week they expect to have all the windows done & the kitchen cupboards built, except for the doors. I asked him how he liked the looks of the place. He thought for a minute, obviously never having considered this, or maybe, just not used to be asked his opinion on things generally. —It's fine, he said, adding, I like the high porch.

10.45pm. Sunny all day today, & in the 50s this afternoon. Wind only dropped late this afternoon.

March 7, 1964

7.45am. House quite cold this morning, as it is freezing outside. This up & down temperature means the house is too hot or too cold all the time at the moment.

2pm. Worn out now. What a busy morning. Went to the C Burr Artz again on a mission for local history, & was justly rewarded, as I have brought home another stack of books & many notes. Also, went to the Market Street bookstore & bought a novel by Richard Yates, called Revolutionary Road. Frivolously, I then went to the Blue Ridge News Agency & bought a Vogue magazine. I got back to the car, ravenous, & had one of those huge stinky White Star hotdogs, leafing greasily through the magazine. I then put more money in the meter & went down the street to J C Penney where I bought a boat neck shirt & a pair of penny loafers. Spring is definitely in the air.

*Went to A & P, where feeling funny after the hot dog, I only spent $14. I have probably forgotten things.

5.30pm. Now tired & dirty in an honorable way, as I have been gardening. Vegetable beds are now shaping up among the string alleys I've laid out.

10.30pm. Had a good scrub, a light dinner & then lay in bed, I'm ashamed to say, reading the Yates novel. Very impressed.

10.45pm. Almost 70 this afternoon, & beautiful sunshine again.

March 8, 1964

8am. Dull gray & cold this morning, near freezing. Fog. Glad I gardened yesterday, though my arms ache, my knees are like tarpaper & unaccountably there is a tender apple-shaped bruise on my elbow.

12.45pm. Walked back with the ladies today. Much talk of their success yesterday selling "the eats" at a public auction, raising money for the church. I'm sorry I missed it. There was a good crowd, they said. I asked Cinch what she bought, & she said, –Aw, just some ole junk. Agassy spoke up & said she got some "real nice flat irons". I said I could remember seeing these when I was a girl (though I didn't say they belonged to the woman who did our ironing). All the women, including Edna, chuckled.

*They also said that there is going to be "a big feed" (ie dinner) over at Myersville at the Fire Department to raise money for the volunteers. It is to be near Easter. I must make an effort to go.

5pm. Drinking tea too long & brooding over Alex. Sometimes, in the autumn, I thought when I was outside, that if a leaf fell & touched me that it was a sign that he was thinking of me. Naturally, I stood sometimes, hoping as hard as I could that the falling leaves would strike me. But they seldom did. Now there are no more leaves.

*No mother dares to be a fatalist.

10pm. Drizzle & some rain today. Mid 50s though. Through the fuzz I watched a little of the "DuPont Show of the Week". If this is the highlight, I wonder what the other six days have been like.

March 9, 1964

6.45am. Not sure whether to light the fire today. Over 40 already outside. Quite wet looking though, & foggy.

9am. Men busy already. Davy & Dicky Bird on the top floor, undercoating windows. Rip seems to be finishing kitchen windows & also helping Marce with cupboards, especially holding sheets of plywood.

    *When I went outside, I nearly tripped as someone has put a flat iron on my porch. Honestly, these women are as shy as deer.

1.30pm. Have let the fire die out as it is 75 degrees outside! Rain a little gusty, or I'd have the windows open. From the windows, my vegetable beds are like rectangular dormant volcanoes.

    *Work at Corner as expected. Rip now on his own on upper middle floor, also undercoating windows. Marce seems to be working on lower cupboards, all of which seems to be managed with a low stream of bitten-off expletives.

5pm. John John as usual this evening. I couldn't help but notice the sorry state of his clothing. How have I not seen this before? He was wearing cheap blue sneakers, white socks, tan pants, a yellow shirt, white t shirt & a green baseball cap. With his plainly unwashed greasy hair & thick black-framed glasses, I can only think what a terrible time he must have at school. Especially as his pants are about three inches too short. "High water pants" Alex used to call them. No child, whose parents respect him, would let him look this way. What can I do?

    *Forgot to look at how far work had got today. Entire place stinks of paint fumes.

10.15pm. Cooler this evening, but still drizzling. Watched nearly all of "Wagon Train" though I missed the beginning. Enjoying Yates.

I'm chopping in the new ground -

I never forget that Fall when they had the big battles. Lord a-mercy. Folks more scared then I ever seen 'em 'fore or since.

General Lee and the Sesesh fellas all crossed the river and 'bout half the folks took to the roads a-carrying all they could. I ain't never seen nothing like it, no sir, I ain't. Folks with children and everything up and flung in the waggons and the horses and all get out. They was Yankee soldiers too, but they was mostly boogered up and sick and just a-trying to get out of them places down Frederick where they was being nursed, all walking best they could to get theyselves out of the way 'fore the Sesesh could catch 'em. And it didn't feel like no Fall yet or nothing neither. Hot as a skillet and not a breeze for your money nowhere. 'Bout the only thing look like Fall was the walnuts a-dropping on the ground with a thump on the ole Mary House roof and on The Corner and a-rolling down into the road, and up on the Big House. Corn all a-dying too, and folks getting ready for the cutting. We hear the Yankees burn all they things down Frederick, a-blowing up they stuff 'fore the Sesesh get it. When the Sesesh get into town, umnh umnh, how the folks goes hog wild. They say they flags and a-shouting and a-singing and a-laughing to beat the band all out in the streets and everywhere. They went and burned down the office of the 'zaminer, and they ain't no paper 'gain like that till after the war. Things sure different when they gone. The Sesesh bust up the train tracks everywhere they find em, and The Corner got waggons outside it all day everyday with people coming to get theyselves some flour and cornmeal. All them folks that did the dancing and the jumping when the Sesesh fellas come 'round singing a different tune then. No sir, they down in they holes like groundhogs then. They run they big mouths folks get the law 'round like they wouldn't have done 'fore. No, sir.

It 'fect most everybody. Up the ole road 'fore you get to the Fisher's Hollow, back in there where the ole cave is and the little falls, you wouldn't believe it, but that mountain flat right out like a mantelpiece, and they a little farm back there. It belong to some people called Doub, a brother and a sister that got it from they daddy. I don't know what he was called, but the sister was named Miss Dewey. It just the two of them and the one field hand they get when they daddy die, a fool young fella name Elias.

Well, soon as the war gets declared, even 'fore you could smell the gunpowder, Miss Dewey's brother run off down the county and cross the river to join up with the Sesesh and do his fighting with them. She in charge of the farm, and she got that fool Elias to do the outside work for her, and nobody 'spect no harm, cause Elias too dumb to lick the trouble off his own fingers.

Now for 'bout the first year year and a half of the war, Miss Dewey and Elias get on fine up there. He doing the work like he oughta, and she left him get on with it and don't say too much. Pretty soon though, ole Elias he starting to feel hisself a little. He start to thinking what if Miss Dewey brother don't come back from the war? 'Spose he up and catch a bullet his own? Ole Elias, he start to thinking he a mighty big and important thing on that farm now. Yes, he did. He start thinking, maybe that farm his own. Maybe he thinking 'fore long, Miss Dewey his own too, and then he ain't hern no more.

So he start getting ideas. He say, Miss Dewey, how it be if I was to go down to the creek and get some that good clay and fix up the foundations on the smokehouse, like it oughta be? And Miss Dewey, she say, Well, that fine with me. And then he do it, and she say, It looks mighty good, 'Lias, mighty good. 'Fore long, he done whitewash the hogpen, roof up the chickenhouse, split all the kindling and I don't know what all. And ole Miss Dewey, she just go on a-saying, That look mighty good to me, 'Lias, mighty good.

Well, when General Lee his own self and all them Sesesh come over the river, Miss Dewey get 'cited 'cause she think she gonna see that brother of hern again. So she get Elias to take the ole mule and ride on down to Middletown where they say the

Sesesh is a-coming in big, and tell him to ask all the soldiers and they officers where her brother is.

Now 'Lias, he don't want to go none, but he do it 'cause she told him, and all them Sesesh fellas ain't got no time for no field hand with questions, and he don't learn nothing. All happen is they fellas take that mule from him, and say if he don't shut up they gonna take him too, and Elias have to walk all the way from Middletwon back home time it get dark. Miss Dewey didn't like it none, for sure and certain, and she say Elias some kind of ole fool for a-losing her mule like he did. And Elias, he start to feeling mighty poorly his own self, and while she a-telling him how dumb he is, he jump up and start to do some shouting of his own.

Don't you see what I do? he say. Don't you see me a-busting my gut trying to do ya right? Can't ya see what I'm a-doing? I done it all for you. That's why I done it. 'Spose ain't nobody come back from this war? What y'all gonna do then? What y'all gonna do then, honey?

Now Miss Dewey, she hear them words, and she know what they mean. She tell ole Elias to hush up and get hisself back out to his quarters 'bove the springhouse and don't bother her no more. She say she got a gun and anybody make her any trouble she use it to lay them out dead, if they Yankee or if they ain't.

Now ole Elias, he don't take it too good. After that he goes to working again just like he used to, but 'thout no 'nitative. Miss Dewey, she keep in the house far as he see, and she put his meals on the porch, and she don't talk to him at all. Then the days when the big battles happening comes, and we all hear the cannons a-booming 'cross the valley. Miss Dewey, she lean out the window and she tell ole Elias to get hisself down the road to The Corner or somewhere and see if he can find out what's a-happening. He come back and he say the roads is got broke-up soldiers everywhere, and they a-fighting over South Mountain. Miss Dewey, she sitting on the porch with a shotgun, and she tell

Elias to get hisself 'bout his chores, and let out if he see anything 'spicious.

Well, they ain't nothing 'spicious for 'bout a week, 'cept bleeding soldiers everywhere, and folks sending they clothes and they sheets and everything they don't want to eat in waggons off to the churches in Frederick and Middletown and Myersville and everywhere in creation. They ain't no paper no more, but the folks come back with the story that the Sesesh is beat, and they all running like dogs back over the Potomac again.

Now Miss Dewey, she get scared, 'cause everybody in Harmony know her brother maybe one of them Seseshes, and she ain't got no man 'round the house case they looking for trouble.

So in the morning, she get up and she call Elias to the porch for his breakfast and she say, Look here, Elias, I 'preciate all ya done 'round here, I surely do. I didn't mean nothing 'bout that mule, 'cause I know you couldn't've helped it none. But we got to get ourselves something straight sorted out 'round here till this ole war ends. Now she say, look here, this what we gonna do. And she tell Elias that 'bout the best thing she can think of is to hire him out till the war over. Who gonna tend them fields? he say. Ain't nobody gonna, she say. It's all gonna have to wait till the war over.

So she send ole Elias with a paper she wrote all the way over the mountain and down Shookstown way till he get to Frederick, and she tell him to find a white man and hire hisself out, and get the white man to send her the money he get. Now Elias, he ain't never been nowhere like Frederick before, and now they Yankees everywhere, and they need all the help they can get for to bury them dead soldiers, and Elias he get a job a-digging graves. That last till Christmas, and then the Yankees tell him far as they concerned, he now a free man. And just like that, he go off, and Miss Dewey, she don't hear from him no more at all.

She didn't hear nothing from her brother no more neither. But after the war one of them Doub boys over Myersville come home, and he say he hear that that brother of hern died in Richmond, sick with something made him bleed from the mouth and other places he didn't like to say. Miss Dewey sell the farm after that and live with her sister up Emmittsburg.

March 10, 1964

8.45am. Just back. Davy & Dicky Bird still undercoating, Rip gone to the top alone to paint windows. Marce to battle with kitchen alone. Achilles with a pencil over his ear.

2pm. Back after collecting lunch tray. Smell of fumes is enough to choke anyone but Dicky Bird, who is in the front room on the middle floor, tiredly intoning that everybody is going out & having fun while he is just a fool for staying home & having none. Marce seems to have got several of the big kitchen cupboards in place now.

5pm. Men driven off. One wall of kitchen cupboards in place, top & bottom. Windows on all floors looking either white or silver white, so I cannot tell what is finished & what isn't.

10.30pm. Weather much like yesterday, but not quite as warm. Still over 70 this afternoon. House cold this morning, but I risked not having a fire. Very windy tonight. Watched some of "The Fugitive". It must be a tricky thing to write & not have it be the same every week. I mean, he can't take a week off, can he? Visit the folks, learn to water ski…

March 11, 1964

7.45am. Have already made a fire, as it is freezing outside again. Quite windy, but a pretty sunrise.

10am. Only noise across the road coming from the kitchen as the last of the kitchen cupboards seems to be going in. No counter tops or doors yet. Others painting.

1pm. Dicky Bird now working with Marce in kitchen, holding plywood. Rip & Davy somewhere upstairs with light hammering. Not sure what they are up to.

6pm. Back from a look around. Upstairs three doors taken down. Kitchen cupboards all in place, & what I think are several doors sit propped around the kitchen. Each of these is very well made, bevelled & smooth all around. I didn't see John John this evening, but as it all looks swept, I suspect he has been here.

10.30pm. In the 40s today, & nice sunshine. Spent a little time after dinner working in the garden. Forgot that it is quite a thing to get clean at the moment; likewise, clothes made dirty with gardening do not wash easily. Finished Yates's RR. Enviable.

March 12, 1964

9am. Role change over the road. Now Rip helping Marce to make & fit kitchen cupboard doors. Dicky Bird & Davy upstairs removing & scraping doors. Huffing & puffing just a little, Dicky Bird is describing his sweet dreams of his baby but wondering just how long he'll have to dream.

1pm. Progress at The Corner seems easier to see now. Doors getting cleaned up very quickly (at least compared to windows). Likewise, there are kitchen cupboard doors going up as Rip fits them while Marce makes & sands them.

5pm. All the upper cupboard doors on now. Spent a few minutes opening & shutting them, just for fun. Also went upstairs, as the air is now breathable again, & opened & shut every window on the middle floor. They glide like they are brand new, although the glass looks like it must be 200 years old. What a house we will have.

10.15pm. Colder this morning than yesterday, so kept the fire up all day. Quite windy, & even some snow on the air this morning. "My Three Sons" could be a good program if only the answers weren't so easy.

11pm. Have been gritting my teeth & wishing I could shout at Alex just once, just once to tell him how hard this has been. Like a mother who pulls her child back from the roadway just in time, who quenches the threat to her love with pained anger, & then lets the love flood uncontrollably. If only I could pull him back.

*I had so many opportunities to pull him back; why didn't I?

March 13, 1964

9.30am. Work much as yesterday, with kitchen-door brigade forging ahead downstairs. Looks like Davy & Dicky Bird will finish taking down & cleaning doors today.

12.45pm. Just back. Half the lower kitchen doors now up, catches fitted, handles on etc. Dicky Bird & Davy struggling to get old back door down as something wrong with the hinges, evidently.

5.15pm. Men left just a little later than usual as all four joined in on back door issue. Marce chirping away at poor Davy as he struggled to hold the thing in place for Rip to fix up temporarily. Couldn't hear his actual words, but judging from the faces of the others, it is probably best I didn't. John John was outside waiting, so I asked him how school was this week. (I noticed he had a great big tear above the knee on his pants. He had had one before, I think, & the pants had been patched on the inside & sewn up, but this new tear was above the patch.) Pretty good, he said, though he got in trouble on Wednesday for talking in math class. He said the teacher told him because his voice was now getting deeper, she could hear him above the other children. He said he thought his dad & the others would finish the doors & kitchen next week. I asked him what he was doing this weekend & he said he didn't know, though his father had told him that on Saturday they were "pulling stumps". I wished him luck.

10.45pm. Weather about like yesterday but felt colder to me. Over 50 this afternoon. Very dark tonight, but clear. Stars like white spiders all over the sky. Watched "Route 66". I really shouldn't watch anything else.

Young man, young man, you too young to pray!

I don't know what to say 'bout some folks. Ya know 'em 'fore the war and ya know 'em after. Maybe they change, maybe they don't. Somehow, ya think ya know 'em, but ya don't. After the war, the womenfolk that works like me mostly gets paid 'bout seven eight dollars a month. So we all 'bout the same like that. 'Fore the war, they ain't nothing the same.

Y'all go down the ole Harmony Road, like you going to Middletown and just where the creek come up to the road, 'fore ya get to the big turning, there a little ole place used to be the quarters for the Flook farm back when they had it. They lost it when the ole man start up his drinking and it get sold to a big family called Somers, and they all Brethrens so they don't believe in keeping no servants, so they ain't nobody wants to live in no old quarters, so they hire it out to a freewoman name Pres. She get a little money making and dyeing wool and clothes and goods all kind. She use the walnut hulls for the black, and the apple moss for the orange, and folks likes 'em both. Maple for the blue and poke for the red and oak for the green. I seen her sometimes, and I tell her 'bout stuff that ole Red Mary told me, stuff help her making ends meet. Like she can't have no gun or nothing, but

I show her how ya can use ya ole hair and all to twist up a real hard ole string so that you can snare youself rabbits. I show her how you can pile up the stickle burrs too 'round they holes so the can't run and you can catch 'em. She eat rabbit all the time then. She can't 'ford no 'lasses, so I tell how you can cook up the birch sap and the elder sap to make sugar. Lord, she do too. She sell some when she can.

She still don't got 'nough money though, she say. She say she think she need a man. Trouble is, all the free men is mostly down Middletown and Frederick, so they don't know nothing 'bout her. Most of the servants on the farms is either hired out or half-scared of anybody with free papers. Nobody left but the white men, she say. I say, They ain't no good. And she say, Hell, they ain't. I say, What y'all gone do? And she say, I show you what I gon' do.

Well, they's a fella down Middletown that come up to Harmony buying them clothes she make for speculating to the farmers with servants and field hands. He mostly buy up them things and travel 'em round to the farmers and sell 'em right at they own places. Well, this fella, he had a son named Mister Dorsey, and he a nice shy kinda boy, mostly keep hisself to hisself. Time he finish school and all he come the one that go out to the women like Pres that makes the clothes and then he the one that takes 'em round to the farmers for buying. He come up to The Corner sometimes and buy the hats and the brooms and the gunny sacks I making for sale. I cut up all the ole clothes into clothes for the children too, and the white folks buy for they servants, if they good. Anyhow, I don't pay ole Dorsey no never mind. But I tell you one thing. Y'all just know he ain't the kinda boy gonna put his hand on no woman no colour less she say something awful nice to him.

Well, I don't know what ole Pres must've say to that white boy, but she get him in that shack of hern in two shakes of a lamb's tail, and next thing ya know, she got the bug up her back. Yes, sir, she does.

I say, Girl, y'all can't 'ford nothing now. How you gonna 'ford to keep no child of you own?

She say, y'all just wait and see what I'm gon' do.

Well, she have that baby girl, and she don't do nothing. Not nothing. I'm thinking, I done told you that. And I start to thinking maybe she find out she a good mother after all. But she is sure as shooting not that. No, she the worse. What she do but wait till that child start to walking and talking but ask one of them speculators how much he give her for that child of hern? Can you believe that? She sell her own baby girl right off herself. Speculator say she pretty little, but she look healthy. He give her three hundred dollar cash money. She say she got to think about it.

Lord, she think about it, all right. She still thinking when next time ole Mister Dorsey come long. She say, How come y'all don't come 'round here no more? You done tired of this already? Look what you done left behind. And she show him that baby girl and tell him he the daddy. Ole Dorsey like to die. He say he ain't come 'round no more 'cause in the winter, his daddy up and die of convulsions, and now he got to look after his mama and sister. Pres, she say, that ain't none of my 'fair. But then she say, I don't 'spect y'all to do nothing for me. No, 'deed, I don't. But that girl child, she costing me money. Money I ain't got. He say, How much you want?

She say, she can't keep no child nohow, 'cause all she does is interfere with the work, and she getting poorer and poorer. Only thing she can think to do is to take her down to Licksville or maybe give her to the speculator. Speculator say he give her four hundred for her, easy. Mister Dorsey, he looking sicker and sicker. He say, Don't you sell that girl now. That's my girl just as much as she yourn. Pres say, Y'all gon' give me four hundred dollar? Mister Dorsey say, I get you money. But don't you sell that girl 'fore I get here with it.

That's how she done it. Couple days later, ole Mister Dorsey, he come 'round and give Pres four hundred dollar for that child and take her down Middletown with his mama and his sister. When the war come, he start to selling blankets and bags and shirts to the Yankees, and 'fore it ends he make hisself a rich man. His mama live with him, and his sister don't never get married, but he does to a woman name Miss Rose from Hagerstown. Pres take her four hundred dollar and move to Hagerstown too. But I never hear nothing 'bout her. Don't want to neither.

March 14, 1964

2pm. Cold in the house, so made up the fire as soon as I got home. In the 40s now & looks like rain.

*Last week's busy day had some results this week. Took library books back, vowed never to eat another hot dog, & spent $21 at A & P. Bought seeds & peat moss at grocery store. Also little flowerpots.

*Bought two hyacinths, one for myself & one for Cinch to say thank you for the flatiron.

*Also went to book store again & bought James Baldwin's Another Country.

3.30pm. Have just had a thunderstorm roll by! Not much rain, not much lightning, but shaking in the trees & ominous air.

10.15pm. Tried watching the movie but quit when I found myself trying to remember the middle names of the girls I went to school with.

March 15, 1964

8.15am. Warmer today, but so gloomy I've made a fire just for company. Very foggy again. 40s.

1.15pm. Well, a surprise. Walked home with the ladies again, giving Cinch her hyacinth. She said, –Well, ain't that purr dee! I thanked her for the flatiron, & she notched her head back & looked confused. Then she rolled her eyes at Agassy, who laughed. –Glad y'all found it, she said. Realizing my mistake, I got them as far as the Mary House porch (they wouldn't come in, they said, as they'd let all my heat out & "track wet" on my floor), but I got the other hyacinth & gave it to Agassy. They wobbled off like little round sisters, looking like they'd won the church prizes for prettiest dresses.

2.45pm. Have just finished a delicious goulash.

5pm. Read some of Baldwin. This is what we need more of, yet it is so harrowing I can hardly continue.

8.45pm. We seek to forget the badness in memories of loving, countering it with the ecstasy. We love in the moments we know, in idleness, loving the moments of accidental bliss, that in memory become that ecstasy. The greatest pain is in the desire to know whether those accidents, or rather ones like them, will come tomorrow. When love ends, the acceptance comes in knowing there will be no more such moments. That is why, right now, I am like a bird that cannot tell whether it is soaring, or simply falling.

*I know that I could accept Alex's death, if I knew it to be certain. Yet that is a terrible guilty stain on my conscious, as I know I should reject it. Isn't it the duty of anyone who loves someone to reject even the suspicion that that someone might be dead? Reject it & keep on rejecting it until it no longer makes sense to do so?

*A fool prepares for the worst, as if there is always worse to come when, in fact, this may be the worst.

*Alex will come home, bearing his traumas, surviving his mother's threats of despair. Outliving the anger that damaged us all.

11pm. Not much above 50 today. Wind blew about some showers.

March 16, 1964

7.15am. Cannot decide about fire! Nearly 40 now. Will it warm up?

8.45am. Marce & Rip in the kitchen making & attaching cupboard doors. Dicky Bird & Davy painting doors.

10am. Ingalls truck just left. A short stay. Delivering kitchen countertops, I think. Same men as usual.

1.15pm. Decided against fire, & this paid off as it is nearly 60 now. Hands are cold.

1.45pm. Painting going on upstairs. Back door down again which improves ventilation. All the kitchen cupboard doors now seem to be in working order. Rip & Marce in consultation over counter tops.

4.45pm. Men gone now. Small piece of kitchen counter attached, pencil marks on other pieces. All upstairs doors now either silver white or white.

10.45pm. Warm day, a little windy. Very bright sun. Watched "Wagon Train" & played a game whereby I tried to guess what was going to be said by each character after a different character spoke. Decided my failure was not based upon my own misjudgements, but rather upon the lack of realism in the program. Men do not talk the way they are shown to talk in shows like this. One by one they do, but not in groups.

March 17, 1964

7am. Temperature like yesterday, so may build a fire after all.

9.45am. Lots of noise downstairs at Corner as work goes on counter tops. Door-painting upstairs. Dicky Bird enriching the air with the fact that he can't stop loving her, though he has made up his mind to live in memory of old lonesome times.

11.15am. In the paper this morning that President Johnson has asked Congress for a billion dollars for his war on poverty. Holy smoke! Does this mean he thinks he'll win the war, or that he's afraid he won't?

2pm. Kitchen counter pieces going in now, one with a big hole for the sink, which has, I've just noticed, been gathering dust under the stairs since I don't know when. Quiet upstairs.

5.15pm. Kitchen counters all look to be in place now. I walked upstairs, which is fever high with fumes, & found some of the doors now back on the frames. Painted or undercoated ones are propped around.

10.30pm. 60 degrees this afternoon & sunny, so I opened the upstairs windows. The house smells nice now.

Took her on the hillside

I, LittleWound, tell this story.

It was at the time when the railway was being built and the mill was selling flour and cornmeal by the waggonload to the drivers who came from Fredericktowne, Berlin and even Point of Rocks. The circles of tar and berries had come to the back of my hands, and I only smoked the redwillow in the mornings. The Washechu had spread themselves over the land and people we did not know seldom came to Harmony. There was one, his beard like straw, who came from across the mountain towards the Furnace, and he was called Stottlemyer, also known as Josef.

He found work as a hand with a farmer named Delauter, who lived on the flat beyond Harp Hill. Delauter had a child, and her name was Gaetha.

Josef joined the father and daughter, and he lived in the room above the kitchen and pantry, working with Delauter all day in the fields and in the barn. Delauter esteemed Josef and praised his work to his neighbours, most of whom, if they had help at all, used slaves, either their own or ones they hired. But Delauter had no patience for those who worked with slaves, and he treated Josef with kindness and shared his meals with him, bought his shirts, and allowed him to raise a few animals of his own. It surprised no one when Josef asked Delauter whether he could make Gaetha his wife. They were married in the church at Wolfsville, not the meeting house, but the church with the bell.

Delauter was satisfied with his son-in-law, and Josef was satisfied with his wife. As for Gaetha, she thought herself to have been charmed with fortune that a man of this estimate should come to her without trouble on her part. She liked his straw hair, the movement of the muscles in his arms and chest, the way his legs swung when he walked and that his eyes were the colour of a jay's wing. He touched her as a man touches a baby, his face blind with wonder and with a will to show her kindness and entitle her to a woman's pride.

The only sadness that kept itself at their windows was that Gaetha did not conceive a child. Nights drew them together as it draws together husbands and wives who find joy in one another, and while their passion shone like that of the stars in summer, no child made its way to them. They exchanged no bitterness on this account and, if anything, their love towards one another closed them as one, like trees intertwining.

The seasons passed, and it happened that Delauter died. He had been walking behind his horses, ploughing the arc of a hill, when he fell, first upon his back and then upon his side. The reins were looped around his arm and shoulder and the horses walked for a time dragging him, not realizing he no longer held the reins in his fingers. He was buried with his wife in the plot among the poplars, above the corncrib.

Now no one lived in the house except Gaetha and Josef. Gaetha questioned Josef, thinking it would be a help to him if he were to find another man to come and live above the kitchen and pantry as he, himself, had done – a man to help with the chores. But Josef would not agree. His stubbornness on this was something Gaetha could not understand. She could not know those things about which Josef never spoke. For when he was in that time between boyhood and manhood, it had been the time when the Washechu battled with the warriors in the sunset coats. Josef had seen how soldiers had behaved, and he distrusted men and their designs. He had seen them bring their own slaves to his father's farm, steal his father's horses, and beat his mother until his father agreed to become their guide. Josef wanted little to do with men.

And so, as the seasons changed one upon another, Gaetha saw little and less of Josef. He scythed the hay, picked the apples, broke the ice from the stream, planted the corn. His days hung about him in chains and the joy in his hands slackened, until even the hyacinth of his eyes dimmed. The farm that sustained them shone like a stone over which the water pours, and all things were as they should be. But time silenced the music of their nerves and the hearts within them beat without longing. Still, no strife ever came upon them, and they left this world without a struggle, neither one understanding how love had deserted them.

March 18, 1964

7.30am. Just over 20 degrees this morning! Fire already lit.

9.30am. Everyone at work as usual. Marce & Rip now in utility room, or rather in & out, starting to work on shelves & cupboards. Upstairs, the doors are being fastened, I think.

10am. Snowing wantonly at the moment.

1.30pm. Strange sight over the road. Peace as Rip & Marce are fitting lower cupboard beside place where washing machine is to go. Dicky Bird attaching door knobs & key hole things as Davy, looking like a giant toddler, is wire-brushing workings of old locks & knobs.

2pm. Windy now, & temperature in the 40s.

5.30pm. Men gone & didn't bother to go over to inspect.

10.30pm. Strange day. Enough to make a hare mad.

March 19, 1964

9am. In the 20s & windy positively howling out there. Sunshine amid clouds racing by.

*Utility room shelves seem to be the lower project at the moment. Doors getting the attention upstairs.

1pm. Doors all look done now. Shelves up. Davy carrying wood upstairs, while others debate closets in bedrooms.

5.15pm. Wood scattered in bedrooms & some work done on bedroom closets in two rooms. Saw John John moving here & there, & he seemed to be doing his best to get something cleaned up (or maybe everything cleaned up as he seems to be quite a neat sort of boy) without interesting anyone's attention. I was tempted to speak to him, but I thought he seemed to be enjoying the anonymity.

10.15pm. Windy all day today but warmed up a little. Sun got better towards evening. Thought I might watch "ABC News Reports" but just too sleepy.

March 20, 1964

9.45am. Closet building today for everyone except Davy. The others are up & down the stairs using the power saws

& other things, while he is in the kitchen, wiping down & varnishing the kitchen cupboards.

1pm. Just witnessed Davy getting a telling off. He was, it seems, varnishing the kitchen doors while they were shut, accidently causing them to stick to their frames. Marce asked him whether he didn't have the brains of p[]ss ant, & told him that when the ones he'd finished dried, he'd have to sand them & start over. Davy looked like he had the will of a murderer, but not the courage of one & he stared into space for a full two minutes after Marce left him.

5pm. Men gone now. I noticed that Davy had got a first coat on the whole kitchen, & that only two cupboards will require a sanding & re-doing. Still, I suppose it is a nuisance & a time loss. Upstairs, four of the bedrooms have very pretty closets.

 *No sign of John John, so not sure what the plan is next week, as no one else thinks to tell me.

10.30pm. Colder today, so nice steady fire. Dry feeling on the air, & sunshine feels more Spring-like.

Jesus gonna make up my dyin' bed.

So, you haven't been down here for years? Really? Rich asked.
 No, she said. Just never got 'round to it.
 Rich was driving them both south from their town near Albany. It was very good of him, considering the weather. It had been snowing when they left, and most of the way across Pennsylvania it got worse, and now, as the afternoon faded into a flat zinc-coloured shimmer, it was coming down hard again. Rich was driving well, but he really had to concentrate, like someone trying to walk on ice, pressing each foot firmly down as levelly as possible. They rolled into Myersville at about 3.30 in the afternoon.

There it is, Amy said, pointing.

It was a tall white house, more than a century old, wide porches, pointed gables, big lawns, small outbuildings. The tips of picket fencing could be seen above the snow. Rich pulled the car up on to what was probably the curb in front of the path. He sighed, rubbed his eyes and stretched, too strained and feeble to leap out. Amy opened her door and stood in the little vee it made with the car and listened.

It's so quiet, she said.

Rich got out and stood listening. Yeah, he said. Are you sure anyone's home? I can't see any lights.

My Uncle Den is supposed to be waiting until we arrive. I hope he hasn't abandoned us. He's probably in the apartment.

The 'apartment'? Rich said. He was dragging their suitcases off the back seat.

Yeah. Mom had a live-in nurse the last couple years. She had the corner of the house made into a place just for her. It was so like her to do that.

Rich looked over at Amy, hoping to match the tone of voice to some look on her face. But Amy had gone around the car and was now waddling ahead of him through the snow towards the front porch.

It was the first time in five years Amy had stood on the front porch. She had come home the first two Christmases when she was at college, but after that she started going to Rich's house for Christmas, preferring his family to her own. Her sisters still lived close to Myersville, and they kept her up-to-date on their mother's health. There was no urgency, they said. Then, after Amy and Rich graduated, there was his Master's degree to finish, and now that they were living together money was pretty tight, and so that kept them away. After that, it was the year he was due to take up the fellowship in Syracuse, and they decided to have a big blow-out and drive all the way across Canada to Vancouver. That was the trip when Amy's mother died suddenly, a bit unexpectedly, Amy's sisters said. They had tried their best to reach Amy, phoned every number they knew, but they just couldn't track her down. Not until well after the funeral. Now her mother's life was recorded on a stone just up the road from her old house, at the Methodist cemetery. Amy thought she'd go and see it soon, maybe take some flowers, all on this visit. Maybe both the sisters would come too.

So here she was. She and Rich stood pressing footprints into the snow that had blown on to the porch, hoping someone would answer the door. At last there was a light, and a scuttle of keys, and the inner door swung back.

Hello! Hello! You made it! So good to see you!

It was Amy's Uncle Den, her mother's brother. He drew them in to the hallway, where it wasn't exactly as warm as either of them hoped. Den was wearing plaid trousers and slippers, a collared shirt and a cardigan. He hugged them both and stuffed his hands back in his pockets.

It's cold out there, he said.

It sure is, Rich said.

Uncle Den, this is my husband Rich. Rich, this is Uncle Den.

Dennis Fulton, he said, pulling out his right hand and holding it towards Rich.

Richard O'Connell, Rich said.

Both men put their hands back into their pockets and looked at Amy.

Shall we get settled? she said.

Uncle Den nodded and led them towards the stairs. Rich took both suitcases and followed. Amy was looking at everything.

Guess it's been a while for you, honey? Uncle Den said as they rounded the corner on the stairs. Your mom sure talked about you though. Yep, she sure did.

The came out into the big hallway upstairs. Uncle Den opened the door to a bedroom and walked in.

Will this one do for you? he said.

Just fine, Amy said, without really looking.

Well, Uncle Den said, y'all get yourselves settled. I'll see you downstairs directly, and we can have a good chin wag then. I guess there's a lot you'll want to know.

Rich edged over a little, and Uncle Den smiled at him, and then disappeared back down the stairs. Rich went into the bedroom where Amy was standing, and he sat the suitcases down on the floor.

Freezing in here, he said. Amy was quiet and he looked at her looking at things. Was this your old room? he said.

No, she said, unlacing the scarf from around her neck. None of them were. She took her hat off and feeling the melted snow on it, put it on the back of a chair. Mom didn't let us have our own rooms, she said. Rich sat on the bed.

What do you mean? he said.

Amy took off her coat and sat down beside him. Mom believed, that if we could say that any of the rooms were 'ours' then it would change the way we thought about ourselves and the things we lived with. She wanted us to be free of all that. So she kept us moving about.

Moving about? he said.

I've slept in every bedroom in the house, she said.

Huh, he said. What are there, four, at least?

Six, she said.

Which one was your mother's? he asked.

She was the same as us, Amy said. She liked to move about too.

Huh, Rich said. Wonder which one was, you know, the last one.

Amy looked at him but didn't say anything.

A little while later they were sitting in the big parlour where it was, at least, quite a bit warmer. Uncle Den had fed them soup and bread and talked to them a while in the kitchen while they finished it up. He didn't seem as inclined to chat as he promised and, if anything, looked a little sleepy. He said he'd leave them in peace to sit in the parlour, while he went back to the apartment. He had hoped the weather wouldn't be so bad as this, as he had hoped to go home; but now it looked like he was staying too. He had things to do, he said.

So Rich and Amy sat on the big 1920s sofa, all cream and mahogany. Rich looked around the room.

Your mom liked books, he said, breathing in the slight odour of leather and camphor.

And music, Amy said.

She pointed, and Rich jumped up.

Wow, he said. Would you look at that.

He walked over to the old wind-up phonograph and touched it gingerly. My grandmother had one of these, he said. He seemed to know what he was doing. He bent down and opened two little swinging doors. Inside, there were ranks of 78rpm records in browning paper sleeves. He drew a few out and looked at them.

Wow, he said. Hang on.

He slid one of the records out and steadied it on the turntable. He reached down and twisted the small crank slowly, then briskly. He lowered the heavy needle and there was a hiss, inside of which were the sounds of a Mendelsohn concerto.

How about that? he said.

Amy was looking at the striped curtains on the tall windows and wondering whether she remembered them.

Has she got anything to drink around here? Rich asked.

I don't think so, Amy said. Mom didn't drink.

He was opening and shutting doors under the bookshelves. Ah, he said, pointing. Someone did.

Amy looked and there were several bottles of bourbon and scotch, all of them open.

Maybe the nurse, Rich said.

In a moment, he came back from the kitchen with two glasses and poured them each a small one.

What do you want to do now? he said.

Amy wished she knew. Sit still and wonder why I don't feel more guilty? she thought. She could do that anywhere. It was one of the last few weeks that the house would continue to look like this. As soon as the weather turned warmer the contents would be parcelled out between her and her sisters, or auctioned off, and the house sold. They would split the money between them, as none of them wanted the house itself. Perhaps, Amy thought, I should look for traces of Mom somewhere? But then, she was everywhere, nowhere in particular.

It's getting dark, Amy said. Let's go to bed.

Seriously? Rich said. He looked at his Timex. It's only just after six.

I'm going to bed, Amy said.

She got up and Rich followed.

A quarter of an hour later they were both naked between the stiff sheets and under four quilts. Well, Rich was naked. Amy had on a tee shirt and panties. They pressed their cold feet together, their cold thighs. Each tried carefully to warm their hands on some part of the other's body without chilling them too much. They lay still a long time, quietly warming up. At last, Rich kissed Amy's head. She turned and he kissed her cheeks and neck. He ran his hands along her back, her arms and her breasts. She could feel him rising.

Amy's eyes roamed around the room. The ceiling with its shadowed wooden pockets, the walls with their soft yellow paper. The curtains were open and through the wide windows she could now see the moonlight very brightly. The snow had stopped and the reflection lighted the corner of the room where their clothes lay. It shone strangely in the silver-framed mirror on the dressing table, a white oval, a pearl shell, a shimmering opal.

Rich's thumbs slid under the corners of her panties at her hips. She raised her back from the sheets and felt his hands slide down the length of her legs, over her ankles and feet. She watched the moonlight in the mirror as it darkened with a passing cloud, and raised her arms, letting the tee shirt slip off her torso, and through the weight of her hair. Rich's face disappeared beneath her chin, his hands moved over her body, practiced with her shape, knowing her desires. Amy saw the light on the mirror brighten. Had it been her mother's mirror? she wondered. Had it always been hers? She felt Rich's body ease into hers, and she drew an involuntary breath. She watched the light on the mirror change and grow dim, then brighten again. She felt the sway of her legs, the tensions in her shoulders and feet. And then the warmth growing in her pelvis, the fire burning in her spine, through her ribs, down her arms and to her fingertips. She watched the moonlight in the mirror, wondering at its changes and at its constancy.

Later, folded into Rich's arms, she listened to the sounds of the house. The wind had picked up a little and she thought she could hear the curtains rustling. Sometimes there were little clicks, little noises, like the soft mechanism of a very slow clock that someone has set in motion.

What are those noises? Rich whispered.

Just the house, Amy said. Old houses are always settling.

March 21, 1964

8am. Not sure what to do. Have bathed (freezing!) & no fire, as I want to go to Frederick. Foggy & raining now, but will it snow?

2.30pm. Snowed hard in Frederick & most of the way home, but it doesn't seem to be sticking. Hard to see when driving.

*Did not go to library or bookstore as worried about the weather. Planning ahead, I spent a wad of green stamps

& got myself a wheelbarrow. Hurrying, I only spent $15 at
A & P.

8pm. Had beef stew. Meat delicious, but carrots overdone.
Read more Baldwin. Such unhappiness.

10pm. Tired this evening. No more snow, but weather still
wet & rainy.

March 22, 1964

9am. Weather looks like yesterday.

12.30pm. Not so many church walkers today. Got details
about Fire Dept meal next week.

4pm. Tea. Have countered The Blues by picturing myself
& Alex living here in various scenes when The Corner is
finished. Hard not to let Tom into the pictures (& conversations). That fact made it all feel foolish. Though
why should it? All futures are equally real & unreal, in a
way. There must be a line between imagining & simply
dreaming.
   *I like imagining & must do more of it.

11pm. Weather just like yesterday. Not such hard snow
showers, but each one longer & gentler.

March 23, 1964

9.45. Davy penitently re-varnishing kitchen cupboards,
having evidently sanded them first. Ripping & hammering
upstairs, as the men seem to be inspecting, removing &
replacing any of the wood around doors & windows that
looks damaged or needs replacing.

11.45am. Hardly above freezing now. Pretty sunshine, but
fire feels nice.

1.30pm. Work over the road seems low-key today. Davy now assisting Rip to replace window work, scrape paint here & there. All seem pretty much on the same projects now.

5pm. Men gone. Had to go over the road, as they accidentally left a light on upstairs. Most everything (everything wooden) looking new or repaired now.

10.30pm. Nice day today. Very sunny. Watched "Wagon Train" & everyone did just what I wanted them to do. This frightened me a little.

March 24, 1964

10am. Terrible sounds from the kitchen in The Corner this morning, as Rip is down there sanding the varnished cupboards. There is to be a second coat, Marce says. Likewise, the utility room. Davy is with Marce, painting & varnishing woodwork. Dicky Bird is alone on the upper middle floor. He was singing, but I couldn't pick out the words.

2.30pm. Rip & Marce now varnishing kitchen & utility room, others upstairs.

5.30pm. Everyone gone. Corner stinks so badly, I couldn't bear to look around.

10.45pm. Gloomy fog ALL day today. Below freezing this morning, & over 60 this afternoon.

March 25, 1964

7.45am. Nearly 40 this morning, so not sure about fire.

9am. Everyone but Marce at work, sanding, painting & varnishing woodwork. Air putrid with fumes. Dicky Bird more like a Stuffed Bird, as totally without song.

11am. No fire after all today. Not bad in here.

*Marce late for work this morning, as he went to Myersville. I asked if everything was okay, & he reached out his hand to give me something. He dropped a coin in my hand. It is the brand-new President Kennedy 50 cent piece. –Got you one too, he said. (He had gone to the bank in Myersville, to make sure he got some.) What a curious thing he is.

5pm. All done over the road. They left two windows open on each floor. Birds dropping out of the sky, killed by the fumes… I had a look 'round, my eyes watering. Skirting boards, door frames, sills etc all look fresh & bright.

10.30pm. Dry, sunny & 70 degrees this afternoon. After dinner I walked around The Patch, imagining how I want it. I want Alex to be proud to be here.

March 26, 1964

9.15am. Rain blowing hard against the window & down the chimney. Fire sputtering.

*Men at work as usual. They showed up with armloads of small things today & it seems pretty quiet.

12.45pm. I have discovered that they are busy fitting clothes rails, hooks, shelf rollers & umpteen internal fittings into all the new cupboards all over the house. All of them seem to be working alone, no one seems at all uptight, & even Marce is whistling. Dicky Bird has found whole new regions to explore vocally, echoing what I think must be Frank Sinatra, who asserts that when someone loves you it's no good unless he loves you all the way.

4pm. Marce's truck has gone, so I think they've left early today.

4.45pm. Yes, they've gone. House is in a strange state now, sometimes really beautiful, otherwise not finished. An adolescent love affair.

10.30pm. Windy & rainy all day, though warmer (nearly 70). Watched "Rawhide".

The elements will turn

I, LittleWound, tell this story.

It was in the time before the Washechu came, crossing the rivers and tying the mountain to the sky with the ropes of their smoke. In those times the Catoctin boys grew to manhood with their palms turned towards the sun, their hearts gathered within them like the eagle. They rose when the stars could still be seen, beginning their duties before the heat could tempt their spirits to retire. And when the days hung like the willow over the stream, they practised with their bows, they wrestled, swam and chased bees. And when they loved they wore the robes that fitted them to esteem, dancing with their arms upon one another like brothers and raising the call of joy until even the pines shook above them. The girls braided their hair into a plait that shimmered even in the darkness. Each one knew when the day came her friends would make her the maiden-feast so that the warriors would know she might become a wife. Only then did the chaperones come, and only then did she put on the feathers of the hawk, celebrating her love.

There was such a maiden named Wahcheewin, or Dancing-Woman, and she was loved by a warrior named Hahkaydah, or LastBorn. Love stood in their eyes and they saw as one another saw. The only impediment was that DancingWoman's adopted father wished her to marry his nephew, a man for whom she felt nothing. But her stepfather was a man who sought no dishonour for anyone, and he refused to compel DancingWoman to abide by his choice. But neither could he refuse the pleas of his nephew or the boy's father, his own brother. And so for this reason, he proposed a contest be held between the warriors, with the winner gaining DancingWoman for a wife. As there was no other way to avoid trouble, both DancingWoman and LastBorn agreed to this contest.

There were to be three challenges. In the first, the warriors were made to race in the centre of the stream that leads from the floor of the valley towards the rising sun, up the mountainside to where it rises at the base of the greenstone falls. Because it was the season of weddings, and the earth was like buckskin and the air clotted like spiders-webs, the stream too had water only at its base. Most of the stream-bed lay like bones and the men had to leap from rock to rock, sliding in the dust, grating in the sand, clambering on the boulders. It happened that LastBorn won the challenge when his rival stumbled over the roots of sumacs and scrub-oaks.

The next challenge was wrestling, and this they undertook in the midst of the lodges where everyone might see. This time, it was LastBorn who lost his grip on his opponent's chest and fell first.

The last test would be archery, but because DancingWoman's stepfather knew that LastBorn was sure to win an ordinary task, like shooting at a target, or even a bird in the air, he proposed that this challenge include a test of bravery. He asked each warrior whether he might shoot an arrow into the sky and wait for its descent, catching the falling arrow in his hand before it struck the ground. Both warriors accepted the challenge and walked to the edge of the village where there was space for all to see without crowding the archers or being near where the arrows might fall.

LastBorn said that as he had lost the last test, he should go first, but his rival said no, thinking that honour lay with him who stood foremost. He drew his arrow from its quiver and fired it into the air. All the heads of the people turned towards the heavens, but few could see the arrow's flight. All at once they saw it descend and they saw the warrior's arm dart forth to grasp it. But he missed, and the arrow stroked into the ground, quaking.

All eyes turned to LastBorn, and DancingWoman could feel her breath heat inside her, and her heart drum in her ears. She watched as LastBorn drew his arrow, one she and all the Catoctins recognized, because he always stained his arrows with the juice of the blackberry, so that everyone might know which ones he had fired. He bent his bow and let fly, and the arrow sped upwards as a breeze shook through the valley, stirring the sycamore leaves like the hands of children. This breeze was just enough to move LastBorn's arrow in its flight, so that as it came down it struck into the elbow of one of the sycamores, where it hung vibrating. Everyone gasped.

DancingWoman's stepfather spoke up and declared that while neither warrior had completed the task, at least LastBorn's rival had come closest to success, and therefore he deserved to marry the bride he had chosen. DancingWoman bowed her head and said nothing. The wedding was fixed for the day of the next full-moon.

That night LastBorn could not sleep. He lay in his blankets and wished to curse the sky that had betrayed him. He picked up his bow and his quiver once more and went once again to the place on the edge of the village where the contest had taken place, and he lay down, staring at the clouds above him, thinking he might try to kill the sky itself. As if mocking him, he saw the branches of the tree overhead, the one where his arrow fell, obscuring his view. He looked at the pattern of these branches. Beside him lay his arrows. He picked up one that he thought sharp and lay its edge against his face. He dragged the arrow back and forth, again and again, cutting into his skin the pattern of the branches where his other arrow had fallen. When the blood clouded his eyes, he returned to his lodge, at peace because he knew he was now a man that no woman might love.

When the people rose in the morning, they did not count LastBorn among them as he always was. Some went to call on him, and what they found they told their neighbours. More days and nights passed before DancingWoman saw him for herself. By then the blood had washed away and only the scars remained. But she knew what his scars meant, and she recognized the pattern of his sorrow. Her spirit came to her hands and she lifted them to the Thunderbird and asked that he might deliver her from her fate.

The time of her marriage was approaching, and still Dancing-Woman had received no answer to her prayers. But then it came. The night before she was due to be wed, the Thunderbird clapped his wings over the mountains and the sky caught fire in creases and bursts. She ran to the ground by the edge of the village where the archery contest had taken place and as she approached the thunderstone fell raging against the tree where LastBorn's arrow still hung. With a crash, the limb of the tree fell to earth, and in it she saw LastBorn's arrow, the colour of the lightning itself. She pulled the arrow from the trunk and with it a handful of leaves. In the flashes of light she looked at the veins in the leaves and copied their pattern, using the blade of the arrow to cut the design into her own face.

The day of her wedding dawned, and as expected, Dancing-Woman emerged from her lodge, dressed like a bride. But the whole village looked upon her, and in her scars they read the story of her love. They knew that now no man would make her his wife.

And so no man did. In his anger over her actions, Dancing-Woman's stepfather still forbade her marriage to LastBorn, blaming him for the tragedy that had befallen her. Yet while they could not become husband and wife, and feel the joy of their people, or the pride of their embrace, both knew that the love they had each felt was unchanging, even as the abundance of the skies.

March 27, 1964

7.45am. Not sure whether to expect the men today as it is Good Friday. Tray ready, but no drinks yet. Windy outside,

& fireplace, or rather chimney, humming like someone blowing over a bottle.

8.30am. No, men evidently not coming today. Dismantled tray till next week.

11am. Went outside to walk around the whole place, just to clear my head & get the image of Michelangelo's grieving Virgin Mary out of my mind.

*I wondered whether it was all right to garden a bit today, though it was awfully windy. As I have no religious duties to attend to, I decided this might count. Will go out after lunch.

2.15pm. Marked out many things in the vegetable garden outside the north side of the house, but grew a little self-conscious, lest I lose traction with the opinion of my neighbors, as no one else seems to be doing anything.

*Had my bath, such as it is. Will read some.

5pm. Finished my tea. Also finished Baldwin, though I confess that I had to read quickly so that too many of the words didn't sink in beneath my eyes.

10.30pm. Nice sun all day today, nearly 50 this afternoon. Still windy. Moon like a silver dollar.

*Watched "Route 66".

March 28, 1964

8.15am. Cold bath again this morning. Below freezing outside.

11.30am. Back from quick trip to Acme ($16). Bought gardening gloves & apron too.

12pm. Sad story in the paper. Huge earthquake in Alaska yesterday brought about fires & a tidal wave. Not sure how that happens. Over 100 dead.

*Just on my way to Myersville for Fire Dept meal.

3.30pm. Back from Fire Dept fundraiser. Food was plentiful & simple – lots of meat, potatoes & vegetables. Fruit pies. After eating, I astonished the church ladies by putting on my (new!) apron & getting into the kitchen to wash dishes along with them. I hope I can remember all their names.

*I don't know why I did that, but it feels very good.

7.30pm. Having second thoughts about my work at the Fire Dept kitchen. I hope none of them thinks I was butting in. I hope I wasn't.

10.30pm. Sunny & dry all day today, though the wind was cold. Over 60 this afternoon.

March 29, 1964

8.45am. Easter Sunday. Slow riser this morning. Listened to the radio. Alaska earthquake brought a tidal wave to California, killing 11.

12.45pm. Windy & rainy, but fire warming house at last.

*Without knowing why, I went to church today. It is the first time since I was married. I didn't expect to, I just did. I dressed up (Cinch, who was in a yellow dress with yellow beads, said she liked my ear rings), & just went. I sat & stood with the others, listened to the sermon (not long, not gloomy), & struggled to sing a little. Cinch, I discovered, has a most terrible voice, like an animal choking. I saw all the couples, & all the women without men (only VERY old men come without women). Lots of children. I have come home, hungry & dazed & I must admit, just a little uplifted.

*Ironically, the weather was so bad that no one was really walking home. Several offered me a ride, but I refused, as it felt absolutely right to walk, in spite of the umbrella-bending rain.

4pm. Enjoyed my lunch & my tea this afternoon. A little dreamy now.

10pm. Still raining a little tonight.

March 30, 1964

8.15am. Lazy again today. Easter Monday. Evidently the gospels don't record what Peter & the others got up to today. Probably the stores were closed though.

*Foggy out there & cold. A little snow blowing about.

2.45pm. Snowing heroically now.

4pm. Just back from a walk over the road. I sat down, actually down, one by one, in every room in The Corner, just to see what each one felt like. They felt nice. Will now make some tea.

10.45pm. Temperature in the 30s all day. No real snow.

March 31, 1964

9.30am. Spirit of merriment in The Corner today. It looks as though they are packing up & clearing away things. Davy & Rip carrying machinery, Marce sorting supplies & re-stacking. Dicky Bird likewise everywhere clearing away, sweeping.

2pm. Truck has come & gone off & on all day, as the men are evidently entering a new phase of work. No one there but Dicky Bird when I collected the tray. I asked him whether he sings at home. He said his kids don't like it. I asked whether his wife does & I'm sure he blushed. He grinned & carried on working.

5pm. Work over the road done now. Place looks very tidy & ship shape, large machinery gone, floors swept. Several stepladders seem to have appeared & some blue tool boxes I haven't seen before. Also some more painting tools.

11pm. Weather about the same as yesterday, though a little colder. Fire very good all day. Fog left by afternoon. Looked like it was about to snow but didn't do much. Fuzzy or not, I watched the "Richard Boone Show". Very interesting.

April 1, 1964

7.30am. Wish I were better at April Fool's jokes. I think it would be wonderful to catch Marce out. How would he respond?

*Below freezing & foggy this morning again, so already lit a fire.

9am. Men at work as usual this morning. There seems to be preparation going on. Rip & Marce are looking up and down at different rooms & how they connect. I wanted to ask why but didn't like to intrude. (Also didn't like to become someone who needed something explained.) Dicky Bird & Davy are busy sorting out lengths of pipe.

9.30am. Ingalls truck has just arrived. I'm going over to watch.

10.30am. Just back. Ingalls van piled high with all sorts of things. Fittings for the bathrooms, kitchen (including my new automatic dishwasher), lengths of pipes & lots of big lights in boxes.

*Listened to the banter, as usual. Mostly, Rip, Dicky Bird & Davy listen as the Ingalls driver talks. He likes to talk. The weather. Spring training for baseball. His children. His wife. They all nod, look knowing & offer virtually nothing in return. But Marce just has to make conversation with the young black man. –Hey, y'all have a good Easter down there? –Yes, sir, sure did. –Bet you did. What ya get up to then? –Well, sir, them kids all eatin' eggs like they ain't never seen 'em before. –You dye 'em colors? –Yes, sir, my wife, she dyes 'em up. –Uh huh. Now listen, Marce said. –You enjoy them kids while they're little, ya hear? It goes faster than Hell, I'm tellin' ya. –Yes, sir, I know it. I surely know that. –Uh huh.

*I went away thinking about this. Marce, for all his racist bravado and bullying of his own son, telling this kind-looking young man to enjoy his children?

*They piled everything in the kitchen, so I suspect it will be Davy's job to deliver it all as it is needed.

1pm. Snow flurries twice so far today & snowing now. Radio says not to expect anything. Didn't see anyone when I got the tray, & it all seems pretty quiet. All upstairs.

5pm. Men gone. I was interested to see John John this evening. His father, far from "enjoying him" greeted him with "fold up them God-d[]mn pasteboard boxes & put 'em by the backdoor". John John used a kind of flat razor-blade holding thing to cut them up.

*I walked around while they were finishing. They have put up the lights in the four upper middle bedrooms, & there seems to be something going on in the top floor about the lights, which are pretty complicated. Otherwise, there were some holes cut in the floor for the "hallway" bathroom upstairs, & copper pipes going into the floor.

10.30pm. Warmed up this evening to about 40. No real snow.

April 2, 1964

9am. Colder than yesterday & just as foggy. Snow & drizzle now. Men all at work this morning. There is a degree of copper-pipe-running going on with regard to the upper middle, or hallway bathroom. This seems to belong to Rip & Marce. Davy & Dicky Bird on ladders on the top floor, mounting the many small lights. Dicky Bird, his ladder like a lighthouse, is looking out tunefully at a sea of heartbreak, lost love & loneliness.

1pm. Back after lunch tray. Dicky Bird & Davy assisting with the copper piping. A lot of joshing going on here, most of which I cannot follow. It seems to be about bringing pipes in from hot & cold water, for the bath, shower, basin & commode. Best I don't know, I think.

3pm. Just had a knock at the door from the Amway man, who said he was sent over from across the road by one of the men. Bought mix for making pie filling.

4.45pm. Back from The Corner. Something going on with John John & Marce. Marce was barking at him when I arrived & threatening to drive home without him. As they got near the truck, all the men looked abashed, while Marce said something to him I couldn't hear. John John said something back, & Marce, fast as lightning, slapped him across the face so hard that the boy spun all the way around. I gripped the window sill & wanted to scream, but I didn't. Marce got into the truck, & John John leapt in beside of Davy, who looked to see whether there was a mark on JJ's face. Oh, my, I feel like crying & shouting.

*Small pipes all now seem to be in place for bathroom, & big "soil pipes" connected too, I think.

10.45pm. Drizzle turned to rain this evening. Around 40 degrees. Watched "Rawhide".

*Why didn't I say anything to Marce? Will I ever say anything? How far does he have to go before I speak up?

April 3, 1964

8.30am. Left the tray this morning & came away quickly. Davy already bringing the heavy boxes upstairs, Marce & Rip unpacking them. Dicky Bird up a ladder working on lights in the large bedroom on the lower middle floor.

1.30pm. Davy & Dicky Bird working on lower middle floor lights. They seem peaceful. Dicky Bird gently lilting through a song about Abilene, which is, after all, the prettiest town he's ever seen. Women there don't treat him mean either. Rip & Marce on the top floor.

5pm. Watched them all leave. John John came to my door, where I tried to look composed while he spoke. He seemed to be his usual self. Maybe, he is. (Oh, how I hope not. How I hope this is not usual.) He said they would finish the lighting fixtures next week & should get "that big bathroom done". I was desperate to ask what happened the other night, but instead, I said something vague, in the how-are-things family, so all I got was a vague answer. Then an inspiration. I asked whether his dad was looking forward to finishing the place. He said he "ain't heard nothing". Then I did it. I asked whether his face was OK. He looked at me a long moment & said it was just fine. I said I was glad. Then he ran to the truck & hopped in with Davy.

10.30pm. Above freezing this morning, & much windier. Started to rain this afternoon, temperature nearly 70. Watched another good episode of "Route 66".

April 4, 1964

7.30am. Why do I wake up early when I don't have to? Looked outside & saw two rabbits in the garden. I may need a closer fence than I had hoped.

12.30pm. Back from Frederick. Spent $17 at A & P. Bought some seed potatoes & sweet peas. More library books, especially slave narratives. Making vegetable soup for lunch, & cornbread & molasses to have with tea later.

3pm. Walked up the Harmony Road as far as Ellerton. Lots of birds around now, including three male robins. Thought I heard a hawk but couldn't see it. Forsythia past its prime; crocuses out, daffodils up but not out, bluebells opening; dogwoods set to open; buds everywhere.

7pm. Just had a strange moment. I was re-reading some of my own pages when I suddenly became conscious of the pattern of the white spaces between the words. I immediately thought that they formed a portrait of Alex's face. I put the papers down for ten minutes, & when I looked again, I could still see it (or see why I had seen it), but the impression was much more faint, not so clutching at the heart. I have just looked again & can barely see it at all now. I don't know what I feel.

10.15pm. Cold again this morning, so another session of washing goose pimples. Nearly 50 this afternoon with good sunshine.

Foggy Mountain Special

His family came originally from the Eastern Shore; originally, meaning the past few generations, as far as anyone cared or bothered to remember. They had been fishermen, working the eastern side of the Bay. After the Civil War they crossed over to the western side, where the living was better, then moved northwards a few times. When the war with the Kaiser started, they gave up fishing, moved to Baltimore and got involved with marine supplies. Harmon had grown up in Baltimore, on the streets of Baltimore, he liked to say. His accent, and the fact that his family hadn't been in the city long, got him some bullying in school, but that bullying gave him a kind of fast-talking savvy that later stood him in good stead. He was able to get a few indoor jobs, offices and such, pretty early and eventually he went to work as a salesman for Friends Home Mutual Insurance. The pay was liveable, and his rise in the company was slow, but after a number of years working, he married a pretty woman named Sandra, who grew bored easily and left him after only two years of marriage. This scarred him deeper than he might have admitted to anyone, but his bosses saw the state of things, and for his own good – and theirs – arranged for him to be transferred west, out to Frederick County, up to Emmitsburg. He became their man in Emmitsburg, their only man there, running an office of his own. It was there that he met and married Genevieve. She was fifteen years younger than him, a real baby, he said. She was also short, stocky, with curly red-brown hair, small dark eyes, flat cheeks and a double-chin. She was easily pleased and found him very amusing. Not the kind of woman, he thought, he needed to worry much about. Not this time.

Harmon spent his days, sometimes going about with cold calls, but usually driving from house to house up and down the country roads, collecting premiums from the farmers and writing them down in his little account book. He liked to socialize with the working men and women inside and outside the town. They thought him a flashy dresser and they liked his stories of the famous people he'd met in his days living in Baltimore – celebrities, socialites, and baseball players.

Harmon knew a lot about baseball, and he liked to talk about the game with all the men he met. He also liked to attend the local games, not much better than sand-lot, he said, compared to the Big Leagues in Baltimore, but still, there was some talent. Sometimes. He liked to go on Saturdays and eat hotdogs and sit in the bleachers, and shout with his mouth full – at good plays, bad plays, blind umpires. He was a loud and colourful supporter, a real character that the wives, girlfriends, parents, sisters and brothers of the players, the people who made up half the spectators, recognized.

This was good for business, he told Genevieve, who sometimes came along with him. He got to meet new people, got to chat to them, find out about their lives, find out what they longed for and what they were afraid of. Then he could sell them small policies, small promises that for small sums gave them the feeling that the things that mattered to them were safe from loss or harm.

Genevieve was with him one Saturday and watched how he worked. Harmon had just met a nice-looking young man sitting out the game because the previous Saturday he had pulled a muscle in his arm from pitching. He was a few rows up in the bleachers behind home plate, and Genevieve watched them from the end of the row where they sat. The young man's name was Paul Ziegler. He was a farmer who lived alone just southwest of town. He was slim and had a healthy tan that almost overcame the freckles he was obviously prone to. His hair was thick and auburn and had a stiff wave to it, locking it into place. His eyes were green and his smile drew sharp lines up and down his chin and cheeks. Harmon kept him talking, and the young man was polite, not quite realizing how Harmon could manoeuvre him into a sense of responsibility towards the things that made him feel vulnerable, make him fairly crave insurance. When she saw Harmon raise his hand, smiling, tilting his head, she could practically feel the words in the air – *Have we got a deal?* – she edged towards them.

Paul's hand hung still a moment, about to meet Harmon's, when his eyes met Genevieve's. He hesitated, and Harmon looked at them both.

Ah, he said. Mr Zeigler, Paul, this is my wife, Genevieve. Genevieve, this is Paul. He's a man knows a good deal when he hears one.

Paul smiled slightly at Genevieve and shook Harmon's hand.

I'll come out and see you Monday, Harmon said to him. We can settle up then.

Driving to Paul's farm on Monday, Harmon got to thinking. He was formulating a plan. These countryfolk, he thought, are tight as the bark on a tree, but they're trusting. And they know a lot about what they don't know, and they're all pleased to trust you with things. There was an opportunity.

The brief meeting Harmon had with Paul, Paul in his overalls, leaning against the tyre of his tractor, had gone just as Harmon hoped. Paul took out a policy on his barn, insuring it against fire or storm damage. He paid Harmon in cash and agreed that it was probably best for Harmon to keep the paperwork filed at his office, so Paul wouldn't run the risk of losing it. There was no need for him to sign anything.

That was where it started. Harmon kept up his acquaintance with Paul as opportunity afforded. He wrote him notes and messages and summaries on company stationery, gave him business cards, calendars, and yardsticks with the company logo on them; but he never produced any policy documents for Paul to read or sign. In this way, Harmon insured Paul's house, life, outbuildings, livestock, equipment, household goods, well, silo, fences and land against potential mining claims. Within two years, if he'd chosen to, Paul might have thought the only threat to his happiness could come from the sky directly above him. And, totalling up all the premiums he'd collected, Harmon had put away quite a sum in his savings account; a sum about which the home office in Baltimore had no knowledge, no record, and for which it would bear no liability.

All through that time, Harmon's love of baseball had never waned. He could be seen in the bleachers, behind the dugouts, near the concessions, every Saturday. He made new acquaintances, made new deals, struck new bargains. He also kept his reputation for being a noisy, rambunctious fan, fully alive. It might have been that, he thought, or the tediousness of his business-related conversations, that gradually kept Genevieve from coming along to the games any more. She had stopped coming altogether only a few weeks after Harmon had introduced her to his new client Paul Ziegler. Paul himself continued to come for a time, taking his place on the mound, sometimes as a starter, sometimes in relief. After a while though, he stopped coming to games too. Harmon asked him about it sometimes, when he was visiting Paul to collect premiums, or to try to induce him to agree to more policies. Work, Paul told him. Too much work to do on the farm, Paul said. Too much insurance to pay. They both laughed.

The following August was a hot one. Harmon had had a long week, driving all around, grinding dollars and cents out of people who were never sure just what they were paying for. The office steamed underneath the ceiling fan. It had been too hot to eat, too hot to sleep. On Saturday though, he went to the game as usual, though he was a little late in arriving, and the only seats remaining were in the sun. He sat down, balancing two hot dogs and two Coca Colas. He wasn't expecting anyone to join him, but he didn't want to have to get up again and walk all the way to the concession stand. It had been a rough year, and Harmon had put on some weight, and he just wanted to rest and enjoy the game.

To his surprise, Paul Zeigler was on the mound for the Emmitsburg team. Harmon looked at the scoreboard. It was the third inning, and Paul hadn't given up any runs. He sat back and took a bite.

By the sixth inning Paul was starting to fade a little. He hadn't given up any runs yet, but he had loaded the bases with only one man out. When the count stretched to three-and-two, Harmon stood up. His gut felt a little queasy, but then it often did these days. He was determined he was going to watch the angle of Paul's next pitch and decide it for himself. Paul went into his half-windup and let fly a fastball. The batter fouled it high, up over the chain fence and well over Harmon's head. Harmon looked up and felt the sun drying the sweat on his forehead. Paul went into his windup and laid down what can only have been a curve. To Harmon, the pitch looked clearly like it caught the inside corner of the plate.

Ball four! shouted the umpire.

The batter tossed the bat to one side and trotted towards first base. The crowd let go a moan and watched as the third-base runner trotted home.

God Almighty, Ump! Harmon shouted. What in the Hell's wrong with you? Call that a god-damn ball?

The umpire knew better than to look around at the bleachers. The crowd, long-used to Harmon, ignored him. Harmon walked, or rather wobbled, down the bleacher steps to the chain fence.

Hey! he shouted, his fingers laced in the fencing. I'm talking to you, he said.

The homeplate umpire turned towards Harmon and looked at him through his black steel mask. Harmon saw the umpire's eyes, and felt his fingers weaken on the fence. He sunk down and heard the pain grow under his ribs and press up through his arm, his neck and into his ears. Then the blue sky sank in darkness.

Harmon's death was a surprise to his employers. It took them almost two weeks to appoint a replacement for him. He had made good provision for Genevieve though; his will was detailed, and his papers in order. She had everything that had been his, including the bank accounts. His funeral was reasonably well-attended, though Paul didn't come. It hadn't seemed right to him or to Genevieve that he should. They even waited six months to be married, though it meant that their son was born only eight months after the wedding.

April 5, 1964

8am. Looked out the window, thinking there would be rabbits, but instead I saw a very proud groundhog; the sort who could be wearing a bow tie & glasses. I would have offered him coffee, but he seemed to be thinking of something important.

    *Determined to go outside & do some more digging, whether the church ladies like it or not.

12.15pm. Greeted my neighbours on their walk back, my face streaked with dirt & my new gloves looking worse for wear. (I found two silver coins in what will be my asparagus bed!) Cinch said, –How come you weren't in church? I told ya what's gonna happen if you don't get your tail up that road and outta that garden a-yourn. She was wearing a pink-flowered dress & red beads & earrings. –Here, she said. I brung ya something. It was a newspaper called Grit. –Y'all ever read one of them? I told her I hadn't seen one in years. She said to have that one, & if I liked it to let her know, as she was the one that sold them. I asked her whether she thought she could forgive me, digging on a Sunday. –It ain't up to me none, she said. The others all grinned. I asked her whether she wanted me to order anything for her from the Amway man, as he was now coming 'round. –He been to see ya, huh? He's always a-mopin' 'round.

4.30pm. Finished last of the cornbread.

10.30pm. Weather about like yesterday, though even warmer this afternoon. Sunshine has dried the soil. Watched "Arrest & Trial". 90 minutes. Chuck Connors's face just gets longer & longer.

April 6, 1964

7.30am. So much lighter in the mornings now. Temperature above freezing, but foggy & breezy.

9.30am. Men at work. Bathroom going together now. Commode in place. (Marce's opener: –Hey, your throne works.)

Shower looking like the tray is fitted. Rip busy tiling the wall. Marce working on the bathtub. Dicky Bird & Davy, now in the smaller room on the lower middle floor, working on lights. Davy constantly drawn off to carry or hold things for the others. Dicky Bird filled with a kind of rapture over a snow-white dove who sends his pure sweet love (which is a sign from Above).

1.15pm. Brought the tray back. Dicky Bird & Davy now in the kitchen working on the lights. Bathtub looks in place to me. Rip still tiling. Marce finishing sides of the bathtub. Dicky Bird gone from Heaven to Hell, as he is now complaining that he has fallen into a burning ring of fire where he has gone down down down, though the flames have gone higher.

4pm. Raining now. Amway man brought pie filling. I told him I'd see him next month. Cinch was right: he mopes.

5pm. Men gone now. Davy & John John riding off with their hoods held over their heads & pinched over their faces to keep the rain off. Lights in the kitchen look finished to me. All the big features, apart from the shower, look attached upstairs.

10.45pm. Over 50 this afternoon. Rain tapered to drizzle this evening. Watched "Wagon Train".

April 7, 1964

8.45am. Men at work this morning as expected. Marce gone down to the lower middle floor to start the half bath. Davy bringing him things. Rip & Dicky Bird both in the upper bathroom, Rip fitting shower & doors, Dicky Bird at work on the lights. Dicky Bird impassioned over thinking that his lips will kiss her one more time & his arms hold her one more time.

2pm. Other than the floor, the main bathroom looks finished. Quite fumey in there now though. Marce & Davy handling pipes for the half bath. Dicky Bird & Rip gone down to the kitchen to get something going on pipes for sink & dishwasher.

5pm. Can't see a lot of changes over the road. Some pipes in place, I guess. John John there, clearing up as usual. He & Davy both looked sullen as the truck pulled away.

7pm. Just finished reading Grit, or at least as much as I need to. I will buy them from Cinch, as they & she share a kind of magic.

10.30pm. Such a dull day. 40s this morning, 60s this afternoon. Fog, then drizzle then rain tonight.

April 8, 1964

9am. Men at work as expected. Davy still with Marce. They are fitting pipes for commode. Dicky Bird & Rip reading instructions about dishwasher. Quite a new thing for them, I think.

1.45pm. Dishwasher looks to be in place to me. Likewise, commode on lower middle floor. Rip & Dicky Bird now plumbing sink & waste disposal. More instruction reading going on. Marce & Davy working on basin upstairs.

5pm. Men gone now. Basin looks workable (I'm afraid to try it without "permission", in case I make a mess.) Kitchen sink either is workable, or nearly so. John John not here tonight.

5pm. Cloudy all day & in the 40s. Air went funny, & now thunderstorm towards Wolfsville.

10.30pm. In the mid 50s this afternoon. No more storms.

April 9, 1964

9am. Breezy this morning & the occasional snowflake. Men here as expected. Davy now with Dicky Bird in the utility room. Dicky Bird getting ready to fit washing machine & dryer. He is surprised because he thought he was only dreamin' but now he hears them screamin' to come & join the parade of broken hearts. Meanwhile, above them, Rip & Marce are working on the bathroom suite for the lower middle bedroom.

2pm. Very peaceful over the road. Dicky Bird singing, but so far away I couldn't hear the words. Peaceful over the new bathroom suite.

5pm. John John a little bit later this evening. He seems in a very good mood. I caught up to him near the Harmony Road side gate & asked him how school was. He said he won every race at the track meet. He looked pleased with himself. I wondered whether he would tell Marce but didn't like to ask. They left on time, & as they were leaving, I asked Marce whether he was proud that John John was so fast. He looked at me & shook his head. –He oughta be good at runnin', he said. John John looked like he wanted to say something, but he didn't.

11pm. Hardly above 40 today. Watched "Rawhide".

I'll settle down and quit my rowdy ways

They were probably cousins. They both thought they were, though neither one could think of just how they were related. Wayne lived in one of the old houses on the Brethren Church Road, where there always seemed to be Frushours living, and Bob lived about two hundred yards away, on the Harmony Road, where there had always been Whipps living. They grew up together, went to school together and married their wives at around the same time. Those wives even had had children at about the same time. For years, both Wayne and Bob had worked for a big concern called Southern Republic. It was a company that had a small line in tractor parts and general farming equipment, but its main business was in bulk items, and they ran a string of feed stores, and delivered fuel oil directly to people's doorsteps. That was what Bob did for a living, driving one of the big tankers up and down the county, refilling tanks at houses in towns, the countryside and on the farms. The success of that trade encouraged the bosses to open a plumbing-and-heating division, and they kept a small team of plumbers and furnace-fitters busy installing and maintaining heating systems, as more and more people were getting them fitted. This was what Wayne did for a living. The two men seldom saw one another at work but, of course, living so closely together, they often socialized at weekends and sometimes on weekday evenings.

That was how things stood when they were joined down at the depot by Elvin Kunkle. Elvin was a mechanic from Minnesota. He was about the same age as Bob and Wayne, and because he repaired and maintained the trucks they drove, he saw them both occasionally. Though not from the area himself, Elvin's mother was, and when Elvin inherited her house up near Fisher's Lodge, he moved east and settled in. He had a skinny, nervous wife and two children, a boy and a girl. Long before they moved east, Elvin had convinced all of them that they were pretty unintelligent, and that they should be grateful for him for taking as much care of them as he did, which was little enough.

Elvin's wife and children weren't seen much around Harmony, though Elvin decided early on that he'd better get himself involved with the local men, if he was ever going to fit in. He helped them hide eggs at Easter for the children to gather. He helped shore up the old stands in the meadow for the annual

Festival in the summer. He raked the infield for the baseball season. He played bingo in the Band Hall on Saturday evenings, and pitched horseshoes with them on Sunday afternoons. In the winter, he shovelled the snow from the paths where old folks lived. In the summer, he sat around on the benches under the walnut trees near the Mary House and shot the breeze.

It was doing these things in that first long year when Elvin caught sight of Wayne's wife Madeline. Elvin had always thought he would have been a man for the ladies if only he hadn't have done the right thing and married the woman he actually did marry, taking pity on her, he felt. But now in early middle age, and in a new place, this old knowledge of his that he had kept subdued, began to reassert itself, and he began to watch Madeline a little more closely.

He decided early that she was as hot as a pistol. You could see it in the sultry blank look on her face so much of the time, the way she listened without speaking. You could see it in the way she walked, her heels striking the ground first, her toes following – especially in summer when she walked around her lawns bare-foot, bringing cold drinks to Wayne when he worked outside, or played badminton with his kids. Elvin thought the bare skin on her arms looked very soft, and he liked the fullness in her calves when she hung out laundry. He knew what he wanted to do, he just wasn't sure how to get started.

Elvin was in the depot on a June afternoon, just over a year after he'd started work, when Bob brought his tanker in for the mechanics to have a look at. Bob had a suspicion that the radiator might be leaking, as the engine's temperature kept rising too quickly. Elvin was already busy changing the front tyres on a feed truck, so the job fell to two of the men he worked with. But Elvin was close enough to hear their conversation.

You still getting any of that good stuff? one of the mechanics asked Bob.

Hell, yes, he said. She's always ready for it, that one.

They all laughed. It was clear that the whole crew already knew the story – had probably heard it many times – but they liked to hear Bob tell it, so he told them again. There were, Bob said, a lot of lonely women out there, and he was damn lucky to have a job that put him in the way of seeing to it that they had a little fun in their lives. Maybe it was his uniform, maybe it was the fumes, but every year since he'd started driving, there had been one or two who could hardly wait for him to get parked up beside their houses before they'd be having him in for coffee and getting their hands on him.

Well, there was this one, he said, didn't live far from him. He knew her husband. Well, God Almighty, she practically tore his pants getting them off him. The boys all laughed at this. Even the hair on her head was hot, he said. And she knew what to do, she did. Yes, sir. That woman was something else.

Elvin went home that night thinking. It had to be Madeline Bob was talking about. Who else could it be? She was about the only woman in three miles who didn't go to church most Sundays, not that he thought that might matter much. But he let his mind go in and out of every door up and down the roads both Wayne and Bob lived on, and he just couldn't believe it could be anybody else. He had to think what he could do about this. He was losing sleep.

He started spending more time down on the commons around The Corner, watching out, in case Madeline ever came outside. Sometimes, she came down and joined the women talking in their separate group, a circle that formed around one of the benches a little way from the one where the men usually congregated. Mostly though, she didn't. He would glimpse her walking around her house or sitting on her porch. He listened for any gossip, but there never was any. He watched Bob and Wayne, how they looked and spoke with one another. There were no signs between them, no recognitions, no secrets. None of the other men paid any special attention to Madeline, near them, or up at her own house, where the sunshine fell on her bare legs.

Elvin thought of plan after plan. He thought of sabotaging either Wayne's truck or Bob's, partly just to be mean, but also in case either stunt could open up a way for him to be alone with Madeline. He thought of trying to find a way to get one of the other mechanics to keep Wayne tied up with something long enough for Elvin to race back to Harmony and knock on Madeline's door. But it would have to be when her children were in school. What excuses would he use? He thought of somehow blackmailing either Bob or Madeline with what he knew, but he couldn't quite see how that would work. He thought about trying to become a tanker driver like Bob.

When the summer ended, Madeline went back into long sleeves. She was also about the only woman in Harmony who wore slacks. There were fewer get-togethers on the benches. Days were shorter, evenings cooler. Elvin's wife began to wonder out-loud when it might be possible for them to get one of those new oil-fired boilers. The children weren't looking forward to another winter in those cold bedrooms. Elvin thought and thought. He wondered about whether it would be possible to move the whole family down to Florida. He had heard that things were booming down there. Maybe he'd give that a try.

April 10, 1964

9.15am. Everyone busy over the road. Pipes growing into place for the suite bathroom. Davy & Dicky Bird moving the washer & dryer into place. Looks like they'll work on the laundry sink too.

2.15pm. Business as usual across the road.

5.15pm. Men just gone. John John came to visit, a little earlier than usual. He said the washer & dryer are in & the sink attached. So the downstairs is done. He said the suite bath is getting finished & should be done nest week. All the lights work. He said there will be inspections of the plumbing & the lights next week too. I asked him what was new, & he told me baseball practice starts next week after school. I asked him what position he played. First base, he said. Just like his dad. My heart sank a little. I asked what batter he was. He said eighth. Oh, my. I said I'd come to the games if he told me when they were, & he promised he would. I really hope he does. I really hope he does.

10.15pm. Not much more than freezing this morning, but in the 60s this afternoon. Beautiful sunshine. Watched "Route 66".

April 11, 1964

7.45am. Three rabbits this morning! I walked out after they'd gone to see what they'd been nibbling at (couldn't tell), but I discovered that just below the top of the bank, on the Hollow Road side, the bank has clusters of daffodils! They get the sun until about 12.

1.30pm. Frederick again. Library first, replaced books with what I could find on the Indians. Very little. Went to bookstore & bought Maxwell's The Chateau. Went to A & P ($15). Went to Blue Ridge News Agency & got a "Saturday Evening Post" because I am in the mood for it.

4pm. Outside all afternoon, & have two blisters, one broken. Going to read now.

5pm. Robin on the place where I was digging earlier.

10.45pm. Weather today just like yesterday. No real chance of making it through the movie tonight.

April 12, 1964

8.15am. Going for early walk to see what I can see.

1pm. Tired & strangely hot. Walked all the way to Myersville this morning, & the air smelled wonderful. Everything going lime green now. Birds galore & blossom on trees waiting to burst. Back in time to join walk-home from church. Cinch wearing orange & brown with turquoise beads & earrings. –Where ya been? was her opener. I explained. –Well, she said. You'll get run over on them roads. (I saw four cars.) I told her I'd buy some more of Grit. –Well, she said. Then all at once she took my arm & leaned over very close. –You ain't heard nothing 'bout your boy, have ya? No, I said. Then she squeezed my arm. Suddenly, she said, –You ain't planted your peas yet, have ya?

    *I made two BLTs for lunch & had both, walking around & looking out the windows, first at The Corner, then The Patch, then The Commons, then I went outside to look at whatever the other bit is called on the far bank of the little stream. I own the four sides of a crossroads & I don't even know why.

4.45pm. Just finished the last of the Earl Grey tea Sis sent. Have spent time outside. Everything in the garden is neat now. Even the banks to the streams are smooth, except for the flowers.

10.30pm. Weather like yesterday, though warmer this afternoon & a bit breezier. Very dark tonight & no moon that I can see. Maxwell is a graceful American.

April 13, 1964

7.15am. Have built a fire, mostly for company. 54, I think, & foggy.

9.30am. Hartsock knocked on my door at nine, asking me to come over the road for an inspection. He has told Marce (now evidently not speaking to him) that dryer ventilation will need changing as it needs to connect to outside wall. Despite weather, Davy now outside chiselling at mortar in stonework to make a new hole. Marce very unhappy, has gone back to work on suite bathroom. Hartsock generally satisfied with things.

*Dicky Bird with Marce, Rip overseeing Davy & dryer business.

10am. Damp & drizzling rain.

1pm. Things much as before, although Davy & Rip gone to Middletown for something at Ingalls.

5pm. Wall outside near wash house now repaired with an aluminium vent fitted. Things moved around in the utility room. No signs of John John. Practice rained out, I imagine. Suite bathtub in place with tiling to be finished above. Commode works (flushed it!) & basin looks ready. Floor still not done.

10.45pm. Climbed over 60 today, but so dark & dismal. Watched "Wagon Train". Read some more Maxwell earlier. So full of sighs.

You can bury me in some deep valley

I, LittleWound, tell this story.

It was around the time when, though I was a woman, teeth grew in my jaws, pushing aside those already there. The Washechu too had changed the style of their hats, so that they now stood like stumps above their ears. It happened on the side of the mountain towards the rising sun, where the HomeWind does not blow, above the pits where they dig for iron for the furnaces, where the Washechu planted the slopes with forests of peaches, cherries, plums, apples and pears.

It was here that there lived a woman who inherited a forest of such trees when her parents died of fever. She sought and married a man named Zimmerman, who was by trade a carpenter, and who knew nothing of trees and fruit. She married him because he loved her and because he placed everything in her hands, for on such a farm the jobs are not like those on other farms, and for this work she hired slaves by the season. Men and women did this work for her, sometimes by themselves and sometimes in gangs. It was to her liking that as much as possible, Zimmerman moved from village to village and town to town, building the things that were needed as the Washechu grew upon the land. He came home as often as he could, but when the days lengthened beneath the sun, these visits could be scattered like leaves on the water.

There was a man who oversaw the slaves for Zimmerman's wife, and his name was Gouker. Like the slaves in his charge, he came and went as he pleased. Or rather as she pleased, because it was not hard for him to discover that she regarded him with more joy than she afforded her husband. This was in spite of his cruelty to the slaves and his contempt for work. He could be seen approaching the farm when the sun was already like a youth in stature, and when others were already aching to rest their limbs. The slaves, like fingers on a hand, would be bound together with rods so that they could not come together or lean upon one another. Sometimes he hired those who had been inherited and whose owners did not know what else to do with them. Sometimes he hired those who had been caught seeking their families on other farms. Sometimes he hired those whose beauty had made them like mares to their masters, but whose looks broke down after their babies had been born and sold. His trade seemed to be in unhappiness, and this he controlled through isolating these slaves on farms where there was no one to whom they might tell their sorrows. But while his slaves grew to be like cornstalks, Gouker ate until his stomach hung before him like a sack of pumpkins.

When she thought no one was looking, Zimmerman's wife liked to lay her hands all over Gouker and she took him to her bed whenever Zimmerman was away working. But before long she found Gouker's weight to be more than her bones could welcome, and so she forbade him to enter her bed again until he became more the shape of a man with muscles she could feel and count.

Because Gouker did not want to lose the privilege of her bed, he agreed even to this, and so Zimmerman's wife decided to help him. While he sat in the shade shouting orders at the slaves picking the fruit or trimming the trees or scything the grass or carrying the baskets, she picked him a meal from the Manitoes' table, from the crops not planted by her hands, but by those of the gods themselves. She chose for him the asparagus, onions and ramp, nettles, dock, horseradish, mustard and turnips, the sorrel, rhubarb, pigweed, lamb's quarters, purslane, chickweed, peppergrass, and shepherd's purse; she picked the radishes, watercress, toothwort, brooklettuce, violets, milkweed, chicory and dandelions. These things she cooked or made into salads for him, and while his face did not blossom over his plate, the promise of her body enticed him to eat with relish. So every meal she sweetened with a bowl of raspberries, blackberries, strawberries and, of course, the fruit from her trees. In this way the days passed, and Gouker's lust and temper grew to be as one, though the fires of his heart were no longer matched by the strength in his limbs.

It happened then that Zimmerman's wife heard that she had a cousin nearing death – a cousin who had slaves of her own, and ones she hoped to inherit. She sent a message to Zimmerman, telling him to return to the farm at once, long enough for her to visit this cousin. Zimmerman came when he could, and his wife left him in charge, telling him that whatever else he did, he must make sure that he allowed Gouker to eat only those things she had specified. She even showed Zimmerman where to find the greens and roots he would need, although she said he might choose whatever fruit he thought best to give him as a finish to the meal. She then left her husband to himself in the house, expecting Gouker to return the next day.

As Zimmerman expected, Gouker came with his slaves when the sun hung in the sky and he put them to work while he himself watched from the shade of the waggon. Hoping to please his wife, and to cause no strife, Zimmerman busied himself harvesting all the things she had described and preparing them as they needed. Alongside this he sat a plate of raspberries, blackberries and peaches.

The next day was the same, and Zimmerman spent his time mending the porch of his wife's house, while the others tended the trees and fields. When Gouker was ready, he came into the porch as before, and had the same food to which he was now accustomed.

The next day came and looked like it would be just the same. But this time, though Zimmerman gathered the greens and the roots, slicing and cooking them and dressing them as he ought, he could find no berries to put with the peaches that followed them. He looked in the cellar and in the springhouse and on the canes, but there were none to be found. He decided then that he would look for some in the same way that he looked for the greens, finding what he could along the fence-rows and at the edge of the fields. He walked in the sun and the shade, and after a while he came upon some plants with leaves like bruises and berries like grapes. These, he thought, must be huckleberries. He picked a half a peck of them and brought them back to the farmhouse where he washed them carefully. He put a bowlful of the fruit doused with milk beside the plate of greens and roots and waited for Gouker to come in for his meal.

Just as the breeze was licking his face like steam, Zimmerman saw Gouker approach the porch and sit down to his meal. He swung his hand in the air, shooing flies. Behind him, Zimmerman could see the slaves sitting in the shade of their ladders and baskets, eating their corncakes and drinking their water. Gouker drank cups full of water himself and chewed through the roots and greens, all the while looking around to see whether Zimmerman was watching, and wondering how soon Zimmerman's wife would return, calling him again into her bed, the one where Zimmerman had slept since his return.

When the plate was empty, Gouker picked up the bowl of berries and milk. He lifted a spoonful and buried it in his mouth, swallowing the juice and the milk together. He spooned the rest and wiped his face on his sleeve. Then he stood up, held the heel of his hand to his nose and shot a stream of snot into the dust beside the porch-steps, shouting out to the slaves to get back to work or he'd skin them.

Zimmerman watched from the window while Gouker walked towards the waggonload of baskets and stumbled. He grabbed the side of the waggon to steady himself, but then let go and grabbed his stomach. Then he grabbed his head and began turning around. He grabbed at his throat, his chest, his jaws and then his chest again. He sank to his knees and ran his hands all over his body, just as Zimmerman's wife used to do. Then he stopped and fell forward, striking his shoulder on the rim of the waggon's wheel. His face lay in the thistles and orchard-grass, and he did not move again.

Zimmerman saw this without moving. Gouker's slaves looked on, their faces as open as their mouths, their tools still in their hands. Their shoulders sank in front of them and they licked their lips as Zimmerman ran to Gouker's side and turned him over. The dead man's eyes looked swollen in their sockets and there were weeds in his mouth.

That night Zimmerman quartered the slaves in the barn, not knowing whether he could trust them to make their own way back to their quarters in Mechanicstown. He closed Gouker's eyes himself, wrapped him in a quilt and got the slave-men to carry him into the cellar, where he thought the body would keep best. He then changed his mind, and got them to carry Gouker upstairs again, laying him on boards between chairs in the parlour. Before the sun set, he collected his tools and built a pine coffin. He sent the oldest of the slave women into town to fetch the sheriff.

Zimmerman was stacking firewood in the barn on the day his wife returned. He pointed out the grave the slave-men had dug for Gouker underneath a plumtree, the grave itself marked by a locust-wood cross he had carved himself. Zimmerman's wife looked at the grave and wondered. She did not, as it happened, inherit her cousin's slaves. While she had been away her husband had used Gouker's slaves to haul the harvest all the way to Fredericktowne, where it was sold for double what she might have sold it for herself. When the frosts came, she asked Zimmerman not to travel and work as a carpenter as much as he used to. When the blossom returned to their trees, she gave birth to a daughter.

April 14, 1964

8.45am. Everyone busy over the road. Davy & Dicky Bird finishing utility room. Marce & Rip working on suite bathroom.

12.30pm. Just back with tray. Rip, a little shyly, told me that electrical inspector had come this morning, though I hadn't seen him. He has requested some work on bathrooms needs fixing as "the breakers ain't right" somehow. Marce is livid & has gone to Ingalls for parts. Meanwhile, Rip is tiling suite bathroom. Dicky Bird is upstairs starting hall bathroom floor, Davy with him. Couldn't hear the words of the song.

5pm. Men left on time, Marce spinning away, scattering gravel all over The Common.

*I would like to meet Marce's mother & ask her what he was like at 16.

10.30pm. Temperature like yesterday, though warmer this afternoon. Thunderstorms to the east, probably over Frederick.

April 15, 1964

9am. Men busy over the road. Marce handling remedial adjustments to bathroom wiring. Rip tiling, Dicky Bird tiling & Davy helping everybody. Dicky Bird singing & telling everyone not to worry 'bout him, 'cause it's all over now, & though he may be blue, he'll manage somehow.

11am. In the paper today that they are opening a tunnel underneath the Chesapeake Bay, connecting the two bits of Virginia. It is 20 miles long & I cannot imagine ever going inside it.

11.45am. Just back from taking tray over. Met plumbing inspector on his way out. He did not look happy. He said he had to tell Marce that there was a slight problem with "the grounding" in the bathrooms. Marce evidently lost what little cool he possesses & must have been offensive. I offered the inspector tea, but he declined.

2pm. Collected tray. Marce back from swift unhappy trip to Ingalls for something else. Glad John John is otherwise engaged this evening.
    * Bathroom floor looks splendid. Now working on suite one & Davy cleaning floor in lower middle (the one they evidently use themselves) making it ready to tile.

5.15pm. Men gone. Didn't go over again. A little tired this evening.

10.45pm. Temperature like yesterday, though not as warm & much windier. Thunderstorms towards the mountains again tonight. Devoted 30 minutes to "The Eleventh Hour". It is one of those dramas where everyone delivers their lines pointing accusingly at someone else.

April 16, 1964

9am. Men busy this morning. Lots of floor tiles in bathrooms now. Marce out of sight, clipping & snipping wires. A low electric buzz of swearing on the air from his direction.

1pm. Bathroom floors nearly all done now, & other repairs look completed. Marce under sink in kitchen. Strangely, Davy helping Dicky Bird drill holes in the wall near the floor upstairs.

5pm. Everyone gone. Things shaping up nicely at Corner now. Maxwell book has slowed to a crawl.

10pm. Freezing again this morning & 60s this afternoon. Woodpile is getting low again. Nice sunshine all day.

April 17, 1964

6.45am. Wonderful sunrise today, temperature over 40 already.

9.15am. Ingalls delivery already this morning. Small amount of cement, some steel poles & boxes. Gone before I could scuttle over the road to watch.

11am. Inspector for electricity just gone, I think.

12.45pm. Just back from taking tray over. Yes, electricity has passed inspection. Marce can collect the permit next week. His verdict? —What a crock of sh[]t.
 *The plumbing inspector is due at two.

2pm. Downright hot now! 82 degrees, out there. Cloudless sky. No sign of inspector.

2.45pm. Plumbing inspector has gone. According to Marce, –That sh[]thead got all he wanted. Marce can pick up the permit for this too next week.

*Meantime, Davy has dug a hole near the chimney on the wash house side of the building, & they are mixing concrete. Davy looks as hot as a melting candle. From somewhere he had produced a Truade that he kept close to him at all times.

4.30pm. Men wrapping up early, so Rip came to tell me. Next week, they are fitting the TV aerial (thus the poles & boxes & concrete base). Then he looked embarrassed & couldn't remember what else he was supposed to tell me. I asked how Marce was handling the setbacks. –Aw, Rip said, He's got more frets than a guitar.

*I asked Rip what he would be doing this weekend. His wife wants him to do some gardening, he said. I asked him whether he liked to garden. He looked like he'd never considered this. Yes, he decided, he did. If it wasn't too hot.

6.45pm. Joanie & Paul outside. Joanie on the autoharp, Paul on the mandolin. I wanted to walk up to say hello, but I was afraid of interrupting. Why am I always afraid of such things?

11.30pm. Radio said the high today was 84. Watched Jack Paar, though only thinking about my upbringing. Being "brought up". What an idea! Sis, "brought up". Bought up, I'd say. Did they make us afraid? Tom was too afraid of being afraid, so I can't blame him. God knows I would if I could, eh Tom? I was afraid for Alex, but not because of him. Not until later.

I looked over Jordan, Lord

Over the hill, 'hind the Mary House, up the ole Hollow Road, ya keep going till ya get to the Hawbottom Road, and ya turn left, up towards the mountain. 'Fore ya get in the ruts pointing up to the Ridge Road they used to be a little steam-power sawmill, belong to a fella name Clyde Hartsock. He married to a woman might have been nice some time, but time I knowed her she 'bout as mean as a ole bobcat. Her name Miss Maybelle. Now I don't know nothing, but what I think is she a nice person inside but being married to ole Mister Clyde ruin her for people. I do. He got a temper on him like you ain't never seen, and he ain't had but nobody much to use it on 'cept her, and she ain't had nobody at all. She couldn't have no children, and Mister Clyde, he think they something more than that wrong with her, and he tell her so more than once. Anyway, that's how things was till Mister Clyde up and have one his brothers die. He got 'bout four brothers, and the one that died owned a big farm down New Market way, and he left most of that farm to his next brother as kin, then he divide up the other belongings to his other brothers. Mister Clyde don't get much, but what he do get is a house servant name Sheba. She 'bout half-growed when she come, and they put her in the ole storeroom out the back 'bove the summer kitchen.

Well, Mister Clyde, he working mostly to cut up the logs that they bringing down from the Point, mostly pine, and up 'bove Hawbottom where it mostly chestnut. They drug 'em down with horses and roll 'em up like cigars, and that's how he get 'stablished, taking the mill to the logs, stead of asking folks to bring the logs to the mill, like the do up in Fisher's Hollow and Crow Rock and them places. He busy as all get out most the time. Then when he get home he start in a-bossing 'round Miss Maybelle, and she don't like it much when it's just the two of 'em, but she don't like it at all now she got that Sheba a-listening and a-looking at her. She spend most her days just a-thinking of things to keep Sheba busy. And Sheba ain't no bad girl or nothing, but she ain't been showed everything yet, and Miss Maybelle start to thinking how much she like bossing her 'round, just same as she get bossed by Mister Clyde. Ask me, she got any sense, she make a friend out of Sheba, but Miss Maybelle don't see it like that. No, sir. 'Stead, she take to chasing and shouting and telling that Sheba she ain't worth nothing to nobody.

Well, one day, Miss Maybelle send Sheba out from the summer kitchen to take the peelings out to the hogs. She get there and all the hogs is down in the wallow cooling theyselves. So Sheba, she open the gate and take the peelings on in and drop 'em on the trough. One of them shoats see her a-moving and jump to his feet. Now Sheba ain't spend no time with hogs before and she scared, so she run off. Thing is, she forget the gate. By evening, Mister Clyde coming home and what he see but 'bout six hogs a-rooting round, trying to get in to the patch 'mong the vegetables. He like to be tied then. He grub a piece a firewood and chase them hogs back to the pen, then he come a-busting in to the house. Maybelle, he say. What the Hell gone on 'round yare, woman? Can't I 'spect nothing out of you?

Now Miss Maybelle, she done seen him out there a-hog-chasing, and she too scared her own self to do nothing. But she up and say, Listen here. That ain't me done that. That was thisn right here. And she point at Sheba. Mister Clyde, he just look at the both of 'em. Well, he say, it's your 'sponsibility to keep her under control. How I 'sposed to do that, Miss Maybelle say, when y'all don't give me nothing to control her with? What you want? he say. Miss Maybelle look at Sheba, and I don't know what she see, but she say, What I want is for you to take her outside and take 'bout an inch off her hide with that bull whip of yourn.

Mister Clyde, he just look at 'em both a minute. Come on, girl, he say, and take ole Sheba by the arm and drag her outside. He get her up to the barn where Miss Maybelle can't see, and he give Sheba a shake. He look at her up and down. How old are you? he say. 'Deed, I don't know, Sheba say. He just look at her some more. He stick out them big ole hands of hisn and start to squeezing her. Uh huh, he say. I tell you something, he say. Y'all let me do what I wanna, and don't say nothing to nobody 'bout it, I let you off 'thout the whipping. Ya hear me? Ya hear me? he say. Ya keep ya mouth shut, I make things easy. You deny me, and I take you down there and skin you good, ya hear?

Yes, sir, I hear, she say.

So Mister Clyde, he fling ole Sheba down on the hay and he interfere with her all he wanna, then he get up and drag her up with him. Now y'all get down to that house, he say. Member what I told ya, he say.

When Sheba get down to the house, Miss Maybelle is a-waiting on the porch for her. Look at me, girl, she say. Mister Clyde beat you like I say? But Sheba, she don't say nothing. You hear me, girl? Miss Maybelle say. Sheba crying a little now. Show me where he beat you, Miss Maybelle say. Sheba, she try to get away, but Miss Maybelle grab her, just as Mister Clyde coming towards the house.

Y'all didn't do nothing up there, did ya? she say to Mister Clyde, and he look like he could just eat her.

I show you, he say. He go off to one of them sleds where they got the logs pile up, and he reach in there and pull out hisself a bull whip. He come back up there, and Sheba she start to shaking. No, sir, no, sir, no, sir, she say, and Miss Maybelle she step back towards the door. That's when Sheba run. But Mister Clyde too big and too quick and he bring that ole bull whip down cross her legs, and down she go on the ground, a-rolling 'round like a chicken with its head cut off. And he stand there a cracking that bull whip on her till her dress and her hands and her neck red as blood. Then he fling that whip down, and he say to Miss Maybelle, Now who ain't done nothing, huh?

After that Sheba don't talk much to nobody no more. Mister Clyde go on a sawing boards and a-getting money in the Farmers and Mechanics bank till he hear that the war starting, and he take all that money out and move hisself and Miss Maybelle up to Pennsylvania. 'Fore they go, he sell ole Sheba to a speculator and tell him to be careful, 'cause he say she healthy but she lazy and like the boys a little too much.

April 18, 1964

8am. Warm today (55 degrees). May be like yesterday. Sleepy from late night & stupid dreams. The bus station in Baltimore & the fish hatchery at Thurmont.

11.30am. Only went to Acme this morning ($15). Strawberries from California on sale. Ridiculous.

4.30pm. Just remembered I haven't heard from Sis in ages. Will phone later. Finished Maxwell. He is so conclusive, so final, so feeling.

10.30pm. Today was as warm as yesterday, though breezier. Forgot to phone Sis. Hope she's OK. Poor Sissy.

April 19, 1964

8am. A bit gray this morning, though still in the 50s.

8.45am. Rabbits have eaten the potato peels I put out. Or something has, anyway.

10am. Walked along to church this morning, defiant & downright strident. Three, if not four women (& one man named George!) said I ought to come in. I said I had already made my plans, (though I haven't really) & said they'd just better think the best of me. Cinch called me a rascal (!), which I liked, & said I didn't know just what I was missing.

*I am baking an applesauce cake with a recipe I got from Grit.

1pm. A first! Cinch, Agassy, Edna, Irene & Carrie ALL came inside the Mary House, sat down, drank cups of tea & had pieces of warm applesauce cake. I have no idea at all about what changed their minds about doing so. I mentioned the new cake, the tea, & in they came. All the chairs were full. They said how cosy the place is, they said the cake was good & they talked about the sermon, who was pregnant, whose hips were getting bad, how much newspapers cost nowadays & whether Spring were truly here. Cinch left me a Grit. They all said they liked my garden, & that if I needed any cuttings, I am to just help myself, & not to worry about asking.

3pm. Windy now, & over 70. Feeling funny, having had cake & no lunch. Eaten UTZ chips, which was a mistake.

7pm. Thunderstorms have blown across us, bringing some sudden rain, but not for long. Had a nice dinner on salad & tuna fish.

10.45pm. Strange day today, weather-wise. Too stirred up to sleep.

April 20, 1964

8am. Have made a fire this morning, as it is very gray. Temperature in the upper 40s.

8.45am. Marce dropped off the others & has gone to Frederick alone in order to collect the permits. Davy, supervised by Rip is making a hole in the back wall towards the upper yard. Dicky Bird is doing the same thing on the opposite side of the back door. Now what?

10.30am. Marce's truck is now parked on The Commons. Not sure when he arrived.

1pm. Work on the back of the house is a setting up of an outside faucet for my future gardening there. The other side is a pair of outside plug sockets, for power tools or lights or similar. Marce is 'round the corner, helping Davy position the pipes that will become the TV aerial.

2pm. Thunderstorms to the west & south. Lightning visible, but little sound. Men have given up on aerial. Faucet now works, sockets too. They are now on the high porch & the porch below doing something.

5pm. Men gone now. They have put in the wires for porch lights above & below. I suspect another is going near the back door.

10pm. House felt stuffy today. Too chilly to be comfortable, too warm to need heating. Fell asleep during "Wagon Train". Finished with library books.

April 21, 1964

9am. Men working as usual today. All outside. Dicky Bird finishing light on high porch & strangely seems to be singing "Hello Walls", asking how things have gone for them today. Words muffled down at the road level, so can't quite tell what he's saying. Rip & Marce busy with TV aerial mounting. Davy, bizarrely, seems to be digging a trench leading from the house to the uppermost corner of the yard.

12.45pm. Dicky Bird now helping Davy. Not enough puff to sing as well as dig. Marce on the ground, passing things up to Rip who is climbing up the three-sided TV aerial tower they are attaching to the chimney.

5pm. Tower now extends to the top of the chimney, ditch to the corner of the yard. I wonder if these things are connected? Men gone, so cannot ask.

*Must ask Marce when John John's first baseball game is.

10.30pm. Temperature in the 40s all day today. Heard one clap of thunder & some rumbling, but that was all. Watched "The Greatest Show on Earth". I'm certain they are mistaken. Fairly certain. Hopeful.

Won't you spare me over for another year?

I, LittleWound, tell this story.

It was in the time when the menses were stopping, and my sleep was ruined by sweat. BlackMary had not yet come to Harmony, and the mill sold more rye-flour than barley.

There was a man named Ahalt who owned a farm near Burkittsville, a day's walk in the valley from Harmony, beyond Middletown. He had a wife named Susannah, and they were married at the season when the slaughtering begins, just as the moon turns the colour of water. Now Ahalt had slaves that lived in cabins under the oaks and sycamores behind his barns, stables, pigpens and chicken-coops. His appetite for slaves was known to his neighbours, and some were pleased by this and some were not. Those who were, invited him into their own slaves' quarters where he fathered children that their owners might keep or sell as they chose. Some even made sure that the women marked with beauty be shown to him so that the invitation would be understood. Sometimes, he sought others out himself, courting them with presents of food or clothing. Sometimes he inherited them, took them in trade, or waited for that day when the frost lay on the fields, and the hiring of slaves was agreed. Regardless of how he came to them, he knew, as did the slaves, that women could be killed for naming the father of their children. All of this happened before his marriage to Susannah.

When Susannah came to live under his roof, the neighbours watched to see what would happen. For a time, they were disappointed. Ahalt kept himself to his farm, to his wife and to his duties, and it looked as though he had become a man with honour again.

It happened though that Ahalt was a man who guarded his interests on the farm and in his business with insight and temper. After one such deal with a neighbour over some land he wished to purchase the neighbour let slip a remark that fell on Susannah's ear, causing her to think over something she had never considered. She began to watch Ahalt in his dealings and to take note of how he spoke to the slaves that were his own, those he hired, and those he saw in the village. She began to have ideas that troubled her.

Whatever she may have thought in her bed at night, or in her parlour in the daytime, she decided that she would act so that whatever happened, the truth would be known to everyone. She began to make calls on the wives who lived in the valley and on the mountainside, listening to the words they used, the tone they spoke in, the gestures they made or failed to make, and she came to see that they both pitied and despised her. For this reason, Susannah decided to take her revenge on Ahalt.

In her visits, Susannah had called on a couple whose farm lay at the ankle of the mountain, the place where the land slopes toward the sky, and the stones are like the hairs on the head. The wife treated her like a sister, and Susannah saw that this woman and her husband shared their farm with slaves who lived as husband and wife. Together this couple lived in peace, and the chores seemed to be divided amongst them all, slave and free. But what Susannah also recalled about the household was that the slave-wife had skin like a blossom, and eyes like coal. Her hair glistened like sun on water, and her movements were like those of a deer.

Thinking she might use this woman to tempt Ahalt, Susannah wrote her a letter. In the letter, she described to the woman how Ahalt fancied her for his own, where she might meet him, and the rewards she might be given. She did not sign the letter, so there was no way to know who had sent it. What Susannah did not know is that it is against the Washechu law for slaves to receive letters, and so the letter was given to the wife, who showed it to her husband. Between them they knew anger and remorse that anyone should so seek to bring turmoil to the happiness of their lives. They took the decision to warn both their slaves that there was a man whose eyes had found the woman, and who was seeking her for his own. Though there was no proof, all the household suspected that the man behind the writing of the letter was Ahalt.

Now it happened that the slave-woman's husband was not a man in whom fear dwelt. Instead, his heart was like the muscles in his arms, and he was determined that no other man, Washechu or slave, would find his way to the wife he loved. Day after day, throughout his working, and as often as he was able, he kept his eyes in her direction, just in case there was anyone seeking to confront her with enticements or with threats.

At about this time it happened that Ahalt himself had taken his horse to ride through the village in the direction of that place where the road rises on to the slopes of the mountainside. His business was his own, and he had no other plans than to visit a neighbouring farm and ask after the farmer's son, who owed him some money for a pony he had bought. Because it was a day when the sky shone like the centre of a flame, Ahalt rested his horse in the shade of the maples at the side of the road, taking himself off to have a nap where the breeze blew. As Ahalt slept, the horse, who came to be in the sun as the time passed, could smell the water in the stream, and pulled at his reins until they loosened. The horse walked to the stream, drank, and then moved towards the field on the other side, where the clover hung in tufts through the rails.

When Ahalt awoke and discovered his horse was missing, he failed to guess the direction it had taken. He wanted to keep his appointment with the farmer's son, so he decided to walk down the nearest lane and borrow a horse until he found his own. This lane was the one that led to the farm where Susannah had sent her letter.

As Ahalt walked up the lane towards the house, he looked around and saw no one. He called out, and the first one to hear him was the slave-wife, who was in the patch hoeing beans. Thinking he had come for her, she screamed and screamed again. Across the field behind the house her husband was using a cornchopper to cut thistles from the edge of the hayfield. He heard his wife's screams and ran towards them, still carrying the cornchopper.

Ahalt thought something must be frightening the slave-wife, and his guess was that she had seen a snake. Ahalt ran towards her to try to help. Seeing Ahalt run towards her, his knife in his hand, as he thought, ready to kill a snake, the slave-wife panicked and tried to run towards the house, but she tripped over her bucket, and fell into the row in front of her. Ahalt sensed now that there was nothing threatening her, so he stopped near her, and took off his hat, wiping the sweat from his face on the same sleeve. He was standing like this when the slave-wife's husband came up behind him. Ahalt turned, and the slave saw the knife in his hand. With the speed and strength of a bear, the slave swung the cornchopper at Ahalt and struck him in the side of the ribs, just where the heart is. The blade disappeared, and Ahalt swayed, falling to the ground in the row next to where the slave-wife lay.

I cannot be certain whether Susannah ever learned the truth about why her neighbours' slave killed Ahalt, or even that Ahalt himself knew. In the days that followed, Susannah claimed the farm where she lived, as was expected of her. She remained a widow until her eyes began to dim, and then she married a man from Williamsport. At that time, she sold her slaves and with her husband managed the farm with labourers who had come from Germany to dig canals and mine coal. After Ahalt's death, the slave who killed him ran away to Pennsylvania, but he was caught by a Methodist who sold him to the sheriff in Fredericktowne for $50. The sheriff had him beaten and hanged. His wife stayed on the farm where the murder had happened, and the farmers bought another slave, already with no hair except at the temples, to help with the chores.

April 22, 1964

9am. Only in the mid 40s again today. No wind at all & a creamy fog everywhere, especially towards Myersville.

*Davy & Dicky Bird seem to be burying a wire in the ditch. Marce still passing things up to the heights where Rip is attaching them to the TV aerial.

1pm. Rip & Marce now inside dealing with TV wires. Davy & Dicky Bird filling in the ditch.

5pm. All four of them have spent the last hour digging a big hole in the corner of the yard. I went inside at The Corner & see that the TV wires look ready for a TV.

*Marce too sweaty & mean-looking to ask about John John's baseball. Will try tomorrow.

10.30pm. Rained off & on today. Windows still drizzled.

April 23, 1964

9.15am. Marce showed up this morning with the other three sitting in the back of his truck, evidently weighting down the long telephone pole he had sticking out the back. The four of them have just carried it up the hill behind The Corner. What is going on?

12.45pm. Just back. They have put the huge pole into the hole they dug & are filling in the hole. I asked what this was for, & they tell me it is to be for my outside light. —Pertek-shun, Marce said. —You bein' a woman on your own and all.

*There is a big box on the ground near them, inside of which, I imagine, is the light.

5.15pm. One way & another, it took the four of them all afternoon to get that light on that pole & check that it was working. There was some swearing & teasing, but eventually it seemed to work.

*Before they left, I asked about the baseball game. Saturday at one, Marce said. –But it ain't gonna be much, he says. I asked whether he was going. –Like H[]ll, he said.

10.45pm. Temperature started in the 40s this morning & then about 70 this afternoon. Fog ALL day though.

April 24, 1964

9am. To my surprise, the men arrived this morning with one of their big ladders again. They set it up on the wash house side.

12.45pm. They have been attaching a lightning rod to the end of the house, Rip doing the high work, Dicky Bird holding the ladder. Davy & Marce nowhere to be seen. Inside, I think.

3.30pm. Dicky Bird & Rip repeated the lightning-rod exercise on the road side of the house this afternoon. Rip is quietly fearless up there, while at the bottom of the ladder, Dicky Bird slowly singing that in time, his dear will understand him and shed a tear, because she'll know she's been living in her tender years.

4.30pm. Davy & Marce have reappeared to help load the ladder. They all left with no one saying what the plan is for next week.

10.30pm. Weather bleak all day with rain mostly. Between about 50 & 70 all day. Watched "Burke's Law". I'm ready to confess, plead guilty & deny even the likeliest alibi.

April 25, 1964

8.15am. Cold again this morning, in the upper 30s. Will make what may be my last fire when I come home.

11.45am. Back from Middletown Acme ($14). To my shame, I bought strawberries. Will make lunch before going to baseball game. Bought hamburger, just to get into the spirit of things.

3pm. Back from baseball. No sign of Marce, though JJ's mother Jean was there. I don't think she raised her eyes to the boys' play even once that I could see. She spent the whole time talking to the people around her. I sat in the bleachers with a box of cracker jacks & shouted at the umpire whenever the home team batted. John John struck out once, got hit with the ball once, & walked once. He made some ordinary plays at first base & did nothing outstanding or terrible. I made it a point to walk behind the bench during a half inning when they were seated, (ostensibly to buy a Coke from the stand behind their bench) & patted him on the shoulder. I wished him good luck. –Yes, ma'am, he said. I tried to see him after the game, after the long parade of hand-smacking "good games" they say to the other team, but he went off over the right field fence & up the field (towards home?) before I could catch him. They lost 11-2.

3.45pm. Once again, the woodpile is filled to capacity. No signs of anyone, so probably John John did the stacking after his father delivered the wood this morning. Will thank them both next week. John John must have been worn out before the game even started.

10.45pm. Beautiful sunshine this afternoon, & temperature up to almost 60.

April 26, 1964

8am. Already had breakfast & mean to mark out some flowerbeds before church crowd comes home.

12.15pm. Met church ladies while still relatively clean. No takers for tea today, as all claim to be going home for "dinner". I asked Cinch why she didn't come to see John John play yesterday, then immediately regretted it. She didn't exactly answer. –You go? she said. I said I did. –Uh huh, she said. They win? she asked. I answered. –Well, she said. That was all. She showed no interest in the boy at all. Why? Why why why? What has he got to do?

11pm. Weather like yesterday. Glorious moon tonight, green as a pale apple.

*I think girls are lonely for lots of reasons, but I think boys are only lonely for girls. I think if a boy has a girl he believes in, who he believes loves him, then he is never ever lonely at all. That girl may, for a while, be his mother (or grandmother), but after that she is the girl for whom he is the only boy who matters. This is why infidelity hurts boys as it does. It hurts girls for so many reasons, so many reasons that disgust & frighten us. But for boys, the abandonment is total. The one thing they have left unguarded about them-selves is struck to bloodiness, burnt, stolen, scattered. A boy who grows up feeling unloved will spend the remainder of his life looking for a land to call home, a port where no storms come, a peace that no war threatens. And he will never find it. That boy will go where he is able to hate him-self without feeling guilty; to where the punishments & hu-miliations disgrace him before himself; to where his screams cannot be heard. There he will die by inches, pleading for the love of all the women in the world, one by one, who never loved him.

*Alex is that boy. John John is that boy.

*Tom, who was loved from his first cry, to whom girls pledged their virgin bodies, & for whom I made suffering a vow, was never that boy.

Ain't gonna work on the railroad

Oh, I do remember the day them big battles got going. Yes, sir, I do. We could hear the boom of them cannons coming up the valley in the morning, 'bout the time we get the washing hung out. Down Middletown I hear they was all a-coming on the horses first, and then they don't get nowhere and give up. Next thing ya know the Sesesh was a-shooting up Braddock and a-half-riding backwards. They was even shooting up the mountain yare at Hamburg, but I didn't hear none of that. I set myself down and got to piecing a ole quilt for the missus – one of them nine diamonds ones she like. The white men that wasn't a-running away was all on they horses going back and forth 'tween the towns trying to find out what was going on. They all standing on the porch at The Corner waving they hands about and a-shouting. I don't know nothing, but I hear they say the Sesesh blowed up the bridge down the low end of Middletown. I seen the junk down in the creek 'bout a month later when we was down there delivering the flour to the soldiers and I go long with the missus for the nursing. They blowed up the bridge sure 'nough, and they burnt some houses and barns too.

They was one belonged ole Mister Koogle. I don't know his right name, but he had the big place down the ole road run up along the creek towards Myersville, the one right after the bridge they blowed up. He had a brother name Mister Amos Koogle that wasn't no farmer. He make clothes for the men, and he left Middletown when they daddy died and move hisself over Myersville, and set up a-making clothes there. He had a wife name Miss Irene, and she sew too, 'cept she make shirts for the men. She get a whole lot more business than he do, 'cause them folks round there and all the way up to Pleasant Walk and the Monument and them places wear they pants till they too poor to wear 'em no more, but they buy shirts like other folks. Miss Irene so busy she got to get help to make them shirts.

Now Mister Amos brother Mister Koogle got hisself some servants down his farm, and he mostly got just the menfolk for the working in the fields. He buy one though name Rex, a good big fella work hard and come with a good reputation, but he come with a wife of his own, a gal name Liddy. So Mister Koogle, he get the idea to keep the peace, he buy her too and hire her out to somebody close by, so least she and ole Rex still pretty close. Well, 'course when Miss Irene need some help, she up and hire Liddy from Mister Koogle. The way they fix it is she got to live in they house in Myersville, and Rex he stay on the farm down the end of Middletown, and Mister Amos and Miss Irene, they let Liddy go down with Rex Saturday nights and come back early on Mondays. The walk 'bout seven eight mile. Liddy, she already sew good, and she sew shirts 'bout as good as Miss Irene 'fore long.

Things ain't too bad for most of a year. Liddy miss Rex and Rex miss Liddy, but things a lot worse for a lot of folks. Anyhow, 'bout that time Miss Irene's mama down Middletown her own self get sick and fall down, and then she can't use her arm no more, and half her face hang like it's asleep or something. So Miss Irene, she got to go down and do for her till she get better 'gain. When she go, she take Liddy with her. Pretty soon though, Mister Amos, he start to say he need somebody round the house to do for him, do his cooking and cleaning and washing. And anyway, they folks 'round there still want the shirts Liddy making to sell. So Miss Irene, 'bout once a week send Liddy back up to they house in Myersville, toting shirts to sell, and while she there, she got to do the chores for Mister Amos. That's where the trouble get started.

Miss Irene's mama ain't getting no better real fast, and ole Liddy back up to Myersville 'bout as often as she ain't. Pretty soon she working in that house and Mister Amos start to chasing her 'round. He saying things like she better do like he say or he gonna tell his brother Mister Koogle to sell her to the speculators or hire her out to somebody down Frederick or Berlin or Prince George's and she ain't never gonna see Rex no more. He get her all scared and they ain't nothing she can do. She tell Rex what Mister Amos say, and Rex think he ought to tell Mister Koogle, but Liddy scared if he do, Mister Koogle don't believe it none, or anyhow, he take Liddy back home and sell her or hire out anyways. So all they can do is to try and talk Mister Amos out of interfering with Liddy when she got to go to Myersville. So Liddy she try to tell Mister Amos, but he don't want to listen none. So Liddy she say she gonna tell Miss Irene, and Mister Amos say she tell Miss Irene Miss Irene gonna fix her for good and they sell her down to Georgia or somewhere. They ain't nothing Liddy can do, so it's 'bout then that Mister Amos start his interfering with her. Liddy like to die she so scared, and she scared Rex ain't gonna want her no more. But Rex, he don't give it no never mind, and he just hold on to her and they cries like babies the pair of 'em.

Pretty soon, ole Miss Irene's mama start to recover herself, and she start to talk again, but she sound like a girl child with her mouth full. She say to Miss Irene, Where that girl of yourn go when she not here? And Miss Irene say she got to back home and do the chores and take the shirts for selling. And Miss Irene's mama say she crazy. You letting that girl 'lone up there with that man? You surely gonna regret that, you surely is. Miss Irene like to be tied when she hear that. So when Liddy get back next time, Miss Irene don't say nothing to her, but she just look at her like she scratch her eyes out, and she say she gonna go back to Myersville her own self from now on, and see what her own house looking like.

Sure 'nough, she go back in the hire buggy, and she see Mister Amos hisself. What y'all doing here, he say? What you mean, what I doing here? My house too, ain't it? she say. She grow 'bout as grouchy as a bear with a burr under his tail now. And she watching him like she looking for something, and he knows it. What y'all watching me all the time for? he say. I got a 'spicion, she say. I got a 'spicion you been a-messing with that girl and a-making a dirty fool of youself, she say. I ain't done nothing, he say. Ain't done nothing at all. But she just look at him like she knows he's a-lying. Honey, y'all got to believe me, he say. What I want with a little ole wench like her for anyhow? And he retch out to try and grab her some, and she say, Don't y'all be coming near me with them dirty ole hands a yourn. And I tell you another thing, she say. That girl ain't coming back her in this house no more if I got to burn it down myself and shoot you besides.

Miss Irene then get back to her mama's in Middletown and she say, Where's that Liddy gone now? And her mama say, She gone down to the springhouse to get me the nice cold water, 'cause I'm powerful hot. And Miss Irene she go out that house just like she shot from a gun, and she see Liddy a-coming with a bucket. Miss Irene reach down and snatch that bucket and pour all the water out. You gonna tell me what you been doing, girl? she say. You gonna tell me right now or I'm gonna skin you alive.

Now Liddy don't know what to do, she a-shaking so bad. She know just what Miss Irene thinking, but she say anyhow, 'Deed, Miss Irene, I don't know nothing 'bout what y'all saying. I just getting a drink of water for the missus. And Miss Irene, she haul off and slap Liddy cross the face like she gonna kill her dead. You damn fool, she say. You think I don't know what you been doing with Mister Amos? You think I don't know? she say. I don't know nothing 'bout what y'all saying, Miss Irene, I surely don't, Liddy say. Don't you lie to me, girl, Miss Irene say. Y'all lie to me, I gonna see Mister Koogle done sell you down to Georgia. You best believe I am, she say.

Now ole Liddy she a-shaking so hard she fall down scareder than a hen in a fox's jaw. Lord, lord, Miss Irene, I don't know nothing 'bout it, 'deed I don't, she say. I ain't done nothing, I ain't done nothing. I like to die if I'm lying, Miss Irene. You got to believe me. You got to.

Miss Irene give her a kick like she gonna put her foot clean through her and she go back 'round to the house. Next thing you know, she getting the hire buggy again and she march herself off to see Mister Koogle. When she get to the farm the sun 'bout to go down, and the field hands all gather up to the porch to get they supper, and Miss Irene, she say, Where I find Mister Koogle? And the hands, they say Mister Koogle done gone out looking for coons that been in the corn down by the creek. And Miss Irene she look like she gonna kill somebody sure as shooting.

Which one of you boys called Rex? she say. Ole Rex get up from the porch and he say, That's me, ma'am. Something the matter? he say. Get over here, boy, she say, I wanna talk to you. So they go on down to the dooryard and stand in the shade and Miss Irene say, Y'all know me, boy? No, ma'am, Rex say. I ain't never seen you 'fore. Uh huh, she say. That girl Liddy, she say, she your woman? Yes, ma'am, he say. We married 'bout four years now, he say. Uh huh, she say. Well, she been living at my house. You Miss Irene? he say. Hush up, now boy, I'm talking to you, she say. Liddy tell you what she been doing? she say. And ole Rex, he a big fella, but he start to get a scared look in his eye. Don't believe I know what you mean, ma'am, Miss Irene, he say. And Miss Irene, she point her finger.

Now you listen to me, you dumb buck. Y'all lie to me I have Mister Koogle overseer rip the hide clean off ya, ya hear me? You gonna look like a skun hog, she say. Now I wanna know what that girl tell you she been doing up there at my house. My house! she say.

Ole Rex he worry sick now 'bout what gonna happen to Liddy and he don't know what to do. He shaking his head 'bout as fast he can, and he saying, Lord, Miss Irene, I don't know nothing. I don't know nothing, indeed. I don't. Y'all got to believe me. And Miss Irene, she start to kicking him hard as she can all over his legs and he a big fella and all, and he keep standing there like to bust hisself with worry. I don't know nothing, he say. Y'all got to believe me. Liddy don't say nothing. They ain't nothing.

Don't you lie to me, Miss Irene say. And Rex, his legs all barked up from the kicking sit down on the ground, and Miss Irene grab up a pick handle and start to beating him on the shoulders and a-shouting, Y'all gotta tell me! Don't you lie to me no more! And he keep a-saying, I don't know nothing, lord, lord, I don't know nothing.

And she bring that ole handle down cross his head and make a cracking and the blood run in his eyes and he shaking his head. And Miss Irene done wear herself out a-beating him like she done.

Next thing you know Liddy get sent back from Miss Irene's mama, and she and Rex stay there with Mister Koogle to the sores on Rex heals up. Mister Koogle then, folks say, hire out Rex and Liddy both to a fella up Hancock and Rex he work in the lathe shop and Liddy keep house. Ole Mister Amos give up trying to make clothes in Myersville and he and Miss Irene go on back to Middletown till the war starts. Then she break her arm falling in the cellar and the gangrene kill her 'cause she won't let 'em cut it off. Mister Amos 'herit the farm when Mister Koogle die, but he sell it 'bout the time of the 'mancipation. I don't know where he went then.

April 27, 1964

7am. Foggy with drizzle now. About 40.

9am. Men scattered all over the house across the road. Mixture of machines & elbow grease as they are sanding woodwork on every floor. Rip is using a sander on the wainscoting. Marce the same. Dicky Bird & Davy are hand-sanding doorframes, skirting boards etc.

1pm. Work as before over the road.

4.45pm. Men gone now. They were walking pretty slowly when they came out. Tired, I imagine.

10.30pm. Rained in spells all day but warmed up to the upper 50s. Watched some of the "Night at the Movies". Channel 4 picture better this evening. No leaves, no snow, no wind, no birds, no sunspots…

April 28, 1964

7.30am. Much warmer this morning. Over 50. But still very gray & showery.

9.15am. Work at The Corner like yesterday. Air filthy with dust. No singing that I could hear.

2pm. Work same as before.

5pm. Saw them before they left. Davy sweeping up. Marce says he will be getting the paint tomorrow.

10pm. Made it into the 60s today. Rain died down to drizzle later.

April 29, 1964

9.30am. Men showed up just a little late this morning. Spent quite a while unloading cans of paint, brushes, cloths & so on. All piled in the kitchen.

1pm. Still sanding going on.

5.30pm. Had a slight to-do with Marce. I was in the kitchen looking at the cans of paint when I noticed some were for an olive green. I asked him where this was going, as I certainly never asked for that color. —Bedroom, he said. That big one. I explained that that one was to be rose pink. He looked at me half-puzzled & half-disgusted & then picked up the tin & stared at it. Then the half-puzzled bit joined the half-disgusted part for a completely disgusted look. —Aw, H[]ll, he said. It seems he got the wrong one. Davy saw what was going on & spoke up. —Ain't y'all noticed he's color-blind as H[]ll? Marce fired him a look. —Least I ain't dumb as H[]ll, he said. So that's it. He said he'd replace it tomorrow.

*I'm sure Davy was grinning as the truck drove away.

10.45pm. Temperature in the upper 40s to low 60s today. Sticky & thundery this afternoon for a while.

April 30, 1964

9.15am. Men at work as expected. Not sure whether new paint is with them yet or not. They are sanding their way around the kitchen, so I didn't like to look.

1pm. Rip & Davy are in the kitchen with masking tape & caulking guns. Marce & Dicky Bird on the top floor. Already the fumes are strong.

5pm. Men gone for the day. Place is looking brighter, & smelling worse, already. This seems like such a coming together of things now. Utility room walls look good, as do some of the kitchen walls. Cracks filled. Top floor too is coming along & may be finished.

10.30pm. Weather looked like yesterday all day but stayed only in the 40s. More thunder tonight.

May 1, 1964

8.45am. All four at work today. Marce & Rip caulking & painting the kitchen. Davy & Dicky Bird caulking the smaller room on the lower middle. Dicky Bird singing that if he could see her just one time, oh how it would ease his troubled mind.

1pm. All pretty peaceful over the road. Same as before, but upstairs room looks finished & they are in the bedroom. Both Marce & Rip now painting.

*Dicky Bird has moved on, singing now that every time he's with her he vows that it will be the last time, but then (just like now!) she comes back, & he's falling one more time.

*Another case of needing to be careful what you pray for.

5.30pm. Men left slightly later tonight, each pair finishing off what they had started. Kitchen & utility room are caulked, some areas of kitchen painted. It is a really big space & very complicated. The utility room painting will take a long time, I think. Both smaller rooms upstairs ready to paint, & they've done a bit in the big room. John John joined them (no practice tonight, too wet). He cleaned up, gathering caulking tubes, newspapers, rags etc (–Don't get none of that sh[]t on ya! Marce.) He didn't wash the brushes as they soaked these. He didn't mention their plans for next week. He didn't need to.

10.30pm. What a gloomy May Day. 40s all day. Foggy this morning, then drizzly rain. Fire all day to keep the chill off. Watched "Destry". A strange feeling. Like my eyes have eaten too much.

May 2, 1964

7am. Only mid 40s this morning. Cold bathing again. Didn't sleep very well & feel oddly frustrated with myself on account of this; like I've let myself down.

11.15am. Back after a trip to Acme in Middletown ($15). Still feeling perplexed by my own grouchiness. Bought myself a "flair" pen (a kind of ink-soaked hard felt thing that writes very softly & swiftly). Turquoise blue.

*Will make myself an omelette for lunch.

1.30pm. Feeling unaccountably better now. May go outside & cut weeds around the edge of the garden.

4.30pm. Back in & having tea, which has left me feeling hotter than I thought I would be. Nails quite green, so must see to them.

*Neighbour Maureen stopped to chat with me over the space that will become my garden fence. She asked me whether I'd heard anything about where the ambulance went last night. I said no, I hadn't. (Didn't say, I couldn't recall hearing the ambulance.) She said it sounded as though it went over the bridge at Coxey Brown Road, & she only hoped it wasn't to see Danny's wife (who?) as she had been awfully ill with morning sickness. I said I hoped not too, though I've no idea who she is talking about. She asked me what I'd planted so far, & I told her. She told me I'd be lucky if the coons didn't eat everything except the onions. I told her I'd already spoken to them about this, & we'd agreed a deal. She thought for a moment & then laughed. She left shaking her head.

7pm. Have been watching for racoons, but none have appeared.

10.45pm. Just over 60 this afternoon. Fog most of the day.

May 3, 1964

7.30am. Cold again this morning, though not much below 40. Will build a fire.

*Didn't sleep well again. Dreamed I was arguing through a barred window with someone over the price of a bus ticket. Odd, given that I never ride buses.

10am. Such a pretty morning, I joined the churchgoers in the walk to church. Cinch (dressed in a royal blue dress, white sweater & glass-coloured beads) gave me my copy of

Grit. She asked me what I was going to do this morning (no one ever asks me that) so I had to think of something. I told her I was going to plant some flowers, pull up some weeds, & look for racoon tracks.

12.30pm. Met the churchgoers on their way home. They stopped at the benches for a session in the sunshine & in the dappled light of the walnut leaves. The talk of the day was not on the sermon, but on the new number codes we've all got to start adding on to our addresses. Nobody thinks they can remember them, or that it will help the mailmen who know everybody anyway. I asked Cinch what she was cooking for her dinner, & she told me roast chicken, hominy, corn & carrots with rhubarb cobbler.

　　*I also asked her whether she ever went to see John John's baseball games. She said she did, –If neither his Mammy or Daddy was coming. I wonder what she means?

5pm. Enjoyed my tea & homemade cookies today. Thought I'd try to remember to buy myself some hominy.

10.15pm. Made it into the 60s this afternoon. Sunshine nice all day. Watched "Bonanza".

May 4, 1964

7.45am. Slept better. Dreamed about the bench near Tom's old office.

9am. Usual crew, usual places this morning. Both Marce & Rip now painting kitchen & utility. Dicky Bird painting the smaller lower middle room (must think of a name for this one…). Davy, a little forlornly, I suspect, on his own caulking the larger living room on the lower middle.

　　*Dicky Bird, with a whole room to echo in, is singing that still, though she broke his heart, still, though they are far apart, he loves her. Still.

1.15pm. All going apace over the road. Kitchen looking brighter & fresher, though air unbreathable now. They've opened the large windows. Quiet upstairs. Perhaps, Dicky Bird has passed out.

5pm. Men finished now. Kitchen nearly done, utility room at least half. Couldn't linger, as I value my lungs. Upstairs, bedroom painted, small living room (a name!) underway, & large living room caulked or nearly so. Wainscoting on crooked walls has created job security for Davy's caulking enterprise.

10.30pm. Started the day in the mid 40s, but over 70 this afternoon. Sunshine all day & no wind at all. Watched "Wagon Train", where no mood is unpredictable, no retort unspoken, no promise unkept.

May 5, 1964

8.45am. Nice weather has put everyone in a cheerful mood. Marce & Rip look likely to finish the kitchen today, & maybe utility too. Davy must be getting through caulking by now, & Dicky Bird in smaller living room, painting.

1.30pm. Kitchen is painted & both Rip & Marce in utility room. Dicky Bird & Davy now both painting in large living room. Dicky Bird merry with singing how he's been everywhere, man, he's been everywhere. From the Great Lakes & Chicago to the San Francisco fair. Man, he's been everywhere.

4.45pm. Windows shut at The Corner, & the men gone. It smells like the combined dreams of the whole DuPont family over there. Large living room ¾ done. No John John again.

6.30pm. Joan & Paul playing on their porch. Autoharp & violin.

8pm. Walked over to see J & P. Both well, P a little heavier than I remember. J let me hold her autoharp. I simply cannot imagine knowing how to play a thing like this.

*They were very kind & asked after the work on The Corner.

10.45pm. Weather just like yesterday, but even warmer this afternoon.

Oh, hallelujah, when the world's on fire!

I, LittleWound, tell this story.

It was around the time when the Washechu stopped journeying to Annapolis and Baltimore to buy slaves, but before the seasons of the stealing of horses.

A day's walk towards Wolfsville, then another day's walk towards Foxville, to where the mountain lay like the lap of a woman when she sits, there was a farm with stones the colour of clouds, which covered the ground like leaves on the birch. The farmer's name was Lutz and his wife was called EstherLutz. She had his child within her when Lutz died, his intestines spilling beneath his skin, hanging down to his thighs. She spent the money they had on seeing him buried near the church in Foxville. In the season that remained to her before the birth of her child, she thought of ways to make her living. She got in chickens and geese for eggs. She made butter and cream from the milk her cow produced. She gathered and cracked walnuts, picked huckleberries, dried herbs and dyed wool and cotton. The people who went to the church alongside her recognized her condition, and bought her wares, or traded with her for the goods she needed. She made all the provisions that a widow might make.

The thing she could not prepare was the time of her child's birth. It is a custom among the Washechu that women who have no other women in their house to rely on, to take themselves to live with family or neighbours when their time approaches. But EstherLutz had had no other children and had never seen a woman give birth. She had no family on the mountainside, and her pride and fear made walls around her. So that when her time came to give birth, she could only make herself go to the room in her house where there was a fireplace and wait until the baby came, handling it as best she could. Some would say that fortune looked upon her as a daughter, for the birth was over in the time it took the sun to crest the mountain and reach the shoulder of the trees on the hills beyond which the sun sleeps. All that was inside her came out as it should, and she used her knife to cut the cord that binds mother and child. But then, after she washed her child and herself, and put the child into the bed beside her, she slept. When she awoke she discovered that the child's throat had filled, and it lay chilling and the same colour as the veins in her hands.

She thought over what she must do. She counted the money she had and thought to the times that lay before her. The season of snows was yet to come, and there would not be ways to re-place the money she would have to spend if she took the child to the church to be buried with her husband. Besides that, the baby had rested next to her heart for so long, had been the only person whose face she longed to see for the whole season after her husband had gone, that she could not bear the idea that the child should be taken away from the house where she knew she must go on living. And so, after three days, she wrapped the child in a blanket that she had made with the hands of a woman quenching her grief, and dug a grave beneath the laurels, on the side of the house facing the morning. She prayed to her god that his hands might find her child's spirit, guiding it to its home.

It was not until the dogwoods flowered that she returned to the church and the village where her people went about with their lives unbending with sorrows like her own. It seemed that no one had thought to inquire what had happened to her and her child when the snow lay upon their roofs and fields. She prayed alongside them, and still no one questioned her fate or that of the child she was known to have been carrying. Once more, as the foxtails began to ripen, she sold her wares to her neighbours, and it seemed that the village life had swallowed her story, like a pond swallows a stone.

It happened then, as she counted the money and goods she collected throughout the greening season, that she reckoned that her farm could not prosper without some help – help of the sort given by a man. It was not that she sought a man of her own, but only the labour of a man's hands. She could not afford to hire such labour, but instead she sought to acquire help through barter. Near the crossroads where the forge lay, she made a deal with Stephen, a slave belonging to the Freshour farm. Like the other farmers, the Freshours did not over-supply Stephen in his cabin, but they did allow him to hire his time to anyone who wanted it, so long as he was fit to do his chores when they needed him. EstherLutz bargained with Stephen, that if he were to cut the hickories and ashes that lay along her stone-ridges, he could keep all the wood that was smaller than his arm for himself, while she would keep or sell the heartwood. Both Stephen and Esther-Lutz were pleased by this arrangement, and in this way the season when the sun burnt the hayfields passed in peace and simplicity.

It was in the time that the leaves loosened on the trees and the fruit ripened in the orchards that the women who sat beside EstherLutz in church began to gossip about her and speculate about the ways in which she lived. What had happened to her child, they asked? Why had she not given it to the earth where her husband lay? Why had no woman attended her? Why did she never speak its name?

Seeing that she had befriended Stephen, a story began to form itself in their minds and on their lips. To the women inside her church, the reason that EstherLutz's child had never been seen among them, was that it looked as much like a slave as it did a Washechu. This they would not forgive. Before long they stopped buying her wares. They stopped sharing the gifts from their garden-patches, letting the collards, the mustard, and the cabbages be fed to their hogs rather than give them to a widow who was, in their eyes, a disgrace and a figure of contempt.

All of this created confusion, anger and sorrow for Esther-Lutz. A day came when Stephen himself refused to come to her farm as the day ended to chop down the hickories and ashes and claim his portion of the wood. Why, she said, have the women chosen to spurn me? she asked. And Stephen told her, It is because they believe that your child, the one whose body lay beneath the laurels, was not the child of yourself and your husband, but rather one born to you of a slave. I am afraid, he said, that they might think that I am he.

EstherLutz forgave Stephen, for she understood his pain and the fear that belonged to him. But she did not forgive the women who sat with her at church. Instead, she waited as the nights grew and the stars shone like ice in the sky. When the ground deadened in frost, she gathered together the brushwood that Stephen would no longer use and carried it by the armload to the church where her neighbours prayed. Throughout the night she took all the kindling and some of the heartwood and she tucked it beneath the risers of the floor. Then, just as the notes of the rooks and crows started in the valley, she struck the tinder and set the flames to work on the church. By the time dawn rose in mist on the mountaintop, the fires had shrunken to ash and there was nothing left of the church but the stones on which it had risen.

By the time the magnolias came again into flower, Esther-Lutz had eaten her chickens, geese and cow, and moved no one knew where. The marker over her husband's grave remains, but the stones over her child were scattered when the Freshours claimed her fields and used her house to quarter slaves.

May 6, 1964

8.30am. Still quite a happy crew over the road, though they have spread out now. Davy is now caulking the corner bedroom on the upper middle floor. Rip is doing the same to the walls up the stairs. Marce is painting with Dicky Bird in the large living room.

2pm. Marce now painting walls by stairs; others each caulking a bedroom on the upper middle.

5.15pm. Stair walls painted, smallest bedroom caulked. Two others may be finished too. The biggest one still not started.

    *I wonder whether Davy misses John John beside him in the truck?

10.45pm. Weather continues to be beautiful, sunny, dry, still, 40s in the morning, 70s in the afternoon. Didn't hear J & P this evening. Finished reading Grit.

May 7, 1964

9.30am. When I left them, Davy was alone, caulking the largest upper middle bedroom. The other three were each painting, or about to paint one of the other three.

1pm. I'm not sure, but there seems to be a spirit of competition over the road between Marce, Rip & Dicky Bird, each painting a bedroom. Dicky Bird is getting the worst teasing as he has the smallest room to paint. —His is just a little one, Marce said. Ask his wife, he said to Rip. Rip remained emotionless, not sure whether I'd heard Marce's comment. Or understood it, anyway.

5pm. Men gone now & entire Corner is lethal with fumes. Upstairs windows left open overnight. Three smaller bedrooms painted. Someone may have helped Davy, or he worked fast, as largest one looks ready to paint. Hallway not started or started much.

11pm. Weather still perfect. Over 80 this afternoon. Joan & Paul had a long session tonight, violin & dulcimer. Not really sleepy now.

May 8, 1964

8.45am. Change of rota, it seems. Now Davy caulking the big upper middle hallway; Rip & Dicky Bird painting the larger bedroom; Marce starting to give the kitchen a second coat.

 *I have finally noticed that they have not done the lower middle hallway (the prettiest one) as this is where they have piled their tools & ladders.

1.30pm. Dicky Bird & Rip look like they've finishing the bigger bedroom. Davy now painting hallway. Marce still in kitchen.

5.15pm. All finished over the road. Windows upstairs open again. Looks like the upper hallway is nearly ½ done. Can't tell about kitchen.

 *Watering plants every day now.

 *No one comes to update me now that John John isn't with them. Hope he is all right.

10.45pm. No fire today. Over 60 by breakfast time, & mid 80s this afternoon. Warm breeze too. Is it summer? Watched "Route 66". Sat waiting for it to start like a girl waiting for her date to arrive.

I'll fly away, oh glory

He was the sort of man who always looks young for his age. His face was thin, bluish around the lower half, where he was clean-shaven, though his beard looked as though it would have come up far on his cheeks. His hair was thick and boyish and the colour of oxblood shoe-polish. Like all the male teachers, he wore a suit to school every day, although he seemed to like to take his jacket off early, to be seen in his tie and shirtsleeves, as if the work were strenuous and he was giving it his all. The students all called him Mr Krantz, though it seemed as if he would have liked them to call him Jim. He had been called Slim Jim when he was in high school.

He became the school's Vice Principal just after he turned thirty. He liked the job, liked being able to go to meetings with the Principal to which the other teachers weren't invited, and he liked being able to call meetings with any of them whenever it suited him. He liked it when parents asked to speak with him. Parents of high-schoolers can need a lot of reassurance, and he was always happy to give it, even though he wasn't old enough to be the father of any of the pupils and, in fact, had no children of his own.

His appointment had come at what he recognized, looking back, to have been a turning point in his life. A year before he had been the younger of the school's two English teachers, meaning he taught the freshmen and sophomores. His room was on the colder side of the building, towards the football field, and the pipes rumbled sometimes, but, on the whole, he couldn't complain. Occasionally, there were some strange smells that blew in from the Chemistry labs next door, but not that often. Anyway, he quite liked Chemistry, and had always had some interest in it at school. This made a good talking point after the old Chem teacher retired and Mrs Trimble was hired as his replacement. Slim Jim Krantz was often looking for a pretext to chat with Mrs Trimble who, though married, was about his age. She too seemed younger than she probably was. She wore her hair long, her dresses and shoes showing the influence of a youthful taste in fashion. She was not fat either, not at all. No, she had a very fine figure, one made better, he imagined, because of her hobby of horseback riding. She and her husband, she said, liked to ride every weekend, and sometimes in the evenings after work, if there weren't too much marking piling up on her desk. Ha ha! Jim said. He knew all about that. Yes, they had a lot in common.

It was after Christmas vacation that year that Mrs Trimble started to change. She seemed more solemn, more focussed, maybe, more distant from everyone. Though not so much to him, Jim thought. She started carrying her lunch tray over to sit with Jim at lunch, telling him about the things on her mind, the big things, about life, about marriage, about growing older. Before long, Jim found himself going around to the Chem lab after the bell, just to see how she was doing, he told himself. Just to see whether she needed anything.

One Friday afternoon, Jim went into the quiet lab a little later than usual, and Mrs Trimble wasn't anywhere to be seen. Jim thought she must have already gone home, but then he heard knocking noises coming from behind the cupboard along the wall, near the far end of the room. He walked towards the noises, and to his surprise, he saw an open door in the wall. There was evidently a storeroom here he had never noticed; not that he paid much attention to other teachers' classrooms. Jim stuck his head in the door and looked around. The room was bigger than he thought. There was a mixture of wooden and steel shelves, filing cabinets, racks and cupboards. The light was on, and the knocking was coming from behind the shelves. Jim looked around the corner, and on the floor sat Mrs Trimble, in tears. The knocking sound was the occasional rapping of her foot against one of the cupboards.

Oh, he said. I'm sorry.

Oh, she said.

Mrs Trimble didn't seem all that surprised to see him. He thought she was going to move as though to stand, but she didn't. He sat down beside her.

Are you all right? he said, and then thought it a very stupid question. What's wrong? he asked.

To his astonishment, Mrs Trimble lay her head on Jim's shoulder and sobbed. For most of the next hour she told Jim all about the problems of her marriage. Her husband was a busy man, with little time to spare for her. He could be quite rough sometimes. (Jim wondered what that meant.) She was very very lonely. She was afraid she was getting old.

Then Mrs Trimble wrapped her arms around Jim's neck and kissed him. Not lustfully, not sisterly, but passionately; letting the kiss speak for all the fury and anguish she felt at being a woman that no one was loving as they ought.

The next day at school, Mrs Trimble was not in the lab in time for homeroom. The roll-call was not taken. One of the senior girls went to the office to enquire. The receptionist then found a letter among the morning's mail that had been delivered by hand. Mrs Trimble had resigned. Slim Jim Krantz never saw her again.

Two months after his appointment as Vice Principal, Jim's boss, Mr Hicks, took a short leave to enable him to recover from a hernia operation that hadn't gone all that well. In his absence, Jim was in charge of the school's affairs, and that included hiring a permanent replacement for the absent Mrs Trimble. Since her departure, the post had been occupied by a series of substitute teachers, some of whom had been very good. But the students needed someone to bring consistency to their lessons, and Jim had his boss's okay to hire a replacement Chemistry teacher.

Jim hired a young woman named Miss Huffer who, he felt, had eyes exactly like Mrs Trimble's. Apart from her slim figure, the physical resemblance ended there. Miss Huffer's hair was straight and mousy, her clothes tending more towards the fashion of the last generation than to the rising one. But she was friendly, and Jim assured her that he would look out for her in any way he could.

By Easter, Miss Huffer had made herself very popular with the students and their parents. The other teachers liked her charm, and the older ones treated her like a favourite daughter. Jim had gone around to her classroom on a number of occasions, 'to see how things were going', he said, and always seemed to find them going perfectly well. He thought he was pleased by this. Professionally, he had made a good choice. Still, in a way, he missed Mrs Trimble.

As the month of June started, Jim began to think about Miss Huffer more and more. How little he knew about her! He went into the Chem lab a couple of times after school, 'just to get to know her', he said. Sometimes he had to follow her around the room as she prepared the lab for the next day's experiments. She never seemed to mind his being there. She liked his jokes. She spoke sometimes about her parents, and about the man she was seeing. She didn't seem in love, Jim thought. Not at all.

As the last few days of school were passing by so quickly, Jim began to feel as though he should say something about this to Miss Huffer. He had grown used to giving advice, and he began to feel that if he didn't speak up, something just might happen. Miss Huffer could find herself pretty unhappy indeed. And with the school year ending so soon, who would she have to talk to about it all then? He began to think of speaking to her about his feelings as an important duty, one he mustn't neglect.

Jim's opportunity came on the very last day of school. Miss Huffer's final class was in the early afternoon, and Jim knew that she would have the last two periods of the day free. No doubt she'd use the time to pack up her classroom, tidy up, sort things. She'd probably welcome a hand. He thought he'd go along near the beginning of the first free period, just in case, by any chance, she was thinking of going home early.

When Jim got to the Chem lab it was empty. His heart began to beat a little faster, just a little harder. He walked towards the cupboard beside which he knew was the doorway to the storage room. The door was open, and Jim caught his breath. He went inside and looked around. There was no one to be seen. Jim's fingers started to tingle. He walked around the shelving and looked. There on the floor, in the same spot where he had once found Mrs Trimble, knelt Miss Huffer. She seemed to be reading from a book, a pile of which were on the floor, and a matching set already on the shelf. She snapped the book shut and looked up at him.

Oh, she said. You startled me.

Are you all right? he said. What's wrong?

But Miss Huffer just looked at Jim for a moment. Why, nothing at all, thank you, she said. I'm just so glad that it's all over now.

Jim looked as deeply as he could into Miss Huffer's eyes. No, he realized, they were not the same as Mrs Trimble's. Not at all.

May 9, 1964

7am. Thought for sure I'd sleep well last night but didn't. Dreamed I was on an airplane & that my suitcase had been left behind. I couldn't get my seatbelt open, & the stewardesses wouldn't come down the aisle any more as there was water flooding in from somewhere.

2.30pm. Just home. Hungrily, had some of the lunchmeat I bought in a sandwich & a tin of Campbell's Cream of Chicken already.

*Went to library & looked at collections of old newspapers. Boy, are the librarians frustrated when you ask for things like this!

*Went to bookstore & bought The Tin Drum. Older (male) customer looked at me as if he were offended. I suspect he is a WW2 veteran. I took my change & said Danke! A priceless look crossed his face.

*$18 at A & P as out of everything.

5.15pm. Spent two hours in the garden & feel good for it.

8pm. Sat on my own porch until it got too dark to see & the mosquitoes were making fing fing noises, listening to Joan & Paul. Guitar & dulcimer tonight. It is so quiet, it could be any century out there.

11pm. Even warmer today! Nearly 90. Windier though. Tired but not sleepy.

May 10, 1964

8.30am. Woke up very early & lay in bed trying to imagine life a year from now, & then fell asleep until 20 minutes ago. It is Mothers' Day.

9.45am. I watched from my window as everyone walked to church. I counted at least 11 mothers with children, ranging from tiny to adults. There they all are, close, religious & tolerant. They will probably have their lunches together later, the younger ones doing the cooking.

12pm. I went outside & talked for a bit to everyone as they came home. Cinch, resplendent in peach & sapphire blue, said she was on her way home, as she had 'em all coming for lunch with her. Most of the other women agreed, they shared her lucky burden. She gave me this week's Grit. Then I came inside & stamped my feet until my legs hurt & I bit back the rage I felt.

*I am alone & it is my own fault. If Alex were here, what would we be doing? Living in the same house where we used to live, attempting to forget everything, or ½ of everything we'd ever said or heard said, & hoping the other person wouldn't bring up anything too uncomfortable. I would cook & he would eat & we would talk about what was wrong with Russia, Republicans & the Chesapeake Bay. If he were here right now, in this house, he'd shake his head, tell me I'm a dreamer, ask me what I thought he was supposed to do in his life now that we'd moved to this place. I would feel that nothing I do was ever going to make him happy. I would wonder over all the stupid things I'd ever done, ever said yes to, ever been afraid to deny him, & join him in his hopelessness. So now here I am, wondering whether it is justice that his shadow is with me, doubting me, doubting my motives, or whether it is his ghost, so angry with me that he is laughing uncontrollably. Alex is missing in Southeast Asia, lost to America, the army, me & himself because somehow I should have seen it coming & told him that sometimes he is a fool who takes himself too seriously. My mistake was thinking that he'd remember what I wanted him to remember, & that the rest wouldn't matter. Instead, I will never know what he remembers & all of it mattered. I know now that the pain I feel is because, like a good foolish mother, I wanted to save my child the pain I knew threatened him, & so I swallowed all his medicine myself, sparing him the bitterness, the lonely cramping fever of growing up & wanting to fit in. I cannot forgive myself for getting between him & the dangers he should have known, & likewise for allowing him to feel ashamed & isolated when he heard the cracking of his bones, all those times when the weight of living with Tom & me took me away from him.

*Mothers' Day is the loneliest day of the year.

5pm. Gardened, read, drank tea. Told myself that Alex is alive & will be back soon, & the rest of this is nonsense.

10.30pm. The weather was glorious today. Mid 60s to upper 70s. Strong warm breeze.

Foggy Mountain Breakdown

I, LittleWound, tell this story.

In the days before the Washechu came to the Catoctins, the mountain shone with the brightness of eyes, and even the shadows were like the darkness of a woman's hair. The water leapt from the rocks and rainbowed in the sky. The breezes sang with the wingbeat of the hawks, and the days warmed against the skin like an embrace.

There lived a woman named ManyLightnings and she loved a man named SpottedDeer. Their love met the expectations of all who knew them, and they were to be married at that time when the daylight fears nothing and finds its joy upon the earth. The people began to celebrate the impending wedding with the games they cherished. The men took it in turns to shoot an arrow into the forest and guess where it came down; the next man trying to make his own arrow fall beside the first. There was feasting and there were songs.

There came to the wedding-day brothers not from the side of the mountain where the sun slipped into night, but from that same direction from whence the Washechu would one day come. One was named WhiteHawk and the other was called Shuntokecha, or Wolf. They were travellers and they were on a quest to find the GreatRoad to the land where the Tuscarora lived, because they believed it was their destiny to return to their own people with gifts that showed their kinship with the Tusca-rora. As was the custom, they were given a place at the feasting, and they were shown the honour due to those who have travelled.

When the vows between ManyLightnings and SpottedDeer were completed and the gifts exchanged, they took their places beside the people who looked upon them and felt their happiness. Shuntokecha and WhiteHawk saw too how the couple agreed like the right-hand agrees with the left, but they felt nothing of the esteem that the villagers felt. Though they expressed no contempt for SpottedDeer, they saw in ManyLightnings a woman whose virtues shone like the moon above the frost. And there was something in the way that she looked at SpottedDeer that stirred the blood-rage in Wolf, a rage that could not be quenched without proof that he might do as he pleased with her.

So the eating and drinking continued and Shuntokecha waited until ManyLightnings rose from SpottedDeer's side to fetch him more of the meat that hung dripping into the fire, and he followed her. Although there were people coming and going all around, and children played in front of the lodges and in the trees, he approached her as she leaned towards the turning spit with her knife. As she held her hands in front of her, trimming the meat from the bones, he grabbed her from behind, putting his hands upon her breasts and then upon her hips, thrusting his body at her as a man thrusts at a woman. ManyLightnings quivered in horror and turned suddenly, swinging at Wolf's face with her knife. Though she scratched his cheek, he knocked the knife from her hand, and it fell into the coals. As no one else had seen what happened, he began to laugh, and walked again towards the feast, as if to sit again among his hosts. ManyLightnings sunk to her knees and screamed.

SpottedDeer turned and saw his bride kneeling by the fire, her face in her hands and her body shaking. He also glimpsed the look on Wolf's face and the streak of blood below his eye, and he guessed something of what happened. He rose and ran towards them.

There might still have been some doubt in SpottedDeer's mind over what had happened, had Shuntokecha not poised himself ready to fight in his own defence. SpottedDeer hesitated, not sure whether to attack Shuntokecha, or see what it was that afflicted ManyLightnings. His mind was made up when he saw Shuntokecha glance towards the fire where the knife still lay at the edge of the coals. SpottedDeer lunged and seized the knife, the blade of which had taken on the heat of the fire. Instead of plunging or stabbing it at Shuntokecha, as Shuntokecha expected, they came together struggling and SpottedDeer pressed the knife against Shuntokecha's collarbone, where it hissed against his skin. His arms slackened, and SpottedDeer drew the knife across Shuntokecha's throat and the blood sprung from him on to his chest.

Hearing ManyLightning's scream, and seeing his brother fall brought WhiteHawk to his feet. Before SpottedDeer could turn to face him, WhiteHawk had struck him on the head with his axe. He raised the axe over ManyLightning, so that he might strike her dead, but before he could make the blow, arrows from the Catoctins who had come from their games broke into his heart and lungs, and he fell to the ground beside Shuntokecha and SpottedDeer. The women circled 'round ManyLightnings, pulling her away from the place where the men lay. Her grief rang through the night.

In the days that followed, stories grew around ManyLight-nings. Some said that she could not bear to know that anyone stood or walked behind her back, and so she always turned at the sound of steps. Some said she would eat no food that cooked in a fire. But even after she had gone to walk the SpiritRoad, it was said that if a bride wished it, she could hear ManyLightning's scream inside the noise of her own wedding-feast.

May 11, 1964

9am. The foursome all at work. Davy & Rip on the upper hallway, painting. Dicky Bird working in the utility room, Marce in the kitchen. Both painting.

1.30pm. Lowest floor still the same. Dicky Bird & Davy now gone down a floor, each painting a room.
   *Amway man came. Didn't order anything.

5pm. All gone now. Can't really tell what's been done, other than to produce a gasping fiendish eye-watering smog of fumes. Also, the place looks messier, I think, without John John to sweep & straighten up.

10.30pm. A little bit cooler today, & not so breezy. Very dark tonight, but stars like 1000 pearl buttons.

May 12, 1964

8.30am. Plan in The Corner looks to be the same as yesterday. Dicky Bird, now working on his own, is belting out that there's gonna be no more loneliness, only happiness, 'cause love's gonna live here again.

    *I hope he's right.

12.45pm. Rip has joined Marce in the kitchen, so I assume that means the utility room is now second-coated. Upstairs, Dicky Bird has joined Davy in the smaller living room. Heard this: Marce –How d'ya drive a Polack crazy? Rip –How? Marce –Put him in a round room & tell him to p[]ss in the corner.

4pm. Men gone just a little early today. Must have reached a good place to stop. All the house is brightening up now. At least I think it is, as the fumes are so strong I can't really open my eyes.

10.30pm. Weather like yesterday, though no breeze today. Too dry for a gardener, as I'm having to water things now every day.

May 13, 1964

6.45am. Slept unevenly. Dreamed that Alex & Tom were talking about the California Gold Rush.

9am. Downstairs is finished now, it seems. Marce is now in the big living room, the other three each working on an upper middle bedroom. More banter. With some people a joke is never old.

1.30pm. Much the same over the road. Smallest bedroom finished, Rip now in the biggest one. Marce alone.

4.30pm. I'm not sure, but I think all the smaller bedrooms are now finished. Biggest upstairs one must be almost so. Hallway looks dry. Choking fumes, as they have left the windows shut, probably because it looks like rain.

5.15pm. Smashing thunderstorm now. Purple & blue flashes. Rain like stones on the roof.

10.30pm. Grayer all day today. High 70s. Cooler after the storm. Storm ended in time to let me watch "The Virginian". Lee J Cobb is such a talent.

*Thinking about the storm & remembering. When I was a girl, when a storm came at night, Mother used to make us all get out of bed & sit in the dark parlour, in case lightning struck the house.

*About ¼ way through Tin Drum. Hard going.

May 14, 1964

6.30am. Still sleeping badly. Lay in bed an hour imagining Alex living in The Corner, working in Frederick, going out with friends, describing a girl he likes. This is a gift to me, & I hope to him. But I cannot allow myself to feel in any way that I have earned it as a privilege.

9.15am. Davy & Dicky Bird on the upper middle floor, DB in the bedroom, D in the hallway. Rip & Marce now together in the large living room.

1pm. Something afoot over the road. Marce & Rip outside poking around the wash house. Davy & Dicky Bird upstairs still.

2.15pm. Shouts & laughter over the road. Sounds like all four are outside.

3pm. Just back from having a look. They have decided to empty out some of the old wash house in order to store things from the lower middle hallway that they think they might still want (in order to clear the hallway for painting). The squawking has to do with the discovery of snakeskins, fur-trappers' traps &, frankly, junk.

*More simple-minded bantering, now about snakes (length, girth, stiffness). Honestly. I'm sure Dicky Bird blushed when I walked up the outside stairs.

*Men's anatomies, if not their personalities, seem built to accommodate this one feature of their bodies.

*They seem to be sorting the stuff they find into the combustible & the dumpable.

5pm. Men gone now. Davy was once again relegated to the truck's tailgate, as the truck was piled high with things, no doubt, soon to be dumped down some mountain ravine. They have piled the things for burning over the road in The Patch.

10.30pm. Much cooler today & very foggy this morning. Ground looks like it has steam rising off it. Mid 60s this afternoon.

May 15, 1964

6.45am. Awake early again. Alex will come back now, because Tom is gone. That thought occurred to me this morning. It may be that he was not captured, but gone AWOL, missing illegally. He will return, chastened, ready to start again. We will find peace in our mutual penitence.

9.30am. All sorts of things going on at The Corner. Marce seems to be supervising the removal of tools & some supplies to the upper & lower floors of the wash house, while Dicky Bird & Rip are carrying. Davy is in The Patch supervising the fire he's started with the dry junk. The fire is twisting in an acrid greasy smoke.

11.30am. Fire is nothing but smouldering ash. They have loaded some things on to the truck.

1pm. Back with the lunch tray. The Corner looks neater inside, as they've swept up and straightened it a bit. The centre hallway is now clear.

*Have decided not to think about Alex now, & not to try & understand anything.

4.30pm. Men just gone. Looks like the hallway is being caulked. Fresh fumes on the air, though I couldn't detect where they were coming from.

8pm. Re-reading Alex's last letter to me. Again. No clues to anything. No impatience, no anger, no remorse & no promises.

10.45pm. Weather like yesterday, but cooler this morning (and no fog), but a little warmer this afternoon (nearly 70). Watched "Route 66". I would like to see an episode, just one episode, without a single car in it.

May 16, 1964

6am. So peaceful. Foggy & chilled, only 44. No dreams. Slept well but feeling tired.

1.30pm. Took library books back & got two more on slavery. Spent some green stamps on new dishtowels & pot holders. Filled up at H L Mills. Spent $14 at A & P.

5pm. Finished tea. Read some more. Dull now. Joan & Paul tuning up, I think.

*Went to little league game. John John struck out once, flied out & mysteriously bunted once when he shouldn't have (got a telling off from the manager). His mother in the bleachers again. I watched her for a while, & she seldom looked at the game, or her son's play. He made some good catches on first base, & even picked off a runner once.

8.15pm. J & P gone in now, too dark tonight. Guitar & dulcimer.

10.15pm. Wind picked up this afternoon, & temperature went over 80. I thought for sure there would be a storm, but none came.

Standing on the corner with the low-down blues

Both families lived above Zittlestown, their farms running against the ridge and into the valley along Dahlgren, and both families went down to the Baptist church in Boonsboro every Sunday. It was natural that they should meet and know something about one another. The Baptist preacher was an old-fashioned zealot, named Wilbur Zink, and he had built-up a congregation with his hellfire-and-buckets-of-blood style. His eyes shone blue up on the pulpit, and his hands seemed to be reaching out to people one by one. It was a surprise, all that power emanating from a small man, with his grey hair closely cut and brushed back, his head and face always glistening, his hands, small and red, his shoulders as lean as a boy's.

One of the two families was made up of Cyril Ridenour and his daughter Hannah. Cyril was a clean, proud, poor man who kept up his farm with sense of careful duty. His wife, Hannah's mother, had died when Hannah was just eight. She got a tumour in her throat that grew until she lost her voice, and by then it was too late to save her life. Cyril had done his best to raise Hannah, the same way he had done his best with everything else, but he found a growing girl hard to understand, hard to discipline, easy to love. Hannah grew up strong, an outdoor girl, long and lanky, brown eyes and hair the colour of coffee-and-milk. Cyril was proud of her, but he worried too.

The other family consisted chiefly of Edna Bidle and her son Eugene. After Edna was widowed, her farm was mostly run by her brother-in-law, Casey Shank. Edna's husband Luther had been killed when he was out using his Farmall H tractor and the sicklebar to mow the side of hill, and the sicklebar caught on a stump that he'd forgotten to avoid, and the tractor upset and rolled over on him. It was a common accident, everyone said. The weight of the tractor crushed his chest and he was dead by the time Edna sent Eugene to find him. After that, Edna really did have trouble with Eugene. He had always shown a tendency to be a wild sort of boy, hair flaming around his face, his voice easily raised in laughter, and always prone to be out and down the roads when he could have been working. Edna loved his freedom though, loved that about him, that spirit.

Every Sunday Edna and Eugene and Cyril and Hannah saw one another at church. There didn't seem to be much between them except smiles and nods. Once Cyril gave his umbrella to Edna and Eugene. Once Edna told Hannah how much she liked a dress Hannah was wearing. All four usually sat in their pews among their neighbours, listening to Wilbur Zink speak about Job and Daniel, Lot and Solomon, people they knew had lived a long time ago.

It shocked them all then when after supper one Tuesday night Hannah told her father she was expecting a baby and Eugene was the father. Cyril sat for a minute, his mouth dry and his eyes closing. He awoke from his trance when he felt his fingernails cutting into the palms of his hands. Something primitive in him wanted violence, wanted to shout a battle-cry and wreak vengeance on someone, on everyone. Part of him felt as though everything in his world that hadn't been broken when his wife died and left him had suddenly shattered. He knew what he had to do.

By the time he got to Wilbur Zink's house in Boonsboro, Edna Bidle was already inside, alone with the preacher, talking earnestly. Obviously, Eugene and Hannah had timed their revelations to their parents beforehand. Cyril stood holding the stained sweatband of his hat when the preacher introduced him to Edna, as if the two of them had never met. Reverend Zink told Cyril to sit down and they'd talk about this whole thing. Cyril sat down, not sure whether he was allowed to look at Edna. He noticed her eyes were red and that she had wrung her hands to dryness.

The three of them talked about an hour, agreeing that the only thing to do was to get Eugene and Hannah married and back inside the bosom of the church as soon as it could be managed. That much was clear. What was less certain was what would happen after that. Both Eugene and Hannah were seventeen years old, and while both had already quit school, they would need a place to live, and some kind of way to make a living. Did either Cyril or Edna have any ideas about that? the preacher asked.

Edna looked at Cyril. She was shy and she was desperate and she was as poor as he was. Cyril thought he ought to speak up, but he wasn't sure how much he could offer. He wasn't sure whether he could live with Eugene under his roof. Maybe, he said, it would be time for Eugene to take on his own daddy's farm, the one being run by Edna's brother-in-law.

Edna looked at Cyril. Somehow, she thought, though he does everything on that place of his by himself, he manages to keep himself looking decent. His shirt wasn't ironed, she noticed, and he was missing a button on the side of his overalls. Could she live with Hannah and a new baby in her house? Suppose Eugene didn't know how to be a man yet? What would she do if

she learned to love Hannah and her grandchild, and then Eugene
and Hannah fell out?

Edna nodded. It made sense, she said, for them to live with
her.

Cyril looked at her. No word of accusation had come from
Edna. A lot of women would have said terrible things about
Hannah by this time, about what a loose, slutty girl she was; how
she had seduced a good-looking healthy boy like Eugene. Or
even how she'd given way to him, if the whole thing had started
with Eugene. Cyril looked at the small wrinkles around Edna's
eyes, the loosened flesh on her arms, her thin legs. She needs to
be better looked after, he thought.

Cyril looked at the preacher and said it didn't seem right to
him that Hannah and her child would be a burden on Edna and
her kin, and that if he could, Cyril himself would make some kind
of contribution to keeping them. He had ten acres still in rocks
and trees that he had been waiting to clear. He could cut and sell
the timber, clear off the rocks, maybe graze some more hogs.

Edna watched Cyril's face as he explained this to the preacher.
These were the longest sentences she'd ever heard him say. She pictured his big arms and his big legs and his aging back up there
clearing that ten acres, and she wanted to rest her hand on him
and tell him not to do it. He hadn't said a word against Eugene,
not one word in her hearing. When he came into the preacher's
parlour and she saw who it was she half-expected him to admit he
was on his way to knock some sense into Eugene the first chance
he got. A lot of men would have been. She saw his flat square
hands hang down between his knees when he finished talking.

Ain't there no other way? Edna spoke up.

She seemed to be speaking to the preacher, but she was
looking at Cyril. He looked back at her and a sound like a wa-
terfall rushed in his ears. A vibration like the walls falling shook
him. At that moment, he looked at Edna and his heart thundered.

I guess, he said, looking at the floor, I guess there might be. He looked at the preacher, who had stood up and walked over to the window where he watched the rainclouds forming overhead. Cyril's eyes were on the preacher's back.

I guess, if me and Miss Edna was, well, if we was to get married our own selves, that would be all right. That would bring everybody together fair and square.

Edna stopped breathing. Was it possible? Something far down inside her screamed with joy, laughed and was reborn. She trembled uncontrollably and tears came to her eyes.

Framed by the window, Wilbur Zink turned softly and looked at them both. Cyril was standing up, though he had turned and was looking at Edna, whose face looked up to his.

No, Zink said. We can't do that. That can't be allowed. If the two of you were to be married that would make Eugene and Hannah sister and brother, and the result would be an abomination in the face of the Lord. No, sir, he said. It just can't be done.

Wilbur Zink turned back towards his window, which was now streaking with rain. Cyril and Edna looked at one another a while longer. Cyril licked his lips and turned towards the preacher, as if he wanted to say something, but he couldn't. He turned back towards Edna, who still seemed to be holding her breath, and he smiled very faintly and nodded his head a few times. She had never seen a man look so sad.

Cyril put on his hat and moved towards the door. I'll let you know what I think on Sunday, the preacher called to him. After church is over.

Cyril was pulling the front door shut when he thought he heard a noise, a woman's noise from the other room. He walked outside and was a few steps down the brick path when he felt Edna walking beside him. They were alone, having turned the corner from where Zink still stood in his window watching the rain. Edna looked up at Cyril and fought the urge to put her hand on his shoulder.

This thing, she said, it ain't over. Not for me.

Cyril stopped walking and turned back towards her.

No, he said. No, sir. Me neither. I guess it ain't never gonna be over, now it's started.

Cyril opened his umbrella, the one his grandfather had bought and the only one the family had ever owned, and they both stood under it.

It's gonna be all right, Edna said.

Sure it is, Cyril says. Folks like us is always all right. We gotta be, ain't we?

Yes, we have, she said. We sure indeed have.

May 17, 1964

7.15am. Warm 50s this morning, but cloudy. No dreams but feel tired.

9.45am. Walked to church with the ladies, all gossiping merrily, mostly about health & husbands. Some personal abuse of a woman named Dorothy who they all think looks like Minnie Pearl. New Grit.

*Making hominy, fried chicken & sweet potatoes for lunch.

2pm. Lunch delicious, though hominy as dull as I remembered. Church ladies discussing a rumor they'd heard this morning that someone on the Easterday Road had committed suicide. No one knew who, which licensed them all to make grim speculations. Quite gruesome in their reasoning. Cinch wearing pale yellow with straw beads today.

5pm. Gardening & watering as usual. Radishes looking ready.

10.30pm. Sky never brightened today, but the temperature went into the 70s. Heat lightning all over the west beyond South Mountain. No signs of J & P tonight.

May 18, 1964

7.30am. Fantastic amber & fuchsia sunrise & a cool low 50s.

8.45am. Dicky Bird painting in the hallway while Davy caulks, mostly the edges of the wainscoting. The other two are upstairs. I went up to see & found them varnishing woodwork in two of the bedrooms.

1.15pm. Same as before over the road, only now Davy is painting too. Dicky Bird singing about how he reached out his arms & he touched her, & then with soft words he whispered her name. He held her right on the tip of his fingers. (Which are now speckled with paint, ironically. Maybe they were then & that's why she left. Wouldn't surprise me.)

2pm. 80 degrees out there! Sun is everywhere.

5pm. Men left just slightly later. The problem of needing everyone to find a good stopping place at the same time. Hallway now brightly painted. Sunlight through it is beautiful.

    *Davy, who looks like he's been boiling fat on a whale ship, is the lucky one, I think, as they drove off, he'd have the best supply of fresh air.

10.45pm. Such a beautiful day. Watched "Wagon Train".

    *More optimistic today. I am here with a good purpose, with honest aims & with decent yearning to do the best for my only son. He is not my victim, & I won't be his, mine or anyone else's.

May 19, 1964

7.30am. Another sky like yesterday, beeswax & pink roses. Light breeze shaking the trees.

8.45am. Everyone varnishing on the upper middle floor now. Light chatter up there. No singing.

11.15am. Marce has driven off.

12.30pm. Didn't see his arrival, but Marce is back.

2.15pm. It is 90 degrees. Back with lunch tray. Tea & coffee less welcome this time. Drinks cans dotted around the floor. Cokes, RCs, Truades. Rip was showing his can to Davy, as it is one of those with a pop top opener. I looked at it too, & said I thought it looked dangerous & that I'd be afraid I'd cut my lip on such a thing. Rip & Davy looked at one another silently. But I could hear them thinking, "Women!"

4.30pm. Men just gone. The Corner smells of finely burned nylons. They are, I think, now varnishing some of the trim on the lower middle floor. All of them looked soaking in sweat when they left.

11pm. A fine summer day, a perfect blessing. Watered plants this evening. Peas, beans, onions, cabbages, marigolds, zinnias etc. I have things to be proud of here.

May 20, 1964

7.45am. Nearly 70 degrees already. Stunning sunshine & a warm breeze. Slept much better.

9am. Dicky Bird & Davy painting the hallway another coat. Rip & Marce varnishing in the rooms on the same floor. Dicky Bird looks too tired to sing. I wish Davy would.

*Wouldn't it be wonderful if he suddenly opened his mouth on a voice like Mario Lanza?

1pm. Work still the same over the road.

5pm. Everything shipshape as the men left today. I had a walk around. The upper three floors glisten with newness. Except for the doors, which they seem to be leaving, inexplicably. The smell is horrendous, like a plastic lava on the air.

10.30pm. A beautiful sunny day. Lower 80s this afternoon. Watched "The Virginian".

Thinking of Alex again & learning to forgive myself. I fear his death, & so prepare myself, just in case. I yearn for his life, & so fear death even more. I possess guilt over that life (maybe all mothers do?) & so my yearning mixes with selfishness. But I forgive even this, as my heartache is for him, really is for him, & these amends are to say that I understand his selfishness as I have accepted my own. I am asking for him to accept it too. I am offering a kind of equality, the kind that parents find it hardest to offer to their children, but the kind that sets the children free. It cannot be offered too soon.

May 21, 1964

6.30am. Only 44 this morning. Ridiculous. I'm tempted to build a fire. Sunshine looks promising though.

9.30am. A change in the line-up again. Now Dicky Bird & Davy in the kitchen & utility room, where they are varnishing woodwork. Marce & Rip are on the upper middle floor, varnishing the doors. Evidently, that is quite skilled, though I'm not sure why.

1pm. Work over the road still the same.

4.45pm. Not sure what is finished, though it looks like the upper middle doors are done, & the lowest floor woodwork too. They left looking easy with one another.

9pm. Joanie & Paul finished. Fiddle & autoharp tonight.

11pm. Mid 70s this afternoon, & sunny all day. I am tired but my mood is so like still water I am afraid to let it go.

In the sky, Lord, in the sky.

I don't know. Seem like too many folks dies like they ought not to done. They was a fella down Walkersville, hand on a big farm down there. He was taking a waggon full of chicken crates up to the auction in Woodsboro, and he gone all day. He get home in the evening, and all the servants is gathered together outside the quarters a-looking for him. He say, What y'all doing standing round yare for? And they say, We come to tell ya. While y'all out at the auction, the boss done sell you wife and son to the speculators. Now this hand, he just look at them and he don't want to believe 'em or nothing, and he look all 'round they quarters and they ain't no sign of 'em. Just 'bout all they things gone. And he come out and he sit hisself down on the ground and he look up at the sky just like he gonna pray, but he don't say nothing. All he say is, I gonna fix 'em. I gonna fix 'em so they ain't gonna get nothing over on me no more. And he look at the other servants and he say, Y'all do what you wanna, stay or go. But I'm a-staying right yare. And he retch in his pocket and he took out a ole harmonica he got there, and he start to playing. And the folks all sat down, 'cause it's a-getting dark early, and he just kept on a-playing and not saying nothing. Some folks went to they bed, but some just sat a-listening. Some time in the night, they all gone to sleep 'cept for the lonesome fella. When the sun come up he still sitting with that harmonica in his lap, stone dead. Just like he took the poison. Die with his heart broke.

When them big battles was a-starting, the Sesesh come down the hill from Braddock on they horses into Middletown, right down the main street. The cannons was a-going off and the Yankees, such as they was, was a-shooting at 'em. Some them Sesesh boys get up in the houses and stick they guns out the windows to shoot the Yankees. But what they don't see is some of them white boys in Middletown, they on the side of the Yankees too and they gets up in the windows and starts to shooting the Seseshes in they windows. Bet they didn't think of that. Down near the bridge, where the burning and the blowing up fixing to go on, they was a servant girl 'bout seven year ole. Her mammy stuck her up in the bedroom and lock the door to keep her safe. Well, when the Seseshes is all gone up the pike towards the ole inn on the top of the mountain, and the Yankees is all over the town, the mammy go back up to the bedroom to fetch the girl, and there she is, dead. They look all over that room for a bullet hole or something, but they never did find nothing. That girl just died of being scared, I guess.

Well, y'all go down 'yond Middletown and 'yond Burkittsville like you going to Point of Rocks and there where the road run down after the big woods there is a bunch a little ole houses. I don't know where they come from or nothing. Maybe they was the quarters or something for them big farms 'fore the war, or maybe they was where the free folk live 'fore the 'mancipation. Anyhow, when the war done, that's sure where the folks go, making theyselves a little town of they own. They so many of 'em 'fore long, they 'points one fella a preacher. His name was Cicero, and he got hisself a wife called Shanty and a son they call Boy-Yes. They good ole folks as good as they can be, and the new town getting 'long fine after the war, 'cause the men all goes down to work on the trains in Point of Rocks and Berlin, and the women takes in the washing and the sewing and the cleaning for the missuses in the big farms in the valley.

What folks talks about is how ole Cicero 'bout the generousest man ya ever did see. He give you the shirt off his back, you ask him. Even if you don't. He grow corn and sweet taters and lima beans and pole beans and biggest damn onions of anybody 'cept me, and he always a-giving 'em 'way to the folks too old or too sick to grow they own. That time when Mister Harrison president, and Harper's Ferry like to flood itself half gone, all the white folks get theyselves somewhere to go, and all the others ain't got no kin to run to. So ole Cicero borrow some horses, and he go up there his own self and bring back all the folks he can find, and take 'em down the valley. He strip all the blankets off they own beds to wrap them people up. I hear he took and carry a child hisself all the way from Sandy Hook. Whenever they was a burying or a baby come he speak out to the people and they all come to listen. 'Fore long, folk saying they ought to build theyselves a church of they own, and that's just what they do. It took 'bout two years for 'em to get all the money together, and the white folks is saying they done stole half what they used to build it from the ruins up Gapland where some of the battles was, but they get it built sure 'nough.

Anyway, things gone too good to last, and the Klan, cross the mountain down 'round Rohrsville, getting ideas in they heads that the folks with they new church and all is getting too big for they britches and needs to be shown something. So one night a pack of them boys on horses come a-riding down the ole road down the mountain and light in there 'mong the houses a-looking for that new church. It's getting dark by then, and them boys ain't got no genius 'tween 'em, so they just decides to burn theyselves the biggest house they find. Well, that was the one where the preacher hisself live. 'Fore ya know it, they got the whole damn porch a-smoking, and they bust the windows and throw they torches in the room where Cicero and Boy-Yes is a-sitting. The Klan boys a-screaming like the war on again, and Cicero got to grab on to Boy-Yes to keep him from running outside. Ole Shanty, she in the kitchen with the chores, and she too scared even to scream. So Cicero grab 'em both and run out the back towards the woods and the little barns and them Klan boys done scare theyselves thinking all the men in them houses gonna come running out looking for 'em, and some of 'em bring they guns, so they ride off back down the road towards Knoxville cause it's too dark to go up the mountain again.

Well, the men and the women all come out, but they ain't nothing they can do to save ole Cicero and Shanty's house none. Next day they ain't nothing left for a chicken to scratch. So y'all know what them people do? They told ole Cicero to get his own self down there, and they gonna make that church they house from now on. The folks bring 'em all they got to spare, and 'fore ya know it, Cicero and Shanty and Boy-Yes is living in the new church. Every Sunday they still go on with the sermons and the singing, and folks say won't be long 'fore Cicero get to build hisself a new house again, but he never does no more. Ain't got enough money, and never gonna. But it don't seem to matter none. They go on living there till Boy-Yes a grown man, and get hisself a job on the railroad, and 'fore the next war start move hisself to Baltimore and marry a gal down there. His mama cry 'cause she miss 'em, but she just so proud. She and Cicero on they own till after that war when the soldiers come back with influenza and ole Shanty catch it and die. Cicero get it too, but he don't die. He an ole man finally die in his sleep, and they bury him long with Shanty just near the windows on the south side of they church.

May 22, 1964

7am. Only 50 degrees again. I must learn to bathe in mid afternoons. Glorious sunrise. Slept all right, but dreamed of the dentist chair, waiting while numbed up, for the dentist to arrive.

9.45am. Marce & Rip working on lower middle floor doors. Davy & Dicky Bird one floor above them: sanding the doors the others did yesterday?

1pm. Davy watching Dicky Bird (it seems) varnish a door in the kitchen. The others still working a floor above them.

1.30pm. Temperature has topped 90.

4.30pm. Men just left. Dicky Bird sitting with Davy in the back! Haven't gone inside & may not.

11.15pm. Beautiful hot sunny day. Watched "Route 66". Anxious mood tonight. I don't know why.

May 23, 1964

8.00am. A little warmer this morning. Sun streaming in every window since dawn. Dreamed, but have forgotten them all.

1pm. I think it is now 91 degrees. Feels like it.

*In the paper today that the president made a speech in Michigan yesterday, describing his goal as to see the rise of a Great Society. For this, I think, we will need great citizens. Inspiration is its own reward, when it feels like inspiration.

*Returned library books & didn't get any more. Too hot to walk about much, so went to A & P ($13) & came home before the milk curdled.

4.30pm. Drank tea as it cooled today. Must make ice tea if this happens again. Or when it does. Struggling with Tin Drum. Not a book for warm days. Or warm minds.

10pm. Spent the evening house-cleaning. Wedged between the bedpost & the wall, I found a small thin cookbook dated 1841. It looks new, unstained & no fingerprints. Not sure of its provenance but may try to cook some of these things. Fried cucumbers?

*Sleepy tonight. Feeling better about Alex. In a way. Almost like he is a boy I had had a crush on, argued with, & now decided to see as a friend. I think this is probably a good feeling. But I am eager to get started on it.

May 24, 1964

8.30am. Slept soundly, though dreamed of walking in corridors, as if in a hospital. Not sure about doors or turnings.

12pm. Hurriedly dressed this morning & joined the walk to the Brethren Church & attended service. No one took any extra notice of me, & it all went pleasantly. I remain unconverted, but the fellowship feeling was warm & filled me with a kind of peace. Nice walk back to the benches with the others, & it felt good to be dressed like them, & to have shared their morning. Cinch looked cool in a sleeveless cream dress with coral beads. If anyone felt anything special about my being in church, they didn't say a word on the subject.

2pm. Had salad & Alaska salmon for lunch. Men are now over the stream playing horseshoes, & women are gathering under the walnut trees.

5pm. Drank ice tea & took some out to the ladies. They all praised my garden, which was nice. Cinch walked back with me, carrying glasses. She put them beside my sink & looked out my windows. She suddenly asked, —Ya heard anything 'bout your boy? I said no. —Well, she said, summer's a-coming, so ya never know. I have no idea what she thinks that may mean, but the real message of hopefulness wasn't lost on me. She said she'd give me some geranium cuttings.

8.30pm. Have been crying for about 30 minutes. I have been thinking about how much I just want Alex to come home. I feel very relaxed thinking this, as it feels completely wholesome that I should. If he never lives here, it is still right that I made it a place to welcome him. He must feel that.

10.45pm. A gentle, beautiful day, from 60 this morning to almost 90 this afternoon. The days are like a slow flowing river without a horizon.

May 25, 1964

9am. Athos, Porthos, Aramis & d'Artagnan all at work. Now Marce & Rip back on upper middle floor, re-varnishing doors. Dicky Bird & Davy sanding off the ones they did last week.

1pm. Davy & Dicky Bird not here, having gone in Marce's truck (to Ingall's?). The other two varnishing doors still. Faster the second time.

    *In the news today that that awful Barry Goldwater has recommended that we use nuclear bombs to flatten North Vietnam. I am horrified at so many levels. Mercifully, all sides seem ready to condemn this appalling idea.

    *Someone should interview the mother of an American soldier currently missing in North Vietnam to hear her point of view on the grotesque threat BG treats so flippantly.

3pm. Truck returned & being unloaded. Lots of boxes.

4.45pm. Men gone now. Not sure about boxes, though there seem to be some piled in most rooms. I suspect all the doors are finished. Their lungs must be slippery with shellac fumes.

10.30pm. Weather like yesterday, but cooled by a breeze this afternoon, & not quite so hot. Watched a rerun of "Andy Griffith". I don't know why. My life is a re-run of "Andy Griffith". I would assign roles to all the neighbours, but then I'd have to assign one to myself. Too sleepy to read.

May 26, 1964

9am. They have set up a kind of outdoor workshop with benches & tools outside the back door. They are all going back & forth carrying things.

10am. Curious, I made as though I was strolling up the Harmony Road, & so peeked over the old iron fencing to see what they are up to. Cutting things, I think are curtain rails.

12.45pm. Just back. Yes, they are all four scattered over the upper middle floor fitting curtain rails, handles, knobs &

fittings like that. It all seems quite light-hearted. Dicky Bird advising energetically for someone to walk on by, but to wait on the corner, because they have to be strangers when they meet.

4.45pm. Men gone now, looking more at ease than they have recently. A quick look upstairs shows all the rails & small things fitted. It is now starting to look like an empty house, not a project.

11pm. Weather like yesterday, but cooler in the morning. A most capacious moon this evening. A white pumpkin. I am sleepy & happy tonight.

Well, the days are long

I, LittleWound, tell this story.

When there was silence upon the hillsides and in the valleys, and there were days when no one knew the noise of the Washechu, the sound of their axes or the cries of their slaves, then there was kinship and honour among the Catoctins, brotherhood and sisterhood, and the rearing of families who walked as gods walk.

There lived in the village a woman named CloudCatcher, and she was esteemed by her neighbours as a woman of understanding. She lived her girlhood respecting the traditions, and she married a man named GreyOwl, who brought gifts to her parents' threshold. They lived together as husband and wife through the seasons, and no one saw pain or anguish grow between them. But neither did her neighbours see love in her eyes or in his. She pursued her tasks as a wife, and he had no cause to complain. His bow was strung with the hair from her brush. His clothes hung with the beads she sewed. His meals made him give thanks. He had no cause to doubt her loyalty or to speak of her in any way that could suggest dishonour. To her, he was as a man might be expected to be. He never asked for what was not due to him. He never hurried her in her tasks or chided her for anything that she did. His provision for them both allowed them comfort, even when the winds bruised the trees with ice. Together they had one child – a boy they named Sunlit. They fed him as parents fed their sons, on food not burning, and yet not chilled. They gave of their own to him, feeding him, before they fed themselves. It happened though that when the leaves bore their weight upon the branches, and the streams dried in their beds, and the walnuts and pecans hung like acorns in the trees, that Sunlit fell upon a hive of swarming bees, and the stings poisoned him, turning his steps towards those of his ancestors. After his death, though CloudCatcher had another son and another daughter, neither came into the world living, and so she had no more children.

Without children to love, it seemed to CloudCatcher that she could see the steps of her days already drawn in the dust before her. Seasons marked off in her mind mingled, with nothing to distinguish them. She saw the breasts of her friends fatten with the milk they fed their children. She saw those children learn to walk, to fish, to play with dolls, to court and to marry. She saw the lives of her people, though she felt no life of her own. GreyOwl, though a man of character, never rose in the esteem of the people, and before the hair on his head thinned or frosted, he was dead. He had been hunting when he fell and broke his leg near the place where it joins his hip. In the days that followed, he weakened, and his lips paled. CloudCatcher held his hand even as his eyes turned away and his pain ended. She grieved as a wife ought to grieve, and through the season of her loneliness, she was looked after by her husband's brothers and nephews, their wives and sisters.

At this time there grew to manhood one who was called ConqueringBear. Above all things, he held in his heart a belief that kindness was the treasure all men and women sought. All his life he had been a witness to the marriage between CloudCatcher and GreyOwl, confused by the calm that set them apart. He looked upon CloudCatcher and he wondered how it was that GreyOwl had never climbed into the oaks to bring down for her a basket of stars. He thought that among the women in the village it was her whose voice hung in the air like meadowsweet and whose hands wove like the hands of the flames. He did not count the wrinkles beside her eyes or the lines above her brows. He did not think to seek her as a bride, but only to give her the treasure of his kindness.

So when the daffodils and crocuses came into flower, he brought to her threshold gifts ready for cooking – chipmunks and rabbits – the gifts that a boy might give to his mother's friends. And at night he played the Pib-e-gwnn, imagining her as she slept.

But he never neglected his work as a man, and no one knew of his affection for CloudCatcher. She spoke to no one of the gifts she had received, the music she heard, or the things she suspected. And so the seasons might have turned their circle, and their destinies flown like birds in the sky, had it not been for an illness that befell CloudCatcher. As she lay in her clothes, troubled and coughing, she saw the eyes of those who attended her. She saw the duty in the things they said and did. But as she looked out upon the people in the village going about their chores she saw and felt the tenderness that lay on ConqueringBear's back, burdening his tasks with care. He did not join his friends or his brothers in their sport, or let his eyes fall on any woman whose steps passed by him. When he looked her way, which he did more than she expected, his eyes sharpened with sorrow at her pain, and his will reached out to her that she might find the strength of her spirits again. In this way, faith in his kindness towards her brought her once again into health. And in this way the truth between them sealed.

When once again the arrows of the sun poured upon the Catoctin's mountain, ConqueringBear sought CloudCatcher for his wife. It was not a marriage that anyone had foretold. Nor was it one that others understood. But at night, as they rested in one another's arms, they felt the treasure of kindness, and they knew the joy of being.

May 27, 1964

7.30am. Rested this morning. Dreamed of Tom & the kite he made the time we went to Ocean City.

9.15am. They have just finished setting up their outdoor workshop again. All four much the same as yesterday. Arguing about baseball & someone named "Harmon Killibrew" (sp?)

1pm. Most of the small hardware now in place on the lower middle floor too.

5pm. Everyone gone. A walk 'round & it looks like they have got everything done now except the kitchen & utility, but they've started the utility.

10.30pm. A day now like the others. Beautiful, warm, dry, sunny, & a graceful breeze. 82 this afternoon.

May 28, 1964

9am. Marce & Dicky Bird in the lowest floor. Davy & Rip clearing up & carrying things into The Patch for another fire, it looks like.

11am. Davy tending a fire in The Patch.

1.15pm. Kitchen fittings nearly done. No sign of Rip or Dicky Bird, but voices in the utility room.

4.30pm. Everyone gone & everything cleared up & straightened. Kitchen looks finished. I poked around the utility room & discovered what they'd been doing. They've put some kind of insulation around a lot of the pipes.

10.30pm. Weather just the same as the past week, but cooler this afternoon (78).

May 29, 1964

7.30am. Cooler this morning. Only 45.

8.15am. No sign of Marce's truck. Have they gone for supplies?

9am. Just had a call from Hartsock. The men are having the day off today. Tomorrow is Decoration Day. He asked how everything is going, & I told him I was very satisfied. I asked when he was coming to inspect it all, & he vaguely intimated very soon.

9.30am. Drank some of the coffee & some of the tea I made for the men. Feeling very worked up now.

12pm. Hoed & raked this morning & watched three of my neighbours hang out their washing. Very hungry, so am making a toasted sandwich for lunch.

4pm. Finished Grass novel. Head feels like a tin drum. Hoping for tea cure.

8.15pm. Walked up to listen to Joanie & Paul playing to-night (dulcimer & fiddle). P spoke a little about his experiences as a soldier. He will not be participating in any celebrations tomorrow. I wanted to ask him what he thought Alex's chances are, but I was too afraid. I wish now that I had.

11pm. Perhaps a change is coming, as although sunny all day, it was only about 70 this afternoon. Watched "Route 66". Of course, all reruns now, but still new to me.

May 30, 1964

7.30am. Woke up usual weekday time. Decoration Day. I wish I knew what to feel.

11.30am. Only went to Middletown Acme ($15). Will spend some time in the garden, I think. May read magazines later. Write letters?

2pm. Full after lunch on homegrown salad!

5pm. Have kept busy all day. Tired but well feeling now. Resisted picturing Alex in his uniform, parading.

7pm. Wrote several letters, balanced checkbook, made lists.

10.45pm. Weather just like yesterday. So still. No cars went up the Harmony Road for more than two hours this after-noon. Probably double that on the Brethren Church Road. Harmony has become a dry backwater.

May 31, 1964

7am. Wide awake this morning. Cannot put down thoughts of Alex's homecoming. I believe that here will be the place of so much healing. That thought makes me so happy I could dance.

9.45am. Watched everyone go to church today, but from indoors, as I didn't want to join them. So much work to do!

1pm. Met everyone after church & strolled home with them. One of the ladies had her hand bandaged, having burnt it on her stove. They all agreed this was her husband's fault, for several different reasons. I agreed, as that seemed politic.

*Cinch told me to come 'round any time to get some geranium cuttings. This is the first time she has, in any way, invited me to her house. She was wearing a pale blue dress, white sweater & ruby-like beads.

3pm. Had small roast beef for lunch which was tasty, but which took so long to cook I became so hungry that I finally ate too fast to leave me comfortable afterwards. Hm.

5.30pm. Went for a walk towards Hawbottom this after-noon, as the temperature was perfect. Lovely views but didn't go the whole way as the road wasn't very good.

10.15pm. Weather continues like a dream. Cool & crisp this morning, upper 70s this afternoon.

PART III:

Blue Note

Hog Wild

June 1, 1964

7am. Cool 54 this morning & very foggy.

9.15am. Men arrived on time, but to my surprise, Marce has parked his truck in the corner of The Patch nearest the iron bridge. They all got out & carried digging tools across the field to the uppermost end. Here they have been busy running strings & hammering stakes in the ground. I took the tea & coffee tray & put it in the truck bed, then walked over to question them. —This is gonna be your barn or stable & all, Marce said. Then he pulled a nice sketch of Hartsock's out of his back pocket & handed it to me. It is just like I described it more than a year ago. —I thought you were going to work on the wash house, I asked. Marce gave me a slight sneer. —Weather's to get bad, he said. I laid the drawing down on the blade of a shovel & left them.

10am. Ingalls's truck is parked in the gravel road nearest where the men are working. It looks piled high with lumber of all sorts, including some really big pieces.

11am. Back from watching the unloading. White driver on his own today, so unloading took all four men to help. —Where's your boy today? Marce asked the driver. —His kid got an infected splinter a-playing in school. –Uh huh, Marce said. –Everybody loves their kids. –Sure do. –He can't help being what he is, Marce added, a little enigmatically (but only a little). The driver, who was carrying a long heavy piece of wood with Davy at the other end, just stared at the pine trees beyond them. Davy watched them both.

12.45pm. Men sat about having their lunch. I've brought the tray back now. They have dug a series of deep holes. Davy has brought over some tripod-like wooden things, to-gether with a tool box, all from the wash house. Radio is playing.

2.30pm. Raining now. Men have disappeared. Wood looks to be covered up with tarpaulins. Truck still there.

3.45pm. Having been idly pawing away at the pictures I brought with me from the old house & never put up in this one (no room, I had said). There is my favorite one of Tom, the one taken just before the war started, when he was at a conference in Philadelphia. I wasn't sure whether it would "fit" in The Corner somehow, or how I would feel seeing it there (or how Alex would). But looking at it now, I have decided that I should make a place for it. It can be a kind of window through which Tom's eyes can see where we have gone. I know I could never really part with it, & if I left it anywhere else, it would feel disrespectful to Tom (& to me, my memory) & I wish to make peace with both. I think Tom would agree.

5pm. Just back from The Corner. (Part of me imagined Tom's photo on every wall, one by one.) It looks as though the men never went inside at all. I noticed that the doors & windows on the wash house have all been removed, & debris piled in the little courtyard near the spring house steps.

10.30pm. Rained a bit this afternoon, then drizzle. Only upper 60s today. Watched a rerun of "Wagon Train".

June 2, 1964

7.15am. A little foggy again this morning. 50s again.

8.30am. Truck parked like yesterday, & all four men digging & sawing posts (I think). I wanted to ask Marce where his bad weather was but thought better of it.

1pm. Big posts in the ground now, held up with temporary-looking braces.

5pm. More braces in place & lots more posts. They have put a kind of low frame, like a picture frame around the whole thing. No sign of John John tonight.

7.30pm. Looking at pictures again. Mostly of Alex in high school & after. Some of him with girls, before dances, at weekends, a barbecue. I stopped looking at them to imagine him some time bringing home the one he will marry, the one who is nervous to meet me, the one he wants me to love as much as he loves himself. I imagine her coming to The Corner, & Alex showing her around, laughing at some things, impressed by some, embarrassed or confused by others. I will love her if she loves him, I know that. The more she loves him, the more I will love her. The more he loves her, the more peace I will feel. So I will encourage him. I am promising myself that I will encourage him.

10.45pm. Breeze picked up this morning & temperature got up over 70.

June 3, 1964

7.30am. Rain in gusts this morning & a little colder than yesterday. Marce's bad weather at last.

9am. Marce parked on The Common again. Men working on wash house now. Two upstairs & two down, everybody cleaning up, pulling loose, cutting out & generally fixing bad woodwork. Downstairs, they have a woodshop set up for repairs & Marce & Rip seem to be making spare parts for Dicky Bird & Davy to fit. Though Davy seems to be more about dismantling & removing than installing.

1pm. Marce & Davy gone in the truck for some tools, apparently. Rip said –There's things outside we need to fix up, walls & roof (which he pronounces "rough").

2pm. Marce back & what look like trowels & mason's tools in buckets gone up the front steps to the lower porch on The Corner.

5pm. Poked around wash house after the men left. Upstairs floor repaired, rafters & woodwork (except for upper door hatch) all looking repaired. Downstairs ceiling (well, bottom of upper floor) looks good, window frame replaced, & door frame new. No door yet.

11pm. Rain in bursts all morning but slowed this afternoon & got over 70 again.

   *Have been reading this old cookbook I found. Some strange recipes here. I am going to buy some things to try & make some of this stuff. I think if I make it, I will feel just a little closer to whoever it used to belong to. Something in me wants her to accept me, just a little.

June 4, 1964

7am. Not much more than 40 this morning. Tempted to build a fire.

8.45am. Truck parked as before. Just after they arrived the Ingall's truck came & delivered a big pile of blue gravel which it took right up to the edge of where they've been working & dumped. They are all shovelling & raking it inside the big picture frame.

10.15am. A cement mixer (huge!) has come & parked next to the stable site & dumped loads of concrete down a trough into the frame (which I now see is a mold). Also into the holes around the posts. The men are all raking frantically.

*I wish I had seen all this closer.

1.30pm. Everyone now at the wash house again. Davy mixing cement for Dicky Bird & Rip & Marce to point the cracks (I know my terms now!) in the upper-floor bricks & lower-floor stones.

*Dicky Bird back in voice (as they seem to have left the radio somewhere). He is admitting to all of us that he can't help her, 'cause he's falling too.

2.15pm. Amway man came. I ordered a kind of brush to do hard-to-reach places. Should be useful when I'm settled over the road.

4.45pm. Men gone now. They look filthy & worn out. Walls look ½ finished.

*John John joined them tonight. He was given the job of cleaning all the cementing tools (he seems to hate this). The others all went over to look at the new concrete, which they covered with a makeshift tent of tarpaulins. I asked JJ why he hated cleaning the tools so much. They make his skin itch, he said.

*He also said school ends next Wednesday. I asked him what he was doing this summer. —Play, he said.

11pm. Much sunnier today & high of 77.

June 5, 1964

7.30am. Warmer this morning than yesterday, but drizzly.

8.45am. Marce parked on The Common again, & all hands busy pointing the wash house. Davy sometimes uses the wheelbarrow to transport combustible junk to The Patch.

1pm. Pointing seems done now. A good thing as the sky is darkening again. Davy on clean-up duty. The others busy working over the wash house's tin roof.

1.30pm. Raining now.

5pm. Truck gone. Raining again, so didn't go to see what they did this afternoon. No John John to give me an update.

10.30pm. Rain this afternoon & this evening. Still up to 78 mid-afternoon. Watched "Route 66".

　*Determined suddenly, for no real reason, that this Christmas I will send cards to everyone in my address book, giving them all my new address. This feels, somehow, like a very good thing to do.

June 6, 1964

7.30am Warm & sunny today. Over 60 already.

2.15pm. Busy morning in Frederick. Went to the C Burr Artz library & got all the books I'm allowed. All histories. (I feel on fire to know everything, suddenly, as if there is magic in knowing.) Went to the bookstore & bought two novels: The Bell Jar by Sylvia Plath, (a poet) & One Flew Over the Cuckoo's Nest, by Ken Kesey. (Seeing a pattern? I have de-cided to run straight into this tunnel as it is the only way I will find the light. I believe that if I do this, I will find it.) Went to H L Mills, mostly for the green stamps, & looking at catalogue, realize I could have got Amway-like brush for nothing. Live & learn. Then went to A & P & bought things

478

for experimental cooking ($21). I will give back to the Mary House smells it hasn't known for a century! Feeling very energetic & full of plans.

*Also bought some flypaper, as The Corner seems to have too many flies. Smell of paint?

4pm. Thunderstorms moving in from the west, & the trees shaking.

5pm. Raining with thunder now but can't see any lightning.

9pm. Quiet & wet & dripping out there. Enchanting. Movie starting.

11pm. Over 70 today. Plants got a good soak, I think. Watched movie through Channel 4 fuzz. Same characters, same mistakes, same apologies, same redemptions.

*Quite tired tonight after all. Listening to the Mary House & what it says in its supposed silence. Pings on the tin roof. Squeaks in the windows. Creaks in the timbers. Ghostly voices that seem to say, Patience! Patience! A woman's life is patience.

*I know that if I can just listen & answer those voices then all the rewards of patience will be mine.

*Patience is the hardest thing in the world.

June 7, 1964

7.45am. Over 60 & bright sun again. Beautiful morning. Forget church, I am going out for a walk.

1.30pm. Back & fed now. What a walk! I made a bet with myself, stupid as it sounds, that if I could find a fish in a creek, it would be a sign that Alex was alive & would come home. I walked all the way up the Little Hunting Creek to Fisher's Hollow, & then up the Hollow itself. It is a frightening place. Hogs graze under the trees. I saw a shed covered with nailed-up hubcaps & license plates (why?). I saw a field where every ten feet old machinery sat in a pile of rust, though cows grazed among them. Dogs barked, roosters crowed, a woman shouted out what sounded like –Hommy hommy hommy! But. But. There, near where the old bridge is, I stopped & looked down in the water, & I saw two sunfish! Slow, stupid, aimless, inedible barbarians. But a promise kept & a prophecy fulfilled. I thanked them, & came home, my heart pounding.

2.30pm. I wish I had seen Cinch. I wish I had seen John John's baseball game. Am I selfish?

5pm. Gone gray now & storms threatening again.

6.30pm. Lots of distant lightning & some rainfall.

8pm. Storm seems to have passed. Have been reading Plath. I believe in her, though it hurts.

10.45pm. Nearly 80 this afternoon. Watched "Bonanza" rerun.

Hell Among the Yearlings

I don't get 'cross South Mountain much 'fore the war. All them little places up there on the top – Smoketown, Cavetown, Mapleville and that. Down to Boonsboro couple times. They a family there run a hotel 'cause the pike runs through the middle of town. They got servants to do all the chores for the folks a-staying there. Woman that owns it a widow, and she ain't got but the one child, a white-hair boy called Mister Kingman. He a real rip torn boy when he young and he can't leave off his tormenting them servants, telling off the men like they dogs or something and about chasing and touching all the gals, specially the young ones. He weren't no more than 'bout fourteen fifteen, he up and mess with this gal name Susannah, scaring her 'bout what he gon' do if she tell anybody what he like to do to her up and down them empty rooms in that house. Well, sure 'nough, 'fore long she having a baby, and the ole widow woman that runs the place whoop her like the tide come in. Then she change her tune and say that it don't matter whether she have no baby or not, 'cause that baby gonna belong to her anyhow. So ole Susannah, she have the baby and it's a little girl, and 'cause she ain't 'lowed to tell nobody who the daddy is, folk call that baby girl Rumour.

Well, the ole widow, she let Susannah keep on a-working for her, just so long as she don't pay Rumour too much mind, and 'fore long, Rumour be the kind of girl spend her time down in the stables 'mong the men, and they mostly pretty good fellas treat her like she they own. 'Bout that time, Mister Kingman get hisself sent down to 'Napolis for to go to college and get hisself educated, and he gon' be gone for 'bout three four years. Next thing he get hisself some kinda job selling something on off the boats down Ballmore, and he don't so much as come to see his mammy moren 'bout twice in all them years.

Meantime, Rumour growing to be a big gal, and Susannah getting worried 'bout her all the time, out shaming 'round the menfolk. And the widow, she getting mighty put out with 'em both, and she tell Susannah she best make that girl behave herself, or she gonna take 'em both down the road to Hagerstown and sell 'em for sure.

Well, 'fore that happen, Susannah upset the washboiler and the water run all down her legs a-blistering 'em, and she only get 'bout half right again, and that widow take her by her own self and give her to the speculator to take to the pens down in Hagerstown, and she gone for good then. The widow, she think Rumour ain't no good for nothing nohow, but the speculator say he got other idea, and he make a deal for the widow to sell Rumour down the end of the road to the whorehouse, and that's just what he do.

'Bout then the state of Maryland deciding whether it gonna be Sesesh or Yankee and the Yankee army all come down to Frederick and 'rest the legislature. They hundreds and hundreds of Yankees 'round now, coming and going like you never seen, and that whorehouse 'bout as busy as it can be. Well, down where he live, Mister Kingman find out just 'bout everybody down there is Seseshes, and they all fixing to get 'cross the river to Virginia and 'list. But he say 'fore he gone, he better see his mama 'gain, and say goodbye, and then he get 'cross the river easy down Shepherdstown.

So he come up there and he staying at that ole inn with his mama and she got all the rooms full with officers and sutlers and I don't know who all. But night time they all go down to the taverns and get theyselves drunk and then head to the whorehouse. It don't seem to matter to Mister Kingman none that he 'bout to be a Sesesh and all the fellas in his mama's house is Yankees, 'cause he drink with them just like they cousins or something. Then when they all goes off to the whorehouse, he goes with 'em, sure as ya born.

Who you think he see there? 'Fore long, he upstairs messing with the long-leg gal, call herself Rumour. 'Course he don't know nothing 'bout her and she don't know nothing 'bout him. I tell you what though. It ain't long for she 'specting her own baby. It could been anybody's and probably was some of everybody's. But I surely surely hope it ain't got nothing to do with him. He never find out though, 'cause he get hisself killed down in Virginia 'cause a cannonball or something cut him up bad. The widow die 'fore the war end too. Rumour go down Hagerstown herself when the whorehouse shut after the war.

June 8, 1964

7.45am. 60 degrees again, but foggy & damp this morning.

9.15am. Everyone at work in The Patch, dismantling braces from stable posts. Dicky Bird letting it be known that he hopes she will break it to him gently, letting him down the easy way. That way he could believe she loves him, even if it is just for one more day.

10am. Raining lightly now. Men disappeared.

2pm. Over 80 degrees & really humid. Men back in The Patch, cutting & fitting what I suspect are the timbers for the walls in the stable.

    *In the paper today that two of our fighter planes have been shot down. Does this make war more likely? Negotiations harder? Does anyone understand what is going on?

5pm. Men gone now. Everything outside wet, & they all looked a little bedraggled. Davy couldn't find a dry place to sit in the truck bed, so he was driven off slightly squatting. Glad John John not with him.

10.45pm. Not much more than gray with sun streaks today. Watched Channel 4 movie while ironing.

June 9, 1964

7.30am. Over 60 already & humid, damp & foggy.

9am. All the men in The Patch, working on the timbers for the stable. Lots of drilling & long bolts. Davy in charge of holding, Marce cutting, Rip fitting & Dicky Bird sizing up the next piece & singing. Today he says he loves her because she understands (dear!), every single thing he tries to do.

12.30pm. All merry in The Patch. They seem more egalitarian when they all work together. Lots of bracing & beams in place now. Brought them ice tea, & a stack of Dixie cups to encourage them to drink freely, as it is pretty hot out there, as there is no shade. Davy looks like he could be wrung out. Marce had sweat running off his nose.

3pm. Thermometer says 89 degrees. Took them ice water.

5pm. Went over to see them off. It's a little cooler, & so they had smiles this evening. Some of the rafters are going up. Piles of lumber still. Also tin, I think. Buckets of bolts & fittings.

6pm. Breeze picked up this evening a little & had a light shower. I notice there are lots of tiny green walnuts & apples that have come loose, fallen off in the recent wind & rain. I've decided that I will practice making coffee cakes with nuts & apple pies of different kinds. Alex has always liked both. Such a nice thing to welcome him with.
7pm. Shower has grown & can hear some thunder.

June 10, 1964

7.30am. Radio says it is to be a hot day today, & it feels it. I've already got the windows open.

9am. Dicky Bird & Rip fitting rafters on the stable, while Marce cuts & Davy holds. Radio punching the air like a welter weight.

2.45pm. Temperature has topped 90. A warm breeze stirring, at least. Rafters look finished. They are putting up some of the siding. I took over ice tea.

   *Amway man come & gone. His hair was blown straight back from driving with his windows open.

4.30pm. Men just left. They look roasted. John John came tonight & gathered up wood odds & ends for a fire.

5.15pm. Joanie & Paul playing tonight. Fiddle & dulcimer. Sat outside until the mosquitoes exhausted me.

11pm. A hot sultry day, but quite beautiful & summery. No moon tonight. Still reading Plath. Such loneliness.

June 11, 1964

7.45am. Warm & sunny this morning. 62 degrees. Pale cream sunrise earlier.

9.15am. Very busy in The Patch. Dicky Bird & Rip on the roof attaching material stuff & tin. Marce & Davy attaching the siding. And … John John is with them. He is a second pair of Davy hands, assisting everybody, holding, carrying, etc. Very pretty wooden siding. Radio on.

1.15pm. All the same over the road. Took them lemonade. I asked JJ how he liked being off school. Before he could answer, Marce spoke up, —He ain't done sh[]t.

4.45pm. All packed up in The Patch. I went out & watched them load up. JJ looked more bored than tired, I thought. I wish I knew what goes on in his head when he is with them.

10.45pm. Not quite as hot today, mid 80s. Nice breeze & drier feeling. Watched "Rawhide" rerun.

June 12, 1964

7.15am. Overslept just a little as it is cooler this morning (just above 50). Gray & silver sunrise.

9.30am. Working like yesterday over the road. John John here again. He drinks tea with milk & one sugar. His dad has two sugars. Marce & Davy on the siding, Dicky Bird & Rip adding trim etc around the roof.

1pm. Work continues. They are looking a little too hot, but not like French Foreign Legionnaires today. Took them ice tea. Spouting going up now.

4.30pm. Siding finished, or almost. They have stored things inside now. John John made a special point of telling me they'd finish it next week.

*I asked JJ what he was doing tomorrow. —Baling hay, he said. I asked what he liked to do on rainy days, & his answer surprised me. —Play parchese, Monopoly, poker, put together puzzles, draw or read books. —What do you draw? I said. –Buildings, he answered. Houses, factories, mills. –What do you read? –Civil War books. Magazines. Civil War. Trains.

*–Always got his nose in a G[]d-d[]mn book, Marce said.

8pm. Joanie & Paul just gone in. The sound of autoharp & guitar through my open windows until moments ago.

9pm. Finished Bell Jar. It is the scream that all women hear, if they dare to listen.

10.30pm. A beautiful day, with clear light since morning. Hardly a cloud. Watched "Route 66".

June 13, 1964

8.15am. Very warm this morning again & very bright. 65 degrees. Will it storm later?

11.45am. Back from Middletown Acme ($16). Rushing a little as I am going to the baseball game.

3.30pm. Back from the game. John John struck out once, got walked once & got a hit when the short stop dropped the ball. One of the white-haired boys plays third base (& bats first in the line-up). He picked up a ground ball & threw it to JJ on first base to get the runner out, but he threw it so high JJ couldn't reach it. Both he & some of the other boys blamed JJ for this, somehow. Neither Marce nor JJ's mother were at the game. Cinch was there, & so I sat with her. She watched it all keenly, commented on most of the boys' appearance & attitudes, talked constantly, & looked positively disappointed (with the umpire) when JJ struck out. After the game, she gave JJ 15c to buy a Coke.

*It was interesting to see Cinch not dressed for church. Today she was wearing a sleeveless cotton print dress, bare legs & red canvas sneakers.

4pm. Temperature topped 85 earlier. Not so humid though.

7pm. Just back from sitting an hour with Joan & Paul & drinking ice tea while they played (guitar & dulcimer this evening). Paul is a keen local historian who knows a lot of the local stories.

11pm. Another beautiful day. No storm clouds ever came. Watched "Gunsmoke". Was a rerun & felt like a rerun. A re-re-run.

June 14, 1964

8am. Sticky & hot this morning, drizzling & over 70 already. Surely a storm later?

9.45am. Watched the churchgoers go by this morning. Cinch in a lemon-coloured sleeveless dress & white hat.

*Garden too much for me this morning in this hot, wet feeling weather, so wrote letters, hoping to pre-empt one from Sis.

11.45am. Church crowd not in a lingering mood today. Spoke with some of the ladies about the recipes I've discovered & they all gave me some pointers. Cinch said, –It's too durn hot to cook!

2.30pm. 82 degrees & clouds building up over South Mountain. Air pungent & thick as gravy. Reading Kesey novel. Men together find it very hard to preserve one another's dignity, lest it threaten their own.

5.15pm. Pouring with rain now, booming thunder, yellow lightning.

10pm. Still evening with drizzle. I went outside & the storm seems to have sucked the heaviness out of my whole body. It feels all over the way it might feel inside my ears if my ears were ringing.

*It occurred to me that I have always imagined Alex returning exactly as he left, imagining all the scars he may have, old & new, to be healed or healing. But it may be that some never do. That is asking too much, & I must not ask it (of him or of myself). Instead, I must love, promise to love, this young man I no longer really know. It is a deal I have to accept. If he comes back missing a leg I must not mourn the loss. If I can find that strength, I believe, it opens up so many more pathways through which Alex might return, as he may then be anyone he has become, & no longer only what I expected.

Sugarloaf Rag

After the war, Middletown get big. Up on the hill end, they building houses like you ain't never seen. I mean big ole houses. And they got whole bunches of men working on 'em. Lots of 'em doing different things with the sawing and the roofing and the glassing and I don't know what all.

They was two fellas that was friends. One of 'em, name Newt Ballenger was a ole bachelor and he renting a room down the boarding house on the ole road towards Jefferson. Other one was a married man, name Elbert Palmer, and he and his wife Miss Canaan, live on one of them little streets run up the little hill down the main street, other end of town from where all the big building a-going on. Anyhow, them two men work on the new houses together and that's how they knowed each other, one a-working on the outside and one a-working on the inside.

Now in the evenings, when they finish working, they both walk down the main street on they way home, and they like to stop at the big dry goods store on the corner and buy theyselves some cooked bacon and a cold drink to have 'fore they get home. Least that's what they said. Now I don't know nothing, but it sure look like to me like what they want to go in there for is 'cause they a shopgirl in there they both think mighty fine. She a pretty young widow called Miss Agata, and she getting herself a reputation for talking kind to the menfolk a-working on the new houses. Ain't nobody got nothing they can prove, but ole Mister Elbert and Mister Newt think she keeping the mouse in the fiddle case just for them. So what they decide to do is to work together and see if they can both get Miss Agata to let them interfere with her.

But the thing is, Mister Newt was just a-tricking Mister Elbert. Yes, sir, the truth is that Mister Newt got his eye on Miss Canaan, and Miss Canaan knowed it for sure and is already 'greeable. So what Mister Newt decide to do is to do the talking for Mister Elbert when it come to ole Miss Agata, and he start to telling her just how shy his friend Mister Elbert is, but how he hear Miss Canaan a-boasting in private that Mister Elbert know moren anybody how to make a woman smile to her own self. Now that hussy Miss Agata, she licking all that up like the cream, and she starting to get 'greeable. So Mister Newt, he tell ole Mister Elbert that he just 'bout got him fixed up. All Mister Elbert gotta do he say, is to wait till the evening on a Sunday and when they ain't nobody 'bout, he meet with Miss Agata up at the big house they building on the hill.

Now Mister Elbert, he wagging like a dog with two tails, and he can hardly wait for that Sunday night. And Mister Newt, he tell Mister Elbert not to worry none, 'cause same time he going 'round to see Miss Agata, he get his own self up to Mister Elbert's house and make some 'scuses to Miss Canaan 'bout where Mister Elbert gone and what he a-doing. Ole Mister Elbert, fool to his own self, swallow that story and don't even taste the hook.

Well, sir, Sunday night come and it's a-raining to beat the band. The thundering and the lightninging is flying like the Judgement Day, and Miss Agata, just like a ole cat, don't want to get herself rained on, so 'stead of going up the hill to that big empty house, she go on home like nothing happening. But just like he figured, Mister Elbert high tail it up that hill in the dark and he get in a window at the house, and he sit in there a-waiting for Miss Agata, 'cause he don't know she ain't a-coming.

Same time as all that, Mister Newt slip on down the road to Mister Elbert's house and he get right in the kitchen door, and Miss Canaan, she get him up the steps just like they kids in the church-house, and they having a big time upstairs 'fore they both know it.

Course, 'fore long Mister Elbert think Miss Agata ain't a-coming, and he just like a hungry dog, so he come right smart down the hill again to his own house. Now Miss Canaan and Mister Newt still 'bout they business and they don't hear Mister Elbert come in, till he shout out, Canaan? Wheren the Sam Hill are ya?

Now ole Mister Newt sure got hisself a problem. He grab up all the things he ain't got on and climb out the door on the sleeping porch 'fore Mister Elbert can get hisself up them steps. Miss Canaan just 'bout get herself covered up and in the bed when Mister Elbert come in the door.

What y'all doing in bed now? he say.

I just a-waiting for you, honey, she say.

Ole Newt been 'round yare to tell ya bout me a-going up to that big house again? he say.

I ain't seen nothing of him, she say. Why don't y'all just get out of them wet clothes? I get ya something warm to put on.

Now when she get out of that bed and Mister Elbert see she ain't got much on, and she all warm and her hair down, and his own boiler 'bout to bust with the steam, he grab hold of her, and down she go on that bed again. While they in they business, ole Mister Newt climb down the sleeping porch and get hisself on home.

Next day, they both coughing like groundhogs and the fever make they faces red. Mister Elbert say ole Miss Agata never did come to that big house. Mister Newt say maybe they got to try again next Sunday.

June 15, 1964

7.45am. Feels like yesterday all over. Humidity growing & thermometer heading for 70 degrees.

9am. All four men & JJ here today. Too hot for tray, so took them root beer. JJ thrilled. His favorite, he said. They are building racks & shelves & tables etc inside stable & framing doors.

1pm. Stable looking lovely inside. Marce & Rip working on doors. Radio playing. Took them ice water.

2.15pm. 90 degrees out there. Sky mostly blue, but clouds over South Mountain getting higher.

4.45pm. Raining now, but not as hard as yesterday. Less thunder, or farther away, anyhow. Men gone. Davy & John John in the back of the truck holding torn tarpaulin over their heads. I wonder if those two are friends?

10.30pm. Cooler this evening & quite pleasant now.

June 16, 1964

7.45am. Warm & breezy this morning. Quite gray.

9.15am. All working like yesterday. Doors going on now. Radio playing.

1pm. Inside of stable looks done. Marce & Dicky Bird now finishing doors. Rip & Davy & John John gone to wash house for some project or other.

5pm. Stable doors up, & whole building looks ready to paint inside & out. Others were working on door & woodwork at wash house. Door looks like it is completely new.

10.30pm. 60s & 70s all day. A little rain this evening, but not much.

June 17, 1964

7.30am. Only 50 degrees this morning. Lovely sunshine breaking up the clouds.

9am. Men divided up today. Marce & Davy & John John painting the stable walls outside. Dicky Bird & Rip painting the tin roof at the wash house. (Woodwork not done, I think?) Radio is with Marce at the stable, so Rip gets to hear Dicky Bird explaining how he's got the picture she gave to him & that it's signed with love, just like it used to be; but the only thing different, the only thing new, is he's got the picture, but … the other guy has got her.

12.30pm. Wash house roof all painted, Dicky Bird & Rip are now on the stable roof, painting away. The ladders are barely long enough, so Davy & John John are stuck holding them. (I suppose the long ladders have gone back. Too long anyway?)

5pm. Went over to see them off this evening. John John cleaning brushes, others tidying up. All are filthy with paint.

6.30pm. Joanie & Paul playing this evening. Autoharp & fiddle.

10.30pm. Stunning day today. Temperature only in the mid 70s & clear sunshine.

June 18, 1964

9.15am. This morning, Dicky Bird & Davy are painting the stables, DB outside & D inside. Marce & Rip are finishing the woodwork on the wash house. John John is helping his dad, who is making him drive nails & telling him why he looks like a girl doing it.

    *Dicky Bird belting it out in the heavy air how he's had six days on the road, but he's gonna make it home tonight.

492

2pm. 87 degrees now. Took them root beer. John John in The Patch. Woodwork on wash house getting a paint outside.

5.30pm. Men slightly late leaving on account of wash house painting. John John spared clean up as there is more to do tomorrow.

8pm. Just inside from sitting on the Mary House porch, listening to J & P playing. Dulcimer & fiddle tonight. I'm ½ afraid that my clothes will no longer fit, as the mosquito bites have added a dress size to my arms, legs, neck etc.

10.45pm. Weather today much like yesterday but much warmer this afternoon. More humid.

June 19, 1964

7.45am. Going to be a hot one today again. It's 70 degrees out there already. Feels humid too.

9am. Marce & Rip in the wash house painting the interior white, one upstairs & one down. Others in the stable, still painting inside.

*Marce came with a six-pack of Pepsi that he put in the small stream near the wash house.

1pm. Painting everywhere. Doors on stable open. Wash house doors & window open.

*Evidently, without air, Dicky Bird cannot sing.

3pm. 92 degrees now. Too hot to work, I thought I'd read, but cannot concentrate at this hour, as it feels wrong.

5pm. Men gone now. Everything looks painted to me. But John John tells me the stable trim needs doing & the floor. Wash house inside needs a second coat.

*I asked him, almost with mischief, what he's doing tomorrow. —Cleaning out the corn crib, he said. Then I said, what about Sunday (Father's Day)? —Goin' for a drive, prob'ly, he said. Get some cherries, maybe.

11pm. Sunny all day & hot. Sound like very light rain falling now. Watched "Route 66".

June 20, 1964

8.15am. Another hot one in store, I think. Drizzle dying away now. 67 degrees.

2pm. 93 degrees. Got a letter from Sis. She has a good memory. Not much inventiveness, but a good memory.

*I mustn't criticize, as she means to be kind. Her message of hope is welcome, of course it is.

*Went to the A & P ($19). I was going to go to the bookstore but had such a strange experience in the parking lot that I changed my mind & came home. I saw a young man who, I think, looked just like Alex. My heart went straight into my throat & I had to steady myself against the cart. Did he look like Alex? If I saw Alex right now, would he look like Alex to me? Of course, Alex would probably not think this other young man resembled him at all. Then it came to me: Who am I waiting for? Who is Alex? He cannot be who he was. (As I hope not to be the person I was.) Thinking this fills me with the same hope & expectation I felt about him before he was born. I am ready to love my son, whoever he is. I hope he will love me.

4.30pm. Clouds coming in from the southwest.

5.45pm. Thunder thudding from the south & towards Frederick. Shakes the windows sometimes. Rain in sheets.

7.30pm. Storm over. From the window, plants look battered a bit.

10.45pm. Very much the beginning of summer today. Watched Channel 4 movie.

June 21, 1964

7am. Up early this morning. Quite warm, even with windows open. 67 now.

    *Today is Fathers' Day. It is also the one-year anniversary of the day I received the letter telling me of Alex's disappearance. I will write again to Sis, as our letters seem to have crossed, & thank her for remembering me. Us.

    *Happy Fathers' Day, Tom.

9.45am. Watched the churchgoers all go by, clean as a parade, joyful in their duties. Celebrating them, even.

12pm. Spoke to everyone on their walk home. Told the ladies about my cooking plans. They all smiled. —What y'all making good today? Cinch asked. I told her fricassee of chicken with eggs & cream; carrots, green beans & mashed potatoes. I said I was making an apple pie too. —Ain't you something? she said. Then she leaned over close & rolled her eyes to me, —Ya eat all that you're gonna get fat! Then she giggled. She was wearing pale mint green with emerald-colored beads.

2pm. Grown windy & clouds coming again from the southwest. Hot too. Over 90 at lunchtime.

4.45pm. Drizzle blowing on the wind now. Lightning in the distance, but no thunder yet.

    *Lunch later than usual today, which was fine as it was a little cooler. The food was wonderful, but I am prostrate with fullness. I can still hear Cinch giggling.

6pm. Too full still to eat anything this evening. Drank tea.

8.30pm. Wrote letter to Sis & tried not to sentimentalize too much about Alex. Also afraid to say too much about how I feel now, as I don't think she'd understand. Will read some, I think.

11pm. Storm never really developed. Cuckoo's Nest painfully good. What would Tom say about my reading it? Somehow, I think he would find a way to scoff AND to be hurt, thinking that I no longer cared that he had pain of his own. What he wouldn't understand is that though my reading it hurts me, it is a curative of sorts. Like pulling a tooth that needs pulling.

*Sorry, Tom, if I've got that all wrong, today of all days. Go on forgiving me like you used to. I still need it.

June 22, 1964

7.45am. Very hot this morning. 72. Sky the colour of cornflowers.

9.15am. Truck on The Common. Marce (with more Pepsis) painting the inside of the upper floor of the wash house another coat of white (walls, floor, ceiling, wood); Rip doing the same downstairs. Radio blares. Dicky Bird & Davy painting the trim on the stable a bright brick red. John John is tending a junk fire in the other corner of The Patch.

*DB on his ladder sings that he knows she's been foolin' 'round on him right from the start.

1.30pm. Hot out there now. Took them lemonade. Two sets now, as they are separate. Both wash house floors being painted light gray. Stable trim looking well advanced. John John has disappeared. Probably ran off to join the circus. Couldn't blame him.

5pm. Men gone. John John not with them. Marce & Rip helped with stable trim, & it all looks good now.

10.30pm. Beautiful day, dry, sunny & upper 80s. watched "Wagon Train" rerun. J & P played earlier, even after dark. Dulcimer & guitar in the star light.

June 23, 1964

7.45am. Hot again this morning: 70. Quite foggy though.

9am. Marce & Rip second-coating wash house floors. Dicky Bird & Davy second-coating stable trim. John John not with them.

1.15pm. Not quite as hot today. All hands on stable trim except for Davy, who is painting stable floor gray.

4.45pm. Men gone now. Looks like everyone helped on stable floor, which is now uniformly gray, & all the stuff is outside, what is left of it, under a tarpaulin.

11pm. Turned into a nice day, as the fog melted. Humid, but only 83. No music tonight down the road.

June 24, 1964

7.30am. Hot again this morning. 70. Foggy.

9am. Dicky Bird & Rip painting the stable floor a second coat. Davy helping Marce (& John John) measure something around the edge of The Patch. JJ writing down what Marce says to him.

11am. Marce & JJ gone in the truck. Davy digging holes at the far edge of The Patch.

1pm. Marce & JJ back. All four men digging holes, JJ passing them different tools sometimes, & sometimes spearing the holes with a long heavy steel rod. This is part of the process, it seems.

3pm. 88 degrees. Light breeze sometimes puffs. All the men look as though they've been sandpapered & then varnished.

4.15pm. Men left early today. Long line of holes on the far side of The Patch.

7pm. J & P playing happily on the quiet evening air. Guitar & autoharp this time.

*I have asked them, in the past, about the songs, all of which have such haunting names: "Sandy River Belle", "Yellow Barber", "Shelving Rock", "June Apple" etc.

10.15pm. Beautiful almost all day, but pretty hot. Gorgeous round moon tonight, like a soap bubble.

It was a mighty bright light that was shining down.

That second time the Seseshes come on big up from Virginia, in the summer, we seen lots of 'em. They look dirtier than ever and they took to stealing most anything they could find to eat, kicking down the sweet tater hills, pulling up the onions. Trouble was, my garden – I calls it mine 'cause it was me that done the planting and the weeding and the picking, though it was the whole garden for the big house and all – set right side the road, so they could see it when they rode past. Last we seen of 'em that year was 'bout the time they fighting cross the mountain at Funkstown. Cannons a-booming for days and days. Well, it was 'tween them days and the Thanksgiving the next year when the 'mancipation took hold good that Mister Asa Main get his eye on Charlotta.

Now Mister Asa ain't no real bad sort of fella or nothing and I always felt little sorry for him. He and his sister Miss Temperance the only children they mama had for she up and died of the tumours, and they live with they daddy up the Harmony road right 'round the bend from the big house. They daddy a mean ole man and he keep Mister Asa sucking the hind tit his whole life. Miss Temperance don't 'tract no husband of her own, and she busy nursing the ole man till 'bout the time the war start when he died too, and got buried by the Lutherans. Anyway, Mister Asa was the 'countant at The Corner, and every day he set there on the ground floor doing the 'counts and dealing with the folks coming and going to buy the flour and the cornmeal and all, and every day his life he busy falling in love with somebody or other. He don't seem to 'scriminate 'tween 'em at all – widowed or married, pretty or ugly, they all the same to him, 'cause he nice to everybody, and he think every time one of them women so much as smile or nod they head she ready to up and run off with him. He fall in love with half the women in Harmony and up and down the valley, and the time his daddy die they ain't no more women left for him to fall in love with and half the hair on his head gone and the other half greyer than it is black. Miss Temperance 'bout as nice as him too, only she don't take on so lonely. I could see him from the Mary House sometimes, I be sitting on the porch twisting yarn weasels and he be over there a-smiling and a yes-ma'aming all them women that don't think no more of him than they think 'bout the chicken they eat for supper.

Anyway, after they daddy die, Miss Temperance come 'round sometimes and sit in an evening and say how-do, nice as you please, and make a body feel like they got kin when they ain't got none. I give her things I make, like herbs for the pot liquor and a broom for the porch. And she always treat me fine. I see though that 'fore long she starting to get worried 'bout Mister Asa, and she coming 'round moren she used to, just to see him at work. So I starts to looking to. And what do I see?

Well, sir, next house up the road from them is where ole Miss Brandenburg live and she real ole and she ain't got no kin of her own, but what she is got is a servant gal name Charlotta. Charlotta 'bout the same age as me, only she pretty and I ain't, and she do all that Miss Brandenburg needs doing. Now 'bout the time the spring comes, she outside moren she was, and with the days getting longer Mister Asa like to walk home every day and get his dinner for he come back to The Corner till time to go home. Well, 'fore long, Mister Asa lonely eye start to find itself looking at ole

Charlotta. Maybe 'cause he ain't got no daddy a-telling him what to do no more, or 'cause he run out of white women to love, but he start to thinking maybe he done find somebody in Charlotta. 'Fore long, he starting to watch her moren ever, and Charlotta 'bout as innocent as a child, and don't know nothing 'bout it. But I knows it, and I ain't the only one. Miss Temperance begins to know it too. She don't say nothing, but I know she knows it, 'cause she starting to watch him like he a child his own self.

Well, Miss Brandenburg, she like her roses and she got so many of 'em, they climb all over her porch till 'bout half the sun don't get in no more, so she tell Charlotta she got to cut down some they roses or they can't see out no more. Miss Temperance, she see Charlotta out there on a ladder getting her hands cut up like skun rabbits and she don't think nothing 'bout going over cross they fence and letting Charlotta borrow her garden gloves, just to get the job done. 'Bout then, Mister Asa coming home for his dinner and he look and see Charlotta up there on the ladder and he a-looking and a-looking, and what he see but Miss Temperance gloves on that girl? Charlotta, she turn 'round and she give a wave to Mister Asa, and she say, Y'all want some of these here rose clippings? And she get down and gather up some of them roses, and she walk over and hand some to him. He reach down and try to take 'em, but them gloves makes her all clumsy and she drops 'em. She try to pick em up, and he do to, and them gloves touch his hand. Then he just stand there looking for a minute, and don't say nothing, but all a sudden he shake like the wind blowing cold. Miss Temperance, she seen it too, and it give her a idea.

Next morning it's already hot before the sun even up good, and Miss Temperance, she tell Mister Asa he don't need to come home for his dinner, 'cause she bring it down to The Corner, and he have it there, cause it's cool on that floor where he do the 'counting. So when Mister Asa gone, Miss Temperance, she see Charlotta outside and she say, How them hands y'all this morning? And Charlotta say the scratches is good, but her fingers done half green with the juice. And Miss Temperance say, Then I give you a present. And she retch in her pocket and she pulls out some little ole cake of sweet-smelling soap, and she tell Charlotta she gots to wash her hands over and over with that. And Charlotta, she say she do. Next thing, dinner time come, and Miss Temperance, she put Mister Asa dinner in a ole cream can, and she go on out there and she find Charlotta in the pole beans, and she say, Charlotta, y'all do something for me? Y'all take this here can down to The Corner for Mister Asa and give it to him? It's his dinner. Now 'fore y'all take it, make sure you wash them hands of yourn with that soap, ya hear?

And Charlotta did. When she get down to The Corner, she go on in and give that can to Mister Asa and he look real surprised that Miss Temperance don't come her own self. But he look at Charlotta funny for a minute and you can see he thinking something. He took up the can and smelled it, handle and all, and he look at Charlotta. He shuck his head, and smiled polite, and Charlotta, she go on home.

Next day not near as hot as the one before, and while Mister Asa down at The Corner, Miss Temperance sit herself on the porch and start to singing songs to herself. 'Fore long, Charlotta come out with the washing to hang up and she hear that singing. What y'all singing, Miss Temperance? she say. I'm a-singing my favourite song, she say. Y'all want me to teach it to ya? And Miss Temperance, she teach the whole song to Charlotta, and she even 'gree to help her hang out the washing.

That evening, Mister Asa come home, and what you think he hear when he get up that road? Everything quiet, 'cept he hear Charlotta sitting on Miss Brandenburg's porch, shucking the peas and a-singing and a-singing that song Miss Temperance done teach her. He 'most run into that house of hisn.

Next day another hot one, and Miss Temperance say to Charlotta gain, Y'all take Mister Asa his dinner for me 'gain today? And Charlotta say, Something sure smell good? What y'all put in that ole can for him this time? And Miss Temperance, she say, I make us a black raspberry cobbler, cause Mister Asa like it bettern anything.

Same thing happen down The Corner. Charlotta give the can to Mister Asa and he look like a wasp get tween his eyes he a-blinking so hard.

Well, next day a Saturday, and on Saturday all the folks, white folks and servants, works in the morning and takes the afternoon for resting and socializing, 'specially when the days getting hot. Mister Asa, he work all that morning in The Corner like always. Meantime, up the road, Miss Temperance outside on the porch trying to get some ironing done where they might be a breeze blowing, and cross the fence, Charlotta got the same idea on Miss Brandenburg's porch.

What y'all ironing? Charlotta say.

Well, Charlotta, Miss Temperance say, I think I a-wasting my time on this ole thing. And she hold up a calico dress. What y'all think? she say. It's right pretty, I say, Charlotta say. You think so? Miss Temperance say. I tell you what, she say. I'm a-gonna give this dress to you, 'cause I don't like it no more. Charlotta, she bout die, 'cause she love dresses and Miss Brandenburg don't give her none but 'bout two a year.

After dinner, and after folks have they nap, pretty soon they all starts to gather down the common front of the Mary House and The Corner and get the loafing started. White folks like to stand 'round under the walnut trees and under the high porch and talk 'bout they things. The servants all goes down cross the creek side the Mary House in the shade of the walnuts and the maples and pitch horseshoes. Some of the white folks come with lemonade and ice tea and I don't know what all.

Well, Mister Asa, he standing over by the creek a-talking with the others when who he see coming down the road 'cept Charlotta, and she got on that dress that Miss Temperance up and give her. She walk on down and over the bridge front the Mary House, and stand side the folks watching the horseshoes.

Mister Asa, he look like the hand of God His Own Self done retch in his pocket and took hold of him. He look and look and 'fore long, he 'scuse hisself and go on back up the road. Miss Temperance, she come down later and say he got a headache or something.

That's just 'bout the end of it all. That Thanksgiving we all stop being servants. 'Fore that though, Mister Asa start toting his own dinner down to The Corner every day. 'Fore Christmas, Miss Brandenburg die, and Charlotta get her free papers anyhow and a bunch of money from Miss Brandenburg's will, and she take it and move herself to Frederick. 'Bout ten year later, Mister Asa marry a widow whose husband and son die in the war, and they go on living with Miss Temperance up the Harmony road. Miss Temperance outlive 'em all.

June 25, 1964

7.15am. Not quite so hot this morning, but still over 60.

8.30am. Men digging holes & measuring. Sometimes Davy helps John John carry the bigger things inside the stable, as he is clearing up tools & supplies.

9.30am. Ingalls truck has pulled in with a load of posts & boards. Usual driver & assistant. Going over to watch.

11am. Ingalls truck gone. All of that is fencing for The Patch. No conversations to report, but I saw Marce give BOTH (!) the Ingalls men Pepsis to take away.

1pm. Marce busy "planting" posts, as are Rip & Dicky Bird (a job that leaves him no breeze for singing). John John has been sent to scrounge up thin strips of wood, though I don't know why.

5pm. Men gone on time today, & I've had a look around. Rip & John John spent some time piling the fence boards inside the stable, with the strips between layers of planks. The others put in the posts. The stable looks very good, & the wash house is just as good as it can be. Both have some of the men's things piled in them.

*Rolled up in a bucket of tools in the wash house, under some rags, was a Penthouse magazine. I didn't touch it.

10.30pm. Another wonderful day, with the high just over 80. Sunshine into every corner. Watched "Rawhide" rerun. No music tonight.

June 26, 1964

7.15am. Cooler this morning, mid 50s. Cloudless sky.

8.45am. John John not here this morning, but the others in The Patch. Davy digs holes, Dicky Bird & Rip insert posts; Marce seems to be cutting & fitting boards on the corner, including some sort of bracing.

12.45pm. Work the same as before. Marce has done one corner & almost done a second one. I took them ice tea again.

5.15pm. Men left a little later this evening. All four corners now have boards joining up three posts to make right angles.

*John John showed up in time to get a lift home. I saw him arrive & asked what he'd been up to. —Seein' a friend, he said. —What did you do all day? I asked. —Nothing much, he said. Built a fort.

10.30pm. Perfect summer day again, though nearly 90 this afternoon. Watched "Route 66".

June 27, 1964

8am. Cool mid 50s now & drizzling.

2pm. Over 90 degrees now, & air mushroomy with dampness. Back from A & P ($15).

3pm. 95 degrees! Butterflies dancing over the garden; bees whirring near the roof & around the porch; dragonflies hovering robotically over the creeks.

4.30pm. Drinking iced tea.

7.30pm. Just back from a session of sitting on the high porch at The Corner, listening to the music (dulcimer & fiddle) & thinking. Something inside me is waiting for the right moment to move in to that house. That thought has only just come to me tonight. The house itself is as ready as it will ever be. So what am I waiting for? I think I am waiting for the work to finish altogether, as somehow, the outside & inside of all of this feels to me to be connected in a way I hadn't imagined before. I echoed all over these big empty rooms, stuffy with closed windows, smelling new & old at the same time. The whole place waits for me to enliven it. I want so much to enliven it. But I can't do that just yet. I looked down from up there at the tiny Mary House, where I have lived for most of a year. It is a place of spirits, each one dear to me. I know that when I move over the road, they won't move with me. I know I will be left on my own in The Corner until Alex comes home. Maybe even after. So for now I am waiting for the last pieces of the puzzle to be put in place. So far, I have put it together in the darkness, & I am not yet ready to turn the lights on. I have trusted myself this far, so I will a little longer. If I do, then I know it will be all right.

11.15pm. Simply too hot today. Frogs singing in the streams!

8am. A beautiful morning with the sky like a carnation in clouds of pink, lavender & white. 60 degrees.

2pm. Missed the whole usual Sunday morning routine because on an impulse I drove over to Sharpsburg & drove around the Antietam battlefield. I stood at the Dunker Church & the Miller cornfield, I walked down Bloody Lane & over Burnside's Bridge. I was almost the only person there. I did this as a kind of homage to Alex, maybe to men generally. It is a beautiful place, still growing corn, wheat & hay. But there are monuments everywhere, granite statues of sombre men, rigid horses & long lists of sons, fathers, & brothers who died in agony & whose survivors hoped that somehow that agony won't be forgotten. I am an intelligent woman & I cannot understand any of it. Not the fighting, not the remembering. Would I mind if Alex were forgotten? No one who loves him will ever forget him. What is the memory of strangers worth?

*I did this for you, Alex, not even knowing why. Doing it, without knowing why, brought me nearer to you. It has also healed something inside me that I didn't even know was injured. I am grateful, always grateful, for impulses that inspire me to overcome confusion. Someday, we may talk about this.

6pm. Made an elaborate early dinner today from the cookbook. Broiled salmon with walnut catsup; fried potatoes with salt & celery vinegar; green peas & lettuce with flour & sugar. Completely delicious.

8.15pm. Took Joanie & Paul samples of the sago pudding I made, and had it with them on their porch, drinking tea, & listening to them play the guitar & dulcimer. Joanie showed me how to hold the dulcimer, & it is almost like looking at a child. A beautiful evening.

10.30pm. Such a nice day. Only upper 80s & not so sticky.

June 29, 1964

7.30am. Cooler this morning, mid 50s. Sky light beige with the sunrise earlier.

9am. Men & boy all at work, truck parked at the edge of The Patch. Everybody working on the fence. Radio near Marce, as he is working on a gate. At the other end, Dicky Bird is smugly intoning that just because he asks a friend about her, just because he spoke her name somewhere, just because he went all to pieces, she thinks he still cares.

11am. Fence joining up in places. Took them lemonade, as it is getting hot.

2.30pm. 92 degrees.

*Rip was helping Marce lift his new gate up to settle on the upright pins which, I guess, act as hinges, while John John was supposed to steer the gate's other hinge halves (like giant paper clips) on to the upright pegs so that they could lower the gate on to its place. It was tricky because the gate is heavy & the men wobbled it about, & quite rightly, JJ didn't want to get his hands pinched when they released the heavy gate, so he struggled to line them up (especially as there are two hinges that have to go on at the same time precisely). I came up & stood behind them, just in time to hear Marce say to John John, -J[]s[]s Chr[]st! If ya can't do this in the G[]d-d[]mn daylight, how ya ever gonna f[]ck a woman in the dark?

*Both Rip & John John saw me, & then the gate suddenly lined up & fell in place. All three brushed their hands together, to clean them, & restore feeling, I imagine. Rip looked furthest away, John John was watching me & biting his lip, blushing & he walked off. Marce just shook his head, turned enough to see me in the corner of his eye, & muttered to Rip, –That boy ain't worth a good G[]d d[]mn.

4.45pm. Men left a little early today. All look sunburnt. I don't think John John & his father spoke to one another the rest of the afternoon.

10.45pm. Beautiful day again, but much hotter this afternoon. No music tonight.

June 30, 1964

7.45am. Set to be a scorcher today. Radio enthusiastically predicts 100 degrees. 66 at the moment.

9am. Men all at work, minus John John. All working on the fence again. Hammering & sawing. Radio blasts away.

1.30pm. Fence ¾ done now. Took them ice tea.

2.30pm. 96 degrees.

*In the paper that the ridiculous Republicans have issued a statement to say that a victory in Vietnam is "urgently required". Unbelievable. Peace is going to be the only victory we will ever gain there, & no one seems to know what that looks like.

5.30pm. Men slightly late leaving, as they finished the last of the boards. Marce pulled the truck out, & Davy latched the gate. All built now.

11pm. Fiery in the sun this afternoon, & humidity getting worse again. J & P played fiddle & autoharp tonight. Finished Cuckoo's Nest. Cried for them & everyone else I know & have ever known. Such beauty in them all.

July 1, 1964

7am. Going to be very hot today. Already 72 degrees! I woke up earlier & saw a groundhog in the garden.

8.30am. Marce arrived on time & parked the truck on the edge of The Patch, unloading dozens of cans of paint, brushes etc. John John is with them this morning, & they are organizing themselves. I brought their usual tray, which they seemed to welcome.

9.15am. Ingalls truck just arrived & has parked on the land just opposite the Mary House, beside the iron bridge. Going to watch.

10.00am. Just back. Marce, Rip & Dicky Bird helped to unload posts, siding, lumber & coils of wire fencing. Marce up to his usual standard. He asked the young black man, —Hey. Y'all got chickens down your way? —No, sir, he said. My wife'd like to get some, but we ain't got any yet. —Uh huh, Marce said. —She fry chicken? Marce asked. —Yes, sir, she does. —Uh huh. Then Marce looked around trying to make eye contact with everyone he could. —I bet she does, he said. Neither Rip nor Dicky Bird acknowledged him, but I thought I saw Rip look at DB with warning in his eyes. The driver shot Marce a glance & then caught the young black man's eye with a look I read as let it go, let it go.

12.30pm. Hot in the sun now. Just back after delivering lemonade. Davy & John John have been joined by Dicky Bird & all three are painting the fence around The Patch a black-brown color. It looks like hard work, as the wood is rough. Meanwhile, Marce & Rip have got a kind of workshop set up under the shade of the maple, apple & walnut trees & are building my new chicken coop.

2.30pm. 93 degrees out there now. Sky like a tight blue sheet. Dicky Bird, on his own at his bit of fence, sings winsomely about cool clear water (?).

*Have been thinking of ways to keep myself involved with the local ladies. I must ask about quilting. I think that if I took up quilting, my time would seem (to them) less like it was spent simply waiting for Alex to come home. Perhaps, it would be.

4.45pm. Men just left. John John has surely got sunburn, as must Davy. I walked over to visit Davy & John John before they left. I asked Davy how his wife was. —Fine, he said. Fixin' to can peaches. I had moved in JJ's direction when Marce arrived. He snapped the brush from JJ's hand, telling him to look at the G[]d-d[]mn thing & how much G[]d-d[] mn paint he was wasting. John John is a slower painter than both Davy & Dicky Bird.

11pm. Beautiful sultry day. Gardened in the shade when I could find any. Leaves stick to the skin. Saw a lovely tortoise! Brownish orange. Quite a shy fellow.

July 2, 1964

6.45am. Sunny, no breeze & 71 out there. Another hot one coming. No groundhog, but birds singing everywhere.

9am. Everyone working like yesterday. John John wearing a baseball cap today.

11.00am. Overheard Rip & Dicky Bird through the window. Rip —Stable looks pretty don't it? Bet there ain't been a horse there'n fifty years. Dicky Bird – Wonder when she'll move ole Trigger in?

1pm. Back with tray, having taken over a pitcher of ice tea. Dicky Bird giving musical advice, telling the whole of Harmony that when they feel like they're in love, they shouldn't just stand there.

4pm. Tea in spite of the heat. I think it would be a very good thing to coax as many stories of old times out of the locals as I can. They seem very willing to talk. I think if I knew more of what they know, they'd feel a little safer with me. It also might explain their outlook & actions a little better.

5pm. Everyone gone now. Chicken coop panels all look done & ready to put together. Also there seems to be a set of roosts & laying boxes built. Patch fence about half-painted.

6.45pm. Joanie & Paul strumming away. Paul's guitar sounds so soothing on the warm air, an instrument of the valleys. Joanie's dulcimer has come down from the hills, more shy, lighter of foot.

11pm. Sunshine all day & 90 this afternoon.

July 3, 1964

8.15am. Men not working today, as it is a holiday (4th of July tomorrow). Hot again today. Already 70.

1.45pm. Just back, sticky & tired in the feet & legs. Made a fool deal with myself that I would walk to the top of one of the mountainside roads, thinking it would be something to talk about. So I went all the way up the Coxey Brown. Very steep in places. The view 1/3 the way up is breath-taking. At least, I had no breath. I'm pretty sure I could see all the way to Harper's Ferry. There is a plateau about ½ way along, & a big farm. Cabins in the woods in places, barking dogs, hub caps, tyres, rusting cars, galvanized tubs, ropes, hoses, woodpiles. I saw a bushel-sized hornets' nest, but only one human to speak to. He was an old man with only two teeth in his lower jaw. He told me not to go down "the Fishers

Lodge t'wards the holla, cowse there was a bear'n her cub down n'are". There was nothing to see at the top of the mountain itself, as the trees are taller than houses. I thought I heard a snake once.

2.15pm. 92 degrees now. I've cleaned up, but too hot to eat still.

   *In the paper today that yesterday the president has signed the Civil Rights Bill into law. Let this be the sunrise on a new day for all of us.

11.15pm. Sunny & dry all day. Watering everything now, especially peas, lettuce, beans & tomatoes (where that tortoise has taken some bites of the low ones…). Spinach is shot. Everything else looks great.
   *Watched "Route 66".

July 4, 1964

7.30am. Another warm start & the air greasy with humidity. 70 degrees. Stiff legs this morning.

8.15am. Drizzling.

2pm. Came home to find everything wet from rain. Garden is sprinkled with opalescent & rainbow pearls in this light.
   *Went to bookstore & got two from the display: A Death in the Family by James Agee & The Edge of Sadness by Edwin O'Connor. Time I caught up with these, & I'm in the mood for both.
   *Went to A & P ($15) & found a hardware store called Quinn's. Bought some more flower pots.

4.15pm. Tea tastes good this afternoon.

10pm. Fireworks sounding above South Mountain, fired off the old Washington Monument. Easy to see from the hill on the Hollow Road.

*When I walked over the iron bridge on the Hollow Road, just before the Common, I looked up at The Corner. I thought that if I wanted to, I could go in there at that moment, walk around, turn on all the lights, dance, sing, take off my clothes. All this in a second. Then my heart gave a thud, & my throat magically tightened. I think it was fear. But of what? I came into the Mary House & the smallness welcomed me. Somehow, I need to move this peacefulness over the road.

*Not quite as hot today. Upper 80s.

July 5, 1964

7.15am. Cooler & less humid today, though over 60 now.

8am. Perfect morning to garden, so not going to miss it.

10am. Break for coffee. Saw the ladies & gents on their way to church. I made a point of speaking to all & sundry, waving my dirty gardening gloves, courting their patient disapproval. I am the Edna Pontellier of Harmony. My sin is non-conformity. Cinch, resplendent in lime-green with sapphire-like beads, said, –Y'ain't come to get your geraniums yet. I told her to look after them for me, & I'd get them soon.

12.30pm. Couldn't resist washing myself up presentably & making a tray of lemonade for them on their walk home. Three of the men had some (one downing it in a shot), but about ½ the women did. The talk is all about hay, corn growth ("knee-high by the 4th of July"), spoiled children, raspberries, the price of sandals, best pickle recipes, hair that won't curl in the humidity, & whether it is acceptable to sell kerosene for hurricane lamps when it's getting harder to find wicks (evidently, some people are hoarding).

*Cinch told me –'Deed, I better get up there & get them geraniums or them cats a-his'n (her husband?) is gonna dig 'em all up. I said, I'd get them tomorrow morning.

3pm. Made myself another fine meal from my cookbook: Rock fish battered with a hint of nutmeg; horseradish sauce; buttered turnips & beet tops. Delicious. I hope the previous owner of the book, is as pleased as I am. Have these walls smelled these smells before?

5pm. Just in. The locals got together for an impromptu horse-shoe match in the little field beside where my chickens will live. I joined the ladies, while the children stoned anything that would float in the two creeks. I took some teasing about the chicken coop: –Gonna re-name this road Pennsylvania Avenue! –Where them chickens gonna park their cars? Then they started on the stable, mostly wanting to know whether I really could ride a horse, & what kind was I going to get.

  *They also wanted to know how soon I'm moving in to The Corner. I was so stunned by the question, I couldn't quite speak. Cinch came to my rescue, –Soon as she's durn good'n ready. Maybe when her boy comes. They'll be a big time then. The others nodded & she looked at them all one by one. For a small woman (5' or so) there was a fierceness about her eyes, just above a smile, that made me think suddenly how deeply she felt all this. I answered, finally, that I hadn't decided, but I was waiting until it all felt right. Their glances met fleetingly, each one communicating that I was to be thought of like a town-bred eccentric, handicapped but not dangerous.

8.30pm. Joanie & Paul just gone in. Auto-harp & fiddle.

10.45pm. Wonderful day, only just over 80, & a soft breeze.

  *I am almost ashamed to say, because of the kooky sound of this, that I don't think I can move in to The Corner until the Mary House is ready to let me go. Perhaps, now that I think this, I will remember to look out for the signs that the time is right.

July 6, 1964

7am. Much cooler today, only 52. Still less humid too, like yesterday.

9am. Everyone at work as usual this morning. Marce parked on The Common. Rip & Marce assembling chicken coop, Dicky Bird, Davy & John John painting.

12pm. Just back from my first visit to Cinch's house. Not at all what I expected. The gravel road (behind my new stable) climbs up the hill & is so rutted I cannot see how anyone could get a car up there. The house itself is wood & bricks, every part of it looking as though it was left 4/5 finished before whoever was working on it quit & went fishing. There is an open porch with a washing machine, tables & shelves of flowers (the whole thing draped with huge purple climbing blossoms of some kind), & about 4-10 cats (they keep moving about!), all of which set up a terrible meow when they saw me approach. There were chickens scratching about the flat field, & Cinch, in brown cotton print dress & a pink bonnet (!) was taking dry clothes off a line on the hillside behind us. There were baskets of strawberries, just picked on a bench, in the shade by the porch. She saw me coming, finished taking down the clothes, & came to join me. She saw me looking at the strawberries. –Ain't they purdy? Y'all better take some them with ya. She sat the clothes basket down, laid her hand on top of a huge tabby & said, –Ya can have any them cats ya want to, 'cept this'n. Then she took the two best looking geraniums from the table & handed them to me. –Y'are, she said. –Give 'em a drink when ya get 'em home. She didn't invite me inside, but I knew she wouldn't. With my hands full, & though I'd already said goodbye & walked 10 feet away, she called, –You keep them fellas a-workin, ya hear?

1.15pm. Chicken coop assembled. Marce & Rip measuring perimeter & marking out with string for fencing. Painting goes on in The Patch. Dicky Bird singing a very strange song about how he has a hole in his pocket & he can't go to the fair, & now he's blue because he had a date to meet his baby there. DB painting the gate.

5pm. Men gone now. Dicky Bird joined JJ & D in the truck bed tonight, maybe to cool off. Fence nearly painted. Posts all in.

10.30pm. Another nice day, though a little warmer than yesterday (upper 80s). Watched the channel 4 movie & sorted files of papers.

July 7, 1964

6.45am. Cooler start again today, but the humidity is creeping back. 55 now.

9.15am. All five at work again. Davy & John John are finishing the fence first coat; Dicky Bird is, apparently, giving the fence a second coat. Marce & Rip (in the shade) are painting the chicken coop, Rip painting the inside white, Marce painting the outside red.

1.30pm. 89 degrees now. All three now painting Patch fence a second coat. The three of them have skin a shade between redwood & tea-without-milk. Dicky Bird intoning how he wants to go home to Detroit city. Oh, how he wants to go home. Marce & Rip as before.

5pm. Men gone on time tonight. They look tired. Aching, if that's possible.

*Out of Marce's hearing, I asked John John if he minds working for his dad. —I'd rather be doing other stuff, he said. —What stuff? —Reading, drawing. —When do you get to do those things? I asked. —When it rains, he said. I asked him if he gets paid to help. —I get a allowance, he said. —Do you get more when you help? —No, ma'am, he said. —What do you spend your money on? I asked. —Nothing, he said. I never buy anything.

8pm. Just gone inside. J & P playing tonight, fiddle & dulcimer.

11pm. Sunny & hot & quite humid all day today.

You got to hurry hurry

Sometimes people is wild and sometimes they is forgetful. Now I don't know nothing, but I tell you this: what you don't wanna be is wild and forgetful. No, sir. They was a fella named Josiah Beachley, and he was both. He got one of them big farms up 'yond Harp Hill. They is big farms before and they is big ones after, and his was after. He was wild when he was young and wild when he got old. 'Fore he was married he was one of a bunch of fellas thought they'd have theyselves a horse race down the ole Harmony Road from Ellerton to Harmony. Well, they running for all they worth up that hill from Ellerton till the road flatten out, then she rise again after Fisher's Hollow, and just there where ya top that hill, one them ole mountain roads comes out, and just as them fellas get there another ole man was a turning his spring waggon up the hill and he was blocking the road. All the racing men pull they horses up to a stop, but not ole Mister Josiah. No, sir. He lean up and take that horse a-flying right over that waggon. He and the horse both make it all right, 'cept the horse's hooves done smash up the side of the waggon pretty bad. 'Bout a month later he come down to The Corner on a Saturday afternoon, and the folks all see him, and one of 'em hollers out, Well, sir, Josiah, I hear folks say y'all done killed youself 'bout a month ago jumping a waggon. And Mister Josiah, he just smile and say, I hear that rumour too, 'cept I knowed 'mediately it ain't true.

Anyhow, the wildness never leave him, and when he a ole man he taking some horses in to Frederick to sell em, and he get out there on the East Side, where the trains all is, and he got a foal tied to his own horse with a rope. Well, that foal hear all the whistling and the steaming, and he breaks loose from the rope and runs out on the tracks. So Mister Josiah, he let go his own horse and set off after that foal, only he don't see they a train coming. He grab the foal, sure 'nough, but down he go, and that train run right over his leg, a-cutting it clean off. The tie it up and sew it and that, but he dead 'fore the morning.

Now up on the farm 'bove Harp Hill, they all sad like folk ought to be and that. And they have the funeral at the meeting house and all the folks come and say how sorry they are. Then long come the lawyer fella out of Frederick and he say he got Mister Josiah's will to read. Mister Josiah left behind a widow and two daughters, both of 'em married to farmers somewhere in the county, but I don't know where. So the lawyer, he read the will to the widow and the daughters and they husbands, and they don't know what to do. First thing is, Mister Josiah leave free papers for all the servants, 'bout four five outside, and two in the house. Then they hear he leave five hundred dollar to the meeting house for they cemetery tendance. Then the biggest thing of all, they find that he done mortgage that farm to a family in Myersville, and they got to either find all that money, or up and sell the farm and move theyselves. They ain't nothing else to do.

Now I don't know, but it sure look like Mister Josiah clean forgot either he got a family at all or that some day he have to die, but he sure forgot something, you ask me. The field hands all hires theyselves out for the rest of the year, then most of 'em goes into Frederick for work, and the widow, she move into the house with one of them daughters. The farm got bought by a fella from cross the line, and he don't keep no servants of his own, and he hire men wherever he can find 'em. He not wild at all.

July 8, 1964

7am. Very warm this morning, but foggy too. 67 degrees.

9am. Drizzling now. Dicky Bird, on his own, is painting the inside of the new chicken coop a second coat. The others are setting up a kind of workshop in the stable (where there is already lumber piled). John John is not with them. DB is singing, but I couldn't hear the words.

2.45pm. Drizzle has turned to rain. Took a tray with tea & coffee over to the stable. They are busy making pieces for the picket fence that will surround the garden.

4.15pm. Men already gone. Stable quite cleaned up & straightened. Probably Davy's work. Doors propped open on the chicken coop.

10.45pm. Such a gray day. Just above 80 this afternoon.

*I have thought that I cannot leave the Mary House until I know what it's fate will be. It must not be left alone to wait for my, or anyone else's return. I must feel that it is secure.

July 9, 1964

7.15am. Humid again this morning, mid 60s. Very strange sight this morning. Two turkey buzzards sunning themselves on the stable roof. Huge wings outspread, drying their feathers, I imagine.

9.15am. Dicky Bird, Davy & John John back to work painting the fence around The Patch. Rip is painting the posts for the chicken run (white), while Marce is painting the outside of the coop red. Dicky Bird gilds the air with the lightest mournful lyric of how he's making believe that she still loves him, though she has left him alone & so blue.

*Took a chance & brought them ice tea this morning.

1.45pm. Rip now helping Marce finish the red on the chicken coop.

3.15pm. Marce & Rip are now in The Patch helping with the fence-painting.

4.30pm. Everyone gone now. In his usual clean-up duties, John John gets to be the one to wrap all the brushes in kerosene-soaked rags. Glad he doesn't smoke.

*It's just occurred to me, that none of them smoke. How is it, that after all this time, I've just noticed this?

10.30pm. After a very hazy sunny day a dark moonless night. Over 80 this afternoon.

July 10, 1964

6.30am. Foggy & 61 degrees.

8.45am. Looks like Davy, Dicky Bird & John John are painting the fence, while Rip & Marce second-coat the chicken coop & posts.

*Took them tea & coffee this morning, which seemed to be welcome.

1.45pm. Still a little gloomy looking, but humid & 87 degrees. Took lemonade this time.

5pm. John John came to see me before they left. He said, a little to my surprise, that the fence around The Patch is done now. There is still the trim & the wiring to be done on the chicken coop. But mostly, next week they want to be working on the garden fencing.

*I asked JJ whether he had a dog. He said his mother has. —Named Lady, he said. I asked if they had cats. —Six in the barn & two in the house. He said he likes cats. I asked whether he liked Cinch's cats. He grinned. —You should see them play, he said.

11pm. Very uncomfortable day, like being in a hot damp attic since sun up. Watched "Route 66".

July 11, 1964

7.45am. Much less humid this morning, but over 60.

10.30am. Back from Middletown A & P ($17). Going for another walk this morning, before it gets too hot.

1.30pm. Back from walking. Took my camera up the Hollow Road, then up through Harmony to Fishers' Hollow, then back & up the Brethren Church Road as far as the grave-yard. I'm not sure why I want these pictures, but it seems important to take them. They belong in The Corner & I think Alex would like them there.

   *Only had a light lunch, but I'm making an extravagant dinner.

4pm. Drinking tea & finally reading O'Connor. Mild, long & important.

6.30pm. Having just finished eating. Another cookbook recipe: Baked beef & potatoes (that is, beef pot-roasted with onions & cloves, then sliced & layered with mashed potatoes, swished in gravy & baked); & delicately battered & fried cucumbers & sweetcorn. Absolutely wonderful, & enough left over for days to come. Can't walk!

10.45pm. Sunshine ripe all day today, & only about 80 this afternoon. Some nice gardening time this afternoon, but slightly tired & no breeze at all. Watched the channel 4 movie.

July 12, 1964

7am. A sticky gloomy morning. Gray, foggy & already 70 degrees. The perfect day to read O'Connor.

9.45am. Raining now, but not hard. Few church walkers.

12pm. No real church walkers coming home. A shame, as I wanted to show Cinch how happy her geraniums are.

*Leftovers for lunch.

4pm. Drizzling again. More tea & reading.

*Thinking about church. Thinking I may start going. Not for the sake of my own faith, but for the sake of others', if that makes sense. So many people who have lived with so little hope, other than in their religion. It feels right that I should honor that. So much hopefulness, if given with kindness, is inspiring.

11pm. Such a dull day. Never really dried off, very humid, & temperature upper 70s mostly.

July 13, 1964

9.15am. Men at work, minus John John today. They are all in the stable at the moment, deciding what to do, I think. Lingering over coffee.

10am. Marce has driven off with Davy. (It is the only time he gets to ride in the front of the truck...) Rip & Dicky Bird seem to be cutting lumber for the garden fence.

1pm. Marce & Davy came back early, & the whole gang has split up into different duties. As it has dried up somewhat, Dicky Bird is helping Marce tie the chicken run posts together at the corners with heavy wire, bracing them, I think. Rip is second-coating the white trim. Davy, with embarrassed courage, knocked on my door & asked whether he could pile some of the garden fence on my porch. I agreed (of course) & asked him where he & Marce went earlier. — Down to Ingalls, he said. Ordering your stuff for your path & all. He blushed at the sound of his own voice.

5pm. Men gone now. It looks to me as though the chicken coop is fully painted & the snug wire fencing is all in place. They have built a cunning gate, which I didn't see them working on. Maybe in the stable? Davy has piled the porch corner high with fence posts.

10.45pm. Weather today exactly like yesterday. Slightly breezier, I think.

July 14, 1964

7.15am. Glorious sunrise this morning. Already 60 degrees. Hope it stays clear like this.

9am. Men at work today & John John with them. So nice out there, that I've got the windows open, & I can hear them. Rip, Dicky Bird & Marce are busy measuring around the edge & driving stakes in the ground in places. Davy & John John are carrying things over from the stable & piling them on the lower porch at The Corner.

    *I heard Marce tell Rip —Don't y'all step on nuthin' or she'll tan your hide.

1pm. Inside now. Feels strange to me, suddenly, to be in the Mary House, with the others so close. All four men are now digging holes for the garden fence posts, putting them up one by one around the edge of the garden & up to the Mary House itself.

    *John John, for once the lucky one, is sitting in the shade on the lower porch at The Corner, sanding the pickets for the fence.

2.15pm. Took them all a drink of root beer, as it looks like awful work. (Centuries of stones have been tossed to the edge of the garden, making the digging slow.) Walked over to The Corner & spoke to John John. It is so quiet that our voices carried a bit. I told him he was the lucky one today, just as Dicky Bird went by carrying a post. A few minutes later, I could hear DB singing something about walking five miles and winning a daub of cotton. JJ appeared to take no notice of it.

5pm. Everyone gone. Porches all left straight & swept (JJ). About half the posts look to be in place. Not much damage to the garden, as expecting this day, I kept things back from the edges. Davy & John John laughing at something as they drove off.

7.30pm. Joanie & Paul just gone silent. Guitar & dulcimer tonight.

10.45pm. Sunny all day, & so much nicer. But still a little too humid. 84 this afternoon.

July 15, 1964

7am. Not so humid this morning, a light breeze in the curtains. Not quite 60.

9am. Working like yesterday out there. Took them ice tea this morning.

10.15am. Too intimidating to sit inside the Mary House with them all just outside the windows. I took my papers, a book, notepad, magazine etc over to the high porch on The Corner & sat in the shade. JJ down below sanding away.

10.45am. The men have changed roles, a bit, specializing now. Rip & Marce seem to be setting up trestles just below the high porch, actually at the edge of the road. Davy & Dicky Bird continue to fix the posts & holes opposite.

11.15am. Rip & Marce are attaching the pickets to slim boards to make panels for the fence. Marce has been chiding

JJ to sand faster & "to get his thumb out of his []ss as we ain't a-gonna wait all day for them things".

2.15pm. Hot now. 86 degrees. I took them lemonade this time. About 2/3 of the posts in place, I think.

4.45pm. Everything put away & the men driven off.

*Just as they were leaving the porch, JJ bumped a post that was propped in the corner & it fell over. –What in the H[]ll's the matter with you? Marce barked. John John knelt to pick up the post, & Dicky Bird gave him a hand. –Aw, ain't that purdy? Marce said.

*In the paper that it was announced yesterday that we are sending 600 more troops to Vietnam. Who will protect them while they hope to protect others?

10.30pm. Lovely sun all day.

Gonna whittle myself a little wooden gun

The Reverend Grayson Hargreaves looked down at the faces of his congregation. Three out of every four faces he saw were people older than him. In the two years since he was first installed in the town's Methodist Church, he had seen the number of attenders shrink slowly but relentlessly as the seasons passed. Some of this was undoubtedly due to the Lutherans enlarging and revitalizing their church halfway down the Main Street. After all, the locals did not have very fixed ideas about the doctrines of the different Protestant churches and were just as likely to go to one as another, depending upon which was closest (and Grayson's church *was* closer to the farms on the west side of the town) or which made them feel the most comfortable about their spiritual health. Grayson had gravitated naturally towards a more relaxed, family-oriented style, while the Lutherans – at least, in his neighbours' church – were more inclined to the primitive, threatening style that many people favoured, no doubt feeling that they got their money's worth in a service that was more dramatic.

But the truth, as Grayson knew, lay in a different area, and that was in the cemetery. The Lutherans still had about a quarter acre to spare, and the Methodist graveyard was nearly full. Ever since it started being fashionable for the country families to stop burying their dead on their own land, they had started buying up plots in the town big enough to support all of the family members they could count. The result was that, although the earth wasn't yet filled up, the space had all been committed for years to come. That was why, Grayson knew, as he looked at the dwindling number of faces in the pews, and in spite of their relative ages compared with his own, the crowd was getting younger and younger. He needed to do something.

One of the parishioners who interested Grayson was Mr George Schmidt. George had come from a family that had had money in its pockets for generations, and he owned an attractive farm towards Harmony. But unlike everyone else with a farm, George paid a man to do his farming for him, while he kept himself busy overlooking the stocks and bonds he had bought in local businesses, including banks, insurance and housebuilders. George was a regular church-goer, and by all accounts, had been ever since his wife died ten years previously. George had dutifully bought a family plot in the Methodist cemetery and interred his wife there, leaving additional room for himself, his daughter Margaret and her likely – though as yet undiscovered – future husband. As Grayson looked down at Margaret from the pulpit, he judged her age to be about eighteen, just finishing high school. This gave him an idea.

There had been talk for years about a vague promise George had made to Grayson's predecessor in the pulpit, that one day, probably after George's own death, George would cede a piece of his land to the Methodist church to extend its cemetery. One of

George's hilly meadows ran right up to the wall on the north side of the cemetery, and about the only use the field was ever put to was to graze young cows. One way and another, nothing had ever come of this vague promise, and whenever Grayson mentioned it to George – and he had mentioned it twice in the past two years – George just laughed and said they'd all just have to wait and see what happened.

This particular morning, after church was over, Grayson hurried to the front door to shake hands with the congregation as they filed out – something he always liked to do. This time, however, as he took George's hand, he held it just a little longer than usual and met George's eye.

Congratulations! Grayson said.

Thank you, sir, George said. But for what?

Grayson turned his eyes towards Margaret, who was chatting to one of the older ladies in hat and gloves. He turned back and looked at George, then raised his eyebrows and smiled. George looked confused, his lips not sure whether to erase his smile or broaden it.

Oh, I see, Grayson said. Mum's the word.

Grayson smiled and nodded knowingly, and let go George's hand, reaching for the next person in the line.

The following Sunday had the same pattern as the previous one. This time though, George saw to it that Margaret left the church well before him, and he held himself back until he was last in line. When he came up to Grayson, he extended his hand.

Another good sermon, Preacher, George said.

Thank you.

Say, now. About that thing you said last week. You know something I don't?

Grayson watched as George tipped his head in Margaret's direction. She was standing in the shade of the maple trees, chatting with another girl and her mother.

Oh, I doubt that's possible, Grayson said. I was referring to the impending wedding bells. But I can understand you might be keeping things secret.

George was thunderstruck. He thought Grayson must be joking. He shook his head and brought up something like a laugh, something like a snort.

You're pulling my leg, Reverend. Margaret ain't getting married. You got her mixed up with one of them other girls.

Grayson smiled. Oh, I guess I must have, he said. I just misunderstood. I don't want to betray any secrets or anything. She just seemed to me to be a girl in love, I guess.

George smiled a bit harder, and not being able to think of anything else to say, he walked off.

The following Sunday, George once again made himself the last in line to shake Grayson's hand.

Who do you think she's in love with? he asked, squeezing Grayson's palm.

I can't really say, Grayson said. He tried to loosen George's grasp.

Can't, or won't? George said.

Grayson only smiled and took his hand back. I suppose we'll all find out soon enough, he said.

The next Sunday George looked as though he could hardly wait for the service to be over so that he could get a word with Grayson.

Now look here, George said. I've been watching her, and I can't be sure of anything. If you know something, I'd be damn grateful – excuse me – if you'd say.

Grayson looked at George closely. George, he said. Are you a betting man?

George thought over his success with stocks and bonds and answered quickly. You know I am, he said. What's that got to do with anything?

Grayson looked away to the meadow to the north of them. I'll make you a bet, he said. I'll bet you half that field of yours right there that if you try, you'll find out the truth before next Sunday. If I'm right, you donate that field to this church for a new cemetery. But if I'm wrong, I'll see to it that no preacher in this church ever mentions it to you again. What do you say?

George looked down the church steps to where Margaret was standing amid a family of his neighbours. He looked across the meadow, a little overgrown and with multiflora briars and thistles just popping up here and there.

It's a bet, he said.

Every night that week, as Grayson knelt down to pray, he was troubled in his soul about whether he had done the right thing. He had, likely as not, bet his church's future on the likelihood that a pretty, nubile, eligible young girl had a beau, and was sufficiently in thrall of her father to admit it. He had betted that the father loved his daughter enough to be kind about it, but was just jealous enough, just curious enough, to ask her the straight question and to accept the answer.

When the next Sunday's service finished, Grayson could feel his heartbeat in his throat and in his stomach. He had sweated his way through the lesson, three hymns, the readings and the sermon, and now he would find out how things stood. He had taken a few opportunities to glance at George during the service. Was he different? More relieved? More resigned? He also had stolen glimpses of Margaret. To Grayson, she seemed just the same, possibly more at ease, more radiant.

The moment came when George took Grayson's hand. Guess you were right all along, he said. He seemed to be studying Grayson's chest before looking up at his face. I've asked her to wait a while, till I get to know the boy a little better. Till we all get to know each other a little better.

George met Grayson's eyes. You'll get the papers on that field next week. Don't bury anybody in there till then, will ya? George smiled.

By New Year the Methodist cemetery wall had been extended to include an extra two acres. By Easter, Grayson saw the congregation almost double. His ruse had worked. He was just a little proud. But he was very very thankful. He was also a little confused, as while George and Margaret still came every Sunday, and George still shook Grayson's hand, smiled and chatted as before, George had never spoken a word to Grayson about an impending wedding.

One Sunday, one beautiful June Sunday, Grayson said to him, So George, any date yet for the wedding?

George looked at Grayson and smiled an open smile. No, sir, no plans. There never were any, he said.

Grayson looked perplexed. What? How come?

I figured out what you were doing, George said. I was resentful at first, in case it meant you were prepared to open up an argument between Margaret and me. But then I knew, once I had it figured out, that there couldn't be any harm in it.

And this way, George said, patting Grayson on the shoulder, by letting you win, I don't ever have to hear another word about that god-damn field. Excuse me, Preacher.

July 16, 1964

9am. Hot out there already (over 70) & very little cloud. Work out there just like yesterday. I've decided to stay at my desk today. All the windows are open. Radio by The Corner, Dicky Bird (out of sight & hamming it up a bit) is crooning at Davy that she walked away & said it was goodbye & laughed when she saw teardrops in his eye. Davy just grins from ear to ear & shakes his head.

12.45pm. Fence posts now look like they're in place. Panels of pickets going together. Davy helping Dicky Bird brace the corner posts.

2.15pm. I've been listening to Marce talking with Rip. He was telling Rip how his grandfather & uncle were orphaned as children & sent to the "work farm", where it was so bad that both boys ran off & lived, homeless, on the mountain-side. They earned money picking huckleberries, stripping bark for the tanneries, cutting barrel staves, railroad ties & "running hogs". Eventually, the brothers saved up enough money somehow to buy "a little bitty ole place" of their own on the mountain & scratched out a living on it until the Depression came. At that point, Marce's grandfather turned to moonshining & hired an out-of-work army veteran as his "gunner", that man eventually marrying his boss's daughter, who then became Marce's mother. Marce himself is one of six children born in a place called Smoketown, somewhere the other side of South Mountain.

*Rip listened to all this, his face long & sorrowful. He nodded, but never spoke up. Had he heard all this before?

5pm. Men gone now. Corners of garden fence braced & panels fitted to two, making firm right angels. The other two, nearest the Mary House are not so straight, & one ends where the gate will be, about ten feet from the front door (beside the porch)

10.30pm. Hot & dry all day. Upper 80s this afternoon, the radio said.

*Can't stop recalling Marce's story. Would like to ask him more about it, but do I dare?

July 17, 1964

9.15am. Another hot & humid morning. 70 degrees already, but fog lying about in places like exhausted polar bears.

*Men all at work. Took them ice tea. John John given clean up duty, first in the stable (brushes, sweeping, straightening). Marce & Rip making panels, Davy & Dicky Bird finding ways to strengthen the acute angle of the fence between the little creek (bridge side) & the Mary House. Everyone seems content.

1.30pm. Fog all gone now, but still cloudy & bubbling with humidity. 90 degrees on the thermometer. Davy & John John sanding now. Dicky Bird measuring up pieces to build the odd-size panels; Marce likewise to build the gate; Rip still on ordinary panels. They take it in turns to help him, when he finishes one, to come over the road & attach them.

2pm. Marce storytelling again. How his mother cut up his father's coat to make one for him. How they boiled tea in a pan. How they had no shoes except in winter. How they slept three in a bed, girls in one bed, boys in another, but in the same room. How in the winter there was ice on the floor.
    *Rip still nodding.

4.30pm. Men left a little early this evening. Everything packed up & tidy, some things locked in the bottom of the wash house again. Over half the picket panels now attached. John John not with them this evening. He must have gone earlier this afternoon.

10.45pm. Another coastal-like day, gray & hot & damp. Watched "Route 66".

July 18, 1964

7.45am. Warm but drier this morning. 68 degrees & sunny. Lots of dreams last night but can't remember them.
    *Squirrels in the walnut trees behind The Corner this morning.

12pm. Back from Frederick. Only went to A & P ($13) for the usual.

2.15pm. 90 degrees now. Hardly a cloud to be seen. Reading more of O'Connor. Can't keep my eyes from yawning.

4.30pm. Drinking tea & trying to forgive Marce, although I cannot imagine why. His cruelties are surpassing in their breadth & magnitude, his brutality is nearly limitless. Yet I feel I can't resist pitying him. Maybe that is what people feel in the presence of men like him, & maybe that is why such men cannot help themselves & cannot abide others. So far, it has been enough to subdue my revulsion. But I know that finding peace with myself over what he represents to me, the primitive temper of manhood, will set me free. Can I do it? Can anyone?

9.45pm. On the news this evening that there have been race riots in New York & New Jersey. What does this mean about "civil" rights?

    *Gave up on movie.

July 19, 1964

7am. Been up a little while now. Couldn't sleep very well because, metaphorically at least, I just couldn't stop shaking my head.

    *Sunrise like an explosion & now the sun sits too bright even to glimpse it in a sky that is almost purple with clarity. 68 degrees & climbing.

12.45pm. Went to church with Cinch & the others this morning (wore my gray sleeveless, with white beads; Cinch in cream with rose). Talk on the way there all about preserving food, as all the women are canning, freezing, drying etc. The service was fine, & the sermon friendly. The hymns slow, the offering discreet. Nice walk home, talking about maintaining the graves of family members. This is something the locals take very seriously.

2pm. 93 degrees. Salad with eggs for lunch. Locals collecting for more horseshoes, or seem to be.

5pm. Horseshoes afternoon finished. I persuaded Cinch, Agassy, Irene & Gladys to come over for a glass of lemonade. Lots of talk about children & grandchildren. No questions for me about Alex or moving over the road. Mentioned Tom twice.

11.15pm. Such a true summer's day. Tonight the sky is galaxied with stars. Utterly wonderful.

July 20, 1964

7am. Beautiful sky again but going to be hot & probably humid. Feels clammy & already 70 degrees.

9.30am. Almost everyone in their roles, just like last Friday, sanding, measuring, cutting & attaching. One small exception is that Marce & John John spread out a big tarpaulin in front & to the right of the gate into The Patch, weighting it with bricks.

10.15am. Ingalls truck just arrived & is backing up to the tarpaulins near The Patch. Davy & Rip watching.

11.30am. Davy, Rip & eventually Dicky Bird & John John all watched or helped as the Ingalls men unloaded sand, gravel & a pile of bricks on to the tarpaulins. This, I suspect, will be my garden paths. Marce joined them late & didn't seem to say much. Thank goodness.

1.45pm. Everyone at work on the garden fence now. Very hot. I took them lemonade. Davy's smooth face (and Marce's more angular flat-topped one) look like boxes of brown, pink & blue crayons that have melted. The others don't look quite so bad.

2.15pm. 93 degrees again. Men bantering & telling jokes & stories of what bad boys they were, tipping over outhouses, buying drinks underage.

4.30pm. Men gone on time. John John told Rip his head hurts. Fence almost finished.

10.30pm. Summer day today: hot, humid, immobilizing.

July 21, 1964

9.15am. All four men at work today. John John not with them. Rip, Dicky Bird & Marce making & attaching panels. Davy, unloading cans from the truck, is readying to start painting the picket fence.

1.30pm. Last of the panels up now, gate attached. All four men busy painting the picket fence (white). Much quieter out there today.

4pm. Men left a little early today. Too hot in the sun. They each took breaks sometimes to get into the shade, & straighten up tools, sweep, etc.

10.45pm. Weather exactly like yesterday.

July 22, 1964

9am. All four men working again. No John John. Task today seems to be to continue painting picket fence.

1.45pm. Took them lemonade today. Fence painting like this is slow work. They are about half through, I'd say.

3.45pm. Drinking ice tea myself this afternoon. Sitting here, looking around the house (which I can almost see into, every corner, from here), why does it all feel so womanly? Whose energy am I sharing here? Why does it feel so good? How will I ever leave it? Will it be enough if I promise never to forget what this little house has taught me? If I am truly grateful, will its energy live on inside me, when I do finally move (as I must)?

4.45pm. Men all gone now. Not a lot of progress this afternoon, as the heat slows them down. Dicky Bird only managed one song that I could decipher (when it is humid he sings more quietly, I've noticed). His song apologized that now & then there is a fool such as him.

10.30pm. Weather remains the same, though perhaps not quite 90 this afternoon. Watering ever day now.

July 23, 1964

7am. Foggy, hot & humid. Went outside to smell the air & saw two rabbits near the chicken coop. That house, at least, must be ready.

9.15am. Everyone painting as before. They seem determined to get the whole thing first-coated or else.

1pm. Fence about ¾ finished, I'd say. Lots of banter, as there is less sun in their faces. Dicky Bird's wife wants him to take the whole family to Ocean City. Rip's wife wants to drive up to Deep Creek Lake. Marce's rejoinder? –These d[]mn women!

4pm. Made tea, but don't feel like drinking it. D[]mn women!

5pm. Men finished for the day & gone. Fence looks to be all white now.

10.45pm. Glum, bankrupt sort of day again. Nearly 90, but no genuine sun. Clothes won't even dry in this weather.

July 24, 1964

8.45am. Men all back to fence-painting (second coat). No John John again today.

1.30pm. Painting seems to go much faster now. They look about 1/3 of the way through. Gave them ice tea. Everyone teasing everyone else about their painting skills. Some sort of sex reference again, but I missed some of it.

4pm. Men left slightly earlier again. I think they reached the ½-way point & decided to quit for the week. No update about next week.

10.30pm. Weather just like yesterday, but not quite so hot. Moon pushing through clouds now. Watched "Route 66".

*On the news tonight that there is a race riot going on in Rochester, NY.

We'll make music till the rafters ring

It's the summers that ya remember. Not cause they special or nothing, but because they ain't. They all the same, you 'member one day from one year and another day, maybe from another year, and they seem like they all together. Maybe it's just 'cause the light so bright. I don't know. Maybe it's the working, maybe it's 'cause it too hot to sleep. Maybe 'cause it's when the nights is short and ya feeling lonely ya go out and look at the stars and ya 'member all the questions ya ever wanna ask and nobody nowhere know the answer. 'Cept maybe God. And he ain't saying.

Lord, lord, like everybody else, I spent my days 'fraid of the padarolles, even though I don't go nowhere much, 'cept 'round Harmony or with one of the missuses when they goes to town for something. But at night, I all 'lone down there in the Mary House, and I look out them windows, and it so dark and lonesome, ya wonder why the Lord His Self don't cry for ya. So then I goes walking. Up and down the Harmony Road, the Brethren Church Road, the Hollow Road. They all laying there in the lights of the night like roads to anywhere. And all them places was places I knowed I never get to go. I come back to my own bed 'fore the sun even get the sky whitening up, and I lay there and I listen, but I don't know what for. I'm glad I can hear the birds and even the damn rabbits a-eating my cucumbers. I'm pretty sure I'm gonna miss 'em when I die. Maybe they miss me too.

I ain't the only one can't sleep at nights when the wind still blow hot. Over Myersville they a big house where the doctor live. His name Irving Gladhill and be got a wife called Miss Rebecca and they got a couple children, not too big. They ain't got but the one house servant and when she say she in love with a fella down the wheelwright yard, they let her go hire herself to that family, on condition she give them the money to hire a 'placement for her in they own house. Well, it come 'bout in the summer, and 'bout the only gal the doctor can find that ain't already hired out is a ole field hand come up from Virginia, and the only thing she called is Lil Huntin. She ain't got a mean bone in her body, but she 'bout as quick on the scent as a dog with no nose.

Anyhow, they brung her in the house to mind the chores and keep the children out of mischief, and every day they show her something new, and she learning best she can. She finding out 'bout changing beds and washing plates and getting boys and girls in they clothes.

She think she got the good straw for most June and July, and then the real hot get going in August. Lord, I 'member it. Ya couldn't half draw the breath right down into ya lungs, and ya dress like an ole wet rag 'fore the sun half-cocked. Poor Lil Huntin ain't used to nothing like that. It get hot like that in Virginia too, 'course. But down there, she get to sleep outside when the nights gets hot, and then all she got to tend with is the skeeters and the bugs. She ask ole Doctor Irving how she supposed to sleep in a bed in a house, 'cause she in the room 'bove the kitchen in the back, and he say same as anybody else, he figure.

Well, one night it just like somebody light the whole valley on fire. The birds don't sing and the dogs don't bark, and they ain't a breeze ya could call by name. Doctor Irving and Miss Rebecca sit in they parlour 'bout half the night, and Lil Huntin get the children in they beds to stay, and she go off to her room to try and wait for the morning. Well, after the folks goes to bed, she still laying there like she some kind of boiled ham or something, till last she can't take it no more. She get herself up and goes out into the hall 'bove the kitchen just a-looking for something to cool herself with. She looking 'round and 'round, thinking they gotta be some kind of breeze somewhere, till last she come to the Doctor and Missus's own room. They got they door just a little open, and sure 'nough, they a little breeze blowing down from this side the house.

Ole Lil Huntin almost panting like a fox by now, and she set for almost anything, so she start to looking for that breeze. She give they door a little push and it swing back, and there she it. They got they windows open on two sides of the house, and even the curtain is a-moving. So ole Lil Huntin, she creep in there thinking she gonna lay down on the floor and just cool herself off or something, then when she get good and sleepy, she go on back to her own room. So she creep by the bed, and then she see 'em in the moonlight. The missus is a laying there on top of the covers 'thout a stitch on herself, for love or mercy. Now Lil Huntin ain't seen no naked white woman before and she get her eye full then. But then just as she gone past 'em, she see that ole Doctor Irving ain't but naked too. Now there something she ain't seen before. She get a good look and she fascinated. Thing is, it's a hot night and he done gone to sleep and a-dreaming, and that little man of his a-standing up all proud and big as ya please. And Lil Huntin just stop there looking.

Now like I say, she didn't have the brains of a chaff tick, so what she do, but reach out her finger and give his little man a poke. He don't do nothing, and she think it's just the right time to be learning something else new for herself, so she wrap her whole hand 'round it and rub it just a little. Well, Doctor Irving, he make a noise of some kind and he turn towards Miss Rebecca. Lil Huntin let go quick, and good she did, 'cause Doctor Irving starting to wake up a little, and 'fore ya know it, he reach his own hand over and put it just where he wants to on Miss Rebecca. By then, Lil Huntin duck down to the floor, and she crawling away 'fore Doctor Irving getting too busy 'bout his business with Miss Rebecca. Lil Huntin listen outside the door for a minute and when she hear the squeaking she go back down to the kitchen. She sleep on the cold floor till she wake up and get dressed for making them children they breakfast. She go on working for the doctor and the missus, even after the 'mancipation.

July 25, 1964

7.45am. Hot, humid & foggy now. Depresses me when it is like this.

1.30pm. Back from a shopping trip to Frederick. Walked around downtown, fingering clothes, trying on shoes, doubting mirrors. Had cookies from a bag, and another White Star hot dog. That may be why everyone seemed to be looking at me later at A & P ($16). When will I ever learn about White Star hotdogs & their speed-of-light raw onions?

2.30pm. Locusts like rusty saws in all the trees now.

4pm. Had soup for lunch earlier, so have already started on the cake I bought. Reading O'Connor. Nearly there.

8pm. Sat with J & P while they played (guitar & autoharp). Watched the lightning bugs & listened to the crickets. Beautiful tonight.

    *Paul explained that his father was a miner, until he died of black lung. He taught Paul some dances to go with fiddling, & Paul taught them to Joanie. I asked her to teach me, & she said she would.

11.15pm. Not as hot today, only upper 70s. Not much sun though. Still rioting in Rochester. Watched channel 4 movie.

July 26, 1964

7.30am. Hot again this morning, & air as weighty as gold. Shards of sun sometimes.

9.45am. Didn't feel like church this morning, so I watched them all go by from the window. What am I waiting for?

12pm. Walked them home from church. Cinch looking slightly chilly in a brown-&-pink large paisley print dress & cream sweater thrown over her arm. I asked whether she was ill. – No, Miss Mary, she said. But it's a-gonna rain something powerful in a minute.

12.45pm. 88 degrees & thunder on the air now.

2.15pm. Half-hearted thunderstorm on now. Enough to water everything.

4.15pm. Tea. Always tea & thinking. What am I waiting for? That's today's topic. Suppose I gave up waiting? Told myself (realized?) that there is no such thing as waiting, forgetting (remembering?) that one moment has no genuine relation to another? If I could shake that hand, sign that dotted line, I would be free. Then I would be free.

　*What am I waiting for?

8pm. Whenever I ask myself "Should I?" it is too late. I already have.

　*I think I may have stopped waiting.

10.15pm. Odds & ends sort of day today, weatherwise. Going to fall asleep smiling.

July 27, 1964

7am. Another hot, fetid morning with humidity & fog & little enough sun.

9am. All four men at work this morning & John John with them. All but JJ are painting the fence. He is sweeping & sorting as usual.

12.45pm. Back to painting. End in sight, I think. JJ mostly milling about until Marce sent him to cut weeds down along the sides of the creeks. –Keep your eye open for snakes too! was the advice he got.

2.30pm. Over 90 now. Air like jelly. Windows open, but quite quiet out there.

4.45pm. Painting of fence is finished. All hands helped clean up brushes & tools. They all look worn out.

11pm. Unhappy weather all day today. Riots seem to be over now.

July 28, 1964

8.45am. Men all at work in the garden. (Oh, spare my plants!). Hammering stakes, digging up my paths, loading wheelbarrows. John John fetching & carrying. Here come the paths, I guess.

10.30am. Men laughing over something. Good to hear, as they are all laughing.

1.15pm. I am reeling. It is in the paper today that we are going to send another 5,000 troops to Vietnam. I can't believe it. It is too few for a war, too many to do real good. It is a disaster. Wherever Alex is, no place will remain safe for long now. I just can't believe it.

*Work outside as before. Can't quite see them among the tall plants, ironically.

5pm. Men utterly broken from heavy labor in the scorching sun. JJ & Davy looked a little green, I thought. Marce like the bull near the end of the fight. As angry with the sky as with anything else.

10.30pm. Horrible weather exactly like yesterday again today. 91 this afternoon.

July 29, 1964

6.30am. Still this miserable weather. Hot, moldy feeling, & dark buttery fog.

9.15am. Work going just like yesterday. They are digging down the paths, putting runners along the edge, filling them with sand, & laying bricks on top. Very pretty results.

1pm. Work going on. They are looking so tired already. Drinking water as well as ice tea.

2.45pm. 93 sticky degrees now. Quiet outside. Nothing but the sound of dripping sweat, locusts, grasshoppers & an occasional bout of swearing.

4.45pm. Men gone now. Half the paths look finished, the remainder getting there.

11.15pm. Wind picked up this evening, so perhaps things are set to change a bit.

July 30, 1964

6.45am. Hot feeling & drizzle now. 67 degrees.

8.30am. Just had a call from Hartsock. Marce & the others not coming today. Can't work in the rain, he says. I asked about his plans to visit & see the results. He apologizes for the strain he's been under. Soon, he says.

10am. Finished reading O'Connor. Keen to start Agee. Should really be working. I keep looking out the window, wondering where everyone is.

1pm. Soup for lunch very nice. A good change.

4.15pm. Read a little Agee, just as a taste. So perceptive. So eager. So hurt.

*I am feeling so full of energy now. So alive & willing. I've changed.

7pm. Quiet outside. No music. Some crickets. An owl, I think, though it might be a dove.

10pm. Rained most of the day today, but still in the low 80s.

July 31, 1964

7am. Hot again this morning, but a little less humid. 66 degrees. Sun & no fog. Dreamed last night about the day I moved out of the old house. Saw the things loaded, saw the house as I drove away from it. Slept pretty well.

9am. Men all working today. They look much more rested & ready for it. Dicky Bird wooing the skies, wondering where his dream lover has got to.

1pm. Back now from delivering ice tea. Could almost pass it out the windows. Paths nearly finished, it seems. Lots of calling out, back & forth. Sound like they are making plans about what they're doing next.

1.45pm. In the paper that the navy has fired on North Vietnamese forces yesterday. We may be slipping into an abyss.

3pm. All finished outside, it looks. All of them are going about the wash house, stable, chicken coop, garden, Patch … everywhere … gathering up, stacking & sorting.

5pm. Men left on time. John John came to say that his dad told him that next week they are working on The Patch. I asked if he was looking forward to any trips anywhere this summer. He said he would probably see his "other" grandma, down near Baltimore. (This must be Marce's mother.) I asked what she is like. —She's nice, he said. She's got a jukebox.

10.30pm. Much better day today, being just over 80 this afternoon & less humid. Sun bright but not so scalding today. Watched "Route 66".

Month of Sundays

August 1, 1964

7.30am. Lovely morning with a golden sunrise. 58 degrees.

1.15pm. Nice easy trip this morning. Went to the bookstore & bought The Moviegoer by Walker Percy & Butcher's Crossing by John Williams. Also bought two magazines at the Blue Ridge & a little bag of cookies at the nice Italian shop near the bookstore. Then to A & P ($18) where, already sweetened by cookies, I bought six cream-puff doughnuts. Very nice young man to pack the bags, & people in the line behind me feeling chatty.

4pm. Feeling very ladylike, sitting on the porch with my tea, magazines & new novel. Air is still, & there is the sound & smell of grass being mown. The Corner looks more & more like a present ready to unwrap. One that I am looking forward to.

7.30pm. Made myself a wonderful dinner. The first steak I have cooked for a very long time. Also baby potatoes, turnips & beans from the garden. (I made "fricassee French beans" from the old book.)

8.45pm. Loving the Walker Percy novel, though I may be reading it too fast, & want to savor it.

10.30pm. Such a beautiful day, sunny & bright & about 80 this afternoon. Watched the channel 4 movie, overlooking the fuzz. Quite enjoyable.

August 2, 1964

7.45am. Rained overnight & still drizzly. Feels like it may get humid. Already a hot 70 degrees.

9.45am. Churchgoers looking both hot & damp out there – women like orchids, men like flowering cacti.

12.15pm. Pleasant short chat with the church crowd. Everyone asking when I'm moving in. Cinch in very light blue today, with yellow necklace, ear rings & narrow belt. She asked whether I heard "them boys a-racing their cars" last night. (I didn't.) –'Deed, they ain't fit to be driving nowhere with mufflers like that.

1.30pm. 90 degrees now, gray & humid. In the paper today that our navy has sustained some sort of attack in Vietnam. Oh, no. This is bound to be seen as a kind of definitive gesture.

4.30pm. Still enjoying Percy novel. Creampuff with tea.

7.45pm. Joanie & Paul finished playing now. Guitar & dulcimer tonight.

    *I asked them once how they decide which instruments to play. They looked at one another & shrugged. Obviously, something they never even think of.

10.15pm. Watched a re-run of "Bonanza".

August 3, 1964

7am. Another warm, wet morning. 62 degrees, foggy & a light drizzle.

8.30am. Marce's truck parked on The Common, driven by Rip this morning. Marce evidently due to arrive shortly with a tractor (?) Meantime, Rip & Dicky Bird making a start at small repairs to the long picket fence between the yard behind The Corner and the Band Hall next door. Davy, by himself, is pruning the mallows that grow all along the stone wall between the wash house & the Brethren Church Road.

*As it is so warm, I wasn't sure what to take them this morning, so risked tea and coffee. That seems to have worked.

9am. Marce arrived on a green tractor, evidently from the 1920s, pulling a plow on wheels. John John was perched (I thought precariously) on the skinny steel bit between the tractor & the plow. If he had fallen off, I cannot bear to imagine what the result would have been. They have gone into The Patch & started plowing it.

12pm. Plowing all finished & Marce & John John driven off. Davy, having done the pruning, seems to have spent his time mending & adjusting the old fence along the top of the wall. Dicky Bird & Rip, having finished whatever they were doing to the picket fence, have moved on to the fence along the top of the wall separating The Corner from the Harmony Road. Both this fence & the one Davy is working on are made of arched bits of thick iron pipe which supports elaborately ornate bits of twisted wire decoration. In spite of this fence's evident age, it is in very good shape, & mostly they seem to be tightening & straightening it.

12.30pm. In the paper today that there has been a fresh race riot. This time in Jersey City.

1pm. Marce & John John have returned on the tractor, pulling a very noisy thing which looks like a large collection of moderately sharp thin steel wheels. This they are using to crush the furrows they have plowed.

    *Took them more tea & coffee at lunchtime. Marce & John John were no-shows, but the other three seem very relaxed.

2.30pm. Marce & John John gone again. The others are now busy brushing, scrubbing & even sanding fences, one per man.

3.30pm. Marce & John John are back on the tractor. This time they are pulling something which looks like dozens of tiny hoes fixed to steel squares. They are dragging this around & around on the bit they have been working on, reducing the soil to an ever-smoother consistency.

5pm. Men are all gone now. Davy (still in the truck bed!) left with Dicky Bird & Rip. Marce & John John have gone on the tractor. John John shows that strange, low-level courage that men seem to have facing threats about which they are unconscious. That is, one tiny slip on his part, & there might be an agonizing death or maiming. His father, likewise ignorant or indifferent, lets this go on as the most natural thing in the world.

10.45pm. Weather damp but not rainy all day. High that I saw was about 80. Watched the channel 4 movie, but lost interest at the point when I found myself trying to recall everything I'd ever seen each actor in.

August 4, 1964

7.15am. Weather about the same as yesterday. Foggy again & drizzling.

8.45am. All five arrived in the truck today, & parked beside the gate to The Patch, spent some time unloading sacks of grass seed, which they've put in buckets. They are now all raking (five rakes!) & smoothing the entire thing. Dicky Bird is in a merry mood, whistling away & singing about how much he'd like to be in Charlie's shoes.

10.45am. Lovely sight, as the whole Patch must be raked, & the men are walking about sowing grass seed with great sweeps of their arms. Timeless.

12.15pm. Just about to make the lunchtime tray when I see that the truck is gone & they've all left. Is this an early finish? It is raining lightly…

4.15pm. Men never did return. Called on account of rain, I guess. Last of my creampuffs with tea today. Read some more Percy – beautiful. Nearly finished.

10.45pm. Not as warm today; maybe upper 70s. Not much rain. Soup for dinner. Finished The Moviegoer.

The fields have turned brown

Fire burns, water cools, God's word never lies. And loving ain't what they tell ya.

They was a servant girl name Lizbeth live down on that place belong Mister Upton Keller, on the way up the hill 'tween Middletown and Braddock. He got a big farm, four five hands outside and Lizbeth in the house helping the missus. Mister Upton farm most things, and he got a kind of side dealing with the speculators on servants. He practically a speculator his own self. Anyhow, he finally take it in his head that maybe it's high time Lizbeth get herself a man and get some children 'round the place. Maybe he work 'em, maybe he sell 'em, but he sure think it's time she doing something 'bout it. He don't ask Lizbeth nothing 'bout what she think, and that's why he don't seem to know that Lizbeth already got a man she love, fella name Darius who a free man working for a saddler in Middletown. So Mister Upton come up with a plan for Lizbeth to marry one of Mr Upton's field hands, a fella they all calls Too Tall. Too Tall don't say nothing 'fore or 'gainst, but when Lizbeth hear that news, she take on something powerful. She screaming and a-crying and she tell Mister Upton he got to let her go with her man Darius. But Mister Upton don't like the idea her marrying no free man, 'cause he worried what happen to the babies she like to have, so he say, no, sir, he don't 'gree with that.

Now Lizbeth don't know what to do. So she say she go peaceful if Mister Upton let the marrying wait to the Fall, 'cause with all the working they doing in the summer, they ain't got no time for marrying anyhow. Mister Upton just glad to get the 'greement and the peace, so he say that's what they do then. Now I don't know nothing, but I'm pretty sure that Lizbeth got in her head that 'tween the Summer and the Fall she either gonna run off with Darius somewhere or hang herself in the barn.

But just like that things all change. The hands all out in the field one day in July and they taking it in turns to fork the cut hay off the ground and on to the waggons while one the others rides on top to mash it down. Well, it was ole Too Tall's turn on the top of the waggon, and the waggon done nearly full, and all at once the whole side of that hay roll off and Too Tall come down with it. He hit the ground so hard he bust the top of his leg where the ball joint is and they has to carry him into the house on a gate. Doctor say he put that joint back where it goes, but they something in there so stretched or crooked or something, that ole Too Tall can't walk no more 'thout swinging his leg like a ole fence post tied on a rope. Mister Upton pretty mad 'bout all that, and he say he ain't got no use for no crip-pled-up field hand, so next thing ole Too Tall on his way to the pens down Licksville.

Now, course Lizbeth just as sorry as she can be for ole Too Tall, 'cause he didn't do nothing he oughtn't to. But 'course, she glad too, cause now she think she least got some kind of chance of getting ole Darius for her man.

Then the bad news come again. 'Bout the time September start to show itself in the mornings, she hear Darius at the saddler's just like always, and he got to take some new finished tack up the pike and over the mountain to Boonsboro for a fella there that bought it. So he puts the whole thing in the spring waggon, the saddle and the tack and I don't know what all else, and off he go. Well, when he get there to the stable where the fella s'posed to collect them things, the fella in some kind of mood like the devil. He took out that saddle and half-throwed it on the horse and he say, See here? This thing don't even fit nohow. And Darius, he see they ain't nothing wrong with the saddle, and the only reason it don't fit is 'cause the fella looking at it with too much whiskey in his eyes. So Darius, say, Here sir, they stiff when they new. Y'all best let me try and show ya. And he walk over towards 'em and he reach out for to take the saddle, but the white man like to drop it and Darius jump to catch it so it don't fall down in the straw and the shit on the floor, and he scare that horse, and the horse lit out and give Darius a kick upside his head. Darius fall down like a stone, and they a little blood in his mouth and eyes, and he shake a couple times, but he dead.

Well, they bring him back in the springboard and bury him in the coloured end of the cemetery, 'hind the Baptist church. The boss at the saddler's give his things to charity, 'cause he didn't have no use for 'em, and Darius didn't have no family.

Poor ole Lizbeth like to die her own self now. She don't let nobody touch her and she don't half listen when folks talk. She don't eat much, but she don't do nothing crazy, but she ain't really living no more then.

Mister Upton decide 'gain that it high time he get her a man to take her mind off the dead ones. So he say she got to marry the fella Mister Upton bring home after Too Tall sold. He pretty heavy-set fella with the short arms and the big neck. He say he willing if Lizbeth willing. And Lizbeth, she don't seem to care 'bout nothing no more. That Fall, 'fore Thanksgiving, Mister Upton get the free-man preacher to come and marry 'em up down side the loafing shed and the barn, and they get a room in the quarters to theyselves. Last I knowed, Lizbeth have three babies, and two that lived. She and Napoleon left after the war, and that's all I know.

August 5, 1964

7.15am. Going to be hot again today, I think. Already 64. Gorgeous sunshine though.

 *From upstairs, I can see the little birds enjoying my new grass seed.

9am. Everyone at work today. Dicky Bird, ka-rooning away with evident solitary self-possession about how all of us must face his Waterloo, is busy painting the complicated steel fence a dull silver color. Davy is likewise quietly concentrating on the same job on the other steel fence in front of the wash house. Meanwhile, somewhat alarmingly, Marce, Rip & John John are, it seems, pruning the tall trees in the far corner of the yard behind the house, near the far fencing. Rip, like a circus performer, is held up by ropes in the trees. Marce stands below & shouts orders & cuts up the smaller bits as they fall. John John, when he is not being shouted at, & sometimes when he is, carries the smaller bits down to the truck which is currently parked by the steps near the wash house.

 *I risked ice tea this morning. No one said yea or nay, but they all five had some. That must mean it was acceptable. I think.

1pm. In today's paper that the navy has been fired on again. That must be strike two (at least).

*Work much the same as before, although there was a trip somewhere with a load of the brushwood that filled the truck. John John stayed behind with Davy & Dicky Bird, while Rip & Marce drove off.

*Dicky Bird sharing with everyone the story of a yellow bandanna & a girl named Roseanna.

*When he isn't picking up stray twigs, leaves & branches, John John reads a page or two of an Archie comic. I watched him biting his lip a little (& watching whether the others could see him?) as he read the Charles Atlas ad on the back. When I approached more noisily he turned the page to one about a drawing competition (draw this picture, win something or other…) I asked whether he had done any school-shopping yet. He said his mother picks out all his clothes, but he's allowed to say what kind of notebooks, folders, pens & pencils he needs.

4.45pm. Both steel fences now a uniform gray-silver, which looks better than it sounds. Branches & twigs all cleaned up.

11pm. A beautiful day. Not so humid, upper 80s, so not as hot as I thought. Watched a re-run of "The Virginian".

August 6, 1964

8.45am. Busy as a hive over the road this morning. Davy painting a second coat on "his" steel fence, Dicky Bird on "his". Rip is painting an undercoat of gray on the wooden picket fence. No sign of Marce (truck gone), though John John is there & evidently given the job of straightening up pretty much everything. He is surprisingly adult about this. He sorts, inspects &, I think, makes a kind of game out of every chore he's given. I've heard Marce tell him off for this last part.

*To my wonder & surprise, Dicky Bird is doing his best with a song about Long Tall Sally, who's built for speed & has everything that Uncle John needs.

1.45pm. In today's paper that our forces have started bombing the North Vietnamese. Pray, if you can. Pray for everyone. Pray for families, mothers, & young men.

*Still no sign of Marce. Took them lemonade, which went down well. Positively lively over there, laughing & chatting. John John doing a kind of can-can with Dicky Bird.

3pm. Fences all painted now, the four of them are over at the stable, clearing up & sorting, piling up for loading, I think. Funny to see them walking around the edge of the Patch, so as not to step on their fledging grass.

*Rip, Dicky Bird & Davy are terrific with John John. They were all chipping in, trying to get him to remember Captain Midnight, but JJ isn't quite old enough, I think. Alex used to love CM. Tom used to listen to Alex explaining the storylines to him.

4.15pm. All gone now. Last things from the stable seem to have been loaded.

10.45pm. Weather just like yesterday. Watched a re-run of "Rawhide".

August 7, 1964

7am. Just a bit cooler today. Sunrise earlier this morning a lovely copper-gold.

9am. Marce here with the others this morning. John John sorting & piling near the wash house. Davy painting a second coat (now white) on the last picket fence. They've piled supplies near the entrance to the path across the rear yard behind The Corner, evidently ready to re-lay this path, which is very old concrete. It is to be bricked, like the garden ones, it seems. Marce giving instructions to Dicky Bird & Rip. He is also taking measurements of the area, also concreted, which acts as a rear porch to the building.

10am. Marce gone. Davy painting, the others on the path, John John assisting. Dicky Bird having his wicked way with a song about Mary Lou, & a moonlit night, his arms around her good & tight. Paving seems much easier here, as the foundation is already made.

*Dicky Bird spoke up & asked me whether I knew that there were squirrels all over the place in the trees hereabouts & telling me that if I wanted any of my walnuts, I'd have to get a cat. This sparked a conversation with Rip over whether they oughtn't to have left me some wood to make tables to dry the nuts once I'd hulled them. Davy said he knew where I could get a kitten. He looked at John John, who then spoke up to say that one of their "barn cats" had a litter.

1.30pm. Just back with the tray. All merry over there. Path well along now. John John looking for crayfish in the small creek (& no one seems to mind).

4.45pm. All of the fence is painted. All of the path is laid. Marce came to collect them, but never got out of the truck, even to look at what they'd done. John John was back in time to sweep the path & put away the tools in the wash house. I was talking to the others when he came up the (new) path, telling me they would be building the new back porch next week. How did he know this? Anyway, I liked his authority here, as the others hadn't mentioned it at all, & seemed content, if not proud, to let him tell me. Marce honked his horn to hurry them up.

10.30pm. No moon tonight, but stars aplenty. Not much above 80 today, so just right. I've made a good start on the

John Williams novel. Reading it is like riding in a car driven by someone you trust.

August 8, 1964

7.30am. Such a beautiful morning again, though the royal blue sky has a few clouds skidding about. Already 71 degrees, so may get hot.

*Slept very well. Dreamed of brick paths & music.

11.45am. Only went to Acme in Middletown this morning ($15). Not inspired enough to go to Frederick. Somehow, I want to spend as much time in the Mary House as I can right now, as I know I'll be leaving it soon.

*I brought home two pasteboard boxes, which I am going to use to carry things over the road. That's right: I'm going to start moving in.

2pm. 85 degrees now. I made fishcakes & salad for lunch. Lettuce is so nice this fresh.

*Headlines today that our uncomprehending Congress has passed a resolution about Vietnam that may as well be a declaration of war. It is like each one seizes the hand of his neighbor, & together they hold that hand in the blue light of an impersonal fire. No one will forgive anyone else until the pain is unbearable. Why?

4.30pm. Had my tea on the porch, watching all the little movements – birds, butterflies, dragonflies.

7pm. Paul & Joanie playing tonight. I took them some of my homemade orangeade (from my book), which they pronounced to be very nice. Mandolin & dulcimer tonight.

10.30pm. Another delightful day, with a cool breeze keeping the humidity down. Wonderful crimson sunset. Should have spent the time packing but read Williams instead.

*Thinking of Alex. Will war be what brings him home?

August 9, 1964

7.30am. Quite a bit cooler today, only mid 50s. Sun & breeze like yesterday.

12pm. Went to church this morning. Such a gentle experience. Not so much a wave, as the feeling that water is rising softly up underneath you.

*Cinch pleased to see me there. Well, they all were. She was in emerald green with topaz-like beads.

*Omelette & salad for lunch. Lots of thoughts about Tom today. I wish he were here, seeing me, feeling these many new things.

2pm. Filled both boxes & took them over the road, unpacked them & admired the tiny gains (before coming back to the Mary House & mourning the tiny losses). I have moved all the books, pictures & superficial decorations. The Corner looks like it has been recently occupied by a tremendously short person, who has a family, reads copiously, & has an eye for random decorations. The smells of newness & materials seem so, well, verbose, garrulous, omnipresent, potent, obvious, crowding etc as to be a little overwhelming. The sheer sense of being so much anticipated, so awaited, makes all the minutiae of actual functional living seem trivial, banal & unconsidered as to be too much. At this stage, I feel more like an explorer over there than a settler.

4.45pm. Back from another visit over the road. Even the presence of those little things has ended an epoch. A geological age. An evolutionary cycle. The house has not absorbed them; not rejected them like alien organs. There is room for more. Room for me.

7.30pm. Lonely sounds of dogs barking out there now. The Mary House is the quietest place on Earth.

10.45pm. So much cooler today, only high 70s. Still reading Williams.

11pm. I have asked all the questions I know & feel like I am through asking. It must be what God feels like after a long long Sunday. He has heard & forgiven so much sin, so much sorrow has been revealed, so much grief slaked, so much pain soothed. He does not fear for His creation. He never has. But he knows He can never fully make it know the peace He wishes for it. Instead, He gives it rest. For this, His creation thanks Him. As it should.

    *Alex, if you live, come & live with me. I will be living here. Living will be good. Still good. Still.

Oh, I'll tell my Jesus howdy

The house sat on a steep embankment, about twenty feet back from the road and ten feet above it. It was a slightly smaller version of the usual two-storey wooden rectangle common in the valley and on the hills, but it was just about the only one between Middletown and Myersville which was on its own but wasn't part of a farm. It was painted white with red shutters, and it didn't look too bad, though there was a kind of stale run-of-the-millness about it. In the yard outside there was a tyre swing in the sycamore tree, and the big grassless circle round it was where the family's two daughters, aged nine and eleven, liked to play. They were good girls, who didn't sass their mother, and who usually got to school with their socks clean. Both girls had four dresses and shoes summer and winter. Their mother, Rebecca, was a woman of about average height, bony, thin and strong, with a quiet voice that she didn't use all that much. She kept a neat house indoors and sometimes made the girls treats, like walnut cake or peach pie. Rebecca's husband, Carl Wisner, was just over six foot tall, though he tended to stoop a little. He was narrow across the shoulders and had a very long torso, as if he had an extra pair of ribs, and oddly, his small stomach bulged just a little above his long legs. He wore his hair short, and his mouth a little open, especially when he was listening. During the day, Carl worked as the foreman at the stone crusher on the outskirts of Middletown on the Old National Pike. Carl was called the foreman because he had worked there the longest, though there were only two other men who worked with him. Carl earned eighty cents a day more than his co-workers.

Carl had an old green pick-up truck that he drove to work and it usually did him good service. The floor was rusted through on the passenger's side and the tailgate struts had long since broken off and been replaced with bailer twine. When Carl drove anywhere with his family (they sometimes went into Frederick just to see new things, and once they went all the way to Hagerstown, which thrilled and frightened the girls a little), he drove with Rebecca at the far end of the seat, and the girls wedged between them, wiggling. Every day when he drove to work, he turned left out of his pot-holed gravel lane, drove up the Middletown Road, and then turned left on to Main Street and followed the road straight up the hill and out of town. Every evening, he traced his route back the same way on the same roads. Rebecca could guess his arrival time accurately to within ten minutes. She needed to; he and the girls liked to eat their supper early.

One Thursday evening in September Carl said goodbye to the men at the crusher and got into his truck when the damn thing wouldn't start. He got out and looked under the hood. Carl didn't know much about engines, but he was pretty sure that his wasn't getting any juice from the battery. He'd have to get another one. By the time Carl had figured all this out, the other men had already driven off and he was alone. There wasn't a phone at the crusher, so Carl had no choice but to walk up the track to where the trolley stopped in Braddock Heights (as that was a little closer) and ride the trolley back to Middletown, and then walk the mile-and-a-half home. He thought his luck had turned when he only had to wait fifteen minutes for the westbound trolley to roll in. But then when he got off and started home, the clouds opened up and it began to rain.

Carl got about a quarter mile down the Middletown Road when it started to come down almost too hard to see. There was a house on his left, a big square two-storey one, a little newer than his, with a big porch. There was a woman looking out the window watching the rain. She saw Carl and disappeared. In a moment her door opened and she was waving him up on to the porch. Carl ran up the steps and stood back in the shelter, feeling the water run down his face and drip off his ears. The woman's name was Sally Reeder, though she didn't introduce herself to Carl. She said he was welcome to stay on the porch till the rain eased off a bit. She asked whether he lived around here. Carl looked at Sally. She was shorter than Rebecca and her figure was much fuller – much fuller. It filled her dress extremely. She had small brown eyes and red cheeks and her hair was a colour brown Carl had never seen on anybody else, and it was so thick it didn't seem to move when she shook or nodded her head. Carl explained what had happened, and Sally told him her name and said he was welcome to sit on the worn-out davenport that lay a little gloomily along the house wall. Carl sat down, and Sally went back inside.

As he watched it rain, Carl looked around. Sally's lane was more of a driveway, or had been, as it was rutted now. There was a shed with doors that sagged, and beside it a tall maple tree, ornamental in its day, but under which now sat most of an indiscriminate Ford. The ground was bare under the tree except for scattered bits of metal and oil stains. The car's windows were all open or missing, and its hood was propped against the shed.

Hanging down from the tree's largest limb was a log chain, several ropes and an improvised pulley. The car's engine block sat near the passenger-side door.

As Carl was looking at this, Sally came back on to the porch from the front door. She handed him a threadbare towel and a cup of steaming black coffee. Carl dried his face and smoothed at his hair. He held on to the coffee and drank a little while Sally talked about things.

That car, she said, belonged to her boys. The oldest one, anyway. He was sixteen and desperate to drive. Her other son was fifteen and liked to shadow his brother. She said their father had died a few years ago and it was his pension that they all lived on. They were good boys, but times were hard, and it wasn't easy keeping body and soul together. She told him her name again and asked his.

Carl answered, and looked at Sally as she kept talking, his own mouth now slightly open. Some of Sally's words just stopped sinking in as Carl looked at her. She didn't seem like a widow to him somehow, though she was about ten years older than him, he thought; forty-one to his thirty-one. The rain slowed, Carl drank the last of his cold coffee, and stood up. He handed her the cup, said he was much obliged and started back up the road towards his own house and his cold dinner.

The nest morning, very early, Carl walked past Sally's house on his way into Middletown. He looked around discreetly from the corner of his eye but saw no signs of life. The curtains were closed and nothing outside had changed. He felt a little disappointed. Before he got to the trolley stop, he went to the garage and bought a battery for his truck, carrying it on his lap till he got to work.

That evening as Carl drove home he slowed down as he approached Sally's house. He saw her standing in the yard with a rag rug pegged to her clothesline, and she was using a worn-out broom to beat the dust out of it. On a sudden impulse, Carl beeped the truck's horn. He slowed right down, stuck his arm out the window and waved. Sally turned and shielded her eyes, studying the driver. When she recognized Carl she smiled and waved back.

All that weekend Carl thought about Sally. He had driven past that house every day for years and never noticed her. How long had she lived there? What were her boys like?

On Monday evening as Carl was coming home he slowed down again near Sally's house, hoping she might be outside, but she was nowhere to be seen. In the back of his truck he had a little something for her, something she might use. In the cedar chest that sat unopened for years at the dead-end of their hallway, there had been a small stack of rag rugs that Carl's mother had made for him and Rebecca when they were first married. Rebecca didn't like rag rugs much, and since Carl's mother was now dead, there didn't seem to be any point in keeping them any longer. Then on Sunday Carl managed to be alone just long enough to haul those rugs out and put them under the canvas in the back of his truck. Now if he didn't give them to Sally, he'd have to explain to Rebecca why he'd taken them out.

Carl pulled into Sally's drive, beeped the horn twice and got out. He had got the rugs out and awkwardly into his arms by the time Sally showed up on her front porch. She looked as though she had been asleep. Carl went up on to the porch and explained to her about the rugs. She listened and nodded and said he was very sweet, and that he probably ought to come inside and sit down.

Between then and Thanksgiving, Carl came home late for his supper at least three nights a week. He stopped taking much interest in his daughters and rarely remembered to give Rebecca the kiss on the cheek he usually gave her when leaving for work in the morning, though he did mostly remember the bedtime one. He stopped wearing most of his older shirts, and he began smelling of aftershave even on work days. If Rebecca ever suspected anything, she never let on. Even though he knew that neither she nor the girls were ever likely to walk a mile down the road, he always parked his truck behind Sally's shed, just in case.

One Monday morning around Easter, Rebecca was up early as usual putting together ham sandwiches, cold salted boiled potatoes, and coffee to pack for Carl's dinner. Carl was already up, shaven and in his overalls. He had decided, he said, that that truck of his just wasn't reliable, and until he thought of a solution, the best thing he could think to do was to walk into Middletown and take the trolley up the hill. He would pay the driver to slow down so he could jump off near the lane leading back to the crusher. Meantime, he would take the truck down to some boys he knew who liked to work on these things and see whether they could fix it up for him. He could count on a good price, he said. They were good boys and really knew their stuff.

The rest of that spring and into early July Carl walked the mile-and-a-half into Middletown morning and evening and took the trolley to and from work. Sally's boys, the oldest of whom was now out of school, and the youngest one never there very much anyway, spent their days patching, oiling, painting, greasing, and replacing parts on the truck, when they weren't out driving it up and down the dirt roads.

As the weather grew hotter around the end of July, Rebecca saw that Carl was finding all the walking on the dusty blue roads harder. He had grown a little leaner than he had been in the autumn, a little tanner, a little stronger. But he looked tired in the face and around the eyes.

One evening, after months of not hearing it at all, Rebecca heard their old truck pull in off the road and watched it bounce to a stop near the house. It seemed to be a little different than she remembered it. There were dents she hadn't seen before, some chrome missing and bent, and the suspension wobbled more. Carl was driving and he got out quickly without shutting the door and ran up the steps calling Rebecca's name.

There was an emergency, he said. A woman in trouble. She needed help, and Carl didn't know who else to ask.

Rebecca looked around to where her daughters sat playing cards on the parlour floor. The music on the radio was ending and the voice said it was almost time for Amos and Andy. The girls perked up. Rebecca told them to stay where they were, and if she wasn't back by bedtime they should act just like they always did when she was there. They both promised they would.

Rebecca sat in the truck beside Carl. He started the engine, which made a growl, and pulled the gear shift into reverse. Then he stopped. He told her that this woman they were going to see was the mother of the boys who had been fixing the truck. They were nice folks, he said, but didn't have any money, especially for doctors, and now their mother had got herself into trouble and needed a woman's help.

Where's her husband? Rebecca asked. But by then, Carl had turned the car into Sally's drive, absentmindedly pulling right the way up behind the shed.

Carl led the way up Sally's porch and Rebecca followed. Carl opened the door without knocking and they both went in. Rebecca heard groaning upstairs and then she knew what to expect. She asked Carl how long this had been going on, and he said he didn't know. No one else was home, he said, Sally's boys — that was her name, he said, Sally — were out somewhere. Rebecca told Carl to stay downstairs and wait. Then she turned away and walked up the steps.

When Rebecca came back down to the parlour where Carl sat it was four hours later and starting to get dark. Rebecca's daughters would be getting themselves ready for bed, probably in the dark, as they weren't allowed to light the kerosene lamps by themselves. In her arms, Rebecca carried a bundle of towels and a small blanket wrapped around something. Rebecca looked exhausted and pale and there was some blood on her sleeves. Carl stood up.

The baby's dead, Rebecca said. A little girl.

Carl opened his mouth to say something, but Rebecca spoke up. She'll be all right, she said. The woman.

What are we gonna do about…? Carl said, looking at the bundle Rebecca carried.

I'm gonna wait here, she said, and you're gonna drive back home. In the kitchen, where the cups are, there's a King Syrup can. Inside there's some money. You get it and bring it down here to me.

Carl did as he was told and came back with twelve dollars, which he gave to Rebecca, who took the money in her palm, and had to hold it against the bundle.

You stay here till them boys gets back, she said. I'll take care of this.

Rebecca went out the front door, heading for the big church on Main Street.

Carl sat down, bewildered. He knew where Rebecca was going and what she was going to do. It was the same thing women in this situation had been doing for a very long time. Carl hadn't cried for more than ten years and he badly wanted to cry now, but he couldn't. He thought he ought to go upstairs and see how Sally was doing, but he couldn't do that either. The truth was he was afraid.

An hour after Rebecca left, Sally's boys came home smelling of beer and Carl told them what had happened. They didn't stay to discuss it, but both ran upstairs. Carl listened and heard them talking to their mother. Carl stood up and went outside. He started up his truck and drove down to Main Street and turned right, towards the big white church.

Carl sat in the truck with the motor off until he saw Sally come down the street towards him. She was empty-handed. She spotted Carl's truck, opened the door and got in without looking at Carl. He started it up and they sat there for a minute not talking. Then they drove home. After that, everything went back to being the way it used to be.

August 10, 1964

8.45am. Ingalls truck arrived at 8am, & the men not yet here. Usual driver, usual assistant. I went out & chatted with them until Marce pulled in with the others. The white man stood leaning on the truck, smoking & asked me what I was going to do with such a big house. I told him I would be doing the same things that people did in a smaller house, but bigger. The black driver snorted & laughed. —Um um, he said. He looked as though we shared a joke at the white driver's expense, which started him feeling a little put out, but he just couldn't sustain it, & laughed too. —Maybe you & me & our better halves should get one too, he said to him. —I hear that, the other one answered. Then Marce's gang arrived, & they unloaded lumber for the new porch.

10.30am. All saws & drills & hammering over there as they are covering up the old concrete slab that was once the back porch. All of them seem in on this except John John who is down below, cleaning up the wash house (which is empty now) with a brush.

1pm. Just back with the tray. Porch is now looking very solid indeed with good sides, & a solid floor. They are making a set of railings now.

4.30pm. Everyone gone. Railings seem to be up, sturdy & attractive. Everything swept. I looked in wash house, & no signs of tools there, so they must have loaded them.

*How peaceful it all seems now.

6.45pm. Thinking of Tom again. He does not, after all, belong here. Or anywhere. Tom has lived. His life is a memory to me, & maybe to him. I have brought him here a little like a Roman householder, bringing fire from the old hearth. It is a burning, connected to another time, a burning just as hot because it is always new, always lighting what is new.

*Tom, I think we are at peace.

10.45pm. Weather just like yesterday. Fewer clouds, sunshine the sort that melts butter, but doesn't spoil it.

August 11, 1964

7am. Foggy & drizzly this morning. 62 degrees.

8.30am. Men not at work today. Luckily, though everything on the tray is clean, I hadn't yet made tea or coffee.

9am. Evidently they aren't coming at all today.

11am. Read some more of Williams. Such heart.

4pm. Just off the phone. I have given the movers a date to retrieve the things from the warehouse. I move in on 1 September. Relieved that I finally did it. That I finally felt like doing it. That I can tell people.

*That I am no longer keeping Fortune at bay, telling it to wait for Alex. I will wait, as I must. But the world, & my life inside it, will make these small adjustments.

7pm. A few too many Oreos with tea, so dinner a little spoiled for lack of genuine appetite.

10.30pm. One shower this morning, but otherwise just a dull day. High about 80. Read a bit.

August 12, 1964

7.45am. Much warmer today & much rainier. 69 at the moment, & rain is soft, warm & steady.

9am. Warily, I have watched the time. Men not here again today. Tray looks forlorn. Hope I don't.

10.15am. Taking stock of the Mary House. Cannot decide whether to move "unnecessary" things (such as rugs) over the road or wait until after actual moving day. Already the places vacated by books & such seem a bit forlorn. I cannot decide.

2pm. Breeze has picked up & rain turned to drizzle. 82 now. All the windows open again to catch the breeze. There must be some way I can let this little house know it is loved, even though I must leave it.

    *In the paper today that another race riot broke out in Paterson, NJ. Hatred & fear in our own streets.

4pm. Tea indoors. Nearly finished Williams. I have decided not to take more things into The Corner until after I move there. It is like leaving home again. Perhaps, that is something we should all do: leave home often, as often as we can bear it.

7.45pm. Had a new idea. I will buy some new things, brand-new things, to move into The Corner.

10.45pm. Dull day. Drizzle ended, but not much of a sunset.

August 13, 1964

7.15am. Cooler this morning (57) & much less humid. Nice sun already.

9am. Dicky Bird & Davy at work this morning. No sign of the others. They are painting the new back porch with a gray undercoat. There is a gentle listlessness about them both, echoing the late summer, I felt.

*Dicky Bird half-committed to a song about a woman who slipped a little heartache in on him.

*I walked around & around inside The Corner, no longer trying to fit my things mentally into its spaces, but instead, trying to ask of it what its spaces required. Most of the time the answer was: my things.

2pm. In the paper that there has been a race riot in Elizabeth, NJ. When will this stop?

*Undercoating continues. John John has shown up, but without anything obvious to do. He has been discussing baseball with DB & Rip. More than anything, JJ wants the Yankees to lose. I don't even know why, but so do I.

4.45pm. New wood all painted now. Everyone gone. Once again, Marce didn't bother to get out of the truck. Rip did though, coming up the (new) path to see what the others had done.

10.30pm. Quite a mild day, only just above 70 this afternoon. Watched a bit of the "Jimmy Dean Show", remembering why I am not a fan. The intros to each act are so very very uncomfortable.

Water Boy! Water Boy!

I, LittleWound, tell this story.

When I was a girl there were people who recalled the time before the Washechu came. They remembered the days when the Catoctins had two shadows, one that could be seen by anyone and one that could only be seen by some. One shadow was made of darkness, and this could be seen by anyone. But one shadow was made of light, and for this, one needed the eyes of a spirit.

This was in the era when Caniew, known as WarEagle, was the leader of the Catoctins.

There lived a woman named RainintheFace, and she was the wife of a man esteemed among the people. Her husband had proved himself a warrior of renown and a hunter of prowess. He treated her with kindness and his happiness grew whenever he beheld her. For RainintheFace, no day had regrets and no night passed in loneliness. But it happened that while their bliss was still upon them, her husband went into the forest to bring home deer for their fire, and never returned. WarEagle sent the men of the village on expeditions to search for him, but he was never found, and he never returned.

RainintheFace grieved as a wife grieves, but she grieved too with the agony of a mother who has lost her child, with that of woman who has lost her friend, and with that of a child who has lost a parent. Through the turning of the seasons her grief hung upon her as the willow overhangs the stream, and her sorrow seemed to be without ending. But WarEagle, who had the spirit of the Manitoes within him, had a dream, and in that dream, he saw RainintheFace wedded to a husband. The husband that WarEagle saw was a man named WhiteDog. In the council, WarEagle spoke of his dream, and it was agreed with RainintheFace's father that she should marry WhiteDog. To this, RainintheFace said nothing, for although her heart was hollowed like a tree, she knew that WarEagle would never speak that in which he had no belief. And so, the couple were married and lived in the lodge where RainintheFace had always lived.

It was at this time that RainintheFace began to have visions of her own. In the darkness, as she lay beside WhiteDog, she saw two handprints on the wall near where the doorway entered the lodge. The prints were those of a man, and they shone with light. RainintheFace knew at once that these handprints were the shadow of the husband she had lost.

Night followed night, and the darker each night grew, the more she could see the handprints. WhiteDog questioned her when he saw her eyes shaken with trouble. But she could not speak to him of what she saw, because she feared what he might say, and she feared for what would become of his regard for her. But as the days passed, the life she feared became the life she lived. WhiteDog became like a bear in his movements and like a fox in his habits. He showed no joy in the works of RainintheFace's hands, and no relish for their time alone. He ceased to touch her and his words shrank to the sounds of the branches knocking against one another in the sky. For a while, RainintheFace was pleased by this change, thinking that she had freed herself forever from WhiteDog's esteem, and filling herself instead with yearning for the handprints, whose shadow lightened the walls around her. But soon this did not please her, and her heart no longer seemed to rise to her bidding.

There came a day when the weight of despair became too much to carry, and she sought out WarEagle to speak with him of the things that had happened.

Speak, daughter, he said. And tell me what sorrows you.

Father, she said. I am frightened to tell you my story, for I will seem to contradict your wisdom and your prophecy.

Do not fear, he said. I am not frightened of any words you can speak, for I know that where there is truth, all prophecies agree.

And so she told him her story, of the sadness that had come between her and WhiteDog, and how her spirit longed to feel again the press of the hands whose prints lit the walls of her home.

Daughter, WarEagle said, where there is truth there is wisdom, and where there is wisdom there is always a path to tread. This is what you must do.

And so WarEagle told RainintheFace that she must return to WhiteDog and her lodge and live the life she lived before. But, he said, she must never again look at the walls, expecting to see the light-shadow hands. If she could do this, he said, then she and WhiteDog would come together in harmony.

So RainintheFace returned to her lodge and lived her days as best she could, trying not to think of the light-shadows. Whenever she felt the impulse to look whether they were still there, whether they still reached for her, or beckoned to her, instead, she caused her eyes to seek WhiteDog, to see what it was that moved in him and with him.

In this way the time passed, and WhiteDog saw the peace that had come upon her. Wife, he said, peace enlarges your beauty, and in these days there is a light that shines within you, such as I've never seen, even among the stars, even among the stars of the sky when the snow lay upon the mountainside.

RainintheFace felt his words swim with the blood in her veins and her heart quickened. Night upon night his fingertips matched hers and his chest brushed her chest. In the daylight, wherever she walked his eyes followed, and wherever he went in his duties, her mind pictured him in safety and with joy.

The seasons passed in this way, and by the time the frosts crept into their joints and the gods scored their faces like the branches of trees, RainintheFace could not even remember where the light-shadows had once been, holding her in a dream of the past.

August 14, 1964

7am. So chilly this morning, I am wondering about a fire … Can you believe it? Only 50 degrees! Raining again, a little.

8.30am. No one coming today, it seems. Tray sitting stark as a crewless ship.

10am. Rain has settled in now. Been leafing through all the mail-order catalogues.

4pm. Rain has turned to drizzle. About 70 degrees now. Finished Butcher's Crossing. Beautifully done. Manly rather than mannish.

 *Cannot decide whether to install all of Alex's old furniture or replace it.

10.30pm. A gray, dank day, with everything sagging, darkened & wetted. Watched "Route 66". I wish it had no music.

August 15, 1964

7am. Too cold to wash! Only 44 degrees out there! Sunshine had better hurry.

1.15pm. 78 degrees now. Back from Frederick & A & P ($19). Cold inspired me to buy some Ovaltine. Got more library books but didn't feel like buying any. Have ordered all the curtains for The Corner. Price too much to commit to writing, lest I faint all over again.

2.45pm. Late lunch on pork sausage patties, fried eggs, salsify & samples from new spinach crop. Delicious.

4.30pm. Tea just a little later. Feels very good today as it is still chilly

5.45pm. I am conscious of an urge to live in The Corner now. Not to wait there, but to live there. This feeling does not diminish my love for the Mary House. Something inside me wants every woman I know to live in this little house, to feel its walls surrounding but not enclosing, to hear its voices raise up inside her own. I need to leave it to make way for whoever will live here next. I am so proud of it all.

10.45pm. A very pretty day, but one which left me no choice but to sweep the fireplace & stack the wood in its place. Hope tomorrow is better. Watched the channel 4 movie. Or I think I did. It was like a movie, & yet somehow not.

August 16, 1964

7.30am. Only 51 degrees this morning. Beautiful outside, where at least it still looks like summer.

12.45pm. In the paper that there was a race riot yesterday in Chicago. Despair finds peace in anger.

*Walked home with the church ladies today. They looked so fine in their hats, gloves, beads etc. that when we got to the benches, I went inside & got my camera. Three of them instantly threw their sweaters over their faces, laughing wildly that they were in no state to be photographed. All changed their minds eventually, so I hope the pictures come out. Cinch was dressed in a gray & brown paisley print dress, tan sweater, gray beads & brown pocketbook.

*They asked me again about moving, & I told them it would be on the first. They consulted quickly with their eyes & decided they could all manage to come & help me "settle in". I nearly choked & may have actually felt a tear.

3pm. Just back. I walked all around inside The Corner again, letting it do the talking to me, instead of trying to instruct it. From the high porch I could see & hear the men playing horseshoes. I went over & discovered that word of my moving in had reached everyone. A farmer, known to me only as Junior, asked if I'd heard any news about Alex, & I told him I hadn't. He looked deeply grieved. He said I must be "sore broke up", & I found myself saying that I was ready for whatever news came. —God bless, his wife said, & touched my arm.

4.15pm. Sitting outside with the tea, though it is just a little too cold in the shade.

* "Ready for the news." There is no longer any news. I have felt everything I can feel. Alex's fate is with Alex, as it always has been, though I have wanted so much for it to be

574

with me. My love for him grows the longer I live. So I must live. I will live in The Corner.

10.45pm. High 70s this afternoon. Is summer over?
  *I do wish I had a novel to read.

August 17, 1964

7.15am. Yet another dank, gray start. At least it is 58 degrees, which makes it bearable. Fog on both mountaintops.

8.45am. Drizzling now. Once again, no sign of the men. Tray may need dusting by tomorrow.
  *Reading the phone book & local papers trying to find a good place to see horses for sale. Must ask someone about chickens too.

11am. Drizzle has turned to rain.

2.15pm. Clouds have gone dry & temperature 82 degrees. Very muggy. Various inconclusive calls about horses.

11pm. Uncooperative day, weather-wise. Still damp feeling. Have sorted papers for moving.

There's bound to be a gal somewhere

I, LittleWound, tell this story.

It was in the time when BlackMary had come to live with me. She behaved with kindness and she used her gifts to bring honour to herself in the eyes of those who knew her. I had fallen into sickness, and I lay upon the blankets, though the leaves hung in storms upon the trees. My legs swelled until my ankles were the size of my thighs. I could feel the weight of the blood in my veins, and I rested my eyes, knowing that soon I must seek for the SpiritRoad without a guide. Sometimes, I pondered upon my life, wondering, if it had been my destiny to marry, how I might have recognized my husband. What sound would his tread have made? How would the sunlight have flowed in his hair? How would my hand have felt pressed against his skin? But I found no answers. I knew though, that if I had had a daughter I would have wished her to be like BlackMary. Her goodness gave her wings and I wished to give her the freedom of my soul, because I loved her. So in those days, when the sun lay in blossom upon the slopes and fields, she would bring me my food at the closing of the day, and tell me all that she had heard, for she knew that I found joy in the tales and works of men and women who lived in the village and beyond. It was on such an evening that she told me the news of Frushour, known as Peter, and his wife Martha.

Peter was a cooper in the valley called Fisher's Hollow, and his life was a life of toil. He dealt with the men who harvested the trees and sawed them into planks. He planed and shaped these with tools and with steam, and the barrels and kegs and buckets he made he sold as he could to the farmers and tradesmen, between Hawbottom and Foxville, Mechanicsville and Smoketown. But his life at home never eased, and his garden was a garden of stones, his fields were places where the hogs grazed, and his orchard grew beyond the reach of his ladder.

His marriage with Martha seemed to all who knew them one of tranquillity and there was no one who could speak of witnessing any disturbance between them. And because of this, it surprised everyone in Harmony, everyone in the villages where Peter's name was known, that one day, after journeying as far as Berlin to sell kegs to the nail-forge, he came home to discover that she had run away, wedding her life to another man. This man, it was said, was a dealer in pelts, and he took her beyond the Potomac and beyond the mountains to places where the beavers still swam and the foxes still barked.

All of this happened, before BlackMary came to my house, before her music swung in my afternoons. So it was a surprise to me when, as I lay looking down at my body, grown to the size of a man's, when she told me that Martha had returned to Fisher's Hollow. She came, it was said – for no one saw her – sitting upon a horse with shoes that had no rust upon them, and she rode straight to the cabin where she had lived with Peter. She took the horse to the stream near the place where the road bends, and let it drink from the stream, before taking it back to shed where Peter dried the wood for his coopering, and put it inside. Then she went indoors without knocking. It was said that she did not come out again, and that no one saw her or Peter until the sun rose after nights of rain. When she was seen, she was wearing a bonnet that she had worn before she left, and she hoed with a hoe that she had used years before. Peter worked as he always worked, his life like a stream in its bed. None of the neighbours heard recriminations, and no one spoke to Martha or Peter about the things they saw between them. In the seasons that separated them as husband and wife there had been births and deaths, beginnings and endings, and the valley had become greater in the eyes of both. To me it seemed proof of something about marriage. There had been need and folly in the time they had shared, before Martha ran away. But what they found together in this season when the cold had streaked their faces and their hair was resemblance to something they understood in one another. It gave them peace. Whatever foolishness and hypocrisy their neighbours spoke, they heard nothing. I was glad for them, even as I yearned for wisdom.

August 18, 1964

7.30am. Warm 61 degrees & drizzling.

9am. Men not working again today. Half-expected this.

1.30pm. Dry now, but gray. 82 degrees. Spent much of the morning walking about all sides of my new place, calculating things, making notes, imagining. The emptiness of it all, even though it is about to end, is stifling me, & I cannot wait to fill up these spaces with tomorrow. I want so much tomorrow that I have it to give away, sell wholesale, pack-&-freeze, trade with Japan, etc. I will unwrap such tomorrows that no one will even recall that there ever were todays.

4pm. Tea is such a luxury. Sitting still. Curing time.

*Tom, what there is of him, seems already to have moved to The Corner, as there is little sign of him in the Mary House anymore.

*I have grown to believe that the sooner I get into the house myself, the sooner it becomes possible for Alex to do so. That is, the Mary House could never be his home, as it has been mine. All this time, I have been afraid to move over there, afraid of its becoming necessary or possible for me to move, just in case it was "too soon"; that somehow, if I were ready before Alex were back, I would jinx the likelihood of his returning. But now, I know that whatever life he still has, real life, or only in my memory, his freedom (& mine) to enjoy it, cannot come until I am there, comfortably situated. So now I cannot wait to burn my boats, sink my pontoons, & live as much as I can.

10.15pm. Another humid blank-newsprint sort of day. No patience for "The Fugitive".

August 19, 1964

7.30am. Same sort of day, though cooler mid 50s. Rainy & dull.

8.45am. Guessed correctly, as no one working at The Corner today.

10.30am. Just had a delivery of curtains. So will spend the rest of the morning over the road.

1.15pm. Back in the Mary House. Curtains all in place in The Corner. Just as I'd hoped. Very hungry.

4pm. Such a light lunch (soup & eggs with toast) that I am parched for tea. Look out Oreos!

7pm. Mustn't let myself eat cookies like that. Giddy all evening. Dinner of beef stew with lots of vegetables, so now feeling cleaner in mind & body.

10.30pm. Groaningly obvious sort of behaviour weather-wise again. Not much above 70 this afternoon, & wet.

August 20, 1964

7am. Freezing again out there this morning (well, 51). Raining in bursts.

8.45am. Once again, no sign of Marce & his minions.

10.15am. Put various letters into mailbox today. Sounds of wood being sawn somewhere towards Hawbottom.

11.45am. Mail arrived. Bill for moving day already come!
   *I wonder when & how I will coax my neighbors into visiting inside The Corner?

1.30pm. Made chicken salad today. Nice with green salad.

4pm. Looking out the window over my tea cup, I thought I saw the white-haired boys & their strange chums go down the road. They looked to be going somewhere on purpose.

7pm. Made spaghetti for dinner. Nice change.

10.45pm. Rain stopped this afternoon, & it climbed to a thick, blubbery old seafood-feeling 83.

August 21, 1964

7.15am. Sticky & dismal fog & rain again today. Already 63 degrees.

8.30am. Men didn't show for work again.

*The Patch has grown quite lime-green now. Swathes & sweeps of density & light, heaviness & aridity. Beautiful & random.

10am. Recalled a dream from last night. The Corner was furnished & I'd evidently been living there a while. The phone rang & the caller asked for Alex. I called his name, expecting he'd be there in a moment. Then I woke up.

12pm. Have picked two of the biggest of the little summer squash. Making them into soup for lunch.

4pm. Such an old summer day this afternoon. As if summer itself has grown old, louche & a little untrustworthy. Drinking tea with no milk, just sugar. (Soup at lunchtime was delicious.)

*It's a funny thing to say this, but I have noticed how impossible it is to outrun our own wishes. All the things we want superimpose themselves on to us from somewhere, then just as soon as they are absorbed (forgotten or realized) more come. Now I want to be in The Corner when Alex comes. I have accepted that my life is now there. In his life, if it is to be anywhere on this earth, he is also now bound to call that place his home. This change has caught up to him. To me. I have let it become true for us both. Whether he rejects it, or never even knows it, no longer matters. I have lived this change, & if he lives, he will as well.

10.30pm. Like yesterday, it went dry this afternoon, & thermometer dared credulity by saying 85 degrees. Horrid air, like a pudding skin. Watched "Route 66".

I kissed her while the fiddles played

Everybody thought they were sisters. They were known to their neighbours as 'the Stroup sisters'. The older one, Anne Marie, encouraged this, while the younger one, Mary Beth, thought it was true, and had never known anything different.

The truth was that the girls were from Hagerstown, where Anne Marie had been living with her mother. She had never known her father, though her mother had had quite a few boyfriends living with her at different times, and even more men friends visiting. Anne Marie herself had got pregnant when she was sixteen, and she and her baby Mary Beth had both lived with Anne Marie's mother for just over two years when the older woman died, probably by accident, from mixing sleeping pills and too much alcohol. She had owned her little timber house though, and as there was no one else to say no after her mother died, Anne Marie sold the place and moved a little east to a small house near Myersville.

The house she bought was in the valley where the old Wolfsville Road runs, alongside Middle Creek. The creek is quite wide there, twenty- twenty-five foot in places, though seldom more than a foot deep. Downstream, it bends across the meadows to where the ridge rises and Myersville stands, and upstream it winds through close hills and trees until it opens out near the old Brethren Meeting House. Here the stream goes on northwards, but the valley splits in two, with one branch quickly turning upwards towards Catoctin Mountain and the Ridge Road, while the other wider one rises more slowly towards Wolfsville. Most of the better farms are in the sloping valley, while the narrow one has smaller houses like the one Anne Marie and Mary Beth lived in.

Their house was clapboarded, and painted white with green shutters, and positioned midway between the road and Middle Creek. They had a decent yard and garden – though a little shady – and a small shed outside, where they parked Anne Marie's jalopy. Ever since they had first moved in, and Anne Marie had found a neighbour to look after Mary Beth, Anne Marie had driven the two miles into Myersville where she worked in one of the general stores on Main Street. As soon as Mary Beth was old enough, she took her along in the mornings so she could attend the school there too. When Mary Beth finished elementary school, Anne Marie saw to it that she got her on the school bus in Myersville, which then took Mary Beth to Middletown for high school there. Mary Beth stayed on at high school longer than anyone might have predicted and graduated when she was eighteen. After that, because times were so hard, she got the only job she could find, which was to work in her old elementary school in Myersville. There she dusted, mopped, tidied up, helped cook and serve dinners, and generally helped keep the school presentable. The children liked her and didn't have a nickname for her.

It wasn't long after Anne Marie turned forty that she started to worry about Mary Beth. At twenty-four, Mary Beth still wasn't married, and there didn't seem to be any prospects on the horizon. She wasn't a bad-looking girl, but no one seemed to take any notice of her. She was a little thin, perhaps, slightly jutting bones, and she had a funny way of moving her arms and legs, like jerky machinery that had sat still for too long, and which suddenly came to life. She wore her hair longer than many women her age, and yet this didn't make her look younger. She laughed gently and easily, and people liked to have her around, if only to see her laugh so simply.

Anne Marie couldn't understand it. She understood about herself – a tall, wide-backed, large-hipped woman who looked as though she'd grown up on a farm, eating beef and drinking milk, even though she hadn't. Her hair curled unmanageably, her jawline was too much like a man's. Anne Marie never sought men's attention, and the men she met respected her and spoke to her with the ease and confidentiality that they would have used speaking to their own oldest sisters. But Anne Marie was worried about Mary Beth.

Most Sundays, Anne Marie drove herself and Mary Beth up the valley to the Meeting House to attend the church there. It was a good, cheap, friendly outing for them, gave them a chance to dress up a little and to chat with neighbours about prices, weather, births and deaths. Mary Beth seemed to enjoy it, though Anne Marie thought it a shame that it was the custom for all the men to sit on one side of the aisle while all the women sat on the other. They both sang out for the hymns, and Anne Marie thought Mary Beth had the better voice. Even the preacher, Stace Lushbaugh, had told Mary Beth what a nice voice she had.

Then one afternoon at the store in Myersville, Anne Marie was stacking cans when Mr Lushbaugh came to the counter to pay for a few things. He seemed in a light-hearted mood, lighter than he usually seemed. Anne Marie commented on it, surprising herself a little. He told her he had learned to look beyond his cares. She should do the same, he said. What were her cares? he asked. No one else was in the store at the time, so Anne Marie, still surprising herself, told him her care, her chief care, was to find a man for Mary Beth. Mr Lushbaugh's lips pursed, and he tilted his head slightly, exhaling. He was thinking. He looked at Anne Marie, and said he'd put his mind to it, and see whether he could find some means to chase all her cares away. Then he laughed, as though he had made a good joke.

Two Sundays later there was a new man in the pews at the Meeting House. He was slim, dark-haired and looked as healthy as a farmer, smoother, but not softer. After the service, Mr Lushbaugh introduced him to Anne Marie. He said the man's name was Lester Wentz, and he had just come home to his family farm up towards Wolfsville, after his time in the army. He had been called up in the last year of the European war, and unlike most everyone else, he had stayed in the army after the fighting. He had only gone as far as Texas himself, and then he got moved around a lot, once over to West Virginia when there was trouble with the striking miners, and then to Washington, DC. He was there when he started to get homesick, and as his time was about up, he quit and came home. Anne Marie thought that from his story he would probably be about thirty-one. Mr Lushbaugh put his hand on Lester's shoulder and led him down the church steps to where Mary Beth was talking to some school-age children who were running around their mothers' feet. The children liked seeing her outside of school. Anne Marie saw Lester remove his hat when the preacher introduced him to Mary Beth, saw Lester's face become expectant, and saw Mary Beth lower her eyes in happiness.

Everything else that happened after that, Anne Marie thought, spun around in her mind, like someone stirring a large boiling pot of soup. Too many things to say which one was which, which one came first. It was all just as it ought to have been, as she might have hoped it would be. Might have hoped, she thought, if she had dared. Or if she had been someone else.

Lester was a quiet man, and he never boasted about anything he had done or seen in the army. He wasn't ashamed, but he didn't seem to think that anything that had happened then could possibly matter now, here, in this place. She saw how he thought of others whenever he listened to them, how he tried to help them to say what they wanted to say, no matter if it seemed foolish or vain, or proud or struggling. He was kind that way to the old folks, to the braggart young men, to the fulsome young women, treating all of them seriously, but never solemnly. Anne Marie knew for a fact that he put a dollar in the collection every Sunday, though his family wasn't rich, and his share of the farm was not, or not yet, as large as it could be. She saw him give the children dimes and nickels to put in the collection too, knowing that only about half of what he gave them would end up there. The neighbours told her about his way of learning to farm. He had left home at about the time most of the local men would be taking on more duties. Now he was almost starting over, growing his calluses fresh, as they teased him; forging muscles that added to or replaced the ones he'd got in the army. He also studied books on the new ideas about farming, talking his father and uncle and cousins into buying new machinery, and trying new things. He was there, always, when there was a festival of some kind, smiling, with friends, with family. He was sober, polite, had a good appetite, a good handshake, and knew some clean jokes. And most of all – he loved Mary Beth. His face beamed whenever his eyes found her anywhere. He was joyful and confident, eager and anxious by turns, dressing well for her, giving her small presents, asking her permission even to kiss her cheek.

For Mary Beth, it had all been like a dream. She glided effortlessly into a mood so calm, so serene that Anne Marie began to wonder whether it wasn't, after all, too good to be true. She had never seen anyone fall so easily into a love so easy. It was as if it had been there all the time, somehow waiting, this story, this unfolding. All she had had to do was ask.

On the night of their wedding day, when Mary Beth and Lester at last slept in one another's arms, Anne Marie sat alone in her little house, caught between the road and the running stream. She could hear the sounds outside, and they were different than she remembered them. She looked at her clean, well-run little home, and she was satisfied that she had done the right things, the best things she could have done. Then she had a strange thought. She looked at the walls in her bedroom, the mantelpiece, the shelf, the windowsill. There were no photographs anywhere, none. She listened, and there was no clock ticking – she had never thought to buy one. She lay down on her bed, on top of the quilt that she and Mary Beth had made the winter when Mary Beth was sixteen, or thereabouts, and she saw a light coming through the window. The curtains were drawn, and she couldn't see it well. But she wondered whether it was the moon, bright before setting, or the sun, just rising above the treetops. She closed her eyes and sighed slowly, content that it should be either.

August 22, 1964

7.45am. Muggy & warm this morning. 64 degrees. A light fog near South Mountain. The sky at sunrise began as rich melon color, before sloping to something like ripe figs.

1pm. Back from Frederick. Took back my library books. Bought a copy of a novel called Letting Go by Phillip Roth. Went to A & P ($15) & for the first time in a very long time, didn't buy a can of coffee. Cold sandwich & tomatoes for lunch.

2.15pm. Hot & vile now. 92 degrees & not genuinely sunny.

4.30pm. Drank tea because it seemed I should. Sat on the porch, deciding I ought to get a porch swing put on to the high porch at The Corner.

    *Isn't it strange how much of what we believe to be our feelings are not genuinely our own, but are actually those we respect ourselves for believing we possess? How long & how often has this been true in my life?

6.15pm. Joanie & Paul strumming tonight (guitar & autoharp). Frogs singing in the streams. Laughter & voices through the open screened windows in my neighbors' houses.

8pm. Very quiet now.

11pm. Breeze picked up this evening, & air more cheerful now. Watched the channel 4 movie while ironing.

August 23, 1964

7.30am. Already verging on hot this morning (74 degrees). Breezy & less humid though.

10am. Defiantly saw the churchgoers go by a while ago. Cinch wearing fire-engine red, navy purse, necklace etc.
1.45m. 90 degrees now. Sun still knows what to do.

*Folks in a lazy dozy mood after church. I walked them home, looking, I felt, more cool than any of them, though I didn't have a paper fan to call my own. I asked Cinch (and the others) whether anyone wanted any zucchini or okra. Cinch said her daughter liked zucchini, so I gave her a little bagful. These will, I now imagine, end up on Marce's table. Must ask John John whether he likes them.

4.30pm. Finished my tea, which I had off a tray (!) on the high porch at The Corner, watching the men playing horse-shoes. Bees & wasps seem to be growing more plentiful.

7pm. Listened with the windows open to Joanie & Paul tonight. Mandolin & dulcimer. Every time they start to play, I smile; yet something in me begins to feel sad, knowing that soon, & unexpectedly, they will stop. What folly it is to accept our joys with caveats.

10.45pm. Great round moon tonight, like a snow pie. Warm summer breeze through the windows. Katydids at work.

*I looked at the channel 9 (CBS) line-up tonight, & I positively can't bear it. It is as nutritious as a bag of cream-puffs. A pity, as this is the best reception I can get. Read some of the Roth novel. Too soon to tell. Too much to tell?

August 24, 1964

7.15am. Warm again this morning, low 60s. Not so humid though & sunshine like new pennies.

8.30am. Full crew of men (& boy) working this morning. Something in my spirit is raised by this news. Marce & Rip are giving the new porch its top coat in deep burgundy-brown. Dicky Bird is supervising, & frankly assisting, John John in what may be the last organizing & removal of tools from the wash house, loading them on to Marce's truck. When they aren't talking, Dicky Bird sings once again about Sally, who used to carry his books to school ('cause she was a good ole girl).

*John John must be two inches taller & so much more mature in the face that I'd hardly say he was the boy I met a year ago.

*Davy, who looks as though his every pore is crying out, is digging over what will become my new border flower beds.

*Unexpectedly, Marce pointed to Davy's work (which is very neat, for such a large man) & said, –You're gonna wanna get your bulbs in them. There was a slight challenge in this; as much as to say, You do know you need to plant bulbs, don't you?

1.45pm. 89 degrees. Mellow breeze. Davy looks as though he might drown. He has done a beautiful job, combing out every stone with a rake, & shaping each bed with a firm edge & a slight crest. Where did he learn this? Surely, this is what this gentle giant should be doing ALL day?

4.45pm. Work finished, porch painted, beds dug, wash house empty, yard as clean as can be expected, & everyone gone. As they drove away, both Davy & John John were pointing off at the fields beside the Hollow Road, each wanting the other to see what he saw. I looked too, & was glad I did, though I don't know what they were pointing at.

10.45pm. A beautiful day, clean as a promise. Watched a re-run of "Wagon Train".

August 25, 1964

7.45am. Warm already (61) & sunlight full & expressive. So much to love.

8.30am. No explanation, but men evidently not working today.

*Saw my first V of geese above the pines behind the stable.

9.30am. Marce's truck now parked near the gate to The Patch. They are unloading what I'm pretty sure are young trees, some tools, bags, a lawn mower etc.

10.15am. The mystery unfolds. Marce & John John are in The Patch, working along the far fence, planting what I now know are fruit trees (all sorts: apple, pear, cherry, plum, peach, nectarine). Meanwhile, Davy digs holes along the opposite fence for more. Rip & Dicky Bird each have a mower; Rip handles the bit beside the new chicken coop, DB is behind The Corner.

12.30pm. Mowing is finished. Tree-planting continues. Near the end of The Patch, about the place where so many bonfires have been, there is some debate about the assembly of a grape arbor. This is a project for Rip & Dicky Bird, & the posts & cross pieces (& a few tools) are on the truck.

2pm. Dry as tinder now, & 93 degrees!

2.30pm. Everyone seems to have taken stock, put away or stacked up his things & gone home. Quiet now out there.

4.30pm. Drinking tea from the high porch again. I have worn out my anticipating & will do no more. I will not spoil what is left of the journey. It is so beautiful here I want to sing.

10.30pm. Summer has risen from the cold ashes & made believers of us all. An evening of frogs, katydids, crickets & a solitary owl asking questions over & over.

August 26, 1964

7.30am. Warm & giving again this morning. 63 degrees & transparent light over the horizons.

8.45am. Same crew, same jobs this morning. Lovely to see them all in the sunshine.

*Mysteriously, Dicky Bird seems to be singing what I think is a hymn. He asks whether the circle can be unbroken, by & by, Lord, by & by.

2pm. Back with the tray (root beer, for JJ's sake). The trees are all planted now, staked, formal & somehow looking as dutiful as young people posing for wedding pictures. The grape arbor too is now built. Such a gentle comedy with this. Dicky Bird & Rip, both so harmless, both so mild, lacking Marce to coerce them, bickered sweetly like an old married couple, both doing whatever they wanted & yet finding perfect harmony in the end results. It looks charming, serviceable & as old as The Patch itself.

4pm. Everything straight, tied & braced, they've all gone.

10pm. A perfect day. 80s this afternoon, & air like a caress.

When we've been there ten thousand years

I, LittleWound, tell this story.

It was in my girlhood, when my head was beside my mother's waist, that I learned the nature of being a storyteller. All day I did my chores and played the games with the other girls. We spun the tops and we ran among the trees, shouting, singing, calling to one another, and whispering. In those days, my voice was as the voice of raindrops when the sky goldens beneath the rainbow, before pain silenced me. In the evenings we gathered to listen to the women who spoke of the tales they knew, and what they told us one night, we repeated in the nights after, until all of us could tell every tale. Please, Aunt, we said. Please, Grandmother. Please, tell us what you have heard. Naubesah! Foolishness, my father said, though he never forbade the listening.

We sat in circles, our eyes upon the faces of the women, like whom, we longed to become. The women in whose hearts the tales of our people were written. They told us of what they had seen, and of what they had not witnessed. We learned of the Ininees, people the size of children who lived in the outcroppings of rocks on the mountainside, and who pulled over boys and girls who tried to visit them in their homes, pushing them to their deaths. We learned of the jeebis and the paukauks, who roamed the woods at night, the spirits of those whose unhappiness turned their eyes away from the SpiritRoad, leaving them to wander the mountains in the darkness. Each of us feared for our own soul, our own ochichang, and those of the families we loved.

I collected them all, these stories of the people through whose steps my destiny might lead. I learned of the dying man, RedCloud, who so loved the wife who had married him, though the sun was already above his horizon. He told her that when he was gone, if ever she were hungry, she should stick one of his arrows in the ground, and then look there on the next day, where she would find food waiting for her. This promise he kept, even from his grave. I learned of the brothers, ChargingHawk and DullKnife, and how ChargingHawk had the strength and beauty of the oak, and how DullKnife was twisted and shrunken like a briar. But how when the wife of ChargingHawk was bitten and poisoned by a rattlesnake, it was DullKnife who followed her even along the road of death, to call her back to the living, so that his brother and his bride might enjoy their destiny in happiness, though it cost DullKnife an eternity of pain. I learned of LittleCrow and SpottedTail, the couple whose destiny it was to live their lives in an alternation, so that, on a day when one had the breath of dawn in his or her lungs, the other was sunken in the snows of time. How it was that though one was always bowed beneath the seasons, on the days when the other flew upon the sunbeams, their love shone in the deeds of goodness that each wrought for the other. And I learned of TouchtheCloud and Lit-tleWolf, the couple whose marriage hung about them in rags until their nights were visited by the spirits of a man and a woman, to whom each told her or his troubles, and through whom they gained insight which led them to peace in one another.

There remain stories to tell, and it is in my heart to tell them. It is the nature thus of a gift that it must be given. Receive what is given to you and give it again to those who will benefit from receiving it. Only then will you esteem the love that is born when two journey together on whatever road they find themselves on.

August 27, 1964

8.45am. Men not here today. Something in this upsets me. Will they come back? The tray looks forlorn.

10.45am. Had a sudden knock at the door at 9am. Hart-sock. He was going to once-over the place with Marce & the gang at 9.30 & wanted to see me first. Was I satisfied? Was there anything I wanted fixed, changed or redone? What did I think of them? It all came so unexpectedly, I'm not sure my answers were clear or even relevant. I heard my-self saying what an experience it had all been. What I had learned. He looked confused. But was I satisfied? I hardly knew how to answer. It sounded, somehow, sexual. Was it all what I wanted? How could I say, yes, though it all sur-prised me, without also sounding sexual? So I said it was fine. Just fine. Strong, pliable, ready for living. Like a good marriage, I wanted to say. Luckily, the wheels of Marce's truck on the gravel stopped me before I could explain what I was thinking. With me two paces behind them, Hartsock & Marce walked all over the place: stable, Patch, chicken coop, garden, wash house, yard, Corner. They talked al-ways of problems & solutions, luck & skill, compromise &

ingenuity. No one asked me for my views. When they were finished, Marce went outside & sat with his gang on the benches under the walnut trees. Hartsock found things to say, things to say to a client, a woman, someone he thought wasn't ready to see the last of him without a proper conclusion. He shook my hand, which he seemed to think was a gesture with more dimensions than I might understand. Then he drove off.

*Marce & the others sat in the shade laughing, spitting, scuffing their feet &, I imagine, talking about anything other than what they'd spent the last year doing. Then, with no one giving any obvious clues, they walked over, got into the truck & drove off. I'm not sure whether I'll see any of them again.

4pm. Having opened all the windows in The Corner, I drank my tea walking around, letting the sunshine sweep through each room, & through me. I feel myself living now in each room, meeting myself around every corner. Rooms that will echo with laughter, shout with surprise, shudder with tears. Rooms in which life grows once it has begun.

7.45pm. Paul & Joanie concluded tonight. Fiddle & dulcimer. Every tune one I now know well enough to hum. Such gifts, such unlooked-for gifts.

10.30pm. Weather just like yesterday. Buoying to the spirits. Read some more of Roth before putting it down. One to read on another day. Another very different day.

August 28, 1964

7.30am. Fog crept in from the west this morning. Warm 62 degrees though.

9am. Fog all gone now. As I thought, no signs of the men today. The tray rests on the table.

2.30pm. Marce & his whole gang have parked on The Common.

4pm. What a strange hour or so. Marce, Rip, Dicky Bird, Davy & John John have now gone, piled into & on to the truck as always. They showed up between 2 & 2.30, looking clean & new, as if the working day had just started, & walked all around the place. Everywhere. While they did this they carried a small Brownie camera. Over & over they posed by things, taking pictures. They must have taken several rolls. First one group, then another. Pulling themselves up to full height, full breadth, coping attitudes, laughing. Posing as fully as posing can be. I went over to watch, & then they pulled me in on it all, making me join them, as if I were the little sister to a family of brothers. We stood by the back door, pointed at features of rooms, squinted in sunlight, struck mock attitudes in the garden, looked serious by walls & windows. But then it was done. They decided, a little shamefacedly, that they'd done all anyone could do. They thanked me for the tea & coffee "and everything" & wished me luck with my new house. Marce said he hoped Alex would be home soon. He looked dry-eyed with sincerity. Then they walked towards the truck & all got in. All except John John, who came back up my (new!) path & gave me a hug. A young man's hug. A boy's hug. A friend & stranger's hug. All the hugs we both needed. Then he jumped in with the others & they drove off. I don't even know where. I don't expect I'll ever see any of the pictures.

7.15pm. No music tonight. No novel. Nothing but the stillness of my very old friend The Mary House. I hope all of her moods have become my own.

10.45pm. A nice day, & not as hot, only just 80 this afternoon. Watched "Route 66".

August 29, 1964

7.45am. 62 & foggy out there. A little humid again.

*It is one year ago today that this story began. Who could have foreseen it?

12pm. Back from Acme in Middletown ($14). Saw two people from Harmony, churchgoers, neighbors, new friends. —How do? they said.

3pm. 90 degrees & air like an animal's breath.

*In today's paper that there has now been a race riot in Philadelphia. It is all so hard, so broken, so un-see-able.

4.15pm. Tea on the Mary House porch. Walnuts now hanging heavy in the trees, the sound of both streams soft on the air. The Mary House itself with the face of a mother who knows I am leaving home soon, wanting me to stay, wishing me happiness when I go.

6pm. High time with Paul & Joanie: fiddle & autoharp. Music for dancing, it seems.

10.15pm. Something of an inglorious day today. Imitation summer, acting with no real talent.

August 30, 1964

7.45am. Hot & muggy 69 degrees this morning. Breeze from the west feels used up & second-hand.

12pm. Wore my green dress to church this morning. Cinch said it was pretty. She was in a dark straw-colored dress with jade-looking accessories. As we walked home, she took my hand & drew me aside before we got to the benches. —Y'all get yourself in there now, ya hear? It'll be such a thing, ya won't never have known nuthin' like it. You'll be so busy, the joys'll come down on ya.

*I kissed her cheek. –They already have, I said.

1.30pm. 85 degrees & sky ominous. Piles of unwanted clouds dumped over South Mountain.

3pm. Clashing thunderclaps now, sometimes two at once, & bouncing rain.

5pm. All quiet in the heavens. Humidity left behind a little, so the job not done.

10.30pm. Quiet & dark out there now. May be another storm coming?

August 31, 1964

7.30am. Hot & bitterly humid this morning. Already 74 degrees.

8.30am. I have not taken down the things for the tray, all of them still sitting on the shelf. I know what to expect, but I still look out at The Common once in a while, half-expecting to see them. Wondering what they'll do. Instead, I wonder what they are all doing today. Who has made their tea & coffee? Who wonders at them?

2pm. 90 full-blooded degrees out there again, & air as firm as wax. Thunderclouds like anvils in the west.
 *Hope it is not like this tomorrow.

4.45pm. Wind whipping the walnut trees & tea-cup sized drops of rain smacking the road & rooftop. Here it comes.

5.30pm. Symphonic thunderstorm now. Raindrops raising funnels of spray on the bench in front of The Corner; tin roof drum-rolling above me.

8pm. Storm completely gone, & the peace of sleeping armies has fallen.

10.30pm. Bedtime.

*Outside the door it is peaceful. Tonight the Mary House holds so much life that I feel as though my truest friends have come to say farewell before the journey they know I am about to take. My gratitude to them all wells up inside me. Their strength & endurance has been an example, their kindness like a sunrise over the treetops. Goodnight & good morning. I am ready now. I am ready for this beginning.

Acknowledgements

Besides the writer's centuries-old rootedness in this exact location, a novel of this kind necessarily has many sources beyond those of memory and experiences. Some of these are as follows:

For information about people, events and impressions of the local area in the Civil War period, I am indebted to Merritt Roe Smith, *Harper's Ferry Armory and the New Technology*; Brian Matthew Jordan, *Unholy Sabbath: The Battle of South Mountain*; Kathleen A. Ernst, *Too Afraid to Cry Maryland Civilians in the Antietam Campaign*; and Barbara Jeanne Fields, *Slavery and Freedom on the Middle Ground*.

Background details on the Revolutionary War, War of 1812, the Federalist period, the Mexican War era and the antebellum years more generally, have some nineteenth-century sources in John West, *The Substance of a Journal...*; Z.F. Smith, *The Battle of New Orleans*; A.T. Mahan, *Sea Power and its Relation to the War of 1812*; Ralph Delahaye Paine, *A Chronicle of the War of 1812*; Joseph T. Wilson, *The Black Phalanx: African American Soldiers in the War of Independence*; Ulrich Bonnell Phillips, *American Negro Slavery*; George S. Merriam, *The Negro and the Nation*; Catherine Esther Beecher, *An Essay on Slavery and Abolition*; S.A. Ferrall, *A Ramble of Six Thousand Miles through the United States of America*; George Washington Williams, *History of the Negro Race in America*; G.R. Gleig, *The*

Campaigns of the British Army at Washington and New Orleans 1814-1815;

First-hand accounts of the experience of slavery reflect those of *The Autobiography of James L. Smith*; *The Life and Adventures of James Williams*; *Narrative of the Life of J.D. Green*; *The Life of Isaac Mason as a Slave*; James Wheeler Johnson, *Autobiography of an Ex-Colored Man*; Harriet Jacobs, *Incidents in the Life of a Slave Girl*; Frederick Douglass, *Narrative of the Life of Frederick Douglass* and *Collected Articles*; Solomon Northup, *Twelve Years a Slave*; *Narrative of the Life and Adventures of Henry Bibb*; James W.C. Pennington, *The Fugitive Blacksmith*; Elizabeth Keckley, *Behind the Scenes, or Thirty Years a Slave*; and Harriet E. Wilson, *Our Nig*. There are also many thousands of pages of interviews in the Library of Congress's compendium of the memories of former slaves. A small sample of these can be seen in Norman Yetman (ed.), *When I was a Slave*.

These nineteenth-century descriptions of indigenous American societies included relevant material: H.C. Yarrow, *An Introduction to the Mortuary Customs of North American Indians*; John Wesley Powell, *Sketch of the Mythology of the North American Indians*; Galen Clark, *Indians of the Yosemite Valley*; Francis Parkman, *A Half-Century of Conflict*; Henry Rowe Schoolcraft, *Personal Memoirs of a Residence of Thirty Years with the Indian Tribes of the American Frontiers*, *The Myth of Hiawatha* and *Algic Researches*; Charles Alexander Eastman, *Indian Child Life* and *Indian Boyhood*; Alexander Scott Withers, *Chronicle of Border Warfare*; James Athearn Jones, *Traditions of the North American Indians*; Zitkala-Sa, *American Indian Stories*; Alice C. Fletcher, *Indian Games and Stories* and *Indian Story and Song from North America*; George Bird Grinnell, *Blackfeet Indian Stories*; Charles Godfrey Leland, *Algonquin Legends of New England*; Horatio Hale, *The Iroquois Book of Rites*; Egerton Ryerson Young, *Algonquin Indian Tales*; 'Old Humphrey', *History, Manners and Customs of the North*

American Indians; and Daniel Garrison Brinton, *American Hero Myths: A Study in the Native Religions of the Western Continent.*

Some elements of Appalachian customs, crafts and folklore are drawn from Eliot Wigginton (ed.), *Foxfire* and *Foxfire 2*. For additional insights into local lore from Catoctin Mountain, including some traditional names and expressions, I owe thanks to three privately-printed books by Virginia Draper, *The Smoke Still Rises, The Goose and the Eagle* and *Postscript.*

About the Author

Dr John Ballam is the author of poetry, plays, fiction and academic works. He is best-known for his critically-acclaimed memoir The Road to Harmony (1999; new edition 2009). He has been a script consultant and screenwriter for several major producers in London, Hollywood and Mumbai. He lives in England where he is the Director of the Diploma in Creative Writing at the University of Oxford.

9 781951 214449